Books by Dave Putnam

Nonfiction

The Working American Bulldog

Fiction

The Gamekeeper's Night Dog

The World War

10 Downing St

10 Downing St

By Dave Putnam

10 Downing St

Published by Bulldog Press, PO Box 620358, Woodside, California, 94062

Author: Dave Putnam
Cover design: Travis Baldree
ISBN: 0-9672710-8-8

Chapter 1

The Red Force Discovers Communism

Sunday was Ranking Officer and Senior Scientist Day at Vladimir's barbershop. Every one of his ten barbers got Sunday off, except Vladimir. All day long, he would personally cater to the grooming needs of the Red Force brass. On this particular Sunday, he'd arrived at the shop early to give his long white beard a pruning. He stood in front of a mirror, making himself presentable and listening to the financial news from the mainland on a high-powered radio. The announcer was describing the latest merger. Daimler-Ford had purchased Ashfield Motors, giving the Japanese industrial giant control of 90 percent of the world's automobile market. It wouldn't be long before Daimler-Ford bought Rolls-Royce, and another iron-fisted monopoly would be born. The news program went on to list a few of Daimler-Ford's holdings, starting with its lock on rubber plantations in the tropics, its vast fleet of cargo ships, and its endless miles of globe encircling railroads. The announcer used a word Vladimir had never heard before: supermonopoly.

Vladimir set his clippers down to add a line to one of his HP equations, smirking as the commentator gave the cowardly reaction of the Anglo-American Federal Trade Commission. The FTC was warning the Commonwealth Congress not to pass antitrust legislation. It claimed that only monopolies could curb the glut of industrial overcapacity hamstringing the global market. He picked up his clippers and finished giving himself a haircut.

His shop was located in the Kauaian village of Poipu. It wasn't really Vladimir's shop. The Red Force had purchased it from a Japanese barber in 1926. It was hard to believe that only a single year had passed since Vladimir (and every Red Force recruit) had been grilled by anticommunist census takers with truth-sniffing Bulldogs. He smiled nostalgically, recalling the ease with which he'd fooled the King's lackey. Years of practice with truth-sniffing German Shepherds had made hoodwinking a Bulldog child's play. Thank God O'Brien and the other Marxist cops had passed the test just as easily.

The pane of glass in his front door rattled with a sharp knocking. An officer wanted a haircut and didn't care about posted hours. Vladimir's smirk vanished. It was probably General Patton. The barber unlocked the door after turning off the radio. Without waiting

1

for an invitation, a general officer shoved the door open and strutted inside, an ivory-handled converti-gun swinging from his right hip in a hand-tooled Corinthian leather holster. It was George Patton, Vladimir's most demanding customer.

The general plopped into the nearest chair, not actually the one that Vladimir had intended to use. Patton's red beret was flung across the room. Impressively, it landed on a hat rack peg, a neat bull's-eye that any marksman could be proud of. Vladimir was expecting a difficult assignment. The general didn't disappoint. He wanted his eyebrows trimmed to a specific length. The jungle of nose hair protruding from the general's globular schnozzle must be sculpted and shaped just so. The sides of his head were to be scalped, the top coiffed into a brush cut, long black hairs tweezed off moles, and fingernails manicured and given a gloss finish. Patton said all this in the tone that one would use to describe a precise and complicated military maneuver. He then popped a cigar into his mouth, but didn't light up. Patton wasn't all bad.

With scissors snipping, Vladimir prattled on about the weather, the caliber of young cadets and soldiers passing through his barbershop doors, and other inconsequential small talk. Patton grunted monosyllabic replies to the inane conversation until he'd had enough. The general wanted Vladimir to take up the subject that they'd been discussing during his last haircut. The barber had described a series of Historical Parallelism algorithms designed to plot the growth of global monopolies as they devoured the world economy over the next hundred years. It wasn't unusual for a barber within the Red Force to hold an advanced degree or be conversant in cutting-edge scientific theory, so Patton felt comfortable requesting an update.

Little did the general know that Vladimir was actually the word's foremost Marxist theoretician, under the pen name Spartacus. Nor could he have known that Vladimir's thinking on Marxist theory had come full circle since the advent of HP equations and high-speed computers to run them on. Early twentieth-century Marxists had laughed at the nineteenth-century Marxist prediction concerning a concentration of economic power in fewer and fewer hands. No one was laughing any more. Although it was true that Marx thought a revolution would occur before a single monopoly owned all the means of production, a single all-encompassing global monopoly had always been a possibility in classical Marxist thought and even a first year economic student could see this trend playing itself out as the twentieth-century ground forward, albeit without the disastrous consequences Marx had predicted, not yet at any rate. This was why trust-busting legislation was slowly winding through the musty governmental corridors of the Commonwealth countries that formed the world congress.

Vladimir's equations indicated that trust-busting legislation would not work. The longer he played with his equations, the more convinced he became. A classic HP fork was becoming more and more defined.

On one prong of the HP fork there were the left-wing parties: Labor, Republicans, and the multitudinous socialist parties. Left-wingers had already successfully socialized private monopolies like utilities, aerolines, and telephone companies. Government ownership of a given industry was virtually impossible if it were not first organized into a monopoly. Therefore, this prong in the fork had a powerful incentive to see the monopolization process move forward.

Just as motivated in the same direction, but for other reasons, was the second prong in the fork: right wing parties such as the Tories and Democrats. They were committed to laissez-faire capitalism and wouldn't bust trusts for ideological reasons.

Both prongs of the fork were influenced by the lobbying and outright bribery made possible by the trusts' infinitely deep pockets. Antitrust legislation was a smokescreen to blind the masses. Vladimir's equations predicted several things in the next ten years: state-owned monopolies repurchased by the private sector, supermonopolies consolidating out of dozens of industries, and the destruction of labor unions. It may take a century or more, but eventually a single monopoly, probably a merger of Daimler-Ford and the colossal Alco Company, would rule the Earth. At that point, the nightmarish plutocracy that Marx had foreseen would bear deadly fruit. Karl Marx would be vindicated, but a revolution by armed industrial workers would be impossible because the plutocracy would control advanced CMG technology.

Patton couldn't and wouldn't absorb all this in the course of one haircut, or even two or three. Vladimir could feed the general only small driblets in a single sitting. The Commonwealth Military Game was twenty-three years away. There was plenty of time to convert the Red Force High Command into a legion of Marxist avenging angels.

The most that Patton could handle today was the mathematical formula proving that monopolies would do anything to protect their existence. The general had an excellent mind for math, and the lesson was going down smoothly when chaos erupted on the street outside. A monumental roar shook the windowpanes of the barbershop.

Patton and Vladimir burst onto the plank sidewalk in front of the shop. It had rained the day before. The red dirt road cutting through the town of Poipu was a swamp. A bull war seal was rampaging up the swampy street. Evidently, the seal had broken out of a training pen near the coast. The seal's handler was running behind the finned warrior. He threw a lariat noose around the seven-hundred-pound bull's fleshy neck. This was a mistake.

War seals can move on dry land with more speed and agility than any other type of pinniped. In thick mud, they are startlingly quick. The wayward bull felt the noose tighten around his throat. He put on a burst of speed, galloping almost as effortlessly as a horse for about ten yards. The seal wrangler was jerked off his feet to slide in the mud on his belly, gripping the lariat rope with frenzied strength.

Patton plugged a shotgun shell into his convertible handgun, drew a bead on the rope, and fired. The horsehair rope disintegrated halfway between the man and the seal. The seal's trainer-handler bounced and bumped to a halt. Unfortunately, his head connected with a rock in the process, knocking the man unconscious.

The seal coiled and leaped, landing in the mighty bough of a large Kukui tree that grew across the street from the barbershop. He sat on the low-hanging branch and barked an angry admonition at the gathering crowd: *Get no closer or I'll eat you!* Part of a war seal's training regimen involved attacking humans, theoretically only on command, although in the early stages of training wanton seal attacks were common. With his trainer unconscious, the bull was even more agitated. This made him unpredictable and extremely dangerous. A few off-duty soldiers in the crowd pushed forward with leashed Bulldogs.

Patton sensed that the soldiers were getting ready to set their dogs on the bull seal. He threw his cigar away and bellowed, "Keep those damn Bulldogs leashed!" The crowd was big enough that the soldiers couldn't see where the order had come from. Patton fired a flare from his convertible gun. The crowd parted to give the soldiers a view of old Blood and Guts. The troopers with dogs straightened to attention as they caught a glimpse of their most feared general. Leashes tightened. Dogs went into quivering sit-stays.

Vladimir put a microradio in Patton's hand. The general sent an order to Third Battalion for a squad in combat suits to head toward Poipu immediately. The squad was to put the bull seal in a training pen, without harming the valuable monster. A medevac team was instructed to take care of the unconscious seal trainer. Patton put the radio in his pocket, cupped his hands around his mouth, and ordered the crowd to disperse. When the people didn't move fast enough, he fired a few rounds over their heads.

Before the soldiers with Bulldogs could escape, Patton stationed them in cardinal points around the Kukui tree with instructions to hold the seal at bay until the armored squad arrived. He fired another flare for good measure. The smoking gun barrel wagged back and forth in the direction of the barbershop. "Never did finish my manicure. Get moving, Vlad." The general and the barber went back inside the shop.

Vladimir was applying the final layer of gloss to Patton's fingernails when the most important scientist on the island walked inside: J. Robert Oppenheimer. Patton called out, "Julius, what a pleasure. Pull up a squat. Let's chat."

Oppenheimer glared at Patton stiffly. The scientist hated his first name. Virtually anybody else on the island would have received a sharp reprimand for using it, followed by instructions to address the head of Red Force research as Dr. Oppenheimer, or Robert, never Julius. That would only have played into Patton's hands, providing the general with an opening for more ridicule. The head of research pinched the bridge of his nose to squelch the beginnings of a headache, his usual reaction to General Patton.

Vladimir tried not to look amused as he fanned a portable hair blower over Patton's glossy nails. The barber couldn't understand why Patton and Oppenheimer hated each other. They were so much alike. Both were fastidious with their personal appearance, although Oppenheimer was truly handsome (almost beautiful) while Patton was, on a good day, rugged. On a bad day, the general could be best described as lumpy and pockmarked. Oppenheimer and Patton were both exceptionally intelligent. However, Oppenheimer probably possessed a more powerful intellect than any other human being on Earth, rivaled only by Albert Einstein. Patton was merely brilliant. Both men had a gift for language. Patton could speak four or five languages. Oppenheimer could speak forty. Any objective measure put Oppenheimer above Patton, save one: Patton was much tougher.

Vladimir provided Patton with a hand mirror. The general was pleased. The eyebrows were nicely trimmed. The brush cut was superb. The nose hairs were sculptured. The polish on his fingernails gleamed like jewels. Despite having achieved grooming perfection, Patton decided to hang around the barbershop, to taunt Oppenheimer just a little bit more. The brass traded places. Patton sat in a vinyl-backed waiting chair, picked up a copy of the *Red Force Times,* and pretended to read. Oppenheimer took the barber chair, instructing Vladimir in a loud voice to give him a simple trim. The physicist cast cobalt eyes at Patton, as if to say: *A haircut need not be an exercise in vanity.* The subtlety of the gesture was enough to temporarily silence General Patton.

The silence calmed Oppenheimer's ruffled ego and cooled his hatred for Patton. Perfecting the atom bomb (and other weapons) was only a small part of the reason why he had joined the Red Force. The greater reason was to transform the Red Force into an instrument for Marxist revolution. Patton had to be transformed as well, or the endeavor would fail.

Scissors snipped away. The scientist asked the barber, "Will your HP equations be computer ready in two weeks? My people start building Fat Baby then. We can spare some computer time." This got Patton's attention. He rustled his newspaper and asked, "Giving away computer time to a barber? My, my, my, hardly a proper use of military resources. What does Red Force care about monopoly capitalism?"

Vladimir snipped away happily, eager to hear the scientist's reply. "Patton, you don't know beans. HP equations have applications in explaining Brownian motion, straight physics. I've a hunch that Vlad's equations will have implications in the factors of calculus we're using on the A-bomb, the second and third derivatives," Oppenheimer said in a challenging tone.

The general's hatchet face screwed up in a mask of detestation. "Don't bullshit me, Julius. I know HP equations only helped show why Brownian motion is unpredictable. Second and third derivative, my ass, I smell a rat." Oppenheimer wore an expression of triumph. His voice was bright and eager, as if Patton had endorsed the project. "Wonderful, Georgey, join us then at the computer center when we run Vladimir's equations two weeks from now. The three of us shall pore over them together."

"I'll be there," Patton snarled. "And I'll bring one of my high foreheads. I find out the mainframe is being used for nonmilitary purposes and I will personally tear your head off and shit in the stump." He threw the newspaper to the floor and stomped out of the room. Patton was so agitated that he nearly walked into Supreme Commander Fred Banner. The general apologized to the generalissimo and said, "Not my fault, Sir. That damned Oppenheimer is running HP equations on the mainframe in two weeks, wasting resources, got me agitated."

The renegade war seal was still sitting on the thick, low-hanging branch. He gave out a thunderous warning bark, drawing Fred Banner, Patton, and Vladimir out onto the street. Ten troopers in silver colored powered combat suits were marching up the muddy road, splashing red muck on their shiny titanium suits. The street and sidewalks were deserted except for this squad, Patton, Fred, Vladimir, and the five soldiers with leashed Bulldogs standing around the Kukui tree. Evidently, a medevac team had retrieved the unconscious seal trainer while Patton was getting his manicure.

Fred demanded to know why a war seal was sitting in a tree and a suited squad was marching their way. Patton filled him in. "No way," Fred said firmly, dismissing Patton's plan for dealing with the situation. "Order that squad to stand down. They'll kill this seal. Get rid of those troopers with Bulldogs. Watch an expert seal wrangler at work. Learn a thing or two."

The SC's orders were carried out. Oppenheimer and a few other people came out onto the street to watch the spectacle. Fred walked up to the Kukui tree with his hands spread wide. The soldiers in combat suits watched from a discreet distance, to give assistance if needed. The off-duty troopers with Bulldogs wanted to watch, but fled after Patton barked a few harsh words in their direction. Fred didn't notice them or anything else. He had tunnel vision. The war seal was the light at the end of the tunnel, the only thing that Fred could see.

"Easy, big fellow. That's a good lad," Fred crooned. The bull seal trumpeted a battle cry, but it held a playful note to Fred's trained ear. The SC walked to within five feet of the low hanging branch. From that distance, he could see deep burn marks on the bull's

5

neck, unhealed, leaking blood. Shock collars were an accepted method of putting control on the large sea mammals, if used sparingly. There was no excuse to burn electrical holes through inches of muscle and blubber, a sign of incompetent training. This animal was from Third Battle-lion, under Patton's Second Division and Second Corps. There was some very sloppy training going on in this battle-lion, and, ultimately, it was Patton's fault. Fred would deal with that later. For now, he had a wary seal to contend with.

With exaggerated care, he bent at the knees and leapt onto the branch. The bull seal ducked his head under a flipper, cringing rather than acting aggressively. Fred stroked one of the seal's long, dog-like ears. Patton partially redeemed himself by calling out, "Supreme Commander, just got word from Third Battle-lion. This beast's name is Achilles."

Fred whispered the seal's name into a long, floppy ear. He told the seal to go back home. The gargantuan pinniped sprang to the ground and galloped through the mud, back toward the Third Battle-lion's training pens. The SC also leaped to the ground. He gave Patton a piece of his mind, not shouting or blustering, but in a calm, collected manner.

When Fred was done, he asked what the general's beef with Oppenheimer was about. Patton had wilted under the dressing down. He regained his old fire discussing the unauthorized use of the mainframe computer for social science experiments.

Fred's eyebrows lowered over his eyes until he was squinting. He'd been getting sporadic reports of physicists running Marxist HP equations on the mainframe, supposedly during downtime, when the computer wasn't needed for weapons research. These reports had been coming at more frequent intervals. The scientists on the Fat Baby and Mole projects were a touchy bunch. Fred considered it wise to give them wide latitude. Now he was having some doubts. "Oppenheimer is going over these equations with you in two weeks, eh, George?"

Patton nodded affirmatively, adding, "I plan on bringing Stokes. The geezer is on his last legs, but he has a working knowledge of HP mathematics. He isn't easy to bullshit."

"I will be there as well, if for no other reason then to stop the enmity between Oppenheimer and yourself. After the bombs, missiles, and Mole digging machines are designed, Robert will begin on the next generation of combat suit. At that time, he will work with officers and enlisted personnel, yourself included."

Patton saluted, executed a crisp turn, and sauntered away in a decidedly unmilitary fashion. Fred was always amazed by Patton's arrogance. The American had commanded a Red Force panzer platoon in the 1920 CMG. Soldiers who had fought on the losing side of a war were usually humbler.

The Red Force IBM mainframe digested the last equation in the series and set to work. Vladimir and Oppenheimer sat on one side of the room, while Fred, Patton, and Wilfred Stokes sat on the other. Stokes was by no means ancient at sixty-seven, but he hadn't aged well and looked like he was pushing one hundred. He sat, twisted and gnarled, in a wheelchair, drool leaking from rubbery lips. His body was a wreck, but his mind was still bright. He looked forward to studying the HP predictions that the computer would start spitting out any second now.

Obligingly, the mainframe ejected a sheet of paper. Vladimir ran to retrieve it, spent a minute glancing at the printed symbols, and whooped deliriously. "I feel like a magician at a sideshow," he exclaimed. "Our program is predicting that Alco and Daimler-Ford will merge today." He looked at a wall clock. "The New York Stock Exchange just closed. This is the time that they would announce the merger, if it happened." He rushed toward a table with a radio, clearly intent on turning it on and listening to the financial news.

Oppenheimer stopped the barber in midstride so that he could address the three skeptics. "Gentlemen, validating the simple HP program we are running today with real world events lends credence to the long-range planning that we might see later on with Vladimir's advanced Spartacus software program."

Patton snarled, "Turn on the damn radio, Julius." Fred issued the general a stern warning not to use Oppenheimer's first name. Before Patton could think of a snappy comeback, Vladimir cranked up the radio.

A baritone voice scratched over the speakers. "To repeat the big news of the day, the world's two largest companies announced a merger agreement after the closing bell. In a stock swap worth billions of pounds, Daimler-Ford and Alco agreed to form a single company that will trade under the symbol DFA. Analysts applauded the move, citing strong links between the giant metal producer and the giant metal consumer. Officials from the Anglo-American Federal Trade Commission were unavailable for comment. In other news—"

Vladimir turned off the radio. He quietly handed the sheet of computer paper to Stokes. The wheelchair-bound engineer peered at the sheet through Coke-bottle glasses. He got to the last set of symbols and said, "Mr. Bakunin is not a magician at a sideshow. These conclusions flow straight from the program that he installed earlier. We could all have made a fortune if we'd bought Daimler-Ford or Alco stock last week." He thought of something and coughed. "Except it's illegal for CMG personnel to buy stock. Neither here nor there. My point is this is good science." Vladimir and Oppenheimer grinned like the proud fathers of exceptional children.

Fred asked for the sheet and bent over it. Patton stood up, ranting and raving as he walked back and forth in front of the busy mainframe: "What good is this fucking program? Will it help build atom bombs? How about ballistic missiles? Mole earth machines? Or combat suits? No, it won't. It's as useless as a nun in a whorehouse."

Oppenheimer opened his mouth. Patton took two quick steps, stopping in front of the physicist with balled fists, radiating menace. The general said, "Don't give me any bullshit about Brownian motion, Julius, or so help me, God—" Fred shouted at Patton to back away from the physicist or face disciplinary consequences. Patton took a step backward, but didn't sit down or unclench his fists.

The room was mired in awkward silence for a long moment until Vladimir spoke. "My work has nothing to do with physics. Robert is trying to goad General Patton with that contention. I don't blame George one bit for being angry." The general turned to face the barber and bowed from the waist. Vladimir gestured toward Patton's chair. "Please take your seat. Everyone, please, let me make clear what this program means to the Red Force. Bear with me. Be patient."

Patton sat down with an air of disapproval. Vladimir was about to start his explanation when the computer spit out another sheet of paper. The barber cum Marxist philosopher watched the paper fall into a hopper hungrily. With a show of willpower, he turned away from the mainframe and addressed his colleagues.

"There is a practical reason for charting the course of future history outside the insular environ of the CMG. We are raising two million children on this island. Those who survive the war will need to be integrated into a bizarre new world that we can't begin to imagine without the help of HP equations. Red Force adults born on the outside will face a hard time too. About 99 percent of our training must be geared toward winning the war. Yet the world will not stop changing. We can't wait years and years for the future world to unfold piece by piece and begrudgingly offer assimilation training in a reactionary manner." Vladimir pointed at the mainframe. "This program will show what the world will be like in 1951. We can offer succinct and hard-hitting courses in our schools that will make the transition to civilian life much easier."

"The world won't be that much different in 1951," Patton scoffed. Vladimir walked over to the hopper on the mainframe. He extracted the piece of paper that had been sitting there. As he did so, another sheet emerged from the machine. The Marxist theoretician quickly glanced at the information contained on the two sheets. He gave Patton a cool stare.

"Not that much different, General Patton? Within the next six months, Daimler-Ford-Alco will purchase IBM, the monopoly that manufactured this mainframe." Vladimir gave the computer a pat, as if it were a large, sedentary dog. "IBM also enjoys a monopoly on software. DFA will create viruses to destroy HP programs like the one currently running in this very room. DFA will make it impossible to run Historical Parallel programs charting the course of monopoly capitalism."

Vladimir turned over the top sheet and stared angrily at the one under it. He held that piece of paper over his head as if it were a shield. "Within one decade, DFA will have enough political power to attack all the unions that it has under contract. There will be a round of global strikes, which will fail, destroying unionism forever. After that, wages will go down. Classical Marxist predictions will take shape."

"How can a fucking monopoly get that kind of political power? Unions have plenty of muscle, tons of voters. A monopoly isn't the damn government," Patton asked, with a great deal less animosity than he'd displayed earlier. Another sheet of paper landed in the mainframe's hopper. Vladimir glanced through this missive before responding: "Business and government will increasingly rely on computers and software to run their bureaucracies. Monopoly status in these industries will give DFA power that transcends the economic sphere. Crushing unions will be nothing to the supermonopoly." Vladimir handed all the sheets of paper over to Stokes.

Another awkward silence settled on the room while Stokes devoured the information on the sheets. Fred looked at Oppenheimer and asked, "Robert, do you swear that running Vladimir's program is not cutting into computer time needed to design weapon systems?"

"Every physicist save myself is turning wrenches right now on the Fat Baby bomb and the Mole digging machine. In a few days, we are all sailing to Niihau to field-test the bomb and then back to Kauai to dig our first tunnel. The mainframe will sit idle the whole time."

"Very well, let Vladimir use the IBM for the next few days. I want to be notified if he uses it again. The primary mission of the Red Force is to win a war, not embark on a campaign of social change."

Vladimir watched Fred's face carefully as the SC said his good-byes and left the building. The head honcho's language was very suggestive at the tail end of the meeting. The SC had said something about a campaign for social change. Interestingly, Vladimir had never said anything about the Red Force changing the outside world. Vladimir had couched his request in terms of transitioning Red Force soldiers to a strange new world after the war, innocuous fare. The fact that Fred was even thinking about using Red Force outside the Hawaiian Islands was an immense step in the right direction.

Vladimir and Oppenheimer exchanged happy glances as Patton beat a hasty retreat. Stokes motored his electric wheelchair to the mainframe and placed the computer printouts back in the hopper. He spun around to face the center of the room. His hands shook with palsy. His voice trembled with rage and infirmity. "Right now, we're fiddling while Rome burns. The world is going to hell in a hand basket. The Red Force has to do something about it. I'm not long for this world. It's up to you two to convince the SC and General Hard-Ass." His rheumy eyes moved from the barber to the physicist challengingly. They inclined their heads respectfully toward him, accepting the challenge.

Chapter 2
The Blue Force Discovers Aether Physics

The air at the summit of Mauna Kea was too thin for Albert Einstein, making it nearly impossible to breath. He'd been up there before and knew that he would face respiratory problems when the arrogant astronomers invited him, his assistant, and every Blue Force senior engineer for a conference at the mountaintop astrophysics research center. Pride wouldn't let him decline the invitation or beg the stargazers to come down to sea level to deliver their findings.

The findings of astronomers, he thought angrily, already huffing and puffing as the car swung into the parking lot of the central observatory, *astronomers, not astrophysicists*. Einstein believed there was physics and there was astronomy. Astrophysics did not exist.

The car stopped rolling. Nkosinathi crunched the parking brake and pulled a small oxygen bottle and facemask from her handbag. He waved it away, a stubborn glint in his eye. He would not show weakness in front of the astronomers.

Nkosinathi could be stubborn too. "Flood your system with O^2 now, give yourself the strength to get inside the observatory and sit down quickly. Once seated, you might not need it again." He still looked mulish. She said reasonably, "Nobody is watching out here," and dangled the bottle enticingly. Einstein tried to make a sarcastic remark about her Falasha biochemistry allowing her to breath in near vacuum conditions. He opened his mouth to speak. A mouse-like squeak came out.

She put the O^2 mask over his face, strapped it on, and adjusted the valve. Strength flowed from his lungs out to his limbs. The breathing apparatus returned to Nkosinathi's purse. They entered the central observatory together. Einstein immediately took refuge in a front row seat before a large viewing screen. Nkosinathi sat next to him protectively. The auditorium was packed with impressive electronic equipment, rows of monitors yoked to the central telescope, mass spectrometers, ten-ton spectrographs, and other inspiring devices. By turning his head, Einstein could see that there was also a primitive cast iron bathtub filled with soapy water in the back of the room. A geometric shape made of wire was suspended by a piece of twine over this tub.

He scowled at the tub and the dangling wire shape. The astronomers were playing with Helix Geometry by studying the minimal surfaces created by soap film on wire figures representing galactic architecture. In other words, they were dabbling in physics, which was not part of the job description he'd assigned this research station. It also meant that they were serious about the existence of the Aether. The soap film represented an Aether substratum in their unauthorized helical model. The astronomers were using Helix Geometry to forge a Unified Field Theory based on the existence of an all-encompassing Aether. He looked toward the front of the auditorium, fuming. Forging a Unified Field Theory was Einstein's job.

A panel of astronomers was gathering before the large viewing screen, ready to make their presentation. The chief engineers from the weapon labs and armory had all filtered into the room. Einstein noticed that the astronomers had taken to wearing their hair long. Some of the shoulder length hairstyles were artificially streaked blonde in cunning patterns that accentuated the astronomers' facial features, making big noses look smaller, weak chins stronger. Traditionally, only physicists wore their hair that long. The astronomers weren't quite pulling off the look, assuming that emulating physicists was the goal. Real physicists had unruly long hair, often greasy and dirty, and it wasn't a fashion statement. Real physicists were too busy to get haircuts or groom themselves like poodles at a dog show.

One of the junior astronomers began the presentation by describing the latest technical improvement in telescope design. Laser beams shooting outward from a given telescope measured atmospheric distortion. This distortion was translated into code, rammed through a computer, and used to shape the telescope's outer flex-lens. For all practical purposes this eliminated atmospheric distortion, and....

Nkosinathi stopped the presentation. She told the panel that Professor Einstein did not like the high altitude. Nor was he concerned about the minutia of telescope design. The information on crystal iron molecules must be relayed at once. The weapon engineers sitting next to Nkosinathi gruffly chorused agreement.

Einstein gave his assistant a dirty look as she mentioned the words "high altitude." Admitting weakness in front of the coiffed poodles was not on his playbill. Despite all this, he felt grudgingly grateful when the astronomers danced to her tune and began offering the information that everyone in attendance craved.

Using burrowing mass spectrometry techniques, the astronomers had found entire planets consisting of individual crystal iron molecules. The cluster of micro-blackholes orbiting the galaxy's central blackhole had these crystal iron planets in their own orbits. Gravitron bombardment seemed to be the natural force converting regular iron into crystal iron. Since the soon to be completed supercollider would be able to focus gravitron particle beams, it should be able to manufacture crystal iron machine parts.

The astronomers had a suggestion for configuring the supercollider to this end. One of the junior astronomers passed out pieces of paper with design specifications that would enable the supercollider to create crystal iron and stable super heavy elements, metals four or five times more dense than uranium. Crystal iron and super heavy metals were vital to perfecting an array of military technologies.

Nkosinathi knew Herr Doctor Professor would be outraged that the stargazers were making suggestions concerning his precious supercollider and giving advice on building weapons. He would probably rage at them. She grew alarmed when he didn't say anything. Einstein's lips were turning blue. He was gasping for air. She pulled her personal microradio from her bag, cupped her hand over the mouthpiece, and called her husband. "Wolfgang, please drop everything, fly a chopper to the central telescope. I have a tactful medical emergency involving the Professor."

She announced loudly to the room, "Doctor Einstein will make his own design changes on the supercollider. We've heard enough." She hustled her boss out of the observatory auditorium, inconspicuously grabbing a sheet with the astronomers' recommended design changes and stuffing it into her bag. She clamped the tiny O^2 bottle to Einstein's face as soon as the other scientists were behind closed doors.

He took about five deep breaths and tore the mask off. She gave him the design sheet, folded up into a little square, which he pocketed without comment. Nkosinathi explained that a chopper was on its way. She wanted to know if he required her presence on the ride down to his lab in Hilo.

"No," Einstein wheezed. "Listen to the rest of the conference. Find out exactly what they are doing with Helix Geometry and Aether Physics. If they've made a breakthrough we need to know. Selfish arrogant bastards, keeping it to themselves to wheedle appropriation funds." He put the O^2 mask back on voluntarily.

Nkosinathi patted the great man on the back as Wolfgang's personal chopper descended onto the gravel parking lot, narrowly missing one of the cars. Rotor wash from the spinning blades whipped Einstein's long gray hair back and forth as he stumbled toward the whirlybird. Wolfgang waved at him from the cockpit, signaling for speed. The helicopter interior could be pressurized, restoring Einstein's O^2 balance without a mask and oxygen bottle.

Once they were pressurized and underway, Wolfgang turned to his passenger and asked, "Professor why don't you order those flipping astronomers to your Hilo lab to make their reports? You *are* chief researcher." Einstein removed his facemask, filled his lungs with pressurized air, sunk into the chopper's upholstery gratefully, and said, "Astronomers consider themselves to be the premier scientists on the island. In reality, they are children playing with expensive toys, testing the theories of the real scientists: us physicists. Lately, the children have developed the bad habit of withholding data from the adults, trying to formulate their own theories. If I showed any weakness, they would become insufferable."

"Next time, fly up there in a powered combat suit. Put the fear of God in those A-holes. Wear the suit during the meeting. They're pressurized, nice and comfy too. Tell them it's part of your ongoing weapons research."

"By God, I like it! Could you teach me to use a PCS without anybody else watching?"

"I would be honored. Give the head of research valuable hands on experience to put on a suit. Tell you what, Doc, let's do it right now. The weapon chiefs are all at the conference you just left."

Einstein nodded vigorously, leaning into a steeply banked turn as Wolfgang changed course and worked his radio. The physicist indulged in a little daydream. He saw himself landing in front of the central telescope, clad in the silver splendor of a fully armed PCS Mark I. In his daydream, the ground actually shook under his feet as he slammed down with military power. The pea-brained astronomers inside the observatory scrambled out onto the parking lot, terrified expressions on their rabbit-like faces.

The chopper landed before Einstein could finish his daydream. He was going to kick in the front door of the observatory. He twitched in mild irritation at the lost daydream and then brightened. It would be more satisfying to do it in real life.

Before exiting the chopper, Wolfgang told Einstein that the boys in the armory had a customized training suit, ready to go, that would fit the professor like a second skin. It was odd that a custom suit already existed. Certainly, the Army would like him to devote more time to suit design. Was the Army manipulating him? It made no difference, anything to swat the pseudo-scientists on the mountain into place.

The professor's resolve was tested when a pair of technicians wheeled his customized training suit out of the armory building on a small electric cart. They dumped it on a lawn next to the helicopter and went back inside.

Wolfgang and Einstein hopped out of the chopper. Ducking low to avoid the slow swing of the rotor blades, they sidled up to the training suit. Black letters were embossed on the shiny surface of the breastplate: Albert Einstein, Chief of Research.

The PCS Mark I looked remarkably like a 1920 CMG Charioteer hard suit. It had fat stovepipe arms and legs, a cylindrical torso, a clear plastic helmet tinted blue, a pair of ducted propellers sprouted from the upper back. To the naked eye, the only difference between the original hard suit and the Mark I was the light machineguns extruding from either forearm. A naked eye comparison was misleading. The Mark I was as much like the 1920 hard suit as the latest Wasp fighter jet was to a canvas and wood Fokker biplane.

Having done most of the design work for the PCS Mark I, Einstein knew how to activate the suit. He put his thumb on a sensor pad next to the embossed lettering. Suit computers read his thumbprint. The helmet tilted back and flopped over the right half of the torso, the torso itself creaked open clamshell fashion. With help, he could now step into the lower half of the suit as if he were stepping into a pair of metal trousers.

The two beefy technicians that had abandoned Einstein's suit were wheeling their electric cart across the lawn with a second PCS. Einstein pointed at his suit, a request for help. Wolfgang said, "A modicum of patience, Herr Doctor Professor. We'll both get inside our suits. Then I must give you a tutorial." Einstein wanted to complain that he was the principal designer of the Mark I. If anything, he should give Wolfgang a tutorial. He held his tongue. Besides being the greatest theorist in all of history, besides recently proving that he was also a great engineer, Einstein was a realist. Wolfgang had trained hundreds of cadets in suit operations. Einstein had never even worn a suit. Theory and practice seldom dovetailed exactly.

The second suit was placed next to the first. Under the letters spelling out Wolfgang's name and rank there were more letters delineating this suit as a combat model. Einstein couldn't see any difference between the two models, nor could he remember designing a training model.

Wolfgang told his student that they would get inside their Mark Is and walk carefully around the armory building to a training ground in the back. Remaining earthbound, they would work their way through the par course, only then would they fly the suits. Whether grounded or in flight, they would communicate by carefully aimed tight beam transmissions, a vital precaution to keep suit radio signals from leaving the island boundaries and be intercepted by the Red Force.

The two beefy techs grabbed Einstein by the armpits and plopped him into the trainer. He jammed his arms as far as they would go into the distended suit arms. The clamshell torso automatically closed. The helmet clamped down on his head. A flexible and ultra-slender needle jabbed into his spine at the base of his skull. Einstein's nervous system and the suit's electronic neural network were yoked, connecting the man to suit computers and sensors, making him something more than a mere human being.

He'd always thought that being locked into the titanium confines of a PCS would be claustrophobic. The opposite was true. The suit really did feel like a second skin. Its calf leather padded interior was buttery smooth against his body, the air-conditioned interior deliciously cool. Enhanced vision and hearing combined with neural linked radar gave a God-like awareness of the immediate environment. He stood there drinking in the altered state of consciousness, aching to lift his arms and fly, when a draft tickled his left big toe.

He tilted his chin inside the blue tinted helmet to look at his foot. The suit armor had a hole on the tip of the left boot. His big toe was exposed to the elements. This was the difference between a training suit and a combat suit. *Die Sáche gefält mir nicht*, he thought worriedly, reverting to German because of the uncomfortable situation. *This bothers me.*

Wolfgang confirmed his suspicions by tight beam. The hole in the left boot was deliberate. Raw cadets felt invulnerable when they first put on the PCS Mark I. A hole in the armor taught them to be careful. Einstein continued looking at his naked big toe. An insect actually landed on the toenail, and buzzed away. It could have stung him!

His instructor was walking around the building. Einstein took a step forward. Leg and arm servomotors obeyed the nerve impulses that drove his flesh and blood muscles. He clomped forward with the speed and balance of an unsuited man. He moved a little faster. Internal gyroscopes kicked in. Now his balance was better than an ordinary man's. A feeling of exhilaration set his heart racing. The suited Wolfgang was only a few yards ahead. Einstein could pass the general and get to the par course first. He started running.

A small stone bounced against his exposed left toe. His head tilted down again. The run became a trot. Instead of an Achilles' heel, he had an Achilles' toe. His pace slowed from a trot to an amble. Wolfgang's voice filled his helmet. "At the entrance to the course a boulder is buried. Please dig it up."

The armory was a dome shaped steel-reinforced concrete structure, painted green and camouflaged with plastic foliage. It blended well with the surrounding jungle. The par course was a mowed lawn, bordered by gardens and trees, with a series of obstacles and tasks every twenty yards. An unobtrusive white sign signaled the beginning of the course. The tip of a huge rock protruded from the ground next to this sign. It showed evidence of having been dug up and repacked into the volcanic soil many times.

His instructions called for digging the rock out of the ground. Instead, Einstein clomped up next to the monolith, squatted, pressed titanium alloy claws into the exposed mantle, and tore the thing out of the earth in one fluid movement. He hefted it over his head and tossed it away. The boulder bounced down a path and collided with a tree, flattening it. The feeling of exhilaration returned: Achilles' toe or no Achilles' toe.

Wolfgang whistled with heartfelt appreciation, adding, "That is a record time for accomplishing the first task of the par course. Not bad for an egghead. Let's skip the course and do a little flying, then we talk of other matters. Raise your hands and deliberately think the word *Fliegen*." Most suits were programmed for English commands. Einstein's suit was different, it responded to German.

"After the command is accepted, flex your deltoid muscles, the nerve endings controlling flight motors are within this group. It's not like leg and arm servomotors. You must feel for flight motors with your mind," Wolfgang instructed.

Einstein didn't really need such elementary instructions concerning his own invention. He kept quiet, raised his hands, and thought the word Fliegen. He then felt for the flight motors with the proscribed muscle group. The two ducted fans on his back began spinning, biting into the thick atmosphere of sea level. The professor found that he could control the flight mechanism without tensing any muscles in his back. He gradually ascended, Wolfgang at his side.

Even though the PCS Mark I was largely the offspring of Einstein's genius, he'd never worn a suit before and he should be experiencing the same control problems of any neophyte. But he was having no problems at all. The suit was familiar to him on many levels, a reflection of his thoughts, even his beliefs. Controlling the machine came easy, much easier than a typical trainee.

Wolfgang instructed his student to hover in one spot. They engaged in a hovering contest. The two suits bounced up and down gently over the dome shaped armory building. Einstein considered the motion of the two Mark Is to be an excellent example of classical relativity. Without activating the heads up altimeter display on the inside of the faceplate, there was no way to know who was winning the contest. Was Wolfgang moving up, or was he moving down, or both?

He looked past his instructor to the shoreline of the verdant island protruding from the sparkling sea like a great emerald, a living thing, pulsing with vitality. The whole universe seemed alive, part of a ubiquitous Godhead. *To be alive in a time of technical marvels*, the thought almost made Einstein weep. If he had been born a couple of decades earlier, none of this would be possible.

Power depletion chimes beeped softly in their helmets at about the same time. Wolfgang and Einstein dropped their suits toward the doorstep of the armory building. They both sent a tight beam message to the antennae protruding from the tip of the dome, informing the techs that the training session was over. Their landings were feather light. Wolfgang slowly and deliberately thought the word, *Open*. Einstein thought the word, *Offen*.

The clamshell function tilted the helmet back and split the torso into two halves on either suit. The efficient technical assistants helped Einstein exit his machine. Wolfgang sprang out as nimbly as a gymnast. The suits were carted inside. Trainer and trainee were left alone, sitting on the steps of the round building.

"The batteries lasted for a shorter time than I'd imagined," Einstein remarked. Wolfgang moved toward his chopper, talking and walking at the same time. "They will last half as long once forcefields and electronic camouflage systems are installed. Combat conditions will cut that down further. Three words solve all problems: onboard micro-fusion reactors."

Einstein jumped to his feet and stepped quickly to avoid being left behind. He didn't bother responding to the taunt about fusion reactors. That technology was a long ways off. Before they could do more than tinker with fusion power plants, fission bombs had to be designed, built, and tested. Next, fusion bombs and full-sized ballistic missiles had to be built. Somewhere along the way, the manufacturing of crystal iron machine parts had to occur. When all that was done, they would tackle fusion reactors. The biggest hurtle would be achieving a total understanding of the quixotic plasma bubbles at the heart of any possible fusion generator. So far, these clouds of superheated electrically charged ions and free electrons collapsed at the slightest disturbance, like a soufflé. Total understanding of plasma cloud dynamics would not come until a Grand Unified Field Theory was perfected. He stopped mentally listing all the tasks that lay ahead. It was too daunting.

They entered the chopper. Instead of starting the engine, Wolfgang turned to the professor with a beseeching look, a dangerous look. Einstein suddenly wanted to scramble out of the helicopter, to escape as if his life were in danger. Wolfgang's beseeching look transformed into anger. He asked, "Albert, you know what question I am going to pose, don't you? You are afraid of my question, aren't you?"

"Of course not. I have no idea," Einstein lied, poorly. Wolfgang asked harshly, "Is Nkosinathi sleeping with Supreme Commander Halifax?"

"No, please," Einstein begged. "Do not ask. I am a physical scientist, not a social scientist. I don't deal well with people. I am poorly suited to untangle your love life. Please don't pressgang me into an undertaking I cannot perform."

Wolfgang had his answer. His wife was unfaithful. He'd only wanted information from Einstein, not help dealing with his adulterous wife. Any action or retribution against the adulterers would have to come from Wolfgang and no one else. *Or did it?* The general's train of thought took an abrupt shift. Perhaps he could use Einstein as a cudgel against Nkosinathi and Jeremiah. The great physicist ultimately controlled the fate of the Blue Force and the outcome of the 1950 CMG. The spies were reasonably sure that Blue Force technology was pulling ahead of Red Force at a substantial pace. Einstein was the engine driving the rapid advance. It was probably not an overstatement to say that without Einstein, the Blue Force could not win the war.

What other weapon did Wolfgang have to wield against his superior, the highest-ranking officer in the entire Blue Force? Could he politely ask Halifax to quit screwing his wife? Beg Nkosinathi to be loyal? Grovel on his belly like a worm? How could an Uberman grovel? No, Einstein would be his weapon. Wolfgang wasn't sure how, only that he would think of something. Step one was to befriend the super-genius.

Wolfgang was ready to apologize for causing Einstein any consternation, when it proved unnecessary, or at least impractical. The physicist's attention had wandered and his nose was buried in the design specifications the astronomers had drafted for his pride and joy, the uncompleted superconducting atom-smasher. This got Wolfgang's attention since he'd helped oversee the earthmoving project that pre-staged actual construction.

"They don't even want to find and categorize subatomic particles. The so-called astrophysicists claim my baby shouldn't even be a research tool. The stargazers want to make it into a manufacturing plant for crystal iron machine parts and super heavy elements." Einstein sounded as if the astronomers had proposed killing every infant on the island.

Wolfgang wanted to know why researchers under Einstein's titular command would propose such a radical departure from established plans. The professor said simply, "Aether Physics." The general demanded a fuller explanation.

Einstein puzzled over the best way to explain Aether Physics in simple terms. He then gave Wolfgang what he wanted, perhaps more than he wanted.

The scientists on top the mountain had arrived at a kind of Unified Field Theory based on the premise that the interstellar void was filled with an all-encompassing medium called the Aether. According to this theory, Dynamic Aether fluid was the very fabric of space. Aether Physics (AP) held that a subatomic particle was a concentrated and very tiny vortex within the Aether fabric. The wave/particle phenomenon was a result of subatomic vortex spin. Different particles have different spin phases. Therefore, the number of possible subatomic particles is infinite. Therefore, categorizing the infinite subatomic zoo was an unending task and research-only atom-smashers are a colossal waste of time and money.

Wolfgang wasn't altogether ignorant of the finer points of modern physics. He asked, "Relativity states that gravity bends space, right? Light follows the curve of space?" Einstein replied, "Aether Physics theory states that Aether flows toward mass, thus causing gravity curvature and all gravitic phenomena. Aether flows and swirls away from dark energy, accounting for antigravity, antigravitrons, and so on. AP theory can also account for all the missing mass in the universe, something the standard model cannot."

"Could they be correct?" Wolfgang demanded. Having lied to the general once already, Einstein couldn't lie anymore, not even to himself. "Yes," he breathed. "Except, I haven't fully analyzed their work because I can't live on the mountain. I don't want to beg them to come to sea level and expose my weakness. Within Blue Force so much is made of a man or woman's rate of oxygen utilization. My altitude sickness is seen as a great failing. Efficient oxygen users such as the Falasha warriors are practically worshipped as Gods. And I can't download the data because the astronomers use different software than what we have in Hilo."

Wolfgang could see the pieces to his personal puzzle falling into place. He said firmly, "Nkosinathi is a brilliant physicist. She could live on the mountain for the next three or four weeks and learn everything the stargazers have to teach concerning AP theory."

Einstein's head rose out of the spec sheet, a chary look in his eye. Wolfgang continued: "I'll have you trained in PCS operations in two days. You can make surprise inspections up there any time, completely at random. Tell Nkosinathi to stay on the mountain no matter what, as if it were a death march. There is no greater task before the Blue Force at this moment than to decide if AP theory is valid. That in turn will decide the fate of the supercollider and the direction of all weapon programs."

The general's ulterior motive was glaring to Einstein. Supreme Commander Halifax would never be able to arrange a tryst with his illicit lover under the eyes of the astronomical team. Unfortunately, Wolfgang's proposal made perfect sense from a research and engineering standpoint. It would relieve the head of research of an enormous burden. No matter how loathsome Einstein found the astronomers, the work being done on the mountain had to be dealt with one way or another. It couldn't be dismissed out of hand, not with millions of lives at stake in the coming war.

Chopper blades beat the air. The helicopter's engine throbbed. They rose above the armory and headed down the coast toward the physics lab. Einstein's personal microradio chimed: a call from Nkosinathi. Personal communicators didn't operate on tight beams, so she was forced to be terse and cryptic. Einstein refused to learn Blue Force military codes.

"I've heard the long-hairs out, what they're willing to give anyway, a bit miffed that you aren't here. Shall I come home?"

"No, learn more. More about…" Einstein hesitated, wondering how to describe Helix Geometry and AP theory over open radio waves. "About diners waiting in straight lines that wrap around the lunch counter," he concluded, knowing that she would extrapolate his true meaning. She would ignore the silly reference to a lunch counter and grasp his intent about the decidedly un-straight lines that wrapped around the toroidal planes described by the geometry of Aether Physics.

"I can bully it out of them, given time. Are you sure you can manage without me?"

"Yes, I have a way to visit you. Stay there until I come for a visit in two days. Learn about the lines."

"I understand. Good-bye, Herr Doctor Professor."

"Good-bye, Nkosinathi."

The doorbell rang in Einstein's private residence. He knew an intrusion here didn't bode well. Supreme Commander Halifax was waiting on the other side of the door, even worse. Einstein invited the SC inside, putting a note of false joviality into his voice. "Jeremiah, good to see you. Please come in, take a seat while I break open a bottle of wine."

Jeremiah's suspicions were quickly enflamed. He asked why the professor had to fetch his own wine. Where was Nkosinathi? Einstein joined his guest in the sitting room, poured them both glasses of wine and explained the reason for his assistant's absence.

The supreme commander took in the story with admirable composure. He asked a pointed question, "Is this why construction on the supercollider has come to a halt?" Einstein agreed that this was the reason. Nkosinathi would make a full report on the science of Aether Physics to the chief of research. He would decide whether the collider should primarily hunt for subatomic particles, only manufacturing crystal iron machine parts and super heavy elements as an afterthought, or do nothing but manufacture exotic metal weapon components.

Jeremiah's eyes darted around the room as if he thought his lover might be hiding somewhere close by, perhaps behind the curtains. He drained his wine glass impatiently and held it out for a refill. An aura of pent up frustration permeating his every move.

"I should have been consulted before a decision of this magnitude was made," Jeremiah maintained. Einstein insisted that no decision had been made; the two of them would put their heads together before the final design configuration of the supercollider was set. Jeremiah grimaced and shook his head, disagreeing without stating his reasons. At that moment, Jeremiah was thinking with his penis. The SC was angrier over Nkosinathi's absence than the fate of the atom-smasher. Einstein didn't pick up on this, however. The physicist thought Jeremiah was questioning his scientific judgment.

"Supreme Commander, do you feel qualified to judge the validity of Aether Physics theory?" Einstein asked incredulously. This put the SC in an even fouler mood. "Yes," the military man said acidly. "I oversee every aspect of the Blue Force. And I have a master's degree in high-energy physics. Give me the basics."

Einstein eyelids drooped partway over his eyes, like flags lowering to half-mast. He'd forgotten that the SC's education was formidable. Jeremiah had even sat in on a few of Einstein's classes. The physicist shifted mental gears and became a professor. "Right, Aether Physics. Well, as you know, there is no love lost between the stargazers and myself. With that said, they are on to something. The standard model fails on the question of missing mass in the universe..." Einstein went to explain AP theory in greater detail than he'd used with Wolfgang. Unlike Wolfgang, Jeremiah was able to ask extremely penetrating questions. They discussed the exciting new theory for about a half hour. Jeremiah announced that he was so interested in this new branch of physics he was going to the Mauna Kea observatory to visit Nkosinathi and talk to the astronomical team directly.

Einstein thought, *In for a penny, in for a pound*, took a deep breath and said, "I'd rather not have her disturbed. Shutting down construction on the supercollider is enormously expensive. I need Nkosinathi to finish her work and report to me."

"Disturb her?" Jeremiah asked. "What does that mean? Whose idea was it to send her up the mountain?"

"General Bernhard's," Einstein admitted.

"I see. Hmmm, Herr Doctor Professor has gotten into the middle of a muddle. I guess I knew this day was coming. All right, never mind. Carry on, Albert."

The supreme commander drained what was left of his wine and left Einstein's house in an angry huff. The professor's head sunk until his chin was touching his chest, a gesture of pure anguish. There was nothing on Earth he hated more than dealing with romantic entanglements, especially among people that he had to work with. Human beings in small numbers were entirely unpredictable because HP equations only applied to groups of over one thousand. Human beings in small numbers that were in love were even more unpredictable. They made the uncertainty principle seem like simple arithmetic.

Einstein was willing to make only one prediction concerning his involvement in the Jeremiah/Nkosinathi/Wolfgang love triangle: It would quickly get more complicated than he could ever imagine.

Chapter 3

The First A-bomb: The First Electromagnetic Pulse

It was an important day for the Red Force. The tower on the northeastern point of Niihau was ready to accept its burden, Fat Baby, the world's first atom bomb. Steel cables on the self-propelled crane squealed in protest as the fifteen-ton bomb was lowered into the tower's cradle. Soldier-technicians swarmed up steel girders to wrench the bomb in place and connect it to detonation wires. The crane's caterpillar treads churned, taking it a few hundred yards away from Fat Baby. It would stay there during the explosion, part of the experiment. The crane would either be reduced to a puddle of molten steel or vaporized into super hot gas, depending on how loud the baby cried.

Oppenheimer ordered everyone onto dirt bikes and make for the beach. The electrical team brought up the rear, spooling out reams of detonation cable. Four small skiffs were waiting on the shoreline, transportation to the submarine: the viewing platform for the big show. The electricians were the last to leave the beach, they had to test and double-test the detonation system.

Standing ramrod straight on the submarine's conning tower, dripping from spray after the ride in the skiff, the head scientist waited for the electricians to get on board. Once every man was accounted for, the sub motored a couple miles away from the tiny island. Nobody was sure how strong the atomic blast might be.

Wilfred Stokes climbed up from the sub's interior to stand next to Oppenheimer and the senior staff of the Fat Baby project. After quadriplegia had laid him to waste, the aging inventor had given up his electric wheelchair for a quadruple amputation and a four way prosthetic transplant. Stokes might be as much machine as man, but he was no longer a quadriplegic.

Oppenheimer raised a pair of field glasses and trained them on the distant tower. He spoke to Stokes without lowering the glasses. "Wilfred, I would have thought assisting Vladimir in his Marxist HP equations would have proven more interesting than watching this giant firecracker go boom." He handed the amputee the field glasses. Stokes's mechanical hand crunched down on the casing of the binoculars. He was not yet able to completely control his artificially amplified strength. Luckily, the casing didn't break.

Stokes glanced at Fat Baby and the tower through the field glasses. Nothing had happened yet, the bomb sat in its tower unperturbed, waiting for oblivion.

The glasses were handed back. Stokes coughed wetly and said, "Vladimir's research is indeed more interesting and more important. I only get in his way. So I'll get in your way instead." Stokes coughed again, a racking, unhealthy sound. Science had yet to perfect prosthetic lungs.

One of the engineers on the platform jeered, "Bakunin's boring HP equations more interesting than exploding Fat Baby? I think not." Oppenheimer tapped an unobtrusive earpiece, hissed for silence, and began issuing orders. Sunglasses were passed out to everybody on top of the conning tower. Cameramen began filming Fat Baby through filtered lenses. An array of sensors, from decibel meters to radar dishes, was activated. The men and women huddled behind the blast shield. Instruments, dark glasses, and foreheads peeped over its tungsten steel rim.

A blinding sheet of white flame silently consumed the sky, casting immense shadows as black as night in all directions away from the epicenter. Oppenheimer screamed, "Bigger than we thought, duck!" Instruments were kept trained in the direction of the explosion. Heads were tucked under the blast shield. The initial shock wave hit an instant latter, tearing off hats and sunglasses, breaking some of the instruments, nearly rupturing eardrums. More than a sound, more than a concussion, it was a blow that slammed into the guts of every man and woman on the tower.

A savagely hot wind blew and blew, pushing the submarine away from the island. The stunned soldiers and scientists looked up into the sky. A towering mushroom cloud bulked over the small island, shimmering with yellow, orange, and pink pulses. It grew taller and wider, like a living thing, a sentient storm, an evil God looking down at the puny humans and their sub.

Oppenheimer stood shakily. Staring at the expanding mushroom cloud, he said solemnly, "I am death, the mighty destroyer of the world. All the warriors standing arrayed in the opposing armies shall cease to exist."

Stokes bent his prosthetic limbs a few times as he lay on the conning tower deck. For a couple of seconds, his bio-electronic hardware had gone dead, paralyzing the quadruple amputee. Shrugging off the bizarre (yet thankfully temporary) paralysis, he stood next to the head of Red Force's science division and asked, "Lord Krishna from the Bhagavad-Gita?" Oppenheimer nodded sadly. Stokes said, "Puts me more in mind of the fourth horseman of the apocalypse." He lowered his voice an octave and said, "I looked, and there before me was a pale horse! Its rider was named Death, and Hades was following close behind him."

"What does that put you in the mind of?" Oppenheimer pointed to a shining silver dot, floating above the submarine, drifting toward Kauai on the dying winds of Fat Baby's explosion. The dot disappeared and then reappeared like the sly wink of a celestial eye. Stokes seized his boss's binoculars, adjusted the focus to get a better look at the mysterious dot, and offered a running commentary. "It's a weather balloon. Now it's gone. Some sort of electronic camouflage's hiding it. I can see it again. The bomb blast must've shorted out the camouflage. I'm sure the thing is loaded with telemetric surveillance equipment."

Red Force High Command evidently agreed with Stokes; a pair of Wasp 23 fighters screamed out of Kauai, bent on capturing the Blue Force spy balloon with skyhook collectors. The jets got within a quarter-mile of their target and must have set off a proximity fuse inside the balloon's high-tech gondola because a tiny puff of fire erased the spy device from the sky. The Red Force jets banked hard and screeched away from the tiny puff, entering ever widening combat aero patrol patterns, looking for other Blue Force tricks.

"Don't stand there with your tongues in your mouth," Oppenheimer scolded the men and women on the conning tower. "Get the blast team into the crater. Collect the electronic data. Stow the gear inside the sub. Chop, chop, we're burning daylight."

Stokes and Oppenheimer were left standing alone on the submarine's steel tower. Stokes wondered if they should contact the Royal Navy. Blue Force's spy balloon had violated the pre-war CMG rules against territorial incursions. Oppenheimer stuck his hands in his pockets and muttered impatiently about the supreme commander dealing with CMG rules. In a louder voice he said, "Let's go watch Mole I begin its maiden voyage into the Earth."

Stokes was seized by another coughing jag. Oppenheimer smacked him on the back, grabbed an elbow, and led the sick old man down into the bowels of the sub. Even though it was only a fifteen-mile journey to Kauai, the trip was not comfortable. The submarine was designed to haul ore and dump it on the ocean floor. There was no place to sit comfortably inside the steel tube and no flat surfaces to stand on.

The sub crossed the narrow Kaulakahi Channel and loafed in front of the underwater lock of the rebuilt Waimea Dam. The Poipu coast was heavily patrolled by Red Force war seals in powered combat harnesses, ensuring that the clanking of the lock mechanism and the inevitable scraping of the sub's steel hull as it entered the lock would not be detected by Blue Force spy subs.

A short trip up Lake Waimea brought the submarine to a second underwater lock. This barrier was hurriedly crossed and the sub surfaced on a saltwater lake inside one of the vast concrete caverns left behind by the 1920 CMG Blue Force. Things were much they same here as they'd been in the first CMG, except this cavern was the hub of the world's most sophisticated mining operation, not a combat center. As was the case in 1920, the giant grotto was brightly illuminated by innumerable arc lights bolted into the concrete ceiling, only there were no weapons in sight, only mining cars, rail lines, and excavation equipment.

Stokes and Oppenheimer expected to be greeted by the chief engineer of the Mole project, Rudolf Diesel. In his place, General Patton was waiting on the saltwater lake's concrete shore as their small skiff made landfall. Oppenheimer had been wracked by conflicting emotions after the Fat Baby detonation and was in no mood to deal with General Hard-Ass. Before the two men could start fighting, Stokes asked Patton where Diesel was hiding.

An outstretched arm pointed mutely at Mole I, a machine several times larger than a standard diesel-electric locomotive, so tall it nearly scraped the bank of electric lights covering the ceiling. Mole I looked like a cross between an oversized locomotive and a panzer. Caterpillar treads jutted out from the undercarriage where one would expect to see wheels. The continuous miner was not visible from where Patton, Stokes, and Oppenheimer stood. This spiked cylindrical device was the mechanical equivalent of a pick and shovel, though it was one hundred thousand times more efficient than the traditional muscle power employed by miners everywhere else on the globe.

Diesel appeared on the top of Mole I, stooping low to avoid the electric lights. He was seventy years old, two years older than Stokes. But far from needing all his limbs replaced by prosthetics, the German inventor was as spry and limber as a man half his age. He saw Oppenheimer, gave a whoop, crawled down the back of the mighty digging machine, and walked across the cavern, jumping over the numerous railroad tracks that crosshatched the concrete floor.

While Diesel was still out of earshot, Oppenheimer faced Patton and asked, "George, why are you here? Aren't there soldiers on the island that need abuse?" Patton sneered at the head of the science division and asked blandly, "How did the Fat Baby test go?" Diesel arrived in time to hear Oppenheimer's answer: "Fat Baby cried much stronger than expected. We'll need to massage data to know how much stronger, actually."

Patton's sneer became a granite stare. "Massage it on the mainframe?" he asked. "Will Bakunin be sent packing?" Oppenheimer leaned away from the general and said coldly, "If Vladimir is finished, then he'll be sent packing. If not, the mainframe is his and my people will work with pencil and paper." The granite in Patton's stare became diamond hard as he said, "I'll explain why I'm here. We finish with Mole I, and then we mosey to the computer lab. Supreme Commander Banner wants me to settle the question of running HP equations one way or another."

All Diesel heard was: "finish with Mole I." He began an excited monolog concerning the drill bits in the continuous miner, giving breathless details about the self-sharpening qualities of the boron carbine ceramic tips. Oppenheimer stopped the boyish seventy-year-old and asked if Mole I was ready to go to ground this instant. Diesel informed him that the maiden voyage would begin in about four hours. Much to Diesel's disappointment, he lost his audience. Oppenheimer told the head of the Mole project to proceed as per schedule. They'd all be back before the day was over to check on the progress of his gigantic digging machine.

Stokes, Patton, and Oppenheimer took an elevator out of the mining cavern. Diesel saw to it that a car and driver were at their disposal at the top of the canyon wall. The car sped down from the Waimea heights to the computer lab in the seaside town of Fort Elizabeth, pitching around turns as Patton spoke in a low voice, so low that the driver couldn't hear. "As Red Force monkeys around with Historical Parallelism, Blue Force is building some damn impressive war machines. This spy balloon, it had some kind of electronic camouflage?"

Stokes was sitting on the far side of the backseat, away from the other two, but with his hearing aid turned up to full volume he could hear everything Patton had to say. Oppenheimer sat in the middle, able to hear Patton, yet ignoring his question. Stokes leaned over Oppenheimer and said quietly, "I got a better look at the spy balloon than anybody. This is my theory: a small, wide-angle TV camera was mounted on top of the balloon. An image of the surrounding sky was projected onto the fabric of the hydrogen gasbag from the gondola. The bottom of the gondola must have been a curved television screen made of a non-reflective, radar-absorbing material."

"Bingo," Oppenheimer cried, loud enough for the driver to hear. "And the electromagnetic pulse of the A-bomb knocked out the television projector. Brilliant deduction, Wilfred."

"Yeah, yeah, brilliant," Patton said in a brittle tone. "Maybe you eggheads will get off your asses and figure out why Red Force sensors couldn't pick up the spy balloon's radio transmission once I yank Vladimir back into his barber chair."

Oppenheimer became reticent and withdrawn after Patton brought up the subject of undetectable Blue Force radio transmissions. He had no idea how enemy radio signals could be transmitted from a spy balloon to the Big Island and yet remain undetected by Red Force receivers on Kauai. What really disturbed Oppenheimer was the possibility of enemy technological advances based on superior theoretical physics. He feared Albert Einstein.

Stokes grew as silent and withdrawn as Oppenheimer, rubbing one of his prosthetic arms with a mechanical hand, reliving the crippling effect he'd experienced during the electromagnetic pulse. Here too was a little understood technology, capable of dismantling other technologies, a predatory technology. The pulse would have fried his pacemaker and killed him if it had been any stronger. Stokes hoped that electromagnetic pulses would never be turned into weapons or people like him, people with mechanical implants, would be wiped out in the war.

The car maneuvered through the narrow cobblestone streets of Fort Elizabeth. Italian craftsmen had built the town in the early 1900s, before the first CMG. It was old enough, and close enough to the Pacific, to have acquired a weathered look. They drove past a Mediterranean style town square, complete with a gushing fountain and marble statues. Oppenheimer reflected on the fact that Kauai had suffered virtually no damage in the last war. After the torrent of Commonwealth money poured into the island nation, its infrastructure, public art, and archictecture rivaled many small European nations. The probability that Blue Force nuclear weapons were certain to incinerate the island paradise was disquieting.

The top scientist heard Patton asking something or other about dinner. Oppenheimer looked at his wristwatch. It was six o'clock in the evening. Neither he nor Stokes had eaten anything since breakfast. The car pulled next to a café in the center of Fort Elizabeth, across the street from a Catholic cathedral that could have been transplanted from any part of Italy. The three men took a table on the sidewalk.

The café also had an indoor dining room. Patton looked at the diners inside through a plate glass window. The general's suspicions flared. There were no women, low-ranking officers, or soldiers, only male senior officers. He recognized Danny O'Brien, the former chief of San Francisco's police department. The other tables held officers that had once been police chiefs in the United States, Canada, and Mexico, an odd coincidence. Some of these officers served under Patton's command. He knew they were all radical socialists, competent, tough, hard working, but politically extreme as all hell, a strange gathering.

Patton tapped on the plate glass window, waving at O'Brien, signaling for the major to join them outside. It didn't take the fifth degree to find out what the leftist officers were doing at the café. O'Brien told them flat out that Vladimir Bakunin had finished the first stage of his Marxist HP algorithm and would make a presentation at seven o'clock to a group of representatives from the Communist International, right here at the café.

The faces of Stokes and Oppenheimer went white as sheets. O'Brien looked at the scientists scornfully and addressed their unspoken concerns. "The International has converted Red Force's scientific community. We have most of the common soldiers. Time to let the cat out of the bag and find out if High Command is with us or against us."

Patton gripped the edges of the table to keep from striking O'Brien. The general had suspected something fishy was going on with the Red Force for a while. A thousand tiny clues had slowly built up over the past two years, including whispered conversations abruptly stopped as he walked by, the omnipresent Marxist literature that the men had brought from the mainland, and the plethora of radical policemen filling the ranks of the officer cadre.

Forcing every ounce of self-control he possessed into his voice, the general asked, "A communist cabal wants to hijack Red Force? Instigate a global revolution? Does Banner know?"

Vladimir chose that moment to pull up to the café on a military motorcycle, wearing a neatly pressed dress uniform. Like everyone on the island, he was a soldier. Rather than answer Patton's questions, O'Brien silently followed Vladimir inside. Stokes, Oppenheimer, and Patton trooped in behind O'Brien and found a spot in the back of the crowded room to stand. Steam was practically shooting from Patton's ears as he stood there, seething. Somehow he managed to contain his temper and remain silent.

The short black man found his way to a podium that had been set up near the kitchen. He looked over his audience, eyes lingering on General Patton. Vladimir spoke into a microphone, noting that a representative from the General Staff was present, thanked Patton for being there, and then jumped into his topic by presenting a list of garden variety monopolies that Daimler-Ford-Alco (the supermonopoly) would purchase in the next year: Standard Oil, Maxim Gun Works, Maxim Aviation, International Business Machines, Caterpillar Tractors… The list was extensive and took nearly ten minutes to recite. He gave the date that each company would be purchased and the approximate price. He explained how the purchase of different monopolies awarded different kinds of political power to the supermonopoly.

Example 1: Acquiring IBM would allow DFA to prevent universities from writing Historical Parallel programs like the one Vladimir was running. Example 2: Ownership of Caterpillar Tractors, Acme Fertilizers, and the railroads will give DFA control over regional agricultural production and distribution, allowing it to fight large regional strikes with regional famines. He gave over thirty separate examples.

Some of the Marxist officers were taking notes. Vladimir told them to stop creating a paper trail, even here, among comrades. A complete read-out would be given to Wilfred Stokes. Every HP prediction would be tested (by Stokes) against the daily information flowing into the island from America, Europe, and Asia via radio and television. Once the notes were torn up and notebooks put away, Vladimir gave a broad outline of the next one hundred twenty years of future history.

After DFA seizes the bulk of the world's heavy industry, its next move will be to establish competition within the global supermonopoly. For instance: four or five separate divisions will be carved out of DFA's core automobile business. Old brand names such as Ashfield, Duryea, and Rolls-Royce will be restituted. DFA's auto divisions will truly compete against each other, but in a controlled manner, a rough echo of the capitalism that had come before. DFA will reorder the workings of global capitalism from a decentralized and disorderly free-for-all to a top-heavy command economy run from the supermonopoly's headquarters in Tokyo. Free market capitalism will be replaced by monopoly capitalism.

As long as the Commonwealth's many unions remain intact, worker pay will not be dramatically slashed. Once the supermonopoly breaks the unions around midcentury, labor will get hammered. DFA will never control more than 50 percent of the global means of production through economic means. Its buying spree of other companies will drive up the cost of the purchases. The only economic tactic to counter this trend will be to ruthlessly lower wages and wring greater production from its workforce, triggering global deflation on a consumer level. When economic means are exhausted, the supermonopoly will acquire political power. A highly centralized totalitarian dictatorship will arise, a cruel parody of socialism. HP equations predict that the authoritarian plutocracy will be amazingly stable. A second Dark Age will linger for centuries.

Vladimir stared directly at General Patton and said, "In light of my latest findings I am forced to make a recommendation to the General Staff. By 1950, when the CMG is scheduled to begin, Red Force must attack the Commonwealth capital cities of London, Washington DC, Lsandhlwara, Berlin, and Tokyo with Intercontinental Ballistic Missiles armed with nuclear warheads."

The room erupted in frenzied applause. Patton shouted over the noise, "This is madness. How can we simultaneously beat Blue Force and the combined might of the Commonwealth?" The objection heartened Vladimir. Patton was raising a strategic question, not criticizing the core Marxist strategy of abandoning the war game. Of course, the politically astute military man could be trying to draw the Marxists out and lay bare their plans. *Too late, now or never*, Vladimir thought, deciding to trust Patton and reveal everything.

"The Communist International has shock troops in Asia, Africa, Australia, Europe, and the Americas in the form of secret communist police cells, sleeper cells we can activate and control. The officers in this room painstakingly built those cells after the World War. Blue Force will be preparing to fight the 1950 CMG while Red Force prepares to fight World War II."

The Marxist officers, Vladimir, Oppenheimer, and Stokes held their breath and studied Patton's reaction. The general's face became a storm of emotion when Vladimir threw out the term: "World War II." The hunger for glory, the desire to play a major role in a grand conflagration, had left the normally loquacious Patton unable to speak. Vladimir spoke into the tongue-tied flux of Patton's confusion, "In the Republic, Plato says: 'Until philosophers are kings... and political greatness and wisdom meet in one... will our state have a possibility of life and behold the light of day'. The Communist International seeks to make Red Force Supreme Commander Frederick Banner into the philosopher king of a worldwide Marxist police state. The Communist International's vast network of sleeper cells will form the nucleolus of a dictatorship of the proletariat."

Patton said, "You haven't said how we'll beat the Blue Force. Something else you people haven't thought through: We can't attack Berlin and Lsandhlwara with nuclear weapons. Our Uberman and Impi soldiers have their genetic identities cryogenically stored in these cities. Hell, I'm part of the Uberman program. They've got buckets of my frozen sperm on tap in Berlin. My little guys are one of the only batches they'll use in artificial insemination. I must have two hundred kids I've never seen in Germany. Never mind that. Our strategy must be to threaten nuclear annihilation against great swaths of the globe, not destroy the whole damn planet. Even I know Marxism is predicated on the idea of seizing the means of production, not blowing it to hell and back. We have to hold the civilian world hostage at nuclear gunpoint and defeat enemy armies in detail. And we can't do that from here. We can't fight a world war from this crappy little island. And we sure as hell have to attack Blue Force in Hawaii before they expect it, years before they expect it. If we can't take out Blue Force with nukes, all your plans are nothing more than horseshit."

Vladimir was going to insist that issues like that were a matter for High Command to take up after the decision had been made to fight for a new world order, rather than another CMG. He stopped short when he saw Oppenheimer getting ready to whisper something to Patton. The rest of the room was breathing by now, but just barely.

The top scientist cupped a hand near the general's ear and said quietly, "George, I think the Moles can get the Red Army away from the island by tunneling under the seabed and building sub pens in the Earth's crust. Submarines can take us anywhere." This was the first time that anybody had used the term Red Army rather than Red Force.

Patton whispered in Oppenheimer's ear, "Dammit man, tell me the truth. Is long range Historical Parallelism the real deal?" The scientist assured the general that Vladimir's predictions would come true, one by one. Validation would come as easily as turning on a television set and watching the financial news. Oppenheimer reminded Patton that they'd all seen Vladimir's short range prediction come true before.

Patton told the Red Force officers to wait inside while he had a talk outside with his grandfather, George S. Patton the first. He left the astonished men and walked out onto the street. The sun was sinking into the Pacific behind the cathedral, casting an orange halo into a bank of clouds. Patton saw an image of an officer in a confederate uniform coalesce out of the abstract shapes of backlit clouds. The apparition had the same homely face as the flesh and blood man looking out into the sky. George Patton III either heard or thought he heard George Patton I speak.

"Patton men are warriors. We don't play war games. A choice between real war and a war game is no choice."

"This communist bullshit has me worried. I don't know, Gramps. I hate politics. I crave the clean world of combat."

"Look here, sonny boy, communism will give you that clean world of combat. It will give you a real war, the greatest war ever: World War II. Be a man. Be a Patton. Stand up and embrace your destiny."

His grandfather's ghost could give no more unambiguous advice than that. Patton tasted the words "World War II" in his mouth as if he were sampling a fine wine. World War II would dwarf World War I. It would be bigger than all the wars in history combined because it wouldn't be nation fighting nation, but economic system verse economic system; a war of ideology. To be alive at such a time was a miracle, a blessing. If communism could deliver a miracle, then it was a blessed creed. He saluted the cloud formation that resembled his grandfather, did a military about face, and walked back into the café.

The general marched through the ranks of communist officers, approached the podium, and eased Vladimir aside. The Russian philosopher hesitated and then stepped away graciously, recognizing the look in Patton's face as victory for the cause.

"Listen up, Red Force," Patton growled. "From this day forward we train to conquer the world. We're going to install Supreme Commander Banner as prime minister for life at Ten Downing Street under a red flag."

A cheer arose from the assemblage. Patton said, "Comrades, where is your Marxist discipline? I'd expect an outburst like that from the bourgeois ranks of the lily-livered Blue Force, not from the disciplined cadre of communist police officers that have secretly fanned the flames of revolution for decades."

The officers would have liked to cheer after hearing that kind of praise. But iron Marxist discipline gripped the cadre like a Bulldog on a buffalo. Jaws clamped shut, steely eyes were trained front and center. They sat ramrod straight, attentive to every word spoken by the newly converted general.

"Now I want you to remember that no bastard ever won a war by dying for his cause. You won it by making the other poor dumb bastard die for his cause. I'll tell you why we're going to win this war. Communist ardor gives us a natural advantage over Blue Force and the corrupt capitalist armies of the putrid Commonwealth. The antithesis of communism is individuality. An army lives, sleeps, and fights as a team. Those bilious bastards that write about individuality in combat know as much about real war as they do about fornication.

"I pity the capitalist bastards we're going against. My God, I do. We're not just going to shoot the bastards, we're going to cut out their living guts and grease the fans of our nuclear powered hovercrafts with them. We're going to go through the Blue Force and the Commonwealth like crap through a goose. Blue Force is the enemy. The Commonwealth military machine is the enemy. Wade into them. Smash open their combat suits and shoot them in the belly. Spill their blood.

"When we land in Asia, Africa, America, and Europe there will be a hellacious amount of land to conquer. I don't want to hear anything about holding our positions. The only thing we're going to hold is the bourgeoisie by the nose while we kick him in the ass.

"I will be proud to lead you wonderful guys into battle any time, on any continent, until we win this war and shine the holy light of communism on every dark corner of this blighted globe. That is all."

The officers didn't break into undisciplined cries of approval or hand clapping. Spontaneously, to a man, they broke out into the communist anthem, the Internationale.

Arise ye workers from your slumbers
Arise ye prisoners of want
For reason in revolt now thunders
And at last ends the age of cant.
Away with all your superstition
Servile masses arise, arise
We'll change henceforth the old tradition
And spurn the dust to win the prize.

Patton's bushy eyebrows lowered over cruel glittering eyes. He pointed a finger at Vladimir, then a thumb at the car outside. The general and the philosopher walked out together, to the thunderous chorus of the revolutionary song. They sat in the backseat of the Daimler-Ford. Vladimir said, "Better learn the lyrics to that song, General. We communists put great stock in symbolism."

The driver grinned at Vladimir's taunt. He must have heard the lyrics of the Internationale and formed a pretty good idea of the political undercurrent about to surge through the Red Force.

"Driver, take us to the supreme commander's private residence," Patton said to the obviously communist private in the front seat, ignoring the soldier's smile and Vladimir's admonition. The car pulled away from the curb. Patton asked himself, *Am I the only non-communist on this fucking island?* He unbuttoned his service tunic and stretched his legs. *No, I'm as red as any of them. By God, that little pinko Vladimir is right, we're either all communists or we're all dead.* The general began humming the Internationale. Vladimir and the driver joined the general by softly mouthing the words of the Red Army's battle song.

Mole I had dug far enough into the Earth that Diesel needed to think about calling a halt to the tunneling and finish mapping the overall design of the Red Force tunnel fortress. His goal was to find the Molokai Fracture, a seam in the Earth's crust that ran between the Hawaiian Islands and Mexico's Baja Peninsula.

If not for the Fat Baby explosion, the mapping process would have been impossible. Cartographic seismographs had been set up before the atom bomb test to use its blast waves to pinpoint the eastern mouth of the Molokai fracture, giving Diesel a crude idea of the tectonic features he was up against.

From the bridge of Mole I, Diesel called up the tectonic map from his personal computer, and issued instructions to the bridge crew: "Maintain angle of attack. Bring the Mole two degrees starboard." A chorus of "Aye-ayes" followed the order. He turned in his captain's chair to face the communication specialist. "Ensign, raise the shoring battle-lion and the dispersal battle-lion. I want progress reports on their operations."

Mole I was a spearhead that capped the shoring battle-lion and the dispersal battle-lion: two extensive mechanized support units connecting the digging machine to the surface.

In the lower regions of the mine, right on the tail of the Mole, the shoring battle-lion turned the Mole's crude tunnel into a true industrial mine. It also built and maintained an oxygen pipeline that pumped refrigerated O_2 into the depths of the mine, keeping the air cold enough and oxygen rich enough to sustain human life. Its most involved task was to throw a shoring structure around the exposed rock/earth walls of the burrow and spray this structure with quick hardening concrete.

In the upper regions of the mine, the dispersal battle-lion's first mission was to operate the refrigerated O_2 pumping station, the lifeline that kept the shoring battle-lion alive. Dispersal's next most important mission was separating ore from useless detritus. The former was hauled to smelters on the rim of Waimea Canyon. The latter was loaded into submarines and dispersed onto the ocean floor.

While he waited for shoring and dispersal to make their reports, Diesel wondered why Oppenheimer hadn't been present when the Mole began its epic journey. The top scientist had certainly been there when Fat Baby exploded. Diesel could guess why his project was being snubbed. The atom bomb project had become glamorous and sexy. The officers and men associated with it were acting increasingly snobby, making up slang terms for Mole I like "earth pig" or "tunnel rat." Diesel had a feeling that would all change as the war got closer and Blue Force developed its own nuclear weapons. Earth pigs might not be sexy, but they offered the only defense against the Blue Force hydrogen bombs that were to come. He'd like to hear what the snobs had to say then.

Chapter 4

Horatio, Ever Heard of War Mammoths and Combat Apes?

T he Crown Princess needed to know more about Fred Greystone. She needed to know why Greystone had started breeding gorillas to speak sign language in 1900. She also wanted to understand what had possessed the world's greatest expert on animal husbandry to recreate the extinct Imperial Mammoth a decade later. Something powerful had driven Greystone and it wasn't merely the desire to improve baiting contests. He had even worked from his deathbed in the last days of his life. Perhaps the Princess could find answers in one of the royal family's personal journals.

Thumbing through her late half-brother's diary was a painful exercise. Of all the royal journals, this one was the most difficult for her to read. Princess Victoria knew it was unlikely to yield anything that she hadn't already digested innumerable times before. She read anyway, helpless to stop, like poking a sore tooth with one's tongue. Maybe if she read between the lines a clue to Greystone's behavior would emerge. She buried her nose in the handwritten volume, letting it transport her back to 1910, the year Crown Prince Albert had died, two years before she'd been born...

The World War had been over for a decade and the royal family's rasion de' être continued to be the production of the finest baiting contests. To that end I had been chosen to lead the Project Mammoth expedition, considered the most resilient of King William's many children. Conditions in Siberia convinced me that I would need more than toughness to find the three known pristine bull mammoth carcasses, collect frozen sexual organ tissue, and get my men safely back to Baikal City before winter set in. To do all that I would need extraordinary courage and leadership abilities, qualities a coddled life in English palaces did little to instill. How I wished for a more rigorous upbringing!

Trekking halfway across Mammoth Plain gave rise to a more realistic concern, I simply needed to read my map, something the howling wind, heavy with shards of flying ice, was trying to prevent. "Set up camp. See to the bloodhounds," I shouted in the ear of my head porter, a Buryat tribesman named Kirkuk. The porters were only too happy to escape the unexpected summer storm. They wasted no time jamming aluminum poles into permafrost and erecting felt tents.

Kirkuk made sure that I crawled into a tent with my three bloodhounds while the rest of the camp was still being assembled. The shorthaired hounds were not ideally suited to the harsh climate of Baikal's northern province, nor was I for that matter. The head porter stuck his head inside the tent and informed me that a fishing party would procure fresh food for the hounds as soon as the weather broke. The tent flap closed. Kirkuk vanished.

I wanted to fire an electric torch to study my map. The spirit was more willing than the flesh. I reached out, hugged my hounds close for warmth, and passed out. Late summer in Siberia made for long days. I slept throughout that day and well into the next. The porters fed the bloodhounds without awakening their Liege.

When I finally awoke at noon the next day, my stomach was making dreadful noises. Dried fish and boiled water served to approximate a breakfast. Outside the tent, a pale sun shone on a broad snowy plain, wreathed by lines of rugged, icy hills. Somewhere on this plain, or more precisely under this plain, the pristine carcass of a bull mammoth was frozen in permafrost.

Several porters shook angry fists at the concealing white blanket, cursing it in their native tongue. Signposts marked out on the expedition map were now hidden. I chucked the map back into my tent for I'd noticed something the porters had not: the three bloodhounds were standing at attention, muscles quivering, ears up, licking their noses in anticipation.

Gathering my swiftest porters, scooping up a few tools, I let the hounds free and led a small party after the keen-nosed dogs. The snow wasn't deep; the hounds skimmed over the lightly crusted permafrost, running a scant hundred yards and then went to ground like terriers.

The swift porters stopped in their tracks when they saw the hounds digging. They yelled for the rest of the expedition. Light, portable refrigeration units and shovels and pickaxes were hauled forward to the dogs' excavation site.

I leashed the hounds, calling them away from the emerging hole. My entire crew got busy, hacking into the permafrost with gusto. They'd exposed a sizeable portion of a mammoth foot by afternoon. Judging by its size, the foot belonged to an exceptional adult bull Imperial Mammoth. The Imperial Mammoth was twice the size of other species. I stroked the stiffly frozen fur of the tombstone-like foot and took a photograph. Exposure to atmosphere meant the shaggy black hair would quickly oxidize and turn red. That would be the only thing happening quickly at the excavation site. When he walked the earth, the frozen mammoth must have weighed 17,000 pounds. It would take the better part of a week to carve away enough permafrost to uncover the prehistoric sexual organs.

My men tore at the frozen soil while I looked askance into the pale sky, the Siberian winter wanted to rear its ugly head. There should be no problem getting the frozen sperm of this particular mammoth out of the tundra and into the Project Mammoth laboratory in London. Finding and processing the two other frozen mammoth carcasses on my map might prove problematic. Delaying the rest of the expedition till next summer was not an option. The carcasses had kept their pristine condition for ten or twenty thousand years, they would keep for one or more years; this was true. Unfortunately, Fred Greystone was nearly 100 years old. He wasn't expected to live much longer. No one believed that Asian elephants cows could be artificially inseminated using mammoth sperm without Greystone's expertise.

31

Five days after the massive foot had been uncovered, the entire carcass was exposed, and an aeroplane equipped with tundra tires sat next to the colossal frozen hulk. The portable refrigerator containing the extinct creature's sexual organs lay in the belly of the plane. Supplies for the expedition had been heaped into neat piles on the frozen tundra. My Buryat tribesman made ready to push into the wasteland.

Princess Victoria slammed the diary shut. She knew how the story ended. Albert's expedition succeeded in uncovering two more perfectly preserved mammoth carcasses. The brother that she'd never met did not escape the teeth of Siberia's winter. Two Buryat tribesmen made it back alive to Baikal City, lugging a portable refrigerator containing the most valuable genetic material known to man.

Albert's death had served a noble cause in 1910. Fred Greystone had died one year later, but not before performing one last miracle. Nineteen eleven was the year that Angerbotha had been conceived. She knew the facts behind Angerbotha's conception, but still didn't know what had driven the enigmatic Greystone.

Princess Victoria looked out the window of her second story room in Southwestern Palace #9. Southern England was so lovely this time of year. She'd always been scornful of the Englishmen who constantly flew to Portugal, Spain, and France for holiday when a much lovelier land lay at their doorstep. What could be more beautiful than a countryside that harbored a living, breathing mammoth? And only a few miles from her southern palace there was the Primate Language Center, where gorillas were being bred to speak with humans in sign language, the most mysterious legacy of the late, great Fred Greystone. As far as Victoria was concerned, sitting on a beach and basking in the Mediterranean sun was a waste of time when one could bask in the presence of such marvelous creatures.

Mammoths and sign language speaking gorillas were Victoria's greatest delights. She was wise enough in the ways of the world to comprehend that these exotic creatures were the very height of impracticality and held little attraction to ordinary working people. It had cost millions of pounds to produce the exotic beasts, but they served no useful function that she could discern. Creating living curiosities for no practical purpose was something that a royal might do, and certainly Greystone had relied on royal funds to work his magic. But Greystone was a commoner, a hardheaded pragmatist by all accounts, and his motivation was hard to fathom. She needed to read more of Prince Albert's diary, even if doing so was painful. In the dark recesses of her mind, Victoria suspected that mammoths and signing gorillas were to play a portentous role in the history of mankind and somehow her fate would be wrapped up in theirs.

She bent back over Albert's diary. A hairy trunk snaked through the open window, snuffling curiously at the journal. Angerbotha wondered why her mistress was so interested in this little book. No other book produced negative emotions in the Princess. Angerbotha didn't like the sadness these pieces of paper caused her pet human.

The mammoth snatched the book off the desk, shoved it in her mouth and ate it. Victoria gave a tiny gasp of pain and dismay, as if a dentist had yanked a sore tooth out of her mouth.

The long, hairy trunk reemerged inside her chamber. Somehow the flexible proboscis displayed an apologetic air. It banged on her desk three times. Angerbotha wanted to take Victoria for a ride. The Princess called out the window, "Very well then, a short ride. Very short, as I've not completed my schoolwork for the day." Angerbotha's trunk curled around the slight frame of the teenage girl, nearly knocking over a framed picture of the original Victoria. It was amazing how much the Princess looked like her namesake and great-grandmother, Queen Victoria I. Amazing, because the Princess was half Japanese. There could be only one royal family in the Commonwealth, and the Japanese royals had been assimilated into England's nobility, as had the continental royal families, and the Zulu monarchy.

The mammoth cow, Angerbotha, didn't care about the Princess's royal pedigree or biracial heritage. She only wanted to play. Victoria was tilted at a precise angle so she could pass through the window frame without banging her head. The mammoth held the girl about twenty feet off the ground, and carefully backed away from the palace.

With pigtails flying in the wind, she clung to the furry crown of Angerbotha's head as the mammoth charged up a hill. Victoria buried her nose in the valley between the two peaks of the pachyderm's skull, inhaling the fragrance of musky fur.

Angerbotha glided down the hill and sailed past the castle, intent on reaching the road outside the compound and taking the Princess to the nearby Primate Language Center. Victoria would spend all day playing with the signing gorillas if they made it that far and Angerbotha would get a change of scenery.

The Princess remembered the schoolwork waiting for her inside the palace and called a halt to the mammoth's scheme, gripping her gigantic flapping ears, steering the hairy titan back to the window that Victoria had been extracted from. The unenthusiastic scholar entered her room the same way that she'd left, dangling at the end of Angerbotha's trunk.

There was a visitor waiting inside, Victoria's father, King William. "Vicky, would you be so kind as to clear up a number of mysteries that have been vexing me?" the King asked with deceptive gentleness. She stood there in the center of the room, unsure of what to say, so she kept mum. "Where is Prince Albert's diary? Why are you gallivanting about on your mammoth while scholarly obligations remain unfulfilled?"

The first question had a ready answer and that answer was bizarre enough to throw the King off track, or so Victoria hoped. "Prince Albert's diary was eaten by Angerbotha." William hesitated for a few seconds. It would have been natural for him to ask why the diary had made its way into the Princess's room in the first place and how could the mammoth possibly have eaten it. But he could see that she was leading him down the garden path. He moved on to his second question. Picking up a volume of Shakespeare's Hamlet from her desk, the King asked his daughter if this was her current reading assignment. She nodded contritely. William asked her why she did not have her nose buried in Shakespeare.

"Well, Sire, I've also a problem that is vexing me, to the point where I cannot concentrate on academics. I'm trying to comprehend why mammoths and signing gorillas came to be, even though they serve no useful purpose," she said truthfully. That truthfulness tempered her father and put him in the mood to help. Still holding the volume of Shakespeare he said, "The answer to that question can be found here, in the works of the Bard, more so than in our family's personal scribbling."

Victoria sighed and rolled her eyes. In another life, King William had been Kaiser Wilhelm and had waged war on England and its allies. Victoria's great-grandmother had put William on the English throne to end the World War. In the intervening years, William had become an Anglophile with the zealousness of any convert. He thought that the wisdom of the ages was locked within the pages of Shakespeare.

The King leafed through the volume in his hand. Coming to the quote he'd been searching for, he cleared his throat and said, "There are more things in heaven and earth, Horatio, than are dreamt of in your philosophy." He snapped the book shut and asked what the quote meant to Victoria. She only shrugged her shoulders. William passed the book to his daughter and continued: "Hamlet utters these words in reference to an apparition that his friend Horatio has seen, specifically the ghost of the King of Denmark. Hamlet understands that supernatural phenomena, royal intrigue, and even murder do in fact exist, even if such thing are outside Horatio's experience."

Victoria looked at the book in her hands with newfound interest, turning it over and looking to her father for a fuller explanation. The King did not disappoint. "The forces that drove Fred Greystone to breed gorillas with souls and recreate the extinct Imperial Mammoth are outside your experience, Victoria. There are more things in heaven and earth than you can dream of, currently that is. To dream more fully, your mind must be broadened. Shakespeare is a start." William left his daughter to her studies.

Chapter 5

The Blue Force Creates Superior Power Combat Suits

On the peak of Mauna Kea, under the stars, wrapped in a thermal blanket, the couple cuddled and made pillow talk, slowly cooling from their lovemaking. They'd discovered that a secret rendezvous was possible on the small maintenance platform bolted to the dome of the giant thirty-foot central telescope. Their tryst remained secret because Jeremiah's combat suit was the newly designed Mark II. Among its many improvements over the Mark I was a host of stealth technologies. Baffled flight turbines didn't keen and shriek in the Mark II, they didn't make much noise at all. Jeremiah could land on the hidden platform in the dead of night and nobody below would know he was up there.

The supreme commander's eyes roved across the splash of stars illuminating the night sky. He said, "I can't take it any longer. Wolfgang has gotten you pregnant. Your duty to the Ministry of Eugenics is complete. Leave him and become my wife."

"My duty is not complete. I am to bear at least three children from Ministry approved sires," she said mournfully. Nkosinathi took her obligation to the Ministry of Eugenics very seriously. The quixotic mixture of old-fashioned morality and modern genetics that governed the Ministry frustrated Jeremiah. It wouldn't let her divorce Wolfgang, even though it was willing to let her have children by other men. He said, "I'll raise your children as mine. The only reason Ubermen must be married is to provide a stable home life. Wolfgang can sleep with you once every two years to get you pregnant. Berlin and the Eugenics Ministry is a long way from here."

Nkosinathi exposed the real problem by saying, "I love Wolfgang and can't bear breaking his heart. I love two men and want to continue as Wolfgang's wife and your concubine."

Jeremiah was going to explain why this was impossible when the scream of a PCS Mark I rent the idyllic stillness. They peeked over the guardrail of the maintenance platform. Landing lights cast yellow pools of light on the gravel parking lot below. Most suit pilots personalized their machines by stenciling in their call names onto the flight turbine cowls. The suit that was landing bore the letters $E=MC^2$ on its twin cowls. Albert

Einstein was making a surprise visit to the Mauna Kea observatory, checking up on Nkosinathi. He'd never shown up during the night before and was usually rigid in his routines. Apparently, there was a first time for anything.

Nkosinathi begged Jeremiah to get into his suit and fly away. The stealthy Mark II could probably exit quietly enough to avoid detection by Einstein's suit sensors. The supreme commander refused to retreat, claiming it would undermine his authority. Nkosinathi said hotly, "You should have thought of that before shtooping me."

"Oh, I did all the shtooping? It wasn't a two-way street?"

"I wouldn't have been shtooping back if I hadn't been pursued like a bull in a baiting contest."

"When we first met at Einstein's office, you were wiggling your ass faster than a cabaret dancer. No man could have resisted."

The argument was loud enough to be detectable by Einstein's audio pickup. The lover's quarrel abruptly ceased when the titanium clad Albert Einstein could be heard hovering above them, the bulk of his suit a dark presence in the night sky.

"Nkosinathi, is that you dear?" Einstein's electronically amplified voice boomed over the screech of the Mark I turbines. She answered in the affirmative, asking for a ride to ground level after hastily throwing on her clothes.

Jeremiah crawled into his PCS and joined the two physicists on the ground. The men in suits seemed to square off pugnaciously, suit lights blazing, like titans ready to brawl, but it was an illusion caused by the menacing nature of their exoskeleton weaponry. In reality, they only faced each other to hold a conversation.

"Supreme Commander?" Einstein asked. Jeremiah made the hand sign for "yes." The professor had never bothered to learn sign language. He persisted with his embarrassing questions, amplified voice loud enough to be heard by the astronomers inside. "If that is you SC Halifax? I haven't interrupted anything important?" Jeremiah's amplified voice responded, "Take your assistant to the physics lab. Let's not have this conversation here, shouting through speakers, loud enough to wake the dead. I'll fly beside the two of you."

Nkosinathi stepped onto Einstein's metal boots. He'd long since graduated to a genuine combat suit, so there were no holes in his armor. He wrapped his suit arms around her waist. The professor had achieved true expertise in PCS operation. He had only to reach out with his mind to find the controls for the flight turbines. He revved the blades, adjusted the pitch, and the suit rose into the night. Compensating for Nkosinathi's weight didn't require conscious thought. He flew carefully down the mountain to the physics lab in Hilo. On the way, Einstein considered how much nobler this use for the powered combat suit was than what would come in the 1950 war. The simple act of giving a friend a lift proved that suit technology could have tremendous civilian applications. He hoped the defensive forcefields that would eventually be built into the Mark III would do what SC Halifax promised: make future war impossible. That thought put him in a dreamy state of mind. He didn't notice that Jeremiah had fallen a quarter-mile behind.

The warm glow faded when Einstein touched down in front of a hexagonal building built out of plasteel: the physics research station in Hilo. Wolfgang was waiting there, in a suit, a Mark II. The professor released Nkosinathi and ordered her into the cyclotron control room inside the hexagon. The room was built to withstand errant particle beams if the supercollider malfunctioned. It would be proof against anything that Jeremiah and Wolfgang might do.

She remained stubbornly outside, protesting the professor's demands. Wolfgang and Einstein's suit speakers blasted the same message: she had to get out of harm's way. Nkosinathi retreated. Einstein did not. Wolfgang turned his speakers on the scientist and told him to go into the control room as well. The professor held his ground.

Jeremiah landed with a thud, harder than necessary if his intentions were peaceful, forearm guns extended. Einstein guessed that the supreme commander must have performed a long distance scan. Superior Mark II sensors told Jeremiah what sort of danger was lurking around the physics lab. The radar evading qualities of Wolfgang's Mark II may have actually served as a red flag. Only a handful of the latest model PCS existed. No one in Blue Force would show up at night for a causal visit inside a Mark II. Einstein looked at Wolfgang. The major general's forearm guns were pointing at SC Halifax.

Einstein knew he should power up his flight turbines and get out of there. Curiosity got the better of him. Soldiers had sparred countless times in the PCS Mark I. Never before had two suited men tried to kill each other, let alone wearing Mark IIs. Every engineer seeks to test machinery to the point of failure, only that way can design parameters truly be ascertained. If a suited man killed another suited man, then the suit itself will have been pushed to the point of failure.

What am I thinking? There are men inside those machines. I have to stop this bloodshed, the professor thought, regaining his moral compass. He was about to say something when the SC and the major general opened fire. Einstein hit the deck as bullets ricocheted off the incredibly tough alloy composite of the Mark IIs, splattering against the plasteel walls of the hexagon and ripping apart the shrubbery of the physics lab gardens. The professor tore at the ground with mechanical claws, carving a shallow slit trench in the earth.

The next generation ammunition for the Mark II had been designed, but not manufactured. Eventually, the forearm guns would carry super-dense metallic missile-bullets, powered by both casing charges and internal micro-rockets. For now, Wolfgang and Jeremiah blazed at each other with conventional high velocity 25 caliber uranium slugs that didn't pack enough punch to rupture the composite armor plating of the PCS Mark II.

However, concentrated bursts of 25 caliber shot *could* puncture the Plexiglas helmet of the Mark I. Einstein was pinned to the shallow trench he'd carved while the men fired at point blank range. He stayed there while the combatants sought cover. Gunfire became more sporadic. Bursts erupted from behind palm trees and rocks. They wouldn't keep that up for long. In a short time, Nkosinathi's rivals would figure out that they could only hurt each other with wrestling moves, punches, or kicks.

Nkosinathi voice sounded over Einstein's helmet speakers. "Professor. The MPs are calling. The gunfire has them concerned. What should I tell them?"

"Tell them I am conducting a spur of the moment experiment and don't want to be disturbed."

His helmet speakers remained quiet. She was accepting his instructions, a good thing. Einstein loathed getting involved in politics or interpersonal conflict of any stripe. Since he was deeply involved despite his wishes, he meant to see this thing through to a resolution. Blue Force could not continue with its leadership divided. Tonight, one man would emerge victorious. The victor would claim the girl and command of Blue Force. It wasn't supposed to work that way, no matter, that's how it was shaping up, by his actions

Jeremiah was admitting as much. If the SC wanted to deal with Wolfgang differently, he would call for the MPs himself.

Einstein crawled from his slit trench and scuttled into the heart of the jungle-like garden in a crouch. The Mark I and Mark II had similar visual enhancers: built-in infrared capacity and neural linked radar. The radar image of the fighters was blurry, but infrared gave a crisp picture. He could see both combatants huddling in the thicket and knew that they could see him, as well as each other. Stealth technology was in its infancy. The Mark III would probably have electronic camouflage, and its crystal iron exoskeleton would most likely be layered with radar absorbing carbon fiber, and then there was heat dispersal technology to be considered. Since the Mark III wasn't even on the drawing board yet, Wolfgang and Jeremiah had nowhere to hide.

A small clearing separated their positions. It was the obvious battleground once the futile cat and mouse game was over. Einstein dug another slit trench with a view of the clearing. He flopped on his belly and peered over the top of his little ditch.

One of the fighters, Einstein thought it was Jeremiah, initiated a charge. The other man sprang to his feet and made his own charge. They ran straight at each other. Neither combatant raised his forearms to fire machineguns because they both needed to swing suit arms to achieve maximum sprint speed.

They crashed into each other with a combined speed of about 120 miles-per-hour. A metallic thunderclap shook the jungle. Clashing rhinos would have made a much smaller impact. Both men were thrown back, knocking down trees and shredding the dense foliage. A fraction of a second later and they were charging again. Einstein estimated that the second clash had a combined speed of 60 miles-per-hour. It didn't generate enough energy to throw the men back.

The two rivals grappled, making and breaking jujitsu holds. One of them made a clean hip throw. Both fighters went down. Move and countermove occurred too quickly for the human eye to follow. They abandoned *katamewaza* holding and pinning techniques to pound each other with gauntleted fists as they rolled on the loamy garden soil.

Wing mounts and cowl encased flight turbines were knocked loose on both combat suits under the barrage of kicks and punches, sending showers of sparks into the underbrush as exposed circuits shorted in the dampness of the rainforest soil. The short, stubby wing mounts and cowls bumped against the trunks of different trees and sat there, sparking and hissing. Einstein was surprised that any part of the Mark II could actually break off in combat. On further reflection, maybe it wasn't so surprising. Titanium alloys were notoriously difficult to weld. Evidently, the electron beam welds that fastened the squat wing mounts to the back of the Mark II had cracked. This had never happened when soldiers had sparred with the Mark I. The welding technique for the Mark I and Mark II were identical. The only possible conclusion was that previous tests had not been sufficiently strenuous. Maybe soldiers should only spar if they were in love with the same girl.

The general and the supreme commander continued to roll on the ground, grappling, punching, and kicking each other with unbridled fury, neither man willing to conserve his strength with defensive moves like parries or clenches. The energy expended by both the men and their machines was prodigious. Einstein knew Jeremiah had a worse O^2 utilization rate than Wolfgang. Blue Force suits were airtight, designed to function in the seething hellish aftermath of a nuclear strike. The SC could easily asphyxiate inside his suit while the major general remained fresh as a daisy. Not good. The ideal outcome would be for the SC to kill his rival. That would resolve the matter cleanly. Einstein didn't see any way to interfere or help Jeremiah short of joining the fight, which would outrage both combatants' sense of honor.

They were on their feet now, slugging it out like boxers, titanium fists swinging with more power than wrecking balls. Jeremiah permitted his opponent to punch his helmet while he worked over Wolfgang's body. A chunk of the SC's faceplate crashed into the interior of his helmet. Cat-like reflexes and a supple neck prevented Jeremiah's head from pulping like a ripe pumpkin. Jeremiah now had all the air he could breathe, but was vulnerable to additional blows to the head or gunfire. The SC moved in tight to keep Wolfgang from firing forearm guns into his helmet.

Every member of Blue Force was trained in jujitsu. Jeremiah had always wondered if straight judo was more applicable in hand-to-hand suit combat. He proved his theory correct by executing the extremely challenging *tomoenage* or circle throw as Wolfgang lunged forward to initiate a foot sweep. The supreme commander's metallic claws found purchase on Wolfgang's dented breastplate. Jeremiah fell backwards forcefully and deliberately, his right foot planting on the major general's titanium belly. With arms pulling in and right leg extending out, Jeremiah performed the circle throw.

The major general hurtled through the air, landed on his back, and bounced six feet into the air. Wolfgang landed again, but not on the jungle floor, Jeremiah was under him this time. The SC wrapped arms and legs around the limbs of his stunned opponent. Servomotors ground against servomotors. The two fighters poured power into leg, torso, and arm motors, draining battery reserves, locking up the larger suit motors. As Einstein had noted to himself earlier, there were men inside the machines, and the men were willing to fight, even if their machines were failing. Human muscles strained against human muscles. The two combatants became a biomechanical pretzel, unable to move.

Wolfgang tried to engage the clamshell function in order to escape from his suit, or at least crack it open for air. There either wasn't enough suit power left to break the hermetic seal or the mechanism was damaged. He was trapped inside with a limited O^2 supply.

Einstein shot out of his trench and sprinted into the clearing, skidding to a sliding stop in front of the contorted pair of suit warriors. He locked a tight beam on Jeremiah's shattered helmet and achieved a workable, if scratchy, connection. "Supreme Commander, the intention here is to asphyxiate your opponent, yes?"

The SC's tight beam was non-functional. He answered over a broadband channel, keeping the transmission at a very low setting so it wouldn't carry more than a few feet, which was about all the power he had left in his suit anyway. "Exactly right, Professor. Much like the original Blue Force's starvation campaign at the end of the 1920 CMG, a slow death."

"That will take many hours. General Bernhard has a very efficient metabolism," Einstein observed. Wolfgang lanced a weak tight beam at Einstein's helmet and said, "Doctor, don't let me die this way. Punch in my faceplate and put a bullet between my eyes for God's sake." Jeremiah activated his radio again, "Don't do anything he says, Albert. He's tricking you into puncturing his suit in order to breath. He's not just a man, he's an Uberman, nothing if not crafty."

Wolfgang's clever request clicked a gear in Einstein's mind, putting him into social scientist mode. He established two tight beams, one linked to the helmet of either combatant. "No one is going to die tonight. Blue Force cannot afford the waste of talent.

I have a solution to your knotty love triangle. Stop fighting, I will get you out of your under-powered suits."

A pregnant pause went on for several seconds. With agonizing slowness titanium arms and legs untangled. The exhausted men used the last of their physical strength and suit power reserves to stand the 350-pound Mark IIs upright. Einstein opened a side panel in his Mark I and clamped a power conduit first into Jeremiah's suit and then into Wolfgang's, instructing them to clamshell out of their PCSs. Once the two military leaders were facing each other, sweating and steaming in their underwear, Einstein got out of his own suit. They left the Mark IIs and Mark I in the brutalized garden and made their way to the octagon.

Nkosinathi was waiting for them inside. She handed out terry cloth robes and led them to the cafeteria, the largest room in the building not filled with sensitive instruments and delicate machinery. She didn't trust Wolfgang and Jeremiah to refrain from fighting.

Once his three test subjects were seated, Einstein (thinking like a social scientist) laid out the rough draft of an experiment that should relieve the psychological tension plaguing the dysfunctional love triangle. Wolfgang and Nkosinathi would stay married, raising a brood of genetically superior Blue Force soldiers. Jeremiah would marry Nkosinathi, giving her two husbands. Wolfgang and Jeremiah would be permitted mistresses from the ranks of single women within the Blue Force. As a married woman, Nkosinathi was obligated to obey ancient Jewish and Falasha customs and be faithful to her two husbands.

Nkosinathi's mood darkened seconds after Einstein laid out his plan. Her lower lip trembled when her two lovers exchanged agreeable looks, nodding in unison. She got out of her chair to make tea, an effort to staunch the negative emotions bubbling inside. She gave each man a cup of instant tea and then exploded, "Jewish custom my eye! Wolfgang is a Jew, a modern Jew. He will not stray from the marriage bed. As far Jeremiah, he claims to be a Christian, but faith never stops him from sleeping with every hussy on the island!"

Einstein blew into his teacup and took a sip. He smiled at the taste and said, "I speak of ancient Jewish customs, the bedrock for Christianity." He took a second sip and continued speaking, not bothering to look at his test subjects. "The sixth commandment says, 'Thou shalt not commit adultery,' a term originally defined as sex with a married woman. Married Jewish men were permitted intercourse with single girls in ancient times. Only the Falasha tribes practice these ancient customs today. I propose a variation on your own traditions, my dear, traditions designed to establish paternity, not stifle sexuality. Jeremiah has had a vasectomy. Therefore, no question of paternity can sully the marriage triad or take away the blessing of the Ministry of Eugenics or the money they pay your family in Abyssinia."

Einstein drained his teacup and set it under the table. He looked at the threesome with a benevolent expression. His gentle voice acquired a razor's edge. "If we are done playing romantic games, there is a war to be won. Red Force disabled one of our spy balloons, crippling our intelligence gathering efforts, perhaps stealing the secret to electronic camouflage. They've exploded the world's first nuclear weapon. Unexplained seismic waves have emanated from their island ever since, possibly a new weapon or aftershocks from the A-bomb. Much work to be done."

Wolfgang, Jeremiah, and Nkosinathi squirmed in their chairs, chastised by Einstein's harangue, eager to get away from the tongue-lashing. He wasn't through yet. "If the supreme commander and major general don't mind, I need to confer with my assistant over this Aether Physics matter. So gentlemen, good night, and don't let the door hit you in the ass on the way out."

Nkosinathi and Einstein sat motionless as the military men trooped outside. The two physicists pretended not to hear the soldiers as they murmured something about picking up girls at one of Hilo's hot spots. The door to the lunchroom didn't hit Wolfgang or Jeremiah in the rear as they left the room. Nor did it stop booming laughter from assaulting Nkosinathi's ears as her two husbands made their way out the building. It was incredible to Nkosinathi and Einstein that the two military men were acting like long lost brothers when only minutes earlier they were locked in mortal combat.

Once the scientists were truly alone, Einstein's brain shifted gears and he was a theoretical physicist again. His periodic visits to the mountaintop observatory had brought him current with the astrophysicists' theories on Aether Physics. He took a deep breath and unleashed a heated attack on the stargazer's theories, intellectual passions stoked by the trauma of dealing with the unsavory love triangle.

Einstein took issue with the equations that described string theory in the Aether universe. The astrophysicists (he was now willing to use this term) had done a fine job discovering and explaining cosmic strings or wormholes, incredible structures that were many light years long. They'd dropped the ball at a quantum level, failing to understand that at this size string interactions don't occur at one point but are spread out in a way that lends to logical quantum performance. Their so-called quantum theory of interacting strings was nothing more than warmed over De Broglie electron waves.

"Herr Doctor Professor is personally insulted because astrophysicists are not competent particle physicists?" Nkosinathi asked dryly. "Were you also upset to learn that pigs couldn't fly?" She actually agreed with the flaws Einstein was exposing in AP theory, but couldn't help taking a jab at her mentor after the way he'd interfered in her personal life.

Einstein was about to rise to the bait when Nkosinathi apologized, admitting she was only trying to get his goat. It was Nkosinathi's turn to take a deep breath and let her thoughts pour forth. She wanted Einstein to quit nitpicking at Aether Physics from a distance. The astrophysicists were at the end of their rope, incapable of taking their work in theoretical physics any farther, and to ask them to do something impossible was petty and vengeful. The great scientist must embrace AP theory, straighten out the logical inconsistencies, and use it to produce a Grand Unified Field Theory. He must order the supercollider to be finished as a crystal iron machine parts factory, abandoning all thought of cataloging a hopelessly infinite subatomic zoo. Finally, he must swallow his pride and end the hostility against the astrophysicists on top the mountain. She batted her eyelashes with mock coquettishness and added, "If I must endure two unfaithful husbands, it is the least Herr Doctor Professor can do for the cause."

A wave of irritation washed across Einstein's lugbrious face. *Good, I've stung him, shaken him up. He needed it*, Nkosinathi thought. Irritation transformed into wistfulness as the professor said, "It will be good to work with crystal iron and begin designing the Mark III. I am heartily sick of titanium. Observing your husbands fight has convinced me that the Mark II is already obsolete."

His expression changed again. Now he had a far-seeing look as he gazed across the room without focusing on anything. "I will draft instructions to the collider team tonight, a blueprint that will make it a factory for crystal iron and exotic super heavy metals. I will

41

start designing the Mark III next. Then I will make a stab at the Grand Unified Field Theory, enough to put my micro-fusion reactor people on the right track."

She stood, put her hands on her hips, and asked archly, "Tonight? The great Albert Einstein will do all that before breakfast?"

"Of course, my dear."

Nkosinathi shook her head in wonder. He really was prepared to do all that in one night. Anybody else making such a claim would be indulging in an idle boast. Einstein was merely stating facts. That didn't mean she was going to let him forgo sleep and work all night.

Her look of bemused wonder softened as she stared at Einstein and thought about Wolfgang and Jeremiah. Her husbands were hitting the first bar about now; ready to act like a pair of tomcats in mating season. The contrast to Einstein's noble desires cast a dirty light on the souls of the two military men she was stuck with. She could take solace in the fact that the professor would always be the most important man in her life and she would always be the only woman in his. Suddenly that seemed infinitely more important than anything the roughhewn and uncouth brutes she slept with might do or feel. It also seemed unfair to Einstein. The question wasn't whether Jeremiah and Wolfgang should share Nkosinathi; the question was why should a man of Einstein's nobility have to share her with anybody?

Looking down at him, she said, "While the great Einstein may be the only human being capable of doing all those things in one night, it is not to be. Tonight you sleep." She took her mentor by the hand and led him outside, making sure that his robe was tied around the waist and that he had sandals on his feet. They walked one block to his private residence.

She tucked him into bed and gave him a tender kiss on the cheek. On most nights his assistant tucked him into bed, once in a rare while she kissed his cheek or forehead, so these things did not alarm Einstein. What she said next was quite alarming.

"The Ministry of Eugenics has done extensive research on breeding for scientific genius. Your first wife was a brilliant physicist and your cousin, on paper a perfect line breeding for genius, yet your sons are only mediocre physicists. Other pairings of closely related scientific geniuses yield analogous results. Human genetics is not yet ready for line breeding of complicated traits like scientific genius. The best strategy is outcrossing an unrelated man and woman with the desired traits. In Germany, only a few such crosses have been made, but with spectacular results. The Ministry is eager to sanction more breedings of this type."

For a second he thought she was going to strip off her clothes, crawl under the sheets with him, and tear off his bedclothes. Mercifully, she only kissed him again and left the bedroom. Unexpected feelings of disappointment confused Einstein. He decided that he wasn't as good at social science as he'd originally thought. Despite uncertainty over his own amateur social engineering, despite his disappointment that Nkosinathi hadn't crawled into bed, he knew a love triangle was more stable than a rectangle.

He fell into a troubled sleep, immediately cast into a vivid dream. Two suited men were walking toward him. They were wearing Mark IIIs, the blue glow of atmospheric forcefield radiation shimmered around the dark figures like angels, or demons. The forcefields snapped off. One of the men spoke. "Ready to fight Albert? This time it shall be a three way match." The voice was Supreme Commander Halifax's.

"That's right," a voice from the second suit agreed. It was General Wolfgang Bernhard. "This time no fancy compromises or ancient Jewish custom. This time we fight to the death."

Einstein looked wildly around his dream world. The three of them were standing in the garden in front of the octagon, the same spot where Jeremiah and Wolfgang had originally fought. The supreme commander made a hand gesture, indicating an empty Mark III leaning against a tree. The flight cowls projecting from the empty suit back were inscribed with the professor's call sign: $E=MC^2$.

When the scientist refused to cross the garden and put on the suit, Wolfgang raised a forearm gun and centered the barrel directly between Einstein's eyes. The major general said simply, "We fight for the girl."

Wait a minute, Einstein thought. *He's not pointing a gun barrel at me. Some kind of energy nozzle is integral to Wolfgang's vambrace.* Wolfgang flicked his weapon at the empty suit, impatient to fight to the death to win Nkosinathi once and for all.

"Stop moving your gun," Einstein ordered sternly. "Let me get a clear look at it." He took three steps forward, seized Wolfgang's metallic forearm, and put his face within inches of the adjustable nozzle capping a tube that resembled the conduits of an aquatic forcefield system.

"Albert, stop acting as if you'd never seen a particle beam weapon," Wolfgang ordered. "For crying out loud, you invented the damn thing."

Chapter 6

The Red Force Becomes the Red Army

Information about the rest of Red Force had always been scarce to the men and women of Project Mole. Lately, it had gotten worse. The shoring battle-lion and the Mole crew had been totally out of contact with the surface for the two weeks of the subterranean crisis. Not receiving news or updates from the topsiders had been the least of their concerns while Mole I fought for its life against torrents of raging magma, or so they thought. News from the bulk of Red Force was about to roil the underground project, now that the two-week crisis was over.

Their travails had actually started fifteen days ago when the effectiveness of the seismic map had been exhausted, forcing Mole I to tunnel blindly into the mantle. The digging machine had deliberately outstripped the shoring battle-lion, rapidly backfilling freshly cut tunnel with loose rock, right before disaster struck. At the time, Rudolf Diesel thought he was taking an acceptable risk; if the backfilled tunnel didn't hit the Molokai Fracture, then the Mole could simply loop back, intersect a cleared tunnel, hook up with the battle-lion, and try again in a different direction. In theory, it would be more efficient to speedily create a backfilled tunnel that missed the Molokai Fracture than to painfully creep forward with a perfectly cleared and shored tunnel stretching behind them.

Disaster struck as the Mole's sensors detected a harmonic tremor in the substratum ahead, a sign that magma was flowing close by. Before Diesel could react, the boron carbine ceramic chisels of the continuous miner's cutting head exposed a vein of red-hot magma. The chisels instantly vaporized. Standard procedure would have been for Mole I to jam into reverse and retreat back up the length of the cleared tunnel to its rear. Then it would have shot a salvo of shaped charges into the roof of the threatened tunnel, collapsing tons of rock on the vein of live magma.

The crew had wasted no time backing up as far as they could, smacking into the heap of loose rock in their trace. At the same time, they fired charges into the overhead rock to the front of the Mole, only a few yards from the advancing wall of magma.

An avalanche of rubble caved in on the rush of molten rock, creating a makeshift dam, and saving the Mole from immediate destruction. This maneuver bought time, leaving the digging machine in a relatively small pocket of noxious vapor, but without any chisels on its cutting head. Before a side tunnel could be cut to affect an escape, crewmen had to don powered combat suits and replace the chisels on the damaged cutting head with spares. The job would have been routine on the surface. Three miles under the seabed, with magma puddles seeping under the rubble dam to lap against the repairmen's metal boots, it seemed as if the repair crew were battling Satan and all his hellish minions. Two men had died during the repair job, roasted alive when suit air conditioners failed.

By the time Mole I had dug its way back to a cleared tunnel and reentered the bosom of the shoring battle-lion, fuel and oxygen reserves had been severely depleted. Diesel was congratulating his exhausted crewmen who lay collapsed on the floor of the Mole's bridge, too tired to move, when the phone rang. Oppenheimer was on the other end. The top scientist ordered the chief of Project Mole to the surface, an emergency meeting had been called and it couldn't wait on ceremony. Every military and science officer was being summoned.

Diesel flatly refused. Conditions in the mine were too dangerous to warrant his absence. Any meeting would have to proceed without him. Oppenheimer gave a second direct order, refusing to listen to excuses. The Mole chief had no choice but to comply, which was easier said than done. The only way to quickly reach the surface was to get inside a PCS and ride the conveyor belt of rock and ore up to the mouth of the mine, landing in one of the shuttle cars like a piece of rock.

The initial leg of the journey proved to be unpleasant, but not as bad as Diesel had feared. He bumped and bounced up the belt for hours, jostled by a slew of man-sized boulders along the way, to be callously dumped into a shuttle car. Ten boulders rained down on top of the suited traveler, burying him in the bottom of the car. He lay there for a moment, grumbling to himself over the indignity Oppenheimer and High Command had heaped on him. The Red Force PCS Model A should have been up to the task of extricating its occupant from the laden ore carrier. Thousand pound rocks were tossed aside as easily as pebbles, so far so good. Diesel found that he was pinned by three medium sized boulders that surrounded his legs a foot past the knee, making it difficult to bend his legs. He should have turned on his suit radio to ask for help or figured out how to lift the boulder with his back straight and his legs bent. Instead, he bent from the waist, grabbed one of the boulders and lifted with his back. The boulder was pried free, but a searing pain exploded in his lower back. Torso servomotors did 99 percent of the work lifting the boulder. Unfortunately, 1 percent of one thousand pounds was still enough to injure the back of a seventy-year-old man. The offending boulder was heaved over board, Diesel jumped, landed on the cavern floor, wriggled out of his PCS, and screamed in pain.

With one hand on his aching back, he looked around for Oppenheimer, but saw only workers from the dispersal crew, busily loading submarines and hooking electric locomotives to shuttle cars. Diesel looked forlornly at the orange sweat soaked coveralls that he was wearing. He was forced to borrow a shirt, shorts, and a pair of sandals from one of the workmen. Passing the clothes to his commander, the workman made a request: "Mr. Diesel, Sir, we've been kept in the dark down here about the communist takeover topside. We'd be much obliged if some of the wild rumors could be laid to rest."

Still holding his back with one hand, Diesel grimaced when he heard this bizarre appeal. He wanted to quiz the man about the so-called communist takeover, except Oppenheimer had finally arrived on the cavern floor and was demanding that they make

45

their way to the surface at once. The throbbing pain in his back was preventing Diesel from thinking clearly. He wanted to ask his superior about the rumored communist takeover in the freight elevator while it whisked them to the surface. He opened his mouth, struggling to frame a question through the miasma of pain. Before he could put his question together, Oppenheimer asked how long it had been since the chief of Project Mole had seen daylight. Diesel admitted that months had passed since any member of his project had seen the light of day. Oppenheimer handed his subordinate a pair of sunglasses and said, "Put these on, very dark lenses, same glasses we used to watch Fat Baby explode. You'll need them."

The elevator slowed. Diesel put on the dark glasses. His eyes were sensitive to bright light under normal circumstances. After spending all that time underground with weak artificial lights, normal sunlight would be almost as painful as the unrelenting ache in his lower back. The irony of Oppenheimer's gift wasn't lost on Diesel. The top scientist wanted to shield Diesel's vision, just as everybody in Project Mole had been kept in the dark about some portentous political change involving the whole of Red Force. It wasn't right, but he would wait until everything was made clear before lodging a formal complaint to Supreme Commander Banner.

The elevator reached the surface. The scientist and the engineer stepped into sunlight. Diesel shuffled forward stiffly, as if a board were glued to his back, the only way he could move without pain. He adjusted the filter on the dark glasses and looked around, spying a suspicious flag flapping in the breeze, projecting from the fender of the Science Division staff car. The symbol for Red Force was supposed to be a plain red rectangle, completely unadorned, no heraldry, no emblems, and no decals. The flag on Oppenheimer's car was indeed a red rectangle, except it was not monochromatic. A yellow hammer and sickle dominated the center of the flag.

Oppenheimer noticed the object of Diesel's attention. The top scientist opened the back door and waved Diesel inside. They sat down, the car lurched forward, and the physicist explained the significance of the flag. "Our new communist flag; beautiful, isn't it? The hammer represents state owned industry. The sickle symbolizes collective agricultural."

The car lurched downward at an angle almost as steep as Mole I had taken into the Earth. The Daimler-Ford barreled down a mountain road. Oppenheimer observed Diesel's expression of pain and bewilderment, mistook it for simple confusion over the flag, and said, "The new flag speaks to the post war world, after we've established our global communist regime," as if that made everything clear.

"Robert, I've been underground for months," Diesel explained patiently. "I seriously injured my back to get here. Very little topside information has reached us since we went underground. We've been metaphorically kept in the dark from the beginning. I don't know beans about your communist takeover and would like a clear explanation."

Oppenheimer looked suddenly sheepish. He wasn't sure where to even begin. A lot had happened on Kauai in the past few weeks. Supreme Commander Banner had transformed the Red Force military-industrial complex into an instrument for world revolution. The changes were too extensive to give elaborate details on the short car trip to General Headquarters. The top scientist gave a brief summary and told Diesel it would have to suffice. After the meeting, a fuller explanation would be forthcoming.

The staff car pulled into a reserved parking space that bore the legend: Comrade Oppenheimer. The courtyard in front of the General Headquarters building contained a flagpole with the new communist flag flying boldly above an inscription chiseled into granite block. Diesel didn't bother to read the inscription, because he knew it would say something about workers uniting and throwing off chains. He couldn't avoid looking at the banner over the vestibule doors. Images of Spartacus, Marx, and Engels were painted next to a message advocating the elimination of private property.

Upon entering the great hall, Diesel was overwhelmed by the presence of one thousand officers, senior scientists, and engineering chiefs. The Mole program was underrepresented with only one man present. He couldn't fault that; his people were engaged in the early stages of a grand project, real work, not proletariat posturing. The pain in his back subsided as he sat in one of the ergonomic stadium seats.

On stage, in front of the multitude, were four men: Supreme Commander Banner, General George Patton, General Erwin Rommel, and Vladimir Bakunin. Banner stood a head taller than Patton and positively towered over the German general and the Russian barber. Even though Rommel wasn't a big man, he had a presence that could not be denied as he calmly gazed at the crowd through hazel eyes. On the surface, the presence of Vladimir (a mere barber) made no sense to Diesel. A moment's reflection brought back memories of the barber's pivotal role as a spy in the World War.

SC Banner walked to a standing microphone, adjusted it to suit his height, and addressed the Red Army elite. "Every military and scientific unit has been informed of the change, from the kindergarten instructors teaching our children to the pilots manning stratospheric observation balloons that spy on the Big Island."

Diesel stirred in his seat irritably. No one in the Mole project had been informed of anything. Oppenheimer felt his underling bristling, leaned toward him, and said quietly, "It was my responsibility to notify your people and test their loyalty. The oversight was mine, not High Command's."

Any slight indignation that Diesel might have harbored over the omission evaporated with the supreme commander's next few sentences. Fred Banner described the prison he had established for the soldiers, officers, and technicians unwilling to join the revolution. He promised that these prisoners would be treated humanely until the war started, failing to mention what would happen to them afterward. The audience growled softly, a feral noise. The full impact of the change that the Red Force had undergone hit Diesel like a wall of magma.

He looked down and failed to hear the next few sentences. His head went up as Rommel and Patton stepped forward. Banner announced the creation of three new structures within the Red Army: Groups A, B, and C. The group commandants were Erwin Rommel (A), George Patton (B), and Vladimir Bakunin (C).

Rommel took the microphone from its stand and put in plain words the mission assigned to Group A. It would revamp military strategy and training throughout the Red Army. They would be fighting everywhere on Earth, including the Arctic Circle, major cities, deserts, mountains, forests, jungles, and plains. Strategy and training must be adjusted accordingly. To wage a real war, the start date of 1950 must be revisited by Group A commanders. If they struck first in 1940, or even the late 30s, the element of surprise would be overwhelming, nuclear death would rain down upon the unprepared Blue Force in Hawaii, freeing the Red Army to tackle its larger objective: the Commonwealth.

A low ripple of approval rolled up and down the assemblage. It didn't take a military genius to see the advantage of an early start date and a surprise nuclear bombardment.

Diesel's heart skipped a beat as Rommel asked for him by name. The chief of the Mole project stood. Arrows of pain skewered his lower back, which he ignored. All eyes turned to Rudolf Diesel. Rommel addressed him directly, "Professor Diesel, our entire strategy involves your digging machines. Every man, woman, and machine in the Red Army must be placed in deep caverns, tunnel fortresses, under the Pacific. After our strike on Hawaii in 1940 or 1939, the nuclear genie is out of the bottle. Even if the Blue Force is annihilated to the last man, the possibility of the Commonwealth developing nuclear weapons is still there. Can impregnable tunnel fortresses be dug under the Pacific?"

Someone shoved a microphone into Diesel's hand. His face flushed from the pressure of an unexpected public speaking assignment. The straightforward technical nature of the question helped him formulate an answer. "Comrade General," he began, remembering the legend on Oppenheimer's parking space. The crowd murmured approval. "Comrade General, the tunnel warren will be immune to nuclear bombardment. This is not the problem. Most people believe the ocean consists of water, a thin layer of sand over the seabed, and layers of rock under that. This is not true. Between rock and water there is a two-mile thick layer of primordial ooze. If the Commonwealth were to use nuclear weapons on Kauai, then egress from the island would be no more. We would have to penetrate this ooze to come and go from our tunnel fortress."

Patton grabbed Rommel's microphone, but looked at Fred Banner before speaking. The supreme commander nodded and the Group B commandant said, "Comrade Rommel is already muscling in on my bailiwick. Group B is in charge of all technical changes needed to win the war."

Diesel felt something jog his elbow. He looked down at Oppenheimer. The physicist had just jerked back in his chair as if an electric current had shot through his body. The man's face was as white as a ghost, eyes bugging out, looking at Patton with a horrified expression. Oppenheimer had just realized that he would be directly under Patton's command.

Pushing Rommel aside, standing on the stage in front of the large crowd, Patton didn't notice the effect his words had produced on the top scientist. The American general said, "Comrade Diesel, wouldn't it be possible to combine the function of submarine and mole into a single vehicle to burrow through the miles of primordial ooze, navigate though seawater, and place an expeditionary force in San Francisco Bay or Washington state's Puget Sound?"

"A large submarine that could travel through the primordial ooze would require entirely new technology. We must haul more than suited human beings, but armored hovercrafts and fighters as well. Propellers will not be satisfactory. The continuous mining head of the Mole will be worse than nothing."

"Hasn't everything we've done involved creating entirely new technology? Isn't that what you're being paid to do? Create new technology?"

"Comrade General, your suggestion is feasible. Project Mole will implement your plan soonest." Diesel saluted and sat down. The crowd erupted in applause. The Mole chief had knuckled under shamefully to Patton's bullying. Diesel hadn't wanted to salute or display sycophantic behavior. He wanted even less to make the assurance that the technical challenge of moving tens of thousands of tons worth of submarine through miles of extremely viscous ooze could be easily overcome. He couldn't know whether Patton's idea was feasible or not without months of study. His first inclination was to dismiss the idea out of hand. He was sure of one thing: dissent under these conditions, in this place, was foolhardy. Supreme Commander Banner's oblique reference to indefinite prison terms or worse for non-communists had a powerful leavening influence. Vague hints that political prisoners might be tortured terrified Diesel more than the threat of incarceration. Diesel suddenly remembered that Fred Banner's father had once been in charge of torturing German prisoners during the World War and had acquired a reputation for sadism. The apple seldom rolled far from the tree.

Somebody removed the microphone from his hands. Diesel got a good look at the Red Army elite in the amphitheater. They were all nattily attired, wearing either dress military uniforms or lightweight linen business suits. No surprise there. Most of the men and women that he could see also wore a red armband with the yellow hammer and sickle emblem facing outward. That must signify membership in some kind of communist political party, possibly the notorious Communist International, a semi-mythical organization that supposedly had millions of members across the Commonwealth.

A commotion near the stage caused Diesel to refocus his attention on the men conducting the meeting. Supreme Commander Banner, General Patton, and General Rommel stepped to the back of the stage area, making way for Diesel's old friend Vladimir Bakunin. The crowd grew very still, like a group of Catholics given an audience with the Pope. The military leaders on stage bowed their heads reverently at the wizened old Negro. *Why would they afford so much respect to a mere barber?*

Vladimir put a microphone to his lips, but didn't start speaking right away. He turned to Patton and bowed. "Group B Commandant, Comrade Patton, makes an astute observation. We will need to clandestinely transport our entire force structure to America or Asia in the opening phase of the war, only a small number of years hence. Within one year, Red Army spies must have the capability to move from Kauai to the various continents and back, at will.

"By 1940, The Red Army will number two million. Our Communist International allies on the mainland will number in the tens of millions. They must be well armed, well trained, and ready to fight. To this end Supreme Commander Banner has placed me in charge of Red Army Intelligence and Covert Operations, Group C. In the days and years ahead, I will be making demands on the people in this room. I may demand you give up your children to Group C training camps. I may ask you to undergo plastic surgery and personally carry out Group C missions in Europe, America, Asia, or Africa. When I make these demands, comrades, remember the discipline Marxists are famous for, and comply uncomplainingly. Thank you."

Vladimir walked off the stage to the roar of the approving crowd. SC Banner returned to center stage and a hushed audience. There was something different about Fred Banner as he coldly raised the microphone to his face, something that Diesel couldn't define. The supreme commander said emotionlessly, "The lot of you will meet with the group commandant overseeing your unit once I'm finished speaking. Every military and science battle-lion will have a political officer attached, a commissar answering to Group C. The non-communists that refused to swear an oath to the revolution have been permanently incarcerated under humane conditions in the first round of purges. This gentle approach is a luxury not to be repeated. Going forward, reactionary elements will be summarily executed by battle-lion commissars."

Diesel expected that fire-breathing radicals in the crowd would roar approval at this draconian measure. The great hall remained quiescent. Military and science officers apparently were less than thrilled with the idea of political officers holding the power of life and death over the men and women in their command, especially without the moderating influence of a court-martial. Perhaps the officers should brush up on the works of the communist icons portrayed in the banner over the great hall. Spartacus had been more of a butcher and a thief than a noble revolutionary. Marx and Engels wrote about "Inroads of despotism" and the "Dictatorship of the proletariat." Despotic governments and police states don't hold trials. The officers should have known that. *They've sown the wind, let them reap the whirlwind.*

SC Banner was still speaking. "My final point is this: We are no longer Red Force. The term refers to a military establishment governed by and subservient to the corrupt Commonwealth. Uttering the words Red Force is now illegal. We are the Red Army, governed by the Communist International. Vladimir Bakunin was, at one time, high commissioner of the International. That title has been handed over to me. I now hold two titles: supreme commander of the Red Army and high commissioner of the Communist International. I would, however, prefer to be addressed as Comrade Banner." He stepped back from the microphone stand and bowed to the officers.

The applause was tumultuous. The military and science leaders set aside their trepidation over the independent political officers soon to join their units and clapped their hands, stomped their feet, and screamed praise at the radical ideas set forth. More than anything, they were delighted with the idea of fighting a real war. Shaving ten years off the start date, planning a surprise nuclear strike on Hawaii, fighting in every corner of the globe against the outmatched bourgeois armies of the corrupt capitalist Commonwealth: all these thing were wildly popular with the frontline warriors.

A sergeant-at-arms cranked up the public address system to deafening levels and shouted for silence. He explained that military police were roaming through the auditorium, handing out assignment cards to every man and woman present. These cards bore the time and place that each officer would be required to meet with his or her group commandant, as well as the name of the political officer assigned to their units. As soon as an officer received a card, he or she pushed out of the room. The three group commandants were waiting outside, in the courtyard, for informal audiences with anyone who wanted to speak with them before the formal meeting.

Diesel took a second to open the card that a burly MP shoved in his hand and learned that George Patton was his group leader. He scanned the list of ten commissars that would be attached to the ten battle-lions that made up Project Mole. None of the names looked familiar. He made his way outside the building and into the courtyard, determined to see Patton.

A stampeding crowd jostled the aging engineer, every man or woman eager to gain the ear of either the supreme commander or one of the three group commandants. Not only did the crush of people aggravate his injured back, Diesel really needed to talk to Patton, far more than anyone else in the crowd.

For the first time since he was summoned to participate in the wretched meeting, something appeared to go right. A phalanx of three tough looking military cops battered through the crowd, making their way toward the Mole chief. As they got closer he could see Group B emblems on their shoulder boards. The cops surrounded Diesel, giving him enough room to take a deep breath and rub his aching back. *Maybe being part of Group B wasn't so bad.* Unobtrusive blows to the breadbasket and boot stomps into the feet of the crowd propelled Diesel's phalanx effortlessly to General Patton's staff car.

Before ducking inside the idling automobile, Diesel glanced at two flags planted on either front fender: the red hammer and sickle that symbolized the Red Army/Communist International and a second crimson standard with yellow letters spelling out: Group B. Then Diesel noticed the car itself. The vehicle looked like a rolling piece of modern sculpture, as low-slung and swoopy as a fighter jet. It wouldn't have looked out of place on a racetrack. Red Force, no Red Army, land vehicles usually looked more like panzers than racecars.

He gave an involuntary wheeze of pain as he stooped down to squeeze next to Group Commandant Patton. The low-slung racecar was exceedingly difficult to get in and out of. Patton sounded concerned as he asked, "Group C spies inform me that Herr Diesel sustained a back injury in the mine. Is this true?" Diesel nodded through the pain. Patton handed him a canteen of water and two large blue horse pills. Without asking any questions, the Mole chief downed the big blue pills, guessing that they were muscle relaxants.

Patton spied two men approaching the large racecar. He rolled down a window and yelled, "Ferdinand, Ferdy, get in the back. I'll ride shotgun." Patton got out, ran around the aluminum-skinned vehicle and sat next to his driver in the front. A man in his mid-fifties and a boy of nineteen got in the back with Diesel. The newcomers were small men, dark-haired, neat and trim in white tropical business suits. They looked so much alike that one could immediately tell that they were father and son.

Diesel knew Doctor Ferdinand Porsche and his son Ferdy, but he didn't know them well. The elder Porsche was the chief of Project Beetle, the engineering task force charged with designing and building the Red Army's powered combat suits. The good feeling Diesel had felt about Group B intensified. He didn't like communism. He did like the efficient way that Patton was putting his design chiefs together.

The three engineers exchanged pleasantries. "This car is handmade, one of a kind. I built it specifically for General Patton," Ferdy said proudly, failing to add that the car was designed by Giocchino Colombo, an employee of Enzo Ferrari. The elder Porsche had bought the designs from Ferrari before joining the Red Force. "Comrade Patton, please forgive my impertinence, but I cannot have my father and myself chauffeured in a Porsche Grand Touring Sedan. The GTS is a sports car, not a limousine. With your permission, I will drive us to the Beetle proving grounds in Princeville," the younger Porsche said determinedly.

Patton looked doubtful. Ferdinand insisted that his son was the best driver on the island, and would therefore get them to their destination much quicker than anybody else. The general sensed that the Porsches could not be dissuaded. He gave his driver the day off. Ferdy got behind the wheel of the outlandish GTS. Its primary engine throbbed with lusty power. Ferdy boasted that the dual turbocharged V16 power plant was mid-mounted, all aluminum, and produced 1600 horsepower. The wail of several tiny ground effect engines added a falsetto accompaniment to the baritone of the V16.

All four tires laid long black patches of burnt rubber on the gray asphalt road as Ferdy let out the clutch and mashed the accelerator pedal to the floorboard. Diesel was pressed back into his seat with the mounting G-force. His back would have erupted in pain if not for the muscle relaxants.

They raced to the opposite side of the island, weaving in and out of traffic, darting between lumbering agricultural vehicles and dinosaur-like troop transporters. The Porsche automobile seemed to grab the twisty road and straighten it, aided by the suction of ground effect machinery. If traffic grew too thick to swerve through, its ground effect engines were reversed, turning the racecar into a hovercraft, enabling it to vault over stalled vehicles with the help of solid fueled booster rockets.

By the time they reached the other side of the island, Diesel's hands had cramped from the effort of gripping the armrests. Ferdy jammed the parking brake into place, allowed the GTS to fishtail to a state of rest, and took a moment to observe that if he and his father were still working for Daimler-Ford-Alco, a vehicle like the GTS would be impossible to build. With Gottlieb Daimler dead, Henry Ford cared only for the low end of the market. Diesel nodded in feigned agreement, he wisely didn't say that the prospect of a communist government permitting a blatantly bourgeois car like the GTS was extremely remote. Now would be a bad time to start a fight with the two German designers and there would never be a good time to say anything even remotely negative about communism.

Diesel looked around in surprise. Most of the design centers and research stations on Kauai were plastic and steel buildings of strikingly modern architecture, an esthetic statement to bolster the image of cutting-edge designers, men and women on the forefront, ahead of their time. The Beetle design center consisted of a series of large buildings, in neat rows, made from hardwood logs pulled from the forest with oxen, very rustic. The cutting-edge technology was all inside. Diesel's intuition told him that there was something very interesting inside the closest building. He forced himself to get out of the low-slung racer slowly and carefully. The pills he'd taken had not cured the injury to his back. They'd only eased the pain.

Patton, Ferdinand, Ferdy, and Diesel entered the building, crossed a hallway, and went inside a design lab. Diesel froze in his tracks. A pinniped combat suit sat in the center of the room. While the machine was clearly designed to fit a war seal, the first word it brought to mind was *mole*. The PCS was a mechanical mole. After viewing the war seal combat suit for a few seconds, Diesel felt ashamed that he'd named his bulky burrowing locomotive Mole I. This device was the real mole. Its metallic forelimbs were two oversized biomechanical claws extending from the upper torso. The rest of the sleek design fit the streamlined shape of a war seal. A living breathing mole and a seal were shaped about the same, except a mole had a shorter neck. The extra length of the digging claws compensated for the pinniped suit's long neck. Six antennae projected from the snout of the combat suit, like the muzzle of a European star-nosed mole, sensing devices that would help the seals navigate through dense layers of primordial ooze.

Ferdinand said, "Behold the Talpidae PCS." Diesel grinned. Talpidae was the scientific name for mole. The Porches had picked that name to assuage his feelings. He could keep on calling his gigantic borrowing machines Mole I, II, and III.

Hundreds of thousands of war seals inside Talpidae combat suits would be able to crawl through the miles of primordial ooze, exiting and entering the tunnel fortress that Diesel was digging under the Pacific with ease. They would also be very good at burrowing through regular soil and attacking shoreline installations. The design was geared toward combat within the Hawaiian archipelago, which, of course, had been the Red Force's only projected theater of operation before it had mutated into the Red Army.

Ferdinand was watching Diesel closely, as if he could read the other German engineer's thoughts. "Can this biomechanical design be adapted to work in a submarine as long as a football field? This is your question, Herr Diesel?"

"Correct, Doctor Porsche, that is my question."

"I have designs on the drawing boards that will work. The problem resides in a sufficiently robust power source. Give me small nuclear generators and I will give you submarines with legs and an articulated body."

"I can't envision such a machine. I'm trying and drawing a blank."

"Think of a mechanical crocodile. It swims by moving its body in a serpentine manner. The legs and the body propel it through mud. Our submarines will have to crack open underwater, emulating the clamshell function of a power suit, to expel hovercrafts and fighter jets. The submarine hulls will have jointed seams for serpentine swimming. Let us use this to our advantage for the clamshell function. In open water, we use propellers like a normal submarine. In the ooze: crocodile swimming."

The father and son inventors gave Diesel a tour of the other design rooms, filled with mock-ups of war machines. One outstanding facet of their design philosophy was readily apparent: the Porsches borrowed heavily from nature. There was an animalistic aura to all their creations.

Like all truly devout communists, Vladimir craved the simple life of a proletariat. He missed his barbershop and the easy lifestyle it represented. The Marxist creed: From each according to his ability, to each according to his needs, precluded his ever living the simple life again. His ability made him the only person in the Red Army capable of leading the Group C intelligence service, negating his need to live a simple life.

His doorbell rang. That would be Major O'Brien. Duty called. The former San Francisco police chief bulled into the house, with a padlocked steel-bound notebook under his arm. O'Brien sat down in one of the living room chairs and said, "Comrade Bakunin, here is the political report from my commissars. The number of anti-communist statements made by Red Army soldiers and officers was insane. Gonna have to beat a revolutionary attitude into some of these hard cases. That or get busy with a couple firing squads."

Vladimir nodded unhappily and said, "The commissars have their work cut out. The Red Army is eager to start and win World War II. Building communism and winning the peace are afterthoughts to many of our comrades." His head stopped nodding. His tone went from sad to brisk: "I'll deal with anti-communist statements later. The Mole and Beetle Projects have developed a way to clandestinely place a Red Army operative on the west coast of the United States. You are that operative."

O'Brien cracked his knuckles, patted his pockets until he found a cigar, and popped it into his mouth nervously. Vladimir glared him into not lighting it. The former policeman asked, "Plastic surgery, eh? I hook up with the cells we built in the western United States?"

Vladimir nodded again, fleshing in details. The stronger cells needed to begin recruiting guerilla fighters. Millions of troops must be ready to hit the streets when the balloon went up. And there was a need to gather intelligence well before then. Group A's war plans were being drafted in a near vacuum. The only information of the outside world entering Kauai came filtered through the TV and radio stations owned by Daimler-Ford-Alco. As the global supermonopoly became more powerful, its broadcasts became increasingly less reliable. And finally, the Red Army needed to steal fission reactor technology that DFA was developing on the west coast.

O'Brien smoothed his moustache and chewed his cigar, nervousness shading into excitement. He broke into Vladimir's lengthy rationale for putting agents on the mainland. "No need to convince me, preaching to the choir."

"So, you accept the assignment?"

"Put me in coach."

"American slang is elusive. A simple yes or no will suffice."

"Jesus Christ, Vlad... Yes, I accept the assignment. Cut up my face. Stuff me into an experimental PCS. Get me to the mainland. Put me in the game. I'm ready to play."

Chapter 7

Freedom of Cyber-speech Threatens DFA as a Lesser
Monopoly Moves to Pick Up the Pieces

S ome parts of southern England were subjected to the hideously loud trumpeting of mammoths in the spring, the mating season for the hirsute monsters. Other parts were afflicted with the equally obnoxious hooting and screeching of gorillas bred and trained to speak sign language. Thankfully, in this little corner of the Southland, spring brought only the song of birds, the scamper of small woodland creatures, and the blossom of flowers. Prime Minister Voss and Chief of Staff Churchill strolled through the gardens of Voss's private estate, imbibing the sights and sounds of the new season. The bucolic splendor should have soothed the frayed nerves of Voss, the Commonwealth's second most powerful man, but didn't.

Voss could have been accurately portrayed as the most powerful man on the planet as recently as a year ago. But at the beginning of 1930, most scholars and pundits considered the chairman of the board and majority stockholder of DFA, Henry Ford, to have supplanted the British PM in global political power. About two months ago, Voss had first found it necessary to negotiate with Mr. Ford before introducing an important piece of legislation in the Commonwealth Congress. Since then, Voss had met with Ford three times, wrangling over anti-pollution legislation, minimum wage rates, and mandatory employer funded health plans, essentially garnering Ford's permission to proceed with a specific legislative agenda.

Winston Churchill wanted to stop all face-to-face negotiation between the PM and Chairman Ford. Direct talks of that nature elevated Ford as a political leader in the eyes of the public, eroding the government's authority and strengthening the supermonopoly. Instead, Churchill would bargain with Ford as Voss's proxy, launching the new tactic with a controversial proposal designed to curb DFA's power over the high-tech industry: the Freedom of Cyber-speech bill.

Voss leaned over a flowerbed, plucked an aromatic blossom, sniffed it, and tucked it into his lapel. "I don't know to whom my power has flowed more towards, Henry Ford or Winston Churchill," he said with a second little sniff.

Churchill had to stuff his hands in his trouser pockets to keep from tearing at his hair. "If Ford fights us tooth and nail, the Freedom of Cyber-speech bill will go down in flames," he said. "Please excuse my mixing of metaphors when I say that this bill is the opening broadside in a lengthy campaign to limit the power of DFA. There will be failures in the years ahead. DFA will fight back. The prime minister cannot be the point man in a losing fight with Henry Ford. If the Cyber-speech bill fails, pin it on me."

"If Cyber-speech wins, the credit goes where?"

"To the Voss administration."

"Very well, Winston, pack your bags for a trip to Tokyo. Good luck battling Henry Ford."

Churchill rolled his eyes in exasperation and said, "DFA's headquarters are now in San Jose, California, Silicon Valley. The relocation of the supermonopoly's headquarters underscores the importance of Cyber-speech, the Cybernet, and computers." Voss made an unintelligible noise that sounded like, "Harrumph," and turned back to his contemplation of flowers.

Churchill spent the next three days arranging a meeting with Henry Ford. He considered it shameful that the lead negotiator for the world government had to bow and scrape to receive an audience with the plutocrat, Ford. Actually, the true shame was that the Commonwealth needed to negotiate with this horrible man in the first place. Ford had never run for office. He had no right to meddle in the law-making process.

At least the Chief of Staff didn't have to fly to California in one of those commercial cattle car jet liners that crawled across the Atlantic at a snail's pace. The Crown provided its elite servants with customized supersonic fighter jets, weapons removed and luxury appointments installed by Scuderia Ferrari, an Italian company owned by the famed racecar driver and fledgling auto manufacturer, Enzo Ferrari.

Churchill's private jet touched down at the San Jose aeroport a week before he was scheduled to meet with Henry Ford. That week would be spent learning about computers and the Cybernet. Despite the familiarity he affected with the goings-on in Silicon Valley to R.H. Voss, Churchill had only a vague notion as to how computers really worked.

He walked out of the concourse. Jan Kaplan, an attractive brunette, was standing on the sidewalk, holding a sign with his name on it. Churchill had hired Jan, a coed from Stanford and a computer science major, to tutor him. As a young man, his ability to study and learn had been the stuff of legend. Nowadays, the only way he could master a difficult subject quickly was to have it spoon-fed by a beautiful woman.

The president of Stanford hadn't lied: Jan was an eyeful. But she shook hands like a man, with a crushing grip, too strong for a woman. And she was tall for a woman, a few inches taller than he was. The way she walked around her Ferrari Spyder to open the passenger door was also mannish, or perhaps only athletic, Churchill couldn't decide which. He was decisive about the Spyder: the car was noisy and uncomfortable. The Commonwealth Congress had been excited when a competitor to DFA's auto monopoly emerged last year. Sitting in the cramped low-slung vehicle, Churchill's enthusiasm for trust busting competition waned. He would have much preferred a DFA Rolls-Royce.

The Spyder motored through downtown San Jose, past soaring towers of steel and glass filled with prosperous businesspeople in silk suits or skirts and heels. He wondered how many silk suits worked for Daimler-Ford-Alco. The signs and corporate logos on top the skyscrapers were deceptive. IBM, Silicon Manufacturing Inc., Digital Harmon, they were all partially owned subsidiaries of DFA. Equity shares in each of these companies traded apart from the supermonopoly under various symbols, heightening the illusion of independence, but they were all partially owned DFA subsidiaries. He was drafting legislation that would make it illegal for DFA subsidiaries to hide behind the names of other companies and pretend that they were independent entities. It wasn't much of a curb on supermonopoly power, but it was politically feasible and it was a start.

The little sports car drove through the shadow of the DFA building. It looked like one of many corporate headquarters, no larger or smaller than the others. The semblance of a community of independent businesses was perfect. In reality, each building was like a tree in a forest of quaking aspen, they may all look like separate plants, but all shared the same root system, part and parcel of a single organism. His legislation wouldn't really change all that. At a minimum, it would destroy the illusion and force all these businesses to plaster the DFA logo on their buildings and advertising.

Where would it lead? Would the chairman of DFA eventually become an elected position, stepping into the shoes of the Commonwealth Congress? Would DFA merge with the government? Was that corporate socialism or state capitalism? Churchill stared grumpily out the window of the Spyder. There was no way to answer these questions with DFA squelching any software program that could run Historical Parallel equations.

Jan drove out of the city, up the peninsula, and through a eucalyptus forest. She rolled down the window, permeating the cab with the fragrant aroma of gum trees. Churchill filled his lungs with the refreshing scent. It made him think of South Africa.

The forest thinned. They rolled through a thoroughbred horse ranch, replete with white fences and red barns. A series of long, sinuous earth colored buildings replaced the horse pastures: the outer perimeter of the campus. A cobblestone road took them into the heart of the university, dominated by a terracotta art deco tower, a striking counterpoint to the starkly modern architecture of stainless steel classrooms, dormitories, and gymnasiums pervasive throughout the rest of the campus.

Jan led her middle-aged charge to the ornate door of the art deco tower and said, "Welcome to Cleveland Tower, part of the Cleveland Presidential Library." She pointed to a window near the top of the reddish concrete structure. The windows were barred on the upper floor, either part of the art deco motif, or a safety precaution. "That will be your room, Sir, second window on the left, a suite actually, quite swish."

Churchill experienced a flashback to his days as a prisoner in the Boer War. The prison-like tower, the need to master academic material, the foreign land, the gum tree forest: all these things combined to trigger an uncomfortable déjà vu. He stumbled over the steps leading into the tower. Jan expressed concern, wondering if he felt faint, taking his hand, leading him through the marble lobby.

He reluctantly admitted to a sense of déjà vu from the Boer War. She asked in a puzzled voice, "Grover Cleveland and you built the Commonwealth together. Don't you feel his spirit here? The walls are imbued with Cleveland's presence." Churchill failed to reply. He did not want to be haunted by Grover Cleveland's ghost.

They entered the elevator together. Inside, a portrait of the late American President smiled benignly on the occupants. Churchill forgot the Boer War and remembered his days spent with Cleveland after the World War, recalling how the president had refused to insert antitrust language in the Commonwealth Constitution. Much of the world's maladies could be laid at Grover Cleveland's feet. The elevator whisked them to the top of the building.

Still holding his hand, Jan led the politician into a room, frowning at the way he hadn't answered her question. Churchill's manners returned once he walked free of the odious portrait of Grover Cleveland. He told Jan not to worry about his state of mind. She mustn't listen to the ravings of a nearly senile old man. She grabbed his other hand and said, "You're hardly senile, Mr. Churchill, and not at all what I expected." He asked her to clarify the last statement, what exactly had she expected?

Jan murmured, "I thought you'd be a superman, stepping straight out of the pages of history. I didn't expect you'd be so approachable, so human." Churchill realized the compliment was very left handed. It didn't matter. He invited her to stay for a while, asking if the tower staff offered room service and if she'd eaten dinner yet.

"We can have a meal delivered by ringing the desk. I'm afraid it will originate in the student cafeteria, edible but not very fancy. I would love to join you for dinner. I shall give a brief lecture on the Cybernet after we've eaten, give you something to digest tonight besides overcooked spaghetti."

Jan was serious about giving him a lesson in cybernetics, and nothing else. That was probably better than what he had been hoping for. There really was a tremendous amount for him to learn in the next seven days, and he could tell that by being patient and respectful, the athletic but beautiful coed might eventually offer him more than dry academics. His belly stuffed with pasta, a glass of passable merlot in his hand, Churchill learned about the Cybernet.

Not counting the computers on the Hawaiian Islands used by the Red and Blue Forces, every mainframe on the planet above a series eight was linked via telephone lines. This network comprised the Cybernet. The DFA subsidiary, IBM, would only lease high-powered mainframes, never sell them. Other DFA subsidiaries owned the world's telephone lines. The upshot: DFA owned and controlled the Cybernet.

The world straddling supermonopoly took ownership seriously in regards to the Cybernet. It could and did open files on its leased mainframes and purge any contents threatening the interests of DFA. IBM programmers would send viruses into the mainframes of any company or individual that tried to link non-IBM computers by phone lines. The supermonopoly ruled the Cybernet with an iron fist.

Jan explained how these loathsome cyber crimes were committed, giving technical details in a way that Churchill could understand. She speculated what future actions DFA might foist on the cyber community as it gradually expanded the net into smaller machines. DFA could rig elections, crush labor unions, or force competitors and opponents to rely on pen and paper, denying them the use of computers and thereby regulating enemies or rivals into the digital dark ages.

There was only one thing Jan didn't understand. How could DFA be so brazen? It wasn't yet in a position to truly challenge the Commonwealth. The proof was the Cyber-speech bill before the world congress. Even if it were defeated in this go around, the bill would resurface. DFA seemed to be overstepping its bounds.

Churchill drained the last drop of merlot in his glass and said, "A bargaining chip. I suspect Henry Ford is after something that the Crown possesses. And by the Crown, I don't mean the British government, but the actual King of England."

"Henry Ford is willing to bargain away dominance of the Cybernet to gain something that the King owns? What, a prized polo pony?" Jan asked sarcastically. Churchill filled both of their wine glasses and replied, "The King owns the technology that will emerge from the 1950 CMG. If his Majesty were to sell the bulk of this super advanced CMG technology to the handful of companies able to compete with DFA, Ferrari for instance, the world economic picture might radically change."

She looked at Churchill with awe, visions of David and Goliath filling her head. Her admiring stare was a good indicator that he could sleep with her tonight, with a little more wine and the right banter. He surprised himself by calling it a night, shooing her out of the suite, promising an early start in the morning. If he wanted a long-term relationship with Jan Kaplan, then having sex with her at the very first opportunity might poison the well. And he decided that a long-term relationship would be nice, something to think about at least. He was getting tired of the freewheeling bachelor lifestyle.

Who would have guessed that buying the largest restaurant chain in the world would lead to the creation of an automobile competitor? DFA's acquisition of Speedee Burger had been a carefully planned operation, a textbook example of the supermonopoly expanding into a new niche. When DFA started snapping up shares of Speedee Burger it already owned the meat processing plants, cattle ranches, and farms that the sprawling restaurant chain depended on. Once the intercontinental restaurant conglomerate had been gobbled up, DFA was well placed to put competing fast food chains out of business through predatory pricing policies on a wholesale and retail level.

Where did we go wrong? Henry Ford thought, fingering a brochure for the Ferrari GTS, Spyder, and Spyder convertible. He threw the brochure on his desk and stared at Alfred Sloan as if the president of DFA had personally built the Italian sports cars. Obviously, Sloan had done no such thing. The ten largest shareholders of Speedee Burger bore the blame for that particular tragedy. The fast food moguls had received billions for their stock. They'd dutifully signed contracts to never compete against DFA's Speedee Burger restaurants. They hadn't signed contracts to forgo building and marketing automobiles. The billions Henry Ford had used to buy the thousands and thousands of hamburger joints dotting the toll roads DFA owned on six continents had been funneled into an obscure Italian company that built racecars.

Until recently, the executives at DFA's automotive divisions had been barely aware that Scuderia Ferrari existed. They had a vague notion that it refurbished old racecars for resale as street cars, their only competition in the retail auto market, capturing .0001 percent of the market. No DFA executive in his wildest dreams had guessed that Ferrari could come up with a dynamic marketing scheme. Flush with capital, Ferrari established a dealer network and exclusively advertised the ultra-exotic, ultra-expensive GTS sports car, offering free test-drives to anyone with a license and a job. The majority of these customers were baited and switched to the more affordable four-cylinder Spyder, which was still faster and handled better than anything DFA produced. The GTS was not a direct threat to the auto divisions of the supermonopoly. The Spyder was a deadly threat, its market share growing daily.

DFA's Rolls-Royce division was scrabbling to build both a high-end sports car to compete with the GTS and a low-end sports car to compete with the Spyder. The experience had so far proven humbling to the clumsy and inflexible supermonopoly. Its first instinct, to crush Ferrari with predatory pricing, had been abandoned before getting off the ground. Even the little Spyder was more expensive than most DFA autos. People weren't buying the Italian sports cars because of price. They wanted performance. Six months had gone by since the GTS and Spyder had hit the street and the fumbling Rolls-Royce division had not even designed its answer yet.

Ford continued glaring at Sloan. The president of the largest commercial empire in history gazed back with equanimity. Sloan was a neat and dapper man in a dark blue suit, balding, fleshy without being fat. The president of DFA said, "It's going to happen again, Henry. The price we pay for an acquisition is so high these days that the folks we buy out have no place to park their money other than DFA stock or bonds, neither pays much of a return. They're forced to open shop and compete with one of our divisions or subsidiaries." Sloan thought about comparing this dynamic to the legend of Hercules chopping off the heads of the Hydra, only to see a dozen more heads spring to life, but decided that the literal minded Ford would miss the analogy. Besides, Sloan had an idea that would turn the problem around and possibly make a dent in the deflation problem too, killing two birds with one stone.

The angry fire in Ford's eyes dwindled like a banked firebox. He could tell that Sloan had a solution. The chairman of the board waited silently for his president to elaborate. "What Ferrari is doing to us is our own damn fault." Ford's face immediately flushed with rage, though he managed to hold his tongue. Sloan remained unflappable. "We've no luxury products. DFA makes cheap cars for the masses. Modular homes for the working class. We make commercial jets and ocean liners, but no fancy yachts or swish private jets."

"Hold your horses, Alfred. We convert ocean liners and jetliners into yachts and private planes, customize all sorts of railcars for wealthy clients."

Sloan's solution rolled forth. He scoffed at DFA's maladroit efforts to create luxury products. They didn't need to modify commercial vehicles, they needed to design and build these products from the ground up. More than that, they needed to create a luxury culture, create an indolent luxury class out of the major shareholders from the companies DFA took over.

Sloan gave the full breadth and width of his vision. Private islands would be outfitted with sumptuous mansions, jets, helicopters, and yachts. Hangars on the private islands would include one jet for transporting people and another for transporting a stable of polo ponies. Private jets and helicopters would use artificial intelligence technology to make them as easy to drive as a car.

The chairman caught on right away. Affecting an English accent, Ford said, "I say, Reginald, care for a spot of polo? I'll load my ponies into the jet and fly over to your island."

Sloan smiled broadly and sketched in the fine details. DFA would launch a new division, dedicated to producing luxury goods. They would buy out Scuderia Ferrari and put Enzo Ferrari in charge of the new monopoly. DFA's real estate division would have to switch gears and start buying islands and oceanfront property. Plans to build Rolls-Royce sports cars could be tabled since the Ferrari models would join the DFA product line up.

Ford rocked back in his chair with a calculating look and threw a little cold water on the scheme. "Buying out Ferrari and building a slew of new products will cost a fortune." He didn't finish his thought because the intercom on his desk scratched with static. His secretary said, "Mr. Ford, your one o'clock is here. Chief of Staff Churchill." Ford asked that Churchill be admitted to his office.

Winston walked into Ford's office, took a moment to admire the panoramic view of San Jose's stormy skyline through the picture window comprising one wall of the room, unhurriedly put his raincoat and hat on a rack, and only then greeted Alfred Sloan and Henry Ford. The latter asked Churchill if he'd had lunch.

Taking a chair, declining the luncheon invitation, Churchill leveled a cool gaze at the industrial magnates. He sat there impassively, as if the industrialists had called for the meeting, a stratagem to force them to make the opening gambit.

Sloan obliged by saying, "Free speech in cyberspace and trust busting in high-technology, eh? Ten Downing Street is sticking its beak where it doesn't belong." Sloan paused to see if this would get a rise out of Churchill. When it didn't he continued: "Peachy keen, let's talk monopolies. Here's a juicy tidbit: the combined value of all the DFA auto dealerships roughly equals the value of DFA's auto divisions. The car dealerships are independently owned and operated franchises. How can we have a monopoly in the automobile industry if there are tens of thousands of small independent car dealers?"

Churchill asked sharply, "DFA has no plans to buy the tens of thousands of independent car dealers, turn them into factory outlets?"

"We can't afford to. Not now," Henry Ford said mournfully. That answered Churchill's question, someday DFA would take over its independent dealer network. Churchill fired another question, "How many auto dealerships would I be permitted to purchase, own, and operate, assuming I wanted to change careers?" Without thinking Ford shot back, "Nobody is allowed more than ten." Churchill let that hang without comment. DFA itself would not permit a monopoly in its own backyard.

Ford and Sloan clamped their jaws shut sullenly. They didn't like the direction the negotiations were taking. The last time Ten Downing Street wanted to pass a Commonwealth law, DFA had haggled with Prime Minister Voss. The PM had proven to be easier to bully than his chief of staff.

Sloan tried to swamp his opponent with statistics. "DFA's percentage share of Gross Commonwealth Product increased last year by a paltry .1 percent. At that rate we will control the entire global economy in one thousand years, hardly a cause for alarm."

The chief of staff fired back that last year saw the rise of Scuderia Ferrari, an anomaly to the overall trend of supermonopoly manufacturing growth. Sloan's statistic was misleading in other ways as well, the DFA dealer networks for boats, cars, modular homes, aeroplanes, etc, didn't show up as a percentage of GCP, yet these businesses were obviously under the thumb of the supermonopoly. Churchill didn't want to argue statistical trivia with Sloan. He wanted to speak about what was closest to his heart: Historical Parallelism.

"Projecting the growth rate of DFA and its future percentage of GCP can only be done by running months worth of Historical Parallelism equations on a network of supercomputers. That will happen after we pass the Freedom of Cyber-speech bill. Plotting last year's growth rate and drawing a straight line on a graph to indicate future growth is a fool's errand. Please refrain from insulting my intelligence."

Sloan surprised Churchill by mentioning Heisenberg's uncertainty principle. Scientists with doctorates in HP had been trying to decide if Heisenberg's theory applied to Historical Parallelism. Churchill didn't realize that Sloan possessed that kind of sophistication.

Ford asked Sloan to slow down and put his argument into understandable terms. Sloan gave the salient points of Heisenberg seminal work, namely that the act of observing a phenomena affects the object being observed. Even though Heisenberg had been talking about subatomic particles, his theory applied to HP. Quantifying and describing historical forces through the prism of HP equations changes the course of history. HP equations don't predict the future; they shape the future as self-fulfilling prophecies. This is why DFA outlawed the science of Historical Parallelism.

This wasn't statistical trivia. It was a valid scientific argument, but not one that Churchill wanted to get sucked into. Time to lay the hammer down. "At the conclusion of the 1950 CMG, King William or his designated heir, Crown Princess Victoria, will sell the CMG technology, not to the highest bidder, but to any company or person that I care to name, for any amount I care to choose."

This got their attention. Sloan and Ford sat up very straight in their chairs. Ford had been playing with a letter opener. He set it down to concentrate on whatever Churchill might say next.

"Having the King and the Princess's ear, I could recommend that every CMG patent and invention be sold to Enzo Ferrari for a mere ten million pounds."

The ticking of a wall clock was suddenly the loudest sound in the room. The faint buzz of traffic from the wet streets below the penthouse office could be distinctly heard. He had them over a barrel. Churchill kept any hint of triumph off his face. He let them sweat for a few seconds and said, "Or I could recommend that the CMG technology be sold to DFA."

The wall clock continued to beat like a drum. Churchill struck for the jugular. "This price is not negotiable: ten billion pounds. That's billion with a 'b.' I shall also require DFA's cooperation in passing the Freedom of Cyber-speech bill. The ten billion pounds will be payable in one lump sum at the end of this year."

He let that sink in. The magnates were surely visualizing the contract he would force them to sign. The doors to HP research would be flung wide open. With twenty odd years before Red Force or Blue Force prevailed in Hawaii War II and the dispersal of the resulting CMG technology, there was no way the plutocrats could renege on any agreement.

Ford and Sloan looked as if they'd been sucking on lemons. The ten billion pound price tag was filtering up from their stomachs to their heads. Time to leave and let them stew in their juices.

Churchill grabbed his coat and hat and fled Ford's office, eager to leave before the magnates could recover from their shock and initiate a squabble over the outrageous price he intended to cram down their throats. "I'll let myself out, don't bother to get up. A contract will be faxed from London to San Jose in a fortnight."

He practically sprinted out of DFA headquarters. Jan had her Ferrari Spyder idling against the curb in front of the building like a getaway car, enduring the hostile stares of Daimler-Ford-Alco employees. She had the only non-DFA auto on the street. Churchill hopped inside and planted a kiss on her cheek.

Ford and Sloan watched the bright red getaway car speed into the soggy beginnings of the San Jose rush hour with a mixture of anger and chagrin. Ford returned to his desk. Sloan stayed at the window and observed, "Ten billion pounds. We can't afford to pay it.

We can't afford not to pay it."

"We can afford that much," Ford said firmly.

"How? It will take billions to buy out Ferrari, billions more to create our luxury division. We have to operate Speedee Burger at a loss to kill the competition. Ferrari is forcing us to hold down the price of cars. In the other industries, we aren't strong enough yet to abandon predatory pricing policies, a source of worldwide deflation. Borrowing billions will raise global interest rates and kill retail sales. Cutting salaries more than what we've done will also kill retail sales and make deflation worse. Welcome to the downside of running a supermonopoly. Our employees are our customers."

"There is a third way. We can keep the salaries of the rank and file steady, but increase hours at every factory, farm, and construction site in the company. We go from our standard 60-hour workweek to a 100-hour workweek. Increased output will make up for Churchill's highway robbery."

"That will lead to other problems, especially since we're creating a luxury division. Class warfare, union strife."

"Nothing we can't handle. It'll mean breaking the unions and breaking some skulls. We've always known that someday there would be a showdown with the unions."

The private jet touched down at RAF Base 4, five miles south of London. Churchill wished the thinly disguised fighter jet had been modified more thoroughly for civilian use. With just a pilot and one passenger in its extended cockpit, a transatlantic journey was tolerable. With he and Jan sharing the passenger compartment, the journey was grueling. Naturally, his creaky fifty-something body had suffered more than her supple twenty-four-year-old frame.

Before the flight had even begun, Jan succeeded in shocking Churchill for the umpteenth time. She'd suggested that the RAF pilot take a commercial flight back to England, and that she fly the plane instead. Churchill had questioned her severely to find out if she really was certified to fly a Wasp fighter. Jan rattled off the name of her instructor in the ROTC program where she'd earned her wings. Her last stint in a fighter had been less than one month ago, service with California's Aero National Guard. Churchill declined her offer, which made the flight back home extremely crowded and uncomfortable.

At least the military aerobase wasn't as crowded as a civilian aeroport. Churchill and Jan walked across the tarmac to an electrified fence patrolled by soldiers and Bulldogs. Looking around the base at rows of fighters and bombers, Churchill could almost hear a captious chorus from a legion of tight-fisted taxpayers. *Why does the Crown maintain expensive military bases when war has been banished forever?*

Guards saluted the chief of staff and his companion, de-electrifying the gate to let them out. Jan gave an incredulous gasp when she saw what awaited her outside. A gleaming red Ferrari GTS sat against the curb, simply oozing insolence and style, looking as though it were breaking the sound barrier while standing still. A bright yellow bow graced its sculpted hood.

Jan squealed, "An engagement gift, a Ferrari in lieu of a ring? Oh Winston, you know me so well." She wrapped him in an embrace and planted a kiss on his mouth before he could deny that the gift was a symbol of betrothal. Jan slid behind the wheel and reached for the ignition. Churchill stopped her and said, "I won't be able to shout directions over the sound of the engine. Let me tell you know how to get to the King's estate now." He gave her a series of directions. Jan's memory was both photographic and audiographic, an image of Churchill's proposed route emerged in her mind.

The V16 awoke with a thunderous snarl. Ground effect engines hummed. The Ferrari entered a DFA toll road. In Europe (where citizens sometimes drove street legal racecars) there were no speed limits. Jan crashed through the gears, hugging the fast lane; she was soon speeding along at 150 miles-per-hour. Speedee Burgers and DFA gas stations zipped by like fence posts. She cranked the car up to 175 mph.

She was tempted to reverse the ground effect fans, ignite booster rockets, and hurtle over slower moving cars. A glance at Winston's white knuckled grip on the armrests convinced her otherwise. Sluggish traffic hardly slowed the GTS down in any case. Ground effect technology meant that she could drive on the gravel shoulder to pass and not lose control.

She didn't think any vehicle on the toll road could pass a GTS maintaining a speed of 175 mph. Incredibly, a couple of street bikes cut a middle lane and blew by the Ferrari, threading through clumps of cars effortlessly. DFA hadn't redesigned any of its motorcycles since the 1920 CMG. Unfortunately for Jan, the bike tech from that era was so hot that even a Ferrari could be put to shame by an eleven-year-old motorcycle design. She glared at the taillights of the bikers, revved up the ground effect fans, and passed the slow moving automobile traffic by swerving out onto the shoulder. The Ferrari gained ground on the impudent bikers, but there were still a bunch of dawdling cars in her way.

The third time that she made the hair raising swerve out onto the toll road's shoulder Churchill shouted over the roar of the engine, "Jan, my love, you are destroying the cars of the good citizens of Britain." She'd forgotten that the ground effect fans had exhaust vents that sprayed gravel against the doors, fenders, and windshields of the Ashfield Runabouts she'd been passing. Jan finished the trip at a more sedate speed, with the GE fans turned off. Whether driving at a blistering 175 or a pokey 100 mph, this was still the best day in her life. A marriage proposal and meeting the King of England didn't often happen in the same day. Heck, meeting the King didn't happen to average people ever.

At first glance, the fence surrounding King William's Southwestern Palace #9 appeared to be merely a larger version of the electrified fence surrounding the RAF base. Peering through the steeply slanted front windshield of the GTS, Jan could see that the 25-foot tall fence was laced with forcefield conduits, as if it were designed to repel an armored assault. Just as odd, at least to Jan, the Household cavalrymen patrolling the outer perimeter did not have a single Bulldog with them. What was that old saying about British soldiers being surgically attached to their Bulldogs? Why weren't there any dogs on guard?

She asked Winston to enlighten her. The politician smiled cryptically and said she would find out in good time. The guard at the gate let them in, issuing a strange warning: Angerbotha and Hela were drinking from a spring on the other side of the compound; this meant that the Ferrari would have to slowly idle up the hill to the palace. The engine must be kept quiet, the transmission in first gear. If Hela did appear suddenly and charged at them, race up the hill as fast as possible.

The low-slung sports car would have had a hard time traversing the bumpy gravel road at any speed above 5 mph, warning or no. A squat concrete fortress drew closer very slowly, apparently a remnant of the World War, not a proper palace by any means. Talking over the muted rumble of the V16 proved relatively easy. Jan asked, "Who or what are Angerbotha and Hela?" Churchill's cryptic look intensified. He gave a typically enigmatic answer: "In Norse mythology, Angerbotha is a giantess that spawns fearsome monsters. Hela is one of those monsters. There are no Bulldogs in or near the compound because Hela throws herself at Bulldogs with rampant fury." Jan gave a disgusted snort, pretty sure that they weren't driving into the pages of a mythology storybook.

On closer inspection, the squat concrete structure was indeed an old command post from the World War. A second forcefield fence surrounded the chunky gray building. Another guard (still no Bulldogs) let them into the inner compound, pointing toward a carport with Churchill's name stenciled in the asphalt. They exited the Ferrari, retrieving the small amount of luggage they managed to squeeze into the cramped cargo area of the rakish sports car. A doorman with a tranquilizer gun let them into the palace. Jan asked the doorman, "Why a tranquilizer rifle?" He explained that if Hela broke through the forcefield fence, and Angerbotha couldn't stop her, then he would have to, without harming the furry fiend. This only added another layer of mystery.

Jan wanted to grab her fiancé and strangle the truth out of him. Unfortunately, Jan found herself knee deep in the process of meeting the King of England as soon as she entered the palace. She followed Winston's lead, bowing at the waist, observing the forms of ritual prostration. With that out of the way, King William put a hand to an ear and asked if he heard wedding bells, glancing from the blushing Jan to the bemused Churchill. William knew that Churchill had never brought a female companion to the castle before, and had made an astute guess concerning the chief of staff's intentions.

"Yes, Your Majesty. Winston proposed today, the instant our feet hit English soil. So romantic!" Jan gushed. The King grinned in delight, turning on Churchill, demanding verification.

"Uh, y-y-yes, quite right. We are to be married," Churchill stammered. Oddly enough, he felt at ease and happy the instant he'd made the pronouncement. The King gave the couple his blessing. Churchill felt even better, grateful for Jan's adroit psychological manipulation. He had subconsciously wanted to marry her all along. Perhaps Freud was right after all. Perhaps humans really are ruled by subconscious desires.

King William put his prosthetic hand on Churchill's arm. Squeezing gently he asked, "Will Henry Ford pay Us an adequate amount of money to clone Angerbotha and Hela? Will Our dreams come true?"

"Sire, if cloning is technically possible, there will be sufficient funds. I will give your people billions." The King gave a whoop of delight, exclaiming, "Imagine thousands upon thousands of Angerbothas and Helas battling million of the finest Bulldogs! The 1950 CMG baiting contests will be more exciting than the war itself."

Jan's patience had reached its limit. Ignoring decorum, she bluntly demanded to be told who or what Angerbotha and Hela were. The King pulled a pocket watch from his vest. "My Nordic monsters will have lunch in ten minutes. We can watch from the rooftop. Learn what they are with your own eyes, Mrs. Churchill."

The concrete fortress had a perfectly flat roof, rimmed with an iron guardrail. From this vantage one could see undulating green hills, devoid of trees, a velvety green ocean of close-cropped grass. Jan thought that it must take a fair number of sheep or cattle to mow a lawn so vast, yet no herds were visible.

An agricultural helicopter thumped the air over the palace. It was a DFA Skycrane, a light-lifting chopper often used by farmers to feed livestock in remote locations. A sizeable load dangled from its undercarriage. The Skycrane hovered over a spot of earth, trampled brown by whatever creatures grazed this large pasture.

The cube dangling from the chopper was light green alfalfa hay, very high in protein. The green cube dropped onto the brown patch of earth, exploding on impact into dozens of smaller bails. The helicopter beat a hasty retreat, flying away while simultaneously reeling in the cable that had dropped the hay. Angerbotha had once grabbed the chopper's cable, nearly killing the crew as it whirled around her like a kite on a string.

The countryside grew still. The hay sat there uneaten, no sign of monsters from the pages of Norse mythology. King William muttered, "Bloody unusual. They're generally here seconds after the hay drops. Vicky must be running a bloody training exercise." Jan wanted to ask if "Vicky" was the Crown Princess Victoria. The question died on her lips as a trumpeting rang out from behind a ridge of hills.

Angerbotha's wooly head emerged from behind a hillcrest as slowly and surely as the main mast of a man o' war appearing on the horizon of a distant sea. The rest of Angerbotha's body came into view, nearly as bulky as the hill that had been hiding her. The much smaller Hela trotted behind her mother. The mammoth calf raised her trunk and issued a tinny trumpet blast.

The adult cow glided gracefully and swiftly to the mound of hay. Her trunk immediately began snaking in and out of her mouth, shoveling heaps of alfalfa into her gullet. Hela placed her pink mouth on one of her mother's two teats and gave a hearty suck. The baby mammoth looked so cute and cuddly, Jan couldn't understand why the compound guards were afraid of the adorable little tyke.

The King told Jan how his Nordic monsters had come to be. Twenty-one years ago, the King's late son, Prince Albert, had collected perfectly healthy sperm from the 10,000-year-old frozen carcasses of bull mammoths in Siberia. Fred Greystone had spent the last two years of his life overseeing Project Mammoth. With the King's purse at his disposal, Greystone had selected thousands of female Asian elephants. Most had been chosen for mammoth-like characteristics: gigantic size, profuse body hair, and lung curling tusks. A small number of elephant cows had been selected for their biddable temperament, smaller logging elephants from the teak forests of Thailand. Countless attempts of artificial insemination had been conducted, using the techniques Greystone developed in his war seal program. Ironically, the one successful pregnancy had occurred among the ranks of the tractable logging elephants. Angerbotha was born to an exceptionally well-behaved and hard working Asian logging elephant. Three years ago, Angerbotha had become pregnant with the last vile of 10,000-year-old frozen mammoth sperm, making Hela ¾ mammoth, which accounted for her fiery temperament.

Jan found the story interesting. More interesting still was the tiny human figure perched on Angerbotha's neck hump. King William noticed the direction of her gaze and said grandiloquently, "My youngest daughter, Mistress of Mammoths, future Queen of England and Empress of the British Commonwealth, Crown Princess Victoria II."

Churchill, Jan, and the King watched in awed silence as hundreds of pounds of alfalfa disappeared. Jan tugged Churchill away from the King and whispered in his ear, "Mistress of Mammoths is an official royal title?" He didn't bother responding. Not only was it an official title, the King always mentioned it before his daughter's other titles.

The tiny figure on the adult mammoth's neck hump shouted a command into Angerbotha's gigantic flapping ear. There was really no need to shout since the mammoth's hearing was hundreds of times more acute than a human being's. The Princess wanted the onlookers on the roof of the castle to know that her mammoths were acting under voice command, not wantonly charging the palace. Angerbotha ignored the last few bails of hay and trudged forward. Hela gave an angry squawk as the teat was pulled from her mouth.

Both mammoths stopped walking at the edge of the castle's forcefield fence, shaggy coats rustling in the breeze. A hundred feet separated the fence from the palace. The mammoths were close enough for Jan to catch a whiff of their musky odor. At last she could accurately gauge how big they were. Angerbotha stood over fourteen feet at the shoulder. She must have weighed ten tons. Trophy hunters in Africa reported wild elephants measuring fourteen feet at the shoulder and weighing up to twelve tons, actually a little bit heavier than Angerbotha. But African bulls set those records. Cows were usually half the size of bulls. The calf, Hela, was about the size of a small horse, nearly twice the size of an average elephant of the same age.

The King stood next to Jan and said, "It's not so much the size of Our mammoths that has Us excited. They can run much faster than an elephant, in point of fact gallop like a horse. Their hide is thicker, tougher, not to mention mammoth fur acts like armor. A mammoth's gameness or fighting spirit is much greater than even the most fierce African elephant."

The mammoths raised their trunks. Catching the odor of a stranger (Jan), Hela pawed the ground angrily and brandished her deadly little tusks. Jan took an involuntary step backward and then felt ashamed for displaying fear. Locking eyes with the smaller mammoth helped her feel better for a couple seconds, after that it proved to be a mistake. Hela charged the forcefield fence. Angerbotha aborted the attack by scooping her daughter into the bole of her ten-foot long tusks.

Princess Victoria leaned down over Angerbotha's flank and screamed a command at Hela. The calf walked out of her mother's tusk prison, sullenly eyeing the strange woman on top the castle. Angerbotha calmly stuffed grass shoots down her insatiable maw, keeping an eye on the volatile calf.

The King chuckled, cupped his hands around his mouth and shouted, "Vicky, cease playing with your pets. Come and meet Winston's betrothed." The Mistress of Mammoths whispered a command in Angerbotha's flapping ear. A trunk thicker than an industrial fire hose wrapped around the Princess's torso, setting her gently on the ground.

A minute later and the Princess joined her father and guests on the rooftop. "Quickly, Mrs. Churchill, embrace me," Vicky hissed. The two women fell into each other's arms. Her lips inches from Jan's ear, the Princess explained that Hela must see that a stranger meant no harm to the royal family. The Princess's body radiated energy, maybe even passion, as it pressed closely to Jan. The bemused American was itching to pull away from the passionate young woman when Vicky disengaged and ordered Jan to embrace the King. Jan hugged the Monarch. King William's metal arm leant a strange sensation to the physical contact. The rest of his body seemed very frail. Jan realized with a start that the King was a sick old man. It might not be long and Vicky would be Queen. Was the world ready for a second Queen Victoria?

A loud trumpet blast indicated that Hela was satisfied. Angerbotha wheeled in a tight circle, gave her calf a swat on the rump, and galloped to the uneaten bales of hay. Both mammoths moved more like rhinos than elephants. The pounding of the short gallop could be felt through the steel-reinforced concrete palace. Vicky observed, "Real mammoths may not have been able to move so swiftly. We may have created a new race by back breeding to a common ancestor of the mammoth and Asian elephant. This was the case with war seals. We would know if Fred Greystone were still alive."

The Princess knowingly looked away from her pets and asked Churchill for news concerning his negotiations with Henry Ford. He provided the answer in minute detail, describing the payment he expected to pry from the coffers of the supermonopoly and the boon this money represented to Project Mammoth. Vicky paused for a second, wondering how to phrase her request. "Sir Winston," she began smoothly. "We cannot embark on another great journey into the realm of animal husbandry without a Greystone at the helm. Angerbotha and Hela would not exist without Fred Greystone. My brother died to make sure that Greystone could finish what he started. We need his granddaughter, Lisa, as badly as We need ten billion pounds. Please secure her services for the Crown." She smiled prettily, used to her wishes and whims becoming reality after making the barest request.

Churchill bowed to the Princess, acknowledged her petition, said his good-byes, grabbed Jan by the hand, and walked away from the royals.

Sitting in the Ferrari outside the big forcefield fence, Jan wanted to know where they were headed. Churchill replied, "David and Lisa Banner's house, north of London. You heard the Princess. She says jump, we say how high?"

As it turned out, even the Princess's directive would have to be ignored, for a short while at least. Threading through the maze of the capital city, puttering through Westminster, Churchill decided to check in with his other boss, Prime Minister Voss. Churchill's timing was either incredibly good or indescribably bad, depending on perspective. Once Jan and Winston were inside Ten Downing Street, the prime minister perfunctorily acknowledged her presence and impatiently listened to the news of their betrothal. Then, as quickly as etiquette permitted, he whisked Churchill into a private room and described a pressing matter that required the chief of staff's immediate attention. The emergency involved the world's second biggest monopoly: Halifax Mining Inc.

Voss pulled a briefcase from a locked safe and dumped its contents onto a desk. He announced, "These are financial statements from Lord Halifax's stable of companies in Africa and the Levant." The prime minister looked befuddled for a second. He started over: "Did I mention that Lord Halifax is dead? Old age, natural causes, peaceful departure, all that rot." Voss made a hand gesture to indicate that the way Halifax had died was unimportant. Churchill shook his head irritably; Henry Halifax had been a friend of his.

The chief of staff pawed through the financial information, his eyes widening as he realized what had the prime minister in such a twitter. Deflation. Nothing could be more damaging to the world economy than another round of deflation.

Holding onto the briefcase that Voss had foisted on him, walking across the sidewalk in front of the prime minister's residence, Churchill grabbed Jan by the elbow, preventing her from getting inside the Ferrari. "I'm sorry, my love, being married to me may prove to be a vexing proposition. I'm afraid I've to put you to work. Will you make the trip to the Banner's house and convince them to join Project Mammoth? Other matters require my urgent attention."

Jan looked at her betrothed with adoring eyes and agreed to do whatever he asked, so long as he was forthcoming with all pertinent information. There could be no secrets between them. Churchill eyed the bobby standing outside the plain black door of the unobtrusive mansion. He decided that sitting in the Ferrari was the most secure place to discuss the secret information that had Voss in such a panic. "Lord Henry Halifax is dead," Churchill began. He quickly filled her in on the Commonwealth's foremost state secret, the matter that would require his presence in South Africa.

She heard him out and agreed that he should fly at once to South Africa. Then Jan promised to do everything in her power to convince Lisa Banner to sign on as an employee of Project Mammoth. Churchill looked at his fiancée dotingly. Not only was she marvelously beautiful and intelligent, she allowed him to be in two places at the same time.

A green oasis situated on the desert-like veldt thirty miles outside the capital city of Lsandhlwara, the Halifax family estate overlooked a small mausoleum of cut stone, so new that marble dust still coated the walls and floor. The former president of Zululand, Soga Halifax had just buried her husband. For years, Soga had studiously ignored her husband's South African diamond and gold mines. She had kept herself just as ignorant of Henry's oil fields and refineries in Egypt, Greater Syria, and Arabia. As president of Zululand, the largest country in the world, she was obligated to keep the details of her husband's commercial empire at an arm's length. That was about to change.

She'd arranged to meet with a trusted comptroller from Halifax Mining in order to learn about the companies that she now owned. Yesterday, a British ambassador had informed her that Winston Churchill would arrive at her estate today, not the trusted comptroller that she'd summoned. No reason was given for Churchill acting as a Halifax Mining executive, although it was obvious that a financial concern was causing the Commonwealth to interfere in the operation of a privately owned business. It was common knowledge that Churchill had just initiated a campaign against the DFA supermonopoly. She didn't relish the same actions taken against her monopoly.

Soga was planting a flowerbed in front of Henry's crypt when Churchill's limousine rolled through the lion pillars of her estate. A cacophony of barking dogs erupted. She whistled sharply to call off the pack of Boerbols (South African Bulldogs) that were snapping at the running boards of Churchill's rented Rolls-Royce. Gravel crunched under the tread of the heavy motorcar as brakes were applied. Alarm bells rang in Soga's head when she saw that Churchill was at the wheel. Whatever the chief of staff had to say must be so sensitive that a chauffeur could not be trusted to be even in the vicinity.

Dusting potting soil from her pants, Soga rose to greet Churchill. The politician looked around the grounds of the estate, confused by the lack of gardeners. His eyes landed on her soiled clothes and the garden tools scattered around the flowerbed. Her lips twitched into a smirk; Churchill couldn't believe that a woman of her stature would have dirty hands.

She brought him into the mansion, noting the Englishman's obvious relief at the sight of servants inside. He was probably afraid that he would have to pretend to enjoy her cooking later in the evening. Soga dismissed the servants, including the cook. Churchill's face fell. Waiting for the house to empty, she turned to her guest and said, "I assume we are to discuss matters of the utmost delicacy, nothing suitable for the prying ears of cooks and maids." The chief of staff reluctantly conceded the issue.

They sat on a sofa of crushed velour. Churchill opened the briefcase that he'd been carrying, the one that Voss had given him, and extracted several leather bound ledgers. He launched into an accounting of her petroleum assets in North Africa and the Arabian Peninsula, emphasizing the spectacular cash flow and using the term "black gold" rather than oil.

She grabbed the petroleum ledger and slammed it shut, saying, "Without a doubt, I am a wealthy woman. Unsurprisingly, I have employees to distill this information. Why am I hearing it from one of the highest officials in the world government?"

"My point, Madam President, is that there is no necessity to liquidate any of your assets. Oil revenue from Halifax Petroleum alone generates a yearly income greater than the gross domestic product of most countries."

Soga handed the ledger back, not challenging Churchill's assertion, curious to see where the chief of staff was leading her, willing to make the journey in a typically Churchillian roundabout manner. She had nothing but time and his circumlocution was actually quite amusing.

He'd started to reopen the volume when his hands froze, sensing the former president's amusement and vaguely mocking attitude. He set the ledger down, frowning. She clasped one of his hands and asked, "Am I wealthier than the King? If so, I shall refrain from selling whatever asset it is that the government desires me to retain ownership of."

"Yes and yes," Churchill said dryly, pulling his hand out of her grasp. "Madam President is wealthier than the King and the government does wish her to refrain from selling certain assets." The first ledger disappeared and another took its place. Churchill outlined a brief history of Halifax Mining since the end of the Boer War. Starting in the late 1890s, the majority of Halifax gold output had been diverted from the marketplace and put into storage in a heavily guarded and highly secret shaft in Transvaal's Witwatersrand mine. The World War had seen this stockpile depleted, but as soon as the war ended the stockpiling resumed. Over the decades, the amount of gold that had accumulated in Transvaal was staggering, enough to swamp the Commonwealth's commodities market and exacerbate the deflation plaguing the world economy. Gold was not only a currency in its own right, but a major component in room temperature superconducting wire, the backbone of modern industrialism.

Churchill's historical account fizzled out. He'd made his case, exposed Britain's fear that Henry Halifax's widow would wreck the global economy by dumping tons of gold overnight. He sat there, fidgeting, hoping that his words had been persuasive.

Soga assured the nervous chief of staff that she had no intention of flooding the world in a sea of gold. Churchill let out a long breath and shook out a handkerchief to mop the sweat off his brow. A fresh concern popped into his mind: "I say, there is a cook on the premises, what?"

The cook had left the premises. Luckily, Soga's cooking was better than he'd expected and the politico did not have to feign enjoying his meal. Setting knife and fork aside, patting a napkin gingerly to his mouth, Churchill asked the former president what her policy would be toward the stockpiling of gold. Merely calling a halt to the stockpiling process would be mildly deflationary, and a concern.

Her answer was, on the surface, reassuring. A greater percentage than ever of the yellow metal would be set aside, virtually all production would be stockpiled. Furthermore, diamonds would be added to the cache. Theoretically, this should ease deflationary pressure. Nevertheless, Soga's answer was troubling. An instinctive conservative, Churchill distrusted any move away from the status quo. Worse, he didn't understand why Henry Halifax had wanted to build a huge reserve of gold in the first place, let alone the reason for the widow to accelerate the process. He put the question boldly to his hostess: Why had Henry Halifax stockpiled the gold? A moment's reflection brought a flicker of embarrassment to his face. He withdrew the question, backpedaling with the observation that Soga had deliberately kept herself in the dark concerning Lord Halifax's business dealings.

"Not at all, Winston," she said, patting his hand again. "I can tell you precisely what course my late husband intended for his stockpiled gold, a path I shall assiduously follow." She explained that Henry had been a student of monopoly capitalism, more than a student, a participant with an insider's understanding. Based on this intimate knowledge, Henry had felt that eventually monopoly capitalism would implode, the leading edge of this trend already evident at the time of his death. The deflation that Churchill so feared was part of this progression.

Churchill was baffled, unable to connect the dots between the growing horde of gold and the structural weakness in the world economy. Soga asked the chief of staff if he remembered the English nursery rhyme: Humpty Dumpty. Utterly confused, Churchill answered in the affirmative. Soga said that her mass of gold and diamonds would do what all the King's men and all the King's horses would be unable to do: help put Humpty Dumpty back together again, after the great fall, as expected.

Chapter 8

Spartacus Remains Controversial as the Red Army Acquires Fission Power

S lowly inching through two miles of primordial ooze gave Danny O'Brien plenty of time to visualize what was happening on the surface. The *USS Abraham Lincoln* had probably finished unloading its cargo of enriched uranium ingots on Kauai. The Red Army's masquerade was in full swing. The communist superpower had temporarily transformed itself back into the subservient Red Force: hammer and sickle emblems stowed in boxes, sculptures of Spartacus, Marx, and Engels covered with buntings depicting Queen Victoria and other capitalist figures.

American sailors were combing every square inch of the *Abraham Lincoln*, searching for stowaways, potential Red Force spies. Whether it was called the Red Force or the Red Army, the military organization on Kauai had a very good reason to put a spy on board the American battleship. The *Abraham Lincoln's* next port of call would be San Juan Island in the waters of Washington state. This is where the remainder of its uranium cargo would go. DFA was building the world's first fission reactor on the tiny island in Puget Sound. The communists had immense interest in nuclear reactor design.

The Red Army had another reason for placing an agent in the Pacific Northwest. The islands in Puget Sound were to be a staging ground for the communist invasion of North America. The American sailors would have no luck preventing a stowaway though. They were looking in all the wrong places.

O'Brien's war seal, Xeres, continued digging patiently through the endless mud. A braided plasteel cable connected O'Brien's powered combat suit to the seal's PCS. Xeres not only had to tow his master through the muck, he had to place him on the seabed directly under the path of the *USS Abraham Lincoln* and make sure that there were no British or American submarines lurking anywhere nearby. Even electronically amplified, human senses and spatial orientation were inadequate for the task. A man or a seal in a combat suit could not simply point his head up and rise through the ooze to reach open ocean. The primal goop consisted of layers and currents. The ooze had to be navigated.

The trip through the primordial ooze ended up taking only four hours. It seemed longer to O'Brien because it occurred in a sensory deprivation environment. Popping out on the ocean floor was a sort of rebirth. He could see again. The infrared filters in his faceplate turned the darkness of the depths into undersea daylight. A blue-green rift valley stretched east and west across the murky plain of the Pacific floor. He tilted his helmet up. He could see and hear the *Abraham Lincoln* churning the surface, one thousand feet up and a quarter mile to the north.

The Porsche Model G Marathon suit that O'Brien wore was about to undergo a serious field-test. If the sonar of the American battleship could detect his approach, then O'Brien and the entire Red Army were in serious trouble.

He made a circular hand gesture at Xeres. The seal nodded inside his PCS, disconnected the tow cable, and dove back into the ooze. O'Brien swallowed once, taking in a dollop of liquid nutrient from a helmet nipple, and pushed off the seabed, swimming up to meet the *Abraham Lincoln*. The stealth technology built into the Model G PCS was deceptively simple and tremendously complicated at the same time. The Model G did not possess any propellers and did not create any cavitation noise. The kicking motion of O'Brien's legs automatically caused rubber fins to sprout from his booted feet. He swam up to meet the battleship like a conventional scuba diver, swim kicks aided by ultra-silent servomotors. He made noise, but it was indistinguishable from the natural harmonics of the ocean and its denizens.

A couple more fin kicks brought him even with the hull of the warship. The lower half of the ship was protected with a conventional forcefield conduit grid, covered in barnacles like the hull of any oceanic vessel. O'Brien swallowed more nutrient gloop; it tasted horrible, taking his mind off what was to come next. He hated extremely complicated machines because there were so many ways for them to break down. The next step in the mission involved the most complicated machinery he'd ever dealt with.

He thought a command into the suit's artificial intelligence system: *spider silk*. Metal fingers tapped barnacle after barnacle, like a typist roving across a vast keyboard. Every time he tapped a barnacle, a wad of liquid spider silk shot from a fingertip, plugged the open orifice of the barnacle, and left a trailing strand of liquid silk; which hardened on contact with seawater. The strands naturally tangled with his arms and legs, lashing him to the bottom of the ship the way Gulliver had been pinned by the Lilliputians.

The last strands were laid and O'Brien reflected on the advantages of serving under Fred Greystone's great grandson. Supreme Commander Banner had inherited his ancestor's genius for animal breeding, inventing a method for increasing the rate of mutations in silk spinning spiders one thousand fold by subjecting them to a steady bath of low level radiation. Dozens of different kinds of spider silk had been created this way, each more useful than the next. New kinds of assassin spiders had also been bred under this radiation regimen. O'Brien had never worked with these eight-legged killers and hoped he wouldn't have to in the future. Spiders creeped him out.

Yoked to the underside of an American battleship over the next week gave O'Brien plenty of time to contemplate the technologies evolving within the Red Army, Blue Force, and throughout the Commonwealth. Concentrating the planet's greatest minds on a Pacific island and giving them unlimited funding was one way to radically advance the state of the art; erasing national boundaries and allowing a supermonopoly to plunder every natural and human resource left on Earth was another.

The fact that DFA had perfected the first workable fission reactor design disconcerted the scientific leadership of the Red Army. More and more, the communist faithful were coming to realize that the war would be as much between the Red Army and DFA as between the Red Army and the Commonwealth. O'Brien suspected that the true war would be for the hearts and minds of the DFA work force.

The Model G Marathon suit was programmed to play music and recite works of literature throughout the long journey. A glitch in the software, or some other malfunction, prevented the entertainment program from running. O'Brien was trapped for a week inside the suit with no stimulation to his mind and no exercise for his body other than drinking vitamin fortified liquid protein swill and eliminating into the suit's built in plumbing.

Days of sensory deprivation magnified the dangers to the revolution in his mind, gnawing at him like a rat. He imagined every DFA factory running full tilt to build a mighty arsenal of reactionary weapons, DFA private armies joining the Commonwealth military, and the remnant of Blue Force emerging from the radioactive hell of Hawaii to strangle the revolution like an infant in its crib.

When the vibrations of the ship's engines changed pitch on the seventh day, it felt as if the spikes of an iron maiden had been pulled from his body. Bleary and bloodshot eyes looked through the faceplate with renewed interest. He was in shallow water. Green streamers of light were playing around the edges of the American battleship, darting into the depths to dance in forests of bullhead kelp two hundred feet below.

Screws on one side of the ship reversed their spin. The *Abraham Lincoln* turned sharply. It must be readying to dock in Friday Harbor on San Juan Island. O'Brien wrenched his arms and legs loose from the hull. The spider silk threads did not break, they were as strong as ever. The thousands of barnacles holding him in place had been drastically weakened during the course of the seven-day journey and cracked like eggs. He dropped into a kelp forest and lay there unmoving until the shadow of the battleship passed over him.

The meandering motion of long kelp tendrils helped conceal the disoriented and exhausted spy as he stood on the harbor floor. O'Brien grew aware of his surroundings. The sunbeams were cutting into the water at a steep angle. It must be three or four in the afternoon. A strong tide was moving masses of floating kelp into the harbor from the channel. That would help immensely.

He wrapped himself in clumps of whip-like kelp, aided by the semi-sticky threads of spider silk clinging to the Model G PCS. Three cautious fin kicks put his kelp wrapped helmet above the surface, right next to an especially large mass of floating vegetative matter. Anyone on shore would have to know what to look for to spot him.

O'Brien treaded water and slowly drifted toward the docks until he was three hundred yards off shore. He could see cranes hoisting lead lined boxes of enriched uranium off the dock and into waiting trucks. With the battleship gone, the harbor contained nothing but sleek 150-foot yachts, resplendent with teak wood decks glowing in the afternoon sun. Every yacht had a helicopter pad and a chopper. Rotating radar dishes kept a watchful eye on the constant comings and goings of small private aerocraft. Servants were bringing early suppers to the rich fat cats sitting on the decks of their yachts.

Vladimir said it would be a bourgeoisie nightmare, O'Brien seethed. San Juan Island had once mined and shipped the world's finest lime to cement factories and steel mills along the west coast. Commercial fishing fleets used to leave this harbor daily. The island had once been a hub of industrial activity. Now it was a plaything for the idle rich, a bauble for the fetid leisure class created by Henry Ford.

What's that? A black and white hovercraft flitted across the harbor, heading out to the channel. O'Brien knew a police vehicle when he saw one. He even thought he'd seen Daniel Lam sitting in the hovercraft's driver's seat. Lam had served under O'Brien in the San Francisco police department. A more dedicated communist did not exist. The Red Army spy dropped twenty feet below the surface and kicked as hard as he could.

The police hovercraft could skim across the water five times faster than he could swim in his power suit. The Model G was stealthy, but not very fast. He got into the channel and had to decide which way to go, north or south. Vladimir had told him that proletariat servants and police officers would probably live on the less desirable land to the south, on the wind swept Point Isolation.

He ducked into every cove he came across, scanning the private docks for a black and white hovercraft. He saw plenty of yachts at anchor and huge mansions peeking between the boughs of Douglas fir and madrone trees.

Looking up the wooded slopes of San Juan Island was a revelation. Living on Kauai, O'Brien had grown accustomed to the notion that islands were always tropical, lush with impenetrable jungles. This island had a distinctly alpine feel, beautiful in a different way, somehow more American.

Halfway around San Juan Island, exactly where Vladimir promised, he found the police hovercraft parked next to a white washed cottage. His comrade in arms—Daniel Lam—stood next to the vehicle, a wrench in hand, evidently performing some kind of repair. Bingo.

The mission called for O'Brien to dig an underwater cave in the rocky wall that surrounded the island a few yards offshore. The cave was to be dug at a depth of about seventy-five feet. The Model G spy suit was to be parked in this cave. O'Brien's orders would have him clamshelling out of the Model G, extracting a wet suit and scuba equipment from a storage container in the PCS, and putting on this gear in the frigid forty-degree seawater. Once inside the wet suit, he was supposed to brick up the cave with stones from the ocean floor. Lastly, he was to surface and make landfall under the cover of darkness.

O'Brien knew he didn't have the strength to carry out his orders to the letter. He couldn't face the icy seawater, not after clinging to the bottom of a battleship for a week. The risk of taking the Model G up onto dry land was enormous. If the USA or any of the Commonwealth governments got their hands on the thing, then they would figure out its origins, putting the embryonic revolution in jeopardy. But the risk of him drowning and washing up on the beach posed an even greater threat to the revolution.

Still in the power suit, he swam right onto the shore. Crawling over a jumble of driftwood logs and standing upright on a patch of dark gray sand, O'Brien looked up the hill to Daniel Lam's house. His old friend was bent over the hood of the hovercraft, a feeble mechanic's light dangling from a tree. There would be a police dog somewhere on Lam's property. He dropped to his knees and began digging.

Darkness fell while he was widening the bottom of the hole. His endurance evaporated on the last handful of dirt. O'Brien clamshelled out of the suit and passed out, falling naked into the damp sand at the feet of the Model G.

A single bark awoke the fatigued spy. The dog's voice sounded familiar, one of Tempest's pups. He called weakly into the darkness, "Storm, is that you boy? Good dog!" A flashlight beam probed the dark interior of the hole. O'Brien called out in a stronger voice, "Faith and be gora, if it isn't Daniel Lam. Throw me a rope."

Lam shoved his head into the hole and gave it a thorough inspection, flashlight beam illuminating the bulky power suit and the shivering unclothed figure of Danny O'Brien. The bizarre scene didn't really surprise Lam. He'd been expecting a messenger from the Communist International or a sign of some sort from the incipient revolution every day since he'd become sheriff of San Juan County. He ordered the police dog to fetch a coil of rope. The dog tore off into the night. Lam asked O'Brien if any other communist agents had made landfall on the island. Through chattering teeth, O'Brien informed his old friend that there was only one agent provocateur.

Storm returned to his master, loops of rope clamped in his jaws. The German Shepherd spit the rope out in front of the sheriff's cowboy boots. Lam threw a line down the hole and hauled the pathetic figure out of the earth. With his teeth still chattering, O'Brien demanded they fill in the pit concealing the Model G combat suit immediately. After covering the freshly packed sand with driftwood, they would need to rake over the deep, mechanical footprints that led back to the sea. Lam took one look at the shivering form of his old boss and said firmly, "Not gonna happen, comrade. I'll walk you up into the house. Katie will put you into a hot bath. Let me worry about hiding this high-tech gismo."

A hot steamy bath breathed life back into O'Brien's ailing carcass, knitting body and soul back together, restoring his spirit enough so that he felt embarrassed when Katie Lam walked into the bathroom with a robe and saw him naked. She threw the robe down on a pile of towels, adding that a mug of hot buttered rum had his name on it in the kitchen.

Katie's tonic had a miraculous effect on the weary communist infiltrator. Sitting in the homey kitchen, an alcohol glow warming his innards, O'Brien could imagine a solid Marxist network radiating outward into the continent, starting with the sheriff's department policing the islands in Puget Sound.

"The contraption's buried. Rolled logs and sticks over the fresh earth. Staked Storm on the beach to keep on eye on that wee bit o' coast. Good enough for government work," Lam said, dusting off his hands as he entered the kitchen. The sheriff gave O'Brien's face a searching look. "Plastic surgery is it? You're uglier than ever, Danny boy," Lam joked.

"Plastic surgery it is. And I lost thirty pounds training my ass off for this mission. I'm nothing but nuts, guts, and tiger meat," O'Brien bragged.

"Ooh, sorry for failing to compliment your girlish figure, comrade boss. Instead of fishin' for compliments, howzabout issuing orders? Get the revolution into swing."

Katie set a mug of rum on the kitchen table for her husband. O'Brien got a tray of solid food. Between mouthfuls, the spy gave his comrades an outline of his three missions. Mission one consisted of capturing a pliant nuclear engineer from the DFA San Juan Island reactor team and transporting him to Kauai. The engineer had to be senior enough to possess the knowledge to build a fission reactor from the ground up. Mission two involved contacting every police cell in North America and delivering marching orders for the 1939 revolution.

Lam choked on his drink when the date "1939" issued from O'Brien's mouth. Katie put her hands over her mouth to cover a gasp of amazement and delight. The cadre outside Kauai thought the revolution was scheduled for 1950.

O'Brien described mission three: increasing the number of indigenous communist guerillas on the ground in North America. Red Army High Command thought communist police cells could recruit, arm, and train select prisoners in the county jails that they ran.

Katie's delight rapidly switched to hardheaded pragmatism. She wanted to know how dirt-poor cops were going to finance the outfitting of a gigantic guerilla army. O'Brien told her that inside the Model G PCS that her husband had buried this evening there were sets of perfectly crafted printer's plates to counterfeit hundred pound notes. Counterfeit currency would be the revolution's coin of the realm.

Daniel and Katie Lam raised glasses in salutation, toasting the three mission assignments like revelers at a Saint Patrick's Day parade. They'd been waiting their entire adult lives for this moment. Most Irish Catholics in the North American communist police cells equated the revolution to the second coming of Christ. The wait for the blessed event transcended their own lives, going back hundreds and hundreds of years.

O'Brien was one of the few Irish communists that wasn't Catholic. He was an old-fashioned Marxist, i.e., an atheist. So he changed the subject. He wanted to know the status of Lam's cell and the overall, situation in the Pacific Northwest. Daniel Lam assured his old boss that the islands in Puget Sound were policed exclusively by loyal communists, a fifth column capable of hermetic security. Moreover, the civilian population in Puget Sound consisted entirely of coddled millionaires, greedy little piglets sucking on Henry Ford's teats. DFA had purchased every logging company in the Northwest. It had simultaneously purchased every island in Puget Sound and transformed them into gilded cages to hold the former logging barons. A better staging ground for the invasion of North America could hardly be imagined.

O'Brien asked coolly, "Who said anything about Puget Sound being the primary staging ground for the invasion?" Lam countered with, "Don't teach your old granny how to suck eggs, Danny boy." The three communist conspirators looked at each other happily, huge grins lighting their faces.

"Enough of the lofty rhetoric," Katie admonished. "Chief O'Brien, tell us how your three darling boys are faring in Kauai."

Trigonometry and calculus sucked. The O'Brien brothers hated working with abstract mathematical concepts, bloodless and boring as a dried worm. Sean, Seamus, and Shay O'Brien were happy to be finished with their advanced math class that morning and looked forward to their next class: aquatic combat simulation. Any red-blooded communist youth loved combat over calculus. The coming class should be better than usual. Today, their war seals pups graduated from powered combat harnesses to powered combat suits.

The boys knew their pups would grow into the war seals that would swim into battle. Hard training today meant a better chance of victory tomorrow. Red Army instructors hammered that lesson into the young cadets on a daily basis, and twice on Sunday.

The seal pups: Jason, Thesus, and Oedipus were waiting for the boys in the combat lagoon. Their instructor, Wilfred Stokes, was waiting next to three small pinniped powered combat suits on the beach. Resting in the sun, Stokes glittered with more metal than the power suits. The boys called him "tin-man," which didn't exactly endear them to the grizzled trainer. At least the O'Brien brothers used the nickname to his face.

"Morning, tin-man," Sean said insolently, strolling across the lagoon's beach with his younger brothers.

"Tell me, Sean, are all your instructors greeted in overly familiar terms? My other students call me Sir or Mr. Stokes," the Red Army instructor demanded.

"No, Sir, only the instructors we love." Sean blew a kiss at his teacher. The two younger O'Briens guffawed at Sean's cheeky behavior. Rather than get caught up in the boys' irreverent antics, Stokes told them to bring out the war seal pups.

Nimble as sea-monkeys, the boys dived into the warm, salty water and ordered the pups to heel after a short stint of splattering about. A series of splashes produced three seal pups next to three boys. They stopped playing, quickly wading ashore and forming a line on dry land in front of their instructor, all business.

Stokes handed the boys large plastic bags filled with silvery fish. His voice acquired a pedantic tone. "The pups already know the command, 'enter war harness.' They will learn a new command, 'enter combat suit.' There may be situations in the war when we need seals in harnesses. At other times we'll want them suited. Who can think of a situation where the seals would be better off in harnesses?"

Seamus raised his hand and asked hesitantly, "In a long-running battle where they are out of contact for a long time and need to catch fish and eat?" The instructor responded, "Are you asking me or telling me?"

Stokes's personal microradio buzzed. The supreme commander was on the other end, ordering him to drop everything and make for general headquarters. Erwin Rommel had his invasion plans for North America and Britain essentially completed. The island's top scientists and military officers would listen to Rommel's presentation and make comments.

"Sean," Stokes addressed the oldest boy. "Take over. I want these pups jumping into combat suits on command, that and nothing more. Do not train them to use the suits. In and out, nothing else. Stop after one hour. When you're done training, take them for a swim in the ocean. Put them back in the lagoon. Go to your next class."

The oldest brother saluted and said, "Yes, Sir." Stokes returned the salute, trotted away from the lagoon, and jumped on his motorcycle. The bike roared down the Karl Marx Highway, a stream of staff cars and motorcycles flowing in the same direction. All the bigwigs and brass hats had been mobilized. Parking would be a bitch. His mechanical body had been acting up lately, probably a symptom of the continued deterioration of his meat body. It hurt to walk any distance beyond a few steps. He needed a close parking place.

The bike leaped forward, threading through knots of slower moving armored staff cars. Skillful driving put Stokes near the front of the queue. He caught sight of General Patton's Porsche GTS. An instinct told Stokes to hold back. The GTS blasted upward like a jump jet, hurtling over a line of cars. *The bastard.* Patton didn't have any ailments. Why did he need to steal a coveted close up parking space? Why did any of the members of Group B need to attend Rommel's Group A meeting?

The traffic flow snarled and stalled, degrading into stop-and-go on the side streets leading to the headquarters building. Patton's Porsche GTS couldn't leap over a long row of stalled cars. Stokes drove up onto a sidewalk and pulled ahead of the American general. Despite the forces arrayed against him, Stokes succeeded in rapidly snagging a choice parking space and a seat in the front of the auditorium. The only thing that slowed him down was a group of pushy guards in the doorway. The bullyboys temporarily confiscated his pistol. But that wasn't much of a hindrance since everybody entering the building had to also endure the short-term confiscation of personal weapons, a new rule, apparently. Stokes did feel odd sitting there without the familiar weight of the sidearm on his hip.

Rommel was standing rigidly at center stage, a sculpture of resolution and determination. George Patton sat down next to Stokes, a bland look on his lumpy face. The American general mustn't have been aware that Stokes had been competing with him for a parking place. A good thing too, Patton would have torn the island to pieces if he'd thought a competition was taking place.

The great hall was rapidly filling. Other than Patton, nobody looked bored. A sense of urgency and excitement permeated the crowd. Patton leaned toward Stokes and asked sotto voce, "Ready to receive orders from the tin-plated Teutonic tyrant?" Stokes hushed the crude American. Rommel was getting ready to speak.

The German general tapped his microphone to see if it worked. "Please listen," he told the audience, clicking a remote control device. The recorded voice of Danny O'Brien boomed over the PA system: "John's boat is swamped by a big tsunami."

"Ladies and gentlemen," Rommel began. "The Red Army received this coded message last night from our agent in Puget Sound. He tells us conditions are favorable for Plan Yellow. Better than we hoped." A smattering of polite applause followed Rommel's opening statement. He waited for quiet and said, "In a week or ten days we will have a DFA fission reactor design engineer, ready to spill the beans." This time the applause was deafening. Every man and woman present knew the Red Army could not waste any more time on basic research. They needed working reactor designs and they needed them now.

Rommel went on to outline the plan for establishing beachheads in North America and Britain. In broad brushstrokes he painted a picture of the sort of atomic Armageddon he wanted to inflict on Hawaii. He then challenged Group B to design every weapon needed to win the war within one year. Full-scale mass-production must begin churning out weaponry in a year and a half.

Stokes could hear Patton stirring angrily. The American general hated taking orders from Rommel. Unfortunately, at this point in the process, Commandant Group B had to take direction from Commandant Group A. Stokes was going to remind Patton of this inevitability when Rommel said, "Groups A and B are obsolete the instant mass-production swings into full gear, naturally so. Red Army will then split into two expeditionary forces: NA and E, for North America and England. The first expeditionary force to see action will be NA. General Patton will lead Force NA. I shall lead Force E."

Stokes congratulated Patton, knowing that the American would be ecstatic over the prospect of commanding the first expeditionary force to see action, stealing Rommel's thunder. Patton started to say something, but Vladimir Bakunin had taken center stage. Supreme Commander Banner stood behind the diminutive Russian, towering over him like a tree over a shrub.

Vladimir turned stage left, bowed to Rommel, and faced the audience again. "Historical Parallel projections indicate that a short, fierce conventional war pursued by a protracted guerilla war, especially in the lesser developed countries where DFA is popular, is one possible outcome in the conflict. General Rommel and his planners in Group A quail at the prospect of a lingering guerilla campaign out in the boonies of Africa, Asia, and South America."

Out of the corner of his eyes, Stokes could see Patton gloating over the insult thrown at Rommel. The German general would never characterize his planners as quailing at anything. Rommel considered his planners heroic and fearless. Stokes served in Patton's Group B as a weapon designer, teaching Red Army youth was a sideline for the aging inventor. He liked to see Patton in a good mood; it made life easier for everyone.

Vladimir leaned into the microphone and said softly, "Conventional war, guerilla war, all I hear is war. Let us cease using the word war." He leaned back and roared, "Revolution! We are staging a Marxist revolution. The Red Army cannot go to war against the 1.5 billion citizens of the British Commonwealth, or we will be crushed."

The audience fidgeted and grumbled. Supreme Commander Banner stooped over Vladimir's shoulder until his mouth was close to the microphone. He gave a terse command for silence and straightened. Vladimir continued calmly: "Group B's timetable to finish all weapon design is important for many reasons, not least of which is freeing the mainframe to run the extensive HP equations within my Spartacus program. Only Spartacus can transform the Red Army's war into the proletariat's revolution."

Oh bugger, not another fight over the blasted mainframe. Stokes cringed, knowing that a volcano would erupt momentarily in the seat next to his. He counted, *one, two, three…* Patton shot to his feet and fairly howled, "Wait a God damn minute you Russian bastard! Keep your mother grabbing paws off Group B's supercomputer." An onstage directional mike had captured Patton's outburst and broadcast it to the PA system. The hall fell into an uneasy silence, not only because of Patton's eruption, but also because he used a nationalist slur. Nationalism was as great a sin in the Red Army as it had been in the Red Force. Patton and Vladimir stared at each other across the great hall. SC Banner broke the impasse by saying, "Commandant Group C, please tell us about the Spartacus program."

"A year hence, the instant General Patton's people are through with the mainframe." Vladimir broke eye contact with the American general and spoke to the larger audience. "I shall run a program that re-fights the Spartacus Slave War in ancient Rome. My staff of HP experts will tinker with the virtual Slave War, running it over and over, seeking a different outcome. We will design a program that allows Spartacus to win, takeover Rome, and establish a new world order. The work we've already accomplished tells us that Spartacus needs to capture and control the agricultural breadbasket of ancient Egypt before he invests Rome. The modern parallel to Egypt is the United States. Rome is England. As you can all readily appreciate, the Red Army's initial strategy is based on what we've done so far. The Spartacus program is not an academic exercise. It is the heart and soul of the revolution, taking up where Karl Marx left off."

SC Banner motioned Patton to take his seat. The American cast one last evil eye at Vladimir before complying. The Russian had the attention of every man and woman in the hall. "Bear in mind that we have a general idea of what it will take for Spartacus to win. Besides controlling key geographic regions, he must get every slave in the empire to fight against Rome, as well as all the gladiators. The modern parallel between the vast number of Roman slaves and today's proletariat is patently obvious." Vladimir discussed how long he expected the Spartacus program to run, giving minute analysis of the intricacies of Historical Parallel algorithms. The audience began fidgeting again.

Patton surged back to his feet, leveled a forefinger at Vladimir, and growled, "For the love of God, Vlad, get to the point or I'll tear it out of you with my bare hands." The auditorium snarled agreement with the American general.

The supreme commander ordered Patton to sit down and cease baiting Vladimir. The Russian bowed to Patton in a display of exaggerated civility and said, "Through time and cyberspace, Spartacus will not only lead us to victory, he will show us the nature of true communism."

Much to his surprise, Stokes found himself standing and waving a prosthetic fist at Vladimir, acting almost as aggressively as Patton. "Bugger Spartacus! That's not how Historical Parallelism works," Stokes bellowed. "HP does not seek to influence the future. It is a predictive science, never prescriptive."

The supreme commander took over the presentation, instructing Vladimir to take a seat. SC Banner asked Stokes if he wanted the revolution to fail under the rubric of Historical Parallelism purity. A crimson flush crept up Stokes's cheeks, one of the few body parts he possessed not made of plasteel or titanium. The inventor slowly sank back into his chair, unable to defend his position rhetorically. Patton clamped a meaty hand on Stokes's artificial leg and husked, "Don't let the bastards get you down, Wilfred." The inventor gave Patton a grateful look and set his jaw in a display of English stiff upper lip. Just because Stokes couldn't defend his position didn't mean that he was wrong.

Fred Banner addressed the Red Army leadership. "At war's end we will need prescriptive HP equations as much as we'll need soldiers and weapons. Marx and Engels left no blueprint for a communist society or government, other than to say that it would be a global dictatorship of the proletariat that would gradually fade away until virtually no government survived. The closest modern structure to what we are trying to achieve is the DFA supermonopoly, which from a HP perspective resembles the bureaucracy of Ptolemaic Egypt. We may have to co-opt DFA, not tear it down. Just as Spartacus needs to takeover Rome and Egypt, not destroy them. How can we transform the Commonwealth and the supermonopoly into a global Marxist state? Only the Spartacus program can provide the answer."

He could have set a bomb off in the great hall and caused less consternation. The onstage directional microphone swung wildly around the auditorium, catching angered snatches of protest: "Transform the supermonopoly? No, destroy the supermonopoly! Kill the vampire capitalist oppressors! Kick Ford in the balls!"

SC Banner shouted into the maelstrom: "Think about it God damn you! Don't run your mouths, think." A modicum of discipline returned to the hall. The military and scientific leaders did just that, they thought. In more measured tones the SC continued: "Old Henry Ford owns the lion's share of DFA stock, a significant portion of total global wealth. Of course he is an exploiter of the worst stripe. That goes without saying."

The hall rumbled agreement. That was why they sought to turn the world upside down: to crush the blood-sucking capitalist exploiter. Fred Banner pressed on: "Imagine that the supermonopoly is left in one piece and all the shares of DFA stock are in the hands of the workers running the company. Imagine an expanded DFA owning all the means of production in every Commonwealth country. Imagine its board of directors owning no more shares than anyone else and receiving salaries neither greater nor lesser than a welder on an assembly line. All government would whither away, as Marx and Engels predicted. DFA would evolve into a global communist society."

He let that sink in, and then pointed at Stokes. "Wilfred, give me an educated guess. After destroying Blue Force and the Commonwealth armies, what do we need to do with or to the supermonopoly?"

The directional mike broadcast Stokes's musings throughout the hall: "I can see where you're driving, Supreme Commander. Maybe rather than destroy DFA, we need to take it over, communize it."

"Exactly," Banner concurred. "Communize it. Not destroy it. Along the same lines, we have to communize the Catholic Church, the Anglican Communion, every labor union, every small business, every school, football team, every sizable institution in the Commonwealth. Accounting systems must be created to monitor the performance of all these institutions. Communist profit and loss statements will apply. HP analysis will tell us how. And let me tell you something else..."

The crowd flared restively when Fred Banner used the words: "communist profit and loss." His voice lowered ominously. His bearing became more threatening. A few of the Red Army's political commissars segregated themselves from the audience to stand near the exit points of the hall. The political officers, unlike the men and women in the audience, had personal weapons and wore them prominently. The collective memory of the attendees registered on the supreme commander's promise to shoot insubordinates henceforth, rather than incarcerate them. The audience grew still and silent as Fred continued speaking.

"Let me tell you something else. Communist factories, farms, hospitals, churches, etcetera, will either make a profit or show a loss. Enterprises operating at a chronic loss will be closed, assets redistributed to profitable concerns, workers will lose their jobs and be reshuffled, the equivalent of bankruptcy in a capitalist economy. And there has to be competition among communist commercial enterprises. This is why I say that DFA is a precursor to a communist economy. However imperfectly and crudely, the automobile divisions of DFA compete against each other, even though they are controlled by a single entity. And when they make a profit or a loss, the accounting is unique, unknown anywhere else in the capitalist world.

"When Rolls-Royce makes a profit a certain percentage goes to the parent company (DFA), a percentage goes to retained earnings, and salaries and dividends are paid. In a communist economy, the profit from every enterprise will be divided between workers, the state, and retained earnings for capital improvement, nothing goes to the parasitic bourgeoisie. Accounting principles still apply. There will be profit and loss under communism. Communism does not mean we will all be living in cloud cuckoo land, strumming harps and flitting about on angel wings."

He stopped speaking to gauge the crowd's reaction. A muted and desultory clapping rippled across the auditorium. It wasn't so much agreement as confusion. These people were warriors and scientists, not economists.

The supreme commander exhaled in exasperation. "Right then. The structure of the post war communist economy is not important to Group A and B. Group C and myself will worry about that. This is all you people need to know: Group A has only a few precious weeks to consult with Group B over weapon design. Group B has one year of mainframe use to design said weapons. Vladimir and Group C will take over the mainframe in one year to run their Spartacus program. These timetables are not open to discussion. Disagreement at this juncture is tantamount to treason. Treason equals a firing squad. Am I understood?"

The applause was louder and more positive this time. The military men and scientists were conditioned to take direct orders, rather than ponder abstract philosophical matters. Besides, none of them could deny the SC's assertion that Marx and Engels had never described the structure of a communist economy. Who were they to say that profit and loss accounting did not apply?

Stokes nodded during SC Banner's statements and then gave Patton an inquiring look. It was apparent that High Command had made several key decisions without consulting Commandant Group B. They'd painted Patton into a corner by announcing these decisions in a public forum. SC Banner must have decided that this was the only method to secure the American general's cooperation. It seemed a dangerous game to Stokes.

Fred Banner was about to find out if he was playing the American general correctly. The SC invited Patton to share any final thoughts with the assembly before the meeting was brought to a close.

Patton climbed to his feet. He ascended the stairs leading to the stage and took a position next to the SC. Fred Banner handed Patton the microphone and stepped backward a few paces. Bushy salt and pepper eyebrows lowered over Patton's hot orbs. The supreme commander backed even farther away, cautiously, the way a man moved away from a poisonous snake. Patton cleared his throat and began speaking.

"When the leader of the revolution gives a communist an order, he says, 'Yes, Sir' and by God he follows orders. Group B scientists and engineers, I'm talking to you. Vladimir wants the supercomputer in twelve months to run his Spartacus program, so he gets the supercomputer in twelve months, and Spartacus battles the Romans until rivers of blood inundate cyberspace. We've got one year to design the weapons that will win the revolution. Nothing can stop us. I will be proud to lead you great bunch of bastards in the laboratory, on the factory floor, and on the battlefield!"

The representatives from Groups A, B, and C exploded in gouts of frenzied clapping and cheering. They spontaneously broke into song: the Internationale, of course. From the darkened rear of the stage, Fred Banner smiled. Leave it to good old Blood and Guts to get the Red Army back on track.

Committing a crime as a cop, especially in an isolated little community like San Juan Island, turned out to be easier than O'Brien had imagined. He looked in the backseat of the police hovercraft at the hooded figure of Werner Heisenberg. Kidnapping DFA's head nuclear reactor designer had proven to be a simple matter of smash and grab. No witnesses had seen the police hovercraft intercept Heisenberg's little Duryea coupe, or seen the new deputy sheriff snatch the German atomic engineer.

O'Brien smoothed his deputy sheriff uniform, reached out to adjust the air holes in the hood covering Heisenberg's head, and returned to the controls of the black and white hovercraft. Windshield wipers slapped back and forth across the front windscreen. A salty spray splattered the vehicle every time it crested a wave. A small storm had drifted into Puget Sound from the Pacific, ideal for the task at hand. There were no yachtsmen snooping around this stretch of water today.

There was one yacht in the channel, primed and ready to sail to Kauai. Not every disenfranchised timber baron was a blood-sucking capitalist mercenary. The *Paul Bunyan*, a seagoing vessel capable of crossing the Pacific, belonged to a wealthy resident of the island who'd been carefully cultivated by Sheriff Lam and converted to the cause.

O'Brien fed power into the lifting blades, throttled back the propulsion fan, and expertly skipped the hovercraft onto the pitching deck of the *Paul Bunyan*. The ship's crew quickly tied the hovercraft to the sailboat's top deck. O'Brien glanced nervously at the crew as they worked, reminding himself that Lam had vetted every man aboard. Cut a man on the *Paul Bunyan* and he bled little red bits of the Communist Manifesto.

Lam's vetting process had better be that good. The Model G Marathon suit was in the captain's stateroom. One call to the American or Royal Navy and the jig would be up. After searching the *Paul Bunyan*, the Commonwealth would contact the Blue Force. The whole world would press in on Kauai with guns blazing. The Red Army could not stand that kind of onslaught, not yet anyway.

He tugged the hood off of Heisenberg's head. The befuddled scientist scratched his nose and blinked like a lemur caught in a poacher's flashlight beam. A crewman led the bewildered Heisenberg below deck. The German scientist made no protest, no noise of any sort, numbly following where he was led. He hadn't really been roughed up, certainly nothing compared to the treatment he would receive in Kauai if he refused to cooperate. The rough stuff probably wouldn't be necessary. It shouldn't be hard to break a delicate flower like Heisenberg.

O'Brien crawled out of the hovercraft and found Daniel Lam standing on the forward deck, gazing west into the gathering storm. The pitching subsided as the yacht got underway. Lam observed that he'd better rev up the hovercraft and head back to San Juan Island. Light hovercrafts fared poorly in heavy seas. It looked like a patch of bad weather was blowing in. O'Brien asked the sheriff if he'd be okay activating the police cells in the Northwest alone, or at least until O'Brien returned to Washington state.

Lam hesitated. Actually O'Brien's presence would make the job infinitely easier, lending the moral weight of a man from the Red Army of Kauai to the job. Unfortunately, nobody other than O'Brien knew how to operate the Model G Marathon suit, the only means by which Heisenberg could be spirited through the Commonwealth's naval cordon surrounding Kauai.

"I'll be fine," Lam insisted. "Best see to your special guest, Danny me lad. Don't want to deliver damaged goods to Kauai." O'Brien grunted assent, promised to return as soon as he could, and left to minister to the delicate flower below deck. Lam watched him leave wistfully and grabbed a crewman, ordering the man to unleash the bonds holding the hovercraft in place.

Lam exhaled noisily, regretfully, before climbing inside the police hovercraft. He cranked the engine on, but didn't take off at once. He envied every man on the yacht. They would at least catch sight of the island of Kauai, even if they couldn't set foot on it. *Kauai, birthplace of the revolution, holy ground.*

He popped the hovercraft into the water and headed home, resisting the impulse to watch the *Paul Bunyan* slide slowly toward the Pacific. Maybe he and Katie would visit Kauai someday, assuming the war didn't vaporize the island in the meantime.

Chapter 9

Should Earth Become a Global Sparta and Storm the Heavens?

His detective agency had stolen Queen Victoria's last will and testament from Buckingham Palace one year ago in a daring cat burglary. David Banner had pondered the document ever since, wondering if it represented a valid reason for militarizing human society even more than what had already occurred after the World War. As of late, the manuscript bore more significance than ever. Events within the Commonwealth were forcing his hand, pressing him to make a decision that could push the post war civilization one way or the other. He couldn't ignore the account of Victoria's divinely inspired dream much longer.

Within the last month, his detectives in America had fed a stream of information to the London office that held grave personal implications for David and Lisa Banner, not to mention the world at large. It was becoming increasingly clear that their son, the supreme commander of the Red Force, was poised to launch a communist invasion of North America. The American and Canadian police cells Banner Detectives Ltd. had been tracking for years were showing patterns of heightened activity: stepping up the acquisition of weaponry and assassinating conservative city councilmen wherever leftist politicos could step in and fill the vacuum. A geographic pattern had also emerged. Communist police cell activity in Washington, Oregon, and Vancouver had catalyzed cells in a wave spreading east and south. An underground mobilization was reaching outward from the northern Pacific into the American heartland.

And hard evidence existed. Banner's agents in North America had confiscated reams of counterfeit hundred pound notes. The quality of the bills was better than authentic currency, a tip-off that CMG technology might be involved. Closer examinations demonstrated that the fake bills all contained traces of radioactive isotopes found in the fallout patterns of atom bomb detonations. Beyond a shadow of a doubt, the printing plates that produced the counterfeit notes had existed on the island of Kauai shortly after one of their A-bombs had gone off.

Even the hidebound and ineffective British Secret Service Bureau could prove malfeasance on the part of the Red Force if Banner Detectives grabbed them by their inept bureaucratic noses and dragged them to the budding revolution on Kauai. The Crown would then have to secretly contact the Blue Force and mobilize the Commonwealth militaries. No matter which way one shook the dice, there was going to be another World War. Banner knew his son and he knew the depth of global communism. The Communist International and the Red Force could not be rolled up like an old rug, even if the Commonwealth struck as soon as it could.

He supposed the war would be easier to win now than later. David Banner would lean toward presenting evidence of the communist conspiracy to the world government if all he had to go on were his son's hijacking of the 1950 CMG and the document chronicling Queen Victoria's dream. It was probably within his power to shorten the duration of the coming communist war. At the same time, he would be putting the kibosh on all future CMGs, a cherished goal he'd held for over thirty years.

If only those two factors were all he had to consider. A third factor had turned his worldview upside down: the emergence of two new war animals, sacred beasts, harbingers of a coming crusade: mammoths and sign language speaking gorillas. The new war beasts weren't yet ready to fight. That changed everything and was possibly a sign that the war needed to take place some years from now.

It was a good thing that Lisa was out of the house for a few days. The tempo of work at Project Mammoth had increased lately, requiring her around the clock presence at Southwestern Palace #9. This gave him the peace and quiet necessary for deep soul searching. Lisa's absence also made it easier to ignore the fact that Fred was inextricably wound into the quandary. The elder Banner couldn't weigh paternal feelings for his son when his wife was around. In the long bloody war years that loomed ahead, he might have to replay the ancient role of Abraham and sacrifice the fruit of his loins.

Oh what a tangled web we weave, he anguished, pulling a tobacco pouch from a drawer. Other than the absence of his wife, the second most important ingredient necessary for deep thought could be found in copious quantities of tobacco and his favorite pipe.

He unfolded his copy of Queen Victoria's last will and testament and reread it for the thousandth time. Smoke curled forlornly from his pipe. Banner wondered if the King had ever discovered that his private vault had been broken into and the inflammatory document photographed. Probably not, William would have raised seven kinds of hell if he guessed Banner Detectives Ltd. had pilfered the account of Queen Victoria's divinely inspired dream.

The document gave two warnings, one trivial and mundane, the other Earth-shaking and fantastic. The trivial warning concerned the forward pass in American style football. Many years ago, Queen Victoria had interfered in a proposed rule change that would permit forward passes in the game. In her secret last will and testament, the Queen reversed this decision, claiming that forward passes should be instituted in football. She gave no reason for her change of heart. But she did assert that the rule change would someday be important. American football was the most popular sport on the planet and there were hundreds of millions of fans that would not consider Victoria's posthumous request at all trivial. No one could disagree that her other request or warning was anything except cataclysmic.

Intergalactic war, several centuries in the future, Victoria's dream predicted a war between humanity and a hostile, ultra-advanced alien civilization. After reading countless science fiction books and watching sci-fi movies and TV shows, the concept seemed less laughable now than the first time he'd heard it back in the twenties. *Little green men with laser beams, come to blast Earth into a lifeless cinder.*

The science fiction writers had somehow guessed what was in Victoria's secret testimony before anyone else. Many of their stories started with an exposé on the apparently not so secret last will and testament. Banner could never decided if this was sheer coincidence, or if someone in the palace had leaked the document's contents years before his operatives had photographed it.

He folded his well-worn copy and returned it to the wall safe in his den. His pipe glowed lustily, filling the room with aromatic smoke. Lisa wouldn't let him pollute the house to this extent, denying that saturating his brain and the house with nicotine helped Banner think.

His youngest Bulldog wandered into the den, attracted to the sweet smelling smoke. "Come here, Hacksaw," Banner said, plopping into a reclining chair and smacking a thigh. The pup leaped into his master's lap, nuzzling an age spotted hand, hoping for a treat.

"Hacksaw, do you think the purpose of World War II is for communism or capitalism to prevail? Or perhaps it doesn't matter which economic system comes out on top. Maybe the only reason we are hearing war drums is that Earth must become a gargantuan Sparta, a unified nation-state devoted entirely to battle. Mayhap the Earth is to evolve into a planetary military base that will send armies out to storm the heavens."

The puppy cocked his head at the mention of his name, the only word he understood. Banner scratched the inquisitive pup around the ears. Talking out loud helped the thought process as much as tobacco. He preferred talking to a Bulldog rather than to himself, although it amounted to the same thing.

He peered through the blue haze at the roughhewn timbers above the fireplace. Two photographs were mounted there: a picture of Lisa riding Angerbotha, the mighty cow mammoth, and a second photograph of Nigel Mortimer speaking sign language with a gorilla. The Primate Language Centers in southern England and central Africa were only on their third or fourth generation of gorillas bred for language ability, but they'd already doubled the great apes' capacity for learning vocabulary and manipulating language. Gorillas would have to be given voting rights if they got any smarter. Banner looked down at Hacksaw and said, "The appearance of two new kinds of holy war beasts is what truly gives me pause."

Hacksaw grumbled because Banner had stopped scratching his ears. "I know. I know. You're a sacred war beast too. That is all well and good, it's just that the mammoth/elephant hybrids and signing gorillas are entirely new species, never trod the Earth 'til now. A sign from God… I think." The bull pup's head drooped. His eyes closed. Snores vibrated through his tiny frame.

"I'm sorry if the subject bores you, Hacksaw. I, for one, cannot take the emergence of sacred animals lightly. It doesn't happen every day." Banner set his pipe in an ashtray and turned his eyes back to the photo of his wife riding a mammoth.

The sound of a dog barking floated in from the front yard. Lockjaw IV was greeting Lisa. She'd decided to come home early for some reason. The front door opened and a grizzled older Bulldog burst inside, running circles around his mistress, taking deep snuffling whiffs of her pant legs, drinking in the heady perfume of mammoth musk.

Hacksaw raised a sleepy head and yipped jealously. He wanted to sniff Lisa's pant legs too. Soon, both Bulldogs had their noses pressed into her legs. Lisa gave them swats on the rump, reopened the door, and shooed the dogs outside.

With hands on her hips, Lisa scolded her husband. "Stop sulking like Achilles in his tent. Fred is not trying to take over the world. Ignore the foolish reports from America. I need help training mammoths to fight Bulldogs."

She looked saucy in that pose, a wisp of hair over a dirt smudged face, dried sweat staining her work clothes. Banner ignored the scolding and let his mind drift back to something she'd said forty some years ago, when they'd first met. Lisa had maintained that their age difference would become less important as the years rolled by. But it hadn't worked out like that. In her fifties, Lisa was so strong and vital she could train the largest land animal on Earth. In his seventies, Banner was becoming an old man.

Lisa could sense her husband's drift back in time. Slightly peeved at being ignored, she asked him point blank if he would train dogs and mammoths for the baiting contests the King wanted to stage before the 1950 CMG. She watched her husband's face go blank. Recognizing a trance when she saw one, Lisa quietly slipped out of the room, knowing her question wouldn't be answered until morning.

The idea of mammoth baiting set thoughts spinning in his head. Bull and bear baiting had existed in England thousands of years before the World War. The sole purpose of the blood sport had always been to create hallowed war dogs and deliver victory to Britain in her darkest hour. Banner had yet to interact with Angerbotha, but he was almost certain that she too was a sacred war beast. Like the original Lockjaw and the war seal Zeus, she would give rise to a race of holy creatures, conduits to Godhead. And then there were the gorillas bred for sign language ability, another breeding program that Fred Greystone had started.

A dim impression of how mammoths might serve as war beasts flickered through Banner's reverie. Maybe war mammoths would march into battle with swift horsemen ranging ahead as scouts and foot soldiers marching with Bulldogs in the rear as infantry. Maybe the highly intelligent gorillas Nigel Mortimer was breeding would sit on top of war mammoths. *Was there even a need for humans?* The dogs might walk under the belly of an armored mammoth: infantry protected by a living panzer. Gorillas could toss around artillery shells the way a human could handle a 50 caliber round. *Why am I thinking in terms of Boer War technology?* He smacked his forehead to get his brain working. In a modern war, mammoths would wear gigantic powered combat suits.

The smoke in his den had thinned to near invisibility. Banner squinted nonetheless, trying to peer into the future, an experience in frustration for a man that had once talked directly to God. He saw, or thought he saw, ephemeral images of primitively armored war elephants wearing small fortresses on their backs like saddles. The long-legged pachyderms were striding under the battle standard of the Carthaginian general, Hannibal; climbing out of the snow-filled Alps. It was no scene from the future, but two thousand two hundred years in the past. The vision was so strange as to be hallucinatory, as though he'd ingested psychotropic drugs. He blinked and it was gone. There was no way his shag-leaf tobacco could be salted with opiates. He bought the stuff from a local tobacconist.

He picked up his pipe and thickened the air once again. Lisa had gone to sleep so she couldn't complain about his contribution to indoor air pollution. Further hallucinations failed to materialize. Banner wondered if he had received a sign from above. Or was his imagination simply working overtime? Either way, he needed to take over Project Mammoth.

Lisa awoke to the smell of frying eggs and sausage. She couldn't remember the last time David had risen before her. She didn't think he'd ever cooked her breakfast in all the years they'd been married. Besides the odor of cooking food, she smelled a rat. In a state of mild alarm, she threw on a gown and ran downstairs to the kitchen. An alarming plate of eggs, sausage, and tomatoes sat at her place. More alarming still, David had cut flowers from the garden and placed them in a vase next to her breakfast.

She pierced him with an inquiring look, lifting her eyebrows and lowering her chin. His response only served to ring more alarm bells.

"Upon the death of your grandfather, I became the foremost authority on Bulldogs and baiting contests. No one is more qualified to design mammoth baiting than myself."

Lisa's eyebrows crawled further up her forehead as she said suspiciously, "Last night, I practically dropped to my knees, begging you to get involved in Project Mammoth. This morning it is you doing the begging. Quite an unsettling turn, what?"

He spread his arms wide and put a mask of wounded innocence on his face. "I seek to aid the Crown and Commonwealth. The baiting contests before the 1950 CMG must be the very best. The good citizens of the world government deserve no less."

Lisa's eyebrows fell. Her eyes narrowed in suspicion. "Only you're of the belief there will be no CMG in 1950. Your detectives in America have led you to believe that our son is leading a Marxist insurrection well before then, haven't they?"

Banner's arms dropped to his side. He gave her a clipped nod and said, "I am certain that great mischief shall spring from Frederick and his army. I am also certain that the best counter to our little darling's epic mischievousness has something to do with mammoths and gorillas." She waited for him to say more. He stood mute. She waited, her eggs getting cold. Still nothing. He wouldn't go into details. She knew pressing him would prove fruitless.

Sausage and eggs disappeared. They showered and dressed. The Bulldogs were chained next to water buckets and given triple rations, enough to last them three days comfortably. Lisa got in the passenger side of their brand new car. Banner had purchased a new Rolls-Royce Silver Shadow not long ago. He got in the driver's seat and turned on the electric motor, feeling a little stab of chagrin. The new Silver Shadow was identical to the old one. DFA hadn't updated any of its models in more years than he could remember, which sucked all the joy out of owning a new car. Without competition, the supermonopoly had no incentive to come up with new designs. Maybe Frederick had a point with his talk about capitalism's decay.

The Silver Shadow wound its way out of the warren of narrow medieval roads that comprised their tiny village and rolled silkily and silently toward Southwestern Palace #9 on the other side of London. The trip took longer than the relatively short distance might have suggested. London was the capital of the world government, the largest city on Earth. The traffic flowing into the sprawling megalopolis at the beginning of a workday was staggering.

They'd reached their destination by midday. SW Palace #9 had become a fair imitation of London since the inception of Project Mammoth decades ago. Mammoth cloning had forced it to grow even larger. The palace grounds had developed into a sprawling complex with more animal enclosures than the world's ten largest zoos combined.

Lisa decided that the first order of business was to give her husband a tour of the maternity pens. They walked past row after row of enclosures built from forcefield fences. Each enclosure contained an Asian elephant cow, nursing a mammoth calf. The elephant cows were surrogate mothers to mammoth clones. Half the clones were based on

Angerbotha's DNA. The other half sprang from Hela's DNA.

Although they looked alike, the Angerbotha clones had radically different temperaments from the Hela clones. The Hela clones charged the forcefield fence as Banner walked by, enraged by the odor of an unfamiliar human being. None of the fierce clones actually made contact with the fence, aborting their charges inches away from forcefield conduits, and then trumpeting angrily at the unwelcome stranger, fierce little eyes glowing blood red with barely suppressed rage. Judging by their charred fur, it was evident that they had all ruptured a forcefield conduit at one time or another. Their deep-set eyes continued glaring from shaggy heads as David and Lisa walked away from each enclosure, tracking the movement of the tall stranger furiously. In most cases, the elephant surrogate mothers patiently pulled the savage Hela calves back to the center of their fenced yards.

Lisa explained that every elephant mother had been selected from the most tractable and steady nerved logging elephants of Southwest Asia. The reason: amniotic fluid surrounding the fetus in the womb affected DNA, more so in clones than natural embryos. Because of the placid surrogate mothers, Hela clones were slightly less volatile than the original Hela, but the difference was not great enough to permit handlers the luxury of letting down their guard.

The Angerbotha clone calves had much friendlier dispositions. According to Lisa, they were a pleasure to train. She wanted Banner to interact with her favorite Angerbotha clone, a calf named Skuld. They walked toward a series of enclosures that fed into a huge central yard: the original palace grounds before it had grown into a sprawling city. Banner asked his wife what Skuld meant in Scandinavian mythology. She answered: "In Norse legend, Skuld was a supernatural spirit representing the future." The big man grunted agreeably, a fitting name for the most promising clone in the program.

They came to an enclosure that contained an elephant cow and a mammoth calf, just like all the others. Both cow and calf seemed affable. Lisa deactivated the forcefield fence around this enclosure and opened a gate. The pachyderms trotted into the roomy center square. The adult cow made straight toward a clump of lush grass, her trunk busily tearing green shoots from the ground.

Skuld raised her trunk and blasted a triumphant greeting at Lisa. The young mammoth leveled a steady gaze at Banner, lowered her trunk, and galloped toward the big man, moving much too quickly to be considered an elephant. Skuld stuck out her front legs, dropped her butt, and skidded to a stop in front of Banner, sliding like a quarter horse.

He plunged his salami-thick fingers into the fur around her neck hump, digging into her muscles like a masseuse. He kneaded the muscles down her flank. Skuld wiggled in pleasure. Banner could tell that the calf's body consisted of lean meat almost as dense and hard as steel. The hide along her flank was as stiff as a rhino's or a wild boar's, much stiffer than the skin of a modern elephant, almost plate-like. The armored hide, the superior speed and strength of the mammoth, all this must have been due to their natural enemy: the saber-toothed tiger. Modern elephants didn't really have natural enemies. Even adult lions gave them a wide berth.

Banner stepped aside as Lisa approached the calf. Placing one hand on Skuld's neck hump, Lisa vaulted on to the calf's neck. Her heels dug into armored shoulder muscles. Holding fistfuls of bristly fur in either hand, urging the 800-pound calf to top speed, Lisa rode Skuld over hill and dale, not quite as fast as a horse, but much faster than an elephant.

Lisa guided Skuld back into her enclosure. The placid surrogate mother ambled happily behind her athletic daughter. Lisa sealed the enclosure, shutting the gate, reactivating the forcefield fence. Banner had been watching his wife deal with the elephant/mammoth pair when he felt the thud of titanic footfalls radiate up from the ground, like a series of small earthquakes.

Angerbotha (the adult Angerbotha, not a clone) pounded down from the top of Palace Hill. Like a captain on the deckhouse of a sailing vessel, Princess Victoria stood on the mammoth's head, waving frantically at Lisa and David. Angerbotha couldn't skid to a screeching halt as quickly as Skuld. The adult mammoth did manage to stop fast enough to dig divots in the turf, showering the Banners with dirt clods.

"Thank God you're here, Lisa," Victoria called down from her perch. "This must be your husband, even better. We need your help. The King is listening to unwise council." Victoria ordered Angerbotha to scoop up the two passengers and place them on her broad back.

Lisa was used to being encircled by the pachyderm's hairy trunk and hoisted into the air. Banner experienced a moment of panic as the trunk coiled around his body, jerking him on top the mammoth. The panicky moment quickly passed. At ground level, he'd felt no wind. Riding on Angerbotha's back, thirteen feet off the ground, a small breeze stirred. The mammoth was so tall that the weather was different on her back. Outstanding. Through his marveling and wonderment, Banner heard his wife ask the Princess why Hela was nowhere to be seen. Banner's tourist-like enjoyment vanished as Princess Victoria choked back a sob and said, "A horrible American is preparing to bait Hela with one hundred Bulldogs. This is why We need your help."

Lisa gave the Princess a hug, promising her that no horrible American would get anywhere near Hela. Banner had never opposed any sort of animal bait before. He'd organized hundreds in his day. In fact, he'd come here with the intention of designing just such a baiting contest. A strange intuition told him to agree with the Princess and his wife. He loudly proclaimed that Hela would not be baited. His heart jumped into his throat and he could say no more. After a forty year drought, was the gift of prescience returning? He watched the ground roll by as Angerbotha climbed Palace Hill, suddenly uncertain. Maybe God was speaking to him again. And maybe not. The original divine messages had always come in the form of dreams. Now he was awake. Perhaps he was sensing the beginnings of senile dementia, not holy writ.

With Hela not in the main yard, the gate leading into the palace's small inner courtyard had been left open. The adult mammoth squeezed into the courtyard and one by one set her passengers on the doorstep of the palace's foyer.

Princess Victoria charged into the palace like a general leading reinforcements into battle. She banged open doors, barging into her father's war room, Lisa and David stepping smartly in her turbulent wake. "I've the world's foremost authority on blood sport, Father, David Banner." The Princess stomped her foot angrily, adding, "He shall put an end to your tomfoolery, Sam Houston." She shot daggers through her eyes at a portly and aging American, sitting next to the King around a table cluttered with toy animals.

Lisa and David bowed to the King, not sure how to proceed in the presence of squabbling royals. Sam Houston took charge by rising and shaking Banner's hand. Nodding politely at Lisa, Sam took his seat and said in a voice roughened by years of drinking whiskey, "Begging the Princess's pardon, ain't nobody got more experience in blood sport than yours truly."

Banner had worked with Sam for many years. The Texan had gathered data for the Secret Service Bureau in the World War. More recently, he'd work with Banner Detectives, keeping track of communist police cells in East Texas. Sam had even collected a few of the radioactive counterfeit bills the communist cops used to finance their burgeoning guerilla movement. Banner didn't relish the prospect of upbraiding an old friend and colleague.

Nevertheless, the big man said, "Sam is a good man, an expert in the baiting sports. He is not in my league though. Fred Greystone trained me. I am the master's protégé." The King looked very thoughtful at this pronouncement. He indicated that Lisa, David, and Vicky should sit around the table. Another gesture told Houston to continue the explanation he'd been giving prior to the Princess's outburst.

Sam moved two shoeboxes next to a ten-inch tall cast iron model of a mammoth. A couple dozen toy Bulldogs were scattered on top of either shoebox. Another four-dozen thimble-sized toy dogs sat in between the boxes.

The Texan shoved the iron mammoth into the gap between the two shoeboxes. He flicked toy dogs at the iron mammoth's heads and ears. The toy bulldogs must have been magnetic because they stuck to the iron model. The tiny Bulldogs on the tabletop were placed on the mammoth's trunk and front legs. The front of the toy mammoth was now covered with approximately one hundred magnetic toy dogs.

"Saber-toothed tigers ambushed mammoths from cliffs. Pretend these here shoeboxes are cliffs," Sam rasped. Everyone in the room was reminded of a little boy playing with toys as Sam rocked the iron mammoth back and forth. He scrapped toy dogs off the front legs and had the mammoth stomp them. Other dogs were shaken free, but Sam had them race up the shoebox cliffs to leap on the mammoth's head or trunk.

"When the mammoth cries uncle, if the mammoth cries uncle, a single kill dog is let loose." Sam moved a single toy dog under the mammoth and placed it on the pachyderm's brisket. "Ka-boom! The kill dog's fitted with nitro-fangs. One good bite and the mammoth's dead. I'm fixin' to do a dry run on Hela tomorrow. Natch, I ain't gonna use no nitro-fangs, save that for later."

The King's face wore a hungry expression. Clearly, the Monarch wanted to see the dry run. Princess Victoria cast a beseeching look at Banner. The big man turned his attention to the King and said, "Mr. Houston's conception of a mammoth bait is a fine one, Your Majesty." The Princess glared at Banner, her supposed champion. She reminded him of Queen Victoria at that moment, short tempered yet passionate in her beliefs.

Banner disregarded the Princess's evil eye, concentrating on her father. "I'm sure most of Your Highness's subjects will find—" he passed his hands over the shoeboxes and toy animals "—this sort of baiting contest interesting, a marginal improvement over traditional bull or boar baiting. It might scarcely surpass a bear bait."

Sam frowned at the word "marginal." The King blanched at the word "scarcely." Banner acted as if he found their consternation surprising. "I say 'scarcely' and 'marginal' in light of the overt similarities between traditional bull baiting and Sam Houston's insipid version of mammoth baiting. I mean, really, all he is doing is bull baiting with larger bulls and more dogs. Quite boring, actually." Now Banner pretended to be confused. "Your Majesty, am I mistaken, or are the 1950 CMG baiting contests intended to rival the CMG itself? Perhaps the baiting contests should be mediocre, so as to not detract from the CMG?"

The King reached across the table and knocked over the iron mammoth model, a disgusted expression screwing up his face, long white hairs on his handlebar moustache quivering in anger. Sam opened his mouth. The King waved an imperious finger at the Texan, a warning to keep silent, and motioned Banner to keep talking.

The large man gave the room a history lesson. English blood sport had its roots in ancient Rome. But outside the very smallest villages, the ancient Romans didn't usually stage baiting contests. Instead, specially trained gladiators would fight dangerous animals. It was usually man versus beast, seldom beast versus beast, although gladiators sometimes used trained war beasts to help them kill wild animals in the arena.

For instance, elephants often tangled with gladiator teams that fought on foot armed with long spears. But sometimes gladiators rode on the backs of trained elephants and fought lions with even longer spears. Bulldogs and Wolfhounds fought side by side with gladiators against a variety of wild beasts. Humans were almost always in the mix.

The King's face screwed up again. Banner guessed that the Sovereign would insist that the CMG baiting contests must entail animal on animal combat with no participation from human beings. The King relied on ancient British tradition, not ancient Roman tradition. And there was another problem with using humans in baiting contests: For some years now, the Crown had prohibited lions, hyenas, and tigers in blood sport because their flesh could not be eaten, or would not be eaten by most Commonwealth citizens. A royal edict proclaimed that any animal other than a Bulldog killed in blood sport must be consumed. Minute regulations actually dictated how much of the stricken herbivore or omnivore must be gobbled up by the spectators, everything except hair, hoof, hide, horn, teeth, bones, or specific organs must become part of the baiting feast. According to this edict, if a human died in a baiting contest, he would have to be eaten.

"Lisa, would you be so kind as to fetch twenty or thirty drinking glasses?" Banner asked. "Sam, do you have two more shoe boxes? Yes? Would you please bring them here?" Sam and Lisa did his bidding. The King watched with ill-disguised impatience. The heavy heart in Princess Victoria's chest grew lighter as Banner set up the model for his version of mammoth baiting.

Four shoeboxes were twisted into a C-shape, representing a box canyon. Drinking cups huddled inside the box canyon: a herd of game bred European bison or Cape buffalo. Banner pushed the iron mammoth into the box canyon, moving the toy animals across the tabletop as Sam Houston had done. He painted a vivid word picture of what his vision of a mammoth baiting contest would be like in real life.

A hundred Bulldogs walked under the belly of the titan. A troop of gorilla gladiators rode on top. The silverback leader gave a hooting command (Banner's sound effects made it seems as if a real ape were in the room). The great Bulldog pack charged out from under the mammoth, knifing into the buffalo herd, blood singing for combat. Buffalo bulls fought back like demons, flinging Bulldogs against the cliff walls of the box canyon, only to have the intrepid canines bounce back into the boiling bovine cauldron.

A certain number of game bred bison proved less than game, as was always the case in any sizable herd. Cowardly bulls tried to escape the raving havoc of the Bulldogs. But to reach freedom they had to get through the mammoth. And she was trained to prevent their escape, skipping across the mouth of the canyon as nimbly as a ballerina, skewering crazed buffalo bulls with scimitar tusks, tossing 2000-pound carcasses over her back the way a man might casually toss a handful of salt over his shoulder.

The gorillas on the mammoth's back carried long, heavy throwing spears. They were trained to spear or bayonet any buffalo that submitted to a Bulldog. This meant that the dogs would have to wear spider silk combat harnesses, similar to the ones used in the 1920 CMG. The apes would also be trained to leap from their pachyderm perches and break the necks of bison bulls with bare hands.

Bleachers would be constructed for the wealthy to watch the baiting contest in person. But most Commonwealth citizens would be forced to watch on the telly, because mammoth baits would not be as numerous as traditional bull, boar, and bear baits. Trained camera crews would be stationed at key locations, capturing all the action on videotape. Eventually, movies and TV shows would be produced of the baiting contests, the proceeds going to the Crown.

The King decided to weigh in. "This sounds well and good. We do see one problem. Mr. Banner's innovative baiting contests give Us the impression that mammoths will suffer very little injury. We envision scores of dead buffalo and Bulldogs, perhaps a few dead gorillas. Yet the big shaggy creatures won't get their hair mused. Hardly cricket."

Banner lowered his head in the direction of the Monarch. The time had come for truth to be laid bare. "As Supreme Governor of the Church of England it is incumbent that his Royal Highness consider the religious implications of two new species of sacred war beasts, placed by Providence into the hands of the Crown. I have read Queen Victoria's divinely inspired dream. My detectives broke into Buckingham Palace a year ago, and I have a copy of your grandmother's secret last will and testament."

The King sat straight in his chair and asked in an ominous voice, "What are you saying, Mr. Banner?"

"Mammoth and gorilla baiting must be designed with an eye toward training and breeding these animals as war beasts. We ought to design powered combat suits for them. The time will come, as your grandmother foresaw, when sacred war beasts will be more precious than rivers of gold."

King William didn't relish the idea that Banner had somehow stolen a document out of Buckingham Palace. There wasn't a great deal that the King could do about that right now. That sort of thing was to be expected from the former head of the SSB; more to the point, his grandmother's secret last will and testament had been independently leaked to the intelligentsia by corrupt palace retainers some time ago.

Princess Victoria sprang from her chair, rushed up to her father, and threw her arms around his neck. She didn't say anything, nor did she let go of the old Monarch, squeezing him somewhere between affection and coercion.

William laughed and said, "Vicky, please unlatch yourself. We acquiesce. We surrender. Mr. Banner shall be placed in charge of Project Mammoth. Mrs. Banner and Mr. Houston shall be Mr. Banner's leftenants. Release Hela."

The King, the Princess, Sam Houston, and Lisa Banner decided to watch Hela's reunion with Angerbotha. With David Banner's complicated and exotic mammoth baiting scheme, there was no need for Sam's dry run. The actual dry run would have to be months in the future. Highly trained Bulldogs would have to be siphoned away from the Commonwealth militaries. The Primate Language Centers would have to be conscripted by the Crown. Expert animal trainers, scientists, and engineers would have to be hired.

Princess Victoria noticed that David Banner didn't file out of the war room with the rest of the party. Lisa grabbed Vicky's elbow and steered the Princess outside the palace, explaining that the aging giant had gone into one of his periodic trances.

The die is cast, for better or worse, Banner thought, fatalism erasing any doubts over keeping mum on the communist buildup in Kauai. Fred Banner was secretly preparing to land a high tech communist army on the shores of North America. David Banner was secretly turning the CMG baiting contests into a primitive anti-communist army. The British government and its Commonwealth would receive no advance warning. Fred would get to decide when World War II started. By the time the conflagration burned itself out, mankind will have seen a war hundreds of times bigger than World War I.

David Banner was still sitting there when the others returned. They were bright and breezy after watching the mother and daughter reunion. During his meditation, the old giant had grown morose again. The bracing bout of fatalism had proven short-lived. His mood swung back toward self-doubt. Maybe the safest course of action, he wondered, would be to tell the King about the Red Force communist invasion at this very moment. But then, looking into the Monarch's beaming face, his mind changed for the hundredth time that day. His mind had changed, but the sour mood remained.

The Banners slept in the castle that night. The next day, they hopped into their Rolls-Royce and motored only a few miles down the road to pay a visit to their long time associate, Nigel Mortimer, director of England's Primate Language Center. The prospect of interacting with a new species had shifted the big man's mood yet again. He was actually whistling as the electric car glided silently up a long driveway flanked by rows of plank trees.

The PLC was housed in another World War era fortress, built along the same lines as the Southwestern Palace #9. It too was surrounded by animal enclosures. Rather than corrals or fenced yards, these enclosures resembled heavily built aviaries, complete with fifty-foot high mesh steel walls and roofs. There were no forcefield conduits anywhere in sight. Young gorillas were climbing on the sides of the enclosures or swinging into them from the branches of trees growing inside. Adult females and juveniles of both sexes saw the strange automobile and began screeching and pounding on the fence walls.

Much to the Banners' alarm, not all the gorillas were behind mesh steel walls. Two fearsome silverbacks appeared from behind the concrete building and charged the Rolls-Royce. They stopped charging abruptly in front of the hand polished sterling silver grill and rose upright, standing like men. Unnoticed by either David or Lisa, Nigel Mortimer had appeared on the scene. He walked to the passenger side door and shouted over the hooting apes: "The larger and hairier of the silverbacks is named Kubwa. As you can see, he is a big fellow; seven feet tall and five hundred and fifty pounds, with his ribs showing." Mortimer paused to fill his lungs and then bawled, "Kubwa, lift."

Kubwa, the mountain gorilla, grabbed the front bumper, squatted like a trained weight lifter, and effortlessly hefted the front of the 6,000 pound car several feet off the ground. DFA may not have updated the Silver Shadow in many years, but the original design was incredibly rugged. The bumper was directly connected to the stainless steel, ladder-type frame. Neither the steel beams, nor the sheet metal of fenders, doors, and hood buckled or bent. Henry Ford would have been proud.

Kubwa set the car down and thumped his chest, creating an ear splitting popping noise, not unlike a small automatic artillery piece. The hooting and screeching from the females and juveniles subsided. Mortimer was able to speak in a merely loud voice: "The shorter-haired and smaller silverback is named Bwana. He is average size for an adult male lowland gorilla at six feet and four hundred pounds. He is unusually strong despite his average size, scoring in the upper 1 percent in our strength tests. Kubwa scored even better, as you might imagine." Mortimer told Bwana to lift the car. The lowland gorilla sent the front end of the Rolls-Royce ratcheting skyward as easily as his friend, the mountain gorilla, had.

By the time their car stopped bouncing on its front springs, the Banners were no longer alarmed. The display of simian strength had taken on the aura of a carnival ride. David and Lisa exited the Silver Shadow and tried to greet Mortimer. Bwana stopped the large one-legged man in his tracks with a hairy paw to the shoulder. The lowland silverback stood in front of the Banners and made hand signs. Mortimer was standing a few feet away, next to Kubwa, and offered a translation of the sign language: "Do you want revenge against us for lifting your car?" Banner looked into the ape's liquid amber eyes and replied, "Why yes, I suppose I do, what do you have in mind?" More signing was followed by Mortimer's translation: "Let's play the eyelash game. Only a strong man can beat a gorilla. You are old, but look strong."

"How do we play?"

Mortimer explained the rules. Using only one hand, Bwana would have sixty seconds to pluck a single eyelash from the one-legged man's upper eyelid. The gorilla could not touch any part of the man except the eyelash. The human could do whatever he wanted to stop the ape, including running away, which counter-intuitively often proved the riskiest strategy for the human, usually resulting in a punctured eyeball. If the human was injured, it meant that the large, hairy primate had touched some part of the human's body other than the eyelash, technically a win for the smaller smooth-skinned primate. Mortimer went on to say that beating Bwana in this game would earn Banner respect among the entire gorilla nation. Bwana was the acknowledged leader of all signing gorillas.

Not waiting for Banner to respond, Mortimer pulled a stopwatch from his waistcoat and cried, "Begin the eyelash game!" Lisa jumped back quickly as Bwana made a lunge at the large man's face with his right hand. The apes in the enclosures were all facing the action, hooting maniacally, cheering their simian champion on to victory. Mortimer and Kubwa stood immobile, watching the game intently, taking the measure of David Banner's skill as a gorilla wrangler.

At one point in his life, Banner had been able to bench press six hundred pounds. In those days, he'd been stronger than most professional football players. He could still bench half that amount, a phenomenal feat for a man his age. Bwana could bench press five thousand pounds, ten times more than an all-pro lineman, fifty times more than an average man. This meant that human strength could only be a small factor in the eyelash game.

Banner placed his two hands around the joint of the ape's right thumb and used every ounce of power that he possessed against that single digit. Bwana's hand moved toward the human's face inexorably, a force of nature that could not be stopped. But it moved slowly enough that the man could bob and weave evasively. It helped that Banner was once a prizefighter.

Out of the corner of his eye, Banner saw Kubwa signing. Mortimer offered a translation: "Kubwa says that Bwana is a pussy to let an old man beat him." With an angry grunt the lowland gorilla rapidly shifted hands, swinging his left hand up and his right hand down. Banner tried to bat the ape's left hand aside the way a boxer would deflect a blow. Bwana punched through the parry easily, grabbed a row of eyelashes, and jerked them free. Moving very quickly, so Mortimer couldn't count the number of eyelashes in his hand, the silverback placed the little pieces of hair on his big pink tongue and ate them, thumping his chest afterwards in triumph. Every gorilla in the compound exploded in ear-shattering exaltation. Kubwa squatted onto his haunches and beat the ground furiously with his fists, sending vibrations up into the soles of the humans' shoes, rocking the Silver Shadow on its springs.

With tears streaming down his left eye, Banner bowed to Bwana. He then turned to the gorilla enclosures and made another bow. The hooting and screeching dropped several decibels. Kubwa stopped beating the ground as he considered the alacrity with which the eyelash had vanished into Bwana's mouth. The mountain gorilla smelled a cheat. He ambled over to the bowing Banner, spun him around and scrutinized the human's face. Kubwa rose up to his full height and made a series of hand signs: "Bwana, you pussy. The man has no eyelashes left. The human wins the game."

The catcalls from the enclosures dropped even further in volume. Bwana looked at his feet for several seconds, straightened, and signed to the watching troops of gorillas: "Okay, I admit it. I cheated. The human won. So shoot me." The two yards were now so silent that the wind could be heard whistling through the wire mesh of the enclosure walls. Mortimer told the two silverbacks to return to their respective troops and get busy making more baby gorillas. King William had big plans for them. There would be a need for hundreds of signing gorillas.

Lisa and David blinked in surprise as the two silverbacks strode up to the two different gorilla pens, squatted in front of heavy metal gates, grabbed combination locks, spun dials to unlock the gates, and slipped inside. Mortimer motioned at the Banners to walk toward the concrete blockhouse, explaining that the silverbacks alone knew the combinations to the locks that kept their troops imprisoned in the large pens. Not even the human staff members at England's Primate Language Center were allowed to know these combinations. Mortimer himself did not know what the combinations were. The silverbacks would not have it any other way.

Lisa fell behind the two men as they moved toward the concrete building. As she walked, she turned her head to watch the silverbacks. Both Bwana and Kubwa had relocked the padlocks on their metal gates. In the two different pens, adult females were mobbing the two male gorillas, bowling them off their feet, permitting the multitudinous juveniles to form great dog piles, with the big males on the bottom. *The adult males can come and go as they please,* she thought. *Or they wouldn't voluntarily participate in the breeding program.* The juveniles and females under the command of the silverbacks had no choice but to participate.

Her husband had joked about giving signing gorillas the right to vote. Suddenly, Lisa wasn't sure how jocular the concept might be in the not so distant future. *What would it mean to make them citizens?* Gorilla society seemed even more patriarchal than human society. If the great apes ever received the franchise to vote, it would probably be extended only to the silverback troop leaders. Lisa shook her head in dismay. *Were humans really all that much more advanced?* The Commonwealth had only granted the franchise to women within the last decade. She smiled at the image of female gorilla suffragettes marching with signs and placards in front of government buildings.

She turned toward her husband and Mortimer. The men had already entered the concrete building. She hurried to catch up. Once inside, she realized that the PLC, or at least this particular branch of the PLC, must have a much smaller budget than Project Mammoth. The interior decorating was quite austere in the cold, damp gray office where she found Mortimer and David. It must have changed very little from the days of the World War. One thing was decidedly different: Mortimer was sitting at a desk with a personal computer, one of the new ones hooked up to the Cybernet.

Mortimer was talking to David. Lisa walked closer to be included in the conversation. "King William emailed me last night. Look, I saved it. The King says that David Banner is the new director of England's PLC and Project Mammoth. I am relegated to the role of assistant." Mortimer didn't seem at all upset over the demotion. His pay plan must not have changed.

The former PLC director was in his seventies, but he was amazingly up to speed on the Commonwealth's latest technological marvel: the Cybernet. He invited the Banners to take a look at England's Primate Language Center's website. Images of gorillas playing football filled the screen on the desktop. The simians had invented new rules for the game, which included a forward pass.

The ability to throw a forward pass was a natural extension of simian sign language. Bwana and Kubwa were the third generation of gorillas specifically selected for language ability. The fourth generation apes were about six years old. In another four years, the fourth generation would start producing silverbacks. Each successive generation showed a greater and greater proclivity for tool use. While there was one specialized strain at the Congo facility that was developing mathematical ability, all strains were increasingly able to use their hands to make sign language symbols, which equated to using their hands for other purposes as well. The first time Mortimer had thrown a football at one of the silverbacks, he had immediately caught it and thrown it back, in a tight missile-like spiral. Gorilla football had been inevitable from that day forward.

David Banner was no different from the hundreds of millions of other Commonwealth couch potatoes who glued themselves to a television every Sunday during football season. In other words, he was a typical sports fanatic. He'd never seen anything like the game that was unfolding on the screen before his eyes.

Bwana had lined up behind his center, one of his wives, an adult female that was considered "butch" or masculine. She weighed a hulking four hundred pounds and was built like a male. The other females and juvenile males on the team were equally rugged, if not as large. The silverback quarterback hooted a snap count. The butch female snapped the ball on the third hoot. Bwana held the ball with one hand and backpedaled swiftly in a three-point stance. He saw an open receiver downfield and reared up to his full height, standing like a human quarterback.

The cornerback and the wide receiver were streaking for the end zone on all fours, tearing along at thirty miles-per-hour. They were both mountain gorillas, the most terrestrial of all gorilla subspecies, and therefore the swiftest. The wide receiver was speedy even for a mountain gorilla and had achieved some separation when the ball sailed over his head. The young blackback coiled and leaped, springing twenty feet off the ground. His hairy hands encircled the pigskin, pulling it in tight to his chest. He landed hard, bounced, rolled, and sprinted with one arm and two legs toward the uprights.

The cornerback ran after the wide receiver on all fours, as such he could move much faster than the ape moving on three limbs. He caught up with the ball carrier, made a diving tackle, and brought the wide receiver down. A whistle shrieked and the play was over. The screen went blank as Mortimer turned the computer off.

David Banner was dancing a jig around the damp gray office, hooting in a convincing parody of a gorilla: "Hoo-hoo-hoo. We have to make gorilla football a commercial enterprise, create the GFL, the gorilla football league. This sport can earn the PLC millions. It will free us of the need to beg Parliament for funding."

Mortimer was nodding happily, counting the millions as if they'd already been earned. But Lisa was shaking her head vehemently. She stomped her foot on the concrete floor and said, "David, I forbid this scheme to proceed until the day arrives when gorillas are paid for every game they play and can own property. Someday gorillas will be performing all manner of jobs. And they will *not* be slaves. I will *not* participate in a new form of slavery."

His wife's words and the play he'd just watched on the computer screen triggered a memory in the large man. He recalled the bizarre passage in Queen Victoria's secret last will and testament that dealt with the forward pass in football. Since a ball-carrying gorilla ran on three limbs, and a tackler ran on all four, most plays in gorilla football had to be throws. With superb blocking, perhaps a few well-executed runs would get through, but the ball would be mainly advanced through the air. *Had the Queen foreseen the advent of gorilla football?*

"David, wake up! You've fallen into a trance again." Lisa snapped her fingers in front of her husband's face. His eyes slowly regained their focus as he came out of the daydream. He pinched himself, shook like a horse, and said, "What's that? Salaries? Yes, quite. The gorillas must be paid salaries. In time they must even become citizens. Mortimer, what say you?"

The former director of England's Primate Language Center said, "I'm inclined to agree. This much is irrefutable: Fred Greystone sifted through hundreds of gorillas in Zululand three decades ago. His first breeding produced apes with the verbal language skills of an average ten-year-old British schoolboy or schoolgirl. While the second generation still isn't overly inclined to read or write, if we give them an IQ test in sign language, they score, on average, at the level of a well-educated fifteen-year-old. The third generation has a few rare individuals with adult human level intelligence, but still little inclination for reading or math. Who can say how smart the fourth generation will be? We are seeing reading, writing, and math problem solving ability out of the youngsters from gen. four, especially at the Congo facility. I expect that eventually gorillas will plateau at roughly human level intelligence."

He pointed a cautioning finger at the two Banners and continued: "It is an understatement to say that Bwana and Kubwa have the IQs of adult humans. I trust their judgment over any human being in most situations."

Mortimer turned his computer back on. He tried to log on to the DFA feed store web site in Canterbury, but the website had crashed or suffered some other technical difficulty. He looked up from his desk and said, "Enough with this extravagant philosophical discussion. If the two of you are in charge, then day-to-day problems need to be addressed. The Canterbury feed store is late in delivering the latest load of gorilla chow. I can't raise them on the telephone and their website is dead. Let us take a ride over there and find out where our feed has gone."

They piled into the cab of an ancient three-ton Daimler-Ford pickup truck. As Mortimer was grinding the starter motor, Lisa rolled a window down and shouted in the direction of the gorilla enclosures, "Kubwa, Bwana, jump in the back. We're going for a road trip!" Two mighty thunks nearly collapsed the suspension on the old truck as the troop leaders vaulted into the bed.

The engine coughed and rattled, but kept running. Mortimer turned to Lisa and called out over the rough running diesel, "Expecting trouble, Lisa? Is that why you're bringing the silverbacks?" Lisa arched her eyebrows and replied, "Nigel, I'm afraid you've gotten a bit isolated from the hurly burly of the outside world. A series of strikes have been initiated against DFA subsidiaries ever since the Cybernet went mainstream and universities began running Historical Parallel software again. If we are facing a situation of that nature, the strikers may be prone to violence, and they may be reluctant to relinquish our two tons of gorilla chow."

Mortimer reached into a glove compartment located near the steering wheel. He pulled out four pairs of brass knuckles; the rings of shiny brass were much too large to comfortably fit a human hand. They were exquisitely crafted nonetheless. The inner surfaces that made contact with the gorillas' skin were thickly padded with jute. The flat hitting surface on the outside was crenellated with stud-like projections. Mortimer lowered the back windscreen. Kubwa and Bwana silently reached inside the cab and grabbed the brass knuckles.

Lisa studied the silverbacks' faces as they jammed black, leathery fingers into the welded metal rings. Even their fingernails were as black as polished ebony. The amber fire glowing in their eyes reminded her of the original Lockjaw, as he made ready to tackle a monstrous bovine.

The trip was uneventful until they got inside the city limits and approached the feed store. Angry picketers were holding signs with messages like: "Supermonopoly = Blood-sucking parasite," and, "Obliterate Henry Ford before the 100-hour workweek obliterates you." They were chanting Marxist slogans and throwing eggs at anybody who tried to cross the picket line. Inside the line of strikers, a large brick warehouse was covered with communist graffiti. The DFA logo was blacked out and covered with white skull and cross bone symbols. Rolling steel doors were locked and battened down tight.

Mortimer hopped into the bed of the truck and stood next to the apes. Bwana and Kubwa reared upright and stuck their faces into the wind, which was blowing away from the warehouse and the strikers. Scoop-like nostrils flared. The apes drank in the scent of tons of gorilla chow, only a few hundred yards away. Their mouths filled with spit. Their bellies rumbled with hunger. They'd eaten huge breakfasts, but that was hours ago, and gorillas didn't like to go even a short while without food.

"Is our gorilla chow in there?" Mortimer asked, not bothering to sign. Bwana and Kubwa nodded eagerly. "Go get it. Throw it in the back of the truck. Try not to hurt the human beings." The silverbacks bounced out of the pickup, landing with ominous thumps. They dropped to all fours, brass knuckles clicking on pavement, and waded into the marching crowd of humans like icebreakers plowing into a frozen ocean. The crowd parted nervously, slogans dying on their lips.

One of the rabble-rousers in the back shouted, "It's a management trick. Stop those scab monkeys!" A dozen arms cocked to throw eggs. The fusillade died stillborn as Kubwa whirled on the crowd, let loose a thunderous roar, and beat his chest with the cadence of automatic artillery. The sight of his wicked fangs, more than anything, caused the crowd to surge back away from the simians.

The two silverbacks approached a stretch of wall that their noses told them was close to the pallets of gorilla chow. They began punching the wall. Bricks and powdered mortar exploded inward. Steel reinforcing rod twisted like strands of spaghetti. The section of brick wall evaporated and the roof above it slumped downward. Shots rang out from guards inside the darkened interior of the building. The gorillas knew what guns were and what they could do. A few bounding leaps over bails of hay and bags of feed put them in front of a knot of security staff, men with carbines. Before the stunned rent-a-cops could react, gun barrels were twisted around their necks, wooden stocks splintering like matchsticks. Only now did the apes hoot and roar, eyeing the stricken humans gleefully. Kubwa exposed a mouthful of long, sharp teeth, lowering his head in preparation for a series of killing bites. The lowland gorilla made hand signs at the mountain gorilla, reminding him that humans weren't supposed to be hurt, if at all possible. Reluctantly, Kubwa closed his jaws and let the guards go.

Bwana stationed himself twenty yards from the old pickup truck. Kubwa stood next to a stack of bags containing the food that he and the other gorillas needed. Kubwa grabbed one bag and flung it through the hole in the brick warehouse. It sailed outside in a high arc, toward Bwana. The lowland gorilla caught the first bag and heaved it toward the truck. It landed squarely in the bed. The pickup's long-suffering suspension bounced up and down as bags rained down in rapid succession.

The DFA guards cautiously exited the building from a conventional door, eyeing the bizarre sight of gorillas playing catch with feedbags, steel gun barrels still wrapped tightly around their necks. The striking DFA employees cheered as the management goons beat a hasty retreat. They kept cheering as the gigantic apes didn't miss a beat. One hundred pound bags flew through the air as if jugglers were performing a circus act. The last bag was tossed. The apes sauntered over to the truck, mugging at the crowd. Placards were set down and the strikers cautiously approached the silverbacks. The apes motioned for the humans to touch them. Soon the strikers were stroking the silver, gray, and black fur covering the gorillas' muscle-bound bodies. The silverbacks would have given autographs if they knew how to write. Police cars were pulling up to the shattered feed store. Lisa called out for Bwana and Kubwa to return to the truck.

Mortimer asked the silverbacks what had happened inside the warehouse after the guns had fired. Kubwa took off his brass knuckles and signed, "No trouble. Everything is okay. Bwana acted like a pussy and wouldn't kill the gunmen. He's the boss ape, so I didn't kill the little puffters. I think they crapped their pants." The apes climbed on top the huge stack of feedbags. They opened one bag, jammed their hands into the mass of green pellets and stuffed food into their faces.

The strikers formed a cordon between the Primate Language Center vehicle and the policemen that were gathering near the damaged warehouse wall. Mortimer steered his antique truck away from the crime scene. David Banner remarked that now might be a good time to sell his DFA stock. The small flurry of strikes against the supermonopoly seemed contagious, likely to spread to its core industries.

Lisa was more concerned about the strike affecting Project Mammoth than the price of DFA's stock. She used her radiophone to make a call to Princess Victoria, giving a heads-up about a potential shortage in animal feed and a warning that power shortages, the disruption of water, and the loss of other basic necessities could occur if the strike spread to other DFA industries. The Princess needed to make contingency plans.

Chapter 10

O'Brien Sews the Seeds of Discontent

There'd never been a strike like this. It touched every country in the Commonwealth to one degree or another, depending on how deeply the supermonopoly had entrenched itself. Advanced industrial nations were more affected than backward agricultural nations. DFA headquarters in San Jose looked like a war zone. Rolls of concertina wire cut off the side streets giving access to Ford's skyscraper. Surface to surface missiles jutted out from behind the corporate logo on the building's rooftop. Panzers patrolled the empty streets around this section of the downtown. A fighter jet circled above the supermonopoly headquarters in endless loops. Daimler-Ford-Alco was under siege.

Henry Ford looked out from the window of his penthouse office. The sight of empty streets depressed the plutocrat. The only pedestrians below were private security guards touting machineguns. The municipal police and the California National Guard were nowhere to be seen. Local, state, national, and Commonwealth governments had abandoned DFA in its fight against organized labor. *More like organized crime*, he thought. The nearly empty street may have been depressing, but the presence of a small private army was preferable to striking workers throwing firebombs at his corporate headquarters.

In the old days, Ford had never faced very many strikes. He'd always paid his workers more than the prevailing wage. He hated lowering wages and had done so recently only under duress. High wages meant purchasing power among workers, a bedrock principle for the plutocrat. The hundred-hour workweek had enflamed DFA's global work force much worse than the mild wage reduction, even though it had been made clear from the onset that the increased hours would be temporary.

They've gotten soft, he decided. Government mandated health insurance, workplace safety regulations, mandatory coffee breaks, sixty minute lunch hours, and all the other socialistic coddling had spoiled his workers, turned them into a bunch of sniveling children.

I should have broken the unions years ago. No sense crying over spilled milk. A few other clichés occurred to Ford. Now that labor and management were at each other's throats, industrial violence was like a genie that could never be put back in the bottle. Only violence could break the loggerhead. Maybe he should have broken the unions years ago, but he had to break them now, or they would break DFA.

Ford walked away from the dreary plate glass window to stand in front of a large wall map depicting DFA holdings in Africa, Europe, Asia, Australia, and the Americas. Green pins symbolized factories that had never gone on strike. A beautiful sea of green was centered on Japan, Baikal, and parts of China. East Asia was the heart and soul of the supermonopoly and it was no mystery why the strikes had not taken root there. The Japanese Emperor, Princess Victoria's uncle, had forbidden labor unrest within his Asian hegemony. The Emperor had even reconstituted a forbidden political class to keep economic order: Samurai. The original Samurai had always kept peasants in line, and the Johnny-come-lately feudal warriors were also first class head-breakers.

The rest of the globe was not colored in such benign hues. Red pins showed violent strikes and property damage. Pink pins showed nonviolent strikes. White pins showed strikes that had been broken by local police forces where workers had returned to the job, meekly accepting the hundred-hour workweek.

He lightly touched a clump of white pins around the Seattle area. Most of the white pins were in the Pacific Northwest. He savored the word *strike-break* as if it were a prized delicacy. In Washington state, Oregon, and Western Canada, DFA logging operations and modular home factories were running full tilt because local cops had engaged in strikebreaking. Nobody in DFA knew why these cops had been so accommodating to corporate policy. They actually took fewer bribes than any other police departments in the Commonwealth. And unlike Japan, there had been no political figure cracking down on the labor agitators.

Ford had only one appointment today. In an hour, he would meet with a deputy sheriff from San Juan County, Washington state. Word had it that this low-ranking policeman was largely responsible for the remarkable strike-breaks in the rainy northwest.

He left the lovely white pins and the wall map to sit at his desk. Paging his personal secretary, Ford leaned over an intercom box. "Wendy, what's the skinny on this sheriff fellow?" The box on his desk squawked, "All we know, Mr. Ford, is the guy's a bad ass Irish cop good at breaking strikes."

Ford gave Wendy a wordless grunt for a response. The plutocrat grimaced at the stack of papers on his desk. Just because DFA was embroiled in thousands of strikes across the globe didn't mean the chairman of the board could pretend day-to-day business no longer mattered. He sifted through the pile.

As always, hands needed to be held. The manufacturing divisions and subsidiaries were having problems picking designs for next year's models. The aerocraft subsidiary in Lsandhlwara wanted to know if there was money to proceed with gyro-stabilization research, technology that promised to make helicopters easier to fly, dramatically expanding the market for luxury choppers, a key component in the long range strategy to create a new leisure class and take over the rest of the economy.

His melancholy morphed into anger. The morons in Aero didn't think DFA had money for research? Couldn't they read? He'd sent all division and subsidiary heads a memorandum clearly spelling out that long range planning would not be affected by the strikes.

He pounded on his intercom, demanding that his secretary place a long distance call to Zululand and get hold of the president of the Aero Subsidiary. Wendy put the call through and reminded her boss how to pronounce the man's name: Nqakula, a tongue twister for most Americans.

The connection went through to South Africa. The chairman of the board vented his spleen on the president of DFA's Aero Subsidiary. Ford would have remained calm if his victim had timidly submitted. Instead, Nqakula fought back, wanting to know if capital outlays on pure research were warranted considering the turmoil engulfing worldwide operations. This gave Ford an excuse to shout one of his presidents down, flatly ordering the man to have a working prototype of a gyro-stabilized chopper in six months, warning that it had better be easier to fly than a single-engine plane, or else. Ford slammed the phone down as Nqakula started protesting that the designers were on strike as well as the workers.

The penthouse office grew still as the chairman's labored breathing quieted. He reached for the 1935 new car designs. The first file in the stack was an entirely new car: the Rolls-Royce Cobra, a high performance two-seater powered by a pumped-up, nitro-boosted, big block aluminum V8, designed to go head-to-head against the Ferrari GTS. Skimming through the report, his eyes caught on a sentence warning that to beat Ferrari in the marketplace, Rolls-Royce had to also beat the Italian manufacturer on the racetrack.

The next file described a car that would never be sold, the race version of the Cobra. Ford shook his head in skeptical chagrin. *Would dominating a single race circuit be enough?* Even if the race version of the Cobra kicked butt in the street circuit, there was still the brickyard open wheel circuit, and the fuelie dragsters, and the rocket dragsters. Ferrari dominated all the racing circuits throughout the Commonwealth. This was part of Ferrari's allure and mystique. Even Ferrari's crappy little econo-boxes won races.

With a heavy heart, Ford made a note in the margins of the Cobra report, instructing his people to develop open wheel racers and dragsters as well as Lemans style street machines. He also noted the necessity of hiring and training the best drivers, pit crews, and all the rest. He could practically feel hundreds of millions of pounds draining from corporate coffers as he wrote.

All these extra expenses would come on top of the extra dividends he was forced to shell out on DFA stock lately. Without fatter dividends, DFA's stock price would collapse in the face of global strikes. Another reason for fat dividends: He had to pump money into the world economy or consumer demand would slacken and deflation would get even worse. Unfortunately, much of that demand would soon be satisfied by companies springing up to fill the vacuum left behind by DFA factories idled by strikes.

How he hated competition. There was no comparison between the orderly operation of a monopoly and the chaos of a free market. Why in hell should a passenger car manufacturer be forced to build freaking racecars? He yearned to restore DFA's automobile monopoly. But that damn Dago wouldn't listen to reason. Enzo Ferrari wouldn't even consider a buyout offer. Sometimes in the wee hours of the morning, Ford contemplated hiring people to blow up the Ferrari factories in Italy. Rumor had it that Ferrari was planning on building a line of family cars and was already hiring many of Ford's striking autoworkers, luring them in with promises of higher pay and a sixty-hour workweek. If that happened while the strike still raged, then Ferrari would eat into DFA's market share like a weevil in an ear of corn. And that could be only the tip of the iceberg.

He returned to the Cobra report. The project manager had come up with an ad campaign that featured beautiful women wearing revealing outfits falling for men that purchased the new DFA sports car. Filled with disgust, Ford flipped through pages of ad copy replete with sexy vixens in bikinis and stiletto high heels draped across the muscular hood of the super car. Focus group testing showed that the sexy marketing campaign would sell 26 percent more Cobras than any other type of ad, and there would be spillover to the other automotive brands.

Ford's pen slashed savage notes in the margins of the report. He categorically forbid any ad campaign that promoted gratuitous sex. Daimler-Ford-Alco had always stood for public decency. He didn't care if the sexy ad campaign would sell one million extra Cobras. The pen broke under the pressure of his written tirade. He threw the broken pen in a trashcan and took a moment to calm down.

The intercom box squawked, "I'm buzzing in the Irish cop." Ford cringed when his secretary called his appointment "the Irish cop," guessing that the fellow must be standing within earshot. *Why don't the ones you want to go on strike ever walkout?*

Danny O'Brien sauntered into the penthouse office. Ford rose to greet him, sticking out a hand and apologizing for his secretary's bad manners. The policeman introduced himself as Douglas O'Brady, shrugging off Ford's apology with the observation that he *was* an Irish cop, and proud of it. The two men settled into chairs. Ford got straight to the point by asking, "Why are the strikes breaking in the northwest and where does Officer O'Brady fit into the picture?"

The Irish cop smiled broadly and said, "Up north we're following orders, Bossman." That did nothing to satisfy the chairman of the board. O'Brien decided to be a little more forthright. He gave a list of all the orders Henry Ford had issued to midlevel employees in DFA businesses not on strike. DFA grocery clerks had orders to not sell food to strikers. DFA restaurants were under orders to refuse service to strikers. Doctors and nurses in DFA hospitals were instructed not to treat strikers, even under life threatening conditions. DFA apartment managers were supposed to evict tenants on strike. DFA loan officers had instructions to call in loans for borrowers on strike, repossessing cars and houses. Electricity and water were supposed to be turned off. A lot of things were supposed to be happening to strikers. Except that none of these nasty tricks were occurring outside the Pacific Northwest. In Oregon, Washington, and Vancouver local cops were enforcing Ford's dictums as if they were laws passed by local government. The strikers didn't have a chance against the blue tide.

The plutocrat digested this information. DFA didn't have a formal intelligence network, but the supermonopoly wasn't completely deaf and blind. Ford had an inkling that O'Brien was telling the truth. More than how, he needed to know why.

O'Brien gave a single word answer: "Money." Ford's puzzled mien convinced the communist agent to give a longer answer: "Lotsa money, Henry. Cough up the dough and I'll get my cop buddies to crush the strikes one city at a time, throughout North America. Starting here in San Jose."

Ford's puzzled expression became calculating. "How much to end the strike in San Jose?" O'Brien made a comic show of counting his fingers. He reached the last digit and said, "Ten million pounds ends every strike in Santa Clara County. One month and every DFA employee's back on the job, no demands, happy to work one hundred hours a week."

"How much up front?"

"One million pounds in my hot little hand, today. Nine million when the job is done."

Ford pulled an old skeleton key from his suit vest and unlocked a drawer in his desk. He pulled out bundles of one thousand pound notes. When one million pounds had overwhelmed the surface of his desk, he keyed his intercom, asking Wendy to find a large canvas bag for Officer O'Brady.

Plump moneybag in hand, O'Brien stood to leave, offering Ford a warning framed in the terms of friendly advice. After San Jose had been pacified, the rest of the Bay Area would be next. Detroit and its auto assembly plants were the next logical battleground. Each city would cost more than the last. Ten million pounds was a one time introductory fee. Ford would be wise not to get tightfisted as the strikebreaking proceeded.

The warning (or threat) took the air out of Ford's lungs, preventing him from saying anything to O'Brien's retreating back. Breaking the global strike with corrupt cops in a tedious city-by-city campaign might cost DFA billions of pounds. There would be a return on investment, however; as DFA industrial cities came back on line, they would once again generate revenue for the parent company. Ford returned to the stack of paper on his desk, dreaming of the halcyon days of peaceful monopolistic growth.

Vladimir Bakunin and Max Stephanitz had communized the San Jose Police Department decades ago. San Jose's police dogs were of a uniformly excellent quality, deriving from Stephanitz's training methods and breeding program.

The German Shepherd sitting at O'Brien's side bore testimony to the foundation laid by the fathers of the Communist International. Cyclone growled with subtle menace, staring at the girl behind the cash register. The clerk running the night shift at the First Street DFA Grocery Store had just sold food to another striker. She'd gone through the motions of checking a customer's driver's license against the DFA black book, but she had ignored the fact that the short, middle-aged man with the hungry look was blacklisted. This was her second transgression tonight.

Cyclone walked stiff-legged to the cash register, breathing in the smell of her nervous guilt. The hungry striker made a move to bolt out the door. O'Brien took three quick strides and knocked the bag of groceries from the striker's hands. The short man proved to be tougher than he looked, or more desperate. He raised his fists, facing O'Brien and standing possessively over the sack of spilled groceries. The wild look in his eyes said that the striker hadn't eaten in days.

The police dog engaged, catching the desperate man on the forearm, dragging him down but clamping his teeth with only moderate bite pressure, enough to hurt like hell, not enough to do any real damage. O'Brien ordered the dog to disengage. The striker stood there unbowed, rubbing his arm and threatening to return with a crew of fire-bombers. The Irish cop laughed in the striker's face. Since the shoot to kill orders had gone out, there hadn't been any firebombs or property damage and both men knew it. The striker at last slinked out of the grocery store, defeated and perhaps ready to return to whatever DFA assembly line had originally employed him. Boxes of food were given to any striker crossing a picket line. More important, returning to work took your name off the blacklist.

O'Brien gave the interior of the grocery store a quick once over, his eyes lingering at the dartboard with Henry Ford's picture on it, just outside the view of the security camera. Under the dartboard there was a small portrait of Marx next to a crucifix. The night clerk had probably put both those items up on the far wall of the supermarket. She was a fiery young Mexican woman, clearly possessing strong revolutionary sentiments. O'Brien hated what he had to do to her next.

"Maria, that's the second time a striker almost bought groceries tonight. I gotta teach you a lesson, gotta let Cyclone rip you up." He gave the dog a bite command. If Maria had been a strong, six-foot tall man with attitude, the dog would have attacked in earnest. Since the cashier was a thin, five-foot tall woman with a mild manner, the K9 gave her little more than a couple of quick nips.

She screamed in terror nonetheless. Cyclone let go on command and returned to O'Brien side, tail wagging happily. Maria picked herself up off the floor. Mustering what dignity she could, the cashier scolded O'Brien: "Every cop in San Jose is a socialist. I know: my cousin is a cop. What is wrong with you people? Where is your class consciousness?"

O'Brien pulled a stool from a corner and sat next to her cash register. He told her to use her own stool and take a load off. Cyclone curled up between them and fell asleep. Past midnight, the store was devoid of customers.

"No, we aren't socialists," O'Brien corrected. "We're communists. This trade union mentality will get working people exactly nowhere. Strikers are happy to trade a hundred-hour week for a sixty-hour week. Sell their souls for a nickel. They should want to overthrow the system. Destroy capitalism."

Her tears dried and her backbone stiffened. Maria wanted to know how the embers of trade union mentality could be fanned into the flames of revolution. O'Brien knew that he had just landed a valuable recruit. He told her to obey Henry Ford's edict, stop selling groceries to strikers. Breaking the strike meant breaking the union, ultimately breaking the proletariat's pitiful trade union mentality.

"Damn you communists to hell and back!" She cried. "For the last thirty years it's been: let capitalism triumph over feudalism, the time for revolution is not here. Now it's: break the union, not the right time for revolution. If not now, then when?"

Cyclone awoke to the sound of Maria's wailing. The German Shepherd sat next to the distraught woman, nostrils drinking in the complex brew of her emotions, ready to act as truth seeker.

"Want me to give the date for the revolution?" O'Brien asked. She nodded mutely. Cyclone sat there, whining softly, his ears perked up. The cop told her to answer the question out loud. Maria said distinctly, "Yes, I want to know the date of the revolution." Cyclone barked once, high-pitched, affirmative, she was telling the truth. But O'Brien had only lobbed her a soft ball, everyone wanted to know the date of the revolution. He pitched her a low, fast slider. "Maria Lopez, swear an oath of fealty to the Communist International and I will give the date." He pulled a small booklet from a pocket and looked up the initiation oath.

A bit more cajoling and Maria agreed to take the oath and abide by its every tenet. Cyclone planted his nose into one of her armpits and sucked in the smell of her mental framework. The dog looked at his human partner and barked affirmatively.

O'Brien led her in a pledge of fealty to the International. Cyclone yipped positively whenever the oath takers paused to take a breath. By the time the last word was uttered, the Red Army had recruited another foot soldier for the coming war. Maria learned the year that would bring revolution: 1939. She'd heard that date before in the form of street rumors and gossip, now she gave credence to the word on the street, something miraculous really was going to happen in a little over half a decade.

She needed to have the stars knocked from her eyes. Stars were as bad as tears. O'Brien described the pain and suffering that would come from breaking the strike. Strikers that refused to give in would become destitute, cold and hungry, thrown out of company owned apartments to wander the streets with rags on their feet. Little children, old people, they would all suffer. He laid it on thick, stopping short when the stars threatened to turn back into tears. Switching gears, he told her that all the pain and misery would be worth it at the end of the decade when the long promised revolution swept the old order away. He gave Maria a revolver and an ammo clip, making sure she knew how to use it. Then he gave her a membership card in the International with his personal signature embossed. He told her when and where the next meeting would be held and left the grocery store, Cyclone heeling obediently at his side.

Cop and K9 jumped into an unmarked police cruiser, slipping into the misty night with only fog lights on. A battered old Duryea Roadmaster pulled into a DFA gas station. Something in the nervous way that the driver jerked the wheel triggered O'Brien's law enforcement instincts. He parked on a side street and watched the furtive driver try to buy gas.

The gas station attendant demanded to see a driver's license and checked it against the ubiquitous blacklist. The man behind the wheel of the Roadmaster obviously was on the blacklist because he was refused service. The creaky old car pulled back on to First Street. O'Brien followed at a stealthy distance.

The Roadmaster tried twice more to find fuel. Both times gas station attendants acted as if they were loyal to DFA, refusing to pump even a drop of gasoline. They weren't loyal, of course, but were deathly afraid of San Jose's savage Marxist police department.

O'Brien whipped through the last gas station with his window down. He yelled to the grease monkey at the pump, "Keep the faith, brother, 1939!" The men yelled back with the stiff-armed communist salute, "Revolution, 1939!" The police cruiser resumed tailing the beat-up old car that was searching for gasoline.

After failing to find gas from a DFA station, the Duryea sedan left the downtown area and headed to East San Jose, probably hoping to buy petrol on the black market. It might lead O'Brien to a black market bust. No such luck. The Duryea sputtered to a stop just as it rolled into one of the seedier neighborhoods on the east side.

Cyclone and O'Brien approached the stalled vehicle. The car's window was open, the man inside staring disconsolately at his windshield. He was caught between a rock and a hard place. Abandoning the car at night meant that it would be swiftly stripped to the bone, practically disemboweled. But what was the guy going to do come daylight if nobody was willing to sell any gas? And he would almost certainly get mugged, or worse, in this neighborhood if he sat there all night.

"Need a gallon of gas to get home, buddy?" O'Brien called through an open window of his unmarked cruiser. The blacklisted man was a young Asian with Coke-bottle glasses, a pocket protector, and a raft of pens in his protected shirt pocket. His appearance screamed software engineer. He brightened until he saw O'Brien's uniform and police dog. "You guessed right, sunshine. I'll gas your car if you swear an oath to cross the picket line at IBM or whatever DFA subsidiary you've been striking," O'Brien said, shining a flashlight in the engineer's face and stepping out of the squad car. The man with the Coke-bottle glasses made a gesture at the dog and pointed at his own nose, but didn't speak. "Yeah, that's right, the dog can smell a liar."

Words at last came to the distressed software engineer, pronouncements about the solidarity of the labor movement, the hopelessness of any possible communist revolution. He was smart all right, and knew exactly what O'Brien was driving at. He must have been worked over a few times by other cops.

A gang of street toughs emerged from the darkness, sensing that the cop was going to leave a tasty prey animal on their doorstep. O'Brien made a move to return to his cruiser. The ghetto denizens moved closer like sharks that can smell blood in the water. The timorous engineer shouted a promise to the police officer. The man would return to his job, meekly accept the 100-hour workweek, and forego the solidarity of organized labor.

A single shot from O'Brien's service revolver sent the street toughs scurrying back into the darkness. Gas flowed from a spare can into the crippled Roadmaster. The young Asian man's eyes darted from the Good Samaritan cop to the keys in the ignition of his car, only inches from his right hand, practically drooling at the prospect of getting out of the danger zone.

O'Brien reached into the Roadmaster and pulled the keys loose. A gargled cry rose from the frightened software designer. The keys dangled tantalizing outside the man's reach. "Hey, four-eyes, you need to understand what happened here tonight," the cop said harshly.

"I caved in, sold out to the man. I'll be a mindless wage-slave for the rest of my life. That's what just happened."

"No, what happened is the union lost a striker and the Communist International gained a foot soldier." O'Brien went on to lecture the beaten down engineer on the virtues of communism. It didn't feel right to give this man a card or take him any farther. The grocery clerk, Maria, had been a genuine recruit, a real find. This guy was merely a seed that might someday bear a single flaming red fruit. All in a days work.

O'Brien threw the car keys at the software engineer. The policeman and police dog returned to the cruiser. The night patrol had told the agent provocateur that trade union mentality had been crushed in Silicon Valley. This city was ready to stand on its own feet. The local cops were doing a fine job. He could move on to Detroit with a clear conscience and get the ball rolling there.

The idyllic street scene below Henry Ford's penthouse office held hidden menace. Panzers, gun-touting soldiers, and concertina wire had been replaced by the reassuring sight of commuters driving to jobs in DFA factories and office buildings. On the surface, this was quite reassuring. Bribing cops to crush the strikes in the western United States, western Canada, and Michigan had set off a virtuous chain reaction in other parts of North America, all the way down into the industrialized regions of southern Mexico. Strikers were crossing picket lines in droves. This gave Ford two different clubs to hold over the heads of strikers in the industrialized districts of Europe and Africa. He could threaten to either turn regional police forces loose on the malcontents or shift production to the docile work forces in North America and Asia. Things were beginning to shape up overseas. This turn of events had allayed his worst fear: that every city in the Commonwealth would have to be taken back one corrupt police department at a time.

Traffic began to thin as Ford continued staring out his picture window. Happy noises bubbled up from the building below his feet. White-collar workers were filing into cubicles, turning on computers, brewing coffee, chatting around office coolers. Outside the building, on the street below, pedestrians in business suits had given way to hot dog vendors pushing little carts. Even from this height, he could see plumes of steam venting from the hot dog carts. Ford grinned and took a sip of coffee. The vendors outside were independent businessmen, but they could only sell DFA brand frankfurters. Even their little carts were manufactured by DFA. On the surface, all was right with the world.

Dig below the surface and major problems emerged. Ford's smile faded. DFA's newly created Security Division indicated that half the returning strikers were under the impression that a communist revolution would erupt in 1939. That was the only reason why hardcore radicals had returned to work. Legions of Marxist workers were salivating at the prospect of overthrowing the supermonopoly and its puppet government.

Throughout this city, and others that had been pacified, a strange graffiti message had appeared: the numbers 1939, splashed in red paint, sometimes accompanied by a yellow hammer and sickle. The rank and file actually believed this horse pucky about a world revolution. Ford was certain there wasn't going to be a communist revolt in 1939, or 2039, or ever. What could happen in 1939 was another series of global strikes. That appeared to be the trap the crooked left wing cops were laying for DFA. They would demand some long green to avert a second wave of calamitous strikes. Ford hated being blackmailed.

The Irish cop, O'Brady, was some kind a kingpin in the global police crime syndicate. Ford needed to powwow with the kingpin. The chairman of the board had wiped his appointment schedule clean today to spend all the time he might need to deal with this O'Brady character.

Ford pulled out his pocket watch. O'Brady was late. Nobody made the richest man in the world wait. The intercom box on his desk squawked, "Mr. Ford, your appointment is here." The Irish cop entered the office, oozing joviality, bravado, and insolence. O'Brien took a chair without waiting for an invitation, threw his feet on Ford's desk, and asked, "Got twenty millski on you, Henry? 'Cause I need that much moola, today."

The plutocrat slapped one of O'Brien's shiny black German style jackboots, glaring at the cop red-faced. The boots inched off the desk with insouciant slowness. Ford let the blatant show of disrespect slide and replied, "We talk cash after I get some answers." The chairman of the board walked around his desk, sat down next to O'Brien, and continued: "Why the graffiti with the number 1939? Are you bastards setting me up for more strikes and more blackmail?"

O'Brien put his feet back on the desk and drawled lazily, "Ah heck, Henry, my cops're sweet talkin' the hard cases back on the job." Ford glared at the pair of gleaming boots in distaste, and did nothing but look up at the cop inquiringly. "Look, Bossman, it's like the pablum that preachers spoon feed the masses. Gonna be pie in the sky, by and by." O'Brien made the sign of the cross, turning the gesture into a mockery. Ford was not an especially religious man and wasn't offended. O'Brien expanded on his explanation: "Marx says religion is the opiate of the masses. Preacher man promises a heaven that ain't real to cow the multitudes to the bourgeois authorities. My cops do the same: promise a revolution that ain't gonna ever happen."

This alarmed the richest man on Earth. The Irish cop had never spouted Marxist slogans before. Ford put on a poker face. O'Brien could see that he'd frightened the plutocrat and pulled his feet off the desk to tone it down a notch. Trying to project an aura of sincerity, he said, "My cops won't leave DFA high and dry come 1939. I gotta plan that oughtta keep the radicals from burning your factories to the ground. And it ain't gonna cost DFA all that much."

Ford's poker face dropped. Hope shone through his lean, bony features. O'Brien went on to outline a fiendishly clever plan where the minority of genuinely radical workers, ring leaders and rabble-rousers, would be arrested over the course of the next year on trumped up charges. The sweep would be initiated as soon as the global strikes were well and truly over. DFA would have to cough up enough dough to build and staff private prisons: boot camps that would tame the violent incorrigibles and turn them into loyal and hard working DFA security guards. The guards would eventually become the toughest strikebreakers imaginable. To catch a thief, you must set a thief.

O'Brien wanted Ford to design an academic curriculum to rehabilitate the radical convicts. The Irish cop would draw up plans for the paramilitary aspect of the inmates' training, but Ford would indoctrinate them in the virtues of monopolistic capitalism and essentially teach them how to think. The chairman of the board had very little formal education and no experience as a teacher, yet he'd always considered America and Europe's educational systems deeply flawed and went to great lengths to avoid hiring college graduates whenever he could get away with it. O'Brien knew that Ford would jump at the idea of reinventing academia in the same way that he'd reinvented capitalism.

Ford's hopeful expression gave way to calculation. "Private prisons? Yeah, that's how we'd have to do it. Only the city governments are already giving me hell for putting their cops on my payroll. Your idea has me creating a permanent shadow government."

"Bossman, have I ever let you down?"

Ford shook his head. The Irish cop had always delivered. The man was on the verge of breaking the last few strikes and putting DFA on the path to profitability. Surely he could handle a few niggling politicians. It was in the politicos' self-interest to prevent another economic meltdown. And their palms would be greased along the way. Politicians that proved incorruptible would have to be dealt with violently.

"All right, O'Brady, you've sold me. I've got twenty million here in my wall safe as seed money. We'll negotiate a final amount as the project gets underway." Ford removed a painting from a wall and dialed the safe's combination. He pulled out bundles of bills, something he always ended up doing when O'Brady paid a visit. "Don't spend it all in one place," Ford said with a grin, chucking fat bundles of money at the communist agent.

The Vulcan was the latest luxury product to roll out of the newly invigorated assembly lines of DFA Aero in South Africa. O'Brien had flown choppers for the Red Army in Kauai, but they were nothing like the computer-controlled, gyro-stabilized Vulcan. Not only was it easier to fly than a military helicopter, it was much quieter and practically vibration-free. Flying it was not unlike driving a Rolls-Royce.

The luxury chopper made his job infinitely easier. He had to inspect every private prison in DFA's North American penal system before the year was out. Hopping from one private prison to another at half the speed of sound gave O'Brien a taste of what it must be like to be a fat cat DFA corporate executive, which sent a shiver of self-loathing down his spine. At least he jockeyed the luxury chopper himself, without resorting to a chauffeur-pilot.

He engaged the autopilot and let the helicopter skim over the featureless Arizona desert. Radar and the computer guidance system would pop it over any hills or mountains in the way. As he leaned back in the reclining pilot's chair, the massage program automatically activated. Rollers and heating elements under the supple leather kneaded the kinks out of his back. Decadence, capitalist decadence, but he didn't turn off the program with the manual override. From the copilot's chair, O'Brien heard a blissful grunt. Cyclone had figured out how to lean back and activate the massage program in the same way that a human being would have. The dog enjoyed a good massage as much as any person.

A gentle chime woke both the man and the dog. Time to turn off the autopilot and land. The DFA Phoenix Penal Colony needed inspecting. A radio operator in the prison control tower asked for the day's password, O'Brien gave it. He received permission to land on the small strip outside the perimeter forcefield fence.

The warden's armored limo was waiting between the aero strip and the forcefield fence. O'Brien and Cyclone hopped out of the air-conditioned chopper and into a wall of hellish heat. Sweat immediately flowed out of every pore in the man's body. The dog's tongue curled and uncurled with heavy panting, dripping saliva as they bounded into the limo. The passenger compartment of the Rolls-Royce was blessedly air-conditioned. Cyclone's tongue rolled back into his mouth.

O'Brien had worked with Warden Otto Mueller many years ago when Vladimir Bakunin and Max Stephanitz had helped establish the San Francisco communist police cell. Since then, the two communists had had no additional contact, following the protocol of the Communist International. Otto had been a member of the International for thirty-three years. He was famous among the initiated because he'd fought as a panzerman alongside the great Vladimir Bakunin in the World War.

"Otto, you old fart, how they hanging?" O'Brien asked. The warden made a show of checking his crotch and replied, "Knocking together like two coconuts in a windstorm." The Irish cop pursed his lips, narrowed his eyes, and nodded sagely, as if to say: Of course, all Marxist men are well endowed.

"I will tell you how it is hanging at the DFA Phoenix Penal Colony," Otto said seriously. "We are following Chairman Ford's re-education regimen more diligently than any other prison in the system. Phoenix is number one."

"Ha! Every warden I've met makes the same claim," O'Brien challenged. There was a small cadre of secretly communist wardens in the system and a great number of openly and rabidly anti-communist wardens. They all had one thing in common: a fierce desire to implement Henry Ford's rehabilitation curriculum. Naturally, their motivations for attempting to turn Ford's vision into reality differed. The majority anti-communist wardens believed Ford's regimen was working. The handful of secret communist wardens like Otto knew that it was having the opposite effect. It was hardening the radicals against DFA and creating legions of Red Army shock troops for the coming war.

The armored limo rolled through a series of security gates until it arrived at the heart of the complex: a flat acre of sandy earth ringed by machinegun towers and campus style prisoner housing units. Standing on the sandy field were several hundred men in black and white striped uniforms. The men were chained together in neat rows. All of them wore big floppy sombreros, their heads bowed against the hammering of the Arizona sun.

Otto, O'Brien, and Cyclone sat in the back of the limo in air-conditioned comfort, watching the chained inmates shimmer in the heat waves boiling up from the ground. Loudspeakers blared from nearby guard towers: "Gentlemen, this is Henry Ford, addressing the entire population of the DFA Prison System by landline transmission. The weather is lovely here in San Jose, I trust that it is not overly inclement wherever you find yourself at this moment."

More than one prisoner in the Phoenix yard uttered a sarcastic guffaw at Ford's opening remark. Guards were patrolling the rows of inmates, alert for just this sort of insubordination. Rifle butts were smashed into the bellies of any prisoners showing disrespect. Four disrespectful inmates doubled over in pain and fell to the ground, dragging several of the men they were chained to down as well. O'Brien noticed that two prisoners sustained blows but refused to fall to the ground.

The loudspeaker kept blaring. Henry Ford was discussing the evils of tobacco. For many years, the industrialist had suspected that smoking tobacco was extremely unhealthy. Recently, DFA doctors and researchers had conducted exhaustive studies proving Ford's suspicions correct. In the light of these findings, DFA cigarette factories and tobacco farms were disbanded and the workers relocated to other divisions or subsidiaries. Did the world government take notice? No, it did not. Tobacco production remained a legal activity and non-DFA companies had taken over the market that the supermonopoly had abandoned. Giving up a profitable segment of the economy proved that Ford was not solely motivated by profit. The health and welfare of his workers was paramount.

How about the unions that had tried to destroy DFA? Did they call for strikes to halt the production of cigarettes and other tobacco products? No, they did not. The unions didn't care about the health of the workers. They cared only for political and economic power.

The two men that had sustained blows to the stomach without falling down pretended to take out packs of cigarettes, strike invisible matches, and make a pantomime of smoking. The two had a great deal of skill in the art of pantomime. Their routine was funny, so funny that men within eyesight were soon doubled over laughing. The entire prison population was soon pretending to smoke as Ford's voice blathered over the loudspeakers.

DFA penitentiary regulations called for fire hoses to be turned on large groups that were acting uniformly insubordinate during a rehabilitation lecture, a punishment that would strip a man of dignity, but cause no real harm. Crushing torrents of water blasted into the giant chain gang from ten different directions, knocking the men around like tenpins.

The instant the hoses had run dry, guards and German Shepherd attack dogs flooded the yard. The inmates were unchained and quickly hustled into their cells before they could dry off in the searing heat. The cells were air-conditioned. Throwing sopping wet men into chilly cubicles was another form of punishment that appeared innocuous to the government, but was actually more severe than it sounded.

O'Brien asked Otto who the two hard cases were. The Warden responded: "Antoine Pevsner and Vladimir Tatlin. Russians. You may have heard of them. They founded the constructivist architectural movement. Card carrying communists."

"This evening, during paramilitary training, I want Pevsner and Tatlin to act as platoon commanders."

Otto didn't respond, but flicked his eyes at the driver sitting behind the wheel of the Rolls-Royce. The chauffeurs for all the DFA wardens were spies that reported directly to DFA headquarters in San Jose. The Communist International not only was aware of this fact, it encouraged the spying.

O'Brien explained, "I've been using this procedure at every prison I inspect: giving the hard cases authority over the other men. It has speeded the process of rehabilitation. Men like Pevsner and Tatlin are willing to endure tremendous punishment if they are isolated from the group. Put them in charge, punish their followers, and the hard nuts crack into a million pieces."

The chauffeur was surreptitiously glancing in the mirror at Otto's face. The warden wore a look of thoughtful defiance. While anything was worth a try, he did confess to having reservations. O'Brien coolly informed Otto that Henry Ford was pleased with the results in the other prisons. The chauffeur's scrutiny increased. He was looking for resistance on Otto's part.

The warden's features grew resolute. He promised to make the Russian constructivists buy into the rehabilitation program by putting them in positions of leadership. And he would redouble his efforts to make the entire prison population tow the company line, admitting, regretfully, that not one of Ford's lectures had been completed without an act of insubordination.

O'Brien threw a playful punch at Otto's shoulder and said, "Don't beat yourself up. None of the wardens can get their inmates through Mr. Ford's lessons in perfect order. There's always a need to turn on fire hoses, let loose attack dogs, or something. The secret is to keep trying. We'll pound respect for monopoly capitalism into these leftist whack jobs come hell or high water."

Otto and O'Brien were impressed with the performance of Pevsner and Tatlin that evening during paramilitary training. Cardboard buildings were assembled in the training grounds and used to simulate an urban assault. The two Russian architects had an incredible sense of space and dimension, able to find their way in the dark like cats. They led teams of mock assassins through labyrinthine cardboard structures, achieving 100 percent kill ratios on select targets.

Once the exercise was over and the inmates were locked up, O'Brien and Cyclone left the prison. The Irish cop sat for a moment in his personal helicopter, reflecting on how stupid the capitalists were to permit military training among the people most dedicated to destroying their way of life. On the other hand, the blood-sucking vampires probably couldn't help themselves. Their fate was to be decided by the dialectic: Any class destined for extinction would always sow the seeds of its own destruction.

Chapter 11
Free Market Communism is not Sexy

Every high-ranking officer or scientist in the Red Army was required to perform an hour of proletariat duty every day, to forge solidarity with low-ranking soldiers and workers. Werner Heisenberg's duty was to exercise a German Shepherd for one hour. George Patton had decided that the inventor of Quantum Mechanics was soft and out of shape. Patton was also of the opinion that the only way to reduce Heisenberg's bourgeois snobbery was to have him rub elbows with the Red Army work force during his daily jogging assignment. The only thing Heisenberg liked about running was that the pain in his legs temporarily made him forget the pain in his stomach. Patton had also ordered him to lose ten pounds in one month.

Lately, the runs were more grueling than usual. Usually he ran on the beach. For the past week, he'd been assigned to the sub-oceanic factory complex in order to supervise the installation of the miniature fission reactors that his team had recently assembled. The complex was part of the Red Army's tunnel fortress, buried miles into the Earth's mantle. Factory tunnels were wild tangles of cooling pipes, power cables, support girders, and heavy machinery. Metal causeways with handrails twisted all around the industrial jumble. These causeways were always clogged with technicians scurrying from one job to another. He and the dog he was exercising had to weave through all this human traffic. Whenever he bumped into a worker while jogging, the net result of the encounter was never increased solidarity, but curses and recrimination.

The alarm in his wristwatch buzzed. Good. A half hour had passed. His proletariat duty was half complete. Heisenberg changed direction and trotted back toward one of the fission reactors that his people were hooking up. He didn't know the name of the dog that dutifully paced behind him, and didn't want to know. They all had meteorological names like Typhoon or Snowstorm. He frowned. The naming scheme was inelegant. The war seals were all named after characters in Greco-Roman mythology. Heisenberg's early training had been in the classics and he found the seal nomenclature much more appealing. At a minimum, the meteorological German Shepherd names were better than the bloodthirsty names given to Bulldogs. Those canine brutes always carried handles like

Rip-gut or Massacre. He was never asked to exercise a Bulldog. Thank the Lord for small miracles.

The run complete, Heisenberg dropped to one knee, huffing and puffing. Someone grabbed the leash he was holding and led the German Shepherd away. The animal wasn't even panting, so it was questionable how much exercise it had received. The microradio in his pocket rang. Ferdy Porsche was on the other end, instructing him to come up to the surface. The youth needed help with a design project assigned by General Patton. Heisenberg told Ferdy that he would help him via the Red Army Cybernet. They could send emails back and forth. Traveling to the surface was a difficult undertaking.

"No. I have to brainstorm with you in person," Ferdy demanded. "I checked with Patton. You are instructed to drop everything and come upstairs." Heisenberg tried to argue the point. Ferdy cut him off. "Don't shed crocodile tears, Werner. I know you hate it down there. I'm not fooling around. Get your ass up here."

Heisenberg dusted off his personal combat suit and crawled inside. There was still only one way to reach the surface: bump along the conveyor belt along with tons of boulders and tons of crushed rock. He had time to meditate on his spiritual journey while making the long physical journey.

The level of loyalty that he felt toward the Red Army and its ideals was remarkable in light of his kidnapping and forced servitude. They had threatened to kill him if he didn't cooperate. There had even been a small whiff of torture, which he hadn't withstood very well. Still, he could have slow-walked the development and manufacture of the miniature fission reactors. He could have worked for the Reds half-heartedly. What had convinced him to fully commit was mathematics and science. More than anyone on the planet, Heisenberg understood the importance of quantifiable and observable phenomena. Vladimir Bakunin had presented irrefutable evidence that humanity was being destroyed on the horns of monopolistic capitalism.

He sat up on the conveyor belt and looked at the military parade scrolling by on either side. Thousands of human combat suits were lining the tunnel, stacked for storage, part of the grand buildup. The tunnel's angle of ascent increased and Heisenberg was forced to stand. The mass of stacked human suits gave way to thousands of pinniped PCSs. The tunnel and the original conveyor belt dropped him into a switchback and an even steeper path on a new conveyor belt. He went into a three-point stance, like a football player. The glare of electric lights revealed tens of thousands of eight-legged power suits: arachnid combat armor. *What naming system do they use for spiders? Probably a simple alphanumeric sequence.* It was hard to believe that anybody would personalize the hideous little bugs. Then again, one could not be certain, Red Army soldiers tended to love their animal warriors.

A change in the pitch of the conveyor belt signaled the approach of another switchback. The howling belt dumped Heisenberg and a load of crushed rock onto yet another belt drive. The jolt was almost hard enough to expand the airbags inside his suit. Ferdy Porsche had better have a very good reason for putting him through this inconvenience. He looked left and right, expecting to see canine combat armor but there were no longer any suits rimming the tunnel walls. Another switchback loomed ahead. He was getting close the surface.

He survived being dumped into an ore car and finally stepped out of the power suit, thinking that the worse was over. That assumption was incorrect, the most arduous aspect

117

of the journey was riding in Ferdy's GTS sports car on the way to Princeville. The young Porsche could not get behind the wheel of an automobile and resist the impulse to drive at insane speeds. In due course, Ferdy and Heisenberg arrived at the Design Center. Ferdy hadn't discussed the project on the ride because he needed every bit of concentration while hurtling over slower vehicles, skidding around curves, and burning rubber in the straight-aways.

"What in thunder is this all about, Ferdy?" Heisenberg demanded once the two men were seated inside the Design Center. "There are only five years until the war begins. The Red Army is strictly in the production phase. We are no longer designing new weapons. Banner, Patton, Rommel, Bakunin, all the leaders, agree."

"That is not true. Patton and Rommel have set me on a new design project, with a one-year deadline. I will describe the problem. Then we must perfect the solution." Ferdy recounted a grave challenge that was impeding the entire war effort. The challenge revolved around a growing consensus that the Blue Force had to be wholly destroyed in a nuclear first strike that achieved total surprise and left Kauai unscathed. A ballistic missile barrage would not come close to achieving this end. There will soon be nuclear tipped missiles in Hawaii, ready for action. Without a doubt, Blue Force radar would easily detect a strike originating five hundred miles away in Kauai. The enemy would immediately send their own missiles at Kauai. And there is reason to believe that Blue Force's next gen. combat suits will be impervious to atom bombs anywhere outside of ground zero.

Heisenberg pinched the bridge of his nose. He asked the young Porsche a series of questions in a sarcastic voice. Why doesn't High Command commission a magic spell that would erase the Blue Force by uttering a few archaic words in some ancient language? Why don't the brainiac leaders make voodoo dolls of the Blue Force and then burn them in a fire? Were the morons that had escaped from the stupid factory leading the Red Army? He went along in this vein until Ferdy stopped him by announcing that a technical solution existed, it only needed brilliant engineering to spring to life.

"What might this solution be, pray tell?" Heisenberg asked, as sarcastically as he could. Ferdy walked out of the building, signaling for the physicist to follow. They walked down to the beach together. Ferdy pointed at the ocean and asked Heisenberg what he saw. There was nothing out there except a humpback whale cow and her calf. The adult whale was staying near the surface, spouting regularly, because the calf was too young to dive very deep. A few other tiny whale spouts plumed in the distance. It was winter and the humpbacks were making their annual migration north.

Heisenberg claimed that there was nothing out there. He was beginning to suspect that the long journey up from the bowels of the Earth had been done for no good reason. Perhaps the young Porsche had slipped a mental cog.

"Nothing?" Ferdy asked incredulously. "I see a fifty-foot, forty-ton humpback whale. If it were a blue whale, she might weigh one hundred and fifty tons and swim at thirty miles-per-hour. What would you think if a one hundred and fifty ton foreign submarine were loitering off our coast?"

Heisenberg combed his bushy hair with his fingers thoughtfully, watching the humpback cow and listening to the young Porsche. Ferdy breathlessly described his vision. One hundred mechanical whales (he used the term "animatronic" rather than mechanical) were swimming toward Hawaii. Flexible plastic skin covered plasteel frames. They were artfully constructed, indistinguishable from real whales and piloted by volunteers willing to commit suicide. The whales beached themselves along the shores of the Big Island at strategic points determined by military planners. The mechanical leviathans opened their great jaws and each one fired a short-range missile into the island interior. One hundred nuclear bombs detonated seconds later, before the Blue Force could even think about responding. The only force on Earth capable of harming the Red Army was now a glowing heap of radioactive trash. The revolution could now march on to victory.

"Ferdinand, I do believe that you are on to something," Heisenberg said, deciding that it was time to discard the younger Porsche's silly nickname and call him by his given name. If that created confusion between the elder Porsche and the younger, then the older one could be called Ferdy.

There weren't supposed to be any more demands made on the mainframe now that the Red Army was in its production phase. All weapon systems were supposed to have been designed, and the only technological task left was to build the arsenal. After years of sweating over software programs, Vladimir Bakunin should have been free (at long last) to run the final version of his Spartacus program. But all of a sudden, General Patton had gotten a bur under his saddle and wanted to design one more weapons system, a kind of robotic whale that would constitute a super stealthy delivery system for nuclear weapons. Vladimir asked how long it would take to design this final weapon platform and was told that the mainframe would be tied up for a full year. Commandant Group C had put his foot down and informed all concerned that he was going to take the next three weeks and complete the Spartacus program. Wild horses could not tear him away from the supercomputer. Supreme Commander Banner had gotten involved and Vladimir prevailed. Patton's weapon designers would have to wait a few weeks.

Today was the big day. Vladimir had only to press a single button and the program that he had poured his soul into would begin running. The Spartacus Slave War would be re-fought in cyberspace. With any luck, Rome would be left in tatters and Spartacus' army would be triumphant. More than that, a new socio-economic system would arise from the ashes of the Roman Republic. Historical Parallelism would take Spartacus' economic system and modernize it for the 20th century and beyond. Vladimir hoped to answer the question: What will true communism look like? The results of this program might decide the fate of mankind for thousands of years.

His finger hovered over the computer console, ready to press the button, when a knock on the door interrupted. Supreme Commander Banner stepped into the cool air of the computer center. He looked around expectantly, as if he hoped to see Spartacus and his legions of gladiators clashing with Roman armies right there next to Vladimir.

"Have you initiated the program, Vlad?" the supreme commander wanted to know. Vladimir jammed the button down and the mainframe, or the part of it that they could see and hear, vibrated energetically. "I just did, Supreme Commander. As I sit here on my fat ass, the proletariat slave army is battling the bourgeoisie of ancient Rome in cyberspace."

Fred pulled a chair next to his group commandant and stared expectantly at the blinking lights of the computer console. "You realize that it will take three weeks before the

Spartacus program is finished and we are able to learn anything?" Vladimir asked.

"Of course. I merely wanted to be here at this historic moment."

They sat silently for several minutes until Fred asked, "What's happening now inside the program?"

"Right now, the program is recreating the first year of the Third Slave War as it occurred historically. Spartacus, Crixus, Oenomaus, and seventy gladiators have broken out from the gladiatorial school in Campua. They will quickly gather seventy thousand slaves from the plantations of southern Italy and, in the cyber-months ahead, will crush two Roman armies around Mount Vesuvius."

Banner knew all this already, but he seemed eager for Vladimir to continue. The short black Russian warmed to his subject, speaking fervently: "After the first few victories, the slave army will camp near the coastal village of Thurii. Spartacus encountered the first seeds of dissension at that point, both in the historical account and in the program. His sub-commander and fellow gladiator, Crixus, was intoxicated with victory and hungry for wealth. Crixus pleaded for a chance to lead the slave army into central Italy for plunder. Spartacus wanted to take the army across the Mediterranean and into Sicily."

Vladimir felt a little like an adult telling an eager child a bedtime story that both of them knew by heart. He continued the narrative anyway. "There had been two previous slave wars in Sicily. Tens of thousands of Romans had died at the hands of rebellious Sicilian slaves. The island was still a hotbed of revolution in 73 BC. To defeat Rome, Sicily had to be the home base of the insurrection. The historical Spartacus knew this but in his heart he probably felt that he could never defeat Rome. So Crixus' argument held sway and in the historical account the slave army marched up the boot of Italy. They won nine battles before being crushed. Six thousand gladiator were crucified after the final defeat."

Banner asked, "As I recall, the point of divergence comes during that debate between Spartacus, Crixus, and Oenomaus in the encampment at Thurri?"

"That is correct, Sir. In the Spartacus program phase one, history is distorted at Thurri. The virtual slave army will *not* march into the jaws of Rome. It will instead sail to Sicily. And from there, the program will have the virtual Spartacus borrowing the tactics and strategy of the Carthaginian General Hannibal Barca."

"What does Spartacus say to Crixus to change his mind?"

"I have no idea. We will find out when the program has finished running."

"Very well, carry on. I shall check back at that time and will expect a full report."

Vladimir stood and saluted as the supreme commander left the room. The wizened old man turned back to the computer console and watched the impassive lights blink at him for an hour. He sighed and left the room, desperately wondering what was happening to the virtual Spartacus, as impatient as Supreme Commander Banner to know the course of the virtual Third Slave War and gaze into the face of true communism.

The leaders of the slave army stared moodily into the embers of the campfire. The three commanders: Crixus, Oenomaus, and Spartacus sat on a hillside above the huge encampment below, debating their next move. This slave war, the Third Slave War, was off to a more auspicious start than the two previous slave wars that had occurred decades ago in Sicily. There was no great mystery as to why. Spartacus had only to look at the scarred faces of his two companions to see the answer. Gladiators were leading the Third Slave War. More than that, the gladiators that had broken out of the Campua school were either former legionaries or auxiliary troops in the Roman Army. The three men sitting around the hilltop campfire had over three decades of service fighting for Rome.

He looked down at the beach. The influence of the Roman Army showed in the vast camp beneath their vantage. The campfires were lined up in neat squares. Trenches had been dug around the camp and manned with soldiers who would remain vigilant throughout their rotation. Like a Roman Army camp, it was more a fortified village than a collection of rag tag warriors. There was an even a standard in the center of the encampment, a silver eagle on an ash pole. The letters SPQNR were carved into the board under the metallic eagle's talons. The letters stood for: The Senate and the People of New Rome.

Every soldier in Spartacus' army had sworn an oath to New Rome. At one time, a century or two in the past, Roman soldiers had sworn similar oaths to the Senate and the People of Rome, i.e., to the state. The standard of each legion had born the letters SPQR as a reminder of this oath. No longer, today's Roman soldiers swore an oath of allegiance to the general commanding their legion and marched under that general's personal standard. In turn, the general promised to line the soldiers' pockets with plunder. Today, every Roman soldier was a mercenary, none of them fought for patriotism. The idea of service to the Roman Republic was fading fast. Spartacus believed that this fading idealism was the root cause of the evils he saw all around him.

There was a time when gladiators were freemen and fought in the arena for love of the game. Every modern gladiator was a slave and fought under penalty of crucifixion. There was a time when free peasants, who owned their own small farms, fed Rome, fought for Rome, and marched under the banner of SPQR. Now, virtually every farm on the Italian peninsula and Sicily was a huge plantation operated by slaves. The percentage of freemen decreased every year. Even though Spartacus was a Thracian, not a Roman, he yearned to bring back the days of the free Roman Republic and go a step beyond so the decay could never set in again. He wanted to destroy old Rome and replace it with New Rome, a nation where slavery was illegal. He envisioned a state with only the three classes of citizens: the Senatorial class, the Equestrian class, and the Plebeians, none of them would be slaves or own slaves. Looking down at his army of seventy thousand, and thinking of the millions of slaves that might be willing to join his cause throughout the empire, he knew that it could be done. But first they must sail to Sicily.

Crixus cleared his throat and began the deliberation. He admitted to being intoxicated with the success they'd enjoyed thus far. Smashing two Roman armies was a heady brew. Among themselves, however, it had to be acknowledged that the Senate had only sent soft troops their way, thinking that this was just another slave uprising. There would come a day when real legions from the borders of the empire would be pulled back from their perennial skirmishes with barbarians and thrown at the slave army. When that happened, it wouldn't make any difference if they were in Sicily or Italy. No matter how well they trained and equipped the slaves, battle hardened legions from Gaul and Germany would eventually prevail. The smart thing to do was march north, gathering more fugitive slaves on the way, fight their way to the Alps, collect copious quantities of plunder, and then melt into the barbarian nations, scattering to the eight winds.

Oenomaus gave voice to Spartacus' thoughts by saying, "And what of New Rome? I am loath to abandon our ideals." Crixus spat into the fire and replied hotly, "Ideals will get us killed. I do not crave death. Let us join with the far Germanic tribes, outside the claws of Rome, weighted with sacks of gold and precious stones." Crixus looked away from the fire to stare Spartacus directly in the eye. Light from the flickering flames roved across the mass of scars on either gladiator's face, emphasizing the damage the arena had wrought.

"Death?" Spartacus sneered. "Death is nothing, lighter than a feather. Slavery is as heavy as a mountain. Tomorrow we use some of our plunder to buy ships from the Cilician pirates and sail to Sicily. There we foment rebellion, conquer Sicily, and prepare to invade Egypt. We strike at old Rome once Egypt is subdued and a willing partner. We fight our enemy the way Carthage fought Rome, one nation against the other. We follow the example of Hannibal. At the beginning of the second Punic War, Carthage was little more than a city-state, dwarfed by Rome, analogous to what we may build in Sicily. Hannibal conquered Spain and raised vast armies there before scaling the Alps and marching into Italy. Sicily will be our Carthage. Egypt will be our Spain."

Crixus' eyes acquired a hungry look. He practically drooled as he said. "Alexandria is the wealthiest city in the world. Egypt has wealth beyond the dreams of Midas. We will wallow in oceans of plunder."

"No! By Jupiter, no," Spartacus said, beginning to lose his temper. "The legions of New Rome are paid in silver denarii and when their tours are over, they are to be honorably cashiered with an allotment of land. Every soldier is to be a landowner and a farmer. He will work his own land with his own two hands; land carved from the slave plantations of the old Roman Republic. In the war that beckons, all plunder goes to the state to pay for ongoing operations." At times like these, Spartacus almost regretted sparing Crixus' life in the arena the one time that they'd fought. He'd gotten very little mileage out of the merciful act. He'd been brutally flogged after the incident, and Crixus never acted grateful.

Oenomaus excused himself from the debate, which he'd heard fifty times before. Why bother debating? The Thracian was the undisputed leader of their army; Spartacus should simply give Crixus orders and leave it at that. Oenomaus bowed to Spartacus and informed both gladiator commanders that he would contact the pirates and open the negotiations for enough boats to transport the New Roman Army to Sicily.

The two remaining commanders sat there in angry silence for a minute. It was a delicate balancing act that Spartacus had to perform with his second in command. Crixus was a Gaul and the army was heavy with thousands of Gauls who looked to the most senior Gallic gladiator as their chieftain. Even though the war had just begun, Crixus had already distributed loot to his tribesmen. Spartacus found himself in the same situation as Pandora; once unleashed, evil could not be put back into a box.

"We have work to do, Crixus. There is little plunder to distribute at this moment anyhow. After Alexandria lays supine at our feet, you and I shall revisit this topic. I need you to make your way to Sicily tomorrow. The servile herdsmen of the rugged backcountry are the revolutionaries that started the two earlier slave wars. Make contact with them. They must seize control of the harbors to safeguard the landing of our army."

Spartacus reached inside his tunic and pulled out five small bags of gold. He gave them to the Gaul and warned him that the money must be used to bribe the warlike slave herdsmen and nothing else. Crixus rose, saluted, and made his way into the encampment.

In the coming weeks, thanks in large measure to Crixus, Sicily fell with more of a whimper than a bang. The militant herdsmen that had launched the first two slave wars had already gotten wind that a third anti-slave crusade had exploded on the peninsula and were therefore primed and ready to fight. Before Spartacus' New Roman Army could smash into old Rome's Sicilian garrisons, Crixus and the herdsmen already had the legionaries routed and the town centers in flames. Spartacus' legions marched into the great slave plantations, only to find them in flames as well, slave owners mounted on crosses to die asphyxiating deaths: a grim and ironic message to the outside world, crucifixion was no longer reserved for slaves. Hardly raising a finger, the Thracian commander had secured the first province of New Rome. He spent the next month raising and training a second army from the ranks of the freed Sicilian slaves.

As the second month of the Sicilian occupation dawned, his spies on the peninsula sent word that the old Roman Senate was stirring. Hardened legions were being recalled from the borderlands and were marching down the boot of Italy. The senators were slowly realizing that the Third Slave War was something new and unexpected, much more than a simple rebellion, and it could not be squelched with soft city troops accustomed to light parade duty by day and endless bouts of drinking by night. Spartacus decided to guard his island fortress by harnessing the avarice of Crixus and his band of gladiatorial thieves.

Crixus was given three cohorts composed entirely of veteran gladiators with stellar records in the arena, the toughest fighting men in the world. They landed in southern Italy and immediately went to work, striking major towns in a premeditated pattern. First, they would storm the gladiatorial school, which meant destroying the soft city garrison charged with guarding the arena fighters. Second, with his ranks swelled by an influx of fresh gladiators, Crixus would unleash his men for a berserker rampage of raping, looting, burning, and killing. Third, his guerillas would melt into the hills and mountains.

In the rural regions of southern Italy, the slaves vastly outnumbered the overseers. Many of them were prisoners of war from Rome's frontier campaigns, barbarian ex-soldiers that were not as easily cowed as the traditional Roman slave born and broken to servitude. The huge influx of defeated barbarian soldiers turned into slaves had made the first two slave wars possible. It would have been easy enough for Crixus to raise an army of one hundred thousand in Italy that summer, but he did not. He'd struck a deal with Spartacus, runaway slaves taking advantage of the chaos in southern Italy were sent to Sicily to join the New Roman Army. Quid pro quo, Crixus was permitted to plunder to his heart's content, so long as he tied the old Roman legions into knots and continued functioning as a rearguard to the Spartacan forces gathering in Sicily, preparing to wage war against Egypt.

The storms of fall had not quite engulfed the Mediterranean when Spartacus found himself at the helm of double-masted trireme named after his wife, *Varina*, the flagship of the New Roman Navy, leading a spearhead of swift galleys that protected a landing force of heavy troop ships. The entire fleet was sailing toward the port city of Alexandria. There were six legions packed into the troop ships, roughly the strength of the entire old Roman Army on the peninsula. The New Roman Army was almost as strong as anything its nemesis could field in the boot of Italy, because old Rome was forced to leave huge troop concentrations along its frontiers.

An afternoon breeze filled the sails of the *Varina*. Its captain had ordered the three levels of oarsman to rest and let the sails do all the work. Spartacus turned away from the sea and glanced at the rowers sitting idle on the top deck of the trireme. The oarsmen on the top deck were always the biggest and strongest. They made him think of the heavily muscled Crixus. It was strange to go into battle without Crixus. Spartacus hadn't seen his friend and cobelligerent in months.

Even though Spartacus missed him, the absence of Crixus had proven to be a tremendous boon for the development of the Second New Roman Army that he and Oenomaus had raised in Sicily. Not only had they made every trooper swear allegiance to the New Roman state, the soldiers had also foresworn rape and plunder. The army was satisfied with Spartacus' promise to distribute land to every New Roman legionnaire when his fifteen-year tour was over.

The New Romans had trained hard all summer in Sicily. Every day, handpicked centurions had lectured the former slaves on Alexandrian culture. This was as important as military instruction as far as Spartacus was concerned. Egypt was Alexandria, plain and simple, and the Alexandrians had some peculiar traits. They revered cats. This may have been due to the constant need to eliminate rats in the grain markets of the coastal city, or it might be a holdover from the ancient Egyptian religion that the Alexandrian Greeks had melded to their own Hellenic beliefs. Either way, the centurions had beaten respect for cats into the raw recruits.

The Alexandrians worshipped the written word and books. The great library of Alexandria would be the first building to be secured and safeguarded once the city had been taken. Spartacus had promised to personally cut the throat of any soldier that allowed harm to befall the great library, or any scholar within.

Most of the legionaries had expressed revulsion and nearly mutinied when they'd learned that the Egyptian royal family routinely married brothers to sisters. The centurions had ruthlessly wielded cudgels that day, pounding reverence for the Ptolemaic royal family into the thick heads of their students.

As the former slaves turned soldiers learned more about Egypt, they acquired an appreciation for Spartacus' grand strategy. They learned that of all the cultures in the civilized world, Egypt had the least use for slavery. Only one in ten Egyptians was a slave. A host of legal rights protected slaves from abusive masters in Egypt. It was not uncommon for slaves to receive wages. If they married and had children, their offspring were not automatically enslaved. Free peasants tilled the soil of the Nile valley, and they were four or five times more productive than agricultural slaves in Rome. This is why Egypt was the breadbasket of the Mediterranean. Rome's inefficient slave economy could not exist without Egyptian grain. A few decades ago, Rome had paid for every bushel of grain it received from Egypt with silver and gold. Increasingly, the Romans demanded the grain as tribute, threatening to invade and lay waste to the desert kingdom if insufficient quantities of wheat were not delivered promptly and free of charge. Rome's demands on Egypt's harvest had grown so onerous in recent years that artificial famines had resulted in the Nile Valley.

In their barracks at night, over games of dice, the New Roman legionaries had speculated as to what exactly Spartacus intended to do with Alexandria and Egypt. Even the most dimwitted among them had grasped that a third army was to be raised before the Italian campaign began. Not one of them could fathom just how strange this army would eventually prove to be.

Nor could Spartacus, at least not yet. He turned away from the idle oarsman as hollow footsteps sounded from the ship's bow. Oenomaus was making his way to the helm, clearly desirous of conversation. Spartacus dismissed the steersmen, and grabbed hold of the tiller himself. As the gladiator approached, Spartacus noted the sour look on

Oenomaus' face.

"Talking to the captain just now. He says these water are too empty, not customary this close to Egypt," Oenomaus said, looking even more worried than he had a couple of seconds ago. Spartacus regarded the wine dark sea solemnly. It was red with mud, overflow from the annual flooding of the Nile. They were indeed close to Alexandria. Tonight they would see the distant twinkle of the famous Pharos lighthouse, one of the Seven Wonders of the World. It was said to look like a star come to Earth.

Oenomaus had more to say: "The pirate bastards must have betrayed us and warned the Egyptians of our attack. I fear that come morning we shall be engaged in a naval battle." In the past year, old Rome had launched a war against the multitudinous pirate bands infecting the Mediterranean. The New Roman leadership had negotiated with these cutthroats, hoping that they would make common cause against a mutual enemy. Evidently, this was a forlorn hope. The pirates had no honor and cared only for gold.

"Yes," Spartacus grumbled. "After we crush old Rome, after we master the Mediterranean, we shall clear the seaways of pirates. Perhaps throw them to the lions."

Night fell, and they did in fact see the beacon from the great lighthouse of Alexandria. The fleet of New Roman triremes succeeded in pulling together in a tight formation around the wallowing troop ships that night, riding at anchor on light seas.

The morning sun peered through a crimson sky, a harbinger of a coming storm. A greater threat moved in from the south, a fleet of four hundred Egyptian galleys. The Egyptians used biremes, not triremes: two banks of oars on each side, not three. Biremes were more maneuverable than the New Roman craft, but not as swift in the short burst, less suitable for ramming tactics and better for multifaceted naval evolutions.

The New Roman warships lowered their sails, dislodged their masts, and charged unhesitatingly, three banks of oars churning the muddy water into foam. The Egyptians expected this tactic. Roman sailors and Marines had only one maneuver: they tried to ram their opponents, then throw grappling hooks, lash fighting ships together, and board with their always superior Marines. In essence, Rome tried to turn a sea battle into a land battle.

The Egyptians moved laterally across the path of the charging triremes. Their tactics were more complex than the brutish Romans, or so they thought. Moving into bow range, peppering the New Romans with arrows and flaming spears hurled by ballista catapults, keeping their boats at right angles to the charging triremes, the Egyptian Navy avoided being rammed, yet kept the brutes charging into the coast. Egypt had huge armies of archers hidden on Pharos Island, the harbors of Alexandria, and on the beaches near Alexandria. They hoped to lure the New Romans near the shoreline, allowing Egyptian archers to spring out from under concealing tarps and turn the invaders into pincushions.

New Rome did something astonishing. The Marines on board the ram's head warships answered Egypt's salvo of arrows and catapult missiles with their own fusillade. In and of itself, that was to be expected. The fact that clay pots full of flammable resin had replaced the New Roman arrowheads and spearheads was not foreseeable. Oily rags had been wrapped and tied around these strange clay pots.

A century and a half ago, a comparable tactic had been invented by the military genius, Hannibal. The Carthaginian general had equipped a fleet with clay pot missiles filled with poisonous snakes. Spartacus had come across this astounding tactic while perusing a history book in Sicily's great library. The idea of substituting flammable liquid for snakes had come from Spartacus' own fertile imagination.

On board the *Varina,* three New Roman torchbearers set fire to the line of outstretched arrows and catapult spears. Once ignited, the flaming missiles were sent arcing between the two fleets, leaving trails of smoke in the air. A fresh round of fire-arrows were notched to New Roman bows. Fresh fire-spears were placed onto catapults. These were lighted in turn. Throughout the New Roman fleet, working methodically, thousands of fire-arrows and fire-spears poured into the Egyptian biremes.

From time immemorial, navies had fired flaming arrows and spears at each other; the combustion had inevitably been provided by oily rags or wood soaked in pitch, the resulting damage was usually more psychological than physical. Ancient navies had never gone up in a puff of smoke from such crude incendiary devices. New Rome's inoffensive looking little clay pots were different. They shattered on impact. The flammable resin ignited and splashed liquid fire across wooden surfaces, sails, and even Egyptian sailors. In minutes, the Egyptian Navy was blazing. Since the tactic was something never seen before in naval warfare, the fires did indeed cause psychological damage. The physical damage, however, was more profound. Panicked Egyptian oarsmen, archers, and Marines flailed at burning sails and gunnels while the New Roman triremes charged with a greater purpose than before.

Egyptian warships were easily rammed. Each New Roman trireme was built around a three-ton bronze ramming head, located at the waterline, under the decorative ram's head sculpted into the arching bow. Timbers from the burning biremes exploded on impact, impaling Egyptian sailors on jagged hunks of wood: the first real blood shed thus far. Some Egyptian warships sank outright. New Roman Marines boarded the others. The Marines were either gladiators or had been trained in close fighting techniques by gladiators. The Egyptians were ruthlessly slaughtered: serious bloodshed at last.

"Prisoners!" Spartacus roared as the Marines from his flagship swiftly butchered the enemy on the ship that they'd rammed. Oenomaus leaped onto two New Roman Marines, bowled them over, rescued an Egyptian officer, and dragged the smallish, olive-skinned soldier onto the *Varina*.

Speaking Greek, Spartacus demanded to know which beaches were safe and which ones were traps. The Egyptian officer pointed toward the great lighthouse and the adjacent stretches of coastline, informing the New Roman commander of the danger therein. Spartacus tightened the gold chain of his purple general's cloak and ordered a sailor to climb the mainmast and signal the fleet captains with mirrors.

Landfall was made without incident and before the sun set. It was fortunate indeed that they were able to land unopposed because the New Romans would not have been able to float the two eighty-foot battering rams to shore otherwise, or wheel them any distance inland. The two legions that had secured a foothold on Egyptian soil immediately set to building two fortified camps on either side of Alexandria. During construction, the storm that the red dawn had promised also made landfall. Their tents were lashed by cruel winds, trenches filled with water, and the New Roman fleet suffered losses since it had not anchored in any of Alexandria's harbors.

The invaders clustered inside their tents, whispering fearfully that Neptune must be angry. It seemed as though the Sea-God was favoring the Egyptians. There would be no means of retreat if a sizeable number of New Roman troop ships sank in the storm. Spartacus and Oenomaus circulated throughout the two camps that night, visiting the troops, bucking up their spirits.

The second morning of the invasion promised good weather, heartening the New Romans and making them realize that Neptune must be on their side after all. The storm had prevented an Egyptian night attack. From the two camps on either side of Alexandria, formations coalesced around the two wheeled battering rams and moved toward the east and west gates of the city.

The sky grew black from Egyptian arrows as the two legions approached their respective gates. Centurions hollered "Tortoise!" at the top of their lungs. The Egyptian archers on the battlements of the great city had heard of the Roman technique of assembling shield walls around armies and/or battering rams. They gasped nonetheless as a shell of interlocking shields grew around the men and the siege engines threatening Alexandria. The things moving toward the gates did look like gigantic tortoises. Arrows fell on and around the tortoises, sticking to the two shield walls harmlessly. The Egyptians wished that they had a few of the marvelous fire-arrows that they'd seen in the naval battle.

Then the hammering started. In a short while, the two gates blew open and the fighting was street-to-street, hand-to-hand, throughout the city. As his legions sent rivers of blood gushing into the wonderfully engineered sewage system of Egypt's capital, Spartacus took the time to marvel at the richest city on Earth. Alexandria was the only municipality in the world made entirely out of stone. It was, therefore, fireproof, and the books in the great library could not be accidentally burned. All around the gladiator-turned-general was evidence that this was a more advanced civilization than old Rome.

Obelisks rose in glimmering splendor in city squares. Egyptian architecture fused with Greek in splashing fountains graced by sculptures of Gods from a multitude of religions. A Doric temple stared down from an acropolis, white marble columns standing at attention in a single row around the inner chamber. The snow-colored walls, columns, and sculptures of the major buildings stood proudly in front of mirror bright reflecting pools. This created the illusion that the city was floating on clouds.

Surrounded by his retinue of bodyguards, Spartacus marched through the swirling combat, stepping over severed heads and mangled body parts, moving toward the city center and the royal palace of King Ptolemy XII. The fighting was diminishing and New Rome was consolidating its grip on the capital city when Spartacus' honor guard squared off with the Egyptian Praetorian Guard blocking the entrance to the royal palace.

The New Roman general called to the captain of the King's guard for a parley. The two men stood before the palace watching a stream of Egyptian prisoners marching in chains out of the city, goaded by New Roman troopers. Spartacus told the captain that he wanted to negotiate a truce with King Ptolemy. The city would be sacked if this meeting could not be arranged.

The ease with which the invaders had subdued Alexandria was disheartening to the captain. Moreover, Egypt's military had been in a near state of rebellion prior to the invasion, due to the cowardliness of Ptolemy's slow but steady capitulation to old Rome. The captain allowed his troops to be disarmed and taken prisoner, sensing a great purpose and rightness in the man wearing the purple cape. The palace was emptied of every royal retainer and Egyptian foot soldier.

Spartacus found himself walking alone down a long corridor, hobnail boots ringing against polished marble. He stopped short of the door that led to the throne room. The haunting sound of flute music rolled out from the room. It was a song that spoke of

Egypt's demise. Spartacus could feel thousands of years of brilliant civilization grinding away under the bloody-minded oppression of old Rome. For the first time, he understood that the evil empire not only held countless individual men locked in the shackles of slavery, but entire nations as well. Tears leaked down his battle-scarred cheeks as the flute music wrapped around his soul.

He pushed open the door and strode into the room. King Ptolemy was unattended, a single scrawny, bald-headed man sitting on a golden throne, playing a flute, garbed in a white silk chiamys and sandals made from peacock leather, trimmed with gold thread. Speaking Thracian accented Greek, Spartacus said, "I am here to liberate Egypt and conquer old Rome. I am Spartacus, consul and general of the New Roman Republic."

Ptolemy set down his flute. Looking down his nose at the ex-gladiator, he sneered, "Consul, eh? Aren't you the runaway slave stirring up trouble in Rome?" It was not an accurate assessment, but Spartacus nodded anyway, to keep the King talking. The flute-player continued: "I will thank you to leave my kingdom, slave, you will only bring the real Romans here, as shit draws flies."

Spartacus grabbed the little man by the scruff of the neck and frog-marched him to a window. The last rays of afternoon highlighted a city under occupation. New Roman guards were stationed outside every public building. Out in the harbors, New Roman ships were taking on cargo, grain and other supplies from the Alexandrian warehouses. Already, the New Roman stronghold in Sicily was being made stronger. Already, the flow of grain to old Rome was being cut off.

Although he kept up a brave front before Spartacus the slave, Ptolemy had been shocked when he saw the ease with which the invaders had crushed Alexandria. He was about to be utterly amazed. Spartacus gave a reasoned discourse on why now was the ideal time to pulverize the old Roman government and erect a new, better edifice in its place.

After five hundred years of stable Republican rule, old Rome had recently suffered its first civil war and the subsequent permanent military dictatorship of the wretched General Sulla. A feeble form of Republican rule had timidly asserted itself with Sulla's death. But the senate currently sitting in Rome was exceedingly wobbly; another round of civil war could break out at the drop of a hat. At sea, old Rome was caught in a naval war against innumerable bands of pirates. On land, the Third Mithradatic War was starting. After old Rome dealt with King Mithridates VI for the third and final time, a bevy of bloody wars with other kingdoms farther east loomed. Rome was well pleased that a weak king sat in Alexandria, because its appetite for free Egyptian grain was about to become insatiable.

Ptolemy watched his city sink into a quiet and peaceful darkness. It was hard to believe that there'd been an invasion and occupation. Old Rome had conquered a few of Egypt's lesser cities as an abject lesson to cooperate. Alexandria should be filled with the screams of women and men being raped. Despite the stone buildings, there should be flames as drunken soldiers burned what they could.

The King blinked in surprise as a century of marching legionaries came to a halt in the street below the palace window, hobnail boots clashing against paving stones in lockstep synchronicity. The foremost among them were carrying torches to light the way. They'd come to a halt because a mother cat was crossing the street with a kitten in her mouth. Normal Roman soldiers would have sent an arrow through the mother cat, grabbed the kitten, and harvested the bodies for their cooking pot. These men stood at respectful attention and allowed the tiny animals to seek shelter. Native onlookers at street level whistled appreciatively. New Rome was on its way to winning the hearts and minds of the Alexandrians. Its discipline was mind numbing.

"These troops are slaves?" Ptolemy said in wonder.

"No," Spartacus said flatly. "They are freemen, soldiers in a new nation devoted to abolishing slavery everywhere. Legions of freed slaves will join our army everywhere we march. Egypt can be at the head of this procession, or we can trample it under our boots into nothingness."

The ocean swallowed the sun. Evening was languidly coasting into night. The throne room was nearly dark and Ptolemy had no servants nearby to fire a lamp. Yet he was still able to see the resolve in the ex-gladiator's battle-scarred face. It was unthinkable that Egypt could be conquered in a single day. There was a great deal more to the kingdom than the city of Alexandria. Dozens of cities down the Nile had powerful garrisons that would fight if the King were harmed. And the mighty river was home to a navy that had barely been scratched. On the other hand, in the unlikely event that his military could beat back this powerful entity calling itself New Rome, then old Rome would swoop down and snap up the weakened Egypt like a vulture on a crippled hare.

Ptolemy scrutinized the hard peasant face of his opponent. Maybe this rebel gladiator slave was the modern equivalent of Alexander the Great. Spartacus' burning desire to eliminate slavery meant that the new world rising in the wake of his armies must have an economy based on the Egyptian model. In Ptolemy's kingdom, slaves did not till the land, but the freemen paid a heavy price for their freedom: the highest rate of taxation anywhere in the world. Up to 60 percent of a farmer's harvest and a like percentage of a merchant's till found their way into the royal treasury. Perhaps, if Ptolemy rolled dice skillfully with the gladiator, then someday usurious tax windfalls from all the nations conquered by New Rome would be filtered through Alexandrian coffers. Who else could administer and tax a worldwide empire of freemen except the incorruptible savants and bureaucrats of Egypt? Who else had experience with a free market economy?

It was utterly dark by the time the King had made up his mind. In a hoarse voice he asked Spartacus what should be done to formalize the alliance. The ex-gladiator said, "My centurions will retrain your army and navy. That will begin tomorrow. More importantly, I will lead a team of scholars in the great library. Egypt's greatest strength is not in providing fighting men. Vast armies of slaves will spring from the very soil of Italy as the war reaches its crescendo."

"What then is Egypt's greatest strength?"

"Knowledge."

With that cryptic single-word reply, Spartacus made an abrupt about face, spinning on the iron nails of his right boot, and left the man who had just become a puppet to New Rome. Spartacus stopped halfway down the marble hallway to listen as the haunting flute music started up again.

Over the next two weeks, the ex-gladiator learned that in many ways it was easier to command an army of legionaries than an army of scholars. His team of gray-bearded pendants was tasked with combing the entire collection of the great library for unique weapons that would aid in the coming war with old Rome. As an example of what to look for, he spoke of the second Punic War. Hannibal's greatest advantage came from his invincible Nubian cavalry. The North African horsemen had ridden into battle on mounts equipped with bridles: an invention unknown to the Romans. As a consequence, the

Nubian horse had crushed Rome's equestrian class. The great library contained nearly all the collective knowledge humanity had acquired in five thousand years of civilization. He reminded them that anything and everything the mind of man could conceive of was contained inside the walls of this sacred center of learning. He went on to describe the fire-arrows and fire-spears that had defeated the Egyptian Navy, a direct result of Spartacus' own scholarly research. Then he'd set them loose on the stacks of books.

The agony began almost at once. Every few hours, the scholars brought him scrolls containing strange inventions and devices, but none of them were useful as weapons. At the end of the second week, Spartacus knew that he would need divine inspiration to see his scholars through the campaign. That morning he assembled his team of graybeards at the steps of the great library along with a New Roman priest, a muzzled wolf on leash and a woodpecker in a cage. The priest sacrificed these totems to Mars, the God of war, spilling liberal amounts of blood on the street before building a pyre and sending a beautiful column of white smoke up into the heavens. He also gave an invocation in Coptic, the language of Alexandria, to Horus the Red, the Egyptian God equivalent to Mars. Like old Rome, New Rome believed in blending religions together.

The invisible hand of the War-God guided the scholars that day. By afternoon one of them approached Spartacus, a scroll in his shaking hands, and an excited tremor in his voice. "Esteemed Sir, I believe I have the answer." He unrolled the cylinder and pointed to a drawing of a warrior on horseback. The warrior was not riding bareback or with a simple horse blanket like a normal equestrian, instead his sandaled feet were tightly ensconced in the wooden stirrups of a leather saddle. The drawing was so strange that Spartacus had to have the text explaining what a saddle and stirrups were read to him several times. Even then, he still wasn't sure what a saddle with stirrups signified. He was sure that this device had never been used in any war fought by Rome or any country that he'd ever heard of.

The scholar agreed with Spartacus. Horsemen with saddles had never fought in any war in recorded history. The drawing was based on the obscure antics of a long forgotten troop of acrobats from the steppes of central Asia. Spartacus almost slapped the scroll from the scholar's hands, angrily demanding what equestrian acrobatics had to do with warfare. The scholar insisted that he'd felt the presence of Horus when he'd viewed the drawing of the saddle.

That evening, Spartacus wandered the streets of Alexandria, praying to Mars. The War-God had a special significance to the ex-gladiator. Mars was especially revered in his native Thrace under the Greek name Ares. More significantly, Mars was the father of Romulus and Remus, the founders of Rome. King Romulus had presided over a pristine culture of yeoman farmers, the very culture that Spartacus hoped to recreate.

Clouds obscured the night sky as the ex-gladiator looked upward. A rent in the cloud cover exposed a single star, a red star, Mars. Spartacus looked around the rest of the sky wildly for a couple of seconds. There were no other stars visible. A clearer sign could not be hoped for. The small red eye stared down at him encouragingly.

He knew what he had to do. King Ptolemy would have to be encouraged to loosen his purse strings and buy one hundred thousand warhorses from Parthia, and elsewhere. More than one hundred thousand leather saddles would have to be sewn together in the shops of Alexandria. Cavalry would have to be trained. Extra large troop transporters would have to be built in the shipyards to move the cavalry to Italy.

Spartacus dropped to his knees and bowed before the red star, giving thanks to the Roman and Greek War-God. After living in Alexandria for a few weeks, he'd picked up a smattering of Coptic. He added a few words to Horus in the appropriate tongue. Like an eyelid closing, the hole in the clouds sealed shut. His prayers had been accepted.

Crixus picked meat scraps from a mess of roasted chicken feet doggedly, but with no pleasure. He'd accepted the mission of harassing the old Roman Army on the mainland as a way to acquire riches. He and his cohorts had collected a fair amount of loot earlier in the season, but who would have dreamed that the assignment would ultimately spell a lifestyle of poverty for weeks at a time? As a gladiator in Campua, he had dined on the choicest food. Beautiful women had been brought to him on a regular basis. Other than the risk of dying in the arena, he'd lived like a king back then. Now, he lived like the meanest beggar and faced nearly as much risk.

Forcing his gladiator-soldiers to live as beggars in the teeming slums of Rome was good strategy though. It should make carrying out the biggest raid yet that much easier. And today was the big day. Besides tying the old Roman legions into one big Gordian knot, Crixus' men had spent the fall and winter perfecting the art of breaking gladiators loose from schools. Their skill and technique would be tested to the maximum this day.

In the smaller cities, smash and grab tactics had worked. But Rome called for something different. They'd infiltrated the big city in small bands, spaced days apart, so as not to arouse suspicion. Half the gladiators had familiarized themselves with every commercial livery stable in Rome, some even finding work as groomsmen and manure shovelers. The other half had concentrated on the wooden Circus Maximus. Since any gladiator that had been in the game for more than five years had fought in Rome, younger gladiator-soldiers that wouldn't be recognized by the old hands in the Circus Maximus sought employment there, handling the wild beasts, one of the few jobs not reserved for slaves.

In its arrogance, Rome had not locked down its gladiators or cancelled very many games in the past few months, despite the raids by Crixus' cohorts and the ongoing rule of Sicily by rebellious slaves. The Third Mithridatic War was proving to be a tough slog for old Rome, and the Senate had reversed itself, deciding that veteran legionaries could not be spared to put down a mere slave rebellion after all. The Senate certainly erred in dismissing the Third Slave War as inconsequential, but it had been correct when it considered King Mithridates VI to be a dire threat. At least the senators had something to show for the legions thrown at the Persian upstart. A major battle had been won in the Mithidatic War, a turning point. And starting today, a week was to be devoted to celebrating that victory with massive gladiatorial games, triumphal parades, and public feasting.

Crixus spat out the bones of the chicken feet that he'd been eating and walked away from the food vendor outside the Circus Maximus. A gigantic Roman throng was filing into the structure, buzzing with excitement, making bets with each other over various matched pairs in the coming gladiator games.

A half-dozen mule-drawn wagons pulled up behind the row of food vendors outside the amphitheater entrance where Crixus stood. He knew that similar wagons were pulling up in front of the other entrances. A number of horses appeared next, ridden by hard-faced gladiator-soldiers. A few of the horsemen had spare mounts as well. Crixus could visualize the carnage his troops had left behind at the livery stables. Probably every stable hand in Rome was dead.

Still more horsemen appeared. The wagons were formed into barricades around the clusters of horsemen, wheels chucked and lashed together until small fortresses emerged on the streets outside the stadium. From these wagon barricades, putative workmen unloaded long wooden planks and carried these unwieldy burdens through the arched entranceways of the Circus Maximus.

The vendor that had sold Crixus chicken feet raised his head curiously, blinking at the large number of horsemen and the strange configuration of the wagon barricades. Other vendors nearby watched the gladiator-soldiers disguised as workmen carrying long planks into the arena. Most of them turned away and tended to their food preparation, assuming that the strange goings-on had something to do with the customary parade. It wasn't unusual for exotic birds to be released from cages set up on city streets during triumphal celebrations. If this was the case, the preparations were being carried out decidedly early. Fifteen hundred pairs of gladiators would fight before the parade was scheduled to start, about one weeks' worth of gladiatorial combat.

Hundreds of additional gladiator-soldiers made their way to the Circus Maximus on foot, walking past the wagon barricades without acknowledging their comrades. The food vendors became genuinely alarmed at the arrival of these rough looking characters. Some of them recognized the faces of well-known arena fighters. All of them suddenly remembered that a low-level slave war had been simmering in southern Italy for over a year, a war led by escaped gladiators and characterized by the violent breakout of arena fighters.

Crixus reached between his legs and pulled a sword free that had been tied to an inner thigh. He took three quick steps, cut the throat of a food vendor, and shouted, "Spartacus!" Every vendor perished in the next few seconds. New Roman soldiers swarmed into the amphitheater, swinging swords and shouting Spartacus' name.

New Rome's timing was perfect, largely by chance. The first twenty matched pairs of gladiators entered the arena sand to the roar of the crowd at the exact same moment that Crixus' cohorts raced down stone steps to the lowest bleacher level. The crowd largely ignored the intrusion, despite the repeated shouts of, "Spartacus! Spartacus!"

The gladiator-solders manning the beast cages under the bleachers heard the name of their leader and sprang into action. Hungry lions were lured into the arena sand with chunks of meat. Cage doors were slammed shut. Up above, gladiator-soldiers rapidly threw down ramps that connected the sandy floor of the arena to the wooden stadium where tens of thousands of Romans sat, shocked into temporary paralysis by the bizarre antics of Crixus' men.

The twenty matched pairs of gladiators on the sand heard the shouts of "Spartacus! Spartacus!" Their reactions were better than the crowd of stunned Roman sports fans. The matched pairs scrambled up the wooden planks and leaped into the stadium seating area, followed closely by an equal number of ravenous lions. The big cats zeroed in on the scrambling gladiators, but soon had easier meals thrown their way. The gladiators seized Roman citizens and threw them into the jaws of the raving lions.

There was a surprising amount of meat to be found on the bodies of the well-fed citizens of Rome. Thirty citizens were swiftly devoured and the lions were sated. Bellies full of meat, the big cats could go on a killing spree without slowing down to eat their victims. The sight of savage felines tearing humans apart created an exodus from the

Circus Maximus that could only be described as a stampede. Fewer citizens were trampled to death than one might have supposed. The exit corridors were so wide and so well designed that the stampeding multitude spilled onto the surface streets of Rome with its numbers nearly intact.

The crazed sports fans would have swept the waiting army of gladiator-soldiers and their horses away like leaves in a stream if the wagon barricades had not held. But they did hold, and Crixus' men were able to stand their ground like boulders in a human torrent.

The old Roman garrison tasked with guarding the gladiators of the capital city had emerged from the barracks and were making their way to the Circus Maximus just as the crowd swamped them. Tens of thousands of panicked humans and dozens of savage lions rocked the garrison back on its heels, smashing and defeating it as effectively as a real military offensive from a powerful barbarian army.

Well-organized files of veteran gladiator-soldiers and recently liberated gladiators from both the arena and the nearby school appeared as soon as the crowd had dispersed. With two men per horse and one man per mule, the veteran gladiator-soldiers and the newly liberated gladiators put their mounts into brisk trots and made for the Apian Way, heading south to the coast to rendezvous with Spartacus' main host.

The liberated gladiator clinging to Crixus like a barnacle didn't bother to give his name as the escapees trotted out of Rome, bouncing painfully on their butts in rhythm to the jarring motion of their horses. Looking around at the mass of horsemen, it was easy for Crixus to believe that two thousand or more top-notch arena fighters had been freed in this particular raid: the biggest haul yet. Each liberated gladiator would be worth his weight in gold as an infantryman once the major campaign began in the spring.

Crixus had no way of knowing that he was only half right. The gladiators would be worth their weight in gold, but not as infantry. Sitting on the stable platform of a leather saddle with wooden stirrups, they would be able to swing swords, shoot arrows, and throw spears with much greater effectiveness than they could from an unsaddled horse. At that moment, Crixus and all his mounted soldiers didn't have the slightest notion of how archaic bareback horsemanship truly was, even though they were riding bareback to escape Rome. There wasn't yet a Latin or Greek word for a saddle with stirrups. Some years from now, all the gladiator-soldiers would look back and wonder how they ever got along on a horse's back without a real saddle.

The Spartacus program had generated some very unusual socio-economic factors. Vladimir Bakunin adjusted his glasses, shook his head in puzzlement, and kept on reading. He needed to put his reservations aside so that he could carefully digest the material. Conversely, he didn't have all day. He stopped reading every word and skimmed the salient details of Spartacus' military campaign on the Italian peninsula. This part of the document was about one thousand pages long. He could see that from a purely military standpoint it closely followed the broad outline established by earlier, albeit more primitive programs.

Flipping through pages, he came across a series of maps and diagrams showing the route Spartacus' main host had taken from the southern coast into the city of Rome. The route was designed to avoid narrow valleys and put the New Roman Army on broad plains wherever possible; cavalry worked best when it had some elbowroom. The route was also a reasonably direct path to Rome. The gladiator-soldiers needed to decapitate the old empire before they could conquer the other slave states around the Mediterranean. Old Rome wouldn't permit New Rome a straight shot at the capital, however. Spartacus' horse army was forced to execute great wheeling movements to outflank and surround the old Roman infantry. Within these pockets, New Roman kill ratios were astronomical. The old order died hard with entire legions fighting to the last man. And fresh enemy troops gushed from every nook and cranny of the empire. The ranks of the old Roman infantry swelled with slave owners: knights, patricians, and moderately wealthy plebs. Class-consciousness lent the slave owners courage and recklessness. They weren't just fighting for their lives, but a way of life.

Old Roman generals recognized the tactics of Hannibal. The generals weren't fools and could see history repeating itself when a second invincible North African horse army smashed infantry legion after infantry legion. Old Rome was psychologically incapable of using the delaying tactics that had defeated Hannibal. Delaying tactics involved attacking supply lines and foraging parties, but avoiding set piece battles. Delaying tactics were an admission that the invading army was superior. While this was an admission old Rome had been willing to make when Hannibal's army of freemen roamed the Italian peninsula, it was not an admission they would make in the face of a slave army.

Class-consciousness was devastating in other ways. Virtually every slave, man, woman, and child, on the Italian peninsula rose against his or her master. Slave owners not fighting at the front were murdered in their sleep. A guerilla slave army sprang up behind the front and attacked old Roman supply lines. Vladimir rifled through maps and text, keeping an eye out for anything unexpected.

The overall pattern was clear. New Rome had conquered Egypt, then the city of Rome, then the rest of Italy, and then the world. When Vladimir ran the second phase of the Spartacus program, he knew it would create historical parallels for the Red Army that would have them conquering America first, then London, then Britain, and finally the world. This was called the Ten Downing Street strategy. No surprises there. Vladimir continued skimming the document.

Something odd did jump out from Spartacus' peninsula campaign: halfway through the great battle at the gates of the Roman capital, Spartacus killed Crixus with his own hands. Once the capital city was totally subdued, the body of the fallen Gallic chieftain was heaved into the roaring altar fire in front of the temple of Jupiter on the famous Capitoline Hill, the ancient and sacred citadel of the eternal city. With a mighty bellow, Spartacus offered Crixus to Jupiter as a human sacrifice. The elected Senate of old Rome cheered as Spartacus uttered an invocation honoring the Gods of the city and Rome's state religion.

Vladimir's skin crawled for two reasons: Crixus' parallel in the Red Army was sure to be George Patton and the distinction between New Rome and old Rome was becoming increasingly murky as the virtual Third Slave War wound to its perplexing conclusion. Old Rome and New Rome were fusing. Spartacus had left the old Roman senators in office. He was taking over and modifying the existing Roman Republic, not tearing it down and building something new. It was evolution, not revolution.

Vladimir was taken aback by the disturbing, almost reactionary economic and political undertones in the first thousand pages. *What was this rubbish about New Rome? What would that parallel in today's world? Would the Red Army have to fight under the banner of something called the New British Commonwealth?* The only comforting parallel was the utter destruction of the plantation slave system, which clearly spelled the end of monopoly capitalism. He kept flipping pages until he came to the end of the war and the establishment of New Rome's permanent government.

Spartacus was pretty damn respectful of the traditions of old Rome. He replaced the copper plates etched with the twelve laws of the old Republic with new copper plates and a new twelve-law constitution, part of a ceremony honoring the Roman War-God on the field of Mars, north of the city. There were new laws graven in copper, to be sure. Slavery was abolished and the plantations were broken into a multitude of little farms, with no compensation for the hated slaveholders. Every adult male was a citizen and could vote, no matter where he lived within the borders of New Rome. Legionaries were paid in land as well as silver, for as long as New Rome stood. Every able-bodied man must serve in the army. Every soldier and officer must swear an oath of loyalty to the state, never to the general commanding a legion. No human being could be honored or worshipped as a God; nor could he or she claim divine ancestry, upon penalty of death for claimant and worshipper alike. This appeared to make the rise of Christianity impossible. Jupiter and Mars were to reign over the Roman pantheon in perpetuity. An entire copper tablet was devoted to tax code and business regulations.

He raced through the text, shocked and intrigued by the conservative nature of the society that the Spartacus program had created in the ancient world, or the virtual ancient world. The army of former slaves that had conquered the Mediterranean was transformed into a nation of farmers, tilling small parcels carved from the old slave plantations or torn from conquered lands. Equitable distribution of income was created by a progressive income tax on all businesses and individuals ranging from 5 percent to 50 percent. No distinction was made between earned income, inheritance, or investment income. Ruthless antitrust laws kept businesses numerous and small, chopping up any enterprise that controlled even 10 percent of a given market. *Was this liberal capitalism or conservative communism? Or a new system altogether?* One thing was obvious: the system would be incredibly stable. Another revolution or civil war would be impossible.

Vladimir slowed the pace of his reading, absorbing the information more slowly and carefully. King Ptolemy had mixed feelings concerning the new world order, but managed to land on his feet. The Ptolemaic dynasty was stripped of its riches and harnessed as a bureaucratic workhorse to enforce the antitrust laws. Ptolemy was sure to parallel Henry Ford.

With the help of the Ptolemaic bureaucracy, tax revenue was funneled almost entirely into the Army. Anyone that wouldn't or couldn't work in the cutthroat, ultra-competitive private sector was permanently drafted into the legions. The slums of the Mediterranean were combed for recruits. An army of former ghetto dwellers replaced the army of former slaves. Since every soldier or sailor would be given a land allotment after fifteen years of service, and every scrap of arable land around the Mediterranean was spoken for, the Republic was forced to expand north and east. The virtual history of New Rome ended with its legions crossing the Rhine to wipe out the Germanic tribes and sweeping into India to conquer the Hindu and Buddhist nations of Asia. If the program were allowed to run any longer, it would have New Rome marching into the Americas and crossing the Sahara to take control of the rest of Africa.

The book was slammed shut and shoved aside. Vladimir scooted his chair over to the computer console. He tapped the keyboard, initiating the second phase of the Spartacus program: historical parallels were to be drawn from Spartacus' virtual revolution and applied to the actual revolution that the Red Army hoped to shape in the here and now.

Other than the conservative socio-economic undertones in phase one, the Spartacus program had produced very few surprises for Vladimir. He didn't expect any surprises at all in phase two. As the software designer that had created the program, he knew what it would spit out. The face of true communism was going to be a lot less radical than he had imagined. *How would Supreme Commander Banner react? How would the Red Army radicals react?* Everyone in the Red Army would have to remember that Marx had never predicted what true communism would look like, other than to say that government would whither away. Vladimir recalled one of Marx's few concrete predictions. The great man had said that a draconian and progressive income tax would be instituted after the revolution.

The Spartacus program phase two would have government gradually withering away (outside of the military) as the private sector usurped its day-to-day functions. The program would provide stiff and progressive income taxes and would decentralize the private sector with harsh antitrust laws. It would forcibly redistribute trillions of pounds of wealth when the DFA supermonopoly was broken, as well as the handful of other, smaller monopolies such as Halifax Mining.

Maybe this landscape did resemble the clues Marx had given for a communist utopia. The only real contradiction was Marx's call for a dictatorship of the proletariat. The Spartacus program would call for the retention of the Commonwealth's democratic institutions. But even then, classical Marxism was not really being violated. The dictatorship of the proletariat was always to have been temporary. The Red Army was Marx's prophesied proletariat dictatorship, and, like all governments, the political aspect of the Red Army would whither away, leaving only its military essence.

Vladimir left the mainframe running, grabbed the spiral bound, phonebook-sized document and stepped outside of the computer building. The morning sun was streaming down from an azure sky. He'd worked throughout the night without realizing it. Cramming the document into the cargo carrier of his little street bike, he jumped on the kick-starter. The one cylinder diesel chirped merrily.

To get to Red Army headquarters, he had to ride past his barbershop. Officers and senior scientists were banging impatiently on the front door of the humble structure. Today must be Sunday. He zipped out of Poipu and opened the throttle. The wind of the bike's passage tugged at his long white beard and caused his eyes to tear. Whipping around corners, he could feel how light and frail his aged body had become. The sad facts were that Vladimir was a very old man and he hadn't been taking care of himself lately. There was never enough time, especially with the war drawing so close.

He braked in front of the headquarters building and placed the bike on its kickstand. Clutching the document protectively, he walked by security guards, stopping in front of the supreme commander's secretary. She said, "Go right inside, Commandant. He left standing orders to cancel all appointments the moment you arrived." Vladimir couldn't help swell just a tiny bit at this display of respect.

The SC remained sitting as Vladimir entered the room. Another show of respect: Fred Banner was so tall that he made the commandant feel like a dwarf if they stood side by side. Vladimir plopped the hefty chronicle of the Spartacus military campaign on Banner's desk.

"This is phase one of the Spartacus program. No real shockers. Phase two, now that's going to raise some eyebrows," Vladimir predicted. Fred Banner responded with a single word: "Elaborate."

Vladimir suddenly felt unsure of himself. He decided to buy time by asserting that phase two was not yet complete. The Supreme Commander asked if Vladimir knew what the program would eventually say in the way of historical parallels applicable to the Red Army and the coming war. Reluctantly, Vladimir admitted that he did. Fred Banner looked closely at the frail old man and wondered when he'd eaten last. Without waiting for an answer, the tall military man picked up a phone and ordered a meal.

A tray of sandwiches emerged from the reception area and both men had lunch. Around a mouthful of sandwich, Fred Banner casually asked, "True communism isn't as sexy as we thought, eh Vlad?"

"The program will have us breaking up the supermonopoly and the lesser monopolies into one hundred thousand small publicly traded companies. The majority shares that Henry Ford and his board and the other vampires own will go to the workers in each of the new companies, more shares going to senior workers, I think. A steeply progressive income tax and ruthless antitrust laws will prevent any of these companies from growing back into monopolies. Spartacus will want the duly elected Commonwealth Congress and national democratic governments left in place, even after we make changes to their constitutions. It's going to say that Queen Victoria's dream about fighting outer space aliens parallels New Rome's conquest of Germany, Asia, and other barbarian peoples. The program will want to continue the Commonwealth Military Games and devote tremendous resources to the military. It will want structural changes to prevent another revolution or civil war. It will want to see the melding of all religions into a single worldwide state religion. One worldwide religion will go a long way to making future war impossible."

"Democracy, huh? What, then, is the dictatorship of the proletariat?"

"You are. The Red Army is. But your dictatorship will be temporary. On that score, Marx and Spartacus agree. Once it has won the war, rewritten the tax codes, and broken up the monopolies, the dictatorship of the proletariat dissolves itself and the democratic face of true communism emerges."

"The old Roman Republic permitted dictatorships in emergencies."

"Precisely. *Temporary* dictatorships. The Spartacus program is drawing on the laws and customs of the Roman Republic more than I had anticipated. Essentially, it is perfecting the reforms that the Roman general, Gaius Marius, made and codifying them into law and stamping the imprimatur of democracy on them."

Fred Banner looked shamefaced as he said, "Jog my memory. Who was Gaius Marius?"

Vladimir's self-doubt evaporated. By explaining the likely machinations of Spartacus phase two, the validity of the entire program crystallized in his mind. It made sense on a gut level. Several years seemed to roll off the aged Marxist philosopher as he responded: "Gaius Marius eliminated the requirement that a raw recruit in the Roman Army must be a landowner. He built armies out of the landless slum dwellers of Rome. The original land ownership requirement had worked for centuries because the Roman legionaries literally owned a piece of the system they were defending. To recreate the old esprit de corps, Gaius Marius proposed that his new generation of landless soldiers be given allotments, small farms, upon retirement. This would have broken up the big slave plantations, so the senate blocked this part of his reform. A host of problems followed that eventually devastated Rome. We would be speaking Latin today if Gaius Marius' reforms had not been stymied."

Fred Banner's eyes narrowed shrewdly. "Millions of DFA workers will fight like hell if they believe they're going to own a piece of Henry Ford's pie or a piece of one of the smaller monopolies like Halifax Mining."

Vladimir matched the supreme commander's shrewd expression and observed, "Throughout the Commonwealth, democracy has become corrupt and beholden to monopoly capitalism. That doesn't mean democratic ideals are obsolete. We will have the American workers eating from our hands if we bring back the Jeffersonian notion of a republic comprised of small, independent businesses. And how can our diehard Marxists complain? The means of production will be in the hands of the proletariat."

The supreme commander's visage darkened. "Oh, they'll complain all right. The fire-breathers in the Red Army will complain big-time." Vladimir was instantly crestfallen. Fred Banner laughed and said, "Leave the diehards to me and the commissars. As you say, I am the dictatorship of the proletariat. It will get messy. There will have to be purges, bloodbaths. The revolution will have to eat a few of its children. Don't concern yourself, Vlad. Your mission is to complete the Spartacus program and get Ferdy Porsche set up on the mainframe. There is one last weapon system to build before we attack."

"Yes, yes. Patton has been haranguing me about computer time for Heisenberg and Ferdy Porsche's absurd mechanical whales. I'm not sure whether to laugh or cry."

"Don't laugh or cry. Putting A-bombs in Ferdy's mechanical whales is the only way to eliminate the Blue Force. Let's not kid ourselves. Einstein is creating devilishly advanced weapons in Hawaii. Little Ferdy is going to see that a whopping load of A-bombs are shoved up Einstein's gungus pung."

Chapter 12

The Red Army Gets a Wake-up Call

The superconducting supercollider was now a factory. The modifications were complete. The design parameters for the Mark VII combat suit had been downloaded into the collider's computer. All Einstein had to do was give the word and his team would manufacture the first of many Mark VII super suits. The great physicist stared listlessly out a window in his house, refusing to pick up the phone and give the go-ahead for the manufacturing sequence to begin.

The Blue Force had used the collider as a research tool for only a very short time before the manufacturing modifications made any additional exploration into pure physics impossible. Einstein would have accepted the change to his beloved particle accelerator better if the glimpses afforded by the brief sojourn into pure physics hadn't been so tantalizing. Subatomic particles bombarding carbon 60 targets had demonstrated that Heisenberg's quantum shift could occur on a molecular level. This was enough to loosely tie Quantum Mechanics and General Relativity together into a working Aether-based Unified Field theory. Which, sequentially, laid a sufficient theoretical framework to finish designing small, highly efficient fusion reactors, making the Mark VII combat suit possible. Unfortunately, they only had a working Unified Field Theory, not a true Grand Unified Field Theory.

He'd fought for more research, claiming that even better weapons would result from a genuine, honest-to-God Grand Unified Field Theory. Regrettably, Supreme Commander Halifax was too knowledgeable to swallow Einstein's bluff. The SC knew exactly what could be done and not done with the current state of the art. He wanted fusion powered combat suits, not the grand theory of everything. The brass ring had been pulled from Einstein's grasp when it was only inches away.

His phone rang. He picked it up. Nkosinathi was on the other end. "Pining for your lost experimental particle accelerator, Herr Doctor Professor?" She asked. He shook his head irritably and replied, "No, I am pining for my lost Grand Unified Field Theory."

"Have we permission to manufacture the Mark VII?"

"I no longer care."

He could tell that she'd cupped her hand around the mouthpiece of the phone so that the scientists and engineers in the control room could not hear her. In an urgent whisper she said, "I'm telling everybody that the director of research has given the green light, and that you're very excited." Einstein made a face at the phone as if she could see him and responded, "Tell them anything at all. I no longer care about the Mark VII."

"When the first VII is finished there will be a ceremony. I expect Herr Doctor Professor to be there, and wearing a smile. This combat suit will win or lose the war. All of our lives are at stake." He smoothed the scowl off his face and forced a smile into his voice: "Please build the Mark VII. I am very happy." He wanted to slam the phone down. With a great effort, he succeeded in setting it back on the counter gently. Otherwise, Nkosinathi would have left the supercollider factory, came to Einstein's house, and dragged him to the control room.

Maybe the empty feeling inside was simple hunger. There were two sausage links in the fridge. The floor vibrated while he ate, causing his shoes to perform a little tap dance. Glancing out the window, billows of condensation could be seen above the part of the supercollider that ran around the town of Hilo. Gravitrons were bombarding laboratory-pure iron machine parts, rendering them into single molecules of crystal iron: a technological miracle.

Einstein turned away from the window and debated internally if his depression was a direct result of the Faustian bargain he'd struck with SC Jeremiah Halifax that traded the idealism of pure research for the necessity of building weapons of mass destruction. Nkosinathi would say that his melancholy was not rooted in high ideals, but a result of perceived obsolesce, specifically: his obsolesce. Now that the Mark VII was being manufactured, Einstein thought that the Blue Force no longer needed his genius.

As if being caught in Nkosinathi love triangle had nothing to do with it. And what about the subtle, yet unrelenting pressure she periodically applied for sex? A week didn't go by when she didn't casually mention that the next generation would need a physicist of Einstein's mettle, or something about his DNA being more precious than gold. She acted as though he were indifferent to Jeremiah and Wolfgang, as if the other men in her life didn't exist. At such time the Big Island seemed like a gigantic prison.

There was no permanent escape and he did not know any way to engineer a temporary escape. The shame of it was that right now would be the perfect time to flee, with everybody on his staff preoccupied building the first Mark VII. They would work around the clock until the initial combat suit was complete. The field-test would continue to prove distracting. Nobody would notice he was missing for weeks. He thought for a minute. Maybe there *was* a way to temporarily escape.

Field rations, water containers, purification tablets, a waterproof sleeping bag, and a few other pieces of camping equipment were shoved into a backpack. His portable radiophone was deliberately left in the kitchen. Anger fading slightly, he decided to scribble a note and leave it next to the radiophone, explaining that he was going camping, and needed solitude. He laced on a pair of hiking boots and sneaked out of his house. He rode his scooter uphill until he hit a wall of jungle so thick that the motorbike was useless.

The rainforest clinging to the slopes leading away from Hilo appeared impenetrable to the uninitiated. Einstein knew better. At the base of a certain hill, a few miles from his house, there was a trail, beaten into the dense foliage by wild boar. After hiding the motor scooter with leafy branches, entering the trailhead, and casting anxious glances at the town below, he struck off on a private adventure.

The boot camp training every Blue Force recruit was forced to undergo taught that the best pace for covering long distances was to jog one hundred steps and walk one hundred steps. After four hours of alternating between walking and jogging, it seemed that the drill instructors were correct. He'd covered a tremendous amount of ground. He'd gone miles along the twisty trail leading up the forested slopes of the great volcanic mountain. Hilo looked like a postage stamp next to the ocean when a break in the jungle afforded a view.

Recreational hiking was forbidden in this area. This was where the 1920 Red Force had made their last stand by building a huge jungle redoubt. Back in those days, this region was called the sylvan tangle. It was supposed to be infested with long dormant booby traps and other mysterious dangers.

The sky darkened. Raindrops splattered on the jungle canopy, lightly at first, then harder. His clothes weren't waterproof, not really a problem in this heat. The rain continued pounding the intrepid hiker. Rivulets of water streamed down the hillside he was traversing. Einstein stepped into one of the little streams and walked directly in the path of the flow. If the Blue Force came looking for him, it would use trained Bulldogs. The water flowing around his boots would carry away his scent. The tactic wouldn't throw off bloodhounds. It might work against the less sensitive noses of Bulldogs.

The rain didn't let up and the stream he was slogging through kept flowing. It necessarily took him to higher ground and denser jungle. He crested a hill lush with plant life as evening approached and looked into the misty distance. There were no industrial lights anywhere. This was real backcountry and probably the epicenter of the battle over a decade and a half ago that pitted British Royal Marines against a rebellious remnant of the 1920 Red Force Army. That part of the original CMG hadn't gone according to plan. There wasn't supposed to have been a battle between the English Crown and a CMG Force, yet it had occurred, admittedly on a small scale.

A tiny shiver crawled up Einstein's body. Would the 1950 CMG go according to plan? If Jeremiah's basic plan came to fruition, then the Blue Force's victory would be so overwhelming there could be no mopping up afterward, no Red Force battle with British Royal Marines. Everything depended on the Mark VII, a weapon of mythic proportion. No amount of false modesty could force Einstein to think differently. The Achilles' heel of the Mark VII was the long time it would take to manufacture a single PCS. Each machine part had to be painfully turned into crystal iron in the supercollider. The first Mark VII would take two weeks to build. Once mass-production was in full swing, the most optimistic projections called for a build time of three to four days per suit. In the year 1950, there would be about fifteen hundred suits, if the factory teams worked twenty-four hours a day, seven days a week. But fifteen hundred Mark VIIs should be able to destroy anything that the Red Force possessed. Truthfully, even one hundred Mark VIIs would be unbeatable.

His foot caught on a root and dislodged a strange object in the soupy mud. Daylight was failing, so Einstein pulled out a flashlight and played the beam over the thing he'd disturbed. The lines of a perfect circle were visible in the watery ground. Putting the flashlight in his mouth, he grabbed the root and pulled up with everything he had. A manhole cover popped up from the jungle's surface.

The flashlight beam exposed a perfectly cylindrical tunnel and a rusty iron ladder, dropping straight into the earth. This was it! The sylvan tangle, where the Royal Marines had slaughtered hundreds of Zulu and Uberman troopers, the closest thing to an unscripted war yet seen in the twentieth century. Still holding the flashlight in his mouth, Einstein climbed down the ladder.

The vertical tunnel met a broad horizontal passageway several yards below the surface. It dead-ended into an earthen wall above a strange slit-like defile. Einstein crawled under the defile and entered a roomy cavern. His hair immediately stood on end. The biggest spider that he'd ever seen was guarding the large cave, its outstretched legs would have easily covered a dinner plate. It must have been a descendant of the savage assassin spiders that had helped wipe out the 1920 Red Force. If so, it would probably attack. And its poison was slightly stronger than cobra venom.

Trying to escape by crawling back through the narrow slit didn't seem feasible. Logic dictated using the backpack as a weapon to squash the oversized spider. Einstein stomach turned sour at the thought of violence. He slumped to the dirt floor and pulled a tin of canned meat from his backpack's food compartment. The open tin was put in front of the assassin spider. It purred like a cat and scurried over to the treat, shoveling sticky wet meat into its face with two front legs. When the spider was done eating, it lapped water from a small pool, scuttled next to the human being, and looked up expectantly.

As part of his research on exoskeletons and powered combat suits, Einstein had studied the biomechanics of various insects and arachnids. He knew that spiders couldn't lap up water like a cat, or purr like a cat for that matter. On impulse, he reached out and stroked the soft yellowish fur of the mutant spider. The cat-like purring grew louder. The spider crawled up his body and sat on his shoulder, playfully tangling its long, hairy legs in the damp fleece of his sweater. Einstein turned off his flashlight and fell asleep.

He awoke the next morning and turned the flashlight back on. Emma (his name for the spider) had left the makings of breakfast at his feet, a piglet that must have weighed ten pounds. It was remarkable that a spider could not only catch and kill a mammal that size, but also drag it around so easily.

Carrying the dead porker up the ladder, Einstein saw Emma's head briefly pop into view. The spider was waiting for him on ground level, with bated breath. Her intelligence appeared to be on par with the Bulldogs used by the Blue Force, which would make her many times smarter than a normal arachnid. He built a fire and roasted the piglet, not sure if eating it was a good idea. Could a human safely eat an animal poisoned by a cobra? Did the poison break down inside the body of the dead animal? He rolled a small boulder over to the campfire and sat next to Emma, deciding whether he was willing to eat meat from the poisoned piglet. He wasn't a devout Jew. Still, pork was not something he ate voluntarily, whether poisoned or not.

Yes, he decided, he would eat it. Against all common sense, Einstein was determined not to offend his newly acquired eight-legged girlfriend. He carved off chunks of cooked pork with a hunting knife and flipped them at Emma. She aggressively snapped them out of midair like Bulldog. It was hard to tell with all that hair around her face, but her jaw structure appeared to be more reptilian or mammalian than arachnid.

He ate a piece of meat and waited for ill effects to set in. Nothing. Emma's catch was perfectly safe. By midmorning, man and beast had eaten their fill. Einstein stood and stretched, bones popping with relieved stress. His body wasn't used to sleeping in a cave.

Emma trotted down a trail leading away from the manhole cover. She stopped before disappearing into the tangle, turned her head, and gave Einstein a pleading look. The physicist hurried after the spider, content to follow anywhere she might lead. He was on vacation, after all, and had nothing else to do. They came to a clearing, disturbing a flock of ground dwelling birds. A rush of feathers whirled all around the odd couple. Emma leaped into the air powerfully, almost as if she had a rocket assist. She landed with a crushed bird in her jaws. Now Einstein could clearly see that she had mammalian-style jaws. She must have both an exoskeleton and elements of an inner skeleton. He sat and pondered biomechanics as Emma chewed the bird carcass.

A man, a dog, or a war seal inside a powered combat suit combined exoskeleton and inner skeleton. It was a powerful combination. How could evolution have moved so quickly? Two factors seemed likely. One, the assassin spider's genetic code had already been highly modified by Fred Greystone earlier in the century, genetically scrambled if you will. This probably made further mutagenic changes likely. Two, the 1920 CMG had left plenty of uranium bullets in the warrens of the sylvan tangle, where the big spiders evidently lived. Radiation from these bullets must have accelerated evolution to a breakneck pace.

The Blue Force's electronically camouflaged spy balloons indicated that the Red Force had developed powered combat suits for assassin spiders. Did the enemy force have eight-legged creatures as wondrous as Emma? If Red Force spiders could be trained to operate powered combat suits, then they surely possessed mammalian level intelligence. It was curious that the Blue Force had not developed parallel technology and animals. But then Blue Force had the Mark VII.

That afternoon, Emma and Einstein returned to the spider's underground lair. He knocked out a chunk of the earthen wall to let a beam of daylight inside their cave. Emma pounced on the backpack eagerly and then jumped away. She ran a short distance down the great cavern, leaping in the air and snapping her jaws, as if she were catching bits of imaginary meat.

Einstein was reluctant to blow through all the canned meat. He wanted to stay away from his people at the accelerator as long as possible. Emma wouldn't relent. He threw caution to the wind and let her devour another tin of bully beef.

It grew dark outside and absolutely pitch black inside. Einstein turned on his flashlight and idly followed the spider's movements as she crawled around the interior of the cavern, raiding caches of insects wrapped in silken cocoons: her version of a refrigerator. He hadn't noticed the noise the night before, but crickets trapped in these silk cages made a steady chirping noise as soon as darkness became total. Emma must not be anywhere near as venomous as a cobra if her poison could only knock a cricket unconscious. Or perhaps she was able to minutely regulate the amount of poison she injected into a victim.

"Emma, you're a woman, maybe you will understand the dilemma I find myself in," Einstein said to the industrious arachnid as he followed her movements with his flashlight. "My assistant is also a beautiful woman. She tells me I must make a baby with her for the good of mankind."

He stopped talking when the flashlight exposed the dead bodies of hundreds of spiders, very similar to Emma, yet only a tiny fraction of her size. "Males," Einstein breathed. "They've given their lives for the good of the species. Simply mating with the queen is suicide."

Mating with Nkosinathi would not be a death sentence, even though the prospect was terrifying, exciting but terrifying. Yet here he was, less altruistic than a mere spider, afraid

143

to take the plunge, afraid of the warlike generals that already had Nkosinathi in their beds.

Stuffed full of insects and one tin of bully beef, Emma crawled onto Einstein's lap and fell asleep. He took one last look at the army of heroic dead male spiders before turning off the flashlight. It was absurd to compare oneself to a spider, even more absurd to make a life changing decision on the basis of that comparison. Somehow that didn't deter the physicist from being influenced by the arachnid carnage all around him. The male spiders must have intelligence equal to the giant female. They would not have been acting out of sheer instinct when they'd given their lives to procreate. It must have been a conscious choice, pure valor.

Einstein did not believe that God took a personal interest in humanity, and certainly there could be no divine intercession in the life of a solitary human being such as himself. There was no such thing as an omen. The example presented by the valiant dead male spiders had to be sheer coincidence. It was a wakeup call nonetheless, a horrible lesson, a bitter pill that he was forced to swallow. When he got back to Hilo, he would take his medicine for the good of mankind and sleep with his assistant.

Emma was gone when he awoke the next morning, which was mildly upsetting. There was a much greater unpleasantness waiting outside the cave. General Kwa and his Bulldog, Halberd, were sitting at the entrance to the tunnel. Einstein climbed out of the subterranean lair to tell the general and the Bulldog to leave at once, adding that Halberd would likely kill Emma. A brief account of the domesticated spider followed this demand.

"Fine," Kwa said agreeably. "Walk with us and we'll talk."

Einstein didn't want to be lured back to Hilo. He wanted even less to watch some stupidly savage war dog tear his arachnid friend to shreds. The two men and the one dog quickly moved downhill, away from the spider's lair. The physicist's belly grumbled loud enough for Kwa to hear. Laughing, the general handed Einstein a packet of field rations. The two men sat down on the moist jungle floor.

"So, Albert, you've stumbled across one of those great big mutant assassin spiders?" Einstein could only nod because his mouth was stuffed with a granola bar. "Be careful, those creatures are why this area is off limits to Blue Force personnel."

The scientist swallowed and said, "Are you taking me back to Hilo? Forcing me back?" Kwa made an elaborate hand gesture, as if to say: who am I to force the great Albert Einstein to do anything? Heartened by Kwa's easygoing attitude, Einstein decided to share the epiphany he'd experienced in the underground warren. Unquestionably, the Zulu general had more familiarity with women than the physicist. Also, Kwa had participated in the Zulu eugenics program, which meant that he probably understood the strictures of producing a baby under the Uberman program.

"Let me get this straight, Albert. You intend to inform Nkosinathi that you'll graciously consent to making a baby with her because you saw a bunch of male spiders die while impregnating one of the big females? And this put you into some kind of guilt trip?" Kwa asked incredulously.

"I didn't actually see the male spiders die. I saw their shriveled carcasses and deduced the rest."

"Oh yeah, shriveled male spider carcasses. That'll really sweep her off her feet. How romantic! Exactly what every girl wants to hear in a marriage proposal."

Einstein blinked incuriously at Kwa. The general's sarcasm had gone right over the physicist's head. Kwa shook his head in utter incredulity. Even the Bulldog was looking at the scientist as if he were as dense as an outcropping of granite.

"This is what you say to Nkosinathi: 'I love you and want to marry you and we'll be faithful to each other until we die. Never look at Jeremiah or Wolfgang ever again.' Get it?" Kwa demanded, adding, "And say nothing about spiders." The general's hot, black gaze bore into the scientist, somehow forcing understanding.

"B-b-but what do I do about Supreme Commander Halifax and General Bernhard?" Einstein asked meekly. Kwa pounded his right fist into the palm of his left hand. Halberd stood warily, looking around at the surrounding jungle to see if he could find the object of his master's enmity.

"Bugger Supreme Commander Halifax and General Bernhard. It's time they woke up and smelled the coffee. We've got a freaking war to win." Kwa surged to his feet, looked down at Einstein and asked, "Do you know what's going on in Kauai with the Red Force?" Einstein shook his head silently. Kwa continued: "Nobody knows. The Red Force has taken everything deep underground. A mystery wrapped in an enigma as Churchill would say. Our spy balloons are useless."

Kwa held out a hand and pulled Einstein upright. They walked downhill, toward Hilo. Einstein cast a couple longing glances backward, hoping to catch a glimpse of his friend, the spider. She must have feared the Bulldog and was either hiding at treetop level or deep underground. The scientist asked Kwa again if they were going to Hilo.

By way of an answer, Kwa raised Nkosinathi on his radiophone and told her that Herr Doctor Professor had something to say. As Einstein reached for the phone, Kwa mouthed the words, "I love you. I want to marry you." Einstein dutifully repeated the words that Kwa had mouthed. The general grabbed the phone and said to Nkosinathi, "We will be in town by nightfall. Get hold of the supreme commander's houseboat. Make sure it is well stocked. You and Albert will spend the next twelve days honeymooning off the coast."

Kwa pocketed his phone and turned back to Einstein. "There will be a ceremony on the boat. The supreme commander will officiate. When you and your bride sail back to shore, the first Mark VII will be complete. We need Albert Einstein to participate in the field-testing that very day. Minor design changes will be necessary. You must oversee these alterations."

Einstein tried to say something, but Kwa cut him off by saying, "I'm not through yet." The general spoke of the theoretician's greatest breakthrough: General Relativity. Einstein had coined a term to describe the testing that the theory had undergone inside the great man's mind: *thought experiment*. Many years had gone by before relativity could be tested outside of Einstein's mind. And the real world tests had not changed relativity one iota; they'd only validated the thought experiments.

It was Kwa's opinion that transforming the supercollider from a research tool to a weapons factory was a blessing in disguise for Einstein. The paltry data it would have yielded as a research tool would have only limited Einstein's quest for the Grand Unified Field Theory. The great man needed to set his mind free of the straitjacket of particle beam bombardment and empirical data. Einstein's mind needed to soar like an eagle, unshackled and free. He needed to create a theory that current technology couldn't begin to test. Let future generations grapple with the problem of testing. Maybe they would have to build starships and fly to the blackhole at the center of the galaxy to test Einstein's Grand Unified Field Theory. That was their problem, not his. As far as theoretical physics, he should henceforth live entirely in the realm of Platonic ideals.

At the conclusion of Kwa's impassioned speech, Einstein stumbled on the trail that he'd been walking on. He felt like his soul was an onion with every outer layer stripped away. How could the Zulu general look into his psyche and succinctly offer a course for the rest of his life as easily as a weather forecaster predicting a summer squall?

A gleaming white smile brightened Kwa's dark face. He explained that while Einstein had a gift for science and engineering, the general had a gift for recognizing holy men touched by the divine light of reason. They walked lightly through the jungle, buoyed by a sense of optimism.

As darkness fell, they came to the industrial city of Hilo, and kept walking, straight to the docks. The houseboat was waiting, as were Nkosinathi, Supreme Commander Halifax, and General Wolfgang Bernhard. The officers wore dress uniforms. Nkosinathi was garbed in an Abyssinian wedding dress.

For an instant, Einstein thought that Nkosinathi's former lovers might be consumed with jealousy. Once he was actually inside the boat and shaking their hands, he could see the relief on their faces, glad to finally escape the brutal love triangle that had nearly torn High Command asunder. Nkosinathi hadn't relished her role as Helen of Troy either, the face that launched a war, in this case an internecine war within the ranks of the Blue Force.

She fell into Einstein's arms. Their bodies molded together in the same way that their minds had always meshed. Einstein's fears of being devoured like a male spider vanished. Kwa waited just long enough to see that everything was proceeding smoothly and left. There was a great deal of work to be done besides the production of Mark VII combat suits. When the war started, the fifteen hundred soldiers in the most advanced suits would only be the tip of the spear, the sharp end of a complicated war machine. For every man or woman inside a Mark VII, there would be thousands of personnel in support roles, ranging from secondary and tertiary PCS armies guarding supply lines and flanks to technicians that would keep all the machinery in working order. Kwa set off to supervise the ongoing construction of the vast logistical pipeline that would make the small army of Mark VII soldiers effective.

Jeremiah Halifax and Wolfgang Bernhard completed the marriage ceremony (Wolfgang had walked the bride up the aisle) and made ready to set foot back on the Big Island, roll up their sleeves, and join General Kwa in their duties to perfect the Blue Force's war fighting capabilities. Both the supreme commander and the general noticed tears glistening in the bride's eyes and could guess the reason. The only thing that marred the ceremony for Nkosinathi was that her son was not present. Wolfgang junior was on the other side of the island, attending his first combat camp.

A week and a few days later, the houseboat returned to dock. Einstein and Nkosinathi made their way to the supercollider control center, holding hands like teenagers. There were a few interesting things waiting inside for the chief researcher of the Blue Force: the first ever Mark VII powered combat suit, a bottle of champagne to christen the war machine, and a crowd of technicians eager to party.

Nkosinathi let go of his hand and told him to inspect the combat suit standing like a pregnant tin soldier in the center of the room. Touching the PCS reverently, Einstein knew what it was like to give birth. The outward appearance of this suit was unique, bizarre, and almost comical. Most combat suits had stovepipe limbs and an equally cylindrical torso. Curved surfaces deflected artillery shells and small arms fire. With its hyper-advanced forcefields, the Mark VII could afford a different shape. Its surfaces mimicked the hard flat angles of cut gemstones, a design that deflected radar waves. And then there was its protruding belly.

He traced the diamond-like finish of the lustrous black crystal iron, so cool to the touch. The crowd of onlookers held their breath as Einstein stepped around the upright suit. He saw the call sign E=MC^2 stamped into both of the twin flight cowls protruding from the suit's back. Every Mark VII was to be custom tailored to fit one specific man or woman. Einstein had no idea that the first suit would be his.

The crowd chanted: "Try it on! Try it on!" Einstein stepped in front of the inert machine and cried, "E equals MC squared, open!" Servomotors whirred. The gemstone-like helmet tilted back. The torso cracked open. Einstein climbed inside, displaying considerably more grace than the first time he'd tried on a powered combat suit.

Neural needles connected with his spine. He thought the command that would close the torso and helmet. The suit sealed around him and life support systems kicked in. Supreme Commander Halifax pointed a handheld directional radio at Herr Doctor Professor and opened a comm. link. "Professor, there are Red Force spy blimps one hundred miles windward of the Big Island. If you fire the plasma beam into the ocean, do so on the leeward side of Mauna Kea. Please stay within the wind shadow of the big volcano." Einstein nodded and walked outside on battery power. He raised his arms, basked in the sunlight for a second, and thought the command for the fusion reactor to power up.

Everyone who saw the Mark VII for the first time thought that it looked pregnant. The swollen belly section contained the reactor core. Upon Einstein's command, thousands of tiny lasers ignited the deuterium and tritium composite in the center of the core. Simultaneously, internal forcefields sprang to life to contain the reaction. Hydrogen isotopes fused and energy, prodigious amounts of energy, poured forth. A tiny fraction of this energy heated a network of crystal iron water pipes, which produced steam, powering electrical generators that fed flight turbines and servomotors. The vast majority of the nuclear power was contained within the forcefield bubbles inside the reactor core.

Flight turbines bit into the dense air of sea level. Einstein flew over the Pacific. Forgetting the supreme commander's admonition, he flew into the wind. From his recent boat tour of the coastal waters, he knew a long stretch of ocean that did not harbor whales or large pelagic life forms because of widely scattered volcanic activity. He lowered his left arm and aimed into this stretch of water. His right arm pointed in the opposite direction, roughly at the noonday sun.

Einstein triggered the particle beam projectors protruding from his left and right vambraces. Fusion power surged through forcefield conduits connecting the particle beam projectors to the reactor core. Twin beams of raw plasma erupted from the two projectors. One beam screeched madly upward. The other blasted into the ocean, boiling millions of gallons of water and sending a monstrous storm of superheated steam into the once peaceful tropical sky.

The beams ceased after only a fraction of a second. For that fraction of a second, it was as though a fragment of the sun's interior had been hurtled into the ocean, a thunderbolt to make the Gods on Mount Olympus jealous. The nuclear thunderbolt created a mushroom cloud that towered over the Big Island. Both the Blue Force and the Red Force had produced plenty of mushroom clouds with nuclear bombs. This was something different, although it wouldn't have looked different to Red Army spy blimps if it had towered over the other side of the island. Red Army blimps would have ostensibly recorded just another hydrogen bomb explosion (admittedly with an odd side effect: the skyward particle beam) if the giant volcano had been blocking their view. Einstein had made a horrible mistake.

Every alarm in spook central sounded in unison. Panel lights blinked in a frenzied panic. Off-duty Red Army Intel technicians rushed to the hub room from all parts of the building. Television cameras mounted in the undercarriages of Red Army spy blimps fed monitors in the room. These TV screens showed a wide-angle view of the Big Island and the expanding mushroom cloud. Technicians worked telemetric controls. Telephoto lenses on one blimp zoomed in on the flying combat suit that had generated the searing energy beams. The other blimps recorded the dissipation of the mushroom cloud.

The shockwave from the explosion hit the blimps, destroying the images that they were broadcasting to Kauai. A hot wind blew them out to sea, away from the Big Island. Technicians wrestled with telemetric joysticks to reorient the blimps and restore the live feed of the unusual Blue Force military activity. By the time that they had the blimps back under control, the mysterious flying combat suit was gone and the mushroom cloud had vaporized.

The screeching alarms grew silent. Vladimir picked up a phone to call Robert Oppenheimer and Werner Heisenberg. Both physicists clamed to be too busy to drop everything, jump on motorcycles, ride halfway across the island, and study whatever had the commandant of Group C upset. Rather than argue with them, Vladimir hung up and called the supreme commander. A quick explanation guaranteed not only the presence of the two ranking scientists, but Fred Banner as well.

Waiting for the heavy hitters to arrive, the videotape of the twin energy blasts was run over and over by Group C technicians. A still photograph was printed from the best close-up frame generated by the one blimp that had used its telephoto lens. To prepare for the grilling that they expected from Oppenheimer, the techs squeezed as much data out of the various videotapes as possible. The height and overall volume of the mushroom cloud could be quantified. From that data, the amount of energy that had poured into the ocean could be determined.

Over the furious clatter of calculator keyboards, Vladimir raised his voice and asked the blimp operators to drop their dirigibles to wave top level and get as close to the blast area as possible. One blimp was ordered to keep looking for the vanished combat suit. The others were told to fan out and comb the surface of the ocean for flotsam and jetsam from the explosion.

After creating the mushroom cloud, Einstein wanted to see how high the flight turbines would take him. He shot upward until they couldn't bite into atmosphere any longer, then turned the fans off and looked at the Earth below. The sight was so overwhelming that he forgot to check his altimeter. The Hawaiian Islands were tiny green jewels flung across a checkerboard of blue and white. The green jewels grew larger as he plummeted earthward.

Feathering the flight turbines, the descent slowed and then shifted into level flight.

Skimming over the industrial city of Hilo, he located the supercollider control center and landed on the lawn outside. A cheering throng swarmed from the building. Supreme Commander Banner and General Bernhard had the assembly form a circle around the $E=MC^2$. Einstein noted with satisfaction that Nkosinathi was standing as far away from her two former lovers as she could and still be part of the crowd.

He shut down the fusion reactor, crawled out of the combat suit, and waded through the adoring assemblage, sustaining slaps on the back and demands for a speech. A microphone was shoved into his hand.

"Ahem, yes, well, the first test was successful. Next, we will shoot missiles with conventional warheads at the Mark VII to test the exterior forcefield. Atom bomb blasts will follow. I don't imagine Supreme Commander Halifax will permit me to fly the $E=MC^2$ for those tests."

A ripple of laughter rose from the crowd. Jeremiah took the microphone and agreed that other, younger pilots would complete the testing regimen, not bothering to add that for all his genius Einstein had forgotten to stay on the leeward side of the island and was better off in a laboratory than on field exercises. The supreme commander made a mental note to never permit Einstein to test any equipment without adult supervision. He dispersed the crowd and told them to get back to work, warning that Red Force technicians probably weren't sitting around drinking champagne.

General Kwa had been standing unobtrusively in the back of the throng. The Zulu general smiled when his supreme commander mentioned the Red Force. It had been a while since Kwa had heard anyone worry publicly about the enemy. Perhaps the era of playing grab ass with other men's wives was over and they could all buckle down and win the war.

The live TV feed showed hundreds of dead fish, floating belly up. Tugging excitedly at his beard, Vladimir called for a marine biologist. A young woman in a white smock was at his elbow in a flash. The commandant wanted to know if the fish were unusually small. The marine biologist confirmed his suspicions. Whoever had been inside the super advanced combat suit had fired energy beams into waters denuded of large aquatic animals by recent volcanic activity.

The young woman in the white smock bowed and asked to be dismissed. Red Army intelligence analysts churned around the commandant as he sat silently, thinking, putting two and two together. A trained test pilot would never have fired a secret weapon in full view of communist spy blimps because the Blue Force always knew where the Red Army spy dirigibles were at all times; only the Blue Force possessed electronic camouflage. The pilot of the super suit had to be an amateur. It had to be one of their top designers performing an ad hoc test flight or simply skylarking. Furthermore, the man or woman that made the flight had to have a soft heart to be so worried about sea creatures.

Technical analysts held magnifying glasses over photographs of the mysterious flying super suit. The call letters on the flight cowls were not clearly discernible. They did look like an equation. To the best of Group C's knowledge, only Albert Einstein used an equation as a call sign: the famous $E=MC^2$. The fuzzy shapes under their magnifying glasses could be that famous equation. And everybody knew that Einstein's heart was soft to the point of being weepy.

Like gears grinding in a transmission, the head of intelligence drew his conclusion: Albert Einstein had taken a powerful new combat suit for a maiden flight. Vladimir was certain that there was, at present, only one super suit in existence. The Blue Force was ahead of the Red Army in developing combat suits that could fly. Flying suits had been photographed many times over Hawaii. Still, there was only one super suit, only one suit powerful enough to boil away half the ocean with directed energy bursts. Vladimir could feel it in his bones.

Visions of Spartacus' horse army wheeling around the clumsy foot soldiers of old Rome galloped through Vladimir's imagination. The Spartacus program had given the good guys superior technology with the ease of a cybernetic genie. What if the magic worked the other way? What if Blue Force soldiers in super suits were able to withstand nuclear explosions? The question went unanswered because the supreme commander and the Red Army's two best physicists had arrived. Intelligence specialists waving charts and photographs quickly surrounded Oppenheimer and Heisenberg. The looks of annoyance on the scientists' faces gave way to amazement. They dived into the data.

Fred Banner left the scientists alone with the techs and drew next to Vladimir's desk. The spy chief rose to greet his boss. Fred looked inquisitively at the short Russian. Vladimir shook his head in mute defiance, refusing to speculate until the physicists had had their say.

Heisenberg broke away from Oppenheimer and the cluster of overly excited technicians. The German looked as if he were caught in the throes of seasickness, barely able to hold down his gorge as he delivered the bad news. "Blue Force has perfected miniature fusion reactors by way of a breakthrough in containment fields that can tame and harness nuclear fusion. The prevailing winds would have blown certain isotopes to Kauai by now if there had been a fission trigger. This has not happened..." His explanation became too technical for Fred or Vladimir to follow.

The supreme commander stopped the guilt-plagued torrent of techno-babble by telling Heisenberg that he was blameless in this latest turn of events. Yes, it was true that miniature nuclear power plants were Heisenberg's specialty. Clearly, Einstein had beaten the Red Army's power plant expert by designing a superior atomic engine, but self-recrimination served no useful purpose.

Oppenheimer sensed the turmoil bubbling within his friend. He tore himself away from the Group C data stream and walked up to the others just as Vladimir was asking a key question: "Can defensive forcefields in the Blue Force super suit withstand blasts from our nuclear bombs?"

Oppenheimer put a cautioning arm on Heisenberg's shoulder and said, "I consider that probable." Vladimir used the awkward silence that followed this chilling pronouncement to recount his theory that Blue Force probably only had one fusion powered super suit.

Fred Banner stated the obvious: "Give Blue Force two or three thousand fusion powered suits and at any given hour of the day or night, there will be hundreds of active suits, powered up by soldiers in training. Fully active suits on field exercises may be impervious to atom bombs."

The supreme commander then made a statement that was only obvious in retrospect. "We should have thrown all resources into Ferdy Porsche's animatronic whale project."

He got no argument from his underlings. Fred added: "Consider resources diverted. Everyone is to work on Ferdy's artificial whales from here on out. Gentlemen, the timetable is advanced by two years. We attack in 1937, earlier if we can."

Chapter 13
Birth of the Queen's Hannibalic Army

The death of King William screamed from the headlines of every newspaper around the globe, followed by the byline that the world now had a second Queen Victoria. Pundits were impressed by the coincidence that Queen Victoria II would ascend the throne at about the same time that the global strikes had died their last gasps, a hopeful sign that her reign would bring less tumultuous times.

Momentous things were expected of Victoria II, and she did not fail to deliver. On the second day after her father's death, her staff contacted the heads of every labor union that had survived the long and crippling strikes against DFA, some three thousand separate organizations. Obeying a royal summons, these men and women were flown to England to meet with the yet-to-be-crowned Queen. In an amazingly short time, she forged an umbrella organization called the Royal Confederation of Labor. The labor leaders ceded virtually all their power to the Monarch, with the understanding that the bottomless royal purse would pay wages to strikers in the event of a second round of global strikes.

Hopes for economic peace were dashed. The chattering classes on TV and the media barons of Fleet Street hauled Victoria over the coals. Stock markets plunged throughout the Commonwealth. The global economy had barely shaken off the chaos brought on by the cataclysmic labor strife of the early thirties and now Victoria was stirring up a fresh round of trouble.

The markets stabilized when she made a single demand, instructing the Commonwealth Congress to pass the 60-hour workweek bill that had been languishing ever since the global strikes had been smashed by the supermonopoly. She didn't even need to threaten lawmakers with an "or else." They all knew what the Royal Confederation of Labor would do if her dictate were ignored. The uncrowned Queen's steely resolve caused the legislators to blink, even though most of them were bought and paid for by DFA. The law passed overnight. Markets surged the next morning.

Buckingham Palace had not wielded this kind of power since the days of the original Queen Victoria. The new Queen's heavy hand not been universally appreciated by political extremists on either side of the spectrum. On the right, there was grumbling that

King William had never dictated policy to legislators in such an undemocratic fashion. On the left, it was noted that monopoly capitalism's potential for oppression and the ongoing reality of political corruption had not vanished just because one law had been passed.

On the fifth day after King William's demise, Buckingham Palace announced a date for Victoria's coronation. Virtually every businessperson, political figure, and self-appointed VIP was clamoring for a royal audience before the coronation. Palace spokespeople told the press that Queen Victoria II would grant only one audience before the ceremony. She would treat with Henry Ford.

The headlines that Ford refused to meet with the Queen were bigger than the ones proclaiming the death of King William. Ford stood his ground, refusing the royal summons, yet also refusing to attack the 60-hour workweek law. The collective attention of the masses moved on to other things. Victoria was content to have pulled at least a couple fangs from the head of the monopolistic serpent. She returned to her primary concern: the increasingly elaborate royal baiting contests involving Bulldogs, mammoths, gorillas and buffaloes that were to proceed the 1950 CMG.

Despite being recognized as a religious figure in some circles, David Banner seldom prayed. Under normal conditions, he was afraid to pray, aware that every bit of divine guidance from God (Ahura Mazda) was accompanied by divine guidance from the satanic deity, Angra Mainyu. With his son, Fred, preparing to invade North America and start World War II, Banner was forced at long last to cast his fears aside, drop to his knees, and pray for all he was worth.

"Lord, grant me a vision, a subtle vision, even a brief glimpse, perhaps something akin to that given the Emperor Constantine before the Milvian Bridge Battle."

He remained kneeling for hours, alone in his backyard. No visions, subtle or obvious, were granted. After exhausting whatever psychic energy he possessed, Banner succumbed to the warmth of the afternoon by stretching a hammock between two trees in his backyard and falling asleep. Divinely inspired dreams were tricky creatures, it was hard to differentiate an earthly dream from a celestial one. His dream that afternoon could have been heaven sent or it could have been a continuation in a series of dreams that he'd been having for the past couple of years involving war elephants from the ancient world.

In this dream, Banner saw the great Carthaginian military leader, Hannibal, as a nine-year-old boy. The boy's father, General Hamilcar, was lecturing the youth on the reasons for Carthage's defeat against Rome, which was also Hamilcar's personal defeat, since he was the leading general in the first Punic War.

"Son, I would've pulverized Rome if I'd only had more war elephants. Not just any elephants, mind you, but trained elephants, with suitable armor. Untrained elephants are as useless as tits on a boar. Worse! They'll turn from battle and trample Carthaginian troops. Let's find out if you've been paying attention. Tell me what anvil and hammer tactics are."

The boy looked his father in the eyes and recited from memory, "The elephant army is the anvil, a slow moving wall. The horse army is the hammer, driving the Roman enemy into the elephants. The Roman soldiers are then beaten like metal trapped between hammer and anvil."

"Very good, Hannibal, I want you to march your little behind outside and spend the rest of the day training that big beautiful bull calf I gave you, Surus. A general of an elephant army must know how to train his own mount. Remember, the general's personal elephant has to be the leader of the whole herd. I've deliberately made your task difficult; in the wild, females are the herd leaders and males are rogue."

In Banner's dream, he saw snapshots of Hannibal's career featuring both the effective use of war elephants and situations like the one Hamilcar had warned against: untrained elephants turning from battle and destroying the Carthaginian troops to their rear. Evidently, the city fathers of Carthage were willing to ship fresh elephants to the Italian peninsula, but not the well-trained and well-equipped brutes that Hannibal needed.

The dream ended with the legendary Roman General, Scipio Africanus, dictating terms of surrender after the Hannibal's final defeat at Zuma. One of Scipio's terms included handing over the last herd of Carthaginian war elephants. This herd had been personally trained by Hannibal for the Battle of Zuma, so they were a genuine threat to Rome. Hannibal complained that Rome would only use the beasts in the arena against gladiators. Scipio was surprisingly conciliatory, agreeing that this would indeed be a travesty. He went on to swear to Mars that Rome would use Carthaginian battle elephants in a new war flaring up against Macedonia. Gladiators would not butcher a single elephant in the arena.

Hannibal asked if at least one elephant, the great Surus, could be spared from both the battlefield and the arena. Surus had fought in every engagement in the long bloody years of warfare on the Italian peninsula. He had survived the perilous journey across the Alps. He had never turned from battle. A nobler warrior never walked the Earth, whether on two legs or four.

Scipio mulled over this request for a long moment and consented. Every Carthaginian war elephant was to be shipped to Rome and used in combat. Carthage must sign a treaty forbidding it to ever raise and train war elephants again. Surus, however, would be given an honorable retirement.

Stretching his arms and yawning, Banner awoke from the reoccurring dream and found that his prosthetic leg was on the blink. It felt like a big piece of wood, unmoving, unbending. The thing had seized up at a strange angle too. The knee was bent at a thirty-degree slant, so he couldn't use it as a peg leg. Like a beached whale, he was unable to move more than a few inches in any direction. He couldn't even get out of the hammock, unless he was willing to flop to the ground. Once aground, he could only get to the house by crawling. Once inside, he would have to keep crawling all over the house until he found his crutches because he didn't remember exactly where they'd been stored, probably in the attic somewhere. Lisa was at the palace and wouldn't be home until late that night.

"Hacksaw, come here boy!" The comforting sight of his Bulldog's friendly head chased away the mild bit of panic welling inside. He'd trained the dog to fetch his slippers. Hacksaw also liked to play fetch with tree branches and knew the word "stick." He even knew to bring an extra large stick if asked. Unfortunately, the dog did not know the word "crutches."

Banner rubbed the Bulldog's ears and said, "Bring me a big stick." Hacksaw raced to the front of the house and the alarming sound of a sapling being torn from the earth became audible. Banner winced. He'd just planted some beautiful and expensive young birch trees.

The Bulldog trotted into the backyard with a fifteen-foot birch sapling clamped between his steel jaws. It was much too big. The root ball on one end and the long skinny branches on the other would have to be removed.

"Tear it up, Hacksaw. Rip it up!"

The yellow fire of violence blazed in Hacksaw's eyes. He smashed the root ball on the ground with a piston-like movement. His jaw muscles flexed and the sapling burst in two. He pounced on the bigger half and tore off the branches.

"Good boy, bring it here." Hacksaw stopped shredding the little tree and brought a perfectly useable five-foot long segment to his master. The dog placed the stick in Banner's outstretched hand and sat on his haunches, tongue lolling from his mouth, tail wagging madly, ready to play fetch.

The stick allowed Banner to ease out of the hammock and hobble indoors. Hacksaw followed with a disgusted expression, cheated out of a game of fetch. Climbing the stairs to the attic was torturous, but worth the effort. Banner saw what he came for in a corner of the room as soon as the light was flicked on. The light bulb exploded before he could get his hands on the aluminum crutches.

Navigating in the dark, stepping on pieces of broken light bulb, Banner got his hands on the elusive crutches. Throwing the crude walking stick aside, placing the crutches under his armpits, he crutched downstairs and into the kitchen, in need of a cup of tea after the ordeal. The electric stove exploded with a huge blue spark the instant he touched the display panel, searing all the hair off the back of one hand. Cursing with quiet intensity, he put a cup of water and a tea bag into the microwave oven, and turned it on for sixty seconds. The door of the microwave oven blew open and sailed across the kitchen to smash against a wall. Another tremendous blue spark flared out into the room like the business end of a flamethrower.

"Jesus Christ on his cross! Why is everything electric going haywire?" The dog growled, casting around for something to attack. Finding nothing, he sat down, keeping an eye on his antagonized master. "I need something stronger than tea. Let's go to the local club." The dog sprang out the front door and streaked to the front passenger door of the Rolls. Banner took a while getting into the car. He had to wrestle the malfunctioning prosthetic leg into position and throw the crutches in the backseat. After those tasks were complete and the troublesome artificial leg was in a position where it could do no harm, the dog and the man took a short breather, clearing their minds to get ready for drinks, darts, and relaxation at their favorite watering hole.

Banner pointed the key at the car's ignition. Before he could even attempt to start the vehicle, another blisteringly blue spark arced between the key and the ignition. He threw the red-hot key on the floorboards and shook his hand painfully, watching small blisters emerge. He nearly turned the air inside the passenger compartment blue a second time with a long string of blasphemous oaths.

Hacksaw covered his head with his paws. Even the Bulldog understood that something was wrong with the manmade devices that his master relied on. "No, it's not a case of flawed electrical devices, Hacksaw. That's not the problem at all." Banner stroked the dog's neck. Hacksaw's tail thumped the fabric of the passenger seat.

"It's a message, I'm reasonably sure, a subtle message from above. Hmm. Let's puzzle it out." He reached down and picked up the key, which by now had cooled. He placed it into the ignition and turned. The electric car was as dead as a doorknob.

"Let's see, the light in the attic is dead, as is the electric stove and the microwave, not to mention the electric car." Hacksaw looked at Banner, not understanding any of these words, but sensing a shift in the man's emotional state.

"I keep trying to start electrical devices, like a dunderhead. And they keep exploding and dying on me." Hacksaw barked, just to participate in the conversation. He enjoyed having the man talk to him as if he were as smart as a human or a gorilla.

"It's as though I were a kind of anti-electrical man, eh?" He was talking more slowly now, more to himself. "General Hannibal, he had to do without electricity, of course." Banner had dreamed of war elephants so many times that he could see armored pachyderms charging insect-like foot soldiers simply by closing his eyes. His eyelids drooped. The darkness filled with elephantine mayhem. "How would a modern mammoth army fight a war if it could not use electricity?" Hacksaw barked again, just to hear his voice echo inside the cabin of the Rolls-Royce.

A modern mammoth army that was forbidden the use of electricity would still need cannons and machineguns. Was Ahura Mazda denying him all modern weapons, or just those relying on electricity? He opened his eyes and asked the Bulldog, "Does the anti-electrical man dampen chemical reactions as well? Let us perform a scientific test." He fished around in a pocket and pulled out a book of matches. He lit a match. It flared obediently. A docile little flame flickered on the match head.

"Here is proof, Hacksaw, that gunpowder and cordite will still explode around the anti-electrical man." He stared into the tiny flame of the match. "Let us assume that I am receiving a message that can be roughly translated as: manmade electricity is a bad thing, at least as far as David Banner is concerned. Furthermore, I keep having these dreams, over and over, of General Hannibal and war elephants. No electricity and an army built around the mammoths we're training for the CMG baiting contests: a strange combination."

Hacksaw tilted his head back and erupted with a thunderclap bark. Banner's ears rang for several seconds before he amended: "Quite right. An army built around mammoths, Bulldogs, gorillas, horses, as few people as possible, and no electricity. That's what God wants. It makes no sense from a strictly rational mindset: such an army would be slaughtered wholesale in the coming World War II, something like the Children's Crusade. But that, my friend, is the will of Jehovah or as I prefer, Ahura Mazda. He or she moves in a mysterious fashion and his or her will shall be done."

The match died. He set it in the ashtray. A tingling sensation surged up from his prosthetic leg. It had turned itself back on and was now functional. He put the key in the ignition. The Rolls-Royce hummed with electrical power.

Slipping the car into gear, he pulled out of the driveway, and continued his conversation with Hacksaw. "We've our answer, old chap. The CMG baiting contests are to be a subterfuge for setting up a low-tech, non-electrical army. So low-tech that General Hannibal would be comfortable as our leader."

Banner stopped talking to Hacksaw, driving and talking required too much effort. He didn't stop thinking about the bizarre request he would have to make to the newly crowned Queen. She'd be furious with him once she learned that he'd known of the coming communist invasion for years and had kept that knowledge confined to a small circle of associates within Banner Detectives.

The Queen would want to know why a primitive mammoth army should be thrown against communists armed with A-bombs. He had no ready answer, except that holy war

156

beasts provided spiritual power. Unless, that is, if communist A-bombs were rendered impotent in the same way that his microwave oven and electric car had been. He pulled into the looping roadway that ran around London to avoid the insane congestion clogging the great city at all hours of the day. Now that the global strikes were over and the economy was booming, traffic was worse than ever.

Green countryside streamed past the Silver Shadow. The reality of the impending global war seeped into Banner's thoughts. Could the mammoth army actually harm the communist army on a practical level, considering the advanced technology of the thirties? After the 1920 CMG, his son had predicted that powered combat suits would combine the function of panzer, fighter jet, and submarine into a single machine little bigger than a human being. The Hannibal-style mammoth army that Banner was envisioning would have been hell on wheels in the Boer War, but only cannon fodder against even a squad of functioning combat suits. Maybe the suits would function and maybe they wouldn't, when the balloon went up. The Commonwealth would need to do a lot more than train mammoths and gorillas to fight men; that might be a sideshow, of spiritual value alone. A crash program for building A-bombs would have to be started at once. New powered combat suit designs would have to be trotted out and mass-produced. The time for secrecy had passed. Banner would present evidence of the communist conspiracy to the high commands of all the big Commonwealth countries to get the ball rolling. Given a year or two, the combined technological prowess of the advanced nations might equal that of the Red Force, even if his Marxist son did have a head start. Plus, he would contact Jeremiah Halifax on Hawaii. The Blue Force would more than tip the balance.

His prosthetic leg froze up again. His mechanical foot was on the accelerator and traffic had thickened ahead. He whipped the car into the fast lane and tried to take his inert foot off the pedal, nearly swerving onto the shoulder in the process. The metallic foot refused to budge. It was like having a cruise control that wouldn't shut off. He put his good foot on the brakes to slow down. *Great, now the brakes'll overheat!* The car slowed, but smoke poured from the brake housings.

"Bleeding hell! Point made. I promise not to alert the Commonwealth or Blue Force to the approaching danger." The prosthetic leg resumed functioning once more. He eased up on the accelerator and switched to a middle lane. Hacksaw sniffed his prosthetic leg suspiciously. Perhaps the dog could catch a whiff of the supernatural forces bludgeoning his master.

There was no room for doubt. Banner knew that he'd received the final word from above. He had another mission and at his age it had to be the last. It meant lying to the Queen, lying to her animal trainers, and lying to everyone else involved in the royal baiting contests, everyone except Lisa, of course. Tooling the Rolls around the great city, he pondered what sort of lie Victoria would swallow.

When he was about five miles from the palace, the only morally correct solution gelled in his mind. He would coax the dominant silverback, Bwana, into lying for him. It shouldn't be a tough sell. Bwana would probably do anything to get his hands on real weapons and lead an animal army into war against humans. Not only did the dominant silverback have an extremely aggressive personality, Banner knew that Bwana was more intelligent than even his handlers supposed and would be able to figure out the most workable falsehood.

The one-legged man parked his car outside the palace gate, leaving Hacksaw inside. He presented a clearance badge to the guards inside the blockhouse, and walked uphill toward the big squatty concrete bunker of Southwest Palace #9. He didn't go straight to the palace, but circled the structure, heading in the direction of the recently built gorilla enclosures. On his way, Banner came across a big pile of rusty steel rails. Each section of railroad steel had been cut in half with a welding torch, which made the rails about twenty feet long apiece.

This had to be part of Nigel Mortimer's simian strength training regimen. While a powerful silverback with no resistance training was about as strong as ten or twelve Olympic weight lifters, the right training could double a gorilla's strength, making him as strong as twenty-four of the strongest humans, as measured by barbell weights. It was difficult to calculate how much stronger a weight-trained silverback was than a human being for everyday jobs. An Olympic super-heavy weight lifter was probably ten times stronger than most people when it came to pumping iron. By that measure, the very strongest weight-trained silverback was two hundred and forty times stronger than an average human. Mortimer believed that figure overstated a trained gorilla's strength because weight and size counted in measuring useable strength: the kind of strength used in day-to-day chores. Gorillas were not two hundred and forty times larger than humans. Regardless, silverbacks that pumped iron possessed unbelievable strength.

In a stroke of good luck, Bwana appeared just as Banner was stooping to examine the rusty rails. The dominant silverback rode a magnificent African bull elephant: an outcross in the mammoth breeding project. Better yet, Bwana and his mount were alone. Providence was smiling on the big man that day.

The bull elephant must have been the largest animal that the Queen's men could find in Africa, a dazzling specimen: fourteen feet tall, superbly muscled, a fantastic sweep of ivory, and an intelligent gleam in his eye. Banner had never seen this particular monster before, but he knew that hunters armed with tranquilizer darts had been looking for a creature such as this for a long time. It was not possible to create a new race from a gene pool consisting of one mother and one daughter.

The great ape sprang off the pachyderm's neck hump, landing at Banner's feet. Bwana made sign language gestures. Banner had learned to read gorilla sign language some time ago, when he'd started working full time on the royal baiting contests.

"Hello, Mr. Banner. This is our new elephant stud. I am training him for buffalo baiting."

"Hello, Bwana. What is the stud's name?"

Bwana switched from the commonly used symbolic sign language to a more precise, but slower method, where he spelled out individual letters: "S-U-R-U-S." The blood in Banner's veins chilled. He gave an involuntary shudder before replying, "Did you know that Surus was the name of General Hannibal's war elephant? The greatest war elephant ever?" Bwana nodded his head and signed, "Yeah, Queen Vicky named him. She said something about Hannibal. It is a good name. Surus kicks ass, only elephant we've seen as tough and strong as a mammoth."

Banner stepped aside as Bwana brushed past him to get at the pile of steel rails. The silverback must have been diligently lifting weights and twisting pieces of steel into pretzels because he'd packed on one hundred pounds of muscle since Banner had seen him last. Kubwa must have added just as much muscle, if so, the mountain silverback would tip the scales with six hundred and fifty pounds of lean body mass, an all time record weight.

The big man leaned against one of Surus's tree trunk legs and watched Bwana's resistance workout. The African bull elephant was certainly well chosen for the breeding program. Not only was he an awesome physical specimen, the bull possessed a calm and steady temperament. He stood there serenely stuffing shoots of grass into his mouth, keeping one eye on Bwana and occasionally scanning the surrounding countryside, ignoring Banner even though the man was making physical contact.

Bwana picked up one of the twenty-foot rails with his left hand. Rearing up onto his back legs, he gripped the steel beam with both hands, took a deep breath, and bent it a V-shape. Flecks of rust popped off the tortured metal like fleas from a dog's back. The steel gave a little scream as it was bent, almost a protest against the gorilla's unnatural strength. The silverback raised the V-shaped rail overhead and plunged the two legs into the ground, burying the thing until only five feet stood above ground.

He picked up a second rail. This piece of steel was rapidly twisted around the inverted V until the shape of a man's torso emerged from Bwana's ferrous permutations. The silverback beat the ground, hooted, and signed, "A scarecrow! I've made a steel scarecrow to scare away steel crows. Original art. Tell that punk, Pablo Picasso, to bite me."

Picasso, eh? Yes indeed. Bwana is much smarter than anyone here credits, Banner thought. The ape faced his human friend and raised both hands. "Sometimes human males see a feat of intelligence and strength by a gorilla and feel inadequate," Bwana observed sadly.

"I can see how it would have that effect."

"The physical weakness of human males is partially offset by their large penises."

"Is that a fact?"

"The average human penis is slightly larger than the average gorilla penis. I mention this to human males that feel inferior to gorillas. It brightens their spirits."

Banner kept a straight face, avoiding laughter by biting his inner lip. Forcing nonchalance into his voice, he responded, "Bwana, tell me, do most human males need to have their spirits buoyed in this fashion?" The ape nodded, gave a sly wink, and signed, "Human penises are larger than a gorilla's *on average*. Penis size varies from one gorilla to another. I never tell humans that Bwana is hung like an elephant. This knowledge would crush most human males considering my superior strength, intelligence, and good looks. I tell you, Mr. Banner, because you are stronger in the mind than most humans."

"I appreciate your confidence and want to ask the strongest, smartest, most well-endowed, and best-looking silverback to help with a secret project."

The mischievous twinkle in Bwana's eye vanished. He dropped into a squat and stared keenly as Banner drew a small notepad and a pen from a pocket. The human rapidly sketched a picture of Surus, the African bull. A war harnesses with a cannon was added to the drawing of the elephant. Gorillas were put on top of the pachyderm. One ape was depicted shoveling shells into the cannon's breech. The other aimed it. Bulldogs with 1920 CMG-style canine machineguns were placed around the elephant's feet. In the distance, horsemen with fish eagles were acting as scouts.

The one-legged old man gave the drawing to the silverback and explained that there was going to be a war. Gorillas, mammoths, elephants, and other animals would fight communist humans that hated Queen Victoria. Unfortunately, the Queen did not believe that communists posed a danger to her Commonwealth. Banner could design and procure weapons for Bwana's animal army. He could help train the war beasts. He could not convince the Queen to fear communists, or even try.

The flash of simian intelligence in Bwana's eyes was as profound as any human being's. He raised his hands to sign. "Queen Vicky does not fear communists. She does fear humaniacs. Heard of them, Mr. Banner? Militant humans dedicated to stopping baiting contests. Humaniacs are violent and dangerous. I watch the news and see that they break fighting bulls loose from corrals at night to stop baiting competitions. Sometimes humaniacs kill human guards to free animals. Vicky is afraid of them."

"I could stage an incident where fake humaniacs attack this compound."

"You do that and I will talk to Queen Vicky about cannons on mammoths and dogs with machineguns."

"Agreed. Only four people are in on the secret: you, me, Kubwa, and my wife."

"Agreed."

Bwana made a sign to Surus. A long gray trunk snaked outward and hoisted Banner onto the elephant's back. The silverback leaped onto the neck hump, not bothering with an elephantine assist. Simian heels were applied to Surus's shoulders. The gorilla grabbed earflaps to steer. The African bull spun gracefully and glided up a hill.

Surus trumpeted when he could see and smell Angerbotha and Hela. Kubwa rode Hela bareback. Lisa sat on a pile of silk cushions in an aluminum howdah strapped to Angerbotha. The mammoth cows raised their trunks and returned Surus's greeting. All three pachyderms twined their trunks together lovingly: Adam and his two Eves.

Kubwa was indeed a sight to behold as he sat on top of Hela. The mountain silverback bulged with muscle, all the more prominently displayed because his long shaggy fur had been trimmed short for summer. He stood upright and made signs at the lowland gorilla: "Did Bwana make another queer-bait sculpture?" Bwana reared fully upright and signed a reply: "Yeah, it's a sculpture of Kubwa bending over and taking it in the rear." The mountain silverback roared his displeasure. The lowland gorilla roared back. But there was no real malice in either threat display and both apes looked at Lisa eagerly once the roaring had quieted.

"Stop signing and stop roaring, the both of you. I'm very disappointed. Today we're to work on teamwork spearing drills. Of all days, this is the one where the two mightiest silverbacks must get along," Lisa shouted. She looked inquiringly at her husband. He nodded and raised his arms like an infant wanting to be picked up by an adult. Lisa told Angerbotha to grab David and place him on her back, inside the howdah. With the personnel transfer complete, Lisa raised her voice again, ordering the two silverbacks to head out to the target range.

Surus and Hela strode side by side in the swift daisy-clipping trot pachyderms use to cover long distances. Angerbotha moved more slowly to give the humans a smoother ride. The net result was that the two pachyderms carrying gorillas outdistanced the one carrying humans. When the distance was great enough for Lisa to lose clear sight of hand signals, the silverbacks began making gestures at each other again, obviously trading insults.

Lisa turned to her husband, who was squeezed into the howdah with his knees near his chin, and said, "A Silverback controls only one troop at a time in the wild. Bwana is able to control two troops, wait and see. He's very good."

"Bwana is going to have to control more than two troops. He is going to have to control an entire army."

"I knew this day was coming. We haven't been training for baiting contests since we got here, now have we?"

"No, we are training for war, a primitive sort of war. I don't fully understand why or how, but advanced technology is going to vanish from the face of the Earth, perhaps with a mere snap of God's fingers."

"With advanced technology gone, gorillas, mammoths, Bulldogs, and Wolfhounds become super-weapons, don't they?"

"Indeed."

The target range was a small valley filled with radio-controlled all terrain vehicles roughly the size of a buffalo. Lashed to the saddle of each small four-wheel-drive ATV was a bail of hay. Over the headlights, a pair of buffalo horns was attached to lend an air of realism to the exercise.

In the center of the valley there was a control tower manned by dozens of engineering students operating radio control consoles. The four-wheelers buzzed around the control tower like bees around a hive.

Two troops of gorillas sat side by side at the entrance to the gorge, behind the two pachyderms and the two mounted silverbacks. Next to each troop there was a pile of long, heavy spears with a few crossbows and bolts alongside the spears. Bwana's elephant pawed the ground like a buffalo bull ready for a bait. The dominant silverback stood, filled his lungs, and let forth a deep bellow that carried an entirely different note than the playful roaring earlier in the day.

Kubwa also stood, gripping Hela's muscular neck hump with his feet. He cupped his hands and beat his chest: a staccato pop pop pop. The females and young male blackbacks on the ground gnashed their teeth, howled savagely, and picked up spears. Each troop member gathered at least a dozen of the steel tipped missiles. The two troops coalesced around their respective silverback and his elephantine mount.

Bwana screamed a snap count. The attack began. The pachyderms waded into the swarm of four-wheelers. Most of the ATVs charged, some tried to escape. The ground-based gorillas chucked spears up to their silverbacks. The big adult males straddled the neck humps of their mounts and heaved spears at the charging four-wheel-drive ATVs, connecting about half the time by placing a spear in the center of a hay bail. Once a four-wheeler was speared, the engineering student controlling it pulled the plug, and the machine lay inert.

The blackbacks on the ground shouldered crossbows and sent bolts into the tires of the charging ATVs that the silverbacks had not been able to spear. The females kept tossing spears up to the silverbacks. Bwana and Kubwa had neatly cut the herd in half, bisecting the valley, controlling the terrain like professional military commanders.

David Banner could imagine aluminum-barreled cannons mounted on the neck humps of the elephant and the mammoth. By squinting his eyes, he could make the spears look like artillery shells. The young male gorillas could easily be holding heavy machineguns rather than crossbows. All he needed to do was add Bulldogs equipped with light machineguns and armed horsemen with eagles, and his primitive Hannibal-style army would be complete. *That and spider silk body armor*, Banner amended.

He looked away from the training exercise, suddenly sick in his heart because he and Lisa were building a war machine that would somehow be used against their son: filicide. Fred Banner was a military genius and the great grandson of Fred Greystone. Maybe he would create his own Hannibalic army and wipe out his parents along with the

161

Commonwealth when God turned off the world's electrical technology. In which case, they might be forcing Fred into committing fratricide and matricide: a dilemma straight out of the Old Testament.

"Nooo!" Lisa screamed. One of the four wheelers had continued charging at Hela and Kubwa despite having multiple spears dangling from its lashed hay bail and arrows projecting at all angles from its front tires. In other words, the engineering student controlling the vehicle was cheating. Kubwa could not countenance a cheater; it was one of his pet peeves. The mountain silverback had launched himself into the control tower and was knocking students around, trying to figure out which one had broken the rules of the game. None of the students could speak sign language and didn't understand what Kubwa was demanding of them.

"Bwana!" Lisa screamed even louder than before. Nobody would be able to stop Kubwa except the dominant silverback. Conceivably, Angerbotha could have grabbed Kubwa with her trunk and pulled him out of the tower. However, the six hundred and fifty pound mountain gorilla would inflict deep wounds on the pachyderm. Worse, that kind of indignity might make him mad enough to swarm up the mammoth's trunk and attack the people in the howdah.

Urged on by his simian rider, Surus achieved a gallop of sorts, not as quick as the true gallop of the mammoths, speedy nonetheless. Bwana leaped into the tower and tackled Kubwa. The lowland gorilla immediately backed off, narrowly avoiding a savage bite as the enraged Kubwa's massive jaws snapped in the air. The mountain gorilla cooled down to a simmer and ceased rampaging at the sight of his leader.

"These pencil-necks aren't worth the sweat off the balls of a silverback," Bwana signed at his subordinate. Kubwa reared up to his full height, roaring and beating his chest. Bwana signed, "That's right. You bad. You bad. You a bad mo-fu." Kubwa signed back, "Damn straight I'm bad, the baddest ape in the jungle. I don't take shit from any human dickhead." Bwana agreed in the main with this sentiment. He knew exactly how to calm Kubwa: "Good job not killing any of the pencil-necks."

Angerbotha set Lisa down in the tower, between the two self-congratulatory silverbacks. She surveyed the carnage, clucking her tongue in only mild disappointment. Seven engineers were unconscious, yet breathing, crumpled in heaps on the floor. The others were cowering in the corners of the room, whimpering like kittens. Lisa's anger at the two silverbacks slowly gave way to disgust at the cowardliness of the humans. She didn't stop to think that this very cowardliness had saved their lives. By running into the corners and not fighting back, the engineering students had gotten off with broken bones, bruises, and scrapes. The tower would have looked like a slaughterhouse if Kubwa had wanted to kill the engineers.

Banner found a radio transmitter in the howdah and called for a helicopter medevac team from the local DFA hospital. Lisa ordered the two silverbacks to return to their respective mounts and then she looked curiously at Hela. The mammoth cow was eating grass, disinterested in Kubwa's mayhem. Something was wrong with this picture. Additional mayhem should have happened, but didn't. The most savage of the pachyderms had stood quietly by while Kubwa went on a berserker rampage. One would have expected Hela to tear down the tower and stomp every human being inside to death. There was a hint of a silver lining to this particular dark cloud. Hela was developing self-control.

Watching the DFA medical chopper lift off with its evacuees, Banner remarked sadly, "Incidents such as this will be much worse after we introduce artillery and machineguns to the mammoth-gorilla mix." Lisa winced, reached out to hold his hand, and added, "Not to mention Bulldogs, Wolfhounds, and men on horseback. They'll be in the mix too. Quite volatile, wouldn't you say?"

Chapter 14

Oscillating Electron Neutrino Pulse: The Fist of God

The submarines of Patton's North American Task Force left the tunnel fortress by spending a whole day clawing up through two miles of primordial ooze. Red Army submarines emerged from the ancient sediment of the ocean floor like titanic crocodiles crawling out of an antediluvian swamp. Shaking off mud and slime and motoring silently into the dark waters of the deep Pacific, the huge submarines were hard to detect, but not genuinely stealthy. The task force's only hope of concealment lay in its ability to operate at two thousand-foot depths, because the Royal Navy and the American Navy were restricted to shallower dives, roughly half that deep. At least the Red Army subs were nuclear powered and didn't have to surface.

General Patton wouldn't leave the bridge of his flag submarine, the *Karl Marx*, for the entire five days that it took to reach Puget Sound. He even set up a cot next to the passive sonar station and slept on the bridge, adding his snores to the soft clatter of the hard working crew during night shifts. The captain of the *Karl Marx* could literally feel Patton's breath on his neck every time he peered into an infrared scope.

Enemy battle groups were detected three times during the first leg of the journey. All three times, British and American ships passed over the communist underwater armada without incident. For whatever reason, the Commonwealth battle groups did not have a single submarine attached. Perhaps after thirty-seven sleepy years of Pax Britannica, the Commonwealth military machine was growing rusty.

If one of the vessels from the Commonwealth battle groups had fired on the Red Army submarine fleet, then counter fire would have been authorized and inevitable. The communist task force could have taken apart anything that the Commonwealth threw their way. But that wasn't the point. The element of surprise would have been lost and the Blue Force with all its technology would be on alert.

Patton didn't relax as the *Karl Marx* entered the strait of San Juan de Fuca, the body of water linking Greater Puget Sound to the Pacific Ocean. Hundreds of Red Army submarines were still motoring through the Pacific, strung out over dozens of miles. Patton couldn't stop grinding his teeth until the last sub had entered the sound and was out of the direct path of a Commonwealth naval patrol.

At an average depth of six hundred feet, Puget Sound was a submariner's dream-come-true. Squadrons consisting of three to five subs converged on their target islands within the sound, slipping quietly under commercial traffic. Lone divers from each squadron were sent ashore, charged with activating the communist police cells within the island communities. The local cops jumped into action, cutting phone lines, confiscating radios, and herding island dwellers into jail. That night, Red Army weaponry began flowing into the islands of Puget Sound: the staging grounds for the invasion of North America.

A week after the task force had left Kauai, two days after it entered the sound, Patton remembered that this was the day that SC Banner's animatronic-whale battle-lion was scheduled to set out for Hawaii. He gathered his officers together that morning before the shipboard activities could begin.

"Men." Patton glanced at the assembled officers, some of whom were women. "And women. I want us all to say a little prayer for the animatronic-whale pilots. They will face a shit load more danger than we will." He bent his head. The officers also bent their heads. "Lord, let the brave souls inside the mechanical whales reach their destination unmolested by the capitalistic navies of the Commonwealth. Let the Red Army's nuclear weapons explode effectively over the island of Hawaii, blowing all the bourgeois evildoers on that blighted island to Hell. Dear God, let the brave soldiers of the animatronic-whale battle-lion make a clean retreat and find their way back safely to our Pacific fortress under the waves. Amen." The other officers chorused, "Amen."

Patton looked up and said, "Listen here, you slackers, we move the main battle 'crafts onto San Juan Island today. We move the fighter jets tomorrow. This gear is loaded with electronics. The animatronic-whales are nuking Hawaii next week. That means a hemispheric electromagnetic pulse is gonna disable every non-hardened piece of electrical gear on the west coast. As you know, we have to install temporary EMP shields over every weapon system. Superconducting shield metal is fragile as a son of a bitch and they're the last things we haul to the island. Our ham handed soldiers will be tired and sloppy on the last day of unloading."

Darts shot from Patton's eyes as he pinned every officer with a savage glare. "I will boil every one of you mother grabbing son of a bitches in oil if the electromagnetic pulse fries even a single Red Army circuit. The EMP is our signal to attack. Every mother loving hovercraft, jet fighter, and powered combat suit had better be ready to fight or I will go medieval on your ass."

There was no element of vainglory in Fred Banner's decision to personally lead the animatronic-whale battle-lion. He had long since abandoned any quest for personal battlefield glory. His decision was based on the simple fact that he had led a similar underwater charge from Kauai to Hawaii in the 1920 CMG and was the only Red Army soldier who intimately knew the topography of the seabed around the archipelago. Actually, Fred wished he didn't have to act as a frontline commander.

The mission was so high risk that the question of succession to the office of supreme command had to be revisited. General Rommel was number two in the chain of command. It had been understood that he was next in line if Fred died. That was not to be. Evolving circumstances forced the SC to designate Vladimir Bakunin as his successor in the event of a catastrophe in the opening battle of the war. Rommel and Patton had been furious after the announcement. Fred didn't have the time or inclination to explain in depth that neither of them possessed sufficient grounding in the Marxist theory of Historical Parallelism to create a new world order when and if the revolution succeeded.

He rubbed his eyes and bit his lip to chase away thoughts of the angry generals. Surviving the mission and remaining supreme commander solved the succession problem. The best way to do that was to not worry about Patton and Rommel. He looked into the monitor connected to the two camera-eyes of his animatronic-whale.

Green water ahead and a break in the corral meant that they were approaching the mouth of a Hawaiian river. The final hour was near. He needed to see if the rest of his battle-lion was still in formation. The animatronic-whales could be described as either highly unconventional submarines or undersea robots, but they were more than that. The machines were designed to so accurately mimic living humpbacks that Fred would have to swim around in a circle to see the other animatronic-whales.

He worked pedals with his feet and levers with his hands. The mechanical flukes beat against the ocean with fluid strokes that were indistinguishable from the motion of a real humpback. Fins adjusted like the ailerons of an aeroplane. The command animatronic-whale executed a somersault. A brief glimpse straight up revealed the prow of a Blue Force ship cleaving the surface like a knife-edge. There wasn't a forcefield grid on its hull; therefore it was most likely a pleasure craft. Fred completed the somersault, straightened out his robotic whale, and turned its huge head left, then right.

Within his field of vision there were twenty animatronic-whales. These mechanical creatures spun around and counted the robots that were not visible to the lead whale. The twenty spun back again and faced the green water flowing off the Big Island: a sign that every member of the battle-lion was present.

The signal to begin the attack was for Fred to take his robotic whale to the surface and perform a breaching maneuver. His teeth clamped down on his inner lip until he tasted blood. The command whale rushed for the surface, blasted into the air, exposed about two thirds of its body, and crashed back into the ocean, sending a huge splash at the Blue Force pleasure craft. For the brief moment that he'd been airborne, the whale's camera eyes had gotten a good look at the Blue Force ship. The vessel was indeed a pleasure craft. An attractive black woman in a green bikini was lounging on deck with four men of different races. All of the men wore swimsuits. The yacht probably had weapons of some sort, but it was clearly not a warship.

Danger to the animatronic-whale battle-lion increased as the mechanical whales performed maneuvers that did not reflect the behavior of real whales. So far, there had been very little artificial behavior. It was perfectly naturally for a pod of whales to swim from Kauai to Hawaii, though they should have had a few calves swimming alongside the huge cows, a minor transgression. What the robotic whales did next was very unnatural.

They took an hour to surround the island, swimming at slightly faster speeds than living humpbacks were capable of. The hour passed and the sound of exploding depth-charges did not fill the ocean. The Blue Force was still asleep, unaware of the mortal danger heading their way.

Every robotic cetacean swam straight at either a beach or the mouth of a river, whipping the blue green ocean a frothy white with mechanical tail strokes that were several times faster than anything a real whale could produce, plowing up onto beaches with unnatural force.

The Blue Force would know something was wrong now. The Red Army battle-lion was no longer using anything even remotely resembling stealth or camouflage. The mechanical whales opened their, gigantic jaws. Hydraulic arms swung missiles into position. Radio antennae popped through the plastic skin on the whales' heads. Fred filled the airwaves with a backward count: "Ten, nine, eight, seven, six, five, four, three, two, one, FIRE!"

Short-range missiles shot seventy-five tried and true A-bombs and twenty-five experimental H-bombs into the heart of the Big Island. The soldiers inside the animatronic-whales worked levers and pedals frantically. Flukes dug into volcanic soil and sand. The whales twisted as sinuously as snakes, got their noses pointed away from the island and swam for all they were worth.

Fred got farther away than most because he'd fired his missile from the inlet of a sizeable river. His whale didn't have to scramble against rock or sand since it was immersed in shallow water during the firing sequence. He'd gotten two hundred yards off shore and was about one hundred feet deep when the nuclear weapons exploded. Even though he was facing the opposite direction of the blast, the sea lit up in a great flash of green through the electronic eyes of the robot. The electromagnetic pulse caused the monitor to go blank. A thermal shock wave of boiling water caught the machine from behind and pulverized it. Fred and every member of the battle-lion were simultaneously crushed and boiled to death. Most would have survived if the Red Army had fired only A-bombs. Oppenheimer's new H-bombs had worked better than expected.

It had been a long week for Jim Pullman. On Monday, a tense meeting with his business manager had caused his ulcer to flare. The two CMG forces had stopped ordering vehicles and spare parts earlier in the year, and the results were only now being felt on the car dealer's bottom line. He hadn't realized how dependent his businesses had become on milking that particular cash cow. Throughout the week, he was forced to refinance his automobile and parts inventories to jumpstart his cash flow. Every trip to the San Francisco DFA Bank office caused his ulcer to growl like a Bulldog on a meat truck.

The only thing that kept him slogging through the torturous week was the thought of Friday and the weekend. Here it was Friday morning and it seemed that the ulcer was the least of his problems. Apparently, he'd lost his marbles and was hallucinating, because as he looked up through the windshield of his car, spiders were raining from the sky in downtown San Francisco. The effect would have resembled a Biblical plague if the spiders weren't encased in titanium body armor. Parachutes billowed as the suited arachnids plummeted past skyscrapers. Chute cords disengaged upon impact. The spiders literally hit the ground running, swarming toward some kind of beacon placed in the fountain at city hall. Some of the metal monsters landed on the roof of his car, leaving dents and scratching the paint.

Pullman had wanted to pull a permit that day, which would have granted permission from the city government to rewire the lighting in his downtown car lots. The night before, there had been a huge blackout and all his outdoor lights had been cooked by an electrical surge. According to the morning paper, the blackout had something to do with a huge explosion out in the Pacific, an accident involving the Blue Force. Pullman had been more worried about thieves hitting a darkened car lot than the exigencies of the CMG. Sitting in the car that morning and watching metal spiders fall from the sky, anxiety over his ulcer and the workaday concerns of keeping vandals off his lots at night vanished. He decided that the mechanically powered bugs must be real. He let the engine idle, not sure whether he should high tail out of there or stick around.

Bloody Paralyzer police troop carriers screeched to a halt next to his parked car. San Francisco's finest stormed the halls of city government, sweeping the mechanical spiders up in their trace. *They must be carrying electronic devices controlling the eight-legged monsters*, Pullman guessed. A pain in his gut indicated that his ulcer was flaring up, comforting in a weird way. The ulcer reminded Pullman that he wasn't crazy, just unhealthy and parked in a dangerous place.

Camera crews from the local DFA media affiliate arrived in white vans. Through all the excitement, Pullman noticed that the vans could use some bodywork. He toyed with the idea of placing a business card for his body shop in the window of one of the banged-up news vans with a note offering a discount.

A phalanx of cops appeared on the top of the stairs, holding guns to the heads of the mayor and members of the city council. One of the cops whipped out a bullhorn and bellowed in an electronically amplified voice: "The 1939 revolution has arrived early. The Communist International has taken control of the city. Monopoly capitalism is—"

Pullman didn't hear the rest of the diatribe. He eased his car into the street and motored deliberately toward his house in Pacific Heights, carefully observing all traffic regulations. His dealerships had sold virtually every armored troop carrier to militaristic communist police cells in all the major cities in North America. At the behest of David Banner, he'd had his top mechanic install micro-sized telemetric devices that could cut power to Bloody Paralyzer drive trains via remote control. The control boxes were hidden in his house.

Minutes later, the car dealer was parked in his own driveway. He jettisoned his car's spare tire and stuffed the control boxes in the wheel well. Even a cursory search would quickly uncover such a blatant hiding spot. Pullman couldn't think of an alternative. He needed to get out of town and hook up with the American Army.

That thought brought a sense of unreality washing over him as he slowly steered his car through streets gone empty. America was at war. There hadn't been combat on American soil since the Civil War, seventy odd years ago. Where should he go? He turned his radio on for a news report. All he got was static. The commie fuzz had knocked broadcasters off the airwaves.

Thankfully, Pullman could rely on his own specialized knowledge. He should not travel up the peninsula and through San Jose, several police departments along that route had purchased Bloody Paralyzers and were as red as Karl Marx and Engels combined. What he needed to do was take the coastal highway south and head out to Arizona on back routes when he got in the vicinity of Los Angeles. The big cities in the Southwestern deserts tended to be politically conservative. Their police departments had not purchased any Paralyzers and would likely be loyal to the federal government and the Commonwealth.

Once he was in Phoenix or Albuquerque, he'd have to get on the horn and have a chat with David Banner. Pullman had to hand it to ol' peg leg: the big one-legged Limey had called the shot on the revolution. The car dealer had been a skeptic until today.

168

Pullman experienced a tinge of regret as he pulled out onto the coast highway. The commies would be hell-bent to rip the supermonopoly to ribbons. Too bad there wasn't time to sell DFA stock short. A guy could make a killing that way, because Henry Ford's company was going to take a nosedive. And it looked like the west coast was the communist beachhead. The commies had been quick to cut off communication with the rest of the country. Someone from the west coast who could travel quickly east might catch the stooges on Wall Street with their pants down. He kept himself entertained on the long winding road south by fantasizing over the bucket loads of money he would have been able to make by ignoring the altruistic impulse to give the telemetric devices to the US Army. Maybe there would be time to do both.

Driving throughout the night, nothing calamitous befell his journey until he began descending into the Los Angeles basin the next morning. The coast highway ran past the DFA Grapevine Penal Colony before it skirted the bedroom communities surrounding Los Angeles proper. A sixth sense told Pullman to park his car several yards off the highway and crawl on his belly to a ridge overlooking the prison complex.

A half-mile below the wooded crest, he could see Bloody Paralyzers knocking down the forcefield fences and smashing into the concrete walls of the supermonopoly's prison. Men in black and white zebra striped jumpsuits spilled out of the broken walls. Machineguns in the Bloody Paralyzers cut down DFA guards in their watchtowers. Communist cops were making a jail breakout, bolstering their ranks with inmates, political prisoners that had been incarcerated by the supermonopoly. Men like that would probably be fanatical fighters.

It occurred to Pullman that the jail breaking cops were acting out a long established plan. Barricades were being erected on the coast highway. The ex-prisoners were being handed weapons and urban gray combat fatigues and hustled into the back of cargo vans. Some of the cops wore powered combat suits. The suited cops were tossing bodies into the ocean, hurtling the corpses of prison guards from seaside cliff tops.

There was no way Pullman would be able to drive into the metro regions of southern California. He would have to backtrack north and find a way to cross the Sierras without getting caught by the surging leftist forces that seemed to be all over the place. Where in hell was the US Army? Maybe he needed to take matters into his own hands.

For a wild moment, Pullman contemplated grabbing one of the telemetric devices from his car and zapping the Bloody Paralyzer troop carriers rumbling around on the highway below. He could be like the Lone Ranger, a hero that paralyzed the Paralyzers. That would shake the commies up. Yeah, for about five minutes, and then they'd nab him. With a weary air of resignation he wormed away from the ledge, got back into his car, and drove north.

It had been a long week for General Kwa. Playing the roles of marriage counselor and shrink were not jobs that he relished, but he knew that the stress Jeremiah and Wolfgang had experienced after Nkosinathi married Einstein was still there. The senior officers had merely papered over their emotions by throwing themselves into their work, toiling night and day over the past year. Their psychic wounds had scabbed over, but hadn't fully healed. Kwa felt obligated to do something about it. After all, the Zulu general had single-handedly destroyed one marriage and cobbled together another.

A vacation was in order, a working vacation where the four members of the love rectangle would be forced to spend time together in something other than an official capacity. Kwa would act as chaperone or referee in case the scabs to the emotional wounds were torn open.

Every one of the five vacationers possessed a custom built Mark VII PCS. As brass hats, they'd been first in line when mass-production had taken off. This was Kwa's excuse to bring them together and initiate the healing process. The five would work out a rudimentary Mark VII battle doctrine on a squad level. They would do this on Jeremiah's houseboat, the *Adam Smith*, in a leisurely and unhurried fashion, unencumbered by the constant nagging details of life on the island.

They'd all seen through Kwa's flimsy rationale, of course. But they'd all agreed to take two weeks out of their schedules and give his idea a chance. Amazingly enough, they'd gotten some real work done on the first few days of the working vacation. The mathematical minds of Einstein and Jeremiah had made some genuine inroads to the problem of Mark VII flying formations.

The physicist and the supreme commander were hashing out their ideas on the deck of the *Adam Smith*, when a humpback whale breached so close to the houseboat that everyone on board got wet. A brief, sharp, hard glint of sunlight caught the glass lens of the camera that served as an eye for the mechanical whale. Jeremiah sprang from the chair he'd been sitting on. Pointing into the ocean, indicating the trail of bubbles left behind by the cetacean, he cried, "There's something not right about that whale!"

Einstein looked up from under his bushy eyebrows and asked, "What could be wrong with a whale? A whale is a whale." Nkosinathi sauntered over to the two men and handed them towels. Sopping up water from the soaking he'd taken after the whale's breach, Jeremiah insisted: "That whale looked like it had a glass eye. I've seen my share of whales and their eyes do not reflect sunlight to any appreciable degree." When this failed to impress either Einstein or Nkosinathi, Jeremiah left them to climb up a ladder to the flying bridge.

Kwa was up there, at the helm, watching the ship's sonar. The two of them peered at the blips on the LED screen, representing several pods of humpbacks. The pod closest to the yacht was ten times as large as any other on this side of the island. This huge pod was acting very strange. Normally humpback pods hung together in a tight knit group, warding off sharks or killer whales. The pod with one hundred whales was scattering at a frantic pace, as if savage predators were chasing them.

Jeremiah studied the sonar screen intently and asked, "Could great white sharks be after these whales?" Kwa shook his head and answered: "There aren't any great whites in these waters. Humpbacks don't run from sharks anyway. They don't really run from anything, maybe orcas. Except I don't see any orcas."

Wolfgang climbed up to the flying bridge and stood next to Kwa and Jeremiah, wanting to know what was so interesting. Kwa pointed to the sonar screen and gave an account of the mysterious whales. Jeremiah told him about the whale's glass eye. Wolfgang ran his hand along the stubble of his chin contemplatively, his gaze riveted to the screen because the blips were elongating into a linear formation.

Kwa sat in the captain's chair, turned the engines over, and got the boat moving, following discreetly behind one of the suspicious whales. "Know what I think?" Wolfgang demanded. The two other officers looked at him expectantly. "Red Force has got itself a new spy device, mechanical whales, their answer to our electronically camouflaged spy balloons."

The Zulu general immediately cut the engines. A robotic whale serving as an intelligence-gathering platform would self-destruct if captured. Rather than capture and destroy the alleged espionage devices, they needed to study them. It might be possible to feed the Red Force disinformation.

Jeremiah got on the ship's radio and sent a tight beam transmission to a coastal watchtower within his line of sight, ordering the entire string of towers guarding the Big Island to scrutinize every humpback within ten miles of the shoreline, and report anything unusual back to him.

The watchtowers had men and women inside with binoculars scanning the horizon. They also had radar dishes on their roofs and sonar arrays in the shallow water near their footings. Several minutes passed as the supreme commander's orders were carried out.

"Sir," the radio-speaker built into the forward bulkhead of the *Adam Smith's* flying bridge crackled. "We are tracking one hundred humpbacks that are swimming at roughly thirty miles-per-hour. I'm told that only blue whales can swim that fast."

Jeremiah picked up the bridge microphone. "What are the fast-swimming humpbacks doing?" The radio-speaker responded, "Supreme Commander, give me five minutes to confer with the other towers." Wolfgang scowled at the ocean and made a comment about the artificially fast whales definitely being spy machines. Kwa looked doubtful. He wondered why the robotic whales would give away their mission by swimming so fast. And why were there so many of them?

Minutes dragged by and at last the radio-speaker crackled again. "Sir, the fast-swimming whales have surrounded the island and are moving inland at sixty miles-per-hour. The fastest recorded speed of a dolphin is fifty miles-per-hour. There is zero possibility that humpbacks can swim that fast."

The hair on Jeremiah's head suddenly itched and his scalp crawled. He understood everything that there was to know about the Red Force mechanical whales. He twisted the dial of the ship's radio to broadcast on a general waveband. "Red alert! This is Supreme Commander Halifax. The island is under attack. Alpha Omega Seven! Mark VII soldiers are ordered to destroy humpback whales closest to the shore."

Wolfgang and Kwa leaped from the flying bridge to the main deck without using the ladder. They told Nkosinathi and Einstein to get inside their powered combat suits and kill humpback whales on the shoreline. The two physicists looked bewildered as they stepped into the crystal iron machines. Jeremiah, Wolfgang, and Kwa rushed to get inside their own fusion powered combat suits.

The five of them stood on deck, in their armor, and activated the lasers in the fusion cores. With agonizing slowness, the reactors came online. The suit warriors watched helplessly as a whale shot from the surf to skid up a beach. There was no question that the thing was a machine. Sections of its rubber hide had peeled away from the friction of the rocky shoreline. A silver colored metallic understructure became visible. The thing opened its mouth.

Jeremiah keyed his helmet mike to a broadband channel and said, "Too late to attack. Fly one thousand feet straight up. Spread out and crank forcefields to maximum! Hawaii's about to get nuked!" The five suits were fully powered when a missile blasted from the hideously gaping mouth of the mechanical whale. Flight fans bit hard and the five suit warriors were almost instantly flying above the doomed island. Training kicked in and the five darkened their faceplates, cranked up forcefields into aerial configurations, and revved flight turbines to maximum.

A blinding white light replaced earth, sea, and sky. A nanosecond later, an electromagnetic pulse threatened to swamp the protective energy shields surrounding the five combat suits. Forcefields shimmered gallantly around the flying Mark VIIs: halos deflecting the effects of the EMP on suit electronics.

Like the fist of an angry God, the first shock wave smashed into suit forcefields. The fireball expanded. The howling voices of one hundred nuclear explosions cast a chorus of thermal energy against air, land, and water, knocking the five suited occupants senseless and scattering them to the eight winds. Thermal energy raged and tore at the Big Island, devouring it, pulverizing it, and sending hundreds of billions of tons of soil, buildings, plants, animals, humans, and machines up into the insatiable maw of the fireball.

The fireball continued to expand into a dome seventy-five miles wide: orange, red, and black, veined with lightning as a secondary (and much more potent) EMP pulsed outward. The fireball boiled upward into a mushroom cloud two hundred miles across and one hundred miles tall, overshadowing the entire Hawaiian Island chain, clawing at the edges of outer space. A titan from the pages of mythology straddled the Pacific, roaring with incoherent rage, spawning hurricanes and tsunamis, and awakening mankind to a world forever changed.

Jeremiah awoke into a deathly silence, with a splitting headache, and to what he thought was the bone-chilling cold of outer space. He thought, *faceplate: lighten*. The photosensitive filters disappeared. It was still pitch black. No stars appeared. He thought, *heads up display: altitude*. Ghostly green numbers on the inside of his faceplate told him that he was underwater at a depth of nineteen hundred feet. That was better than being in orbit above the Earth. He did a system diagnosis. The suit was functional but it was operating on battery power. The reactor core had automatically shut down because of an electrical overload. He remembered the multi-layered external forcefields withstanding one electromagnetic pulse. There must have been another pulse that had stripped away external and internal energy shields after he'd lost consciousness. He sipped water and liquid glucose from the helmet nipple, used the suit's indoor plumbing, and feathered the flight turbines to rise to the surface.

The ocean was calm, there was no mushroom cloud dominating the sky, and it was daytime. Jeremiah could tell that much just by looking around as he bobbed in six-foot seas. The nuclear firestorm must have sent gigantic walls of water crashing into the other islands, perhaps as far as North America and Asia, but here it was tranquil. A quick check of the suit's chronometer told him that the Red Force sneak attack had occurred yesterday. He could see smoke rising from the flattened slagheap that had once been Hawaii, about fifty miles away. He turned in the water and faced Maui. It didn't look much better. The real question was: where are the other four Mark VIIs?

He smiled grimly. *Yeah, that's right, where are the suits? More important than the people inside.* World War II was one day old and there was no room for sentimentality. Everything revolved around the Mark VII suits. Red Force vessels might be nearby, listening to the radio spectrum. Despite the risk of detection, he needed to gather the five Mark VIIs together into a fighting force. The greatest danger facing humanity at this moment was the Red Force acquiring Mark VII powered combat suits.

Jeremiah triggered his helmet microphone and spoke over a high-powered broadband: "Albert, Nkosinathi, Wolfgang, Kwa, proceed directly to Kealaikahiki Point on

Kahoolawe." He was forced to speak in plain English because Einstein refused to memorize any Blue Force codes. He couldn't afford to lose a single suit. Grudgingly, the supreme commander admitted that he couldn't afford to lose Einstein either. Herr Doctor Professor was the one person of the five that could be considered indispensable to the Commonwealth in the war years ahead. Albert Einstein's brain was the only thing more valuable than a Mark VII.

The message was repeated at full volume until his voice grew hoarse. Jeremiah's gut told him that there weren't any Red Force surface ships or planes within radio range. Not yet anyway. The unexpectedly strong electromagnetic pulses would have ranged all the way to the mainland. Within five hundred miles of ground zero, nothing, not even a Mark VII forcefield, had been able to withstand the second pulse. He wasn't sure how far the pulse could travel underwater. The vulnerability of Red Force submarines was an unknown factor. In any case, Red subs wouldn't be able to hear his radio transmission.

He thought, *reactor core: power up.* Thousands of micro-lasers ignited the deuterium/tritium composite. Internal forcefields contained the reaction. A tiny sun burned in the belly of his suit. Jeremiah flew out of the peaceful ocean and circled the ruined Big Island at a low altitude, traveling clockwise, broadcasting continually to his fallen soldiers. He saw something in Kiholo Bay. General Kwa's voice sounded in Jeremiah's helmet, in code. "Kwa here. Joining your search pattern."

A second Mark VII popped out of the ocean. Kwa ranged a mile out from Jeremiah's left flank. Together they swept the channels between Hawaii and Maui, succeeding in adding Wolfgang to their squad. Two more laps around the Big Island failed to produce any signs of Einstein or Nkosinathi.

Jeremiah told his squad to abandon the search and make for Kahoolawe. The three military men landed on a beach that was partially sheeted over with black glass. The thermal blast from the nuclear fireball had extended from the Big Island to scorch the two neighboring islands. Every tree on the little island of Kahoolawe had been transformed into a blackened stump. Here and there, tendrils of smoke curled over the devastated landscape. The tsunami hadn't been as big as the supreme commander had thought. This made him question the assumption that the second EMP had reached all the way to the mainland. He wished Einstein were here to answer technical questions.

A jumble of blackened logs pushed apart fifty yards from the three military men. The suited figures of Einstein and Nkosinathi emerged from hiding. Einstein jogged toward the supreme commander, established helmet-to-helmet communication and said, "Jeremiah, the fallout is much worse than anything we've planned for. Please follow my lead for the next two hours, or we may die."

Jeremiah agreed to the professor's request. He pulled away from Einstein and made a tight beam link with the others, informing them of the temporary shift in the command structure. Einstein led the group into a forest of charred palm trees. He made them stand in a row and pointed his right particle beam projector at them. A soft pearly glow bathed the four Mark VIIs. Einstein walked around his friends and hit them from all angles with the lowest setting and widest beam angle that the projector was capable of. Once he was finished, he motioned for Nkosinathi to bathe his suit with an equally mild dose of energy.

His suit cleansed of dust and radioactive minerals, Einstein began digging, scooping handfuls of blasted volcanic soil with fusion powered suit hands and arms. The others followed his lead, shoveling the backfill he was creating to hollow out a steeply angled tunnel under the charcoal stumps of the incinerated palm forest.

They gave each other a second low intensity particle beam bath before crawling into Einstein's cavern. The professor was the last man to enter the fallout shelter; he placed a large rock over the entrance to plug the tunnel, fusing sand and rock with a final mini-burst of plasma.

Einstein touched his helmet briefly against the helmets of each of the other suit warriors, instructing them to power down their Mark VII reactor cores, exit their machines, and seal them tight. Still inside his own suit, Einstein injected half of the $E=MC^2$'s drinking water supply into a bag of adhesive molecular detergent. The professor shut down his suit's reactor core. He clamshelled out of his Mark VII and manually slathered the four other suits with soapy water. He clambered back into his suit and heated the helmets of the other suits with a low level beam until the air trapped inside was warm enough to double internal air pressure. Soap bubbles failed to appear along joint seams. Suit seals had not been damaged by the nuclear explosion. He didn't test his own suit, satisfied that none of the five had ruptured seals.

Grinning sheepishly, the professor apologized because the Mark VII didn't have a built-in piezometer, which would have automatically discovered broken seals. There were a great many features he would have designed into the definitive PCS if weight and simplicity hadn't been overriding considerations. He didn't want to even contemplate the lack of electronic camouflage. Nkosinathi quickly accepted the apology before Einstein could start explaining the many design problems he'd faced.

Jeremiah was reluctant to have all five soldiers remain out of their suits for any length of time because the Red Force could come searching for survivors at any moment. He grudgingly ordered them to remain unsuited because he had to talk to his squad as human beings, not half-machine-cyborgs. They'd all been through a lot in a short time period and emotions could be running high.

His assessment was proven correct as soon as everybody was sitting next to his or her suit. Nkosinathi took a moment to let her eyes fully adjust to the feeble light illuminating the rocky cave from the display panels of the five faceplates and then sprang forward, bodily attacking the supreme commander, screaming, "You bastard! My son is dead! Everyone I know and love except Albert is dead!" She beat his chest with her fists.

Wolfgang jumped to his feet and pulled his ex-wife off the supreme commander, shouting, "Bitch! You're the only one who's lost loved ones? Wolfgang junior was my son too, you slut-tramp-whore." Einstein made a move to attack Wolfgang. An iron grip on the professor's shoulder aborted the potential fight. Kwa shoved Einstein back into a sitting position, took two steps, and separated Wolfgang and Nkosinathi as if he were breaking apart a pair of squabbling children.

The five survivors of the decimated Blue Force returned to their original places. The cave was filled with labored breathing. Jeremiah announced that the temporary change of command was over. Einstein was demoted. The supreme commander was back in charge.

Kwa balled his fists, stood upright again, and glared at the group. Einstein and Nkosinathi dropped their eyes, genuinely afraid of the powerful Zulu. Satisfied that he'd shocked them into acting sensibly, Kwa sat back down. Jeremiah cleared his throat and said, "Albert, tell us about the fallout. How long until we can fly safely?"

The professor raised his head and said glumly, "It is worse than one might suppose. The fireball consumed the nuclear weapons and fission power plants on Hawaii. This will add to the fallout. Virtually all of the contaminated dust will have fallen to the ground or into the sea within the next sixteen hours. The surface of this island will remain dangerously radioactive for six weeks. Fallout radiation cannot penetrate a sealed Mark VII. Even now we could fly through the clouds of fallout dust if we carefully decontaminated after landing in a safe location. Simply washing our suits thoroughly would be sufficient, although the wastewater would have to be carefully disposed. At all cost, our flesh must not come into contact with radioactive dust."

"How far away is safe? Where is the closest safe landmass?" Jeremiah asked.

"If prevailing winds do not shift, the fallout will drift northeast into America and Canada. There is a corral atoll eight hundred miles west-southwest of here: Johnston Island. It is the closest safe landmass, assuming the granddaddy detonation didn't disrupt normal weather patterns and reverse the trade winds."

Jeremiah sat there for several minutes, thinking. He shook himself and started explaining to the group that the Red Force was unlikely to do more than aerial surveillance around Hawaii until the fallout had ceased to be dangerous. At this moment, the enemy was certainly attacking the western United States. The only way the Red Force could capture the five Mark VIIs in combat would be to overwhelm them with wave after wave of fighter jets and missiles, killing the suit warriors inside and leaving the exoskeletons functional. In the absence of hard intelligence that a Blue Force threat had survived the devastating nuclear inferno, the enemy was unlikely to siphon assets away from its nascent front lines in America and Canada.

Silence returned to the miserable little cave. Jeremiah formulated his immediate strategy. "We'll sleep here tonight. In the morning we fly south-southwest until we hit Johnston Island, which is actually an island chain where a small group of guano harvesters live. We'll figure out how to contact the American or British Navy once we've befriended the guano gatherers."

Nkosinathi's sense of humor seemed to have returned as she smirked and said, "I'm sure they'll be overjoyed to have World War II dumped in their laps like a turd in a punch bowl."

They left Kahoolawe for Johnston Island an hour before sunrise. It took three hours to reach the flat corral island, skimming so low over the waves that the Mark VIIs occasionally were splashed by whitecaps. According to Einstein, this would be enough to decontaminate the suits since trade winds had indeed held steady.

Kwa flew with his belly up and his back down to scan the sky for enemy spy planes or fighter jets, flipping over only occasionally to realign within the Mark VII formation. It was the longest three hours of his life. He thought, *God is looking over fools today.* According to visual and radar, the sky was empty and nobody was pursuing them. Yet he could hear the radio chatter of countless Red Army pilots. They must be combing the waters east of Hawaii.

The five landed on a sandy white beach which showed no signs of having been scorched by Satan's forge. Healthy palm trees waved on a soft breeze. Green plants grew on shallow rolling dunes dotted with the grass huts of guano gatherers. The island looked peaceful and calm, untouched by the opening attack of World War II, except for the fact that it had been hastily abandoned. Mooring ropes were freshly snapped on the island's one dock. A ship must have pulled out in such a panic that the crew hadn't even bothered to untie the lines. Meals were left on plates, uneaten, in the grass huts. Clothing, food, and water had all been left behind. The island inhabitants had obviously seen and heard the granddaddy detonation (as Einstein and Nkosinathi were now calling the nuclear strike) and decided that Johnston Island was too close to the cataclysm for comfort.

It wouldn't do to pretend to be guano gatherers and not have a ship tied to the dock. A derelict vessel was already sitting propped up on the beach with wooden chocks. The suited warriors carefully lifted the old tub into the water and placed it next to the dock. It immediately began to sink. Kwa dived into the lagoon and rapidly built a corral pyre under the creaky old guano boat.

The five power suits were stashed in a hut. The clothes left behind by the guano collectors were none too clean: a small price to pay for effective camouflage. The food left behind wasn't exactly gourmet fare, but it was edible and the exhausted survivors of the granddaddy detonation could at last catch their breath and relax.

Einstein and Nkosinathi wandered off by themselves after Kwa warned them not to get too far away from their combat suits and to keep their faces turned down if spy planes appeared overhead. Jeremiah and Wolfgang turned on an ancient hand-cranked ham radio that they'd found in one of the huts while Kwa stood outside scanning the horizon with a pair of field glasses.

"Better take a break, Kwa. Come in here and listen to this," Wolfgang shouted through the open door as he swung the hand crank and adjusted the dial on the primitive radio set. The three military men huddled around the set, listening to a voice that they would quickly grow to hate.

"Citizens of the Commonwealth, this is Vladimir Bakunin, supreme commander of the Red Army. Leftist intellectuals know me under my pen name, Spartacus. The 1939 revolution has arrived two years early. As you have all no doubt heard by now, the forces of global liberation have destroyed the Blue Force on Hawaii and invaded North America. Communist soldiers are sweeping through the western United States, virtually unopposed by the American Army. I am here to make our first demand. Nuclear bombs will destroy Washington DC within two months if Henry Ford and his executive board do not agree in principle to dissolve Daimler-Ford-Alco and place ownership of the ill-fated supermonopoly in the hands of the millions of DFA employees that it has exploited. Details of our proposal are too complicated to share in a radio address. Suffice it to say that the proletariat will be issued equity shares in the companies that employ them and the Commonwealth's stock markets will remain intact. The supermonopoly will be broken into thousands of publicly traded companies that will operate independent of government control. We do not seek to destroy democracy, micromanage the economy, tear down the Crown, or overthrow governments. All we seek is to break the chains of the working class and put the means of production in their hands. This is the meaning of true communism."

Vladimir's address went on for a few more minutes until the signal was lost and the radio emitted nothing other than static. Wolfgang stopped cranking. The three men looked at each other with comprehension and horror spreading across their faces. Up till now, they'd thought some sort of collective megalomania had overtaken the men and women of the Red Force. Vladimir Bakunin's radio address had dissuaded them of that notion. A cool and calculating mind was directing the madness. There were lofty goals behind this war and, considering the hatred sewn by DFA, huge chunks of the Commonwealth were sure to support Bakunin's Red Army. Unfortunately, this knowledge did nothing to solve their immediate problem, which was to figure out a way to link up with the American or

British Navy and not alert the enemy to their existence and intentions.

Twin sonic booms rattled the hinges of the door in the humble little hut. The three men scrambled outside to see two fighter jets orbit their island. The two enemy planes dipped lower and reduced speed to make another orbit, paying special attention to something interesting at the center of the tiny island. The afternoon sun glinted off the jets as they banked for a final run. Red hammer and sickle emblems blazed proudly on their tails. The communist fighters streaked away on an east-northeast heading: the exact direction of Kauai, a reminder that the enemy stronghold was only one thousand miles away.

Inexplicably, one of the jets lost power and tumbled into the ocean. The other jet hovered over the stricken fighter and slowly lowered into the sea. The advanced fighter's ability to hover and land anywhere, even on water, was more than impressive; it was spectacular. The rescue at sea was completed and the second jet rose to resume its heading toward Kauai.

Kwa looked to the center of Johnston Island. Einstein and Nkosinathi were shoveling guano into a wheelbarrow, sweating and laboring under their wide brimmed coolie hats as if their livelihood depended on scooping up bird crap. With a guilty start, the Zulu general realized that the two physicists had presented a very good picture to the Red Army jets, possibly delaying the arrival of communist soldiers by days. Einstein and Nkosinathi had pulled the squad's chestnuts from the fire.

Standing under the concealing eaves of the grass hut, Kwa swept the oceanic horizon with his binoculars, looking for enemy fighter jets. There was a multitude of tiny dots moving against the hazy line where sea met sky. The dots vanished, perhaps returning to Kauai to refuel, although it did look as if some of the planes had fallen from the sky, very strange. He walked around the hut's lanai until he was facing due east. Another set of dots moved against the horizon. Enemy planes were methodically searching this part of the Pacific. It was only a matter of time before communist troops landed on Johnston Island.

Kwa adjusted the focus on his binoculars to better capture a strange drama involving the roving bands of fighter jets close enough to see clearly. Several of the planes had nose-dived into the drink. Other planes were landing next to the fallen jets and attempting rescues. Some of the rescue jets that had landed on the ocean were unable to take wing again. There was some kind of systemic failure plaguing the enemy's fleet of Wasp fighters; certainly good news, widespread mechanical problems would hamper the communists. But anything inexplicable was troubling. Maybe the Commonwealth navies were similarly afflicted. Maybe it was an aftereffect of the granddaddy detonation.

He let the field glasses dangle from his neck. Sweat dripped down the front of the Aloha shirt that he'd found in one of the huts. His eyes fell on the pair of scientists pretending to be guano gatherers. He'd been too hard on them earlier. Time to mend the broken fence. Kwa wandered over to their wheelbarrow, trying to assume a casual air.

Einstein paid the Zulu general no mind. The physicist was on his hands and knees, tearing into the natural fertilizer with his bare hands. He pulled a silvery cable as thick as a man's arm from the filth and held it over his head. Dancing and shouting, Einstein did a fair imitation of a miner that had struck gold. He motioned for Nkosinathi and Kwa to join the celebration. Nkosinathi started dancing. Her rendition of the hula was better than Einstein's clumsy rumba. Kwa looked into the wheelbarrow and saw several pieces of silvery wire protruding out of clumps of decayed bird feces. The metal looked familiar.

"This is a segment of RTS cable," Einstein said happily, waving the thing under Kwa's nose. "That stands for Room Temperature Superconductor." The braided metallic cable wagged back and forth like the tail of an excited dog. It did not move smoothly though. The cable crunched and stiffened with movement as if it were somehow fundamentally damaged.

"I know what RTS stands for," Kwa said irritably. "What's it doing out here? Don't tell me the shit farmers were building a supercollider."

Nkosinathi grabbed her husband's hand and lowered the stiffening cable before it hit Kwa in the nose. "My dear General Kwa, this is a piece of Blue Force technology, blown here by the granddaddy detonation," she said matter-of-factly.

A cloud of doubt passed over the general's face. "Why was it not consumed in the fireball? I thought temperatures inside a nuclear explosion ran into millions of degrees…" Kwa's voice trailed off uncertainly. Einstein took a deep breath, a prelude to a lengthy and highly technical explanation. Nkosinathi stroked the professor's cheek, distracting him, stifling the lecture. Einstein turned away from Kwa and bowed to his wife, intimating that she could offer a more succinct explanation.

Nkosinathi reached for the slice of non-functional superconducting cable. She used it to gesture with. The thing was now as stiff as a rod. "The supercollider had miles of cable like this, thousands of miles, wrapped around supermagnets, ringing the perimeter of the Big Island. There were two pulses. The earliest pulse was caused by the interaction of the nuclear explosions and the Earth's magnetic field. It then interacted with the thousands of miles of shredded superconducting cable and fomented a second pulse. Blasting from the cloud of superconducting chaff, the second pulse emitted a wave of particles that we are calling Oscillating Electron Neutrinos or OEN. These hitherto unknown fundamental particles are like neutrinos in one respect: they can evidently pass through most material without interacting, except OEN particles cannot travel through billions of miles of solid lead like true neutrinos. The OEN particle can probably pass through only a few miles of solid lead. Another difference between OEN particles and neutrinos is that OEN particles oscillate into fully charged electrons when they encounter undamaged lengths of superconducting wire or cable, creating violent electric charges—"

Kwa made her stop. The watered down explanation was going over his head. Nkosinathi smiled and nodded, understanding what was important to the military man. "Albert believes that we can build small nuclear bombs with outer casings of RTS wire chaff: pulse bombs that can permanently disable advanced technology over entire continents. Let me put it in the simplest terms, we can build bombs that will render inoperative every electrical device on Earth."

"Red Army fighter jets are falling from the sky. Is the OEN pulse the reason?" Kwa asked. Nkosinathi assured the general that it could be the only explanation. The burrowing OEN pulse would have passed through rock and water to fry superconducting circuitry and computer chips throughout the Pacific, anywhere from hundreds of miles to thousands of miles from ground zero. Old-fashioned copper-wired electric engines, generators, and so forth would be minimally impacted, perhaps permanently disabled, perhaps not. Modern equipment with superconductors and chips would be decimated.

"When the Red Army fighters over flew this island, you and the professor weren't pretending to be guano gatherers, were you?" Kwa demanded. Einstein blinked at the Zulu general in a distracted manner and asked, "Was that aeroplane an enemy jet fighter?"

"Of course it was an enemy fighter. Don't tell me that—"

A horrible suspicion germinated in Kwa's mind like a noxious weed. He almost didn't want to ask the next question. "Don't tell me that you raised your face to stare at it?" Einstein looked even more distracted. "Did I stare at the aeroplane?" He uttered the question as if he was uncertain of its meaning.

Kwa's voice shook with anger. "The enemy fighter was photographing the two of you during its flyby, with telephoto lenses. Red Army intelligence officers will study these photographs. They will recognize the faces of the great Herr Doctor Professor Einstein and his famous girl Friday."

The towering Zulu glared down at the scientists in exasperation when they failed to respond. The eggheads weren't even contrite. Disgust and anger leaked out of the general like an old inner tube. He told the Einsteins to go inside and talk to Jeremiah about electromagnetic pulse bombs.

Chapter 15

The Red Army Begins to Respond to the EMP Threat

The heat inside the tunnel fortress was unbearable. Half the pumps running the cooling system were still on the fritz a week after the damned electromagnetic pulse had nearly disabled everything that Rudolf Diesel had painstakingly built. The engineer still fumed about it when he had a few seconds to spare. Oppenheimer hadn't warned him that the pulse would be able to travel underwater and through miles of muck and rock to disable the electronics in what was supposed to be the most protected slice of military real estate on the planet. To be fair, Oppenheimer claimed that he was taken as much by surprise as anybody, asserting that there was an unforeseen qualitative difference between the super-pulse and the smaller pulses that the Red Army had generated in its A-bomb tests. The super-pulse wasn't just bigger; it was different in a way that defied explanation.

Oppenheimer didn't cotton to phenomena that defied explanation. He wanted help studying another EMP that was slated to occur in the near future, as if Diesel didn't have enough to worry about. Rudolf left the sweltering hovercraft assembly line, ignoring the catcalls of disgruntled workers, walked down a hallway that could have done double-duty as a sauna, and opened a door with the renowned physicist's name on it.

The head of the Red Army Science Division stretched his long body against the cool leather of a reclining chair, took a sip from an iced tea that had been sitting on a marble desk, and waved Diesel to a seat. It was almost chilly in Oppenheimer's office. Special air conditioning vents had been installed there the day after the super-pulse had knocked the AC out everywhere else in the tunnel fortress. The egalitarian philosophy of the Red Army was imperfect, at best. That reminded Diesel of a problem he was having with assembly line workers. Before Oppenheimer could open his mouth, Diesel said, "My people are excited about the shares of stock promised to the proletariat on the mainland by Supreme Commander Bakunin. They want to know when Red Army equity shares are going to be divided up and will there be a dividend."

Oppenheimer squirmed in his buttery soft calf leather easy chair. It was always amusing to watch the great genius fidget whenever he was thrown an intellectual curveball. Despite his astronomical IQ, Oppenheimer clearly hadn't seen this one coming and had, for the moment, forgotten the discussion about studying the next EMP.

"Umm, your workers want to own shares in the Red Army? They do realize that revolution is not a profitable enterprise?"

"It could be profitable. The Red Army could charge the New Commonwealth a fee for ridding the world of the hated DFA supermonopoly in the same way that exterminators charge a fee to kill rats. The fee could be applied to pay dividends on our shares of Red Army stock. The sale of Red Army surplus equipment and patents could also generate dividends for Red Army shareholders, after the war."

Oppenheimer wasn't sure if he was being played or not. As outlandish as the scheme sounded, it was actually the sort of thing that would appeal to Supreme Commander Bakunin. The head scientist's long graceful fingers waved through the air like cranes performing a mating dance, his way of eliminating a vexing problem that he no longer cared to discuss. The dance ended when Oppenheimer's hands were stuffed back into the pockets of his silk pants. "I brought you here to discuss the next EMP. Patton is probably going to nuke Washington DC in a month or less. It won't concern us here in the fortress. Out in the field, our hovercrafts, jets, and powered combat suits will be vulnerable."

"Jesus H. Christ, Robert. One month? We still don't understand why our circuitry shields failed during the last EMP."

"Don't get your panties snarled into a snit. I don't expect the problem solved in one month. You're to join a frontline combat unit and make experimental modifications on their circuit shields. I get the feeling that Patton is more willing to use nuclear weapons now that Bakunin is supreme commander. We're going to have to lick this EMP problem sooner rather than later, because it's not going to go away."

"Heisenberg should go in the field. He is a physicist. I'm only an engineer."

"Heisenberg is a sissy."

"Then you should go, Dr. Oppenheimer."

"I'm a sissy too."

"When and where do I report, Sir?"

"The *Friedrich Engels* is leaving for Puget Sound tonight at nine. I've assigned Sean, Seamus, and Shay O'Brien as bodyguards. Your sub is in Lock Five. Pack your bags and go now."

By afternoon, Rudolf Diesel found himself standing in Lock Five next to the three O'Brien brothers and their three war seals, all of them looking at the magnificent bulk of the Kilo class submarine named after the great architect of communist theory. The thing looked more alive than mechanical. It had four hydraulic legs, each of them one hundred feet long, extending from its hundred yard long cigar-shaped body. The articulated plates in that body were presently configured to give it a slight S-curve. Anyone with even the tiniest bit of imagination looked at a Red Army Kilo class submarine and saw a crocodile.

At seventeen, Shay was the youngest brother, not only young, but in some ways foolish. He climbed up to the knee joint of one of the hydraulic legs. Oedipus, his war seal, barked joyfully, and scurried up after him, the claws of his flippers catching neatly on plasteel girders, short otter-like limbs propelling him upward. Diesel marveled at the agility of the war seal. He was always impressed by their ability to move nimbly on land. Sometimes they even climbed trees.

The oldest brother, Sean, walked up to the engineer, looked down at the shorter man from his imposing height of six-foot-four, and said, "My brother's not as silly or as young as he looks, Mr. Diesel. The three of us have seen action in North America. We helped break communist revolutionaries out of DFA prisons." Sean raised his voice and shouted for Shay and Oedipus to climb down.

The four humans and three war seals trooped up a gangway and into the *Friedrich Engels*. Diesel had been awarded the luxury of a private berth, which he had to share with three strapping young men, three war seals, and seven powered combat suits. There was barely enough room in the so-called private berth to take a deep breathe.

Klaxons sounded the length of the great steel and plastic crocodile. Red lights blinked in every cabin, corridor, and compartment. Internal forcefields within the hull plates crackled, increasing the tensile strength of the plasteel composite fifty fold. Sliding panels in the domed roof of Lock Five slowly peeled away. The primordial ooze flowed down upon the *Friedrich Engels*.

The huge bubble of air that had been inside the lock ballooned upward, aided by the clawing passage of the four-legged submarine. Hydraulic motors whirred and labored against the viscous muck, the decay of one billion years of sea-life. The sub's nose tilted up at a 45-degree angle. The vessel's articulated body undulated in concert with the mechanical beast's hydraulic legs, clawing and worming its way through the slime.

The private berth was anything but a luxury. Since it was located against one of the articulated hull plates, it swung back and forth with the serpentine motion of the sub's body, a recipe for seasickness. And there was no room in the jam-packed cabin. Diesel found a war seal's butt inches from his face. The O'Brien brothers and the fishy smelling seals were crammed all around him. A sardine packed in a tin would have had more room. Sean ordered his brothers to, "Give the old man some space." Powerful young arms pushed against powerful young bodies, creating a little pocket around the engineer. Diesel could still barely take a deep breath. At least the undulating motion ceased once the sub reached open water, a small blessing.

The journey under the Pacific was nothing like the sea cruises that Diesel had taken before joining the Red Force thirteen years ago. There was no opportunity on board the *Friedrich Engels* to be invited to the captain's table for a spot of fine dining. He and the boys ate standing up. They had a choice of protein bars, carbohydrate bars, or veggie bars. During mealtime, the seals were thrown masses of dried fish. The sound of snapping jaws and the horrific odor of processed fish did little to stimulate the appetite. Not only did they eat and sleep with war seals, humans and pinnipeds used the same toilet. Diesel could, at any rate, appreciate the engineering involved in the cross-species water closet.

The trip became even less of a pleasure cruise about one thousand miles from the mainland. The American Navy got lucky and caught the *Friedrich Engels* in a fierce depth-charge barrage. Sirens wailed and red lights flashed as the O'Brien boys hustled Diesel into his combat suit. Only after he was safely ensconced inside the titanium skin and buckled to a bulkhead did they order the war seals into pinniped suits and put on their own personal armor.

A series of concussions rocked the submarine. Diesel banged around the padded interior of his suit with gritted teeth. This shouldn't be happening. American technology was inferior and they shouldn't be able to strike a Red Army war machine. Another sort of vibration could be felt through the titanium soles of his boots. War seal combat suits were being ejected from torpedo tubes. The *Friedrich Engels's* engines revved. The vessel tilted downward and then leveled out. Communist war seals must be attacking American ships and winning a sea battle. There should be battleships plunging into the depths, but Diesel couldn't hear or feel any of that. Nor could he gauge how long the battle lasted. Green lights glowed on the bulkheads and an all-clear signal bleated a soothing note inside his suit helmet. The *Friedrich Engels* had survived.

The aging engineer's euphoria proved to be fleeting. Hours after the successful conclusion of the sea battle, a messenger appeared in the doorway of their compartment, bearing an envelope from the captain, who Diesel still hadn't met. The engineer read the letter out loud to the boys. The sub had been slated to land on one of the islands of the thoroughly pacified Puget Sound region: a milk run. Regrettably, George Patton's siege of San Jose had taken a nasty turn. The *Friedrich Engels* had a new mission. It would be landing under fire in San Francisco Bay. The soldiers on board should sit tight and wait to hear from their battle-lion commanders for more detailed orders.

Diesel expected the gung-ho O'Brien brothers to react with glee. Their gazes dropped to the stamped aluminum deck plating under their boots. Shifting their weight nervously from foot to foot, the three of them made mumbled comments about San Jose being a communist graveyard. They brightened when Diesel remarked that their mission surely hadn't changed, even if the sub's mission had. The engineer still had to make his way safely to land and get his hands on the EMP shields of the hovercrafts, jets, and combat suits in Patton's North American Task Force. The boys still needed to act as his bodyguards, hardly frontline duty.

These reassuring words proved prescient when the boys' battle-lion commander, Leftenant-colonel Wilfred Stokes paid them a visit that evening. Stokes informed them that Foxtrot Battle-lion would be the last to leave the submarine. Its prime directive was to get senior engineer Rudolf Diesel on shore safely. Stokes talked specifics with the young soldiers, describing the conditions in the bay and what he wanted them to do after being launched from torpedo tubes. He turned to leave, in a hurry to get to his next squad. Diesel grabbed the leftenant-colonel by the elbow and begged him to answer a few questions, not about the landing in the bay, but about his experience when the Hawaiian EMP had hit. As far as Diesel knew, nobody in the world had more prosthetic hardware than Stokes or had achieved a more profound integration of machine and flesh.

Stokes nodded brusquely and agreed to the request. He'd heard a great deal of nonsense about the EMP. "For starters, there were two pulses, seconds apart, not one. I felt them distinctly. Pulse number one danced harmlessly around the shielding. Pulse number two burrowed into me electronic innards and nearly tore me guts out." The man that the boys affectionately called "tin man" nodded again and left the compartment.

Diesel was lost in thought until Seamus nudged him and said, "Wanna know what I think about the pulse, Mr. Diesel?" The engineer's head bobbed absentmindedly. "The pulse is a good thing. It saved our bacon. Me and the boys'd parachuted into the Phoenix DFA prison with our battle-lion when the Hawaii pulse hit. Knocked out all the searchlights in the guard towers. Opened all the electromagnetic locks on the cell doors. Shut down the forcefield fences. Made the prison break a piece of cake. I love electromagnetic pulses. Ha, ha, ha."

Sean added, "It did help a lot. Only bad thing that night was tin man getting thrown for a loop." Shay put in his two cents: "I'll bet anything that old Blood and Guts Patton's planning a couple hundred jail breaks around the next pulse. I'm glad, too. Those guys we break out of DFA prisons fight like mother-fuckers!"

Diesel squinted thoughtfully and wondered out loud: "Isn't it a shame the Red Army runs on electric engines powered by nuclear driven steam turbines? If it ran on diesel engines, EMP would have no effect."

"Nope," Sean contradicted. "We tried to crank over some diesel trucks the night we hit the Phoenix prison. Wouldn't crank over worth a shit. Sorry, Mr. Diesel. I know how you invented the diesel engine and all."

"The trick would be to get a diesel engine running without an electric starter motor," Diesel said, more to himself than to the oldest brother. "A hand crank won't work in most applications. One would need superhuman strength to turn over a multi-cylinder diesel engine. The lack of glow plugs is a problem too." He stopped talking, brow furrowed with concentration.

Sean pounded the older man in the back and said, "Invent diesel panzers or hovercrafts that we can hand crank and we could pulse the crap out of the capitalist blood-suckers. The vampires gotta butt load more military hardware than we thought back on the island. Their aeroplanes are nearly as good as ours. You'll find out soon. We hit the LZ tomorrow. It ain't gonna be no picnic."

They slept in their hard suits that night, as per orders from Leftenant-colonel Stokes. The sub motored cautiously between the twisted steel beams of the shattered Golden Gate Bridge without incident as dawn approached. One of the nasty surprises that the Americans had sprung on the communists was the overnight conversion of DFA's huge civilian aeroline fleet into a bomber fleet. DFA pilots had remained loyal to the parent company throughout the global strikes due to their high salaries and government safety regulations prohibiting long work hours. The upshot was that the American Aeroforce was two hundred times larger than Red Army Intelligence and HP equations had predicted.

That morning, DFA bombers practically clogged the sky over the southern part of the San Francisco Bay. And they weren't dropping bombs into the bay, but torpedo equipped and combat suited war seals. The Friedrich Engels began absorbing direct torpedo hits as it churned past the town of Mountain View, three quarters of the way to the Landing Zone in the Alviso Slough. The capitalist barrage was unprecedented in its ferocity, probably because the bourgeois military was defending DFA world headquarters, the rotten heart of monopoly capitalism.

In an attempt to evade the enemy war seals, the sub dug into the mud and silt of the bay. Diesel's private cabin whipped back and forth with the seasickness inducing motion of crocodile mode. Enemy war seals burrowed into the mud in pursuit. Explosions again rocked the sub's hull. Finding no respite, the sub clawed its way back into open water.

The captain of the *Friedrich Engels* ordered most of the sub's complement of war seals into the bay. Diesel was sweating profusely inside his power suit as the deck plating under his feet vibrated and lurched like a bucking bronco. The sub was simultaneously jettisoning friendly war seals and enduring explosions against its hull from suicidal enemy pinnipeds. He looked across the cabin at Sean's faceplate. The oldest of the O'Brien brothers was white-faced, eyes wide with terror, lips nothing more than two thin white lines drawn across sweat soaked skin. To Diesel, the fear on Sean's face was worse than the pounding that the sub was taking.

Enemy torpedoes ruptured the sub's outer skin in a dozen different places. A sudden surge of forcefield energy bled uselessly into the bay water. Forcefield conduits were designed to shut themselves off at the point of contact with water. Normally, this protocol

184

would protect the integrity of the entire energy defensive system in the case of a breach or two. That day, the sub's forcefield system was overwhelmed and it shorted out.

The captain's voice could be heard inside the helmet of every soldier on board. "Initiating self-destruct sequence on count of five. Five. Four. Three. Two. One. Self-destruct." Explosive bolts built into the *Friedrich Engels* at key junctures blew the sub into thousands of pieces.

Clouds of bubbles flowed past Diesel's faceplate. He could feel his body spinning like a pinwheel. Plasteel girders from the sub's mechanical legs were falling all around him as though crazed lumberjacks were knocking down trees. His suit had aquatic propulsion fans, but he didn't think to turn them on.

The metallic shape of a Red Army war seal flew at him from the muddy confusion. Oedipus grabbed Diesel with his front flippers. The seal cranked his propulsion fans and churned southeast through the chaos, heading toward the landing beach.

Diesel's titanium legs sunk into gooey mud. He stood upright. The water was only two feet deep. He slogged forward. On dry land, it looked as though a lightning storm was raging from the shoreline to the city. Hundred-ton Red Army hovercrafts were pounding troop carriers and panzers from the American Army. Forcefield conduits on the American armor were rupturing under the onslaught, sending flashes of sheet lightning and sizzling electrical arcs into the morning air.

Sean and Seamus grabbed Diesel by the armpits and hauled him up the beach. Shay trotted behind his brothers in case an enemy seal arose from the bay and attacked them from the rear. The war seals, Jason, Thesus, and Oedipus, formed a wedge in front of the humans and galloped ahead. There was a crush of Red Army soldiers and seals crawling from the water and running into the communist battle line. The soldiers from the *Friedrich Engels* were unable to join their assigned units, so they merged with the closest formations that they could find.

The O'Brien brothers flung themselves and the old man behind the hulk of a burned out Yankee Panzer. Sean clicked his helmet against Diesel's and said, "Look at the sky." Diesel looked up. The sky was devoid of American bombers and fighters. Sean said, "Look at the bay." Diesel broke helmet contact and glanced in the direction that they'd come from. The tortured and mutilated fuselages of countless aeroplanes stuck up from the shallow water like so many tombstones. The dozen hovercrafts that had been in the submarine's cargo hold were floating on the mirror smooth surface of the water like fat bullfrogs on lily pads, hanging back in reserve. Sean tapped helmets once again with the aging engineer. "Look at the city." The line of American troop carriers and panzers was gone. The fighting had moved into the urban jungle. The enemy was being smashed back. The *Friedrich Engels* had not died in vain. The reinforcements it had supplied to Patton's army had apparently pushed the siege to a tipping point, breaking the capitalist resistance.

The fear and horror of the landing receded. Diesel remembered why he was here. He stood and made hand signs at the boys: "This is no time for a nap. We've to find General Patton."

Henry Ford never thought he'd look out the window of his penthouse and see a war zone again, not after the global strikes had been crushed. Only now was he realizing that the strikes had been a mere dress rehearsal, a prelude to another World War, and this one was not nation verse nation, but a fight between economic systems. The richest man on Earth, the richest man in history, looked out the wall of glass and forced himself to stare unblinkingly. He hadn't gotten to be the richest man ever by avoiding a fight.

The building he was in, DFA headquarters, still stood, but half the structures in San Jose had been flattened. His window faced northwest, toward the bay. At one time, the skyline of San Jose had blocked his view of the bay. Today, he had an unimpeded vista of that once beautiful body of water. What the new landscape had to reveal, he didn't want to see. Armored hovercrafts (with forcefields more powerful than anything his people had designed) were boiling out of the bay. Clouds of Red Army fighter jets clung perniciously above the communist armor. American panzers and fighters were withdrawing, using the rubble of the city to cover their retreat. He could see it all from his picture window, developing like a drama on a movie screen.

Alfred Sloan broke into the office, panic made his voice high-pitched. "Henry, for the love of Pete, let's get moving! A chopper is waiting on the roof. General Eisenhower says he will unleash ten fighter squadrons the instant we're aeroborne. They're going to hold the line at Gilroy. We'll land at Sixth Army Headquarters in Sacramento." Sloan grabbed Ford's arm to physically drag him upstairs. The chairman of the board fought off the efforts of his president and shouted: "God curse Eisenhower to hell! I'm not going anywhere. You want to turn yellow and run, Alfred? Be my guest."

Sloan had an encrypted radiophone in his hand. The voice of the chopper pilot on the roof sounded tinny and indistinct from the phone's small speaker, although it was obvious that the pilot was begging the executives to get on board his craft. The president of DFA brandished the phone at Ford as if it were a weapon. The chairman shook his head and said, "The commies know I'm in this building. That's why they haven't flattened it. They want to negotiate."

Missiles rose from the advancing avalanche of armored hovercrafts, hitting all around the headquarters building, partially burying the retreating American panzers. The headquarters building shook, but didn't sustain any serious damage. A fresh wing of Yankee jets swooped onto the inexorable Red Army advance. Small fireballs dotted the sky as missiles flew back and forth between the two sides. Yankee Panzers crawled from the detritus that had once been a great city and opened fire. Small assault units, Red Army soldiers and war dogs in suits, spilled from their massive hovercrafts and flowed toward pockets of resistance.

The fighting grew closer and closer to Ford's picture window as the pockets were collapsed. Suited enemy combatants seemed to grow larger as they moved into the center of the city. It was possible to distinguish between humans in powered combat suits and their metal-clad dogs. Red Army men, women, and canines scurried from one cairn of blasted rubble to another. When shells or slugs connected with their power suits, flashes of blue energy lanced outward like thunderbolts from a storm cloud. The hovercrafts were no longer firing on Yankee Panzers with main guns. In most cases, communist suit warriors used titanium arms and hands to tear lightly armored American panzers apart like can openers. The capitalist soldiers inside also wore suits, which were no match for the PCSs of the invading Red Army.

Something caught the corner of Ford's eye as he pressed against the plate glass window. Looking straight down, he saw a small eight-legged combat suit shaped like a spider, about as wide a manhole cover. The thing crawled to the middle of First Street at a rapid clip and pried open an actual manhole cover. It peered curiously into the darkness of the storm sewer, decided a capitalist combatant was holed up there, and slipped underground. Ford shuddered. He hated insects, especially insects that could rip a man's head off.

The phone in Sloan's hand kept begging for a response. The president looked at the thing with a bewildered expression, as if he'd forgotten what a radiophone was. "Alfred." Ford's voice was icy calm. "The freaking commies will nuke Washington DC if we retreat. Innocent people will die if we turn yellow. We've got to stand our ground and strike some kind of deal with these maniacs. You and I are the majority shareholders, nobody else can make a bargain."

With his hand shaking, Sloan put the radiophone to his mouth. The pilot was instructed to save himself and fly to Sacramento. Ford resumed his vigil, staring at the action directly below on First Street. Several metallic spiders had swarmed down the storm drain, so there must be American soldiers down there. Dogs in power combat suits were also arriving on the scene. The suited canines could move so fast through the wreckage blocking the congested streets, it was hard to follow their progress. Ford couldn't imagine how any holdouts would survive the night.

The fighting farther away from the headquarters building was dying down. Suited Red Army humans and animals were returning to their hovercrafts and recharging their batteries. Communist spiders and dogs became more numerous on First Street, sniffing here and there throughout the smashed landscape, looking for capitalist survivors. Red Army fighter jets were landing on streets in the downtown area. They had vertical takeoff and landing capability, Ford noted, which DFA fighter jets did not.

Darkness overtook the battlefield. The hovercrafts turned on searchlights and moved forward. Ford could sense that he and Sloan were being surrounded. It was going to be a long night. Ford pounded his intercom and demanded that somebody bring coffee and sandwiches to his office. There was no response. Sloan hesitated to tell his boss that the building held only two occupants. Ford must have figured it out for himself because he returned to the picture window, morose and taciturn.

The chairman of the board and the president of the once mighty supermonopoly watched the lights of Red Army vehicles and suits come and go in the darkened street. They listened to the rattle of sporadic gunfire and the occasional scream, waiting for the new day sleeplessly.

Armored hovercrafts and power combat suits were nowhere in sight as a gray dawn gave way to harsh daylight. The San Jose police department had replaced the Red Army, regular foot patrols resumed where they'd left off, almost as if the battle had not occurred. The local cops directed garbage trucks and city workers. The carnage of the past weeks was slowly whittled away. The normalcy was as frightening to Ford and Sloan as the battle had been. They'd heard news reports that communist police cells controlled hundreds of cities in North America. It was hard to distinguish propaganda from reality. Phone service to San Jose had been cut off since the war began and the airwaves were under the jurisdiction of the Red Army. Watching the methodical police work caused the executives to reevaluate what they'd heard. Maybe there really was a continent-wide mass uprising. Ford had paid those communist police bastards, paid to have his own throat cut.

The biggest chunks of war debris had been cleared off of First Street late in the day. A single main battle hovercraft slid slowly along the key thoroughfare, taking up both lanes.

Scraps of garbage whirled around the sluggish machine in a series of small tornadoes, kicking up pieces of old newspaper fifty floors to where the executives watched. The hovercraft stopped in front of the DFA building, collapsing heavily on woven titanium/ceramic plenum chamber skirts.

A hard-faced officer climbed out of the hovercraft's cupola. He wore a cotton or wool uniform, with a red beret. A large pistol of exotic design dangled from an expensive looking holster and gun belt. Incongruously, he carried a blue-collar worker's lunch pail. A pure white Bulldog jumped out of the war machine and trotted beside the officer. Suited soldiers gushed out of the cupola and took positions on the street. The hard looking officer and his dog entered the DFA building. Ford and Sloan were not looking forward to meeting this particular visitor.

George Patton kicked in the door of Henry Ford's office. Knocking and entering politely would have been too bourgeois. The general did introduce himself and shake hands with the two robber barons after he told Willy (the Bulldog) to take a nap in a corner of the room. Sloan was trembling after the introduction. Ford looked mad, a controlled fury, as he calmly asked the communist military leader what business he had with DFA.

The lunch pail was slammed onto the polished mahogany of Ford's desk. Patton pulled a chair next to the desk, sat down, and pulled out food items: ham and cheese sandwiches on rye bread, coffee, and slices of apple pie wrapped in cellophane. Willy woke from his nap at the smell of food. Patton threw the bulldog a cautionary look, and turned to Ford and Sloan, inviting them to have lunch. While the plutocrats ate, Patton talked. He described the submarines that were even now swinging into place on the eastern seaboard. He gave details about the nuclear-armed missiles that were being targeted on the capital of the United States. Finally, he explained the effect that three hundred-megaton blasts would have on the cities and countryside of Virginia and Maryland, not to mention DC itself.

Ford looked up from his sandwich and growled, "You idiotic Reds have given so much advanced notice, the Congress and President have buried themselves in bunkers. Everyone living in DC has headed for the hills." Willy didn't like the tone in Ford's voice. The Bulldog stood and walked closer to the three men.

Ignoring his dog, Patton took out a nail file and went to work on a hangnail. He held out his hand to judge if the nail gloss had been scuffed, decided it looked okay, and set his hand down. He went on to detail information that the DC metropolitan police had given him earlier in the day, hastening to add that these cops were loyal communists. The Congress and the President were hunkered down inside what would become ground zero of the capital city. Their bunkers would not withstand the coming nuclear blast. They would be vaporized along with hundreds of thousands of other people that had not moved far enough away. Those deaths would be on Ford's conscience.

Sloan wanted to know what kind of terms Patton was offering. Patton asked harshly if the two magnates had listened to Vladimir Bakunin's radio addresses. They nodded unhappily. Patton pulled a small, but old-fashioned, reel-to-reel tape recorder and spoke into the microphone: "If you've heard Red Army Supreme Commander Vladimir Bakunin's demands, then you know what it'll take to abort the nuclear missile strike on Washington DC. What say you?" He held the microphone next to Ford's face. The chairman of the board said coldly, "Suck eggs. I'll die before turning my business over to a pack of commie pinko fags."

Willy grunted softly. Patton gave the dog a questioning look and moved the microphone next to his muzzle. Willy tilted his head back and let out a shrill yip. The Bulldog was a trained lie detector and he'd just confirmed the veracity of Ford's statement. The general turned off the tape recorder and said, "My work here is done. DC will be wiped out in a month. Capitalist America will fight to the last man after we destroy its government. All to the good. We'll get the war over quicker that way."

He tried to push back his chair to stand. Sloan grabbed an armrest, forcing the general to listen to the sweet light of reason: "No. Let's work out a compromise. Put us in front of Bakunin if you have to. His plan amounts to a kind of profit sharing scheme. We already do that on a limited basis."

"Bullshit," Ford said. "It's not profit sharing. It's communism. And it won't work. It will cause more harm in the long run than nuking Washington. Issuing ultimatums is not negotiating."

Patton fumbled to turn his tape recorder back on and jam the microphone into Ford's face. Willy was keyed on the chairman, analyzing everything he said for truthfulness. The dog gave out several soft yips as Ford kept speaking. "The communists think you can take a grease monkey off the assembly line, trade his blue-collar for a white-collar, call him a manager, and bingo he's running the place. What's the first thing the grease monkey's gonna do? Raise wages. What are all the other ignorant grease monkey managers gonna do? Same thing: raise wages. What happens next? Hyperinflation: helluva lot worse than deflation. Global hyper-inflation and the world economy comes tumbling down like a house of cards."

Sloan shook his head. Patton hastily turned off his tape recorder, sensing that Sloan was going to argue the opposite point of view. The general didn't want to give Vladimir an excuse to forgo bombing DC; nor did he want the war to come to a quick end.

The president of DFA argued, "So you don't randomly pluck a grease monkey off the assembly line. You and I run a transition team that either keeps existing managers in place, or we put freaking Harvard MBAs in charge of the new companies. Our transition team will decide where the fault lines lay: break up the supermonopoly in a rational manner. And we'll get paid doing it. This Bakunin character is not your run-of-the-mill commie. He's got a brain. We can reason with him."

Ford turned his back on Sloan after giving him a Bronx cheer. The president of DFA wasn't going to be put off that easily. He stood up, gripped Ford by the shoulders, and spun his swivel chair to face Patton and Willy. Sloan nodded at the general and his Bulldog. "They're going to take our company away from us, Henry. These people have atom bombs. We can either be robbed, or we can create Ford-Sloan Transition International and charge them a hefty fee."

Patton was immensely relieved that he'd turned his tape recorder off and that he hadn't brought any witnesses to this meeting. Bakunin would eat up the idea of Ford and Sloan masterminding the breakup of the supermonopoly. The general got out of his chair and asked the two plutocrats if they had any portable radios on this floor. Silently, Sloan handed over his small radiophone. He made them say out loud that they didn't have any other means of communication. Willy barked affirmatively when Ford and Sloan admitted that they were bereft of contact with the outside world. Patton got on his own radiophone and ordered a squad of soldiers up into the headquarters building. The tycoons were going to be held in the penthouse as prisoners until Washington DC was reduced to smoking ruin. After that, they would be shipped to Kauai where Supreme Commander Bakunin would do whatever he wanted with them.

Willy and Patton marched out of the room: the general whistling a jaunty tune, the dog wagging his tail. Ford walked to his picture window and pounded on the glass impotently.

Rudolf Diesel knew that the Phoenix prison was the ideal facility for testing the effects of the next EMP on circuits, engines, electromagnets, and other electronic components. It had an elaborate electronic command post that monitored and controlled every electric lock, forcefield, TV camera, and light bulb. Also, there was a permanent cyber-record of what had happened during the first EMP when the prison had been under DFA management.

Diesel hungered to gain control of the Phoenix prison and set up various pulse shields around all that electronic hardware before Washington was nuked, which would be in about three days or as soon as the Supreme Commander Bakunin gave the final go-ahead. The major obstacle stymieing Diesel's plans was the unfortunate reality that the Americans had recaptured his prize. It wasn't even a prison any longer, but the largest base for the American Army west of the Mississippi.

Leftenant-colonel Wilfred Stokes listened to Diesel's pleas with a mixture of forbidding and wariness. Any mission to seize the military base would have to be led by Stokes, since he'd led the original Phoenix breakout during the early stages of the war. The two operations would be entirely different. Stokes couldn't make Diesel see that. There would be no element of surprise. There was a gargantuan American garrison in Phoenix, armed to the teeth, not a bunch of limp-wristed prison guards. Worse, like much of the Southwest, the city of Phoenix was not under the control of a communist police cell.

Stokes finally agreed to lead the mission after the O'Brien brothers joined the argument. Stokes's agreement was only half the battle. General Patton had the final word in approving a major offensive. It was no easy matter to secure an interview with the commander of the North American Task Force. They tried bulling past the guards at the entrance to the DFA building (re-christened NATF Headquarters). They tried sweet talking Patton's secretary and then bribing one of his adjutants. Nothing worked. Diesel did pick up a few scraps of information while trying to get past the bureaucratic wall around the four star general: Patton was embroiled in a serious problem that involved the Bloody Paralyzer armored personnel carriers used by communist cops on both sides of the front line. It seemed that these vehicles were stalling out at strategically bad moments. This was a problem in enemy territory because communist police acted as a fifth column, performing various duties such as disrupting the landing of capitalist reinforcements from Britain, Germany, Japan, and Zululand.

Diesel told the adjutant that had refused the bribe that he could solve the mystery of the stalling armored personnel carriers. But he had to have a meeting with Patton. Within a half hour, he was sitting face-to-face with old Blood and Guts. The aging engineer started the meeting by asking if he could get his hands on one of the suspect Bloody Paralyzers. Patton told him that his combat engineers had dismantled four or five of the cursed things, to no avail. Diesel promised that he could do better. He wasn't a combat engineer. He was the most senior engineer in the whole Red Army. Patton made a chopping motion with his right hand and said, "Done. Report to the motor pool tomorrow morning."

"Begging the General's pardon. I'll have to do it after we take Phoenix."

"Explain yourself. And this had better be good."

The senior engineer gave a full account of why he needed to take control of the Phoenix prison before nuclear bombs fell on Washington DC. Of all the high-ranking generals, Patton had the best understanding of technical matters and the need for research. He also had a larger strategic picture to consider. Capitalist resistance was stiffening. It was no longer possible to mount a light raid into enemy territory. Hundreds of main battle hovercrafts, thousands of jet fighters, and one hundred thousand suited dogs and humans would be needed for any push east. An offensive was already planned. Machines and soldiers were already staging on the eastern slope of the Sierras. The Red Army was going to roll across Nevada and Idaho to attack the industrial Midwest and Northeast: union country where communist police cells held local power and the population was militantly opposed to the supermonopoly and the puppet government that kept it in power. By contrast, the Southwest was a hard nut to crack, union membership was weak, antipathy to DFA was lukewarm, patriotism for the US government and the Commonwealth was red hot.

"My guess is that America's A-bomb is being built in the southwestern desert, somewhere along the New Mexico/Mexico border," Diesel said nonchalantly. Patton's jaw immediately jutted outward as he retorted, "Intel says the Commonwealth is working on nuclear weapons in the Gobi desert."

"Britain may well be working on nukes in Asia. America has to be running a separate program. George, you are an American. Will your people be willing to gamble on Britain inventing and building A-bombs in a timely manner, not to mention transporting sufficient quantities across an ocean on the verge of becoming a communist lake?"

Patton sat there, fuming and stewing, not answering Diesel's question. The senior engineer pressed forward with his argument: "Within seconds of the successful test of an American nuke, we will know about it. The Americans will have to strike with their new weapon, hard and fast. As long as the Red Army occupies only the western coast, the Americans can use nuclear weapons against us. They sure as heck have the bombers to get the job done. Considering that A-bombs are America's only hope, it is not going to rely on a tenuous supply line stretching to the Gobi Desert. The Yankees are building large numbers of A-bombs here, on this continent, I'm certain. They are going to want to shovel A-bombs into bombers the way a fireman shovels coal into the firebox of an old steam locomotive."

The imagery of mass-produced American A-bombs caused Patton to swallow convulsively. He then contemplated the advantage of throwing the enemy a slider. Eisenhower was expecting a communist lunge into the heartland. That attack could easily be turned into a diversion and the brunt of the offensive could swing south into Arizona and east into New Mexico.

Old Blood and Guts admitted to changing his mind. Diesel would get his way. The engineer was to report to the motor pool and take a cursory look at one of the balky armored personnel carriers that were causing so much trouble for the Red Army's police allies. Patton warned him not to get overly engaged in this problem though; within a couple days, he and Stokes's battle-lion would be joining the buildup in the eastern Sierra.

Diesel left the meeting with a sense of victory mingled with impending doom. He'd talked General Hard-ass into attacking Phoenix. He'd also put himself into the line of fire.

Diesel's perfunctory examination of the recalcitrant armored personal carrier did no good other than to provide a distraction for two days. On the third day, he found himself in Nevada's Smoky Valley. Diesel, Stokes, and the O'Brien boys piled into a hovercraft and led their battle-lion into formation alongside several armored columns swinging south across Nevada.

The slender ribbon of asphalt leading down into the Grand Canyon State was inadequate for the heavy division. Most of the hovercrafts had to strike cross-country. Diesel could see that the hundred-ton battlewagons were poorly designed for desert warfare. Vertical obstacle clearance was not enough to hurtle over the tree-like saguaro cactus. A true fix would have involved installing taller flexible skirts around the plenum chambers, not a practical option in the field. Fine, but cutting blades could easily be installed on the bows of the 'crafts flexible skirts. The vibrating skirts would transmit a chopping action to the blades. Cactus could be chopped down, rather than laboriously mowed. He held his piece, not wanting to step on the toes of the local engineers.

A more serious problem didn't bear an easy solution out here in the field. While the main battle hovercraft had stealth capabilities that were epic in the Pacific, the battleground they were originally intended for, out here in the desert they were about as stealthy as a herd of stampeding dinosaurs. Monstrous clouds of dust mushroomed outward from the air cushions that the 'crafts rode on, announcing their location miles in advance.

Diesel was still grousing over the great rooster tails of dust kicking up from the armored columns when Stokes's Foxtrot Battle-lion thundered down from the hills surrounding Phoenix. Stokes got Diesel's attention with a command to don personal combat armor. Every canine and human soldier inside the Foxtrot command hovercraft was scrambling to suit up and Diesel needed to stop his wool gathering.

Two miles out from the American Army base that had once been a prison, the 2nd Division's hovercrafts let loose their complement of war dogs. The sight of metal clad Bulldogs sprinting at sixty miles-per-hour cheered Diesel. Here at last was technology suited for the desert. The dogs' tan colored powered armor was practically invisible as the canine teams swerved in between towering saguaro cactus. The amount of dust they kicked up was negligible.

Artillery within the American base fired on the armored air cushion vehicles. The Yankee gunners were unable to see the well-camouflaged war dogs that were only a few hundred yards from the forcefield fence protecting their camp. Explosions erupted around the Red Army 'craft, knocking a handful out of commission. Older model Wasp warplanes took off from an aerofield within the American compound. The 2nd Division's aero arm engaged afterburners, hungry to dogfight. American strumwagens rolled out into the desert to meet the communist land army.

Diesel had no business bothering Stokes while a battle loomed. The engineer tapped his helmet against the leftenant-colonel's helmet anyway, pointing at a pack of Bulldogs visible through a view slit. Whatever Diesel was about to say died stillborn on his lips because Stokes made a violent chopping motion with one of his suit arms, calling for silence.

With his helmet still connected to Stokes, Diesel heard orders for the battle-lion commanders to break off the attack. Spook central had uncovered solid intelligence indicating that America's atom bomb project was located in or near White Sands New Mexico. The 2nd Division had a new and immensely more important mission. A small tactical nuke would be used to take out the enemy's Phoenix base. There was no time to fool around with EMP experiments.

Stokes turned in his chair. Shoving Diesel away, he keyed his helmet mike to the canine channel to order Foxtrot war dogs back into their respective hovercrafts. Breaking helmet-to-helmet contact had been a good idea; it meant that Stokes didn't have to hear Diesel's heated complaints as the senior engineer realized that the EMP from the Washington DC nuclear blast would not be studied or analyzed. Since 2nd Division was going to charge straight into New Mexico after nuking the Phoenix base, Diesel wouldn't even have a chance to study the small EMP from the tactical nuke. He was without a job.

He did have the interesting and vexing problem of Bloody Paralyzer troop carriers stalling out to fall back on, after the combat mission was over. Who knows, that problem might shed light on the EMP question. Some kind of electrical short was plaguing the Paralyzers and it had something to do with chips failing on telemetric command. There was no disputing the ease with which superconducting chips were overloaded by electrical surges. The two problems could be part and parcel of the same failing.

Chapter 16

The Battle of Johnston Island

Either Albert Einstein had a twin brother working as a guano collector on Johnston Island, or a tiny remnant of the Blue Force had survived the first nuclear attack of the war. Vladimir Bakunin set his magnifying glass down and stopped staring at the photo of Einstein pretending to be a guano collector. There was no point in second guessing the decision to throw every available resource at the flyspeck island smack dab in the middle of the Pacific, even if that hampered the reinforcement of Patton's North American Task Force. The die had been cast. Destroying and/or capturing the super suits was worth nearly any risk. What concerned Vladimir was Rommel's decision to lead the assault. After Fred Banner had died leading a similar operation, the Red Army could ill afford to lose any more senior leadership.

Rommel pushed through the heavy steel door, cinctured by a brace of Uberman guards. The general and his guards marched into spook central, where Vladimir still kept his office despite assuming the mantle of supreme command. Rommel saluted crisply, clicked his heels Prussian style and said, "Operation Mole Star shall commence upon your orders, Sir."

Vladimir toyed with the idea of ordering Rommel to find a replacement mission commander. Rommel read the indecision in his leader's body English, took a step forward, returned to attention, and said quietly, "Fred Banner did not die in vain. No one else could have jockeyed the animatronic-whales into position. What we seek to do with Mole Star will be twice as complicated and just as vital. I wouldn't risk my own life if I thought anybody else could fill in."

Vladimir wasn't sure if he believed Rommel. There was a less compelling case to send the German general into battle than there had been when Supreme Commander Banner put his neck on the chopping block. While brilliant and ferociously competent, Rommel did not have specialized knowledge of the geography or conditions around Johnston Island.

Rommel displayed an eerie predilection for reading Vladimir's mind by saying, "The plan, Sir, that is where I have specialized knowledge. I crafted the Mole Star battle plan.

It is radical. Too radical to be executed by anyone other than myself."

The intelligence officers in the nerve center abandoned their workstations to watch the theatrics between the high-ranking general and the generalissimo. Vladimir was aware of their eyes on him. He shrugged in resignation. He was a political leader, not a military expert. As such, he had to trust the judgment of the experts serving under his command.

"Very well. Permission granted to launch Mole Star," Vladimir said brusquely. Rommel braced to attention more stiffly than before. His heels came together with a sharp cracking noise. He spun hard and fast, practically goose-stepping out of the room, the fire of countless generations of Teutonic Knights burning in his eyes.

Timing was good for the Red Army. The combat-ready 5th Division was prepared to leave for Puget Sound the day that the spy photos had arrived from Johnston Island. Rommel conceived and perfected the Mole Star battle plan in record time, a few short hours after the photos of Einstein had landed on his desk. One more day was spent briefing the men and women of the division that had been intended to resupply Patton's North American Task Force. They would embark on their new mission today.

Inside the mining cavern, Rommel donned his power combat suit, assisted by his aides. The ride down into the tunnel fortress was as uncomfortable as ever. The conveyor belts designed to haul ore up out of the Earth were a clumsy method to haul people, war beasts, and equipment down into the bowels of the planet. With World War II raging, it seemed unlikely that the Red Army would find the time or resources to build an escalator or elevator.

Achilles was waiting by one of the gangways leading into Rommel's flag submarine, the Red Army *Proudhorn*, suited and ready to fight. Rommel had adopted the war seal after Fred Banner's death. War seals were very conscious of their handlers' status within the military hierarchy. Achilles' spirit would have been crushed if he hadn't been assigned to a high-ranking officer. The benefit worked both ways. Achilles was a better fighting animal than the seal that he had replaced.

Rommel walked up and down the flagship submarine's cavernous interior, personally inspecting its hovercrafts and fighter jets. The disc-shaped armored hovercrafts were securely bolted to their rubberized body mounts. Like flies bunched together in a web, the fighter jets quivered overhead in spider silk tethers. Hovercraft drivers and Wasp pilots were suited and sitting in front of their controls. Infantrymen and their seals were also encased in titanium exoskeletons and jammed tight inside the 'crafts. This would not be the slow and steady marathon to the North American mainland that had been originally planned. The subs were going to sprint to Johnston Island. The division would be fighting by noon tomorrow.

Achilles leaped onto the hull of Rommel's hovercraft, the *Bismarck*, and dived through an open hatch. The general carefully climbed up the slippery rounded contours of the war machine and joined his war seal inside. Also waiting in there were Achilles' pod and three crewmen. Rommel clanked across deck plate, plopped into his skipper's chair, and raised a comm. link with the *Proudhorn's* captain. "Captain Ito, launch the offensive. Full military power once we are free of the ooze."

Every one of the tunnel fortress locks opened, exposing 5th Division to the miles of decomposed goop stretching upward to the open ocean. Tons of goop cascaded down on the waiting submarines. Looking at a monitor hooked into the *Proudhorn's* sensor array, Rommel could see the mud-like substance fill the enormous chamber that his sub was in.

Hydraulic motors whirred in the *Proudhorn's* front legs. It pushed off from the floor of the inundated lock. The articulated plates of the sub's hull twisted sinuously. The row of hovercrafts in the belly of the metal beast undulated in S-shaped waves. The submarine slithered upward through the muck. Hours ticked by. It pulled itself from the slime, shook free of the clinging gunk, folded legs against hull, and slid forward under propeller power. The forty-nine other subs in the 5th Division made the same journey.

One thousand miles was a long distance for the Kilo class subs to travel under full military power. Operation Mole Star depended on speed. The Blue Force survivors and their super suits could not be expected to remain on the miniscule corral atoll for long. Sitting inside his hovercraft, Rommel couldn't hear the howl of the sub's redlined steam engines or feel the excess heat from its over burdened cooling systems. The mechanical stress was there nonetheless, and in all fifty subs. He could only pray that none of them broke down before the battle. Intuition told him that they would need everything they had to knock out and hopefully capture the super suits.

He keyed the comm. link to a general channel and told the platoon on board the *Bismarck* to initiate their autohypnosis training and catch fifty winks. Following his own orders, he modulated his breathing pattern and counted backward from one hundred. He muttered the last number and slumped against the padded interior of the combat suit. Rommel usually slept fitfully under the spell of autohypnosis. For him, a self-induced trance seldom lasted more than an hour. His body must have craved rest, because he slept nearly twelve hours, awakening only when Captain Ito chimed the platoon into a state of alertness, five miles off Johnston Island. Suited war seals dived into hovercraft torpedo tubes.

Ito's voice sounded in Rommel's helmet. "General Rommel, Sir. The fleet has the island surrounded."

"Captain Ito, issue general order seven dash gee."

Fifty crocodilian Kilo-class submarines cracked open, flooding cargo holds with a deluge of seawater, permitting hovercrafts and fighter jets to float up to the surface. The hovercrafts wallowed heavily in the roiling seas like titanic sea turtles, only the cupolas projecting above water, making them very hard to see by a topside observer. Compressed air hissed into plenum chambers and inflated flexible skirts. Fans ramped up. The hundred-ton turtles trundled forward. As they gained speed, they became less turtle-like and much more agile.

The fighter jets were also forced to bob in the waves for several seconds until their engines warmed. They sprang from the water en masse. Engines tilted from vertical flight configuration to level. The jets screamed over the rampaging hovercrafts, knifing into the flyspeck island.

Because of its size, Johnston Island was easy to surround and attack from all angles. The Wasp pilots were under orders to conserve missiles in the opening minutes of the battle and rely on 50 caliber slugs to catch unsuited Blue Force combatants in the open or in their grass shacks.

Armor piercing uranium slugs tore into the island's motley collection of huts. In response, particle beams blazed outward from the humble little houses, turning them into puffs of smoke and a few stray embers floating on the ocean breeze. Jet fighters hit by the beams did not prove to be much more durable than the grass shacks. Dozens of planes were so thoroughly destroyed that virtually no debris rained down on the land below.

The Red Army aerial assault had not achieved the element of surprise. Three men in Mark VII combat suits stood along the spine of the corral atoll at intervals of one or two hundred yards. Forcefields shimmered around the suit warriors like the sun's corona, blinking off and on when one of them fired an energy weapon. Suit software compensated for the irregularities of the terrain, giving the dome shaped energy shields a tight seal against the ground.

Wasp pilots switched off their machineguns and loosed missile after missile. Fireballs bubbled up from Mark VII forcefields, obscuring the vision and ruining the aim of the Blue Force combatants. Red Army pilots kept pouring missiles into the three suit warriors, attacking from all angles.

Phase two of Operation Mole Star was initiated. Radar guided proximity alarms shrilled in the Blue Force warriors' Mark VII helmets, warning them of the encirclement and approach of two hundred main battle hovercrafts.

The *Bismarck* charged as hard as any of the other 'craft. Rommel keyed his comm. link to the hovercraft general channel, ordering every war seal fired from torpedo tubes. There wasn't any time to glance at the wakes of the seals' passage to make sure they'd gotten out okay. Land roared toward the air cushion vehicles at a breakneck pace. The hovercrafts slammed into beaches and barreled into the three suit warriors, firing main guns and loosing surface-to-surface missiles. The men in the Mark VIIs were awash in walls of fire. Then the elephantine hovercrafts simultaneously collided into the three mountainous bonfires, hammering the three Mark VII forcefields, sending shockwaves into the suit warriors, and shorting out hovercraft forcefields. The hundred-ton behemoths bounced jarringly away from the epicenter of the battle like so many billiard balls. Missiles sheeted down into the three Mark VII forcefields, from jet fighters. The Blue Force forcefields continued blinking off and on. Particle beams continued picking off individual hovercrafts and jet fighters.

Four command hovercrafts, including the *Bismarck*, careened away from the skirmish, returning to the sea, turning and hovering in place one half mile off shore. The command hovercrafts disengaged lift fans. Air leaked out from under their plenum skirts and the vessels once again became turtle-like, sinking into the Pacific until only their cupolas peeked out from under the rolling waves.

Half the fleet of Wasp fighters had survived the opening engagement. They were now orbiting the battlefield, lobbing missiles to pin the three super suits to earth for the war seal attack, flying swiftly and erratically to avoid the slash of particle beams. The communist pilots were attentive to the possibility of the suits taking to the air, holding back a reserve of avian guided missiles in case this happened. Communist bio-missiles were smart enough and adaptable enough to fly into the gaps in Mark VII forcefields where air would have to be vented to let propellers function.

The Wasp pilots were too preoccupied to notice that during the heat of the battle two Mark VIIs did just that: they flew, emerging from the sea and streaking for the Asian mainland. Seven hundred miles east of Johnston Island, Einstein and Nkosinathi ended their long and exhausting swim by taking to the air, embarking on an even more grueling journey, one that the combat suits were not designed for. Their ultimate goal: Southwest Palace #9 in southern England.

The ordnance battering the three suit warriors burned so brightly that Achilles could clearly see the enemy's position even as he raced toward the island at a depth of ten feet. He fixed their locations firmly in mind and dove at the sandy slope a few feet below the waterline where the beach dipped into the lagoon. His five-seal pod moved in concert with the alpha leader like a hand in a glove.

Titanium claws cut into rock and sand more efficiently than a steam shovel. One thousand seals burrowed into the tiny corral atoll from all directions, throwing geysers of sediment and fountains of crushed stone into the lagoon surrounding the miniscule dot of land. The radar and enhanced vision of the three Blue Force warriors inside their Mark VIIs did not register the war seals' underwater advance. The element of surprise was holding for this part of the operation.

Achilles burrowed rapidly and surely, possessing a clear idea of where he wanted his tunnel to wind up. He could hear his pod mates digging madly only a few feet on either side of his small mine. He hoped that they would keep their distance and not permit tunnels to merge. The confusion of several seals in one big sloppy excavation would slow down construction. Speed was everything. Red Army seals were trained to move swiftly in battle, whether swimming, galloping, or digging. This engagement lent a special urgency to the war beasts' efforts. They could all sense that their human partners aboveground were taking a pasting.

Achilles' pod broke through to the surface with their heads poking up in a neat circle around the feet of Wolfgang Bernhard's suit, inside the fierce energy walls of the Mark VII's forcefield. Wolfgang looked down in surprise and saw the crushing metallic jaws of the bull seal's PCS close around the crystal iron greave protecting his calf. Red Army seals spent countless hours honing combat skills against suited humans. The pod leader and his pinniped suit outweighed the human and his suit by a large factor. Wolfgang's suit had a more advanced design and vastly more horsepower, but weight counted for something in a fight like this, and Achilles knew it.

The seal crawled all the way out of his hole, gripping the man's suit leg hard and hoisting him off the ground. Whipsawing his entire body, utilizing muscle and machine strength, Achilles smashed Wolfgang against the top of the ridgeline. Mark VII suit computers rapidly reconfigured the forcefield to keep it snug against the ground, emotionlessly carrying on the job of missile defense. This did Wolfgang little good since his real enemy was inside the forcefield perimeter and bodily hammering him. The man suffered a severe concussion, but gamely hung on to consciousness. Wolfgang was an Uberman, innately tougher than an ordinary human being. He pointed a particle beam projector at the bull seal and opened fire with an abridged power burst, reducing the bull seal and his combat suit to vapor particles, but not packing enough recoil punch to send the man careening across the island.

The other seals in the pod had remained partially buried as Achilles fought the man in the suit. With Achilles gone, the alpha female, Helen, reached out from her tunnel. Grabbing the man by the back and pounding him against the ground, she nearly knocked him senseless.

Wolfgang tried to point his particle beam at the monster gripping him from behind. He missed and zapped the interior of his own forcefield, shorting out the energy shield. With his last bit of strength Wolfgang waved his arms wildly and fired both beam weapons without aiming or moderating the beam's output. Helen and Wolfgang bounced wildly over the length of the island like a nuclear powered rubber ball. Wolfgang's crazily gyrating particle beams destroyed hundreds of war seals and dozens of hovercrafts. They also blew away Jeremiah and Kwa's forcefields, leaving the Blue Force combatants exposed to Wasp aero-to-surface missiles. Dimly realizing what he'd done, Wolfgang ceased firing. Helen and Wolfgang landed hard on the eastern tip of the coral atoll. Filled with rage, she battered the Uberman until he was at last unconscious. She relinquished her grip, roaring inside her helmet with frustration. She could sense that her opponent was knocked out but still alive.

Jeremiah and Kwa each had a demonic war seal attached to their combat suits and were struggling against an animal antagonist that had, like Helen, gripped them from behind. And like Wolfgang, they decided to indiscriminately fire particle beam projectors as a desperation ploy.

Wasp fighter pilots saw the forcefields go down and quickly unleashed their ultra-accurate avian-guided missiles at the Blue Force combatants before they could go on beam powered Nantucket sleigh rides. Fireballs temporarily erased the images of the two suit warriors and the war seals locked onto them with merciless death grips. When the balls of flame dissipated, all three Mark VII soldiers were prone and unmoving.

Rommel's voice screamed in the ear of every Red Army soldier and officer: "Ceasefire! Ceasefire! Call off seals. Combat engineers, get the enemy out of those suits. Corpsmen, administer medical attention to the three prisoners. Take them alive!"

Helen heard her handler's voice over the speakers in her helmet, an order to cease attacking and guard her prisoner. The order had come none to soon for Wolfgang, the alpha female was girding herself to deliver the coup de grace. She was going to swim to the edge of the lagoon, dragging her opponent to a projecting clump of corral for another thrashing. The sandy soil of the island was too soft to properly pulp a human being inside a PCS. It was a good plan and would have surely killed the Uberman who clung so stubbornly to life.

Helen's handler arrived at about the same time as the corpsmen and the combat engineers. The alpha female spit out her opponent and watched Red Army technicians labor over the Mark VII. Wolfgang was pulled free of the super suit. Without a conscious human sending signals to its computers, with its major electrical systems shorted out, the exoskeleton had automatically powered down its fusion reactor. The female war seal nudged the bloody and bruised body of Wolfgang Bernhard curiously. He appeared to be an ordinary man, even though he'd fought with extraordinary ability.

Helen backed away from the unconscious warrior, giving corpsmen room to administer an intravenous drip. A Wasp fighter landed next to the laboring medical team. Men with a stretcher emerged from the jet. Watching the aftermath of battle was boring to the alpha female. She looked at her handler earnestly through the faceplate of her helmet. He helped her out of the powered armor and gave permission to take a short swim in the lagoon.

Rommel's shoulders stooped in despair after he'd looked the last of the three suit warriors in the face. He recognized the Blue Force supreme commander despite the fact that Halifax had lost an eye and his face was a mass of bruises. The other two were recognizable as Blue Force high-ranking generals. None of them were Albert Einstein. The enemy had staged the battle as a rearguard action to protect the escape of Einstein and possibly others. Obviously, one or more super advanced combat suits had left the island with the Blue Force's foremost scientist. Jeremiah Halifax had been willing to trade the most potent weapon ever devised by man for Einstein's escape: a chilling thought. Rommel would not have made the same trade for Oppenheimer or Heisenberg.

The Red Army general's demeanor became defeatist as he gazed around the island. Wrecked fighter jets and hovercrafts littered the island battlefield. Broken pinniped combat suits were everywhere. The fractured and bloody remains of war seals were visible through rends in metallic suit skin. Half of 5th Division was gone. The only reason they'd gotten off that lightly was that Johnston Island had provided ideal terrain for the Red Army. The burrowing tactic was unlikely to be anywhere near as effective on the mainland. Three of the super advanced suits had decimated an entire Red Army division. At least one super suit, probably two, had escaped.

Part of him wanted to cobble together an expeditionary force from the decimated 5th Division and immediately strike out for Asia in an effort to capture Einstein and whoever else was with him. Rommel's thoughts were interrupted by the passage of corpsmen bearing one of the wounded enemy warriors into a Wasp fighter. His palms itched as he looked at the three super suits laid out in a neat row, exposed and unprotected, the most valuable objects in the world. He couldn't risk transporting them back to the tunnel fortress in a fighter jet, not when one of the existing Blue Force super suits could vaporize that jet, scoop the suit up, and carry it away. The entire fleet of submarines moored around the island would be needed to get the job done.

An optimistic thought caused the general's shoulders to square and the worry lines on his face to relax. To a man, Red Army scientists agreed that the Blue Force had used its supercollider to build the super suits out of crystal iron. The supercollider was no more. It didn't seem plausible that more super suits could be built in the foreseeable future. Rommel's gut told him that the Commonwealth and the Red Army would be evenly matched as far as super suits were concerned for the North America campaign. Of course, his gut was no oracle. Accurate information would have to be extracted from the three prisoners. The spooks would have to find out how many super suits had escaped and where they were headed. It would take extremely skilled interrogation technique; mere brutality would not suffice, especially with these three. Bakunin would want to handle it himself.

Jeremiah regained consciousness surrounded by darkness. He experienced a moment of déjà vu. The experience was much like the one he'd gone through after the nuclear explosion, or maybe not. He was resting on a mattress and wearing loose fabric clothes, not a power suit. A weak light bulb flickered on, showing him a damp concrete cell, about ten feet by twenty feet, with a plain looking steel door including a standard prison issue food slot. There was a mirror on one wall and a chamber pot in one of the corners. He could be in any prison anywhere in the Commonwealth, but was probably on or under the island of Kauai.

An arm and a leg were in plaster casts. *I must have broken them fighting the damn war seal.* He touched his head. A none-too-sanitary dressing was stuck to a crusty wound on his face that covered his left eye. He somehow knew that the eye was gone for good.

He rubbed a hand along his jaw. The stubble on his face was now a short beard, maybe two weeks worth of growth. He inhaled a deep lungful of air and nearly choked. His body odor was like a second person in the cell.

Footsteps could be heard from outside. He sat upright in the bed. Pain shot through every part of his body. The empty eye socket throbbed. The steel door creaked open. A short, elderly black man with a white beard stepped inside. The man wore a uniform with hammer and sickle emblems on the shoulder boards next to the stars of a supreme commander. At his side, a large German Shepherd padded silently, shadow-like, not taking his eyes off Jeremiah.

The short black man stuck out his hand and introduced himself: "Supreme Commander of the Red Army Vladimir Bakunin." Feeling foolish, Jeremiah shook hands from bed, giving his own name and rank. He let his hand fall away and asked what had happened to Fred Banner. Vladimir recounted the story of the animatronic-whale battle-lion. Jeremiah nodded dumbly.

Vladimir raised his voice and told an unseen listener to begin General Kwa's interrogation. The light bulb in Jeremiah's concrete cell went dark. The mirror on the wall became a clear sheet of glass that looked into a brightly illuminated cell similar to Jeremiah's. Impi Kwa was in the other cell, naked, strapped to a heavy wooden chair, electrodes attached to various parts of his body. Jeremiah dropped his glance to the moldy concrete floor, knowing what was about to happen to Kwa.

A powerful man in a Red Army sergeant's uniform entered Kwa's torture chamber. Speakers in Jeremiah's cell caught the ring of the sergeant's hobnailed boots. Even though the Blue Force SC was unwilling to raise his one good eye off the floor and see what was happening in the other cell, he couldn't help listening. The speakers caught the sergeant's words: "General Kwa, where did Doctor Einstein flee? How many Blue Force personnel besides Einstein left Johnston Island? How many of the advanced suits did they have with them?" A crunching sound indicated that the electrodes were being tightened on Kwa's body.

Jeremiah jerked his head up to watch Kwa's expression as the Zulu warrior said woodenly, "Eat shit and die." Voltage flowed into the defiant Blue Force general. Convulsions wracked his body. In an amazing display of will power, Kwa swallowed his tongue as the last spasm contorted his frame. His fingernails and lips instantly started turning blue. The sergeant screamed for a doctor.

Vladimir cursed and made his own request to the unseen workers monitoring the interrogation cells. He asked that the audio feed be turned off from Kwa's grilling and the two-way mirror deactivated. The light bulb in Jeremiah's cell blazed. Isolated from the botched attempt to break the resolute Zulu warrior, Vladimir regarded Jeremiah balefully. "In a stupid sort of way, your man's defiance is admirable. Nevertheless, you people are doing the Commonwealth no good." The leader of the Red Army went on to detail his plans for transforming the world economy and the structure of the one world government, emphasizing the retention of democratic institutions and private property, albeit forcibly divided into the hands of the many by way of antitrust laws.

Jeremiah gave a long, low whistle, impressed that the man before him was as brilliant as he was evil. "Assuming your forces prevail: the communist dictatorship will surely flourish," he said wonderingly. "I'm surprised at the intense cunning. Temporarily harnessing market forces and democracy is a stroke of genius. The totalitarian dictatorship that replaces your worker's paradise will function all the better because of the excellent groundwork. My hat is off to you, Sir."

Vladimir sat on the cot next to the prisoner. The German Shepherd crawled up there as well. The Red Army supreme commander said smoothly, "The supermonopoly and the lesser monopolies like the one owned by your mother have to be destroyed. Any right thinking human being knows as much. Only my people can destroy these cancers and put together something better. We are not going to establish a permanent dictatorship. Help me end the bloodshed. Where is Einstein? How many super suits does he have?"

Jeremiah laughed, shook his head, and said, "The dictatorship will come after your death, Comrade Bakunin. You want me to help destroy monopolies like Halifax Mining? Someday I will own Halifax Mining, you idiot. Better ramp up your information extraction technique. I'm sure a regimen of sleep deprivation is in store for me. Try again after I've been kept awake for a week. Good luck."

"Why sleep deprivation?"

"I'm too banged up to withstand electroshock. The Red Army will quickly discover that I don't care if Kwa and Bernhard are tortured. It's a waste of time to make me watch them suffer. And time is something you don't have. It would be prudent to initiate sleep deprivation on me immediately."

"Why don't we have time?"

"You don't have time to spare as far as Einstein is concerned. Every second he is at large within the Commonwealth scientific community is another coffin nail in your revolution."

"Einstein is only one man."

"According to your worldview, Einstein is an insignificant singularity. One man is nothing against the collectivist forces of Historical Parallelism and Dialectical Materialism, right? Marxian philosophy preaches the insignificance of the individual. It denigrates free will and personal ability. That is its fatal flaw."

"Historical Parallelism is backed by scientific research and empirical data."

"The Red Army's collectivist ideology is a big log blithely rolling down the conveyor belt of a sawmill. Albert Einstein is the buzz saw that will turn communism into a useless heap of sawdust that will be swept into the dustbin of history. Or as children on the playground say: You're a bunch of morons about to get dipped in idiot sauce."

The German Shepherd barked happily. Jeremiah was telling the truth as he saw it. The Blue Force supreme commander continued: "Better kill me now. As soon as Einstein has destroyed communism, the war crimes trials are over, and I'm running the family business, I'll put you morons to work digging diamonds in South Africa, slave labor, no pay. Hip-hip-hooray for monopoly capitalism."

Vladimir's visage set into lines of grim determination. He got up and moved to leave the cell, whistling for his dog. Before calling for a guard, the Red Army SC said, "Mr. Halifax, much of what you say is nonsense. One thing is quite accurate. We will institute a sleep deprivation regimen on you and the two others. Please don't struggle when my people install electrodes in your skull."

Jeremiah flipped Bakunin the bird. The Red Army leader paused at the cell door, realizing that he'd let the interrogation spiral out of control by being overly emotional. Taking an entirely different approach, Vladimir sat back on the cot and outlined the communist war strategy, openly and honestly, trying to convince Jeremiah that capitalism was doomed.

Capitalist America would be conquered and communized. The war would temporarily stop, pausing for about one year. During that year a supercollider would be built in Texas, using the firm that had designed the original Blue Force collider. Crystal iron super suits would be mass-produced in the Lone Star state. The suits would be used to attack Britain…

Vladimir gave a detailed, point-by-point account of the Red Army grand strategy. When he was done, Jeremiah flipped the bird a second time, unimpressed and uncowed. Jeremiah knew that Einstein's EMP bombs could (potentially) throw Bakunin's strategy into a cocked hat. But no amount of torture or sleep deprivation could get Jeremiah, Kwa, or Wolfgang to admit as much.

Chapter 17

The Red Army Stumbles Across America's A-bomb Program

The Red Army's 2nd Division crossed state lines, entering New Mexico from Arizona north of where they'd originally planned. The featureless desert was giving way to an equally arid land characterized by dry gorges cut into reddish hills and rocky spires sculpted by centuries of sandstorms. Diesel sat in a corner of the cargo hold, staring moodily out a narrow view slit, trying to avoid getting sucked into the inane conversations of the younger men and women comprising the infantry complement of Stokes's command hovercraft.

Earlier in the week, the division hadn't slowed or given him any time to study the tiny pulse created by the tactical nuke that had destroyed the enemy's Phoenix base. A second, much larger pulse was scheduled for today: the Washington DC nuclear event. Diesel was receiving no cooperation in studying this one either. Standard issue pulse shields were wrapped around the division's electronic components like so much tin foil, and that was that. The hunt for America's experimental nuke facility trumped everything else.

It had been relatively bright in the cargo hold. It got suddenly darker; then lighter; then darker. Lights flickered off and on in the belly of the titanium beast. This was it! The next big pulse had hit. Diesel stood and ran up a flight of stairs leading to the control cabin. When he got there, the crew was struggling to hold the reins of a bucking bronco that had seconds ago been a well-behaved war machine. He grabbed the handrail in the stairwell to ride out the hovercraft's gyrations.

The luminescent display panels and lights in the upper cabin winked on and off for seven seconds. Radio communication roared with static for roughly one minute. Engines continued to stutter, stall, and catch again as electronics died, came alive, died, and returned to normal. A steady flow of air returned to the cushion under the vehicle. Static cleared from the airwaves, replaced by the confused babble of dozens of battle-lion commanders, all asking the same question: were they experiencing a pulse or something more sinister?

Division Commander Brigadier Zhukov's voice cut through the chatter, calmly informing his people that they were experiencing nothing more than the aftereffects of the nuclear bombardment of Washington DC. By all indications, this EMP was mild: a mere nuisance.

Leftenant-colonel Stokes was undergoing a dizzying loss of biomechanical motor functions. It came and went swiftly, but it also knocked him senseless. When Stokes regained consciousness, Diesel was hovering over the tin man, concerned, asking questions: "Tell me your subjective analysis of this pulse, while it is fresh in your mind?" Diesel waited a beat and decided to add the word "Sir."

Stokes looked at him irritably, but decided to play along. "Umm. This one was stronger than the tactical nuke. It was weaker than the Hawaiian EMP by a wide margin."

"Is there any way to quantify those values?" Diesel begged. Stokes shook his head, adding, "The big difference is that this time there was no secondary pulse as in Hawaii. The secondary pulse is what tears through EMP shielding. Looks like only truly huge explosions do that. These small and medium nukes don't amount to a hill of beans for causing pulse damage. The Red Army is unlikely to ever use one hundred nuclear warheads in concert again. Looks like you're out of a job, soldier." Stokes jerked a thumb at the cargo hold, indicating that the senior engineer should rejoin the young troopers below.

One of the hovercraft's radar operators said, "Entering injun country. Fighter jets spotted ahead." Alarms sounded in every hovercraft in the division. Men, women, and war dogs tumbled into personal combat armor. The division's fighters had been riding piggyback on the air cushion vehicles to conserve fuel. They rose from their mobile platforms to meet the American threat.

Second Division had been filing in between a series of red rock canyons, avoiding major highways in an attempt at creating a slight element of surprise, although billowing clouds of dust mitigated the effort. The flattened mesas topping the canyon walls unexpectedly sprouted twenty-one inch guns, scores of them, lining the passageway leading down to White Sands. The big guns spoke with authoritative voices, spitting shells the size of motorcars into the naked columns. Communist forcefield conduits sizzled to life.

The American shells had proximity fuses that issued mild pops one hundred feet above the passing file of communist armor, releasing dense clouds of vaporized explosives. The clouds merged into a single long haze that ran the length of the canyon containing the bulk of the division's armor. Polymerized aerosols congealed inside the hazy cloud like clotting blood. Micro-charges within the fuel-air mixture ignited, resulting in an explosion that nearly equaled the tactical nuke the communists had used earlier in the week.

American helicopter gunships shed concealing tarps, swooped down from the heights, and hosed the communist juggernauts with armor piercing slugs. Undamaged hovercrafts fired back, splattering choppers against the rust-colored rock walls.

A number of hovercrafts were knocked out of commission. Rubble rolled down from the canyon walls, forcing the air cushion war machines to blast their way out of the arroyo with main guns. A handful of American panzers met the Red Army in the flatland. Under normal circumstances, the panzers wouldn't have posed more than a pinprick to the nuclear powered hovercrafts. Unfortunately, the fuel-air bombing had degraded communist forcefields, enabling the enemy to annihilate three armored platoons before being overpowered and destroyed.

Dogfights stormed above the struggling communist armored column. The Red Army Wasp fighters were only marginally better than the American version. The fight lasted for the better part of that day. The division's aero arm managed to wipe the sky clean of enemy fighter jets, paying a heavy price for their victory.

Once the division had fully debouched from the rocky defile to an open plain, Zhukov ordered his wounded expeditionary force to strike camp. The brigadier warned them to dig in extra deep. Reconnaissance in force operations would begin tomorrow. Parties would be sent back into the blasted canyon this evening to recover the wounded and cannibalize wrecked armor and fighters. In other words, the camp would be home for a while. Stokes could tell by the tone in Zhukov's voice that reinforcements would not be forthcoming from Red Army headquarters in San Jose any time soon. There also seemed to be a problem with mundane resupply. The war must be getting hot in the northern Rockies and on the Great Plains. Perhaps, the enemy's new fuel-air bombs were taking a toll up and down the extended front line. Second Division would have to move more cautiously from here on out.

Diesel was happy to get out of his PCS, hop out of the hovercraft, and stretch his legs once a lager had been formed. He seemed to be the only soldier to shed personal armor that afternoon. He idly watched suited humans and dogs busily dig pits and pack earth around war machines. Other troopers were slipping away to the deadly canyon they'd recently come from or out into the desert to search for evidence of the American Army. The division was taking care of itself just fine without any help from the aging engineer. Which was only fair. It had done nothing to help him study the spate of EMPs.

Diesel jumped when a voice spoke directly behind him, inches away: "I've a bit of work for you, Rudolf. Put your expertise at building underground factories to use." It was Stokes, the only other person in the battle-lion not wearing combat armor. The Leftenant-colonel went on to explain that the firepower concentrated in the canyon was odd, suspiciously potent for a useless stretch of desert, possibly an indication of a hidden laboratory or munitions factory, maybe even a sentinel for the elusive American A-bomb project.

Diesel scratched his head doubtfully. It would be truly odd for a well-hidden underground factory to call attention to itself by staging an ambush. He voiced his concerns to Stokes. The Leftenant-colonel informed Diesel that native communists had probably infiltrated America's A-bomb program. One of them may have ordered the ambush as a signal to 2nd Division to take action.

The three O'Brien brothers appeared from nowhere, along with three German Shepherds, all six garbed in dun-colored PCSs. Sean saluted the befuddled engineer. The dogs went into crisp sit-stays, displaying an eagerness to take orders. Diesel regarded Stokes mournfully and protested, "Me? Lead an assault squad. I don't think so." Stokes clapped the obstinate engineer on the shoulder and said, "It won't be an assault squad. You're to poke around in that canyon and figure out if they've built something like what you've built under Kauai."

Diesel quickly found himself looking through the infrared filters of his PCS faceplate, threading through the chaparral of a high desert evening. The recovery squads had filtered back to 2nd Division's base camp, leaving his squad alone in the gathering twilight.

Covering the same terrain hours before, peering through a two-inch wide view slit from the interior of an armored main battle hovercraft, Diesel hadn't noticed the network of wagon ruts leading to the valley where the Yankees had set up the ambush. That was the problem with the hulking war machines: they insulated you from the environment.

He tapped helmets with Sean and asked the youth if the dogs could smell rubber tire tracks while wearing combat armor. They could, so the boys ordered the dogs to "find rubber." The canines picked up a promising scent and led the party to a jumble of boulders near the entrance to the dry gulch, snug against a steep cliff.

Diesel dropped to his knees, placing his faceplate to within inches of the ground supporting the jumble of boulders. What looked like a slab of rock embedded in the desert floor was actually high quality concrete, cunningly wrought to resemble stone. One at a time, he tapped helmets with each of the three boys, asking them to remove the pile of boulders, quietly and carefully.

With that done, Diesel was unsurprised when a six-foot wide tunnel yawned at them from the side of the precipice. The dogs entered first, followed by the O'Brien brothers and the elderly engineer. Under their metal shod feet, a narrow gauge rail line wound into the hillside. This was mining country and the two ribbons of steel bore all the hallmarks of belonging to an old silver mine. Except that the rails were shiny from recent use. The mine wasn't abandoned. So why was the entrance blocked? More tellingly, why would anyone go to the trouble of putting a concrete pad under the cairn of stones blocking the entrance? The only reason that made sense was to facilitate the assembling and disassembling of the jumble of boulders. Easy to get in. Easy to get out.

The shaft descended gradually, snaking around and branching off several times. It was not difficult to follow the true trail, however, because the underground rail tracks became rusty when they deviated from the beaten path. Diesel had the boys scour the ground for the tailings of minerals. They found nothing of the sort. They did find a new pair of fingernail clippers and a plastic comb, items that miners would never carry.

Their infrared sight told them that the mine was getting wider and wider, too wide for it to be a commercial silver mine, or any kind of working mine. This was the final straw for Diesel. From the beginning of their underground journey, the place smelled of American military. Now he was certain, somewhere under this mountain, Americans were designing nuclear weapons.

The lead dog froze in midstride, alerting on something ahead. Diesel activated his radio, ordering the three boys and the three dogs out of the mine, not wanting to fall victim to a second American ambush. They retraced their steps as silently as church mice. Once outside on the canyon floor, they stacked the boulders back over the entrance of the mine before returning to camp.

On the way back, Diesel recalled that the land under the mountains and deserts of New Mexico was riddled with an extensive complex of natural caverns, some of the largest in the world. A few of the older mines must connect with these naturally occurring underground chambers. With very little work, the Americans could have installed their A-bomb program somewhere under the so-called land of enchantment. Evidently, he'd found where that somewhere was.

Stokes accepted Diesel's report with detached composure, telling the squad to reassemble near the command hovercraft at oh eight hundred hours, tomorrow morning, warning them that being late would carry dire consequences.

They made it on time. A good thing too, because George S. Patton was there, standing next to three of the strangest looking powered combat suits that any of them had ever seen. The suits were almost comical, with swollen bellies, as if they were pregnant. Patton dismissed Diesel and locked his eyes on the three O'Brien brothers. He gave them a rundown on the capabilities of the Mark VII, followed by a long lecture on the importance of keeping the suits out of American hands. Then he gave them operational instructions. Other than the fact that it could fly and possessed particle beams and forcefields, the Mark VII functioned like a standard Red Army PCS. The boys had trained all their lives on various kinds of power suits and attack helicopters. The mission that George Patton gave them seemed to be destined by Providence. Two of the suits were the right size for the average height of Seamus and Shay. The third suit was perfect for Sean's long and lanky frame.

The boys spent the remainder of the daylight hours practicing with their new combat armor. Patton warned them to concentrate on emitting the weakest possible particle beam blasts. During the mission, if they needed to use anything approaching full force, a counter beam had to be pointed in the opposite direction as the weapon beam. They absorbed all this and more, familiarizing themselves with the ultra-advanced machines as the sun coasted down beyond the desert's horizon.

On the trip out the day before, Sean had painstakingly memorized landmarks that would lead the brothers back to the entrance of the American weapons lab, a necessity since they would have no dogs with them to sniff a path. Sean's memory proved effectual, by midnight they were standing in front of the familiar jumble of boulders.

The brothers tromped down into the mine, keeping enough distance between one another to prevent forcefields from clashing if they came under fire. The mine's twists and bends took them to the place where they'd turned around last night, where it widened into a cavern.

Patton had warned the suit warriors to use particle beams only as a last resort. They strode into a spectacular cavern, dripping with rainbow hued stalactites, and encountered suited American guards. Sean leaped on an enemy soldier and broke his neck, utilizing the superior power of the Mark VII.

A shower of bullets rained down upon the three brothers from all directions. They were well placed inside the monster cave for the use of forcefields. High velocity lead bullets with tungsten cores disintegrated against the energy shields like bugs against a zapper. The art of blinking the forcefields off and on to permit the firing of particle beams was not a skill that they'd yet mastered. Fortunately, in the confined battlefield of the underground research center, the forcefields were effective as battering rams. American shooters were fried as the boys smashed into their enemies.

They lowered shields when the shooting stopped and methodically wrecked every piece of machinery in this particular cavern. A blast door had closed during the firefight. It must lead to other parts of the complex. Seamus and Shay flattened out on their stomachs as Sean carefully lined one particle beam projector on the blast door and the other into the cavern. He fired both beams. Two searing shafts of energy lanced outward in opposite directions. The blast door dematerialized and the cavern was even more thoroughly wrecked than it had been before.

The brothers pounded down the open corridor. Their augmented hearing told them that trouble was headed their way. Dozens of suited American Bulldogs boiled up out of the subterranean cauldron. Again, Seamus and Shay threw themselves prone. Sean whipped both arms up like Jesus on his cross and sent two more particle beams roaring in opposite directions. The metal clad dogs were atomized. The frontward facing beam had created a new tunnel, but it was easy to differentiate it from the real tunnel carved by bourgeois

American scientists bent on strangling the revolution.

The boys tumbled into a second cavern filled with men and equipment. Oddly enough, the men not wearing combat armor were wearing military fatigues, none of them looked like scientists. The American soldiers in this chamber opened fire on the intruders. There wasn't enough room to activate forcefields, but the crystal iron exoskeletons easily absorbed the armor piercing rounds.

Sean was growing increasingly comfortable with his beam weapons and felt that speed was essential to get the job done. For the third time, the two younger brothers got out of his line of fire and the oldest O'Brien inundated an American laboratory with the devouring fury of raw plasma.

Three blast doors stared implacably at the suit warriors. Sean ordered the team to split up. Beam weapons fired upon three more steel blast doors. The energy discharges were causing more structural damage to the mountain's interior than Sean anticipated, collapsing the upper tunnels that had led the boys down this far. The three blast doors were evaporated though, as if they'd been constructed of tissue paper.

The boys regrouped in the deeper caverns, where they at last found scientists, though only a handful. Like whirling dervishes, they fought through packs of suited dogs and humans, destroying uranium centrifuges, metal forges, and most importantly, capitalist physicists with the skill and knowledge to build nuclear warheads. Sean radioed a message to his brothers, instructing them to split up again and inflict maximum damage on the rest of the facility and its personnel.

The night wore on and blurred into a kaleidoscope of carnage. The three rejoined forces in the last cavern, a barrack's worth of civilians, mostly young Hispanics: janitors, cooks, and maintenance men. Sick in his heart at the mayhem and murder he'd wreaked thus far, Sean was forced to scorch the blue-collar workers in case a scientist was hiding among them. Grimacing inside his helmet, he used his beam weaponry one last time, pointing both projectors straight up, and burning a passageway hundreds of yards through the tortured mountain. When the dust, molten rock, and debris had settled, nothing, not even an ameba, was alive under the mountain, except the suit warriors.

They engaged flight turbines and flew up the vertical shaft that Sean had carved to land on the pinnacle of the mesa, beam projectors extended, ready to fight. Only a short while ago, the flattened mountaintop had been host to substantial American forces, strong enough to deal a serious blow to Zhukov's 2nd Division. But now, in the waning hours of the night, the boys looked through infrared faceplates to survey a smoking junkyard slick with the greasy residue of burnt napalm. The artillery pieces that had demonstrated such devastating firepower during the ambush were nothing more than military garbage, twisted beyond recognition. The corpses of Yankee fighter jets were dispersed across the mesa and the plain below. A fierce battle had transpired aboveground while the boys battled below. Poking through the debris, they found charred corpses: human and canine, cooked to death inside combat armor. The adrenaline of combat ebbed from the boys' bodies and the stark horror of what they'd done throbbed like a migraine. They'd been told since they were toddlers that their lives would be devoted to destroying capitalist oppressors. Nothing that noble had occurred under the mesa. It had seemed more like slaughter than liberation.

Standing there on shattered rock, the O'Brien brothers listlessly watched as a dusty yellow dawn spread across the tortured land. Diesel's voice crackled over their helmet speakers. "Tango, are you whole and hearty?" Sean sent a coded message back, answering in the affirmative. Diesel expressed his relief and quickly got down to business. Geiger counters within the base camp were ringing like fire alarms. The hole they'd blasted through the top of the mountain was spewing radioactive particles. The boys needed to plug it and take a swim in the Rio Grande before rejoining 2nd Division.

They wedged boulders and packed gravel into the radioactive chimney. Flying away from the sepulchral nightmare and plunging into the great river did more for the boys than cleanse them of radioactive contamination, it helped them psychologically. Their young minds were nothing if not resilient. And they'd seen combat before. They emerged from the water reborn.

Skimming back to camp at sagebrush height, it occurred to Shay that he and his brothers had dealt the enemy a grave blow. Without nuclear weapons, the Americans were helpless. An accomplishment of this magnitude surely warranted medals, perhaps the Order of Spartacus. By the time the trio landed in the center of the semi-permanent camp, Shay had convinced himself that a brass band and the army's top leadership would be waiting for them, medals in hand.

Rather than an adoring crowd and a glittering ceremony, stone-faced military police waved Geiger counters around the Mark VIIs. Radiation readings were acceptable, so the military cops hustled the boys out of the precious super advanced combat suits, gruffly telling them to report to their battle-lion commander. The cops used powered gurneys to load the suits into a hovercraft that sat in the middle of the camp. An entire platoon was stationed around this 'craft.

Stokes did offer brief congratulations to the squad, shaking each of their hands and telling them that they should be proud of the job they'd done. But no medals were offered and he immediately asked for a description of the equipment they'd destroyed in the cavern complex. Seamus began relating the specifics of an American uranium enrichment centrifuge that he'd slagged, emphasizing the difference between what he'd seen under the mesa and the centrifuges the Red Army used in the tunnel fortress under Kauai. He went on to depict the scene they'd encountered in the depth of the mine, the soldiers roasted alive. Shay broke into his brother's narrative, demanding to know where General Patton was and did he know about the brothers' exploits. Would there be any sort of commendation?

Chuckling dryly, Stokes told Shay that Patton had been called away by High Command while the boys were still underground wrecking American hardware. Although the general knew about the mission's success, he didn't know the boys by name.

Not only did Shay drop his eyes in disappointment, the two other brothers looked crestfallen as well. Stokes's eyes twinkled with amusement. He told them that a picture was becoming apparent: the nuclear research facility under the mesa had very few scientists and engineers. It seemed to have been staffed primarily by soldiers. The core of America's atomic researchers was probably holed up in Santa Fe. By all rights, 2nd Division should be hauling ass for the mountainous hideaway. And they would be too, if not for the losses incurred during the ambush.

The tin man glared at the boys from under shaggy white eyebrows, asking if they wanted career advice. Sean looked puzzled for a few seconds and then enlightened, as though he'd eaten fruit from the tree of knowledge. He stared his mentor in the eye and said, "General Zhukov thinks our division has lost combat potential. He isn't factoring in the Mark VIIs. We're actually stronger than ever."

Stokes nodded and acquired the tone that he'd used when teaching the boys back in Kauai. "Which one of you can draw up an operational doctrine that will integrate the three Mark VII power suits with 2nd Division's other weapons?" He paused, watching the wheels turn in the two older boys' heads. "Which one of you has the guts to present the doctrine to General Zhukov? Who will lead the charge into Santa Fe?"

Sean wanted to know if Zhukov would be willing to use the super suits again in battle, or would he be afraid of the Americans capturing them. Stokes beamed at his prize student, informing him that this was the crux of the issue. There was a lot of pressure to remove the Mark VIIs from the line of fire, for the reason that Sean had cited and another: Red Army scientists were eager to tear the suits down and figure out how to reverse engineer them, eventually mass-producing them in quantity.

"This is what politics is all about, boys," Stokes said helpfully. "If the brass is determined to take these Mark VIIs out of the line of fire no matter what anybody says, then it would hurt your careers to speak out in favor of using them." He waited to let that sink in and then continued: "But if you could persuade the fat cats to use the suits in the Battle of Santa Fe and you boys were the suit operators, then your careers would get a huge boost. Something to think about."

Other than guards, there had been no visitors to the top floor of the North American Task Force Headquarters building in San Jose for several weeks. Henry Ford and Alfred Sloan were slowly going stir crazy. The erstwhile industrialists hated George Patton, yet they were glad to see him if for no other reason than to have someone intelligent to talk to.

"We're taking a trip, the three of us," Patton said, crossing his legs and sipping an espresso. Ford and Sloan perked up, like dogs whose master had just picked up a leash. "The big kahuna, Supreme Commander Bakunin, has summoned us for a command performance."

Ford asked, "When do we leave?" Patton set his espresso cup down and said, "Right now. Seeing as how the Pacific's been pacified." The general smirked at his play on words. "We can to take one of your plush DFA corporate jets, not one of my ass-busting military jets."

The plane that Patton selected for the trip was as opulent as promised. Patton and his Bulldog, Willy, luxuriated on silk cushions while sampling an assortment of drinks and snacks. Ford and Sloan relaxed on a sofa, eating the same snacks and drinking the same drinks. As quiet and smooth as a maglev train, the corporate jet dashed across the ocean, secure within a wing of Red Army Wasp fighters.

Patton pointed at a TV set hanging from a forward bulkhead. "Gentlemen, shall we watch the DFA war channel out of London? Get an update?" Sloan's eyebrows shot up in shock as he asked, "The commies consider our news channel accurate?"

The general held up a remote control device and turned on the television. He clicked around until he found the channel that he wanted and said, "Oh yeah. It's about half accurate. I'll pipe up when your employees start lying."

The screen flashed to a view of the Statue of Liberty. A fleet of Commonwealth troopships was sailing past lady liberty, proudly flying the Union Jack. The newest model

DFA Wasp fighters from Zululand were hovering protectively over the ships. The procession steamed by Ellis Island and made its way to the American Army's Jersey City Terminus Station.

Patton noticed that the volume was too low, so he increased it. The announcer's resonant voice could be heard over stirring strands of patriotic music: "Witness the latest weapon from London. William the Conqueror main battle panzers: a gift from Her Majesty Queen Victoria II." The screen showed dark gray panzers hurtling off the decks of the massive British warships, plunging into the Hudson River, sinking from sight, and then cheerfully churning up the concrete banks of the Terminus Station, guns swiveling hungrily, already questing for communist targets.

Willy's ears sprang forward when he heard the announcer say "William the Conqueror." This was the dog's full name, and his tail wagged as the man inside the TV repeated it, claiming that Britain had landed two thousand William the Conqueror panzers in New Jersey in the last week alone.

Patton nodded at Ford and Sloan, informing them that the news broadcaster had uttered the first piece of disinformation. Britain had actually landed one thousand panzers.

The TV now showed soldiers in dark gray combat suits wading ashore. The powered body armor was clearly a new design, although the announcer did not mention this fact or give any details. The suit soldiers were carrying bulky 50 caliber machineguns in their right hands, waving them around like revolvers. Bazooka style rocket launchers were slung around their metallic shoulders and they toted huge backpacks bristling with missiles. Obviously, the new PCS design gave them the ability to carry heavier weapons.

Patton pulled out a cigar and lit it, his eyes never leaving the screen. The announcer asserted that the soldiers slogging up out of the Hudson River were Impi warriors from Zululand, born and bred for battle. Through a curtain of smoke, Patton conceded that this was probably true. The announcer said that two hundred thousand Zulu warriors would be sent into the fierce battle raging on the outskirts of Santa Fe shortly. Patton disagreed. The number was less. Not that many troopships had punctured the Red Army's Atlantic submarine blockade. Most of the Commonwealth soldiers and equipment had arrived via aeroplane. Zululand's new fighter jets had created an aerobridge. It was working, up to a point: personnel and material were trickling into America, but not fast enough to staunch the red tide. And the Red Army could always use nuclear weapons against eastern seaports and aeroports any time it felt truly threatened. Patton reluctantly admitted that there would be unpleasant political ramifications among local communist parties if they hit America with a second batch of nukes. The Red Army was beginning to think about winning the peace in the USA, not just winning the war.

"What's stopping you from declaring a ceasefire?" Ford wanted to know. Patton bit down hard on his cigar, breaking off a piece. He spit it out onto the Persian carpet and said, "You are." Sloan and Ford looked at each other in confusion. "The big kahuna thinks he can negotiate a truce in the USA with you two bozos."

Willy jumped off his silk cushion, ran up to the tattered chunk of cigar, and ate it. The dog looked belatedly at his master, realizing that the boss was angry at something. Patton looked like a bull facing a red cape. He actually snorted and cast an evil glance at Ford and Sloan, which only mystified them. Why should old Blood and Guts hate the humbled industrialists?

The dog stalked back to his cushion and sat facing in the direction of his master's glare. Willy took the same bearing as Patton toward the plutocrats. Lips curling back against pearly white fangs, he gave them a low rumbling growl.

Sloan was an expert on bureaucracy: tables of organization in the private sector weren't much different from chains of command in the military. For their own safety, he and Ford needed to reshuffle Patton in the Red Army's deck of cards. Cautiously, Sloan asked, "Bakunin will stop the war in North America if we help turn DFA's North American subsidiaries and divisions into his vision of communism?" Patton snuffed out his cigar in disgust, refusing to answer the question. Sloan continued: "Your supreme commander's ambitions for economic reform stop at this continent, for the time being. Communism will be perfected in Mexico, America, and Canada. Then, and only then, will the war move overseas, to Britain or Zululand."

Ford punched an armrest of the sofa and agreed: "Talk about hitting the nail on the head! I'm no military man. But I'll bet my last pound Bakunin's planning to hold a communist North America up as a shining example for everywhere else. Sure as hell, he wants a pause in the war, a long breather. He needs a red USA that's hitting on all cylinders, or I ain't the man that invented mass-production."

Sloan spoke as though Patton wasn't in the cabin: "Old Blood and Guts must have a very distinct command: North America, and that's it. Some other commie general will lead the Red Army into Africa or Britain."

Willy fixed his amber gaze on the capitalists, sinking into his cushion like a hovercraft with a defective plenum skirt. The Bulldog let out another growl, responding to his master's muted enmity. Ford worried briefly that old Blood and Guts might turn the dog loose on them, but dismissed the notion after a moment's thought. Bakunin would be well aware of Patton's desires to keep the war raging in America. If he and Sloan were suddenly killed, immediate suspicion would fall on the commander of the North American Task Force.

Sloan seized on Ford's last pronouncement: "Yes indeed, a red USA, Mexico, and Canada complete with a booming economy based on Bakunin's ideas. A peaceful and prosperous communist North America would serve as a beacon to rally the working classes across the globe before the war hops the pond. His timing could be perfect. The US federal government was decapitated in the DC nuclear strike. DFA North America is holding together with rubber bands. Bakunin's version of communism calls for an extremely decentralized government and economy—" Sloan stopped talking abruptly, suddenly cognizant of Patton, glowering at him from the other side of the jet's cabin.

The general's eyes narrowed dangerously into razor thin slits. Ford's prominent Adam's apple bobbed up and down like a yo-yo. The two capitalists looked at each other fretfully, as if they'd said too much. Sloan did some hard and fast thinking. He knew that the only way for he and Ford to avoid a firing squad was to play ball with the leader of the communist revolution. But it was a two way street. Bakunin's goal of turning the supermonopoly into thousands of smoothly functioning, worker-owned, independent companies would flounder in the absence of active participation by Ford and himself. Now, a new wrinkle occurred to the industrial genius. Patton could throw a monkey wrench into the embryonic economic structure in a number of ways. He could clandestinely organize opposition from either the far left or far right, or both. Guerilla war would derail the fusion of Jefferson and Marx that Bakunin was trying to stitch together. Sloan's guess was that Patton wanted World War II to last for a long time, maybe decades.

"General Patton," Sloan began his pitch tentatively, wanting to probe his opponent like a cautious boxer in the opening round of a long match. Patton leaned back into his pile of cushions and nodded for Sloan to keep talking. "I gather that another general will be designated for the big push into Britain or Africa, whichever comes next. Assuming Ford and I can strike a deal with Bakunin and end the war in North America."

Patton spat out a single word: "Rommel."

Sloan was quick enough to figure out that this was the name of Patton's chief rival. The president of DFA exposed the main line of his plan carefully: "Neither Henry, nor myself are military men. We do know a thing or two about industrial production." He stopped talking. Patton had to agree to this point before Sloan could try to reel him in. The general made a circular motion with one of his hands, affecting an air of boredom, yet asking the industrial magnate to proceed. The hook had been set. It was time to fish or cut bait.

"There is zero chance that the Commonwealth had only one A-bomb development program. Even locked up in our penthouse, Henry and I've heard rumors on the telly about a second program in the Gobi Desert. There's also talk that the Sahara is the best place to test atom bombs. There can be no doubt that the Red Army will do what it can to snuff out the Commonwealth's nuclear bomb program, wherever it might be. This will be the next big military adventure for your people. The invasion of Britain or Zululand has got to be a year or more away."

Patton stopped Sloan and said, "From each according to his ability. To each according to his needs. Ever hear that one, Alfred?" Sloan conceded that he had; communists repeated the insipid slogan ad nauseam. Patton continued: "I'm considered an administrative genius. No one's better than good ol' Patton at running an occupying force in a pacified North America. That is my ability and the Red Army's need. General Georgi Konstantinovich Zhukov and his 2nd Division eradicated America's nuclear weapons program. That is his supposed ability. Bakunin believes that the Red Army's need is to have Georgi Zhukov and 2nd Division sent to the Gobi Desert. Like you said, the only other place in the Commonwealth any good for nuke building is the Sahara. Rommel is gearing up 5th Division for a junket into North Africa. Those two ass-wipes will see combat hunting down nukes."

Ford decided to stick a needle in Patton: "Gonna have you flying a desk, eh George? Shuffling paper? Counting beans and bullets?" Sloan gave his boss a warning glance. Ford shut up. Patton's face turned crimson, but he held his tongue, glowering and refusing to rise to the bait. A menacing silence descended on the plane's cabin. In the absence of conversation, the DFA news report could be heard. All three men glanced at the TV.

The screen showed a weatherman standing before a map of the United States. His pointer was indicating swaths of land, mostly stretching northward from Washington DC. The man was describing radioactive fallout patterns from the nuclear attack. He went on to give advice to American and Canadian citizens in the afflicted areas, starting with a warning to consume the potassium iodine tablets that the Red Army was handing out to communist police forces throughout the area.

"It's already started," Ford gloated. "The great George Patton is running the iodine tablet dispersal program." Sloan jabbed his boss with a sharp elbow to make him shut up. However, the chairman of the board's comment had the desired effect. Patton glared at the industrialists and growled, "What're the likes of you going to do about it?" When that failed to produce an answer, all pretense and bravado fell away from the general like autumn leaves. "How can I help you? How can you help me?"

Sloan knew he was about to land a big fish. He made a key demand on the general: Radical communist elements in the North American occupying force had to be purged and soon. In return, as a price for their cooperation with the Red Army, Sloan and Ford would tell Supreme Commander Vladimir Bakunin that Patton must take Zhukov's place as commander of 2nd Division and sent to the Gobi Desert. If Bakunin refused, then the industrialists would withhold their expertise.

Patton expressed doubts that their plan could work. In his opinion, Georgi Zhukov was a rising star for one reason: He was born in Strelkovka, a poverty stricken village not far from Moscow. By overarching coincidence, this is where Supreme Commander Bakunin was born. The bond between the two Russians would be hard to break. Zhukov had no more desire to run the incipient North American Administrative District than did Patton. And Zhukov could appeal to the SC in his native language, evoking imagery of their shared misery growing up destitute in rural Russia.

Sloan wanted one question answered: Was Zhukov's discovery and subsequent destruction of the American A-bomb program an example of military genius? Patton cradled his aching head in both hands, sick and tired of the hyperbole surrounding the Russian general's most famous achievement. In a weary voice, he told the industrialists that 2nd Division had stumbled on the enemy A-bomb program through the help of American communist moles and Bakunin knew it.

Ford said, "Vladimir Bakunin can't do squat without Alfred and me. The system he wants to build is a kind of free market communism. Alfred and me are key to its success. George, give your word that radicals won't sabotage what we're gonna build in the good old United States and we'll stand firm on your command in the Gobi Desert."

Old Blood and Guts raised his right hand and swore on his grandfather's grave that if he got the combat assignment in Asia, then he'd personally conduct a bloody and hellacious purge that would scour the Red Army in American clean of dangerous radicals.

Willy put his head in Patton's lap and fell asleep with his tail wagging. He couldn't know that they would be in the field soon, on the front lines, battling for revolutionary ideals. He did know that his master was happy, which meant that he was happy.

The humans returned their attention to the TV screen, which showed two images: one of Queen Victoria II, the other of Dwight D. Eisenhower. The announcer said, "Her Majesty has today appointed General Eisenhower supreme commander of the combined armies, navies, and aeroforces of the British Commonwealth; sacking General Montgomery. The move is expected to better coordinate the various national armies fighting the communists in the United States. It will mark the first time that a modern British army has fought under a foreign commander and highlights the ever closer integration of the American and British governments since the total destruction of Washington DC."

Patton clicked off the television and rubbed his hands together gleefully. He cast a taunting glance at the industrialists and asked for their reaction to the latest news item. Ford thought that it presaged an outright annexation of North America by the Crown, extending the boundaries of the United Kingdom across the Atlantic. The general shook his head as if reprimanding a student for failing a pop quiz and said, "That may be so, but forget politics. Think about military implications. Eisenhower's in London, why? The US, Canadian, and Mexican militaries will begin a phased withdrawal to Britain within weeks, maybe sooner. The war on this continent is about to become a rearguard action for the

Commonwealth."

Ford wagged a finger at Patton and said, "I'll not forget politics when it comes to purging Red Army fanatics here in America. Alfred and me'll need you to clean house, Georgey, and by God, you'd better deliver."

Red Army storm troopers kicked in the door of Danny O'Brien's San Francisco apartment. His German Shepherd coiled and sprang at the suited soldiers. Although the apartment was dark, enough light streamed in from the hallway for O'Brien to see that the intruders wore powered combat armor. Cyclone would only break his teeth against their titanium arms or legs.

"Cyclone, aus!" O'Brien hollered. The dog put on the brakes, skidding across a hardwood floor and nearly slamming into the interlopers. The two storm troopers leveled guns at the dog and the man inside the high-rise dwelling. O'Brien called the police dog to his side. The faceless men inside the combat armor spoke simultaneously, German accented voices distorted by electronic speakers. "Police Chief O'Brien?" The chief nodded silently, knowing that they could see in the dark with their infrared faceplate enhancements. "We are Red Army secret police. Come with us." The two suits stood there unmoving for three or four seconds, and then added, "Bring the dog. He is a trained killer and could cause harm unattended."

On the street below the apartment building, an unmarked police car was waiting. O'Brien was amazed to see that George Patton, a white Bulldog, and a red bloodhound were all sitting in the back seat. The two storm troopers piled into the front seat. The car's springs collapsed under their suited weight. O'Brien and Cyclone crammed themselves into the back, a tight squeeze.

The squad car rolled into the light nighttime traffic and Patton launched his interrogation. The general warned that the bloodhound would definitely catch any lies that might slip past a German Shepherd or a Bulldog. The big red dog bayed noisily, assuring the prisoner that the tiniest whiff of mendacity would surely be detected.

Patton described the role that Henry Ford and Alfred Sloan would be playing in the formation of free market communism. He went on to illustrate the similarities between the emerging economic system and free market capitalism before the monopolies took over, dwelling on the fact that some people would get rich in the brave new world, economic egalitarianism would not be a high priority after the war ended and the Red Army was triumphant, which would stick in the craw of the Marxist hard-liners.

The bloodhound leaned across Patton's body to jam his nose into O'Brien's armpit. The hound snuffled aggressively as the police chief answered a series of questions. Patton wanted to know if O'Brien objected to the establishment of thousands of non-governmental companies from the breakup of the supermonopoly and the lesser monopolies.

"Look, General," O'Brien began, "I may be an old-time Marxist, but I ain't no dinosaur. Who am I to disagree when Vladimir Bakunin says that this is what the face of modern communism looks like?" The bloodhound sniffed so hard that the fabric from O'Brien's shirt traveled up his nose several inches. The hound woofed affirmatively, a testimony to the chief's honesty.

"That pleases the holy shit out of me, Danny," Patton said brightly. "Because I want you to head up the Red Army secret police. There are dinosaurs in our ranks that aren't as liberal-minded as you and me. We need these fossils eliminated, bodies disposed of, no public trials, no muss and no fuss. Up for a promotion and a fat pay raise?"

"Put me in coach."

Chapter 18
Eisenhower is no Hannibal

Angerbotha saw Einstein and Nkosinathi's combat suits pop over the forcefield fence before any of the other animals. She raised her trunk and trumpeted an alarm. Angerbotha, Surus, and Hela had been patiently waiting while the three silverbacks: Kubwa, Erevu, and Bwana cinched their war harnesses tight and adjusted the aluminum barreled artillery pieces on their backs. The two mammoth cows and the one bull elephant pulled away from the adult male gorillas and stampeded toward the sinister suited figures walking inside the compound. Cannons and machineguns in the howdahs had not been secured, so they swung wildly back and forth. Worse, the belly straps holding the howdahs in place were loose.

The three silverbacks raced after the rampaging pachyderms, leaped onto their backs, and, with typically heroic strength, pulled the listing weapons platforms upright before they could slide under the big beasts' bellies and trip them up. The gorillas were so focused on preventing injuries to their beloved pachyderms that they failed to notice the two ambulatory gatecrashers and their exotic personal armor.

Angerbotha and Hela galloped more quickly than Surus, reaching the intruders first. Hairy trunks lashed out, encircled the two Mark VII power suits, and hoisted them twenty feet off the ground. At last, the three silverbacks saw what had the big monsters so riled.

To Bwana and the two other apes, it looked as though the smallish humans in power suits were not carrying weapons. One on one, the adult male gorillas had always been able to hold their own against an unarmed human in a PCS. Three against two, it should be no contest, and their troops were marching down the hill as back up. Bwana signaled the mammoths to lower the offending interlopers. As Einstein and Nkosinathi slowly sank to earth, Kubwa made hand signs to Bwana and Erevu: "I'm gonna open me a can of whoop-ass on these pinko faggots." The mountain gorilla beat his chest for emphasis. Three separate gorilla troops formed a circle around the brawny male apes and the titanic pachyderms, screeching and hooting, eager to see that can of whoop-ass get opened.

"Cease and desist!" Queen Victoria belted out the command while standing on a small racing style howdah strapped to the shoulder hump of Skuld, her favorite Angerbotha clone. The Queen's mammoth galloped over a hillock and skidded to a halt. The Monarch gave Skuld a command. A hirsute trunk wrapped around Victoria's trim body and set her between the strangers in suits and the three angry silverbacks.

Victoria faced the strangers. "Get out of your armor this instant!" She fastened the silverbacks with a reproving eye. "Do not harm these people. They are not communists." Kubwa raised his hands and signed to the Queen: "We wait for the faggots to get unsuited, then beat the shit out of them, right Vicky?" Victoria shook her head and said firmly, "We've been expecting two humans in combat suits. We shall ascertain their business and proceed from there. We have a strong premonition that these two are friends, not foes. And, Kubwa, We've warned you numerous times not to make homophobic remarks. It is unseemly."

Nkosinathi and Einstein clamshelled out of their Mark VIIs to collapse at Victoria's feet. They did not look their normal selves. Einstein's hair and moustache were shaved and he had body makeup that gave him a much darker complexion. Nkosinathi was wearing a greasy brown wig and body makeup gave her the skin color of a Caucasian.

Kubwa cast sympathetic eyes at the sick old man wheezing pathetically on the ground and the bedraggled woman so weak that she could barely kneel. The mountain gorilla squatted next to Einstein and signed, "Old geezer, I'm sorry for calling you a commie pinko fag. Let me carry you inside." Scooping the professor up like a baby, Kubwa tenderly carried him toward the palace. The youngest silverback leader, the newcomer from the Congo facility, Erevu, cradled Nkosinathi in his arms, following closely behind Kubwa.

Bwana squatted next to the pachyderms, watching Victoria and the two adult male gorillas make their way toward the concrete structure. The Queen was acting very solicitous toward the woebegone visitors, leaning over the hairy arms of the silverbacks, asking the humans questions. She suddenly straightened, reacting to something that the dark-skinned, baldheaded man had said. Victoria turned to face the dominant silverback. Cupping her hands to her mouth the Queen shouted, "Bwana, please bring those power suits inside! Store them in the armory under lock and key! That's a good fellow." The top gorilla raised his hands over his head, acknowledging her command with sign language. Before dealing with the suits, Bwana told the adult female gorillas in each of the three troops to take care of the four pachyderms, stow the howdahs, and unload all the weapons. Weapon practice was cancelled for today.

He stood there and pondered for a few seconds before grabbing a suit. Vicky had obviously been expecting these people. The human guards on the perimeter fence had not fired on them. Yet the gates had not been opened either. It was a mystery how their combat suits had crested the forcefield fence. A man in a power suit could jump higher than an unsuited man, but not that high.

Bwana was also curious as to why the arrival of the mysterious strangers had been kept deliberately low key, secretive actually. He turned one of the Mark VIIs over and fingered the flight cowls connected to the back. He'd never seen PCSs with flight cowls before, but had seen them on helicopters. Sniffing the suit interiors, Bwana's face crinkled into a mask of disgust. The smell of unwashed human was hard to stomach. They'd been in these things for a long time. He closed the torsos of both suits and snapped the helmets back in place.

Placing his hands under the armpits of a Mark VII, he hoisted it up, grunting with effort. The suits were unbelievably heavy, so heavy that he would have to carry them one at a time. He jockeyed the suit onto his back and knuckle-walked to the palace on all fours, transporting the thing as if it were an oversized saddle.

Once inside the palace, he paused at the heavy oak door of the armory room and listened. The creaky old pipes of the fortress were vibrating with running water. Kubwa and Erevu were drawing hot baths for the visitors. The number two and three silverback leaders had acquired pets. Next, they would feed their pets hot chicken soup. Sick humans always required chicken soup.

Bwana sloughed the heavy combat suit onto the stone floor of the palace basement. He pulled a set of keys from a loop around his neck and unlocked the ancient and rusty lock on the armory door. He dragged the thing next to a row of royal combat suits and pushed them aside to make room for the Mark VII. None of the body armor stored in the palace was powered. Gorillas and pachyderms didn't fight with power assistance. Their protective garments were made of leather, hardened aluminum alloy, and spider silk. PCSs were reserved for human weaklings, to compensate for their puny bodies. Next to the unpowered mammoth and gorilla body armor, the room contained gorilla-sized battle-axes, spears, flamethrowers, machineguns, hand grenades, and a host of seemingly medieval weapons including a variety of shields and swords, many of which would be too heavy for a human to even lift, let alone wield.

Trekking from the palace back to the training field, glancing at the mammoth barn, Bwana was happy to see that the pachyderms had been led to their stalls and hay had been placed in their mangers. The adult female gorillas were always conscientious. He wrestled the second suit onto his back, got on all fours, and slogged it to the big concrete blockhouse. The second exotic power suit was placed next to the first. The armory was locked. Bwana ambled back to the training field, ready to execute his usual round of inspections.

His two partners were also out there, tired of playing with their newly acquired pet humans, set to patrol the grounds of the compound. Kubwa was carrying three machineguns. Which was unusual. The mountain gorilla handed Bwana one of the fifty cals. Erevu grabbed one as well. Signing with his free hand, Kubwa said, "I didn't like the perimeter breach, even if they were friendly. Today we patrol packing heat." Bwana agreed, happy to see the unimaginative Kubwa showing some initiative.

They started with the long row of mammoth corrals that ran behind the barn. The Angerbotha and Hela clones were all doing fine. Every trough was filled with clean water. Piles of grain and heaps of alfalfa hay plumped their feed bins. Erevu pulled a wad of hay from one of the feeders and tasted it suspiciously. He signed at Bwana, "This hay is getting moldy. Mammoths will get sick if it gets any worse." Bwana took a bite of hay and nodded disagreeably. He would have to take it up with Nigel Mortimer. Humans were always cutting corners. Probably a new manager at the DFA feed store was trying to pull a fast one. Maybe they should drive into town and punch in the walls of the feed store.

The Bulldog kennels were next. The slab-like canines threw themselves repeatedly against cyclone fences in a rapturous assiduity to come out and play with the silverbacks. Ignoring the dogs' cries for attention, the gorillas inspected water bowls and the packed earthen surface of the kennels for cleanliness. The Wolfhounds were better behaved, leaning against the cyclone fences to be scratched by the simians. Satisfied, the apes moved on to the guard post at the main gate.

"Hey, limp-dick, how come nobody told us about the visitors?" Kubwa signaled through the forcefield fence to the man in the guardhouse. The captain of the Queen's

Household Cavalry eyed the gorillas' hulking fifty cals anxiously and shouted, "These visitors are very hush-hush. I don't even know who they are." Kubwa reared up onto his hind legs and gave the captain the one-fingered salute. The man turned away from the apes, not wanting to antagonize them, well aware of their proclivity to fire weapons if angered. He disapproved of giving gorillas unlimited access to machineguns and hand grenades. The Queen saw it otherwise, citing the rush of radical humaniac attacks, effectively closing the possibility of debate.

Bwana led his partners away from the main gate in disgust. Kubwa signed, "Know what cheeses me the most about humans and chimps? So many are homos. Rump rangers make me puke." Erevu agreed: "Up to 5 percent of male humans and chimpanzees are homosexual. In the Congo PLC, I saw a sizeable percentage of queer chimpanzees." Kubwa scratched his head in befuddlement. Erevu was a fourth generation technical-strain signing gorilla, bred at the Congo Primate Language Center. The two older silverbacks were third generation general-purpose strain, bred in England. Most of the apes from gen. four tech peppered their conversation with references to mathematical concepts like percentages. Anything beyond basic arithmetic was difficult for gen. three general-purpose apes.

Bwana gestured at Kubwa, "Whatever you think about homosexual men, when the war starts, some humans in our army will be pufffers. We have to judge humans on fighting ability alone. Winning the war takes precedence over social engineering."

"I don't like male human homos. Lesbians are different," Kubwa signed stubbornly. As usual, Erevu agreed with Kubwa: "Gorilla lesbians turn me on. Human lesbians make good soldiers." On this topic, Bwana was of the same opinion as his junior partners: "Lesbian humans and lesbian gorillas make fine soldiers." The silverbacks had speculated in the past many times as to whether Queen Victoria was a lesbian or not. Usually, their conversation would turn to that subject whenever the subject of lesbians cropped up. However, they were now striding next to the palace, and any member of the royal staff or the Queen herself could be peeking out a window and might see their hand signs, so they changed the subject to an old standby: half-hearted threats to steal prize females from each other's troops. Kubwa stopped walking and sniffed the breeze. "I smell the approach of our weasel boss: Nigel Mortimer."

Mortimer stepped around a corner of a palace courtyard and made a beeline toward the three male gorillas. Before Mortimer could get a word in, Kubwa accused him of being a weasel and wanted to know why the silverbacks had been kept in the dark about the two human visitors. Mortimer responded, "Never mind that. You're in the loop now. Actually, I need your troops and mammoths to create a diversion tomorrow morning, a bone to throw at any communist spies in the area. Scientific equipment is to be smuggled here inside a load of hay. Your job is to take the gorillas and all the adult mammoths down the road to the Primate Language Center in a very showy procession." Mortimer paused to let that sink in and added, "There is also a need to get the apes over at PLC some time on mammoth back. Once you are there, I expect some effective training of the PLC troops and junior silverbacks. They haven't fired the cannons or machineguns very much and their aim is below par."

Bwana signed, "We'll do it, Boss. By the way, I hope there is a real load of hay in that delivery, because the garbage we're feeding the mammoths sucks." Mortimer promised to check the quality of the hay being delivered tomorrow. He spun on his heel and dashed into the palace, clearly in a twitter over all the changes ushered in by the mysterious visitors' arrival.

The silverbacks watched his departure suspiciously. Despite what their superior had asserted, they weren't truly in the loop yet. Gorillas consider withholding information tantamount to lying. And they hated being lied to. There was one person that they could always turn to for straight talk. Bwana asked the other two if they'd noticed whether Hacksaw was amongst the other Bulldogs. Erevu thought that he was. They ran back to the kennels after swinging by their individual enclosures to grab the bags of peanut butter and celery sandwiches that their females routinely prepared at this time of day.

Hacksaw was there all right, whining and then smashing into his kennel gate, trying to get out. One of the kennel boys was scraping dog dirt out of the runs. Bwana made signs at the boy, asking him to tell Hacksaw to find David Banner. It was hard to give orders to war dogs in sign language. The boy was only too happy to stop working for a while. The Bulldog was turned loose. The boy gave him the command. Hacksaw sprinted away at top speed. The silverbacks bounded after him, wishing that they'd had the foresight to hook the fleet-footed Bulldog to a leash.

Hacksaw raced over hill and dale. Puffing mightily through flaring nostrils, sandwich bags gripped between their teeth, the massive apes struggled to keep up. The extra muscle they'd packed on during weight training was both an asset and a liability. They were stronger than any wild gorilla, yet they had less endurance. Long runs like this were especially exhausting to the bulky apes.

The gorillas and the Bulldog drew steadily away from the buildings and pens of the complex, out into the open grazing lands where the mammoths and Surus were occasionally permitted to run wild. There, between two trees, a hammock was strung. A tall, heavy boned horse was cropping lush grass next to a very old and very large man with a wooden leg. The snoring of the old man sounded like boulders grinding together.

Hacksaw refused to awaken his master, going instead into a down-stay under the hammock. The gorillas slowed to a walk once their quarry had been spotted. Squatting on either side of the sleeping invalid, the silverbacks were no more willing to rouse David Banner than Hacksaw had been. They carefully peeled back their paper bags and extracted stacks of sandwiches as wide as roofing shingles. Gorillas can do anything silently if they choose. They ate their sandwiches as quietly as silkworms chewing mulberry leaves, slipping the Bulldog a few bits to keep him from whining.

Banner's eyes fluttered open. He was mildly amused to see the silverback trio and Hacksaw waiting there. Bwana asked the holy man what he'd been dreaming about. The answer: Hannibal's great victory over the Romans at Cannae. The apes grunted knowingly. Banner almost always dreamed about General Hannibal, for this reason the ancient Carthaginian military genius was a totem for the gorillas. The mathematically minded Erevu signed brightly, "After Cannae, the Carthaginian city fathers gave Hannibal forty more elephants."

Hastily, Bwana steered the discussion to the mysterious visitors, not wanting to bog down in a David Banner lecture on classical history. The one-legged man sat upright in his hammock, rubbing the five o'clock shadow on his cheeks, and then rubbing the sleep out of his eyes. He peered fuzzily at the shaggy Goliaths and said wonderingly, "Albert Einstein is here. The final piece of the puzzle has fallen into place. I must get to him before he talks to Churchill and Eisenhower."

222

Kubwa signed, "The old man wearing makeup is a sweet little guy, not a mighty warrior." Banner was now fully awake. He told the mountain gorilla that Einstein was the greatest warrior of their age. The aging cripple hobbled to his horse and swung into the saddle. Neck-reining the warm blood until he'd wheeled around and was facing the palace, Banner asked the silverbacks to please put Hacksaw back in his kennel and stay out of trouble themselves. He clucked the horse into a brisk trot and was gone.

Einstein couldn't believe that he had to wear makeup even inside the palace. He pushed the half eaten bowl of chicken soup away. Nkosinathi scolded him, insisting that he finish it, adding that chicken soup had chemical compounds that resembled penicillin. It was not an old wives' tale that chicken soup was good for people suffering from colds or the flu.

"Dammit, woman, I'm not sick, just tired. It's getting late. We should go to bed," Einstein said irritably, getting up and crossing the room, making for the bed. A knock on the door brought another grumble from the exhausted physicist. There was no excuse for the palace staff to bother him further. He'd already told these people what he needed in the way of scientific equipment. Until it arrived, there was nothing he could do, and he needed his rest. Queen Victoria's voice called from the other side of the door, announcing a visitor: David Banner. Einstein quickly recrossed the room and whispered in his wife's ear, "Why does that name sound familiar?" She whispered back, "David Banner is that fellow that started the Boer War. Considered a religious figure in England. Has a sort of cult following, something to do with animals. He's the reason for all the war beasts around here."

The door creaked open. Banner gimped into the room and slammed the door shut, practically in the Queen's face. Einstein immediately told him that the hour was late, too late for chitchat. Banner took a seat near the room's one window as if the professor had invited him in, cold gray eyes alighting on the pair of itinerate scientists. "I agree. Please sleep. Both of you will think more clearly after resting. I will be here in the morning. We'll talk then," he said in a tone that broached no compromise. Mr. and Mrs. Einstein were already wearing pajamas and a dressing room joined the bedroom. Still, Banner's suggestion was highly irregular.

Nkosinathi wanted to protest the bizarre imposition. Something about the one-legged man stopped her. He was a caricature of the immoveable object as he sat there framed by the large picture window: a granite boulder that no force could pry from their chamber. In some odd way, his presence was comforting. The Einsteins pulled blankets up around their necks and succumbed to fatigue, passing out into a dreamless sleep. Moonlight poured through the window, casting a pale glow on the somnolent couple. Banner watched them without moving a muscle, his mind a blank, locked on to a single purpose to the exclusion of all else, even proper decorum. The final piece of the puzzle had to fall in place or his whole life had been wasted. He'd waited decades for the talk that would come in the morrow. Churchill and Eisenhower could not get to the brilliant couple before he did and poison their minds.

There would be a conference. The future course of the war would be plotted. He'd always failed to persuade the powers-that-be in conferences. He always felt like Oliver Cromwell addressing the Church of Scotland: *I beseech you in the bowels of Christ think it possible you may be mistaken*. But the powerful politicians never thought it possible that they might be mistaken. This time it would be different. Albert Einstein would spell that difference.

Moonlight waned. The morning sun turned a black sky gray. Stable hands and kennel boys began the long process of feeding breakfast to the army of war beasts. Barnyard noises filtered up to the palace. Einstein and Nkosinathi stirred. Banner rose stiffly from his séance, the one-legged man offered to bring a tray of crumpets and tea up to their room. A curt nod from Mrs. Einstein sent him shambling downstairs, to the kitchen.

He met Lisa while preparing the tray of victuals. She helped carry it upstairs. Upon entering the bedchamber, they found the two physicists glued to the room's window, staring at the pageant Nigel Mortimer had planned the day before. One hundred mammoths and one African elephant were decked out in unpowered body armor. An aluminum howdah swayed on the back of each marching pachyderm, full up with a hefty cannon and two swivel mounted heavy machineguns. The gorillas inside the howdahs also wore unpowered body armor, like King Arthur's knights on steroids. Metal shields were strapped to their backs, battle-axes dangled from their belts.

Behind the mammoths, packs of Bulldogs trotted jauntily in heavy war harnesses, light machineguns rotating between their shoulder blades as if they were tiny dreadnaughts. Sprinkled among the Bulldogs were human riders on mustangs: the leaders of the mobile canine infantry. On the flanks of the animal army were additional horsemen riding long-legged thoroughbreds, directing leggy Wolfhounds garbed in very light armor and carrying only a few clips for their light machineguns: the cavalry.

Angerbotha climbed the knoll closest to the palace and posed for the onlookers inside. On her back, Kubwa climbed from his aluminum howdah, placed his feet squarely on the twin crowns of Angerbotha's mighty skull, rose to his full height of seven feet, and clashed his battle-axe against his shield. The silverback raised his chin. His helmet tilted back. Through the air holes in his visor, a leonine roar reverberated. In the military parade funneling toward the main gate, Bulldogs and Wolfhounds barked, gorillas roared, horses whinnied, humans shouted, and mammoths trumpeted. The sound of the animal army's battle cry shook every window frame in the castle.

David and Lisa Banner walked all the way into the Einsteins' room. David took the tray from Lisa and set it on a table. Lisa pulled out silverware and napkins. The Banners pulled back to give the hungry travelers some room. While they ate, David remarked, "The army outside your window, it contains no electronic or electrical devices. It is, therefore, immune to—" He experienced a senior moment, searching for a word and coming up blank. He paused and asked, "What is it called again, the energy blast which disables electrical components?"

Einstein took a sip of tea and said, "An electromagnetic pulse." Banner nodded, his tired old brain bouncing back onto track. He and Lisa sat on the bed and the one-legged man seemingly changed the subject by quoting a famous saying of Einstein's: "God doesn't play dice with the universe."

Nkosinathi frowned, but Einstein smiled nostalgically and responded, "I said that to cast doubt on Heisenberg's Quantum Mechanics." Banner massaged his stump where flesh and the wooden peg leg joined and continued: "A very different approach, the one Heisenberg takes, compared to Herr Doctor Professor. Heisenberg will only countenance that which is directly observable, a stratagem that is, under most circumstance, inimical

224

to perceiving or even discussing the existence of God."

Neither Einstein nor Nkosinathi responded. Their faces bore the stamp of calculation, as if they could guess where Banner was leading them. The professor broke the logjam by pointing at the window, indicating the war beasts outside. "Somehow, Mr. Banner, you've been inspired to make guesses about my theories and designs concerning electromagnetic pulse weapons. There would be two very distinct phases to warfare if such weapons existed: a pre-pulse environment and a post-pulse environment. The army parading outside this window would dominate a post-EMP environment, I imagine."

"Professor Einstein, I can barely spell the words electromagnetic pulse, let alone anticipate the mind of history's greatest theoretician," Banner asserted. "It's true," Lisa echoed, "David has no formal scientific training. He started building the Hannibalic Army with no knowledge of EMP technology. He only knew that something like EMP weapons would someday exist."

"How could he have known?" Nkosinathi wondered. Rather than delve into raw mysticism, a topic sure to make scientists squirm, Banner decided to set out the performance criteria that the pulse weapons would have to deliver.

"My wife uses the term 'Hannibalic.' Our post-EMP army is based on the military of the great Carthaginian general, Hannibal Barca, the most effective strategist, tactician, and technical innovator to have existed in ancient times. It is a myth that Hannibal's elephants only arrived in large numbers onto the Italian peninsula by crossing the Alps. Many of his elephants sailed across the Mediterranean." Banner stopped talking to gauge the mood of the two scientific geniuses.

Nkosinathi and Einstein were wearing expression of distaste under their makeup. It wasn't clear what was bothering them, so Banner resumed speaking. "The Commonwealth's Hannibalic Army will have to sail across the Pacific and Atlantic and hit either coast of the American continent. And I do mean sail. The Banner family fortune is being used to secretly build ships with sails and nineteenth century coal-fired steam engines. Commonwealth EMP weapons will have to not only render every continent electrically impotent, the surface and depths of the oceans will have to be similarly affected. Pulse weapons must have a global reach."

The scientists' looked pained. Yet the continental and oceanic requirement for pulse weaponry didn't seem to be upsetting them. Banner wished that he had brought Hacksaw to the tête-à-tête. The dog could have sniffed out the strange emotions percolating inside Nkosinathi and Einstein. Luckily, the good doctor made the presence of a canine mood detector unnecessary by saying, "We were hoping that pulse weapons would end all war, swords beaten into plowshares. My wife and I are pacifists."

Banner stood and limped painfully to the window. The noisy procession of gorillas, Bulldogs, and mammoths was gone. Semi-trucks were quietly unloading bails of hay. The gleam of scientific instruments flashed occasionally between blocks of hay being moved with forklifts. Among the innocuous hay bails there were lead encased ingots of uranium and the components needed to build enrichment centrifuges.

The crippled old man said, "My wife and I are also pacifists. The only valid purpose of war is to create lasting peace. Britain had the chance at the end of World War I, and blew it with the cursed CMG. When that war ended, the original Queen Victoria held untrammeled power over humanity and could have secured a lasting peace. Dr. Einstein, Mrs. Einstein, Lisa, between the four of us, Victoria II can be put in that position again.

The Crown must not and will not fail a second time. Pulse weapons combined with the Hannibalic Army will make for true peace."

Banner faced the interior of the room. The two physicists were about to learn why the strange one-legged man had spent the night at their bedside. He was unleashing a kind of preemptive strike in an upcoming debate. He warned them of the impending visit of Commonwealth military brass. Winston Churchill and Dwight Eisenhower would be arriving at the castle sometime today. They would try to convince Einstein to build more Mark VII power suits and put the quest for pulse technology on the back burner. According to Banner, that path led toward years of war. Pulse weapons would permit a speedy Hannibalic victory pursued by a negotiated settlement.

Lisa and David Banner finished their pitch and left the room and the palace to care for their animal charges. Einstein collapsed into the bed in exasperation. Nkosinathi wandered to the window to watch the unloading of nuclear weapon components. She hoped that the ranks of stable hands and kennel boys milling about were not riddled with communist spies. The high-tech components imported from the London A-bomb program were encased in hay bails. How long would that rouse work? For that matter, would the disguises and makeup that they were wearing fool enemy spies determined to sleuth out the secret of the great scientist's whereabouts?

Two dented old cars pulled up the long driveway between the palace and the main gate. Civilians and men in uniform exited the vehicles. From the mammoth barn, David and Lisa Banner emerged. The big man was leaning heavily on his wife as they hurried to intercept the new arrivals. A Bulldog circled the Banners excitedly. The Queen and a small retinue came out of the castle. All these groups converged in one of the courtyards. Nkosinathi didn't like the look of the augury below.

A knock at their door produced a royal messenger and a request for the couple to proceed to the Queen's throne room. Nkosinathi told the messenger to wait outside for a moment. She and her husband were dressed too casually. There were more formal clothes in the dressing room. She clothed Herr Doctor Professor in a somber gray suit and a bright red bow tie. The outfit radiated respect for the Queen, yet said Einstein was not an old fogy. For herself, a black dress and pearls. It took them quite a while to dress due to the need to readjust their elaborate disguises.

Walking down the stairs behind the messenger, Nkosinathi put her mouth close to Einstein's ear and whispered, "They are expecting you to make a military decision that only Jeremiah Halifax is qualified to make." He hissed back at her, "Jeremiah did not earn three Noble Prizes when he was twenty-six years old." She bowed her head deferentially, conceding the veracity of the statement and hiding a grin at the same time. Nkosinathi had lit a fire under Herr Doctor Professor's belly, negating his natural inclination to defer military judgment to professionals. She knew that the professionals lacked the technical knowledge to choose between EMP weapons and Mark VII combat suits. To paraphrase David Banner: the military experts couldn't even spell electromagnetic pulse.

The Queen was sitting on her throne, perched on a dais behind a balustrade of transparent plasteel. Two Gurkha female bodyguards stood on either side of the throne. The two women from Nepal looked as tough as any man in the room. Household cavalrymen in purple tunics stood in a line against the balustrade. A rough-hewn table carved from a solid granite boulder dominated the center of the room. It must have been bolted to the castle's concrete foundation. Almost floating above the boulder table on her ethereal throne, screened by her guards, Victoria appeared as distant and removed from the proceedings as if she were on another planet. The effect was deliberate. She wanted open debate, not a ritual in royal prostration.

Winston Churchill, Dwight Eisenhower, and a gaggle of military aides pushed back chairs and stood as the two scientists entered the room. Lisa helped David to struggle up onto his feet. Everyone took a seat after acknowledging the Queen's presence. Nkosinathi noticed that Prime Minister Voss was not in attendance. While on Hawaii, she'd tried to keep up with world politics by listening to DFA news broadcasts. Nothing in those broadcasts indicated that the PM's chief of staff (Churchill) had usurped the real power at Ten Downing Street. There was no other explanation for the obvious authority that the tubby little man was wielding.

Churchill began the meeting by congratulating Einstein and Nkosinathi on surviving the long and perilous journey from Johnston Island to England, which was, according to Churchill, an odyssey worthy of Homer. He noted that for security reasons there were no representatives from Japan here today. Nevertheless, the Japanese secret service was owed a debt of eternal gratitude for overseeing the rail transport of the two scientists and the Mark VIIs across Asia, over the Urals, and eventually to this very palace, all the while employing the concealment skills of their ninja ancestors. The Japanese had expertly disguised Einstein and Nkosinathi, providing cover stories and false identities. They had also made up two of their agents to look like the professor and his wife and sent them to the ersatz A-bomb program in the Gobi Desert. With any luck, communist spies would be converging on the Chinese city of Pao-t'ou any day now, sniffing blindly down the false trail that the Japanese had so expertly blazed. One would have almost thought that Churchill was Japanese from the praise that he was heaping on the island kingdom.

The chief of staff didn't give any more details concerning the fake A-bomb program in China. That information was on a need to know basis. It was only important for Einstein and his wife to appreciate that they needed to continue wearing their disguises while they worked on wonder weapons at SW Palace #9. Churchill would have liked to chastise the two physicists for losing patience with their Japanese escorts and completing the last leg of their journey by flying the Mark VIIs directly into the Queens' compound. That had not been part of the plan. However, nothing would be gained by belaboring the point now.

He moved on to an update of the overall military situation. The American Army and its allies on the other side of the pond had been evacuated to Britain and were being integrated into the Queen's Army under Eisenhower's command. The communists had consolidated their grip on the United States and were pushing into Mexico and Canada with impunity. Spy plane photos revealed that construction of a superconducting supercollider in Texas was well underway. The Red Army's three Mark VII suits that had last seen combat in the Battle of Santa Fe had temporarily disappeared, probably to be taken apart for reverse engineering by Marxist technicians.

Alfred Sloan and Henry Ford were actively cooperating with the communists. DFA companies in North America were being broken up into smaller competing units. Shares of stock formerly belonging to the DFA board of directors were being issued to workers. The beginning of a powerful industrial boom was underway. DFA holdings in Europe, Asia, South America, Australia, and Africa were in a quandary without direction from the home office in San Jose. For the moment, the Commonwealth was directing supermonopoly industrial policy toward military ends. Ironically, Commonwealth controlled DFA companies bore a closer resemblance to traditional socialism than the strange new system emerging across the Atlantic. Pressure was mounting for the Commonwealth to break up the supermonopoly outside of North America and follow the model Ford himself was establishing, i.e., foster fierce economic competition through antitrust laws and employee share transfers, a move that was being resisted because it would disrupt military production.

The good news was that the enemy had taken the bait concerning the faux A-bomb program in the Gobi Desert. The Red Army's dreaded 2nd Division was assembling on America's west coast for a push into Asia. That, combined with the communists' need to consolidate their gains, should buy the Commonwealth critical time to build its own Mark VII power suits and finish the real A-bomb project in England. The Red Army could not invade Britain for at least one year.

All eyes turned to Einstein. He took a pair of eyeglasses from a breast pocket and nervously polished them on a handkerchief. "My wife remarked this morning after breakfast that a choice lies before us that would best be made by a man possessing acumen in both military matters and advanced technology. Blue Force Supreme Commander Halifax had such credentials, alas, he perished defending Nkosinathi and myself on Johnston Island."

Einstein's normally dreamy gaze sharpened as it swung across Churchill and Eisenhower. Nkosinathi reached out and grabbed the professor's hand, squeezing hard to lend him strength. His gaze softened as it alighted on David Banner. "It will take years to build an army of Mark VII suits. In months, I can build pulse weapons that will disable every scrap of electronics on Earth, scaling the heights of the stratosphere, plunging to the depths of the Marianna Trench."

Eisenhower began to object. Einstein showed uncharacteristic backbone by cutting the supreme commander off with a curt question: "Can the Commonwealth hold off the communists for three years while we laboriously build a supercollider?"

Eisenhower retorted hotly, "We can hold them off by rapidly finishing the A-bomb project. Atom bombs can keep the enemy at bay while Mark VII combat suits are cranked out here in England."

"I'm told that British atomic weapons are almost ready for combat," Churchill added hopefully. All eyes turned to Einstein. With his expertise on tap, there may be no need to explode nuclear weapons for testing purposes, retaining the element of surprise for the Commonwealth, magnifying the duplicity of the fake A-bomb program in China.

"The Hawaiian supercollider was built by a Texas firm many years ago," Einstein said sadly. "They have the design on file, I am sure. We will have to start from scratch. Your British uranium enrichment program is indeed producing weapons grade fissile material. We can build A-bombs in a matter of weeks. H-bombs in months." He paused to sigh and drop his head in the posture of defeat.

The last two sentences sounded extremely hopeful. The military men wanted to take heart but could see that the professor wasn't going to let them. They held their tongues and waited for the great scientist to resume talking. "There is no point in trading H-bomb attacks. If we stand toe-to-toe and slug it out in a nuclear war, both sides will be utterly destroyed," he said, his noble cranium still hanging in wretched failure.

Slowly, he raised his head to judge the temper of the crowd. Eisenhower and Churchill were angry, but trying to conceal it. Their military aides were pensive, fearful of the gloomy picture that Einstein had painted. The Banners appeared hopeful. The Queen was stone-faced. A Bulldog stuck his nose up between David and Lisa Banner to sniff the mood of the humans around the block-like table, taking the same kind of inventory as Einstein.

"The situation would indeed be dire, if not for the advanced state of Britain's A-bomb and soon its H-bomb program." This seemed to contradict Einstein's earlier assessment. The anger drained a bit from Churchill and Eisenhower's faces. Everyone else looked confused. "Nkosinathi and I will very quickly transform H-bombs into P-bombs. Electromagnetic pulse bombs will be able to deep-fry the circuitry and electrical components of every machine in the Red Army, in the world, actually." He stopped and let that sink in.

Nkosinathi released her husband's hand and gave a brief lesson, in layman's terms, on pulse weapons and their effects. She summed up her explanation by citing the analogy of a global switch that could turn off every machine on the planet that used electricity, from aeroplanes in the stratosphere to submarines at the bottom of the ocean. Refineries would stop producing fuel. Munitions plants would stop producing bullets. H-bombs would not explode. Radios would fall silent.

She went on to list the technology that would remain functional. Cordite would still explode. Non-electrical chemical reactions would be largely unaffected. Small arms, turn of the century hand grenades, primitive flamethrowers, and old-fashioned breech-loading artillery would remain operative in the post-EMP environment, although ammunition would rapidly dwindle because factories would be totally disabled. Very small, kick-started diesel motorcycles would also be effective until their fuel supply dried up. Wood-burning or coal-fired steamships would function effectively. Steam locomotives would run on wood, but the advent of maglev trains had necessitated the removal of old style rail lines in most countries, this meant animal power would be the only reliable military option in advanced countries, once the war was well and truly into the post-EMP era.

"No, you people can't be serious!" Eisenhower shouted as he at last connected the dots. "The big monkeys and hairy elephants are a joke!" He looked around wildly as if he were trapped in a surreal nightmare. The Queen's statute-like detachment fell away. In icy tones the Monarch asked if the supreme commander was referring to the royal mammoths and royal gorillas. Did he know how many centuries the apes of Gibraltar had been a part of the royal menagerie? Was he aware of the holy status of Bulldogs in the Anglican Church?

The Amazon Gurkha bodyguards had drawn handguns from their baggy shirtsleeves during the Queen's icy questioning. The guns weren't pointed directly at the supreme commander, but the Nepalese warriors were staring straight at him. The Queen's cavalrymen had their hands on holstered forty-fives and were also looking at the American general, who was beginning to comprehend the difference between serving under an elected commander-and-chief and operating under the heavy thumb of the Queen of England. If he didn't apologize for defaming the royal menagerie, the Gurkhas would kill him and the only repercussion would be the Crown selecting another supreme commander.

Eisenhower was not a man to be put off by the mere threat of physical violence. He stubbornly pushed ahead: "I cannot imagine an army that fights with elephants like Alexander or Hannibal did thousands of years ago." Victoria's icy tone took on a mystical quality: "There are more things in heaven and earth, General Eisenhower, than are dreamt of in your philosophy." The Queen's statement was sheer gibberish to the American. He looked wildly from one English face to another around the table. Every freaking Limey wore an expression of comprehension and approval. These island-dwelling aliens understood exactly what the Monarch was driving at.

The terrain of the debate was so unfamiliar that Eisenhower was forced into a tactical retreat. He nodded respectfully at his Liege and said, "Her Royal Highness's point is well taken. Let's set aside the question, for the moment, of H-bombs verse P-bombs and war beast verse machine. The two Mark VIIs here in the palace, they're going to be needed to attack communist convoys crossing the Atlantic."

Nkosinathi glanced at her husband from the corners of her eyes. Einstein was hunched over the table with his hands spread along the smooth granite expanse, lost to the discussion, in a trance, probably running equations through his mind that might or might not have anything to do with pulse weapons. She slapped the palms of her hands on the polished granite of the weighty table as hard as she could, startling everyone in the room except Albert Einstein, who remained oblivious. Nkosinathi said, "The two Mark VIIs here in the palace will be modified to serve as space transporters, to place the P-bombs in orbit. We cannot afford to lose them in combat; there is no time to design and build conventional rockets."

Nkosinathi's hands remained on the stone slab after she'd punctured Eisenhower's last hope. Her eyes suddenly grew wide with wonder. She asked the others to place their hands, palms down, on the table. Some of the mammoths were returning from their sojourn. Tremors from elephantine footfalls vibrated up into the granite table, and into the hands and arms of the symposium participants. The tramp, tramp, tramp of the mammoth's heavy tread hypnotized the members of the conference, putting them in the same trance that was enthralling the professor, effectively ending the discussion.

Einstein raised his hands, bowed to the Queen, and said, "I will not create electromagnetic pulse weapons unless the Crown meets one demand of mine—" He faltered, losing his nerve, mumbling something about begging Her Majesty's pardon. Banner pinned the scientist with a scathing look. When this failed to infuse him with the requisite backbone, Banner glared at Nkosinathi, who boldly picked up the ball and ran with it. "My husband, and myself, will not develop pulse weapons unless the Crown promises to permanently ban the Commonwealth Military Games, when and if the war is won. Mankind is ready for peace."

Victoria smiled blandly and informed Nkosinathi that there was no stomach anywhere in the Commonwealth for another CMG. This pronouncement received universal approval from every man and woman in the assembly room, the only sentiment meeting with universal favor that day.

Chapter 19

The War gives Way to an Uneasy Sitzkrieg

ommunism was taking root in America. Jim Pullman had a huge portrait of Karl Marx hanging in his office and Vladimir Bakunin's little red book in his pocket. Pullman loved the rough and tumble of free market communism. He was making more money now than he'd ever dreamed of under the stupefying inertia of monopoly capitalism. It was a different ballgame nowadays, an entrepreneur had to play by a whole new set of rules. Not only was competition fierce between the thousands of companies spawned by the breakup of DFA North America, within a given company workers counted for more and had to be listened to. Every publicly traded corporation had its own workforce as majority stockholders. Their permission had to be granted before any major decision could be implemented. If the chairman of the board couldn't intelligently guide and direct the primal urges of the unwashed masses on the payroll, then the whole enterprise would get flushed right down the crapper because some other lean and hungry outfit would leap into your market and snap up your customers.

Pullman had sold his car dealerships and purchased every outstanding share in Constructivist Archangel Inc., one of the innumerable DFA spin-offs. A 20 percent stake made the former car dealer the largest single shareholder. This hadn't automatically made him chairman of the board. There had to be an election, which meant schmoozing the other 80 percent of the shareholders (all of whom worked for the company), plus he had to get the nod from Henry Ford: the Red Army's industrial Czar. Pullman would retain his leadership position and continue raking in fat bonuses if, and only if, he kept making money for the shareholder/employees.

The workers still had a union. Although it had morphed into an owner's association for political reasons the organization still liked to call itself a union. Pullman had a meeting scheduled with the two union reps. Under discussion was whether or not to hire Antoine Pevsner and Vladimir Tatlin as Constructivist Archangel's chief architects, and whether or not to pay them the exorbitant salaries that the Russian geniuses were demanding.

Danny O'Brien and Otto Mueller swaggered into Pullman's office. O'Brien had his faithful German Shepherd, Cyclone, on a leash. The union reps doffed their caps and tipped their heads respectfully to the portrait of Karl Marx. Cyclone curled up in a corner of the plush office. Since the war had ended in North America, Mueller had gotten quite fat, nearly as fat as Pullman. The erstwhile prison warden heaved his stocky carcass into a chair and made a motion for O'Brien to take the other seat. O'Brien didn't sit down. He wandered over to an abstract sculpture on the other side of Pullman's office. It took the chief of the secret police a few seconds to realize that the objet d'art was actually a scale model for a building: a lofty skyscraper. Most skyscrapers were steel and glass boxes. This building was shaped like a sine wave, a coiling entity that lovingly enclosed negative space between sensuously twisting girders and glassed in rooms, a building that looked in on itself introspectively while looking out at the larger universe. O'Brien tried to tear himself away from the model, but couldn't take his eyes off the thing. It symbolized the dynamic forces transforming North America in a way that made rhetoric and words pale in comparison.

"Yeah, that's right, Chief. That building is something else. The Russkes' best ever," Pullman said, ignoring Otto and speaking directly to O'Brien. "I'm not gonna to tell you what you already know. I'm not gonna to tell you that Pevsner and Tatlin founded the constructivist movement and every other architect is a hack compared to these two guys. I'm not gonna to tell you how they were lead architects when this company was owned by DFA. That's old news. What I am gonna tell you about is that building." He pointed at the model that had so captivated O'Brien. "The Communist International World Headquarters. We're gonna tear down the old DFA headquarters and build that baby right here in San Jose."

Otto adjusted his bulk so that he could see the object that had the other two men in a twitter. He turned away from the bizarre steel and glass curves and said, "It's ugly and impossible to build."

"No," Pullman corrected, "impossible to build without technology from the Red Army. With transparent plasteel windows that can bear the same loads as conventional steel girders, building the CIWH will be a snap." O'Brien's eyes shone brightly. Otto looked grumpy and unconvinced. The chunky union rep weighed in with his real complaint: "Even if we land this building project, one million pounds a year is too much salary for these fancy pants avant-garde Russkes. Paying that kind of bread goes against communist principles. At least it did in my day, back when I was locked in a filthy British prison cell alongside Vladimir Bakunin and Max Stephanitz, sweating under interrogation lights. Yeah, we were real communists back then. Anyone said 'free market communism' in those days, we would have kicked the crap out of him. Those were the days."

O'Brien walked up behind the seated Otto and put meaty hands on his friend's shoulders, pinching a nerve with his grip. In a low and dangerous voice O'Brien said, "My dear, dear friend, please don't forget who you're talking to. I am the head of the secret police and could have you shot for making seditious remarks against free market communism." Otto shrugged off the nerve pinch and snorted in derision, obviously unmoved by the threat. The Red Army secret police had killed men for making disparaging remarks about the new economic order, but none of them had been old acquaintances of Vladimir Bakunin.

Jim Pullman hoisted his fat body out of his chair and waddled over to a liquor cabinet. He poured three drinks, lifted a glass, and offered a toast to free market communism. They downed the fiery spirits: vodka from Russia, expensive stuff in light of the embargo.

Pullman smacked his lips and looked at O'Brien, who had given up pinching Otto's nerves and was sitting down. "Danny, your sons are fighting in the Gobi Desert. Pretty hairy out there, or so I here." The secret police chief's face darkened. He nodded without saying anything, afraid that his voice might crack.

Pullman picked up a pocket calculator from his desk and started punching buttons, murmuring as if to himself, but loud enough for the others to hear. "Hmm, let's see. Pevsner and Tatlin are demanding a million each, per annum. The latest model PCS suit with jump jets costs three hundred thousand. Income tax rates in the top bracket are 50 percent. In 3.6 months the Russkes've bought one of your boys the best combat armor on the market." He set the calculator down, glared at Otto, and asked angrily, "What's the matter, Mueller? Don't want O'Brien's kids to have the best combat armor? That's what high salaries do: pay taxes that buy the good gear for our fighting boys and girls."

Otto said nothing, holding up an empty tumbler for a second shot of vodka. Pullman decided that another round was in order, so he filled everybody's glass. After downing the fiery liquid, the ex-car dealer took another tack. "Let's at least pretend we're free market communists and give a shit about profitability, shall we? The CIWH building pencils out to one hundred million pounds profit. It'll take five years to build. The salaries of the two Russians will hardly show on our balance sheet. Whatever firm hires them captures the project. Bakunin won't want students trained by Pevsner and Tatlin designing the most prestigious building in the world, he'll want the real McCoy." Otto's glass had become empty during this recital. Pullman filled the German's glass a third time, but left his own and O'Brien's dry. "The architectural style known as Russian Constructivism is gaining favor among the communist intellectual elite. Blow this contract and we lose buildings in New York, Mexico City, and Toronto. When our side wins the war, we'll lose big projects in London, Tokyo, Berlin, and Lsandhlwara."

Pullman gave Otto's glass one final topping off and said, "It's a no-brainer. I need to, yet today, sign employment contracts with Antoine Pevsner and Vladimir Tatlin. Sure as hell, one of our competitors will beat me to them if we wait even one day."

"I'm one step ahead of you, Jim," O'Brien said, standing and putting his Red Army beret back on his head. "You need to know if we can deliver the rank and file when the voting starts." O'Brien gave Otto a pointed look. Otto pushed against the armrests of his chair, gained his feet, and said sourly, "We can do it if you're so damned fired up to pay these Slavic bastards the moon and the stars. The rank and file will go along with whatever we say. I'll tell you what, we don't land the headquarters building and Pevsner and Tatlin will be albatrosses around our necks." The former warden trundled to the door.

O'Brien walked back to the model of the CIWH building. He asked Pullman if Tatlin and Pevsner had personally installed the maquette. Pullman told him that the two Russian constructivists had a difficult time delegating routine tasks, so naturally they were the ones that had placed the model in that spot, making a big production out of it, obsessing over the play of light and shadow from the artificial lighting and other trivial details.

Cyclone was whistled over to the mock-up and ordered to give it a good sniff. The dog's large nostrils snuffled all over the steel and glass construct. O'Brien tapped the miniature building and repeated the names of the two architects. He then walked to Pullman and handed over Cyclone's leash, explaining that the Russians were probably not patiently waiting in their south-of-market loft for Constructivist Archangel Inc. to make up its mind and produce an offer. Another construction firm had, by now, jabbed its avaricious claws into the prize, probably schmoozing the two Russkes at this very moment in one of the bars dotting the Southside ghetto that masqueraded as an artist neighborhood. In other words, Pullman would have to hunt the architects down.

O'Brien gave Cyclone the "look" command and placed a hand on Pullman's shoulder. He told the war dog that Jim Pullman was his new boss. The German Shepherd's nostrils widened and closed rapidly, drinking in Pullman's scent, taking the measure of the man. Temporary handler transfers were part of the Red Army's canine training course and posed no problem if the temporary handler smelled okay and knew a thing or two about dogs.

Pullman waited for the union reps to leave before making a cup of strong black instant coffee, needing to counter the alcohol he'd consumed. Suitably fortified, the tycoon and the war dog pushed outside, got in a Ferrari waiting at the curb, and rumbled through the dense evening traffic of world communism's capital city. The street legal racecar was poorly suited for city driving. It was also hard to get in and out of for a fat man. Pullman liked it anyway. Ferraris had always held their value far better than the DFA brands, even the spin-offs. With all trade to Europe blockaded by the war, the Italian sports car was actually appreciating in value.

Pullman's Ferrari pulled in front of an industrial building on the Southside. In this part of town, the war had left most buildings standing, although Red Army missiles had gutted quite a few, leaving empty shells. The day that the defeated caretaker US government signed its peace treaty with the communists, artists had flocked into this neighborhood to build living spaces over kilns, forges, foundries, and wood shops. Pevsner and Tatlin had been leaders in this movement, determined to embrace the bohemian lifestyle of sculpting rather than design buildings for corporate America. Pullman had tracked them down and began the process of extricating them from the grubby industrial area and the world of fine art by throwing money at them.

Cyclone knew that he was supposed to track the two men whose odor he had acquired from the maquette. He caught their scent on the sidewalk in front of Pevsner and Tatlin's grimy industrial building. The dog tugged against his leash. The scent trail lay along the sidewalk and led away from the building. The fat man understood full well what the dog was trying to do. Nevertheless, he had to make an attempt to find the artists in their loft.

A minute's worth of banging and shouting on the Russians' door proved the canine correct: no one was home. Cyclone put his nose to the steel grating in the stairwell leading to the loft and made exaggerated snuffling noises, eyeing the man sarcastically. "I get it. I get it. Go ahead and track," Pullman said in exasperation. Red Army war dogs were nearly as smart as humans and could be just as sardonic.

Sensing that Pullman was not an experienced handler, Cyclone did not lean into his collar and pull with his usual gusto. He did pull hard enough to get the fat man jogging down the sidewalk and into a warren of alleys that fronted a series of greasy spoon cafés and seedy bars. Not sure if their quarry was armed and dangerous, Cyclone sat in front of the establishment where the trail ended, prick-eared, alert, and showing a little fang.

"Easy, Cyclone, take it easy," Pullman said soothingly. "Easy" was a command that the dog was trained to obey. His tail started wagging and his fangs disappeared as the war dog dropped out of attack mode.

Cyclone and Pullman entered the bar and grill. The Russian constructivists were seated in a private booth in the back, shrouded by the dim and smoky atmosphere of the dive, staring raptly at a tall, attractive, olive-skinned woman with long black hair streaked with gray. She wore a Hawaiian dress and a Red Army beret with the supreme commander rank insignia next to the hammer and sickle.

Pullman knew that he could be in serious trouble. The woman was Aniki Banner, widow of the original (and revered) Red Army supreme commander. Aniki was a sales rep for Modular Homes Amalgamated. Her status as a communist icon could be disastrous for Constructivist Archangel. While Pevsner was only reasonably devoted to communism, Tatlin was a red fanatic and probably had a shrine to Fred Banner in his loft, which he prayed to daily. The company that Aniki represented was dangerous for another reason: MHA was a DFA spin-off that had specialized in factory built homes. Dozens of smaller companies were raiding its core market, forcing it to move into big commercial buildings and raid Constructivist Archangel's core market. Welcome to the cutthroat world of free market communism.

"Mind if I sit down?" Pullman bowed to Aniki and introduced himself. Fred Banner's widow responded enthusiastically, exclaiming that a great deal of time could be saved by both companies if they all laid their secrets bare right here and now. The issue of hiring Tatlin and Pevsner could be settled this evening. Cyclone curled up at Pullman's feet, ready to act as a canine lie detector.

Antoine Pevsner looked sharp and stylish, evidently spending his share of the money Constructivist Archangel had paid for the maquette of the headquarters building on a custom tailored suit. A toothy grin spread across a face that would have been movie star handsome if he weren't bald. The Russian satyr's eyes darted between Aniki and Pullman, looking at them the way he would two sacks of gold, clearly relishing the prospect of a bidding war between the two construction companies.

Vladimir Tatlin did not look happy. His grease stained Red Army beret was pulled low over his deep-set eyes, making it hard to see the features of his long, sallow face. He was shabbily dressed, his jacket was a leather welding-apron bearing burn marks from a recent project, pants torn and burned in places, shoes: scuffed and ratty. Tatlin pulled out a cheap hand rolled cigarette, lit it, and said, "I don't care about money or architecture. Only reason I want to build communist headquarters with Antoine is to work with transparent plasteel. Mrs. Banner is widow of supreme commander. I want to work for her. Either company will build with plasteel."

Pullman bummed a cigarette from the founder of Russian Constructivism. A waitress came by to take their orders. Pullman asked for a milkshake to soothe his ulcer while the others ordered real food. The portly businessman launched his pitch: "My company has built skyscrapers, Mrs. Banner's company has not. There's a lotta red tape they don't know how to cut. We all understand this because Antoine and Vladimir use to work for Archangel. I'm gonna make this real easy. Archangel will hire Aniki Banner as project manager. Everybody's happy."

Aniki fanned cigarette smoke from her face and asked why she should take the offer. Pullman said, "I'll double your salary. I am a personal friend of your father-in-law. I'll get him to come to America and visit your kids."

"My father-in-law is a capitalist pig, the last person I would want to see."

"I'm sure your sons would disagree. David Banner is very influential in British business and politics. He could be the Crown's ambassador to the People's Republic of North America. If we got him face-to-face with Bakunin, it might open the way for a peaceful settlement."

"I find that highly unlikely."

"Look, the Limeys don't know jack about how smoothly the economy is running in the People's Republic. Ol' peg leg will like what he sees over here. It could be the start of something good. And your sons will appreciate meeting their grandfather."

Aniki knew that Vladimir Bakunin's grand strategy called for a mass uprising against the old order in Europe, Asia, and Africa, as much as an invasion by the Red Army. The spark that was supposed to ignite the popular unrest was to be good economic news from North America, verifiable evidence that worker's chains could be thrown off. Her father-in-law could be one of the messengers that delivered the message of deliverance to the old world.

She asked what Archangel was willing to pay the Russians. Pullman gave the figure of one million pounds, apiece. She regarded the designers coolly and said, "They want 1.5 mill each and I need three hundred grand." Pullman said, "Agreed, with this stipulation: the lot of you sign a contract tonight." Aniki said, "You got a deal, chubby," and reached across the table to shake the overweight wheeler-dealer's hand.

The two Russian were mildly offended that a woman was speaking for them. Pevsner struggled to think of a way to salve his Slavic masculine pride and yet not threaten the fabulous deal that the Hawaiian woman had negotiated for them. Tatlin looked resigned to being carried along on the currents of fate.

Aniki stuck her hand in front of Pevsner's face and asked if they had a deal. He grudgingly nodded, grabbed the offered appendage, and winced as she gripped harder than an average man. Tatlin also shook with the bone-crunching Hawaiian woman, rubbing his hand afterwards in bemusement.

Aniki Banner smiled at the way the Russians rubbed their hands. Her smile faded as she thought about her father-in-law. David Banner might be a one-legged capitalist pig, but she wouldn't dare try to crush his hand, it would be like trying to crush the gauntlet of a power combat suit. Would the Commonwealth and the Communist International agree to David Banner's safe passage? Would Lisa come along? Could her in-laws actually help end the war? Were they bitter about Fred's death?

"Steroids? I decide?" Bwana signed at David and Lisa Banner, looking at the clear liquid in the syringe. Lisa picked up the hypodermic needle and held it up to the skylight. She leveled a sympathetic gaze at the silverback and said, "Since our goal is to make gorillas full-fledged citizens with the right to vote, the time has come for your people to make decisions on matters that affect them. As the dominant silverback, it is your choice whether or not adult males will be enhanced by steroids prior to the start of the post-EMP war."

The two humans and one simian were sitting around the Banners' kitchen table, Bwana in an extremely sturdy chair, constructed specifically for gorillas. Lisa had carefully explained the benefits and liabilities of a steroid regimen to the leading silverback. The anabolic chemicals, affording gains that even weight training could not give, would dramatically increase bone density and musculature. The downside would be a temporary shrinkage in the size of the adult males' testicles.

Bwana knew that steroids would be a boon to the simian warriors in combat and that human psychosexual problems did not apply to his people. He pondered how to explain himself in sign language without offending his friends. The human concern about the size of ape testicles was just that: a human concern, a Freudian concern. Gorillas did not endlessly contemplate their sexual organs the way humans did. David and Lisa Banner failed to realize that the dominant silverback was only joking when he talked about these matters, playing to his insecure human audience, in fact mocking them. Human intelligence was good for building machines and writing long boring mathematical equations, unfortunately, they lacked self-knowledge. Worse, they lacked wisdom.

The ape gave up trying to formulate a diplomatic response. He signed, "Inject me with the steroid." Lisa swabbed one of his puissant crescent-shaped pectoral muscles with alcohol and jabbed in the needle. David Banner asked him if the other silverbacks would be similarly disposed to the anabolic treatment. Big hairy paws moved rapidly: "Let's find out if it makes me stronger."

Bwana bolted into the living room and returned with a fireplace poker. He made a show of straining against the spindly steel rod, grunting with fake exertion. "Holy crap, the steroids have made me weaker. We better sue the manufacturer." The big, bony head tilted back, his mouth opened wide, filling the kitchen with hooting laughter.

The telephone rang. David Banner picked it up. Bwana could smell strong emotions immediately start to radiate from the big man, even though he couldn't follow the rapid clip of the one-sided conversation. Lisa Banner could piece together what was going on better than the gorilla. Her face was growing pale from shock and the welling of emotion. That was odd. Bwana didn't think that the tinny little voice from the other end of the phone was the Queen's. Who could cause the Banners so much consternation other than Vicky?

David Banner's body gave out a new odor: the stench of mendacity. Bwana had learned to recognize the smell by working with Bulldogs. The one-legged man was lying as he spoke into the mouthpiece: "My wife and I would love to meet our grandchildren. I'm sure we can arrange it with our government if you can do the same, Jim. I like your notion of turning our visit into a good will tour. Why don't we show up with our gorillas and mammoths? We can stage a baiting exhibition. Communists love blood sport as much as anyone, eh? Hell, maybe we can end the war, what?"

Bwana watched his friend set the phone down carefully and grin. Something sneaky was afoot. The plot gushed out in a flood of words. Einstein's pulse weapons would soon be ready for action. The communist authorities in America might be persuaded to allow a large-scale baiting contest in the San Jose area, providing cover for the placement of the Commonwealth's animal army in the heart of world communism at about the time that the pulse would hit.

The silverback was quickly lost in a torrent of details. Banner mentioned something about the Trans-Siberian railroad and maglev trains to Vladivostock and an ocean voyage across the Pacific. There was talk about a "peace circus." The one-legged geezer spoke of decking out the mammoths with balloons and dressing the gorillas like clowns, all for the cameras. Bwana caught the gist of the plan, and liked it.

The longer David Banner spoke, the angrier Lisa Banner became. At last she exploded: "Use a meeting with the grandchildren as a pretext to invade America? That's not right, now is it? Staining Fred's memory with a military ploy isn't right either, is it? The grandchildren'll hate us forever, won't they?" Pretending not to notice her anger, Bwana's favorite human went on to say that they needed to meet with Eisenhower and Churchill right away to get the ball rolling. When that didn't work, Banner resorted to pleading with his wife.

Bwana leaned back in his reinforced chair and smirked at the adult male human. It was amazing how men interacted with women. David Banner was several times stronger than his wife, yet he acted as if she were capable of thrashing him. Bwana had seventeen females in his troop. At times, all the females would attack him en masse, and he would still kick their pretty little asses up between their shoulder blades, smashing them against the enclosure walls until they saw stars. The net result was that female and juvenile male gorillas obeyed their silverback without the endless yak, yak, yak. The way humans wasted time debating and talking was crazy. Bwana knew that Banner would get his way eventually, but the geezer would have to verbally convince all the humans, one at a time: yak, yak, yak. It would be much more efficient for the hulking cripple to line up his wife, Churchill, and Eisenhower in a row and bash them upside the head, beat his chest, and shout at them to do as they were told. The only person that Banner should politely try to convince was the Queen. Vicky transcended male and female, age and youth, human and ape. Victoria II was the ultimate silverback.

The adult male gorilla opened his eyes with a start. He'd dozed off during the long boring conversation. The humans were packing bags and heading for the Rolls-Royce. Bwana and Hacksaw got in the back seat. They drove into London, through streets teeming with military personnel from seventy-five nations. The men and women wore as many uniforms as there were countries in the Commonwealth, but the soldiers in combat armor all had the same type, the newest model, their booted feet clustered with the rocket nozzles of jump jets. The Rolls stopped at a florist shop. Lisa went inside and bought a bunch of multi-colored helium balloons. The car then zeroed in on the seat of power: Ten Downing Street.

Bwana was told to tie the string of balloons around one of his hands before they entered the prime minister's residence. Out on the street, the bobby and the Bulldog serving as guards recognized Banner. They let the two humans, one gorilla, and one Bulldog into the mansion. The officer smiled at the sight of the hairy titanthrop holding a bunch of brightly colored balloons. Banner noted the effect the simian camouflage had on the policeman approvingly. The stage prop had transformed Bwana from a fierce jungle creature to a harmless clown, the exact image the one-legged man had been shooting for. The silverback was beginning to understand Banner's plan better and better.

Eisenhower, Churchill, and Prime Minister Voss were waiting for the foursome in one of the residency rooms. The powers-that-be smirked when they saw the silverback and his balloons; again, an ideal reaction. Bwana and Hacksaw sat on a hearthrug near a fireplace, warming their backsides and drowsing through another long, boring human jaw fest.

Bwana's slumber was interrupted when Churchill asked him if he understood the premise behind Banner's peace circus plan. The silverback made hand signs. Lisa translated the symbols into spoken English: "Trojan horse." Churchill rubbed his chin thoughtfully and commented that the silverback was a man of few words, adding that the ape's synopsis was accurate nonetheless. Churchill then asked if the other gorillas would grasp the essence of the plan. Bwana signed a slightly more complex answer, which Lisa translated: "I won't explain why to the gorilla nation. I'll explain how. The gorillas will do what I tell them. I don't waste time debating with my people."

Hacksaw crawled into the silverback's lap and the two drifted off once again. Something caused Bwana to groggily open his eyes. The humans were discussing horses. Besides thousands of warhorses, the smooth-skinned primates needed hundreds of thousands of draft horses in England to effectively farm once the global EMP hit. It was important that the industrial countries of Europe and America had plenty of horses as well. Bwana cared about food and he cared about farming, but this was a strictly human issue that gorillas could do nothing about. Each primate in the human/gorilla partnership had a clearly defined role. The gorillas would fight the post-EMP war. The humans would do everything else. He paid attention anyway as Churchill cited a survey that his office had commissioned. It seemed that there were roughly the same number of draft horses on European and American farms today as there had been in the late 1920s when tractors had begun supplanting horses as the primary motive power for agricultural production. The reason: farmers liked their faithful plow horses and were willing to let them die of old age. Another reason appeared to be a very limited market for horsemeat. Bwana could see how this was an important issue, still he couldn't force himself to stay awake as Churchill recited region by region statistics proving his point that there were plenty of horses and horse drawn implements on the farms in question.

The silverback dreamed about a birthday party that the Queen had thrown him last year. Victoria had given his troop a banana tree in a planter box. Gorillas enjoy eating entire banana trees, not just the fruit. The feast that day had been memorable.

Bwana's eyes remained closed while his jaw muscles bunched and flexed against his cheeks. His arms and hands twitched as he relived the feast. Then his dream took a strange turn. He was still stuffing banana leaves into his mouth, but Lisa Banner was lecturing him on politics. She said, "The animal army will have a moment of triumph if all goes well. A fleeting window of opportunity will exist for gorillas to wield political power. This will be your chance, Bwana, to secure the franchise for gorillas. Do you understand me? The franchise is the right for gorillas to vote in elections and even hold office themselves. Without the franchise, mankind could eventually turn your people into slaves."

His eyes opened fractionally. The dream was volatile enough to cause him to awaken. The human politicians were still wrangling over the number of farm horses needed for the primitive agriculture that would have to be in place prior to the eruption of pulse bombs. His eyes opened all the way. Bwana made an effort to follow the abstruse conversation.

Inexplicably, Churchill sprang from the table and reeled around the room like a drunkard, pumping his fists at the ceiling. "Eureka, I have it!" the politician shouted maniacally. "Yes, yes, yes, horses will be important. Of greater import will be small wood burning steam engines! Post-EMP agriculture and industry shall be based on wood and coal burning steam engines."

"Winston, have you seen the coal-fired steamships I've already constructed on the Thames?" David Banner asked coolly. Churchill stopped spinning, collapsing into a chair and breathing hard, feverish with excitement over his latest brainstorm, in awe of his own brilliance. After catching his breath, the politico ignored Banner's question and went on to delineate an industrial plan that would involve the wide scale production of 19th century style steam tractors, locomotives, and ocean liners. Factories would be built prior to the pulse that would churn out these machines in the post-EMP environment. Iron mines and coalmines in Britain would be modified to operate with coal-fired donkey engines. Nineteenth century style railroad ties and rails would also be manufactured under the same rubric. Then, after the pulse crippled the world's industrial economy, Britain would send wood and coal-burning steamships to every corner of the planet. The ships would have bellies full of small steam engines, primitive cast iron machines, exactly what the planet would need to rebuild.

Churchill's impassioned speech turned to the manner in which the Commonwealth could use 19th century technology to bludgeon humanity out of the grasp of communism. Bwana's eyes were fully open. The silverback carefully weighed Churchill's words and gauged the reaction of the other human beings in the room. The balance of power was shifting more and more in Churchill's favor.

Bwana looked at David Banner. The old geezer was leaning back in his chair, a half-smile tugged at the corners of his mouth. Banner was already building steam engines, yet Churchill was getting credit for the idea and assuming leadership over post-EMP industrial policy. The one-legged man seemed satisfied with this state of affairs, content to exert influence behind the scenes. Bwana scratched his sagittal crest meditatively, as leader of the gorilla nation he would have emulate David Banner and try to pull strings when the humans weren't looking. Human politics would someday be very important to gorillas, but humans would never vote gorillas into office whatever Lisa Banner might say. Gorillas would have to be kingmakers, not kings.

Banner was whispering something in Churchill's ear. Bwana's gorilla hearing could detect what was being said where a human could not. Banner had made a suggestion that Churchill talk about the production of copper wire, which could be used to replace the ruined superconducting wire in some of the larger electrical devices after the pulse hit. This way hydroelectric power plants, electrical transmission cables, and old style telegraph lines could be rapidly brought online. They wouldn't be as efficient with copper wires replacing superconducting wires, but they would work.

Churchill nodded brusquely and made a speech about renovating copper mines and building copper wire plants utilizing 19th century technology, insisting that David Banner had reminded him of an idea that he had formulated already. Bwana sniffed hard and caught a whiff of Churchill's mendacity. The silverback could tell that the idea about copper wire had originated with the old geezer. But Banner was making sure that Churchill received all the credit. This made the smaller man beholden to the big one-legged man.

The silverback grunted in admiration. He didn't understand the technical discussion or the significance of copper wire in the post-EMP world, but he could see exactly how political power was flowing around the room. The putative leader of all mankind was Prime Minister Voss. Yet Voss had less power than his underling, Churchill. A cursory examination of the relationship between Banner and Churchill suggested that the same relationship held: Banner was the power behind Churchill's throne. Bwana knew it wasn't as simple as all that. Churchill could crush Banner in a second if the one-legged man didn't walk a Machiavellian tightrope. And Queen Vicky overmastered them all, even though she generally refused to wield her enormous power.

Bwana was glad that the political culture of signing gorillas was evolving along a different track than the Byzantine jungle of human society. A dictatorial hierarchy was arising in the gorilla nation, where every silverback carried a rank. Naturally, Bwana liked the system that he was helping to create. He was, after all, the dominant silverback.

The leader of the gorilla nation corralled his wandering thoughts back to the human discussion. David Banner was addressing the assemblage, making a demand that would require the full backing of Churchill and the others. Bwana could see that Banner had maneuvered the group all day to make this speech.

"We cannot share Chief of Staff Churchill's plan to develop 19th century technology with the other great powers in the alliance for fear of a security breach. The last thing we want is communist duplication of our efforts. Secrecy is of the utmost importance." Banner's bowling ball head rocked up and down in self-agreement. He didn't start talking again until the other men's heads were also rocking up and down.

Banner said firmly, "With this exception: our closest ally, Japan, must be taken into confidence." The up and down motion of the other's men's heads stopped abruptly.

Bwana watched the wrinkles around Banner's eyes tighten. The old geezer began speaking once more, ticking off points on his thick fingers. "Japan is the most virulently anti-communist nation in the world. It has the best secret police and the highest level of security, better even than Britain's. It is an island, as we are, and Japan can mask industrial actions better than a continental power."

Imperceptibly, Banner's head bounced up and down as he continued giving reasons for sharing Churchill's plan with the Emperor, the Queen's uncle. "Japan's location is strategically critical. After Einstein's pulse, Japan will be well situated to build railroads, string telegraph lines, and renovate mines in the Asian mainland. Japan will be in position to ship troops to America's west coast. The emperor has, perhaps, displayed a fair bit of prescience, considering that he has reconstituted the Samurai class, warriors that are sworn to fight using swords, bows and arrows, knives, and the like. A division of Samurai will, I daresay, be a Godsend in the post-EMP battlefield. "

Still ticking off points on his fingers, Banner's head began to nod more vigorously. The action proved contagious. The other men nodded more aggressively in turn. Bwana decided to play the game, nodding his head vigorously whenever Banner gave another reason for inviting Japan into the fold. To the gorilla's astonishment, the old geezer's ideas did make more sense when one's head was nodding in agreement. He would have to remember this technique when it came time to persuade human politician to give gorillas the franchise.

Churchill jumped up, walked around the room a couple times, and threw himself into an impassioned plea for full disclosure and cooperation with Japan. Bwana's nostrils flared. He could smell strong emotions bubbling off the chief of staff, much stronger than anything coming from Banner. Churchill's faith in Japan was stronger than the one-legged geezer's. Japan was Churchill's baby. Banner had broached the subject to give Churchill an opening and to solidify the little guy's support for stuff that Banner cared about. You scratch my back and I'll scratch yours.

The meeting dragged on. Bwana would have liked to sleep but couldn't afford to. The display of human political interaction was too important to ignore. From across the room, Banner locked eyes with Bwana and winked.

Chapter 20

The Red Army Chases After A-bombs While the Lesser Monopoly Makes Its Move

From a military point of view, China's Yellow River had its advantages. It carried a greater concentration of silt than any other river. Over the centuries, levees had been built around the banks of the constantly silting river, inexorably raising its level, inch by inch, above the surrounding countryside. The hovercrafts of Patton's 2nd Division skimmed along the surface of the Yellow River, twenty feet above the fields and villages of the Huang Ho Valley, enjoying an unimpeded view measured in miles, not hundreds of yards as would have been the case with a normal river.

Another advantage: the river was not navigable by conventional ships. It flowed too swiftly in the lower third, where Patton's division was currently located, and was too shallow in the upper two thirds. Because a traditional navy could not traverse China's second largest river, Commonwealth military bases had not been built in the Huang Ho Valley.

These geographical advantages were more than offset by the political and economic realities of rural East Asia. The DFA supermonopoly had started in Siberia and grown up in Japan. It had developed this part of the world from primitive subsistence agriculture to commercial farming and semi-advanced industrialism. Many of its rural Asian employees believed that Henry Ford was a bodhisattva, a saintly person who was delaying his own personal entrance into nirvana to ease the pain and suffering of others. More than a few would fight to the death for Henry Ford.

Patton and Willy the Bulldog stuck their heads out of the armored cupola of 2nd Division's command hovercraft, the *General Lee*. Patton squinted through the spray of the plenum wash, scanning the entire panorama without using binoculars in order to get a feel for the land that they were passing through. In the distance, a row of green-forested hills marched resolutely to the horizon. The hills were close enough to the river to accurately lob artillery shells at the strung out division. The forest was dense enough to hide big field guns. In the immediate vicinity, Farmers were tilling soil with water buffaloes. These growers were unlikely to instigate much trouble. The fragile levee walls would cause catastrophic flooding if bombs started exploding. There was no question that the locals were enemies, however. The fertile land that they once owned around their villages did indeed belong to the supermonopoly, but these peasants were happy to get a paycheck as opposed to eking out a living that promised nothing more than continued existence.

The general ducked as a stone hurtled over his head. Chinese boys were chucking rocks at the armored column as it skimmed north toward Pao-t'ou: a city on the north bank of the grand bend in the Yellow River. Pao-t'ou straddled the southern border of the Gobi Desert and was purported to be the gateway to the Commonwealth's A-bomb program, hidden somewhere in the heart of the rocky desert.

Patton's right hand shot up. He caught a stone and hurled it back at an Asian youth. Willy barked in delight. The *General Lee* was moving too swiftly for Patton to see if his rock had beaned the impertinent Chinese lad. A voice from the hovercraft's interior called out: "General Patton, radar is picking up hostile fighter jets. Most likely Japs from their Peking base."

"Launch all fighters, every single Goddamn one," Patton hollered, slamming the hatch shut on the cupola and diving for the radar station, Willy in hot pursuit. The *General Lee* shuttered as its own complement of two VTOL Wasp fighters sprang straight up, twisting in flight to face the aerial intruders. The division commander's eyes were glued to one of the radar screens. Green blips were racing along an arc, their terminal point well ahead of the armored column's position. The enemy fighters were bent on dam busting, or more accurately, levee busting.

Willy sat at Patton's side, eyes burning with the excitement of combat. Most of the *General Lee's* control crew got inside combat suits. Only those that needed to maintain maximum flexibility did not. Patton and Willy didn't even look at their personal armor. The soldiers and war dogs in the cargo hold were already suited, but it was unlikely that they would see action, not if the only enemy machines thrown their way were Commonwealth fighter jets.

"Combat engineers, break hovercrafts out of formation and hightail to that forest due west of here. Start cutting trees, get ready to plug a hole in the levee; maybe ten miles ahead. These Goddamn Japs're fixin' to cause a flood," Patton bellowed at his radio operator. He took a breath and ordered the division's fighter pilots to do what they could to keep the Japanese fighters from blowing up the river.

Psychological warfare, Patton rolled the words around inside his head. The Japanese pilots would try to make the coming flood look like the Red Army had caused it, or, at a minimum, that it was the direct result of a firefight between the Commonwealth and the 2nd Division. The locals would be pissed at their communist liberators either way.

Hearts and minds; Japan and the Red Army were fighting to win the loyalty of the peasants of the Middle Kingdom. When and if the enemy's A-bomb program was destroyed, Patton would have to come back and pacify this part of Asia: a Herculean task. While HP equations predicted that breaking up the supermonopoly and installing free market communism would raise the standard of living in advanced industrial countries, out here in the boonies those same equations predicted that living standards would fall, at least in the short run. The peasants getting paychecks didn't need to run HP equations on supercomputers to know that DFA was good for rural Asia. Japan's fiendish psych war tactics played into peasant loyalty toward the supermonopoly, making the pacification job doubly difficult.

He and Willy climbed the short ladder leading to the cupola. Patton undogged the hatch and looked around. To the west, the hovercrafts of the combat engineers' platoon were racing for the hilly woodlands. To the north, 2nd Division fighter jets were lighting afterburners and flying directly up the Yellow River, to head off enemy jets before they could launch aero-to-surface missiles.

Patton watched as the two aerial formations got close enough to tangle. Aero-to-aero missiles crosshatched the sky over the muddy waterway. Explosions thudded like the rapid-fire thunder of an angry storm. Dirty black and orange fireballs blossomed: noxious weeds in an evil garden.

The Japanese pilots veered away to regroup for a bombing run. The odds were stacked against the communist pilots. Nearly every capitalist plane would have to be destroyed or run out of fuel for the engagement to be a complete success for the communists. All the Japanese had to do was either land a few missiles into the levees or connect with a couple of kamikazes and a big section of earthen embankment would pop like a ripe pimple. Previous aerial engagements had taught the division that the Emperor's fighters were more than willing to commit suicide to defend monopoly capitalism, a case of misplaced class consciousness if there ever was one.

"General Patton, Sir, enemy fighters headed our way," the radar operator pleaded, wanting the General to pull his fat head inside the hovercraft's composite armor (reinforced with lovely forcefield conduits) and use the periscope. Patton cursed, pulled Willy down, ducked inside the combat vehicle, but refused to use the periscope.

The *General Lee's* antiaerocraft guns coughed. Its hull rang with the concussion of enemy rounds. The other hovercrafts reported receiving heavy fire. The division commander ordered the column to come to a halt, assemble combat formations by platoon, and fight. Air escaped from plenum skirts. Hovercrafts took on the stealthy disposition of turtles, sinking into the muddy Yellow River until only their guns and radar arrays peeked above the surface. Underwater harpoon guns sent anchors slamming into the riverbed, a precaution that would keep the submerged hovercrafts from being swept away by the powerful current. Antiaerocraft guns yammered up and down the length of the stationary hovercraft platoons. Surface-to-aero missiles shot up into the attacking Japanese fighters. Enemy aerial formations melted away over the partially submerged communist armor. Pressurized air refilled the plenum chambers, hoisting lift blades out of the water so that they could bite air. The turtles hovered. The column reformed and began moving back up the river.

Overhead, the aero battle continued unabated, although it was hardly textbook. The Japanese were more concerned with blasting a hole in one of the embankments and flooding the countryside than killing communist fighter jets. Patton's fighters were more concerned with protecting the levees than killing Japanese. The net result was that the battle ranged far and near, up and down the length of the river.

Patton hovered over the shoulder of the radar/sonar operator. "Can we use sonar to detect a hole in a levee like we did last time?" The nineteen-year-old specialist replied, "The river's narrower now than before. If our hovercraft drops a sonar buoy, the other 'crafts will chew it up, Sir."

"What about the last 'craft in the column?"

"Might work, Sir."

Patton craned his head over his shoulder to growl at the radio operator: "Got that? Give the order!" The young woman working that station replied crisply, "On it, Sir."

Dueling fighter jets roved up and down the long straight expanse of river. Second Division heroically defended the levees and seemed to be winning until the radio operator informed her commander that the Japanese had scored a direct hit. She started to tell him where it was, but he cut her off, snarling, "Don't tell me. Tell the colonel leading the engineering platoon."

Unable to stop himself, Patton climbed up and reopened his cupola. Willy scrambled up there as well; the dog's head popping out of the hatch like a jack in the box. The western embankment was gushing a mile upstream. A violent flow of muddy water poured into mostly empty fields. It could have been worse; the rupture was well away from the nearest village. The general ducked his head and hollered, "Status of enemy fighters?" A voice called up a minute latter, "Enemy fighters routed, survivors heading back to Peking."

He stuck his head back into the open air and noticed the burning hulks of fighter jets dotting the verdant farmland, not all of them were Japanese. A more reassuring scene presented itself to the north. The hovercrafts of the combat engineers were converging on the torrent that was threatening to flood the surrounding lowlands. Their 'crafts had dozens of logs chained to upper hulls. Men in heavy-duty power suits were clambering over these masses of timber, tossing them around like tinker toys. This looked good, but everything wasn't butterflies and rainbows. The bulk of 2nd Division's hovercrafts was barreling straight at the repair job, a train wreck in the making.

The general shouted at the radio operator, "All hovercrafts leave the river, cut cross-country two miles. Then back into the river and collect fighter jets." Hurtling over an earth wall and crashing twenty feet down a dirt embankment to splay out on the flat field below was too jarring a maneuver for even Patton and Willy to remain precariously perched on the tiny steel platform inside the cupola. They bounced down into the cabin below. Patton strapped himself into his commander's chair, gritting his teeth and holding Willy's collar.

The *General Lee* hit the ground hard and sailed out into a bean field. Because of the battle there were no farmers to get sucked into air intakes, chopped up and spit out by the hovercraft's armored lift blades. There were a few abandoned tractors and light trucks scattered about in front of the rampaging division.

Patton reached up with one hand to use the periscope. He swiveled it left and right, counting tractors and small pickup trucks as his war machines chewed them into metallic confetti. He let go of Willy's collar. A notepad appeared in his hands. He made an inventory of the damage. At some time in the near future, the Red Army would make payments to the farmers whose vehicles it had destroyed, even though DFA actually owned the tractors and trucks. *Hearts and minds,* the general reminded himself.

The armored column veered back into the river. Patton and Willy clambered up to the crow's nest. He aimed his field glasses south to gauge the progress of the levee repair crew. Spray from the long line of hovercrafts made it impossible to see how things were going with his own two eyes. He didn't want to radio for a progress report and break the engineering colonel's concentration, not just yet anyway.

The division's fighter jets were returning from the east, hovering over 'crafts, dropping down for landings. The wing commander would be drafting an encrypted radio report that Patton would have to hear soon. He had to know how many aeroplanes had been lost. Replacement pilots and machines would have to be requisitioned from Kauai. The fuel depots on Johnston Island would have to be tapped. Converted aeroliners would parachute in drums of high test. The nuclear powered hovercrafts didn't require fuel, but the jets sure as hell did. While Kauai was parachuting in supplies, he would ask for a case of frozen lobsters and a dozen bottles of champagne.

The *General Lee's* two fighter jets came into view. Old Blood and Guts relinquished his grip on the periscope and hit the recline button on his command chair. Reports began flooding in. Aeroplanes had been lost. Hovercrafts had been damaged. An unexpected amount of ordnance had been expended. Chinese farmers were already clamoring for remuneration with their ham radios. The patch on the banks of the Yellow River had been successfully installed. Whoever was sent to pay the locals for their lost farm equipment would also have to instruct them on maintaining the impromptu log dam. In other words, an engineer would have to be sent, and he or she would have to bring someone along who spoke the local dialect.

George Patton dealt with the mundane tasks left in the aftermath of the battle, unable to even take the time to savor a victory. Darkness fell and a camp had to be struck for the night. The hovercrafts slipped off the river, much slower and more carefully than they had earlier in the day, under combat conditions.

Aware that their commander had had a hard day and loved to watch DFA's English language news broadcasts from Peking, a few of the soldiers set up a reception tower, a portable television, and a camp chair outside the *General Lee* while Patton and Willy's dinners were being prepared. It was the height of summer. The weather outside was fine. A mosquito-net tent was draped from the tower and a homey little environment was created for the hard working combat executive.

The general and his dog relaxed in this cozy den with a bowl of beef stew, a bowl of kibble, and a cold beer. The TV blinked on, showing a train station in Berlin. A maglev train, a very lengthy maglev train, one hundred twenty cars long, was winding its way through the German city, coasting to the station amidst excited crowds of well-wishers. A newscaster's disembodied voice said: "The peace circus is making a whistle stop in Berlin, an interlude to its penultimate destination of Vladivostock, and then on to San Jose, California by cargo ship."

The train slowed and landed. Big metal doors on the forward stock cars swung open. The crowd pulled back as scores of gorillas pedaled out on heavily built bicycles, gaily decorated with helium balloons and colorful horns of varying sizes and shapes. The apes rode through the crowd, honking bicycle horns and passing out balloons to children. Willy cocked his head at the television, not sure what he was watching, curiosity lines etched in his forehead. Patton laughed out loud.

The TV showed mammoths gliding out of another set of stock cars. The pachyderms were stained pink and pale blue with vegetable dye. Rather than howdahs, they had bushels of candy strapped to their backs. The pink and blue circus beasts chased after the gorillas, careful not to trample human beings, tossing bags of candy into the crowd with their trunks.

A tall, gaunt elderly man with a wooden leg climbed painfully from a passenger car, accompanied by a handsome, middle-aged woman. The crippled old man wore the top hat and tails of a circus master. The disembodied voice explained that the viewers were watching David Banner, Her Majesty's newly appointed ambassador to the People's Republic of North America. A microphone appeared in front of Banner's face. A reporter began asking questions. The gist of Banner's replies centered on the peaceful nature of his mission and his desire to discover what the communists wanted in the way of a peace settlement.

The reporter said, "Ambassador Banner, we've been hearing rumors that Henry Ford and Alfred Sloan are willing to break up their supermonopoly and sign over their stockholdings outside of America to DFA employees. Word is that this will be enough for the communists to lay down their arms." Banner nodded at the newsman benignly and asked if there was a question in all that verbiage. The interviewer asked directly, "Is the Queen and the Commonwealth willing to accept those concessions in the interest of peace?" Banner replied, "British law permits Messrs Ford and Sloan to assign stock to whomsoever they please. The war is as good as over if that is all it takes, assuming a gun is not being held to the monopolists' heads. No contract is valid under duress. Bear in mind there are other monopolies besides DFA, Halifax Mining for example. I very much doubt that Soga Halifax is willing to reassign shares."

"Will you be meeting with Ford and Sloan?"

"Absolutely. I will also be meeting with Supreme Commander Vladimir Bakunin."

The next question had something to do with the death of David Banner's son, Fred. Patton turned the volume down and stroked Willy's back, trying to guess what the results of this new round of diplomacy would bring. Free market communism was designed for the world's most advanced economies. If the highly industrialized countries accepted the Red Army's formula for redistributing and restructuring the assets of the supermonopoly and the lesser monopolies, its progressive income tax scheme, its military oriented governmental spending priorities, and its draconian antitrust laws, then the war could end quickly, in the advanced nations.

It was a horse of a different color in the far reaches of DFA's commercial empire. In the city of Pao-t'ou, for instance, peace might not be so easy to achieve. The factories were antiquated out here in the hinterland, many of them built during the first World War, most were barely able to break even, nothing like the modern and bustling coastal cities of China and Japan. DFA spin-offs in north-central China wouldn't be able to effectively compete if the forces of free market communism were unleashed. Who besides Henry Ford was going to invest in sheep stations near the Gobi Desert? The locals weren't that keen to lose their subsidized livelihoods. That's why HP equations predicted years of guerilla warfare in the rural parts of Asia, South America, and the Congo.

This could be either good news or bad news for Patton. He did not want to lead a peacetime army. Conversely, he could easily imagine the Communist International, or whatever political party eventually came to rule the Commonwealth, denying battlefield commanders out in the boonies the necessary resources to win a protracted guerilla war. Out of sight, out of mind.

The TV switched from coverage of the peace circus to financial news. Patton turned up the volume. Stock markets in Europe, Asia, and South America continued their panic stricken slide, losing nearly 90 percent of their value since the start of the war. And the months of combat hiatus (or *sitzkrieg* as the Germans called the cessation of full-scale battles) had done little to dispel the fear of investors, exactly what Bakunin's HP equations had predicted. Most of the bourse losses came from the freefall of DFA and its subsidiaries.

Patton put his beer down and paid closer attention to the television. The announcer said something that conflicted with the Red Army's Historical Parallelism model. The African exchange had stabilized. Patton sat up in his chair, almost elbowing his beer off the armrest. This was real news. The widow of the 1920 Red Force supreme commander, better known as the former president of Zululand, Soga Halifax, had acquired a 49 percent stake in DFA Aero, buying every share not owned by Ford and Sloan. Rumors of other stock acquisitions by the enigmatic widow were firming up share prices south of the Sahara. Patton knew he should try to figure out what this meant, but he was too tired to think clearly.

With a resigned grunt, the commander of 2nd Division clicked off the TV and closed his eyes. Willy put his head in Patton's lap. The two fell asleep. One of Patton's adjutants threw a blanket over the sleeping pair and posted a guard to watch over them. The general was disappointed the next morning to find that his breakfast consisted of another bowl of beef stew, hard tack, vitamin tablets, and black coffee. Earlier in the mission, closer to the coast, local farmers had been willing to sell the division fresh food. As they'd traveled inland, the hostility from the locals had grown. Any food they bought out here might be poisoned. The attitude of regional growers gave a pretty good indication what the reception would be like in Pao-t'ou.

Two days journey placed the division on the outskirts of the desert city, arrayed in a crescent-shaped siege pattern. The place had the same feel as the heavily defended city of Santa Fe, unsurprising considering that both desert locales were support bases for A-bomb programs. Patton ordered a squadron of fighter jets to buzz the perimeter of the metropolis. The roofs of adobe buildings germinated a crop of antiaerocraft guns. A wall of flack was thrown at the communist fighter jets. The explosions were awe-inspiring, knocking three jets out of the sky, rattling components inside the hovercrafts. Advanced Commonwealth technology was at work. Fuel-air ordnance: the poor man's atom bomb. *No*, Patton changed his mind, *the rich man's fuel-air bomb.*

Patton ordered hovercraft main gunners to take out the enemy's AA guns. Thunder rolled from the division's cannons. The probing action of the fighter jets had allowed main gunners to register targets. Dust obscured the city as communist shells obliterated adobe buildings and the human beings inside. Foxtrot Battle-lion, commanded by Alfred Stokes, was ordered into the city, taking advantage of the cover provided by smoke, fire, and dust.

Foxtrot hovercrafts broke from the siege configuration, approached the city, and slipped through the gaping holes left by the division's fighter jet barrage. Foxtrot fighter jets assumed a supporting role, but would operate independent of Foxtrot's advancing 'crafts, landing and refueling within the ranks of the fixed hovercrafts arrayed outside the city. The rest of the division's aero arm would continue patrolling the immediate countryside, ready to bail out the infiltrating battle-lion.

Electing to remain with Stokes's battle-lion had not been an easy decision for Rudolph Diesel. On the one hand, he'd made progress figuring out how telemetric commands were being used by the reactionary capitalists to dismantle Bloody Paralyzer troop carriers. On the other hand, this effort shed no light on the debilitating effect of electromagnetic pulses. Studying EMPs had become a sort of crusade for the aging engineer.

The Red Army was committed to the long-range goal of raising a world dominating army in North America, led by a vanguard of Mark VII super suits. This enormous force wouldn't see combat for a year or more. The only active fronts in the foreseeable future were 2nd Division's foray into the Gobi Desert and 5th Division's mission in the Sahara. Since Patton had tactical nukes at his disposal and held no compunction against using them, 2nd Division represented the best possibility of encountering and studying electromagnetic pulses.

Diesel wouldn't be caught off guard a second time when and if a nuclear explosion rocked the battlefield. He'd turned Alfred Stokes into a walking laboratory for studying pulse shields of varying designs. The hovercrafts of the Foxtrot Battle-lion also had a variety of pulse shields protecting their circuitry and wiring systems. As a consequence, Diesel seldom left Stokes's side, ever ready to monitor the dials and gauges festooning the leftenant-colonel's prosthetic limbs, always hovering over the battle-lion commander like a mother hen.

Within minutes of penetrating the city, Foxtrot Battle-lion hovercrafts could go no farther without blasting a passageway through buildings and homes. They were hemmed in by narrow streets and looming structures. Diesel quietly watched his test subject, Stokes, give the order for an infantry platoon to dismount and establish a foot patrol.

The city streets were empty, too empty. Stokes observed the foot patrol sally forth through his periscope. Scraps of newspaper blew around their feet. Stray dogs bolted at the sight of the metal clad humans and canines. Not one native resident was visible.

The communist foot soldiers melted into alleys and Pao-t'ou regained the semblance of a ghost town. Searing desert wind moaned through canyons of mud brick buildings. Diesel squirmed nervously behind Stokes's command chair. The leftenant-colonel asked, "Worried about your friends, the O'Brien brothers?" Diesel admitted to that exact fear. Stokes did nothing to allay the engineer's concern when he said, "You're right to be afraid. I've a very bad feeling about this city. We don't have the right kind of aero power for investing an urban environment. We should have good old-fashioned Merlin gunships, not aero superiority fighters."

Sean O'Brien kicked in the door of the Buddhist monastery and depressed the trigger of his fifty cal, spraying armor piercing rounds indiscriminately. There weren't saffron robed monks waiting inside, but Japanese soldiers in combat armor, peeking around a gilt edged sculpture of Siddhartha, blazing away with their own heavy machineguns and armor piercing rounds.

The O'Brien brothers, the other seven suit soldiers in their squad, and two armored German Shepherds dove for what cover they could find, piling the shattered remains of furniture between themselves and the fire pit around the statute. Keying his helmet mike, Sean forced himself to speak calmly in combat code one, "Too hot in here. I'm going to call an aero strike. Throw flash-bangs and retreat on my mark. Three, two, one, mark!"

The soldiers of Sean's squad cocked their arms and ten flash-bangs sailed into the Japanese position. A flash of blinding light made the monastery resemble the inside of a ping-pong ball, nothing but white was visible to the enemy for several crucial seconds. The faceplates of Red Army suits possessed superior light filters, which allowed the squad to exit the building without taking any more fire.

They reassembled behind a heap of yellow bricks between two buildings on the other side of the street, a position that afforded a clear angle of fire at the monastery. Sean painted the religious structure with a reflective targeting laser and called in an aero strike. His troops sprayed a steady stream of bullets into the monastery, keeping the enemy pinned long enough for a Wasp fighter to finish them off.

Seamus touched helmets with his older brother and asked chidingly, "Betcha wish we had Mark VIIs now, eh bro?" Sean bit off an angry retort: "Don't waste my time. Got any useful military info? If not, bugger off."

"Yeah, I got useful info. Looky here." Seamus held up his brother's right suit arm, the one not aiming the targeting laser. A small geyser of white vapor was issuing from an invisible puncture in the composite metal around Sean's right forearm. Red lights blinked on the squad leader's heads up display. The suit's software had noticed the problem at the same time that he had, its air conditioning system was totally compromised. Sean would cook to death if he didn't get out of his combat armor. The heat started to increase precipitously, ratcheting up with every blink of the crimson warning lights in the heads up display. And there was nothing he could do about it because the targeting laser had to be held steady until after the aero strike. As squad leader, Sean should have assigned the job of holding the laser to another soldier.

A Wasp fighter screamed over their position, releasing a salvo of missiles into the monastery. The explosion that followed not only pulverized the Buddhist shrine, it brought down the two buildings that had been sheltering Sean's squad. The troopers had to dig their way out of the rubble. As he dug, the temperature inside the squad leader's suit skyrocketed. Room temperature superconductors become less conductive as they warm up. This creates a deadly feedback loop. The less conductivity, the more heat the wiring sheds, which makes them less conductive, which makes them shed more heat...

Standing on the surface of the rubble mound, dripping sweat, Sean read an interior suit temperature of 140 degrees. As quickly as his tired body could move, he clamshelled out of the suit and donned a flak jacket, a plasteel helmet, and holstered a handgun. He named Seamus as the new squad leader. Without a combat suit, Sean couldn't receive orders from battle-lion command or communicate with his troopers. He was essentially excess baggage.

The 100-degree temperature in the open air of Pao-t'ou felt cool, at first. Only a few seconds ticked by and the open air felt like a blast furnace. Sean's fatigues were soon soaked with sweat. He set the self-destruct mechanism on his damaged suit and hurried to catch up with his squad, which had moved out of the rubble and was marching into the heart of the city.

The nine humans and two dogs in powered armor could move tirelessly and swiftly. Sean tried to keep up, puffing and sweating behind the squad, baking in the merciless sun, choking on dust blowing off the desert. He carried no water. He was scantily armored for even small arms fire. The Red Army made few provisions for a soldier that had lost his or her combat suit. His hand strayed to the handgun swinging from his hip. The thing felt like a toy.

The two German Shepherds noticed that he was trailing behind the squad. They double backed and tried to take a rear guard disposition. Seamus gave the dogs a radio command, forcing them to trot back to the front and assume point. The new squad leader was entirely correct in putting the dogs back where they were most needed, although it did make the struggling soldier without a suit feel naked and vulnerable.

Sean realized that in some ways his senses were more effective unshackled by hundreds of pounds of powered combat armor. He could judge the distance and direction of the countless aero strikes erupting all around the city better without electronically amplified hearing. The sound of small arms fire was unrelenting, but he could tell that it was relatively far away. Every now and then, the thump of a fuel-air bomb jiggled his innards. He could hear the scream of dying men and women. Other soldiers must have abandoned their suits. Communist and Japanese soldiers were dying throughout this crummy Chinese burg.

The squad was slowing. Seamus directed the dogs and troopers into an empty building, a saloon or maybe a restaurant, on their left. Sean stumbled inside after his unit, glad to be out of the sun and out from under the scopes of Japanese snipers. His rubber soled boot crunched against the glass of a framed photograph. He probably wouldn't have noticed such a trivial incident in a suit. His unencumbered eyesight zeroed in on the image of Albert Einstein, staring at him from a glossy sheet of paper. The famous capitalist scientist had signed his name to the photograph, using Roman letters, and had also written a short note in Chinese. It probably said something like "the Fat-choy restaurant makes the best noodles in town."

The soldiers of 2nd Division had been trained to look for any traces of the Commonwealth's most celebrated scientist. There were tons of reports that the capitalist genius and his equally brilliant assistant were living somewhere around here. Sean scooped up the photograph, examined it, and shoved it under his shirt. He was about to tell his brother that the squad needed to move back to the hovercraft because of the Intel he'd discovered when Sean began making gestures in sign language: "Yo, Bro. Platoon says we gotta head back to the 'craft."

Sean hurriedly searched the saloon for bottled water. He found only liquor. Fighting through a haze of thirst and exhaustion, he scrambled out into the dusty street. The squad was already two hundred yards down the road, marching double time with artificially enhanced speed. One of the German Shepherds had stopped marching and was looking at him imploringly. He hated the realization that he was a burden, slowing down the squad. Time to dig deep and give a maximum effort.

In his haste to catch up, Sean tripped and lay sprawled, dizzy and unable to stand. His eyelids were closed when the explosion hit. Small rocks, broken bricks, and chunks of metal rained down all around him. He wiped grit from his eyes but couldn't see through the dust cloud. When the ringing in his ears stopped, the silence told him that his squad had been vaporized.

A piece of paper flapped around his ankles. Sean was surprised to find himself upright and walking. He caught the flapping paper and put it close to his face so that he could see it through the dust. It was a second photo of Albert Einstein. In this photograph the bourgeois scientist was wearing different clothes. The signature looked the same. The Chinese letters looked different. He stuffed the second Einstein photo down his shirt and stumbled forward.

His two brothers were dead. This thought weighed more heavily on the unsuited soldier than thirst and fatigue. The entire squad was gone. His staggering gait firmed into a mile-eating trot. One signed photograph of Albert Einstein with a personalized note seemed to be definitive proof that the notorious scientist had recently been in Pao-t'ou. What were the odds of two such photos falling into Sean's hands within minutes of each other? What did that prove?

The tramping of power-suited footsteps sounded somewhere ahead, hard to tell where in the obscuring dust. Sean crawled into an alleyway, unsure if enemy or friendly soldiers were maneuvering nearby. A dog in a PCS nudged him from behind. His reflexes were so dull by now that he hardly reacted to the poke in the rear. There were two survivors from Sean's squad. The dog was Cyclone, his father's German Shepherd. Before the brothers had left for China, Danny O'Brien had pulled some strings to make sure that Cyclone would be a part of whatever fighting unit they might be assigned to. His father's insistence would likely save Sean's life.

"Cyclone, take me back to the hovercraft," Sean hissed at the dog's helmeted head. The unsuited soldier dismantled the machinegun on the dog's titanium back, chucked it aside, wrapped arms and legs around the dog's suited torso, and clung to him like the world's biggest jockey on the world's smallest horse.

Cyclone ran down into the smoking crater in the center of the road, the spot where the squad had been obliterated. The dog tentatively stuck his suit head over the lip of the crater wall. Unlike Sean, or any of the human troopers, the German Shepherd could differentiate between the footfalls of suited Japanese soldiers and suited communist soldiers, even through the distortions of electronic amplification. The enemy was all around them.

The dog judged that waiting would only make the situation worse. He sprinted south, the direction of the friendly siege line. Even carrying Sean, the suited canine was blazingly fast as he looped through the chaos of the war torn city. He slowed to a trot in the vicinity of the 2nd Division's armor and activated a radio beacon that automatically requested a rescue team.

Sean had kept his head down and his handgun holstered throughout the passage from hell to communist controlled territory. He rolled off the dog's back, stood, and told the rescue squad walking his way to hand over a canteen of water. It was an effort to drink only half the canteen, any more and he would be sick. He asked his rescuers to immediately take him to General Patton. He ordered Cyclone to return to Foxtrot Battle-lion.

It was only a short distance to the general's hovercraft, yet Sean found himself fading. He asked the medic in the rescue squad to give him a mild stimulant and more water. The dull sensation of being wrapped in a smothering blanket of fog was replaced by a sharp headache. At least he could think again.

Thankfully, Patton was willing to see the young sergeant. Sean found himself sitting on a canvas chair inside the general's tent, waiting for the great man to set down his radiophone. Sean looked out through the open tent flap. The siege line was taking on a semi-permanent atmosphere. Next to every hovercraft battle-lion there were small collections of tents. He could see the little tent camp erected by Foxtrot Battle-lion. It would have been a good place to bury his brothers, if only the capitalist pigs hadn't incinerated their bodies. Sean rubbed his temples and concentrated on what he wanted to say to General Patton.

The general set down his phone and gave Sean an inquiring look. Pulling the two photos from his shirt, the squad leader recounted, "I found one of these photographs in an eating establishment, Sir. The other was blowing out on the street. My guess is that Pao-t'ou contains hundreds of autographed pictures of Doctor Einstein. The enemy definitely wants us to think he is in this province."

The photos were sweat soaked from pressing against Sean's skin. Patton noticed that the inked messages had not smeared or ran. This drew his eye to the high quality paper used for both photos. Despite having gone through a war zone, the paper was remarkably intact. The lad was correct, either the British SSB or Japan's secret police had planted these pictures. Patton thanked the sergeant and instructed him to return to his battle-lion.

Sitting in his tent with Willy, Patton reviewed all the evidence that had been collected thus far about the Commonwealth's Gobi Desert A-bomb program. High-flying Red Army spy planes had photographed a short white man with long frizzy gray hair walking next to a tall black woman near Pao-t'ou, surrounded by Japanese imperial guards. No other couple was more readily identifiable from the air than Albert Einstein and his assistant, Nkosinathi. Shipments of uranium had been traced to the desert region by rail from Baikal. Machine parts for earthmovers designed to work in sand had also been shipped into the Chinese part of the Gobi. The ferocity of the battle that 2nd Division had just fought suggested that the Commonwealth was protecting a valuable asset. And now there were these photos.

A mountain of evidence pointed to the Gobi Desert for the Commonwealth's second nuclear weapon program. Yet the enemy had kept the secret of the first program in New Mexico airtight. Under Zhukov's command, the 2nd Division had blundered into it along the Arizona border through sheer chance and the help of communist moles.

Patton couldn't yet piece together the Commonwealth's overall strategy. He did sense that Red Army High Command was unwittingly sending his division on a wild goose chase. One fact was indisputable: all roads led to Einstein. Rommel was impressed with the extraordinary choice that Jeremiah Halifax had made: trading three Mark VII combat suits for Albert Einstein's escape. And here Patton was, staring at photos of the most exceptional scientific mind in the capitalist world, probably the whole world. Obviously, the broad question of Einstein's whereabouts and the progress he was making in weapons development was key. But Patton had to answer the narrow question: Was 2nd Division wasting its time in the Gobi?

Second Division couldn't afford to chase its tail up and down this rock-strewn desert. Nor could it afford to simply leave. After all, the Commonwealth could be playing an elaborate game of reverse psychology. They might want Patton to think that the Gobi clues were too barefaced. In that case, the enemy's A-bomb program might actually be hidden under one of the sandy patches in the stony Asian desert, as Red Army Intelligence claimed. That left only one choice and Vladimir Bakunin wasn't going to like it. Each Red Army division was armed with fifty tactical nuclear warheads. Second Division had used only one nuke so far, in Arizona. Patton would use the other forty-nine to expunge the town of Pao-t'ou from the surface of planet Earth and ravage the nearby desert.

While the Gobi was enormous, only 3 percent included sand dunes. Spook central was adamant that the capitalist's A-bomb program was located in a tunnel complex carved under a region of rolling dunes. Second Division's nuclear arsenal was sufficient to obliterate this specific geography. The fallout from the widely dispersed bombardment would inundate the rest of the desert, including grasslands, mountains, and rocky valleys, especially if the division's A-bombs were buried before being set off. A series of deep ground bursts would make the fallout much more deadly, contaminating ground water and the wasteland's one permanent stream, sterilizing the Gobi.

Patton and Willy returned to the *General Lee*. Patton got the ball rolling by calling a meeting of all battle-lion commanders. He told Leftenant-colonel Stokes to bring Rudolf Diesel. The senior engineer would be ecstatic to hear that he would finally be able to test his theories on electromagnetic pulse shielding.

General Erwin Rommel hated the Red Sea. He hated the Sahara Desert. He hated Greater Syria and he despised the Arabian Peninsula. His 5th Division was a miniscule speck floating on the endless waters of the Red Sea. To the east and west, the talc-like powdery sand of the Sahara made hovercraft travel nearly impossible.

The only bright spot he'd encountered in the mission thus far was his ability to buy jet fuel from the Halifax refineries dotting the coast, a surprise in light of the fact that underdeveloped regions like North Africa were notoriously anti-communist. In reality, the natives' willingness to supply his aero arm with fuel was a sign of contempt. They saw his planes making never-ending sweeps over the trackless waste and laughed. Why shouldn't they sell him fuel? The 5th Division was doing them no harm. And they seemed to think he was wasting his time searching the largest desert in the world.

Early on, Rommel had decided that human Intel would prove more effective than aerial surveillance; the search area was simply too vast. The Arabs had proven more than happy to talk to his intelligence officers. The comings and goings of Boer and Zulu petroleum engineers from Halifax Mining had been chronicled. These engineers could, conceivably, have been nuclear scientists in disguise. The lesser monopoly's oil fields had been plumed with Geiger counters for radioactivity. So far, the net result had been zilch. It was looking more and more as though the Sahara did not contain an A-bomb program.

Rommel would make one last effort before begging Vladimir Bakunin for permission to reposition 5th Division in Gibraltar, where it could support the invasion of Britain. He spread topographical maps across the desk in his office that sat in the shadow of Mount Sinai. The Qattra Depression immediately jumped out at him. Here was the largest landmass in the Sahara that resided far below sea level. This was the most logical place to test fire nuclear weapons. He would set up a new field headquarters at El Alamein and have his people pore over the Qattra Depression with a fine toothcomb. If they found nothing after one month of searching, he'd tell Bakunin it was time to throw in the white towel.

The German general glanced at his wristwatch. The evening news would be on shortly. Before he'd left for Asia, George Patton had advised Rommel to stay abreast of world events and financial news. The American general correctly observed that the instant the war was over, top Red Army military commanders would be embroiled in economic matters. Neither Patton nor Rommel could afford to be caught flat-footed.

Rommel pointed a remote control device at a television set in the corner of his office. The image of Soga Halifax shimmered across the screen. He'd remembered her from much younger days, when she ruled Africa with an iron fist. Back then, her hair had been raven black. Today, she wore it like a snowy crown. Character lines were graven in her features like the dried banks of so many rivers. The old gal looked more formidable than ever. Why was she leading the news broadcast?

The anchorman said, "Stock markets in Europe and Asia posted their first gains since the start of the war. This woman, Soga Halifax, who viewers will recognize as the erstwhile president of Zululand, has staunched the monumental financial losses on international exchanges by snapping up outstanding shares of DFA subsidiaries. In a strategy reminiscent of Henry Ford's buying spree in the early part of the century, Mrs. Halifax—"

Rommel turned down the volume and sat thinking. He wished that Patton were here to offer commentary. The German general's gut instinct told him that this development was inimical to communist goals. It could not be a good thing to have a second supermonopoly arise in the old world just as the original one had been tamed in the new world. Rommel mulled over the source of Soga Halifax's wealth: she owned the diamond and gold mines of South Africa, as well as the oil fields in the Levant. Soga was supplying his division with aviation fuel. He knew this was somehow significant, but couldn't quite see how. It was almost as if Soga Halifax and the Commonwealth welcomed 5th Division's presence in North Africa.

In the privacy of her own mind, Soga thought of World War II as Humpty Dumpty's great fall, the economic cataclysm that would end monopoly capitalism forever. The moment that her far-sighted husband had planned for was at hand. Her mountain of gold bullion, crates of uncut diamonds, and countless barrels of oil would shape and massage a global economic landscape that had come to resemble a World War I no-man's-land, preparing it for the orderly demise of the monopolistic era.

Her first big purchase had been every outstanding share in DFA's South African Aero Subsidiary, a 49 percent stake, controlling interest in the absence of Henry Ford and Alfred Sloan's voting bloc. She calculated that the African aeroplane factories would be the most expensive acquisition in light of the swollen backlog of governmental orders for fighters and bombers. Ironically, the price would have been even higher had there been no war and no juicy backlog of military planes. The world's investors were in a panicky mindset after Washington DC had been nuked. They wanted species, precious stones and metals, not paper money.

Her second major purchase had been the DFA Global Media Group, based in London. The price for these shares had been higher than expected. War or no war, the market was aware of her smaller purchases as well as the big ones and it was getting wind of her plan to create a second supermonopoly. Her third significant purchase was in the works: DFA Medical Trust Europe, headquartered in Cologne. Soga had chosen a trusted Halifax Mining executive to accompany her to Germany and help hammer out a deal, Larry Liquidara, a veteran of the 1920 CMG who had served under her late husband.

Soga and Larry boarded a Halifax Star-freighter at Lsandhlwara International Aeroport. The plane had a bellyful of gold bullion and a phalanx of Zulu guards in combat armor. The pilots, guards, and bullion were kept separate from the former president and her trusted aide by soundproof bulkheads.

After making sure that everything had been properly loaded, Larry secured the doors of the bulkheads, sat next to Soga in one of the two chairs bolted to the cabin decking, and waited for take-off. The plane flew north. Soga watched the continent flow by gracefully under the Star-freighter's wings without speaking. Larry was sure that she wanted to discuss ways to lower the share prices on all the companies that she intended to acquire. He had a plan to make this happen, but wasn't so presumptive to speak out of turn.

The plane was entering Congo aero space when Larry tackled the subject. He hesitated, not sure if she could stomach what he had to say. Soga insisted that he speak his mind. "For starters," Larry said, "Madam President owns Halifax Media Group, which controls the news coming from the active theaters in the Gobi and the Sahara. And it controls news of the economic boom in America. Share prices would plunge if the war news took a sudden bad turn and America's economic expansion got a little airtime."

"I will not spread lies to gain commercial advantage!"

"Wouldn't be lies, Madam. Existing news is slanted to make the Commonwealth look good, pure propaganda. Halifax Media is downplaying the American economic miracle and pooh-poohing communist battlefield victories. Simply telling the truth will make it look like the war has turned sour. Stock prices will plunge."

"Such a tactic will demoralize the troops."

"Half the troops are Zulu. Nothing can demoralize them. The truth will eventually buck up the civilians better than pandering."

"An excellent point, Mr. Liquidara. What do we do about Commonwealth censors? That is the reason for the propaganda in the first place, to forestall government censorship."

"Unlikely the government'll get too huffy, seeing as how Madam controls the production of Wasp fighters and Colossus bombers. Like I said, most soldiers are Zulu. The Zulu nation will back up their beloved former president. So long as we report the straight truth, the government ain't gonna do squat."

"A penetrating insight."

Larry nodded at the complement. Her gaze returned to the portal and grew distant and dreamy. Larry wanted to talk about gaining 51 percent stakes in the DFA subsidiaries that she was taking over by issuing new shares and buying them up. To do this they would have to add real value to these companies as well as perform some accounting slight of hand. He held his tongue when he saw Soga's hands shake with palsy. The old woman's health wasn't what it had once been. She must be in her nineties. He hoped that she was strong enough to finish her mission of creating a second supermonopoly. It would sure throw a wrench into the plans of the stinking communists to have a supermonopoly controlled by Zulu, who wouldn't back down like those sissies, Ford and Sloan.

Larry's political concerns evaporated when a cabin speaker crackled with the pilot's voice: "Mrs. Halifax, do not be alarmed. The fighter jets to starboard and port are an escort from the Zululand Aero Force. We will be entering territory controlled by the Red Army in five minutes."

Soga did not stir from her trance-like stare out the portal. She didn't seem to see the squadrons of needle-nose Wasp fighters that had engulfed the Star-freighter in a protective cloud. Larry looked down at the ground. The lush vegetation of the Congo was yielding to the starkness of the northern desert. He did a double take. Aggressive little dots were rising from the sea of sand.

Three hands of Zululand fighters dropped out of the main defensive formation to tackle the communist jets. Fiery puffs of death ripped through the small Zulu offensive formations. Larry fumbled wildly for a pen and a scrap of paper. He needed to record the exact details of the aero battle. The good guys were taking it on the chin. This could be one of the realistic news stories that would help drive down share prices.

Pen in hand, Larry watched a communist avian guided missile zig and zag through the cloud of friendly fighters encapsulating the Star-freighter. The ultra-agile missile reminded him of a Ferrari racecar. He jotted down words along those lines. The enemy missile connected with the outer port engine of their transport plane, sending shock waves into the passenger compartment. Flames spouted from the stricken engine. Larry scribbled furiously in his notebook.

The pilot spoke over the intercom in Zulu accented English. "Not to worry, Madam President. The Aero Force is sending reinforcements. We can make it to Europe on two engines, if need be." Larry didn't stop writing as he looked out a porthole. The aero space below was animated with dozens of dogfights. Communist fighters were achieving a two-to-one kill ratio, but reinforcements were indeed arriving and the aerial combat was moving away from the Star-freighter.

The affable blue Mediterranean smiled up at the plane, replacing the sandy frown of the Sahara. The pilot announced that the danger had passed and the rest of the journey should be uneventful. Larry glanced at the damaged engine. It was stone cold, free of flames. He wondered if he could get away with a little embellishment and claim that the engine trailed flames all the way to Germany.

Mrs. Halifax woke up and asked what had happened. Larry read her the news copy that he had penned. When he was done, she agreed that the story deserved a headline in the morning papers. Larry grinned. He could see the price of equities plunging.

Chapter 21

The Three Horsemen of the Apocalypse

"Albert, as a boy, did you think you might be the first man in outer space?" Nkosinathi asked, admiring the sleek lines of the two partially completed Mark VII spaceships. The scientist's shoulders rose and fell in a dismissive gesture as he said, "My boyhood dreams were entirely cerebral." He too stood there, admiring the spaceships. Footfalls caused them to look away from the fusion powered rocket hulls.

Through the hangar doors of the barn, the couple saw Dwight D. Eisenhower marching their way. The general's movements were as stiff and precise as his starched uniform, button down collar, and the neat row of gleaming stars on his hat. Eisenhower appeared too polished and formal to be in anything other than a bad mood. The Einsteins needed to avoid his wrath. They needed to escape.

With the departure of the peace circus, the mammoth barn had been cleared of pachyderms and modified into a factory that produced pulse bombs and converted Mark VII suits into spaceships. General Eisenhower was unfamiliar with the maze-like passages and hiding holes in the ramshackle structure. Nkosinathi batted her eyes at the two Royal Marines standing guard around the spaceships, begging them to keep mum when the general asked which way they'd gone. The two scientists opened a door and slipped into the tangle of pipes in the tritium processing room.

Eisenhower got to the spaceships. His head snapped left and then right. He didn't bother asking the guards to give the location of the two illusive scientists. Sniffing the air like a bloodhound, he grunted, and stalked away, defeated. When the supreme commander was out of the building, one of the Marines whistled a merry tune, a sign that the coast was clear.

The couple inched out of their hiding hole like mice wary of a particularly aggressive cat. They timidly returned to the spaceships and resumed their conversation. Einstein told a story about his boyhood concerns. At three years old, he was obsessed with a game that he and his uncle use to play called "what is X?" Latter on, he learned that the rest of the world called the game "algebra." Nkosinathi laughed. Her childhood had been spent obsessing over mathematics as well, much to the chagrin of everyone else in her family.

Einstein gave details over his next great boyhood interest besides mathematics: playing the violin. It had occurred to the young Einstein that someday he might grow up and become a famous concert violinist. Alas, his talent was not sufficient.

A human silhouette became visible against the backlight of the open hangar door. Instantly, the Einsteins cringed. One of the guards told them that the silhouette belonged to Jan Churchill, the chief of staff's wife, and the second person scheduled to reach outer space. Einstein had tested higher on the Mark VII spaceship than any other candidate. Jan had also tested reasonably high, although several Zulu fighter pilots had scored higher. Zulu warriors intimidated Einstein and made him feel uncomfortable, so he had insisted on Jan as the second Mark VII spaceship pilot. They were to be mankind's first astronauts and would place the pulse bombs in orbit. Nkosinathi wanted to fly into outer space alongside her husband so badly it hurt. Unfortunately, she'd failed the physical tests.

Trying not to show any jealousy or rancor towards Jan, Nkosinathi invited her to join them, asking if she knew where General Eisenhower was. The American software engineer told the two physicists that the general had gotten into his staff car and left the compound. A sense of liberation overwhelmed the pair. With the mission only days away, they couldn't stand Eisenhower's hectoring any longer. Lately, the general had been preoccupied with the possibility of the Red Army using its Mark VII combat suits against England. Before the Commonwealth's two Mark VIIs had been sheathed in plasteel casings and turned into spaceships, Eisenhower had been calm, secure in the knowledge that his side could counter the ultra-advanced weapons of the communists. With the Commonwealth Mark VIIs locked inside confining straitjackets and unable to fight, Eisenhower was a caged tiger, someone to be avoided.

Nkosinathi wanted to know about the other caged tiger, Jan's husband. A tone of exasperation crept into Mrs. Churchill's voice as she said, "Winston remains unreconciled to my flying the second spaceship. He cannot accept that I am the most qualified person for the job. I'm afraid that traditional male chauvinism has him by the short and curlies."

Nkosinathi felt a strong pang of jealousy. It would have been easier if the other astronaut had not been a woman. She could at least blame her being passed over on the military's patriarchal attitude. As it was, she had no one to blame but herself, her lack of eye-hand coordination and balance. Chocking back the envy, Nkosinathi put a consoling arm around her friend. "Don't be overly hard on Winston, Jan. I'm not exactly thrilled that Albert shall be risking life and limb thousands of miles above the planet. You will look out for the professor up there, yes?"

"I'll bring him back in one piece."

"Speaking of Winston's short and curlies, how did you ever get him to agree to your participation in Operation Pegasus?"

"There is a reciprocal agreement in play. Winston is, at this very minute, flying to Vladivostock to join the peace circus on its journey to America. Both of us shall be in danger zones at about the same time."

Nkosinathi needed a second or two to digest that tidbit. It seemed that everyone was going into a war zone, except her. There was no helping that. Her skill as a pilot was not great. Yet her competence running mission control on Earth was considerable. *What was it that the communists were always saying, from each according to his or her ability?*

Einstein suggested that they retire to their guest quarters inside the palace and watch the news before having a spot of dinner with the Queen. The grounds between the mammoth barn (or rather the spaceship hangar) and the palace were lonely and desolate. The hooting of gorillas, barking of war dogs, and trumpeting of mammoths had been ingrained into the very fabric of the compound for years. Even the chirping of insects seemed loud with the Hannibalic Army gone.

There was a quick fix for their animal nostalgia. The DFA evening news featured the peace circus's arrival in Vladivostock. All the larger towns and cities along the six thousand mile route from France to Baikal had been treated to a parade and a circus. Baikal's major port would see something more: Bwana and Kubwa's troops were going to play one of their legendary games of football.

The TV screen revealed simians flying through the air to catch long passes and gorillas butting heads at the line of scrimmage. Five plays were shown, far more exciting than human athletics. But all good things must come to an end. The news broadcast moved onto the most serious problem afflicting the long-suffering planet Earth: the impending war between the new world and the old. There were indications that the sitzkrieg was drawing to a close.

Images from Utah's Bonneville Salt Flats appeared on screen, courtesy of videotape from the Communist International. The monochrome plain heaved and bunched with movement, like a tabletop completely covered by a colony of angry ants. One million suited soldiers were shown drilling across the salty wasteland. Hovercrafts circulated among the teeming mass. Wasp fighters and Viper helicopters churned the sky. Communist America was mobilizing and the Commonwealth's outmoded industrial base was not able to match the Yankee colossus.

Einstein suppressed a sob and leaped to his feet, rushing across the room to turn off the television. "All those young boys and girls will die in their suits when the pulse hits. Heat prostration and suffocation, a most horrendous death." He looked as though he were on the verge of tearing at his own face or gouging his own eyes out. Jan's gaze dropped to the carpet, tears leaking down her cheeks. Once they were in Earth orbit, she would be as much responsible for the pulse as Herr Doctor Professor. Not only would military personnel perish, aeroplanes would fall from the sky, cars would lose power on freeways and crash into each other, patients would die in surgery, miners would expire in the depths of their shafts, water pumps for drinking water and sewage treatment plants would fail, the list of calamities was endless. Deaths would number in the millions.

Nkosinathi pushed Albert back into his chair and faced off against the two would be astronauts, hands on her hips, black fire sparking from her eyes. "Look at the two of you! As if the barbaric war communists have not already floated diplomatic trial balloons. We know what they will be demanding: a civilization based on Commonwealth Military Games. They've created this ultra-efficient economic machine for the sole purpose of fueling military spending, millennial warfare, and armed conflict throughout the ages. Any one of the CMGs could spiral out of control into another world war. And this will happen time and time again if the war communists win."

Mrs. Einstein asked them to consider the frozen eggs and sperm in cryogenic vats in Zululand and Germany. Most of the men from her tribe, the Falashas, had been wiped out in the Hawaiian nuclear event. Their DNA existed in the frozen vats of the eugenics programs in Berlin and Lsandhlwara. The pulse might spell genocide for the Falashas. Everyone was being forced to make tremendous sacrifices. The burden was only worthwhile if this was the war to end all wars.

Lately, Bwana had taken great pains to get involved in technical discussions that might have an impact on his Hannibalic Army. He'd never enjoyed these discussions, but he soldiered on like a true silverback by forcing himself to participate. It always helped to have Erevu there at his side. The younger silverback had a nimble mind that could easily grasp the nuances of human technology.

The Captain of the *RMS Titanic*, William McMaster Murdoch, was not having a good day. The white whiskered old sea dog was venting his spleen on Winston Churchill while Bwana and Erevu listened attentively.

"The *Titanic* and *Britannic* may be old and rusty, Mr. Churchill, but that was no cause for your mechanics to've butchered 'em. These old ships are ladies, what you did was tantamount to rape." Murdoch blew an angry exhalation through his fluffy white mustache. He was angry that Churchill's minions had removed the electric engines, batteries, and generators from the two venerable ships, jerry-rigging a direct drive between the remaining diesel engines and the props, a crude and unnecessary modification that would hurt performance. Like many ocean-going commercial vessels built since the World War, the *Titanic* and *Britannic* were diesel-electric. Nowadays, there were DFA spin-off shipyards in America building nuclear powered ships and oil-fired steam turbines had been around for a while, other than that, there was no substitute for diesel-electric technology, certainly not straight diesel engines.

"Another item that's been vexing me," Murdoch raged on, "your big chimpanzees loaded maglev railcars in the lower hold that my people have yet to inspect. The chimps won't let my sailors get near the cars." Gleaming white fangs were suddenly protruding from the massive jaws of the two silverbacks. The gorillas might have ostensibly been there to gain an appreciation for technical matters, but no ape in the sign language breeding program would tolerate being called a chimpanzee.

Taking no heed of the simian threat display, Captain Murdoch steamed ahead into uncharted waters: "The Red Army will be boarding and inspecting our ships near Hawaii. If they find weapons, we're likely to be sunk. It's not a game were playing here, Mr. Churchill."

Bwana seized the old salt by the lapels of his pea coat and elevated him off the ground with effortless strength. Erevu signed at Churchill, the chief of staff translated the signs into spoken English for Murdoch's benefit: "Who you calling a chimpanzee, hairless house ape? Did they dip you in idiot sauce or were you born stupid?" When the captain did not respond, Bwana shook him, calling for a response. Churchill advised Murdoch to answer the silverback's questions.

"Ah, I meant no harm with the chimp jibe. You're the finest examples of gorilla flesh that I've ever the pleasure of seeing. Spectacular, truly. He, he, he." Bwana set the captain down, mockingly adjusting his navy blue uniform. The dominant silverback signed at Erevu, telling his subordinate that human crane operators had loaded hay, grain, and water, it was time for gorillas to load mammoths.

The two silverbacks knuckle-walked over to the maglev train. A chill wind was whipping off the Pacific, swirling throughout the harbor and train station. Both lowland gorillas shivered. The weather pattern drifting down from Siberia was not conducive to creatures that had evolved in the low-lying African tropics.

Kubwa joined his fellow silverbacks. He took stock of their chattering teeth and shivering bodies and signed, "Pussies. A little chill in the air and you're shivering like hairless house apes, pitiful." The mountain gorilla patted his thick layer of fur, grunting contently. The icy wind was cool and delicious as far as he was concerned.

Long hairy trunks snaked out of air vents in the stock cars. Mammoths tasted the frosty sea breeze blissfully. Having evolved in Siberia, to the mammoths, the wind smelled like home. A low rumble emanated from one of the stock cars. Erevu's sensitive hearing told him that Surus's stomach was grumbling. The weather was much too cold for the African elephant.

Erevu signed, "I'm getting Surus's battle armor from the ship. He's freezing to death." The junior silverback attempted to bound away but Bwana grabbed him by the bicep and spun him around, signing, "Jesus Christ! How many times have I told you morons? No armor and no weapons until the pulse hits! Red Army spy planes could photograph us at any time." The dominant silverback looked hastily around the deserted train station to make sure that no stray humans had seen his hand signs. Erevu complained, "Surus is freezing. I can't let him ice up. Remember the story about Hannibal's elephants in the Alps? Elephants can't take cold weather." Underscoring his point, another rumbling noise vibrated out of Surus's stock car.

Bwana and Kubwa gave Erevu a hard look. The older silverbacks were clearly of one mind. Kubwa signed, "Look, punk, you're a fourth generation tech ape, means you're bred to use tools and build stuff. Get off your ass and make Surus a coat." Erevu glared back at the senior silverbacks and demanded: "Where do I find raw materials?"

Bwana patiently explained that the junior silverback was going to have to seek help from the captain of the *Titanic*, adding that it shouldn't be hard to get cooperation from the man after the dominant silverback had expertly roughed him up.

Erevu nodded uncertainly, left the other gorillas, and opened Surus's stock car. The African bull charged out onto the street, followed by two mammoth cows, Hela clones. Erevu leaped onto the bull's neck hump, guiding him up to the *Titanic* with hands and feet. Surus trumpeted his displeasure at the cold climate, but led the two cows out of the railway station and down the pier where the *Titanic* and *Britannic* were moored. Behind him, a monstrous procession of mammoths was filing out of the other maglev railroad cars.

Surus crossed the ramp between the pier and the rusty old ship confidently, crossing narrow bridges was part of his training, elephants and mammoths were a lot more agile than they appeared to the uninitiated. There were bails of hay waiting for the pachyderms on the deck of either ocean liner. Surus trotted up to a mound of hay on Deck B and began stuffing green shoots into his mouth. A low seismic rumbling escaped from his belly that had nothing to do with hunger. The icy claws of the Siberian wind slashed harder and more savagely into the harbor.

A flow of mammoths inundated the main deck area of both ocean liners. As they glided aboard, they kept their trunks up, waving happily at the northern breeze as it ruffled their dense fur. Surus's stomach protested all the louder. Erevu sprang from the elephant's back and ran to a reader-board fastened to one of the ship's superstructures: a map giving the location of every cabin on board. Most of the cabins had been cut away to turn the passenger liner into a modern day Noah's Ark. However, the human crew retained normal accommodations. Erevu found Captain William Murdoch's name and cabin number. Only a fourth generation tech gorilla would have been able to make sense of the map and locate one of the cabins, he noted to himself proudly.

Erevu's hairy fist pounded frantically on Murdoch's door, nearly knocking it off the hinges. The knob turned from inside, the door opened fractionally, and Erevu burst into the captain's quarters. The silverback immediately began making hand signs. Murdoch angrily countered, "I don't know how to speak your blasted chimpanzee talk." Erevu's temper flared at the word "chimpanzee," but he kept it in check. There was no way to beat blankets and tools out of this human being.

Looking around the stateroom anxiously, the gorilla's eyes fell on a notepad and pen. He pounced on the writing implements and began penning a list of the things that he needed: blankets, twine, a thick needle, and waterproof tarps. Captain Murdoch's eyes widened as he examined the neat letters and coherent logic of the gorilla's request. "My God," he breathed. "Apes can honestly think like men. I thought it were a parlor trick 'til now." He looked into Erevu's eyes searchingly and saw an unmistakable glimmer of intelligence, a glimmer that he wouldn't allow himself to see when he'd first met the apes.

"What're the blankets and tarps for?" Murdoch asked. Even third generation general-purpose signing gorillas were adept at drawing pictures. Erevu was a virtuoso at portraying his thoughts with two-dimensional images. He sketched Surus. Then he sketched Surus wearing a coat made from blankets and tarps. Under the drawings he wrote a caption: *my elephant is freezing*.

Murdoch closed the notebook and set it down decisively. "I won't have a freezing elephant on my ship," the captain declared. He worked the ship's intercom and mobilized a small contingent of sailors. In a short while, Erevu and Murdoch were supervising a gang of sailors cum tailors as they stitched together a custom fitted coat for the chilled African bull.

The last stitch was sewn and the sailors backed away from Surus, admiring their handiwork. Surus raised his trunk and let loose a grateful trumpeting. Erevu patted Captain Murdoch affectionately, jumped onto the back of the bull elephant, beat his chest, and let out a distinctive roar, one that his troop would recognize.

All around the deck, dozens of silverbacks were standing on top their mammoths, beating their chests, and crying out to their troops. Adult female gorillas and juveniles of both sexes were riding young mammoth cows onto the *Titanic*, congregating around their silverback leaders, forming up into battle units for the trip to California.

Captain Murdoch looked past the marvelous sight of the congealing gorilla/mammoth troops and cast his eye at the heavily reinforced gangplanks connecting ship to shore. Men and women on mustangs were now riding aboard, leading huge packs of Bulldogs and Wolfhounds. There were thousands of dogs, but that wasn't what caught the captain's eye. The dogs were marching in formation, four abreast, in perfectly straight lines. The Bulldogs and Wolfhounds advanced in separate columns, winding through the knots of gorillas and mammoths to the lower decks, where their kennels were located.

Murdoch came from a long line of British seamen, countless generations serving the Royal Navy. He could tell the difference between circus performers and a trained military force. The animals boarding his ship were definitely in the latter category.

The Mark VII spaceships resembled the suits that they were based on the way a butterfly resembled a caterpillar. Since the 1920 CMG, missiles that could exceed the speed of sound had been shaped like fifty-caliber bullets, the only other object at the time that could also travel at supersonic velocity. Since then, various supersonic fighter jets had been configured differently. The latest generation of Halifax Wasp fighter was tucked in around the waist, like a Coca-Cola bottle. Einstein mistrusted wind tunnel testing and had not been convinced that the Coca-Cola bottle shape was aerodynamically correct. And then there was the problem of leaving the atmosphere, which could not be tested in a wind tunnel. The long and the short was that Einstein felt compelled to pick the most conservative design for his two spaceships: the tried and true shape of the pointy nosed fifty-caliber bullet.

Jan Churchill and Albert Einstein had been walking side by side. They split up, approached their separate launch pads, stepped onto their own concrete platforms, and stared up at the towering bullet shapes of their individual spaceships. A small army of assistants helped the astronauts through the open hatches at the base of the space vehicles. Jan and Einstein slid into their respective combat suits, deep in the hearts of the plasteel and aluminum towers.

Their suited arms were pointed rigidly straight down, an integral design feature of the spacecraft. The particle beam projectors on the vambraces of the suits fed plasma combustion chambers which were connected to gimbaled thrusters: exhaust points for the energy streams that would power the spaceships.

The two suits clamshelled shut. Hatches on the hulls of the spaceships closed. Fusion reactors in the bellies of the suits came to life. The two astronauts could hear Nkosinathi's voice in their helmet speakers. She was assuring them that all vehicular systems were functional and wanted to know if the suits were in a similar state of readiness. The integration between suit and spaceship had not reached the level that Einstein had hoped for. The astronauts could not monitor any of the vehicular systems outside their suits and had to rely on mission control to keep on eye on the internal workings of the spacecrafts.

Once mission control declared the spaceships, suits, and pulse bombs ready to go, Nkosinathi gave the astronauts a countdown: "Three, two, one, fire!" Particle beam projectors blasted into the forcefield lined plasma chambers. The secondary fusion reaction sent superheated ionized gas into the thrusters, which vibrated on gimbaled grooves as nuclear fire scorched the launch pads. Chunks of frozen nitrogen floated off the spaceships' fuselages. *Freedom* and *Liberty*, the two spaceships, rose slowly into the air. They gained speed and were soon rocketing out of the atmosphere.

The crushing G-force of the incessant acceleration was partially offset by the excellent fit of the suits. Nevertheless, both Einstein and Jan blacked out as blood drained from their heads. Regaining consciousness at about they same time, the astronauts checked helmet chronometers and throttled back their particle beams.

Mission Control sent two tight beam commands to the spaceships when they reached an altitude of 20,000 miles. *Freedom* and *Liberty* powered up their fusion drives for one last burst and assumed closely spaced orbits over the Earth's equator. Explosive bolts sent small shudders traveling up and down the length of the bulky spacecrafts. Aluminum plates peeled off the outer hulls, exposing a latticework of alloy beams that encased ten pulse bombs per ship.

The two astronauts used the strength of their nuclear powered limbs to twist away the alloy girders that had been holding their suits in place. They floated free of the skeletal space vehicles, spider silk ropes reeling out as tethers. Jan looked out at the Earth and the

Milky Way. She was momentarily stunned, star struck by the aching beauty of the blue and white planet against the lustrous diamond studded blackness of outer space. Her breath grew short as the immensity of the universe became overwhelming. She wasn't prepared for the emotional impact, or the raw majesty.

Einstein had imagined the starscape stretching out in all directions many times. It held a homey familiarity for him and wasn't in the least intimidating. He sent Jan a tight beam, "Jan, be very careful using the particle beams as thrusters." It was impossible to use the beam projectors to fly in the atmosphere because of control problems. In the vacuum of space, tiny blips of beam energy could work as a means of locomotion if the suit astronaut held tight to one of the immensely heavy pulse bombs.

"Watch me unload the first bomb." Einstein reeled himself back to the *Freedom*, placing one hand over the other and tugging on the spider silk tether. He spun around before grabbing the spaceship to make sure Jan was watching. She hadn't acknowledged his radio transmissions, but was looking his way, presumably paying attention. He climbed up the filigree of the spaceship until he reached the first pulse bomb, peeled back aluminum girders as if they were taffy, and pulled the bomb free.

"I'm watching, Dr. Einstein," Jan tight beamed. *Good*, he thought, *she had her head in the stars there for a while*. He grabbed a handhold on the bomb and carefully aimed his other arm so that the beam would not hit the *Freedom*, but it would take the bomb in a trajectory along the ship's orbit. Einstein's particle beam stuttered with a tiny blip of energy. The bomb and the astronaut sailed slowly away from the spaceship. Another series of tiny bursts and Einstein released the bomb and sailed back to his spaceship. He tight beamed Jan: "Every ten minutes we take turns and release a bomb. That will take us through one orbit. Then we reenter the atmosphere and touchdown in Britain."

They took turns releasing bombs, working smoothly until they were orbiting above central Asia. The huge brown eye of the Gobi Desert was winking with immense flashes of light. Only nuclear explosions could be visible from outer space. The Red Army was once again employing weapons of mass destruction. But it was not setting off a single nuclear bomb, but scores of them. This time it was Einstein's turn to be paralyzed and Jan who kept her wits.

Jan sent him a tight beam, "Professor, there is nothing we can do about those A-bombs up here. We have to continue deploying pulse bombs." A few seconds ticked by and he didn't respond. "Dr. Einstein, can the electromagnetic pulses of those detonations affect us in orbit?" The technical nature of her inquiry shook Einstein out of his catatonia. "N-no. The pulse will be localized from those relatively small fission explosions. I-I-I'm just feeling shame that we weren't able to deploy our P-bombs sooner. We could have stopped the slaughter below if—"

"It's your turn, Doctor. Deploy your P-bomb. We must stay on schedule," Jan said firmly, burying her own emotions. The two astronauts worked methodically and silently for one complete orbit of the Earth. Once the last bomb was in place, they pointed their helmets at the planet and blasted their particle beam projectors to gain momentum.

Fiery halos writhed and curled around the plummeting suits, friction from atmospheric contact. The suits' air-conditioning systems were soon laboring to keep the interiors cool. Forcefields bloomed around the Mark VIIs and the wicked flames were put an arm's distance away. Even with forcefield protection the PCSs had to use emergency power, ramping up their internal air-conditioning to withstand the fierce thermal forces of reentry.

265

It was hoped that communist ground observers would consider the blazing lines scratched across the sky as nothing more than a couple of harmless, if somewhat large, meteorites. There was little reason for the Red Army to think otherwise. The nose-diving astronauts were absolutely indistinguishable from naturally occurring meteorites and bore little resemblance to the gigantic spaceships that had put them in orbit. Then again, the communists would be on high alert after monitoring the Mark VII spaceships' journey into orbit.

Einstein and Jan intended to keep up the natural appearance of streaking fireballs as long as possible. They didn't want to have to deal with the Red Army's three Mark VII combat suits. And then there was the problem of navigating. Luckily, the cloud cover over the Atlantic wasn't so extensive that Great Britain was completely obscured from ultra-high altitudes.

Collapsing their forcefields into tight fitting sheaths, Jan and Einstein were able to steer by bodysurfing. Jan watched the professor more than she did the ground or the sea, mimicking his every move. When he flipped around and put his feet down and his head pointed at the sun, she executed the same maneuver. Forcefields vanished and lift turbines bit into the increasingly thick air.

The two suits ceased falling and began flying. The green fields and gardens of southern England were soon skimming below their Mark VII boot heels. Whenever there was a break in the clouds, the late afternoon sun turned their shadows into long dragon-like entities that skipped and jumped over the countryside. They landed on the scorched launch pads that had, only a few hours ago, seen their departure into space.

The astronauts clamshelled out of their suits and were surrounded by mission control and the palace staff. The Queen was out there as well, parting the crowd like Moses and moving toward the heroes. Einstein bowed impatiently to the Monarch and mumbled annoyed words of acceptance as she heaped flowery accolades on the two astronauts.

Nkosinathi held a large portable radio over her head. She knew what Einstein wanted to hear. When the Queen had said her piece, Mrs. Einstein turned on the radio and the assembled crowd, as well as people all over the planet, heard mankind's first broadcast from space.

"Citizens of the British Commonwealth, Switzerland, and the People's Republic of North America: fill bathtubs, buckets, and swimming pools with water. Do whatever you can to store clean drinking water. The electric pumps that send potable water into your cities will malfunction in a matter of hours."

The prerecorded voice was Einstein's. Its source was the orbiting pulse bombs. They would beam this message to Earth for the next eight hours. At which time, the three horsemen of the Apocalypse (the initial space pulse, the secondary high-altitude atmospheric OEN super-pulse, and the troposphere tertiary pulses) would shred mankind's industrial civilization, reducing humanity to an 18th century technological base. In the remote event that the Red Army could somehow successfully put one of their Mark VIIs in space to attack the pulse bombs, proximity radar would set them off early.

That wasn't the only military threat posed by broadcasting the Commonwealth's intention to use pulse weapons in advance. From a strictly military viewpoint, it made no sense. Churchill and Eisenhower hated the idea. But Einstein had drawn another line in the sand, and made the warning broadcast a precondition for his participation in Operation Pegasus.

Bwana had a pretty good handle on the dangers that the two ships faced as the hour for the EMP drew near. The *Titanic* and *Britannic* were halfway to the Hawaiian Islands. If the communists figured out the Trojan horse nature of the two ships, then they would send fighter jets roaring across the Pacific and put the Hannibalic Army on the bottom of the sea with impunity.

Hela stood on the upper deck facing west, her trunk wagging lazily in the cool breeze. Bwana was lying on his stomach on Hela's back, feet and hands tangled in her warm fur. Both creatures were looking in the direction of Hawaii, the source of peril. Bwana understood that there was nothing they could do if commie jets, warned by that miserable bleeding-heart-do-gooder Einstein, came screaming over the horizon. As far as the silverback was concerned, human beings could drink water from creeks and lakes and they could do so without being instructed by radio transmitters in outer space. Humans couldn't even drink water without electricity? Gorillas had existed without electricity for millions of years. Maybe Kubwa was right. Maybe humans really were all pussies.

One of the few people that Bwana unreservedly considered to be a non-pussy came limping up to the mammoth, his dog, Hacksaw, trotting jauntily at his side. David Banner called up to the silverback, "See anything?" Bwana arched his back and put a pair of binoculars to his eyes, scanning the horizon. Nothing. He gave two short barks, a way of saying "no" when sign language was inconvenient.

Banner asked Hela to lift him up next to the silverback. Like a living elevator, the mammoth cow's trunk picked up the crippled old man and set him on the flattest portion of her back. Through a combination of leaping and climbing, Hacksaw scaled the mountain of pachyderm flesh to sit next to the primates. The three rested comfortably up there, regarding the activity on the decks below. The man and the ape took turns with the binoculars, sweeping the horizon. Someone on an aft deck shouted, "The P-bombs have stopped broadcasting!"

Bwana asked Banner what was going to happen next. The man explained that pulse bombs would soon fire maneuvering rockets to slide closer to the atmosphere. Then chaff missiles would be fired directly down into the depths of Earth's ocean of air. The missiles would explode in the thermosphere and a ring of superconducting foil would encircle the globe. He was about to continue the explanation when a great fiery line materialized in the southern sky, partly obscured by clouds.

Sailors below called up, "The P-bombs have hit atmosphere. Gorillas cover the elephants' eyes!" Bwana crawled out onto Hela's forehead, placed his furry mitts over her eyes, and closed his own. A bright red light shone through the veins of his eyelids. He kept his eyes shut for ten seconds, opened them, and looked out on a changing world. The post-EMP environment was being born.

The first two horsemen of the Apocalypse had made their run. The last horseman was having a field day. Lightning flashed from cloud to cloud. The electrical storm stretched out to sea as far as the eye could see. The more distant bolts were like tiny blue wires. Closer to the ship, huge electrical shafts oscillated between ocean and sky. Thunder pealed unendingly. An errant bolt hit the *Titanic*. Bwana felt his fur stand on end as the discharge worked its way throughout the ship. The pyrotechnic show lasted a couple more minutes and the world straddling electrical storm degenerated into a few menacing thunderclaps.

The silverback smoothed his fur and looked around. From the bridge deck of the *Titanic*, nothing seemed to have changed. The ocean liner and its sister ship were still plowing through the Pacific, their hard working diesel engines unaffected by the three apocalyptic pulses. Nobody on board had been hurt by the lightning. The sky was still blue, the ocean still wet.

The gorilla made hand signs at Banner, "Everything is the same." Banner held the dial face of his electric watch under Bwana's nose. The hands were frozen in place. The silverback snorted disdainfully. He expected a bigger change than that.

"Yo! ape-shapes, the fridges are out. Eat yer fruit now, or it'll go bad!" This cry came from the *Titanic's* human crew, an admonition to clean out the ship's copious freezers and refrigerators, most of which were filled with perishable fruit.

Bwana's troop had been lazing around on the bridge deck, sunning themselves, enjoying the warmer weather as the ship moved into more temperate climes. He gave the hooting call that meant they were to assemble around their lord and master. A simian circle formed around Hela. The dominant silverback stood where they could all see him and made hand signs, advising them to feed most of the fruit to the mammoths, there was too much there for gorillas to eat, he didn't want the apes to get sick.

Similar circles were taking shape around the other silverbacks. In each case, an adult male gorilla was lecturing his troop from the back of a mammoth. Shipboard life was beginning to undergo a small amount of the far-reaching changes implied by the post-EMP world. And the leaders of the Hannibalic Army had been planning for the calamitous event for months. Banner wondered what was happening in the rest of the world. It wasn't a thought worth pursuing. Death and misery were swirling in the turbulence left behind by the Apocalyptic Horsemen.

Lisa Banner and Captain Murdoch navigated through the hurly burly of gorillas and pachyderms stuffing their faces with apples, watermelons, bananas, strawberries, and other fruit. They climbed up the ramp leading to the bridge deck, stepping carefully over dropped produce.

Bwana, Banner, and Hacksaw were still sitting on top of Hela, observing the pandemonium below. Murdoch called up to the dominant silverback, "The ship needs a course correction. We've to implement the plan talked about earlier." Bwana blinked in disbelief and signed to Banner, "Already? The freaking pulse just hit!" The one-legged man responded, "We are employing Great Circle navigation. Which calls for constant course corrections—" The silverback frantically waved his hands for silence. He couldn't stand listening to explanations concerning Great Circle navigation. The problem was that, unlike the humans' wordy ranting and raving about superconductors and EMPs, he could almost understand the concepts behind Great Circle navigation, and that almost but not quite understanding gave him a headache, as though a tasty melon were inches from his grasp. Erevu understood the navigation technique perfectly and would be steering the ship until they grounded in Monterey Bay, California and attacked the commies.

Bwana hurtled off the mammoth to land on the deck with a resounding thump. Hacksaw leaped off the hairy mountain, landing with less impact than the silverback, but equal panache. Banner had Hela carefully deposit him on Deck A with her trunk. Bwana told his number one female to keep order in the troop until he returned. David Banner, Lisa Banner, Captain Murdoch, Hacksaw, and Bwana walked down to Deck B, where Kubwa and Erevu were waiting patiently. Erevu was already in his harness with two long coils of spider silk rope attached, radiating zeal for the upcoming job.

The enlarged procession marched to the stern of the gigantic ship. They peered into the churning water of the ship's wake. The three gargantuan bronze propellers were spinning cheerfully. Below deck, powerful diesel engines were lustily singing, mocking the EMP that had turned most technology off throughout the world. The massive rudder was locked in one position, the exact position that it had been in when the pulse had struck. It was controlled by electric motors and would have to be turned manually. This could only be done outside the ship, a feat requiring the strength of a weight trained silverback on steroids with the intelligence of the fourth generation tech, a task tailor-made for Erevu.

Captain Murdoch shouted last minute instructions at the young silverback. Erevu nodded eagerly and handed silk ropes to Bwana and Kubwa. The three apes strode upright to the railing around the stern. Erevu leaped off with a gleeful hoot. The two older silverbacks lowered him until he was in place, straddling the hull plates directly above the frozen rudder.

Erevu moved his feet against the hull, seeking the horizontal mullions protecting rear-facing portholes. His feet found purchase and curled around the sturdy metal bars. He looked up at Captain Murdoch inquiringly. The captain held an old-fashioned wind-up pocket watch to his face and bellowed, "Now!" Murdoch put his mouth next to a slender speaking tube projecting from the deck and shouted at the sailors below to unlimber steering cables.

Leathery gorilla hands gripped the slippery surface of the rudder. Spray splashed up into the simian's face. Muscles swelled in Erevu's arms, chest, back, and legs. The rudder groaned and tilted five degrees to starboard. The ship keeled sharply. With gritted teeth, the silverback held the rudder in place for a long time, so long that he lost all sense of duration and seemed to be in another dimension where the only things that existed were muscle pain and the rushing water that he was struggling against. He remembered the Zen training that General Kwa had drilled into the gorilla warriors. Kwa had taught them to find their chi, their center, and let strength flow out from that special spot in the belly. The young silverback felt his strength increase as he found his spiritual center. Power surged out from his chi.

"Time!" Murdoch shouted. "Straighten 'er out!" Simian muscles strained anew. The rudder creaked back to neutral. Cables, gears, and the internal movement of electric motors moved as well. The entire rudder mechanism was locked into place by the hands below deck. The ship stopped listing and took its new heading, steaming bravely into the post-EMP environment, where brawn counted for as much as brains.

Erevu was pulled back up onto Deck B, none the worse for wear. The older silverbacks pounded the young male's back with sledgehammer blows, hooting triumphantly. "Uh-oh," Kubwa signed, "heads-up, Siamese-twins are coming." The gorillas had given Churchill and Eisenhower the combined nickname "Siamese-twins."

Eisenhower inquired as to the efficacy of the course correction. He was gracious enough to congratulate both humans and apes after hearing the good news that all had gone well. With that out of the way, he ordered the gorillas to extract combat howdahs and ammunition from the railcars in the hold. The troops and their pachyderms were to assume a battle station rotation for the remainder of the trip. The Red Army possessed sailboats in their island stronghold. It was entirely conceivable that old style breech loading artillery, machineguns, or other chemically powered weapons could be mounted on schooners and used against the *Titanic* and *Britannic*. Bwana reared up to his full height and gave the supreme commander a crisp salute, casting a warning glance at Kubwa to refrain from signing a sarcastic or insulting comment. Eisenhower returned the salute, nodding approvingly at the dominant gorilla.

"While we're on the subject, Sir. If I may?" David Banner spoke up. Eisenhower bade him to continue. "The mammoths need to be trimmed, given a nice close shave. It's hot in the Hawaiian waters and hot in California. There won't be time latter on." Eisenhower started to say something about the gorillas acting as barbers. Lisa gave Churchill a scathing look. The chief of staff and de facto prime minister gently explained that if the gorillas were well and truly on a combat rotation, then they must be kept ready for battle twenty-four hours a day. Shaving the mammoths involved shearing them with handheld clippers, a time consuming task. There would be no choice but to use sailors and human soldiers, even human officers if need be. He didn't say that the gorillas had to be treated like frontline combat troops from here on out, not large, hirsute laborers. Churchill added that carrier pigeons should probably be sent to the *Britannic* to make sure that the same division of labor prevailed in both warships, trying to make a suggestion rather than give an order. Eisenhower could see through the gentle prodding and didn't like it. The supreme commander could also see that Lisa and Winston were making valid points.

Slowly but surely, the Hannibalic Army found its sea legs. Mammoths were stationed at one hundred forty foot intervals around the railing of Deck B, howdahs brimming with weapons. A silverback stood in front of the cannon inside each howdah. Two senior female gorillas stood next to their mate, covering the two machineguns extending from the sides of the aluminum combat platforms. Behind each mammoth, a troop of young gorillas stood next to mounds of ammo boxes. The younger simians would pitch shells and boxes of bullets up to the silverbacks and senior females in the event of a firefight.

Each of the two warships had fifty mammoths and fifty gorilla troops on board. One hundred forty foot intervals put twelve mammoths and twelve gorilla troops on the front line per twelve-hour shift. Included in the rotation was a reserve of canine mobile infantry, which meant that one thousand Bulldogs were kept in battle harnesses on Deck C during each shift. This put another one thousand light machineguns at Eisenhower's disposal at a moment's notice.

They were loaded for bear as the big ships steamed past the corpse-like remains of the Big Island. The humans on board were solemn and dropped their eyes when the glassy sheets of incinerated land floated by. The two mighty volcanoes that had once stood head and shoulders above all other Pacific peaks had been reduced into pathetic twisted stumps that barely rose out of the waves: a sign of the Red Army's might.

Ninety miles out from the archipelago, a three-masted sailboat appeared from the north, cutting an interception course on the *Titanic* and *Britannic*, racing in front of a stiff breeze. Eisenhower sent runners to the silverbacks on his ship and pigeons to the *Britannic*, warning the senior male gorillas to be ready with cannons. The canine mobile infantry reserves on both ships were called up from their lower deck.

Bwana pressed his binoculars to his eyes. He could see a black man waving a white flag from the crow's nest of the schooner. He dropped the glasses, letting them fall against the cord around his neck. There were no weapons visible on the interloping vessel. He looked up at the *Titanic's* bridge deck. Eisenhower was pacing nervously, stopping every few steps to peer at the sailboat with binoculars. The silverback could guess what was going through the supreme commander's mind. The small ship could be carrying a load of dynamite or some other kind of explosives. It might try to get right next to the *Titanic* and destroy it with a suicide blast. If not, there was little to be gained by rescuing a few stray yachtsmen that were lost at sea. Eisenhower was getting ready to give the command to fire.

The binoculars returned to Bwana's eyes. There was a brown man waving his arms energetically in the bow of the sailboat. Still no weapons visible. The brown man suddenly looked familiar. His outline was very distinctive, with a large beak-like nose. Bwana might have seen him before, in photographs that Nkosinathi had shared back at the palace. Clamping his fangs tight until his jaw muscles hurt and squinting every particle of vision into his eyes, Bwana bored in on the waving brown man, almost crushing his field glasses.

The *Titanic* was closer to the schooner than the *Britannic*. Eisenhower sent runners down from the top deck to the silverbacks on the port side of Deck B with the command to sink the three-masted sailboat. The waving brown man and his boat drew close enough for Bwana to clearly identify him as Jeremiah Halifax. At the same time, Bwana heard the order to open fire. The dominant silverback tilted his head back and barked twice: short, sharp, and piercingly loud. The silverbacks on his left and right echoed the sharp double-bark. In this context it meant, "Belay that order."

Mammoth cannons were lowering on Deck B, turning aside to point into the ocean. On the bridge deck, Eisenhower turned to Churchill and asked what was happening. The chief of staff said, "Bwana just told his troops to stand down." Eisenhower's face contorted angrily. He muttered something about chimpanzees thinking they were human. Churchill infused his voice with a diamond edge and directly ordered the supreme commander to send a runner that understood sign language to find out why Bwana had refused to fire. There was no need; Bwana was bounding up the ramp to the bridge deck.

The dominant silverback had enough political savvy to stand erect and salute the two dominant humans. Churchill said, "As you were, Bwana. I understand sign language well enough. Tell me why you countermanded General Eisenhower's order." A series of hand gestures brought the explanation forth.

Eisenhower thanked Bwana for his quick thinking, adding that under the circumstances the countermand was perfectly justifiable. Pigeons were sent to the *Britannic*, appraising the sister ship of the situation. With that done, the supreme commander looked distinctly uncomfortable and Churchill looked thoughtful. Bwana had a vague notion as to the cause. Nkosinathi routinely referred to her former lover as "Supreme Commander Halifax." The silverback knew that Jeremiah Halifax had once led a formidable army called the Blue Force and that it had been an ally of the Queen's, an enemy to the Red Army. Bwana wondered if this new supreme commander could usurp Eisenhower's authority.

Captain Murdoch threw a dinner that evening in honor of the dignitaries rescued at sea. Bwana recognized that an important corner had been turned in human/gorilla relations when a messenger boy interrupted his vigil on top of Hela with an invitation to attend the power supper.

The meal itself wasn't as enjoyable as he'd hoped. Bwana did not take pleasure in eating peanut butter sandwiches with a knife and fork. Nor did he like sitting next to humans that were wolfing down tins of bully beef. To survive, a starving gorilla might choke down fresh raw meat. Death would be preferable to ingesting the vile processed

271

cow flesh that Englishmen so relished. Merely smelling the food on the humans' plates was nauseating.

Listening to Jeremiah Halifax describe his daring escape from Kauai made up for the odoriferous bully beef. After the pulse hit, the three Blue Force generals were able to easily break from their electromagnetically locked prison cell on the south side of the Garden Island. It hadn't been overly difficult for them to navigate through the chaos of post-EMP Kauai or steal Red Army uniforms. The communist elite kept a stable of sailboats in Lihue. None of these boats were guarded, so the fact that the Blue Force team was able to steal one was unremarkable. The fact that they were able to successfully rig explosive charges and blow every other sloop to smithereens before setting sail was mind-boggling, the best part of the story for Bwana. Furthermore, Supreme Commander Halifax told the tale with flare. Closing his eyes, the silverback imagined that he was setting the charges in the keels of the sailboats, striking old style matches to the improvised explosives.

From the darkness of tightly closed eyes, he called up another image: photos of ancient Carthaginian coins depicting Hannibal Barca. Bwana opened his eyes and stared at Jeremiah Halifax. The Blue Force supreme commander could have been the template for those ancient coins. He had the same prodigious hooked nose, wide at the base with nostrils flaring like the wings of an eagle. The high forehead, the cap of closely cropped curly hair, and most significantly of all: Generalissimo Halifax had only one eye. The man was the living reincarnation of Hannibal.

Next to Jeremiah sat Eisenhower: scrawny, two watery eyes, less hair than most humans, a big head on a small body. Eisenhower was a bureaucrat: soulless, bloodless, uninspiring—an anti-Hannibal. Gorillas, war dogs, and mammoths could not serve under this scrawny man. Bwana would not let them. They must have the one-eyed general: Jeremiah Halifax, the modern day Hannibal Barca.

More than ever, Bwana wanted the meal to end. He must have a private chat with Churchill, to force the issue. The ape suffered through lengthy rounds of drinking. Humans illogically raised glasses of toxic alcohol in toasts to good health. Then they pulled out cancer sticks and puffed away until their lungs rotted. At such moments, it was not hard to believe that they were very closely related to chimpanzees, the only other creature besides man that enjoyed smoking tobacco.

A waiter plunked a half-gallon can of tomato juice at Bwana's table setting. The silverback hoisted the tomato juice can and clicked it against the alcohol-filled glasses of his tablemates. He couldn't afford to appear impatient with the hairless primates. He had to play politics on a human level.

Bwana's patience was rewarded. That night, he found himself sitting on a Persian rug in Churchill's quarters, discussing the need to install Halifax as the supreme commander of the Hannibalic Army. Large leathery hands made gesture after gesture: "Vicky chose Eisenhower to lead a modern army. Ike is not a Hannibal. Halifax is. I can smell it. I can see it. I can taste it. Halifax will be a better leader."

They argued throughout the night, eventually agreeing that Jeremiah was a better tactician and Eisenhower the better strategist and politician. A compromise emerged. Eisenhower would remain supreme commander, operating out of a fixed base behind enemy lines once the war began in earnest in California. Halifax would be appointed field commander, riding with the troops into battle, in charge of day-to-day decisions and tactics.

With that settled, Bwana brought up the subject of the war's aftermath. He wanted Churchill to understand that gorillas would be adamant that two laws must be enshrined in the new Commonwealth constitution: Gorillas must be given the vote and eugenic techniques must quit being used on chimpanzees. Existing chimp sign language breeding programs must be dismantled; the signing chimps put in zoos or returned to the wild. There was room for only two species of sentient primates on planet Earth.

Eisenhower asked Bwana what he thought about eugenics programs geared for orangutans. Bwana hesitated for a long moment and finally signed, "Orangutans are good people, not evil like chimps, they have good hearts, but aren't team players. It wouldn't be a disaster if the red apes were bred to sign. Still, I say no, leave them in their forests. Intelligent chimps are a crime wave waiting to happen, a plague on society." Bwana gave a shutter of revulsion brought on by the mere thought of sentient chimpanzees. The PLC had already done too much with their chimp program.

Churchill tugged an earlobe contemplatively. The chief of staff was a wise enough man to realize that human primatologists were woefully ignorant of the deeper ramifications posed by breeding souls into man's closest relative, the chimpanzee. He would trust the dominant silverback on this score. It would be interesting to see how signing chimps fared after being returned to the wilds of Africa. If the signing chimps took up agriculture and tool making, then a host of legal questions would eventually tangle the courts.

Chapter 22

Hannibal is at the Gates

The EMP had come at the worst possible time for Jim Pullman: right after the Communist International had selected his company to build its world headquarters building, a blockbuster coup. But that wasn't the half of it. Pevsner and Tatlin had applied constructivist principles to designing a new kind of potato chip. The constructivist chip was not flat and brittle like its competitors. It had structural ridges like a piece of corrugated steel. This revolutionary potato chip could hold five times more guacamole dip than a conventional flat chip, and not break. It was, therefore, five times better, and should sell five times better. But it didn't cost one farthing extra to make. With the draconian antitrust laws of free market communism staring at you around every corner, a successful company needed to diversify. The food sector was a promising safety valve in case government fiat broke up Constructivist Archangel's building division.

Pullman had a potato chip assembly line up and running when the damn pulse hit. He'd had semi-trucks loaded with bags of chips, ready to ship to market. Those bags had disappeared in the first day of food riots. The rioters probably hadn't even noticed whether the new chips could hold more dip or not. The pulse and the British blood-sucking capitalist pigs that caused it were to blame. Monopoly capitalism knew it couldn't compete with free market communism. The pulse was the monopolists' way of taking away the football and saying nobody could play if the capitalist pigs weren't guaranteed a win.

No matter what the bloated monopolists did from their London redoubt, there was no holding back the American entrepreneurial spirit unleashed by the new economic system. As soon as the food riots abated, Constructivist Archangel began constructing a gravity-powered aqueduct from the Santa Cruz Mountain Reservoir to San Jose, using hand tools, horses, and elbow grease.

Today, Pullman was riding his horse away from the aqueduct, out into the Salinas Valley, to secure a long-term food source for his workers. The Red Army had lent him two German Shepherds and a light machinegun for the journey. In the aftermath of the EMP, a human life was nothing compared to a horse, especially the big German coach horse that carried Pullman's beefy carcass.

Farmer after farmer turned the entrepreneur down. The price of crops was rising day by day in the city markets of northern California. No one wanted to get tied down by a long-term contract. It occurred to Pullman that he might have better luck on the coast, with the fishermen. It would be impossible to reach Monterey by nightfall. He needed a safe place to camp.

He found a small hay barn on a hill overlooking the bay. There was a small boy guarding the small barn. Pullman approached the gun-toting lad carefully, on foot, hands empty and in plain sight, the horse and dogs trailing behind.

"I'll pay ten pounds for two flakes of hay," Pullman offered, halting and standing still in the direct line of the boy's fire.

"Gotta buncha thugs hidin' in the bushes yonder?" The boy aimed his assault rifle at a likely clump of foliage, clicked it to semi-automatic fire, and squeezed off a round. When that failed to stir up any accomplices, the farm boy decided that the stranger was on the level. A price of twenty pounds for three flakes of hay was agreed upon. Pullman offered to assist in guard duties for the night. The boy looked skeptically at the fat man, but appreciatively at the two powerful German Shepherds, and agreed to the deal. In turn, Pullman shared his meager supply of pork and beans around the campfire that evening. The German Shepherds made due with a few dog biscuits and licking out the cans of half eaten beans. Nowadays, even a journey of just one hundred miles required careful rationing.

The campsite did have clean water. There was a swift running creek nearby that drained a wilderness area, not pastureland with cows pissing in the creek. Although Pullman skipped breakfast the next morning, he did have a mug of cold instant coffee. Sipping the bitter fluid, he straightened the kinks from his spine and stared blearily at the painfully bright waters of Monterey Bay.

He dropped the coffee mug. The German Shepherds' ears shot forward, alarmed at their handler's sudden agitation. Two monstrously huge ocean liners were steaming into the Monterey docks. The cloud of white vapor belching from their smokestacks was not only incongruous, it was jarring, frightening, a sign of military power in the post-EMP world.

The instant the ships were moored, streams of Bulldogs in war harnesses blasted down gangplanks, swamping the coastal hamlet. "What is it Mr. Pullman?" the boy asked, rubbing sleep from his eyes. The youth regarded the ships and exclaimed happily, "The peace circus is in town!" Jumping up and down, he went on: "I saw it on the telly before the blackout: gorillas playing football, really big, hairy elephants doing tricks."

"No, it's not the peace circus," Pullman corrected. "It's Britain's capitalist army. Britain made the blackout. The redcoats are coming to reconquer us and recolonize this continent." Pullman hastily saddled his horse, drawing up the stirrups to fit the young farm boy. He ordered the two German Shepherds to watch over the lad and then gave the youth a series of instructions. The boy was to ride to the Red Army base in Salinas and tell the duty officer that the Commonwealth had landed an army in Monterey. "Keep the gelding at a steady canter. Don't gallop the whole way. Tell any adult you see that the enemy is here. The redcoats have landed. Don't stop and chew the fat. Don't take orders from anybody. Even if you see your dad, keep going. Ride to the Red Army base in Salinas, that's your goal."

Sitting on top the heavy boned coach horse, the boy wailed, "The redcoats'll steal Poppa's hay!" They both looked down at the harbor. Four legged mountains were wading in the shallows of Monterey Bay. Standing on top of the walking mountains were fierce apes brandishing heavy water cooled machineguns: war mammoths and battle gorillas invading the city.

"Yes," Pullman agreed. "The enemy will steal your family's hay and worse. They'll steal the whole hay farm. They'll put the field hands to work growing more hay as slave labor. Remember the midnight ride of Paul Revere?" The boy's head bobbed up and down grimly. Pullman told him to ride like Paul Revere, shout warnings at every passersby, but stop for nothing and nobody. The horse's rump was slapped. The gelding cantered away, the powerful young German Shepherds trotting vigilantly behind.

Pullman studied the rough terrain between the small hay barn on the hill and the invading army in the bay. It was a lot of ground to cover on foot, especially on an empty stomach. The only good thing about the pulse was that Americans were being forced to work off the layers of fat that industrialized living had piled on. He threw away the Red Army issue light machinegun.

Sweating and swearing, crashing through the brush, Pullman slowly worked his way down the slope. An African fish eagle swooped over the portly businessman, screaming fiercely and giving away his position. A Hannibalic dog patrol picked him up in a meadow between two Eucalyptus forests. Ten fierce Bulldogs had him surrounded in the blink of an eye, canine machineguns aimed at his chest, stomach, and head. As long as he remained perfectly still, they were content to hold him in place. The pack leader boomed a thunderous bark. Minutes later, Pullman resisted the urge to twist his head and see the rider that was pounding the turf with a drum of hoof beats somewhere to his rear. The dogs seemed extremely trigger-happy.

A horsewoman in Commonwealth fatigues rode into Pullman's field of vision, the fish eagle perched on her saddle horn. The equestrian soldier dismounted and patted the fat entrepreneur down for weapons, asking if he belonged to the Red Army or was serving as a communist spy. The lead Bulldog sniffed Pullman as he answered: acting as a canine lie detector. Pullman told the scout that he wasn't a spy for the communists, although at one time he had been a spy for the Commonwealth and must be put before a senior officer without delay, all of which was the truth and didn't raise the suspicions of the canine. And it produced the desired result, in a manner of speaking. Handcuffs were clipped around his wrists. A rope was tied to the handcuffs and the scout's saddle. Pullman was tugged, stumblingly, behind the enemy horse.

Aching feet and cramping leg muscles were forgotten when he staggered down Main Street. Thirty mammoths were swinging grandly down the village's principal thoroughfare, decked out in green and brown body armor covering virtually every square inch of their immense bodies. On their backs, camouflaged howdahs were animated with weapons and armored combat gorillas.

Tugging Pullman along, the scout was forced to place her mount, captive, and dog pack in an alley to allow the heavy armor of the battle-lion get by. A horse-drawn baggage train rolled behind the armored pachyderms. For some reason, the sight of gorilla teamsters driving wagons seemed strange, while the sight of gorillas on top of mammoths seemed natural.

Next, the Bulldogs of the Commonwealth canine mobile infantry marched in ranks led by men and women riding doughty little warhorses, equipped in an identical manner to the scout that had found Pullman. At this distance, the chubby businessman could see that every dog wore a 1920 CMG style war harness. How could Red Army foot soldiers outflank four-legged infantry capable of running thirty-five miles-per-hour and scrambling over twenty-foot walls?

Long-legged Wolfhounds, four feet tall at the shoulder, trotted next to lanky thoroughbreds: the redcoat cavalry. The last racehorse and the last Wolfhound stepped smartly past the alley. Pullman looked down Main Street. The battle-lion was debouching from the shelter of the town into the valley: a dagger to strike at San Jose and cut out the heart of world communism.

The scout plopped him down in the room of a hotel that the Hannibalic Army had commandeered in downtown Monterey. He was shuffled from a low-ranking officer to a mid-level officer. All the time, Pullman kept emphasizing his former role as a Commonwealth spy, over a decade ago. This gave the mid-level officer the idea of fobbing off the troublesome prisoner to David Banner, who had once been head of the Secret Service Bureau, back in the old days.

Pullman was ecstatic that the tactic worked. He grinned from ear to ear as David, Lisa, and Hacksaw filed into the dingy hotel room. The Banners recognized Pullman and gave him a hearty greeting. Pullman mentioned that he hadn't eaten since the evening before. The Banners procured copious quantities of food and drink for their fat, famished friend, and a light snack for themselves.

"Gotta be a way to stop this war, 'cause it's nuts. Vladimir Bakunin knows what he's talking about," Pullman said between bites. "Free market communism is the best God damn economic system possible, light years ahead of monopoly capitalism. And it's democratic as a son of a bitch."

David Banner frowned over a steaming bowl of fish chowder, set his spoon down, and said, "Fifty percent income tax is confiscatory. Combining personal and corporate income tax equals a 75 percent bite. Frankly, I don't see how business can operate under that load."

Pullman stuffed a piece of bread in his mouth, chewed, and swallowed. "It's a progressive tax. But, yeah, sure, you and me, we're in the top bracket. Income ain't taxed twice though. Payroll is an expense. Dividends are an expense. Retained earnings are an expense. Income is only taxed twice for inheritance, a once in a lifetime occurrence! Forget that for now. Under free market communism, there is simply income tax, nothing else. No sales tax. No property tax. No license tax. No severance tax. No franchise tax. No excise tax. The whole tax code can be written on the back of a matchbox. Simplicity. I'm telling you, that's what's been supercharging the American economy during the sitzkrieg, the simplicity of the tax code, even more than antitrust laws. Bakunin is a freakin' genius. Know what ol' Queen Victoria One did right? Got rid of the stinking tariffs. Simplified the tax code. Same here. Bakunin has gotten rid of a shit load of taxes. Tax planning is nonexistent under free market communism. So pure, so awesome."

The Banners had no response. The only sound in the room was Hacksaw's snoring. Pullman waved a fork at his captors. "Government spending is just as simple. The lion's share goes to the army, first and foremost, then the cops, and criminal courts. Nothing else."

Lisa asked how government pensions, state health care, and public education were funded. The answer: the free market performed all these functions under government charters and mandates. Truancy laws meant parents had to pay to send their kids to school or the whole family faced jail time, but they had a choice of any number of private institutions. Pullman gave details and the Banners gained an insight into the hyper-efficient economy that had sprung from the mind of Vladimir Bakunin.

Through the window of the hotel room, Pullman saw wagons roll by filled with metal workers and carpenters. Some of the wagons carried hull plates from the ocean liners. He wondered what was going on. David Banner explained that the Hannibalic Army was turning Monterey into a walled town, like ancient Rome or Carthage. The post-EMP war would quickly consume whatever bullets and artillery shells existed and then the fighting would involve swords, spears, bows and arrows. Walled cities would be back in vogue.

There were several things that alarmed Pullman in Banner's cool recitation. The chunky American seized on the term "Hannibalic," noting that Red Army officers also talked about Hannibal a lot, much to the confusion of the civilians in the People's Republic of North America.

Lisa nodded and looked at her husband. "The Red Army employs the strategy of Hannibal Barca. The Commonwealth employs Hannibal's tactics," Banner opined. The statement went over Pullman's head. He was more interested in business and politics than military history.

Pullman steered the conversation back to familiar waters: "The scuttlebutt is that Churchill carries more weight than Prime Minister Voss. Is that right?" Lisa fielded that question, informing Pullman that Churchill enjoyed carte blanche authority in America. The chief of staff could probably end the war if a settlement proved feasible. She covered her mouth in chagrin, realizing that she was admitting that Churchill was in Monterey. David Banner insisted that no faux pas had occurred. He wanted all the cards laid on the table and wanted to hear what Pullman was proposing.

"Look, Churchill is a big time advocate of Historical Parallelism, likes to see HP equations dictate public policy. Bakunin is the same kind of egghead. Get those two yo-yos together and a negotiated settlement is in the bag. End a lotta bloodshed and wind up making guys like you and me a ton of dough."

Erevu had to concentrate to keep his chest from swelling with pride when Field Commander Halifax chose the young silverback's battle-lion to secure the Salinas Valley, which would be the first real battle in the post-EMP phase of the war. His pride deflated slightly on the second day of Surus leading the battle-lion into the valley, away from the cooling breezes wafting off the ocean. By three o'clock, the California sun was baking the inland terrain, raising the temperature into the upper-eighties. Surus scarcely noticed the heat. The mammoths, despite all the fur that had been shaven from their bodies, were on the verge of overheating.

An irrigation canal crossed the path of the struggling battle-lion at an opportune moment, right before they were to attack their first objective, the city of Salinas. General Halifax ordered the mammoths to wade into the water and soak their body armor. The hairy pachyderms slopped up out of the ditch and into the afternoon breezes, refreshed and ready to fight.

On the edge of town, the battle-lion assembled into a fighting formation: armored pachyderms up front and en bloc, canine mobile infantry intermingled with the armor's baggage train as a second tier, and the cavalry spread out in two wings protecting either flank.

The Salinas Red Army had scores of old cars and trucks upended and chained together around their barracks, a wall of steel. Communist foot soldiers were aiming rifles and machineguns from these rusting hulks, ready for the onslaught.

Sitting his horse on a hill outside of the town, Jeremiah signaled a human bugler to sound artillery barrage. Erevu raised his own horn, echoing the human bugling, and clicked his heels into the African bull's neck. Surus jumped forward, seeking favorable ground for the fusillade, twenty-nine mammoth cows following his lead, fanning out into an inviting scope of trees. Erevu unlimbered his cannon, aimed at the center of the automobile body barricade, and yanked the lanyard. Broken automobile carcasses shattered under the explosion, sending shrapnel into the defenders and opening a hole in the steel wall. He fired two more times, rapidly reloading after each shot, exhausting the shells he had stacked in the howdah.

Erevu hopped out of the aluminum combat platform, landed on Surus's butt, and barked at the female gorillas in the baggage train, making a hand gesture for three more artillery shells. He could hear the number one and two females up in his howdah working their machineguns. He could also hear the cannons of the other silverbacks in the battle-lion blasting away. Gorillas in the supply wagon tossed up the three shells, grazing Surus's enormous rear end. Erevu shoved one shell in the chamber of his big gun, stacked the other two, and cast an eye at the front line.

The enemy counter-fire was very weak, sporadic bullet thuds impacting the armor of the pachyderms. The slugs weren't armor piercing and were, so far, causing no difficulties. The weak counter-fire could be a trick to get the battle-lion to charge into some sort of trap, but Erevu had a feeling that this wasn't the case. These humans could not be that calm and calculating facing a completely novel threat that none of them had trained for.

From the general's hill a bugle sounded attack. Surus responded to the bugle charge, leading the mammoth cows into battle, Erevu guiding his movements with a long-handled ankus. The gorillas operating the ammo train kept their position, coughing at the dust kicked up by the pachyderms' headlong charge.

The African bull barreled through a gap in the steel barricade and spun toward the enemy soldiers manning the barrier. Erevu reached out and slapped his number one and number two females. When they looked at him from either side of the howdah, he rapidly signaled that they should not fire their machineguns. He didn't bother to explain that conserving ammo was of paramount importance, trusting that they would open fire if Surus needed help. The three gorillas in the howdah leaned back and let the bull elephant do his thing, keeping their guns elevated and out of the way.

Surus's trunk slipped in and out of the twisted and tortured wall of steel, pulling men and women from their hiding places, violently flinging them to the ground, stomping them with his front feet for good measure. Other pachyderms were punching holes in the wooden barracks buildings, where small arms fire was originating. Field Commander Halifax judged that the time was ripe to let slip the dogs of war. Human handlers in the canine mobile infantry unclipped leashes. Bulldogs flowed around the feet of the rampaging pachyderms, sprinting through the holes in wooden walls of the communist barracks, spraying the interiors with hot lead.

The holes in the barracks were large enough for horsemen and horsewomen to ride through. More than a few lost their lunch at the gory scene awaiting them inside, Commonwealth Bulldogs were not trained to take prisoners. The humans in the mobile infantry ordered their dogs out of the military camp and into the town. The Wolfhound cavalry was already encircling Salinas, hunting down enemy soldiers.

From the vantage of his hilltop, Jeremiah could see that the cavalry and infantry were easily seizing control of the objective. His main concern now was the health of the overheating pachyderms. Bugles blatted a command for a mammoth withdrawal and for gorillas to get ready to remove howdahs and combat armor from the behemoths, all except Surus. The African bull would remain suited and on guard while the mammoths roamed down to the cooling waters of the irrigation ditch.

The gorillas formed two columns around the marching pachyderms, heavy machineguns drawn and ready. On Jeremiah's signal, they stripped the mammoths down. Surus climbed up the knoll that overlooked both the city and the watery ditch to stand next to Jeremiah and his horse. Without being told, the bull elephant spun and faced the city. Erevu kept a tight grip on his cannon, searching the far hills for suspicious enemy troop movements. His number one and two females were equally vigilant with their machineguns.

The mammoths plunged into the ditch, squirting their hot bodies with cool water like fire hoses gone amuck, drinking thousands of gallons. They were clearly not suited for a semi-desert environment. Erevu's gorilla troop organized a bucket brigade to bring water to Surus as he stood guard on the hill.

Field Commander Halifax tapped Surus's trunk, giving the elephant a thumbs up gesture. A smooth gray trunk wrapped around Jeremiah, depositing him in the howdah next to Erevu. The general said, "Bring your people and mammoths inside the compound. I want the gorillas to rebuild the steel wall right away. Establish a gate with two of your best silverbacks as guards. Place about fifty female and juvenile guards at likely spots in the rest of the wall. Infantry will be filtering into camp throughout the night. Do you remember today's password?"

Jeremiah caught the flash of anger that passed over Erevu's face and added, "I would ask the same question if you were a human." Erevu grunted a mollified noise and signed, "The password is Victoria." The field commander saluted and slid down Surus's trunk. He got on his horse and left with an entourage of human aides, riding into the town to gather infantry and cavalry.

Erevu thought of something. The silverback let loose an ear-shattering bark before Jeremiah was out of earshot. To show a modicum of difference, the gorilla jumped off his elephant and sprinted out to the field commander's horse. "Do I detail a party to collect shell casings from the battlefield? Do I send a small convoy back to Monterey with the casings?"

"I'd forgotten how important recovering shell casings is under current conditions," Jeremiah admitted. "Human cavalry scouts will be best suited to that job. I'll see to it myself. Thanks for the reminder. Carry on." Erevu beat his chest triumphantly, reacting with gorilla etiquette, highlighting human stupidity. Jeremiah understood the gesture, but let it go without comment.

Once the stockade was secure, Erevu inspected the mammoths. Four willow trees were growing inside the compound. The pachyderms were reducing these trees to kindling, enough food to tide them over for the night. They would need more water, however, before daybreak.

The silverback ended up working through most of the night. That morning, his head felt fuzzy as he sat through a meeting of the human officers. Scouts with Wolfhounds had ranged as far as Hollister the previous day, the next Red Army garrison that had to be seized.

One of the English officers deduced Erevu's condition and offered him a steaming cup of tea, explaining that it was a stimulant, a means to chase the fog out of the gorilla's head. The silverback downed the scalding beverage and was indeed better able to focus on the problems that lay ahead.

A scout was telling the officers that the road to Hollister was undefended, suspiciously undefended. Erevu's battle-lion would have to pass through the mission town of San Juan Bautista to reach Hollister. As far as reconnaissance could tell the mission town appeared, at least on the surface, to be completely abandoned. Yet the old mission church was built like a fortress and occupied vital strategic real estate. Next to the low hill that held the massive adobe church, there was a slightly taller hill that contained a cemetery. Large tombstones and granite mausoleums, tightly packed together, presented ideal ground to encamp a light communist army. The possibility of an ambush or multiple ambushes could not be discounted.

Jeremiah decided that the battle-lion would be divided in half. The field commander would take two companies and tackle the graveyard. Erevu would command the two remaining companies and smash the church. The human officers exchanged apprehensive glances after hearing that a gorilla would be giving them orders. The battle-lion moved out of Salinas and toward San Juan Bautista.

The sun was hanging straight overhead when the four companies split in half. Erevu's mammoths filed past the ominous looking graveyard and surrounded the mission church. A squad of young male gorillas was getting ready to storm the ancient adobe structure when Erevu saw the ground between the pachyderms and the church crawl with life. Reflexively, he slammed his bugle to his lips and blew the note for machinegun fire.

The female gorilla machinegunners in the howdahs aimed at the only thing that was moving, the indistinct surge of crawling things on the ground. Hundreds of spiders died in the fusillade, hundreds more survived and leaped onto the legs of the foremost ring of mammoths, swarming up the giants to find chinks in their armor. Poison fangs plunged into exposed pachyderm flesh. Venom burned into the mammoths' bloodstreams like streams of lava pouring into the ocean. They reared onto their hind legs, bellowing with anger, and came crashing down on the spiders surging around their feet.

Surus and Erevu were in the rear echelon. A minority of spiders was making it all the way to the back of the armor. Every pachyderm had at least one or two arachnid tormentors. The silverback blew a frantic note on his bugle: "Attack dogs! Attack dogs!"

Humans released Bulldogs. Canine mobile infantry rushed into the frenzy of stomping mammoths, jaws snapping. The spiders weren't as swift or as nimble as the canines but they were willing to snap back and their fangs dripped with poison. Roughly one hundred and fifty dogs were poisoned by the time the last spider bit the dust.

It would take more poison to kill a twelve-ton mammoth than the spiders were capable of delivering that day, but the communist arachnids did inject a big enough chemical cocktail to knock most of the pachyderms out of action. Limbs were already swelling on the brobdingnagian war beasts. Bwana signed at his number one and two females, "Order gorillas to take off mammoth war harnesses and body armor." The females tore into the writhing herd, transmitting Erevu's orders. He also blatted the order on his bugle.

The distant cough of sniper rifles reverberated off the hills surrounding the mission. Jeremiah's two companies were moving toward the mission church and communist marksmen were taking advantage of the confusion in the Commonwealth lines to pick off a few inviting targets. Carbines coughed from a much closer distance. Erevu recognized the report of Commonwealth issued Lee-Enfield rifles. General Halifax had sent scouts into the mission to wipe out the enemy spider wranglers. *He should have told me what he was up to*, Erevu fumed.

The four companies reunited around the fountains of Plaza Square, eighty yards away from the fortress-like church. Pachyderms jostled each other to get at the water in the fountains. The elephantine swelling from the spider bites was diminishing. The mammoths were on the mend. The dogs weren't so lucky. Half would eventually die from multiple spider bites.

The human general reacquired overall command of the mission, informing Erevu that the graveyard had been cleared of enemy soldiers. Jeremiah received an all-clear signal from the leader of the scout commando that had attacked the church. He ordered the pachyderms into the adobe building. The exhausted brutes caved in select walls and tramped inside. The gorillas dragged the howdahs with all their guns into the mission church's nave, careful not to disturb the statues of Christian saints and other religious relics lining the walls of the large chamber. The apes were superstitious when it came to human religion, not sure which objects harbored talismanic power.

The four buildings of Mission San Juan Bautista formed an interior courtyard large enough for the thirty mammoths to into fit comfortably. The double layers of timbered, yard thick adobe walls were reassuring. The courtyard gardens were an oasis, lush and profuse, perfect fodder for mammoth and gorilla alike. The apes especially liked the pear cactus, quite edible after the thorns had been stripped off. The Spanish had built their mission churches to serve as military bases, and this one, the largest and best designed, made a perfect garrison for the battle-lion.

Jeremiah grabbed Erevu by the elbow and ordered him to gather all the silverbacks together immediately. The general sketched out a hurried battle plan for taking Hollister. The groundwork for the campaign against the next target was already underway. As the field commander spoke, Commonwealth scouts were attacking the enemy snipers hidden in the San Juan hills that overlooked the mission church. Most likely the scouts would clear the hills in a few hours and Erevu's battle-lion would have a totally secure base in San Juan Bautista. The enemy would expect a Commonwealth consolidation, a breather before the next attack. They would know that their spiders had proven effective against mammoths and taken a deadly toll on the dogs. It would be only logical for Erevu's battle-lion to regroup. For that very reason, now was the perfect time for a lightning raid by silverback commandoes, without mammoths, horses, dogs, or men.

Hollister was ten miles away, due east. The simian commandoes could be there before sunset. Total surprise could be achieved if they stayed off roads and traveled by foot. Halifax guessed that Hollister was home to a great many more spiders than they'd encountered in San Juan Bautista. He ordered the gorillas to do what they could to capture spiders alive. He then gave Erevu a basket of homing pigeons trained to return to specific mammoths, complete with message capsules, parchment, and pens.

In order to move more swiftly, the thirty silverbacks set off cross-country for the next enemy stronghold with their heavy spider silk combat armor strapped to their backs alongside their machineguns and bandoliers. Whatever the merits of his scheme in its totality, Halifax was right about one thing, Erevu realized, the big male gorillas could move through the dense woodland much more swiftly and silently without humans, horses, and all the rest. The only noise coming from the band was the soft cooing of pigeons, which could have been a natural forest noise.

The sun was slipping below the horizon when the apes caught a whiff of assassin spiders from a clearing ahead. They pulled on their protective suits, readjusted their machineguns straps, and crept ahead, worming their way forward on their bellies. Erevu tied his basket of pigeons to a branch and carefully gave the target a once over. The Hollister barricade was made out of crushed auto bodies, as was the one in Salinas, although this wall of steel was more artfully constructed. Branches and mounds of earth helped it blend into the countryside.

A communist dog patrol was drawing near. One of the German Shepherds caught wind of the gorillas and began barking. Erevu gave his own barking commands. Thirty silverbacks sprinted straight at the Red Army compound, killing the dog patrol barehanded en route. They somersaulted over the barrier, absorbing enemy fire and landing on their feet on the other side. Their guns were set for bursts of three slugs per trigger pull to save ammo. The apes cut down Red Army soldiers like threshing machines.

The commando attack was unfolding so rapidly that the enemy reaction was sloth-like in comparison. The apes heard men stirring in barracks in the center of the compound and charged these buildings. Not bothering with doors, the silverbacks ran through thinly planked walls, shattering boards and bursting in on soldiers fumbling to put on boots and grab rifles. To save ammo, the apes destroyed the human combatants with savage bites to the neck. In some cases, biting so hard their opponents were decapitated. Some of the human soldiers tried to surrender. Unfortunately, the battle apes were incapable of niceties like taking prisoners.

Speed. Speed. Speed. Moving swiftly was everything with such a small force. Erevu reconnoitered the fallen camp, moving as quickly as was simianly possible. The instant that he was sure that no living enemy had been left behind, his commandoes vaulted over the barricade and sprinted into the heart of the town. There were signs leading the way to the police station. As a fourth generation signing gorilla, he could read and write English at a high level of proficiency.

Eliminating the blue-coated bobbies in the cop station was tantamount to swatting flies. Not one gun was fired during the police massacre and the humans living in the adjoining neighborhood were unaware of the mayhem. Actually, the town seemed oblivious to the fact that it had been captured. Darkness had barely fallen and the Hollister garrison was secure. Erevu had also learned a tactical lesson. Mammoths should be held in reserve when conquering these smaller towns. Larger towns might be different. Formidable city walls would not be so easy to jump over. The cannons on the backs of the mammoths were designed to act as siege machines.

The spider baskets interspersed among the crushed car bodies of the Hollister stockade were intact and prime for transport. There were even a few crickets running around inside these baskets, a light snack for the spiders. Erevu sent one gorilla commando back to San

Juan Bautista with a collection of baskets lashed together in such a way that they were easy to transport. He was reluctant to send pigeons because the birds navigated poorly in the dark. Speaking of dark, Erevu struck a match to an oil-burning lamp and illuminated the building that he and his silverbacks were now occupying.

There was a map of California on one of the walls. It drew his attention. He looked away from the map to the darkened yard outside. The camp needed to be secured, a perimeter guard should be mounted on the stockade, but his eyes kept darting back to the town of Gilroy on the map, only fifteen miles distant the way the crow flies or twenty miles the way the gorilla marches.

The element of surprise was the reason why they'd managed to capture assassin spiders alive and kicking. Something inside Erevu told him that capturing more spiders might be crucial to the war effort and the only likely spot would be the Gilroy garrison. The good citizens of Hollister were probably getting suspicious right about now. They would discover the bloodbath in the police station of their fair city sometime tonight. A runner or horseman would be sent to Gilroy and alarm bells would be ringing all the way to San Jose. Could the commandoes steal a march on the enemy?

Erevu extracted five message capsules from his pigeon cage and penned five messages, informing General Halifax that his silverbacks would be attacking Gilroy shortly after dawn. He stuffed the messages into the capsules, tied them to the feet of the birds and released them. The birds would have to deal with the darkness as best they could, surely one would get through.

He then had a powwow with his combat apes, informing them of the change in plans and the need to build strength by eating whatever human food was in the barracks. When a quick search revealed mostly tinned meat, the gorillas protested, much more upset about the orders to eat vile human rubbish than the orders to march all night and fight another battle without sleeping.

The commando leader was adamant. The apes needed their strength. Canned meat was high in calories and would sustain them in the combat ahead, regardless of how hideous it might taste. Grudgingly, the silverbacks shoveled horrid and slimy tendrils of meat into their gullets. They would be in an evil mood when the Gilroy garrison was stormed.

Eisenhower put Lisa Banner in charge of training the captured assassin spiders. The trip from Vladivostock and the early stages of the post-EMP war had taken their toil on her aged husband. Not very many octogenarians could hold up in a war zone. This left Lisa as the only person in the Hannibalic Army with the expertise to retrain captured communist war spiders to defend mammoths. Certainly, she had to do more than that. She had to teach other human trainers to be as proficient, or almost as proficient, as she.

From the corner of her eye, Lisa saw Bwana and Erevu draw near to the mammoth she was sitting on. Erevu was carrying one of his inventions, an oddly shaped metal bar, but Lisa couldn't get a good look at it because the ten spiders she'd been training alerted to the approaching simian threat and scurried down the mammoth's tree trunk legs, stopping at the knee and hissing aggressively at the apes, ready to sink poisonous fangs into any unauthorized creature that touched their mammoth. The silverbacks sensed the spiders' enmity and stopped in their tracks, giving the dinner plate-sized arachnids wary glances.

Bwana reared up on his legs and signed at Lisa, "Mrs. Banner, help us to win hearts and minds. We require a translator." Eisenhower had created a program where the Hannibalic Army worked to gain the support of the citizens of California's central valley, with an eye toward plumping the ranks of fighting men and women. At present, the gorillas were especially gung-ho toward winning over fresh recruits because the army was pausing while it gathered for the big assault on San Jose.

Lisa fobbed off her spider training assignment for the day to an assistant and slid down the trunk of the hairy pachyderm. Refusing to comment on the strange metal bar that Erevu had slung around his back, she stood between the two silverbacks, an inquiring eyebrow arch her only hint of impatience.

Bwana asked Lisa to walk with them to a farm in Coyote Valley, an agricultural region outside of Gilroy, near the front line of the walled city of San Jose. An hour's walk brought them to a weed choked field bordering Coyote Creek and within sight of a mammoth patrol prowling the battlefront. Lisa looked hard as the armored mammoth glided by, straining her eyes to catch a glimpse of the spiders that were performing their own patrol on the body of the hairy titan. Try as she might, the green stained arachnids were invisible against the pachyderm's equally green camouflaged spider silk body armor.

Erevu deliberately blocked her view of the mammoth patrol, tossed his head toward something in the weed filled field and signed, "Here is a more interesting object, a bulldozer full of diesel fuel." There was indeed a bulldozer sitting on the edge of the plot of ground, its blade elevated and a plow attached to its rear.

A middle-aged farmer hopped off the 'dozer, stuck his hands in the pockets of his bib overalls, and walked over to the two apes and the woman. When he got closer, Lisa recognized the grower as an old friend, Tommy Atkins, a World War I veteran who had trained war seals for combat in the North Sea alongside Lisa, her husband, and grandfather. The two veterans shook hands under the watchful gaze of the apes and swapped brief life histories. Tommy, or Thomas as he was now called, had migrated from England in the twenties and set up a truck farm in Coyote Valley.

Bwana broke up the reunion and signed at Lisa: "Erevu is ready to start Thomas Atkins's tractor." The younger silverback proudly brandished his strange steel bar as if it were a war-winning weapon and walked upright to the front of the inert tractor. Lisa studied the bizarre tool closely. It had a head like a blunt trident and a thick shaft with two right angle bends: a cross between a fisherman's spear and the starting crank of a 19th century horseless carriage. Erevu had fashioned this device, like his other inventions, by using an oxyacetylene welding kit from the *Titanic*.

Erevu ripped off the bulldozer's grill, too excited to take the time to unscrew the bolts. He was more careful with the engine, methodically unscrewing every other bolt on the cooling fan, which was connected to the drive shaft and was, like all DFA machinery, over engineered and incredibly rugged. The prongs of Erevu's trident fit neatly into the holes left behind by the three bolts that he'd discarded. There were still three screws left intact to hold the cooling fan snugly in place.

Gripping the handle of his starter crank with one hand, Erevu spit on the other hand and placed it on the lower part of the shaft. He gave a mighty turn. The bulldozer spewed white smoke and lurched forward, caterpillar tracks biting into the rich soil. The big 'dozer blade smacked Erevu in the forehead and the plow bucked up out of the earth. Erevu danced forward with the lurching tractor, cranking and growling angrily. The diesel engine backfired. The starter crank flew out of his hands. Sheepishly, he signaled to Lisa that he'd forgotten that the tractor was still in gear. Lisa translated the hand signs to Thomas Atkins, who muttered, "No shit, Sherlock," but not so loud that Erevu could hear.

Thomas stepped up to the balky machine, sat down in the driver's seat, and threw the transmission into neutral. Erevu reinserted the crank and gave it a second spin. The tractor started, docilely rumbling with throaty power. The simian engineer quickly extracted the rapidly spinning hand crank, gave Thomas a thumbs-up gesture and stepped out of the way. The farmer clicked the 'dozer into low gear and calmly began to plow his field.

Erevu loped away from the bulldozer to watch Bwana tear a tree down and place the trunk alongside a shady bank of Coyote Creek, a crude bench and a place to confer with Mrs. Banner. The senior silverback bowed courteously to Lisa and patted a smooth section of the prone tree trunk. Erevu and Bwana squatted on either side of Lisa after she'd taken her seat. She regarded them curiously, wondering what they were up to and how it might involve her. The apes hadn't really needed a translator to communicate with Thomas Atkins. Some sort of sales pitch was in the offing.

Bwana signed, "I think Thomas Atkins will fight for the Commonwealth in the Battle of San Jose. Other farmer recruits will rally around Atkins if we get diesel tractors running and supply them with fuel." Lisa nodded agreeably, but said nothing, unsure where all this was heading. Erevu took up the story line, "Thousands of gallons of diesel fuel are in the *Titanic* and *Britannic*. Captain Murdoch is greedy with this fuel." Lisa stopped the younger silverback and asked, "The two of you want me to twist Murdoch's arm, do you? Put a stop to his greediness?"

"Thank you for offering to speak to Murdoch," Bwana smoothly slid into the assumptive close. "Please talk to Churchill too. He must convince the recruits rallying around Atkins that the Commonwealth supports free market communism, not monopoly capitalism, a sticking point."

That was a curve ball that Lisa hadn't seen coming. Of course Atkins was a communist. All Americans were communists. She watched the dour little English expatriate happily plow his field. It was late in the summer for planting. Most likely he would raise fodder for the army's multitudinous horses and mammoths.

"The farmers love communism," Bwana explained. "We've promised them that Queen Vicky will keep America commie after the war." Erevu chimed in: "Farmers make good coin under communism. The Red Army provides corporate structure, free land, and equipment." Both apes threw their hands down in chagrin, pain scrunching their leathery faces. Bwana lifted his hands and signed bitterly, "We were taught to hate communism in England. Everyone here was getting rich before the pulse. Communism made them rich. Gorillas want to get rich after the war."

With a start, Lisa realized that Marxism was a seductive philosophy to the impressionable apes. More importantly, Bwana was embracing communism. Whatever the dominant silverback believed, the entire gorilla nation believed. The simians practically thought with a single mind. They would follow their national leader anywhere. She put her hand on Bwana's chin, tilting his colossal head down until their eyes met. If a sentient being's eyes were windows to his soul, then Lisa was looking into a soul writhing in torment. Bwana was suffering a conflict between his loyalty to the Queen and the future well-being of his people.

"Have either of you talked to Jim Pullman?" she asked, still looking Bwana straight in the eyes. The apes shook their heads no. "Jim is a very wise man. He says that after the last battle, Churchill and Bakunin should be put into a room and permitted to hash out the outline of a new world order." Lisa dropped her hand from Bwana's chin, innocently asking, "Who could arrange for such a meeting? Who could put the two men together and force the issue, after the last battle?"

Lisa went on to promise that Murdoch would be forced to relinquish his hold on the precious diesel fuel. As for Winston Churchill, the time was not ripe to meet with the chief of staff. Her recommendation was to tell the farmers what they wanted to hear. She also recommended that Bwana spend some time with Jim Pullman. It wouldn't hurt for gorillas to start talking to businesspeople, start thinking about their place in the world economy after the war.

Thomas Atkins and his bulldozer rumbled by, a big grin on his face, happy to be a mechanized farmer again. He called out to the gorillas, "Yo, ape-shapes, weld a wee bit o' metal, add a gun and me tractor'd make a bonny panzer, what?"

Erevu's head snapped upright. His engineer's mind blazed with excitement. He closed his eyes and saw all the wasted deck plating in the *Titanic* and *Britannic*. The ocean liners had already been partially cannibalized to wall in Monterey. Why not cannibalize them down to nothing and build panzers?

Chapter 23

Preparations for the Final Battle

The Battle of San Jose would end the war, one way or the other, just as the Battle of Zuma had ended the second Punic War, or so everyone said. Jeremiah was heartily sick of the constant comparisons between his plan for San Jose and Hannibal's plan for Zuma, two thousand two hundred years ago. The similarities were superficial, but nobody could see that. The last time an army had paved the way for close combat with one hundred war elephants had been on the plain of Zuma in North Africa, the only major battle that Hannibal had lost and the coffin nail for the Carthaginians. Fueled by the pseudo-science of Historical Parallelism, the superstitious Commonwealth soldiers saw Jeremiah's mammoth corps drilling in formation and whispered fearfully of Hannibal's loss.

Everything changed when Erevu parked his panzer in front of field headquarters in Morgan Hill. Not only would the panzers prove efficacious in battle, they would diminish the morale sapping comparisons to the Battle of Zuma. Even the most feeble-minded Commonwealth soldier knew that Hannibal did not have panzers two hundred years before Christ.

Erevu crawled out of his panzer and entered the general's office to give a glowing update not only on the program to build tracked war machines, but also on efforts to dam all the creeks and rivers that flowed into San Jose. The Constructivist aqueduct had long since been diverted to serve the agricultural needs of the central valley. All the other streams had been similarly redirected. Not one drop of water was entering the big city. It seemed likely that the enemy could be drawn out of their concrete canyons to fight in the open terrain that favored the Commonwealth forces, as per Jeremiah's plan.

The general handed Erevu a basket of strawberries and invited the simian engineer to sit in a specially constructed chair reserved for people weighing four hundred pounds or more. The silverback gratefully accepted the food and sat with a groan. He'd been involved in backbreaking labor all day on the dams and irrigation systems.

"I finished reading a book about the Battle of Zuma," Erevu signed in a conversational manner, cramming strawberries down his throat. Jeremiah rolled his eyes in exasperation.

He was ready to vomit if he heard one more piece of superstitious nonsense about Zuma and Hannibal. "I paid special attention to the tactics of the victorious Roman general, Scipio Africanus," Erevu continued. "Your battle plan is much like Scipio's. Both of you try to draw the enemy out of a walled city."

Jeremiah felt a rush of warmth toward the hairy being sitting on the opposite side of his desk. Virtually none of the humans in his command grasped the elementary point that Erevu had just articulated, proof that intelligence was not restricted to humans.

"Sir, I hesitate to offer military suggestions in light of the paucity of my own martial experience." Erevu looked at his feet shyly, barely able to believe his own audacity. Jeremiah reassured the young silverback, urging him to speak up.

"I made the panzers large enough to hold gorillas for a reason." The ape was signing, but his head was still tilted downward. What he wanted to say was difficult. He wished Bwana were here for moral support. Humans never intimidated the dominant silverback. Without looking up, Erevu signed, "If a panzer stalls out, only a gorilla can restart it. Mammoth artillery shells are very heavy. Humans will have a difficult time loading and firing a cannon designed for gorillas. The extra-thick spider silk body armor we gorillas wear is an additional layer of protection to supplement the steel hull." In his nervousness, Erevu's hands began moving so rapidly that only an expert would have been able to keep up. Jeremiah was barley conversant in sign language.

"Erevu, as Jim Pullman might say, you're talking past the sale. Ask a closing question," Jeremiah said firmly. The American entrepreneur had everyone in the California Commonwealth speaking in marketing and sales terms.

"Can my troop run the first harassing raid? Gorillas and war dogs, no humans."

"How many panzers are ready? Is your troop fully trained in raid protocol?"

"Five panzers ready, a complete platoon. Perfect for raid one."

"And your troop?"

"My troop is 100 percent generation four technical, more experience with hand cranked diesel panzers than any primates, human or gorilla. They know raid protocol backward and forward. You've seen us training. We rock."

"Is Hacksaw's pack attached to your troop?"

"Yes, Sir, Hacksaw, best Bulldog in the Army."

"Very well. We strike now, when the iron is hot. The battle is joined tonight with your raid. You'll strike at dusk, open a hole for the dogs and let the bow-wows do their thing. Report back here with your troop in one hour for a briefing. We'll meet at the debarkation point at nineteen hundred hours."

The queasiness festering in Jeremiah's stomach since the initial planning for the first panzer raid dissipated during the briefing that afternoon. When he was a teenager, he'd racked up an excellent record as a middleweight boxer in the Zulu army. He'd always experienced butterflies in his stomach before a big fight. The butterflies always went away once he stepped in the ring. Briefing the gen. four tech gorillas was akin to stepping in the ring.

Erevu's troop filed outside at the meeting's conclusion. Jeremiah grabbed the silverback's elbow before he could step out the door and said, "I'll be using Surus to monitor the raid. No problems there, eh?" The silverbacks were generally not possessive of their pachyderm mounts, all except Erevu. Over the last couple weeks, he'd refused to let anyone else ride the African bull. The silverback stood, bowed at the waist, and responded, "My elephant is your elephant, Field Commander." With a mischievous twinkle in his eyes, Erevu gave his superior a parting shot: "A one-eyed general riding an elephant named Surus? It will be hard to maintain the illusion that you are Scipio, not Hannibal in the final battle. Ha, ha, ha." The gorilla hustled out the door, not giving Jeremiah a chance for a rejoinder.

Jeremiah spent the remainder of the day putting the finishing touches on the second operation in the Battle of San Jose: a push by Kubwa's battle-lion into the mouth of the Santa Clara Valley, a move designed to cut off San Jose from the San Francisco peninsula, its only source of food and water ever since the Commonwealth seized control of California's huge central valley. Kubwa's troop made its way into his office. This operation would have extensive cavalry support, so humans were included in the briefing.

An aide interrupted the conference to tell the field commander that Surus was waiting to carry him to the marshaling yard to monitor Erevu's raid. Kubwa and the human cavalry officers walked outside, irritated that their meeting had been interrupted. They knew their jobs though and were more than ready to cut off the besieged communist capital.

Sitting bareback on the neck of the African elephant, Jeremiah watched the human officers ride off on horses alongside the big mountain silverback on his mammoth. The officers were shouting comments up to Kubwa. He was signing responses back at them. Neither ape nor man seemed cognizant of the bizarre aspect of the interchange. It had all become so natural. The field commander's head swam for an instant. He briefly wondered if the changes brought on by two sentient primates sharing planet Earth would be the most profound consequence of World War II.

Jeremiah kicked his heels into Surus's neck and steered the elephant by grabbing his ears. Surus glided northwest for an hour, toward the marshaling yard, finally sailing over a hill and coming to a halt in a sheltered ravine where the five panzers sat idling.

The African bull struck his trunk outward and aggressively snuffled the command panzer. He could smell Erevu inside the steel box, a cause for anxiety and concern. An embrasure opened on the hull of the panzer. Erevu peered out and could see that Surus was on the verge of trumpeting. The silverback crawled out of the belly hatch and went over to his beloved war elephant, stroking his trunk and purring a soothing song. Surus rocked his head side-to-side, placated. Erevu returned to his command vehicle. Jeremiah and Surus retreated to the safety of a wooded knoll and waited.

The height of the knoll combined with the height of the elephant gave Jeremiah an unobstructed view of the walls of San Jose. As the evening grew darker, insects began dive-bombing the rows of flickering torches jammed into the rammed earth parapets. The guttering flames highlighted a small swarm of bats, swooping out of the night to devour insects. Communist soldiers were patrolling the ramparts, zigzagging along its confusingly jagged path, following the course of stone-faced bastions that projected into a saw-toothed counterscarp lined with sharpened stakes and hosting its own complement of soldiers, who were hunkered down, probably clutching the grips of heavy machineguns nervously. The Red Army's outer bulwark against the encroaching Commonwealth Army was well designed and formidable. According to Pullman, San Jose's static defenses were the brainchild of Russian constructivists.

The rattle of diesel engines bubbled up to the one-eyed general on top the elephant. The panzers lurched into view. Jeremiah's single eye prevented him from judging the distance between the enemy wall and his trundling panzers. Muzzle flashes from within the walled city screwed up his vision even more. Fountains of earth geysered all around the panzers. Communist machineguns sprayed the war machines, bullets sparking off their hulls, leaving substantial dents in their steel plates. One of the tracked vehicles took a shell squarely on the prow. It shuddered to a stop, burning. They rest crept forward at a painfully sluggish pace. Mammoths could have charged the wall three times as fast and were infinitely more maneuverable. And mammoths could have absorbed the small arms fire nearly as well with their spider silk body armor. Civilian bulldozers could not be transformed into real panzers any more than a sow's ear could be made into a silk purse. Then again, the panzers' psychological effect was enormous and they were immune to spider attacks.

The Commonwealth armor opened fire. Chunks of stone and clouds of dust blasted into the night air. A rhythmic series of explosion walked up and down the stone-faced wall. Soldiers' bodies wheeled upward to be swallowed by the darkness. Torches were blown out. Communist reinforcement moved desultorily into the ruptured defensive line. The dug-in Red Army machineguns kept on twinkling as brightly as a constellation of stars. Fifty-caliber slugs continued spronging off the hull plates that Erevu had hammered and welded together. Panzer cannons lowered until they were aiming at the counterscarp and its maniacally chattering Maxim guns. A second series of explosion assaulted the city defenders. Sharpened stakes, communist soldiers, and machineguns were blown away like straw in a whirlwind.

Panzer cannons elevated their gun sights. Erevu's gorilla-strength lungs helped him blat out a powerful series of bugle notes. Inside the tracked metal boxes, gorillas switched explosive shells for incendiary shells. A third and final volley arced beyond the defensive wall, discharging in and around the communist's primitive and jerry-rigged artillery. Napalm scorched the innermost ring of San Jose's static defensive line. Wicked flames licked against the legs of the towers holding the city's awkward muzzle-loaded heavy guns. Bags of powder in nearby storage depots exploded. The artillery towers collapsed into the spreading fires, feeding the flames with a fresh batch of gunpowder.

Klaxons rang shrilly from deep inside the city. Communist firefighters in horse-drawn wagons raced into the growing walls of flame. Constructivist engineers had retooled the city's network of fire hydrants to feed off water towers they'd built in the very heart of San Jose. Firemen were forced to expend the besieged city's most precious resource: water.

Jeremiah hadn't seen the dogs crawl out from under the panzers. He could deduce that the canines were already infiltrating the city though, because the armored tractors were withdrawing and gorillas were outside their vehicles, firing small arms at anything that moved. The field commander kicked his heels into Surus's neck and steered the African bull to the southeast, climbing into the Coyote Hills to get a better view of the bedlam that the war dogs were about to create in San Jose.

Hacksaw and his pack had been trained to shoot firefighters and fire hydrants as their primary and secondary targets, part of that training involved seeking out fires. The dogs funneled through San Jose's sundered defensive wall and zeroed in on the buildings blazing refulgently on the outskirts of the city, clawing over broken hunks of concrete, ignoring the bodies of dead communist soldiers and the frantic maneuvers of live ones. The pack leader woofed softly at his pack mates when a squad of firemen appeared out of the war-torn chaos, hauling fire hoses, sweating and swearing at the raging inferno, oblivious to the silent threat posed by the Bulldogs.

The pack crouched and fidgeted in the penumbra vacillating between the fire's orange glow and the enveloping darkness of a city devoid of electricity. Worming on their bellies, the dogs wiggled into a crescent formation to facilitate both enfilading and direct fire. Their butts remained pressed to the ground while their chests moved up a few inches, angling their machineguns in such a way as to prevent friendly fire.

Hacksaw gripped the wooden firing bar dangling inches in front of his snout and aimed the gun mounted between the shoulder blades of his war harness, drawing a bead on a fireman gripping a gushing hose. Ten Bulldogs jammed their firing bars forward. Ten light machineguns spat slugs into the communist fire fighting team. Men were ruthlessly cut down. Their fire hoses came loose, undulating wildly like snakes on speed, spraying water everywhere. The instant the last fireman hit the ground, ten canine machineguns swiveled toward the two fire hydrants. Armor piercing rounds cut into the mild steel fireplugs, shattering seals. Water plumed extravagantly out onto pavement, draining the irreplaceable contents of the city's water towers.

The dog pack moved on, searching for another group of firefighters. Red Army soldiers were everywhere, swarming toward the slaughter that the Commonwealth canines had caused. The enemy foot soldiers had German Shepherds and Bulldog at their side. Hacksaw gave the dogmen a wide berth, wanting to kill firemen, not soldiers, whether two-legged or four. By using a tortuously circuitous route, the pack leader was able to assemble a second crescent shaped firing squad around a group of laboring firemen. Men were mowed down, fire hydrants ruptured, and most of the war dogs ran out of ammo. Hacksaw heard the clicking of empty chambers and barked three times. The pack took flight behind its leader.

Veteran war dogs or exceptionally gifted rookies always keep a few rounds in reserve at the end of a mission to facilitate their withdrawal. Every dog was devoid of ammunition, except Hacksaw, as they sprinted through the streets and alleys of the battered metropolis.

Relying on speed and cunning, the pack found itself hiding in a pile of rubble near the hole that their gorilla partners had blown in San Jose's defensive wall. A platoon of communist soldiers stood shoulder to shoulder, plugging the hole, facing the city, guns drawn. Five or six German Shepherds were leashed to Red Army handlers, testing the wind with ultra-sensitive nostrils.

The city's fire roared unabated behind Hacksaw's pack, creating its own miniature weather system, sucking the Bulldog's scent away from the communist German Shepherds. The fire-cast shadows boogied in crazy profusion around the pile of rubble. Hacksaw slunk deeper into a shallow pit, willing himself into invisibility. The other Bulldogs did the same. Statue-like, they lay there, barely breathing, concentrating on their pack leader.

The fire grew, a monster devouring the Southside. Cries for help from within the city reached the platoon guarding the hole. Bucket brigades were transferring well water from hand-powered pumps to the inferno. There was a desperate shortage of men at the wellheads and in the lines of the bucket brigades. A short, tough-looking, bald-headed man wearing a different uniform from the others stomped out of the stygian chaos, surrounded by a squad of guards.

The tough-looking man in the fancy uniform ordered the platoon to help the firefighters. The single squad with its high-ranking officer took over the job of guarding the hole in the wall. With lightning speed, Hacksaw and his pack tore straight at the hole in the wall gang.

The pack leader could not know that the tough, bald-headed officer was the highest ranking general in the Red Army, although his canine sense of pack hierarchy did tell him that the man was an enemy leader. Either way, Hacksaw understood that the officer was a succulent target. The Bulldog waited until his pack was upon the communist soldiers and opened fire, sending his last few rounds at General Georgi Konstantinovich Zhukov. Every bullet missed by a fairly wide margin but two. One of the two bullets creased the Russian general's skull and the other knocked off his beret. Zhukov went down, though he was not seriously hurt.

The pack blasted by the squad of guards. Despite the darkness, the elite Red Army soldiers squeezed off a few rounds of their own and hit their intended targets. The guards' high level of marksmanship was off little use. The Red Army's 25 caliber assault rifle did not use armor piercing rounds. The communist bullets impacted against spider silk war harnesses and did no damage to the fleeing canines.

Hacksaw was the last dog through the hole in the wall. His paws stomped on General Zhukov's bloody beret. The pack leader lowered his head, opened his jaws, and scooped up the beret, carrying it back to Commonwealth controlled territory.

The rest of the Bulldog pack barked as they neared Erevu's armored camp at the base of the Coyote Hills. Hacksaw had to remain mute due to the beret clamped between his jaws. The barks were better than any human code because the gorillas' sensitive ears could distinguish between one dog barking and another.

A mammoth patrol relieved the panzer platoon. Jeremiah rode Surus down from the hills to hear the preliminary report from the silverback. After the field commander was satisfied, Erevu's gorillas hand cranked their diesel engines. Headlights flickered on. Hacksaw butted his head against the field commander's knee. Jeremiah stooped and picked the beret from the dog's mouth, giving a low whistle when he saw the row of stars and hammer and sickle emblem of a Red Army general officer. He gave a second, even lower whistle, as he felt the sticky blood on the beret and fingered the bullet hole. The raiding dogs retired from their exertions, crawling into the strumwagens and resting on the vibrating deck plates inside, drifting off to sleep, blissfully enjoying a couple hours of relaxation.

Hacksaw awoke to the sound of Lisa Banner's voice. He darted out the hatch and into her open arms, bowling her over, slopping his dishtowel tongue across her face, nearly knocking over the kerosene lantern she'd left burning on the ground.

The other dogs piled out of the tracked vehicles and raced into their kennels, where kennel boys had food waiting. Hacksaw tore himself away from his beloved mistress, sniffing at the Banners' tent on the way to his dinner. Snores from within indicated that the one-legged man, the most important person in his life, was sleeping inside. A strange odor tugged at his nose. He crawled under the tent flap, snuffled up and down the long, prone body, and whimpered. Hacksaw carefully put his snout next to the man's nose and smelled his breath. The Bulldog whimpered again. He could smell the early stages of lung cancer every time his master exhaled. David Banner was dying and Hacksaw knew it. Regrettably, there was no way to communicate his knowledge with humans. The dog curled up under his master's cot, refusing to eat or leave the tent.

Erevu inched out from under the command panzer, a tight squeeze. Brushing off his fur, he padded over to Lisa, squatted next to the lantern, put his hands where they would be illuminated, and signed, "Hacksaw kicked ass tonight." He swung a long, hairy arm to the northwest. A false dawn glimmered over San Jose. The communists were only very slowly beating back the fire.

Lisa murmured, "The enemy is severely overmatched." Erevu chortled deep in his chest and signed, "The last battle has begun. The gorilla nation will soon end man's war." Lisa was going to reply when Hacksaw's kennel boy intruded on their conversation, complaining that the pack leader had not eaten his dinner.

Lisa picked up her lantern. She and Erevu entered the Banner's tent. Hacksaw looked up at them with soulful eyes and turned away in bitter resignation. Erevu squatted next to the dog and stroked his back tenderly. A flicker of preternatural Bulldog intelligence coursed through the dog's brain. Gorillas were not human. Hacksaw put his nose next to the still snoring proboscis of David Banner and sucked in a great lungful.

Erevu scratched his head. Lisa said nothing. The one-legged man snored unabated. The dog backed away, inviting the ape to smell the man's breath. Erevu put his huge wind scoop nostrils next to the man's nose and drank in his scent. At first, he smelled nothing unusual. A gorilla's sense of smell is not as keen as a Bulldog's. He concentrated on the training of General Kwa, locating his chi and exhaling softly. Focusing on the spiritual center in his belly, not his nose, he inhaled again. This time he smelled it.

Erevu stepped away from the sleeping man. Putting his hands in the light of the lantern, he signed to Lisa, "Your husband is sick in his lungs. The dog thinks it is serious. So do I." Tears flowed down Lisa's cheeks, catching the rays of the lantern like soft jewels. At his age, David Banner could not survive a serious illness and the beasts seemed to be hinting at cancer. He'd always smoked too much. *I've already lost my son. I can't lose David too.* She stifled a sob so as to not awaken her husband. Then Lisa put her hands near the lantern and signed to Erevu, "David is a prophet, enormously wise in mystical matters. You, Bwana, and Kubwa must spend time with him while he is alive. Your civilization must come to grips with matters of theology."

Hacksaw's head moved from Lisa to Erevu as if he could follow the sign language conversation, but of course he couldn't. The Bulldog could smell strong emotions radiating from the primates. He knew from experience that when primates displayed strong emotions during a conversation, then they were likely to talk a long time. The dog sighed, rested his head on his paws, and fell asleep.

Surus wrapped his trunk around the field commander's torso, placing him carefully on the ground. Through the windows, lanterns could be seen burning in Jeremiah's office. *Who has the gall to invade my headquarters?* He thought. The guard at the door was unperturbed, whoever was in there was a military or civilian leader.

A piercing whistle brought privates scurrying out of the darkness to care for the elephant. Jeremiah brushed past the saluting guard and practically kicked in his own door, although he was careful not to drop the Red Army general's beret that he clutched like a priceless diamond. His features softened at the sight of Generals Kwa and Bernhard sitting around his desk. The field commander would not have been so forgiving if it had been Churchill or Eisenhower.

Wolfgang set a flask of brandy on the desk and nodded significantly. The two generals bore the disquieting manner of men bearing bad news. Jeremiah grabbed the brandy, keeping the beret out of sight from the two while tilting the flask upward and taking a long pull, suspecting that he would need serious fortification for whatever was coming next.

"A steamship landed in Monterey," Kwa began. "Tokyo sends fully outfitted infantry, mammoth artillery shells, portable steam engines, mounted Samurai, and news from London. The Halifax supermonopoly is making terrific strides rebuilding the world with 19th century technology."

Jeremiah reached for the brandy a second time at the words "Halifax supermonopoly" and drained it, still keeping the beret out of sight. Wolfgang and Kwa were too distraught to take notice of the little hat. All three men failed to comment on the arrival of "mounted Samurai."

"Your mother owns a controlling interest in every DFA division and subsidiary outside North America." Kwa faltered, looking to Wolfgang for help. The generals' disconcertion told Jeremiah that his mother was sick, which shouldn't be a shock considering her age, but it hit him like a punch in the breadbasket anyway. Jeremiah fell bonelessly into his chair.

Wolfgang took over the narrative. Soga Halifax's health was indeed precarious. She had signed a power of attorney that made Jeremiah chief executive officer of the economic imperium that Halifax Mining had become. She'd published her will, stating the obvious: her only son would inherit everything, and the not so obvious: Jeremiah would personally own the CMG patents that DFA had bought from the Crown, including Einstein's designs for fusion reactors.

An iron wall slammed into place around Jeremiah's heart. His mother's impending death was going to be worse than his father's passing away, even though he'd spent much more time with his dad. He couldn't think about any of that now. Not only did he have to bring World War II to a conclusion, he would be the architect of the post war economic order. He would have to decide if monopoly capitalism should survive or not.

"Is the report from London here?" Jeremiah asked. Kwa handed it over. The field commander unobtrusively set the bloody beret on his desk and scanned the document. The communist insurgency was dead outside of North America. With mankind on the brink of starvation, workers of the world craved the steam engines and copper wire that his mother and the Crown were doling out. Communist police forces were being offered up wholesale to the Commonwealth in exchange for 19th century technology. After winning the Battle of San Jose, Jeremiah could set himself up as the new Henry Ford, if he wanted to.

He pushed up out of his chair wearily, took a single step, and clasped Kwa by the shoulders. "Impi, take the Japanese steamship and its crew, steam to London, bring Queen Victoria here. Make sure the crew knows how to either navigate or blow through the Nicaragua Canal." Jeremiah spun to face Wolfgang. "Uberman, leave at once for Monterey, finishing drilling the army in the Zuma formation. One final battle beckons. Victoria, myself, Churchill, and Vladimir Bakunin will strike a new world order at its conclusion."

Before saluting with machine-like precision, the two generals sprang to ramrod attention. Their about-faces were parade quality. Wolfgang clicked his heel before marching to the door. Jeremiah called his two top generals back as if he'd forgotten something. They settled into their chairs wearing mystified expressions.

Jeremiah handed Kwa the Red Army general officer's beret and explained how Hacksaw had given him the token. Kwa put his finger through the bullet hole in the bill of the cap and said, "It appears that the round must have entered into Zhukov's forehead, considering this hole and the blood on the fabric. Undoubtedly, Zhukov is dead." Kwa handed the beret to Wolfgang, who gave it a thorough examination, agreed with the Zulu general's assessment, and added: "Patton is stuck in the Gobi Desert. Rommel is lost in the Sahara. Zhukov is dead. The Red Army has no visionary generals."

Jeremiah gave his views on the long-range implications of Zhukov's death. Vladimir Bakunin would assume military command of the Red Army. Bakunin was like Churchill, obsessed with Historical Parallelism. The looming battle was being called the Zuma Battle even by those not enthralled by HP equations. Bakunin would try to duplicate the strategy of the Roman general, Scipio, in a predictable fashion. Scipio had won by funneling Hannibal's war elephants down lanes, separating them from the succor of Carthaginian infantry and then destroying the pachyderms piecemeal. Bakunin would try to do the same thing, turning the boulevards of San Jose into mammoth thoroughfares and deathtraps.

The field commander dismissed his generals. This time, they left without exhibiting parade style military precision, leaving Jeremiah alone with his thoughts. He sat there in the flicker of kerosene lanterns, waiting for dawn, trying not to think about his mother. The morning came at last. Jeremiah pushed outside to check on Erevu's raiders and the unceasing mammoth patrols that kept San Jose hemmed in.

Jeremiah found Erevu and his troop repairing the damage that their panzers had accrued during the fighting the night before. The silverback was lifting an armored tractor by the front, tilting it at a forty-five degree angle. Two adult females were drilling holes in a section of undercarriage deck plate using diamond tipped bits clamped into big, old-fashioned, hand-operated wood drills. The females dropped the drills and held a steel plate with matching holes up to the area that they'd just perforated. A gorilla inside the panzer shoved a length of steel bar through one of the fresh holes. With the help of the ape inside the panzer, the females bent this bar and threaded it through the row of holes, like seamstresses sewing a patch on a steel garment.

The fourth generation tech apes had developed an expertise that worked beautifully in the post-EMP world. Their intelligence was impressive. How would they fare after mankind reindustrialized? Strolling through the panzers, watching the females and juveniles laboring away, Jeremiah knew that he would have to find a way for gorillakind and mankind to coexist as equals. He wanted to get a detailed report from Erevu on last night's raid, but didn't want to delay the repair job.

Beyond the hard working gen. four techs, a mammoth patrol was gliding in from the west. A mile to the east, a wagon was rolling purposefully along the six-lane Monterey Highway, its trotting horses matching the pace of several bicyclists heading in the same direction. The horse-drawn wagon was on an intercept course with the mammoth patrol. It had one female gorilla and one woman on board. Jeremiah started walking to a point where the mammoth patrol and the encroaching wagon would intersect. The mammoth got closer and he could see that Bwana was riding Angerbotha. The wagon got closer. Lisa

Banner was holding the reins, sitting next to a female mountain gorilla that he didn't recognize. *This should prove interesting.*

Bwana, Lisa, and Jeremiah met in the center of the highway that hadn't seen motorcars in months. The human bicyclists had peeled off the road and struck a cross-country route, perhaps sensing a potential conflict. Lisa bowed to the field commander and introduced the female gorilla to Bwana as Kubwa's number three wife. The females in Bwana's troop growled with intent at the newcomer. The silverback flew off his mammoth, roaring at his wives for silence. It was obvious that Lisa wanted to incorporate Kubwa's number three into Bwana's troop. This meant that one of Bwana's females would have to leave and accept Kubwa as troop leader, something that Bwana's wives were reluctant to do because Bwana's troop ranked higher than any other within the gorilla nation.

With his females sufficiently cowed, Bwana knuckle-walked stiffly over to where Lisa, Jeremiah, and Kubwa's number three female were standing. Lisa put her hands on the female mountain gorilla's head and addressed Bwana: "This is Msanifu. There are genetic reasons to place her in your troop. Kubwa is willing to trade her for your number one. Even a rookie primatologist can see why your number one should breed with Kubwa." Bwana's face tightened. His fangs glinted in the sun. He reared up onto his legs, roaring and beating his chest fiercely. The silverback dropped to a three-point stance and signed, "She has a name? Why? We give females numbers, not names." Lisa said, "That is about to change. Never mind numbers and names, watch what Msanifu can do."

Bwana was about to insist that trading away his most prized female, his number one, was out of the question when Msanifu rummaged in the back of the wagon and pulled out several gnarled chunks of sheet metal, old car hoods, piquing the silverback's curiosity. Pounding them with her fists, she flattened the mangled car hoods on the roadway and started tearing at them with her fingers, shredding away pieces of metal, forming and tearing the hoods into the shape of wings. Bwana pushed up alongside her, grunted happily, and grabbed one of the metal sheets. He folded it like origami paper until the head and shoulders of an eagle emerged. Msanifu hooted eagerly and grabbed the sculpted metal from the silverback. Working together, the two apes built a sheet metal bird of prey. Their natural abilities were more than complementary. Together they built a sculpture that was more esthetically pleasing than anything they could have done independently. Jeremiah could see that these two gorillas should breed. It could be the start of a new strain of simian artists.

Lisa told Msanifu to put the completed sculpture in the bed of the wagon. It would go on display in a gallery in Monterey. When it sold, the female gorilla would be paid a percentage of the proceeds, the same percentage as a human artist. Lisa hesitated and then asked Bwana if he wanted to lay a financial claim to the artwork. The silverback was about to sign a reply when his number one female unexpectedly launched an attack on Msanifu. Bwana stepped back quickly, ordering everyone present not to interfere. The battle would decide the fate of the two adult females.

At four hundred pounds, Bwana's number one was the largest and strongest female gorilla in the sign language breeding program. But her reflexes for one-on-one combat had been dulled by the countless games of football that she'd played. In a serious fight, a gorilla's primary weapon is his or her jaws. Biting is illegal in football and number one hesitated to use her fangs. Msanifu did not hesitate. After a few chunks of flesh had been taken out of her hide, number one learned her lesson and applied her teeth with a vengeance. The struggle that followed was protracted and bloody. During the course of combat, Msanifu grabbed the eagle sculpture and battered number one on the head. The sculptural battering turned the tide in favor of the newcomer. Msanifu straddled the prone body of her vanquished foe and beat her chest like a male.

Bwana made an incredible leap, landing next to the crowing victor. He drew back a battering ram fist and punched her in the solar plexus. Msanifu went down like a bag of rocks. Every female was watching the silverback's hand signs. "Number one, leave with Mrs. Banner. You belong to Kubwa. Number two, you are the new number one." He looked at the prone female groveling at his feet. "Msanifu, you are number seventeen, the most junior female in the troop." He glared at the senior female that he'd just promoted to the number one slot, ordering her to take Angerbotha and all the gorillas in the troop back to camp.

Lisa helped the defeated four hundred pound female gorilla into the wagon, consoling her with soothing words and, to Bwana's chagrin, giving her a name, Zuri, or beautiful in Swahili. A flick of the reins and Lisa and Zuri were off to Monterey, where Kubwa's troop was stationed. Zuri would enter the new troop at a very low rank, but her size and strength were such a wonderful complement to Kubwa's that no one could deny the soundness of the breeding.

"Bwana, walk with me," Jeremiah said. The man and the silverback meandered through the camp without conversing, observing Bwana's mammoth patrol stand down, watching Erevu's troop put the panzers back into combat ready condition. They followed the progress of a human company working its way through a series of calisthenics. One of the humans was a twenty something woman, wearing tailored fatigues that showed off her stunning figure.

The shapely young soldier had raven black hair, like molten darkness, and fine Hispanic features, probably a local recruit from the central valley. The company jogged by the field commander and the dominant silverback. Somehow, the raven-haired beauty succeeded in dropping a note near Jeremiah's feet without arousing the ire of her fire-breathing Zulu drill instructor. Jeremiah picked up the note after the company was well out of sight and read it to the gorilla: "Commander. Midnight tonight. Under tower nineteen. Bring a condom." The woman had to have written the note well in advance.

Bwana signed, "Sir, will you make the rendezvous?" Jeremiah nodded contritely, conceding that it was not necessarily a good idea for a ranking general to have sex with a private. But he was helpless to resist. Bwana persisted, wanting to know if Jeremiah would take the woman as a permanent wife. The field commander predicted that he would have a short and fiery love affair with the volcanically hot young Latina.

"If she has a mate, he could try and kill you," Bwana asserted. Jeremiah conceded that the possibility was more like a probability. California's Latinos were more prone to that sort of violence than most men.

"It's a stupid system," Bwana remarked. "Human monogamy doesn't work. The gorilla troop system is more stable. I have seventeen wives. With that number, there is no desire to cheat. And weak silverbacks do not acquire troops and do not reproduce."

"That may be good advice. Actually, I wanted to talk to you about a serious subject along those lines. The war is nearly over. I may be in a position to draft much of the new Commonwealth constitution after the Battle of San Jose." Jeremiah stopped talking, attempting to read the expression on Bwana's face. The field commander didn't have enough experience to read the subtleties of gorilla body language and their expressions were almost always deadpan, only flaring up in rare moments of extreme rage, joy, or sadness. Bwana was unreadable.

The two walked into Jeremiah's office. There was gorilla-sized furniture inside, so Bwana made himself comfortable. Jeremiah took a seat next to the silverback and said, "Gorillas will be given the right to vote. It seems that silverbacks control everything in simian society. My question is this: shall female gorillas also be given the franchise?"

Bwana gave his commanding officer a searching look. The silverback was at an advantage. He could read human body language and smell human emotions. Big hairy hands rose to face level and made signs slowly. "Females gorillas must be given the franchise. We saw today that Lisa Banner is giving them names. Female gorillas' liberation will run a course like human women's liberation."

This pronouncement held a note of disingenuousness to Jeremiah. The field commander didn't know the half of it. Bwana was aware that not only would every female vote in the exact same manner as her silverback, every silverback would vote according to the wishes of the dominant silverback: at this point in time, Bwana. The gorilla nation thought with one mind. All the dominant silverback cared about was magnifying his own personal vote after the war.

"To fit gorillas justly into man's global democracy, distinctions in physiology must be taken into account," Bwana signed. "A gorilla is fully mature at eight years old, not eighteen like humans. The simian voting age should be eight. We are shorter lived, pensions and retirement must start sooner."

Jeremiah was beginning to catch on to Bwana's scheme, but didn't know enough primatology to intelligently play devil's advocate. And the silverback was most likely correct despite his obvious self-interest.

"Human history is filled with examples of ethnic minorities suffering at the hands of the majority," Bwana asserted. "Gorillas will be a tiny minority within the overarching human civilization for many centuries, conceivably forever."

"Those are powerful arguments, Bwana, I shall take them under advisement when the moment arrives. Now, tell me what your patrol encountered last night."

"We ran down a communist foraging party outside the city walls. The hunters had killed a deer. The first thing they did was cut the deer's throat to drink its blood. The communists are dying of thirst."

"The hour for the great skirmish draws near."

"Another thing, we've started to find fresh motorcycle tracks out there. Must be the kick-start little diesel bikes you've been talking about."

"The enemy will use these diesel motorcycles as cavalry, if they hold them in any numbers."

Bwana turned the conversation back to sex. He discussed at some length the surgical procedures used to reverse vasectomies in the various Primate Language Centers' laboratories. There had been several instances where human breed wardens had been too quick to order vasectomies on young male gorillas. Later on, when they'd grown to adulthood, these silverbacks had proven to possess vital genes.

Jeremiah asked coldly what this had to do with him. Bwana met the human's frigid stare with equanimity, responding: "The PLC surgeons are skilled in reversing vasectomies in human and gorillas. Our two species share 95 percent of the same DNA.

Our bodies are not that different. Your vasectomy, Field Commander, can be easily reversed. There may come a day when such a procedure will be essential for the political stability of the Commonwealth."

"I don't see how that could ever be true," Jeremiah said, his lips skinning back against his teeth. Bwana leaned forward, the heavily reinforced chair creaking under his bulk. The leader of the gorilla nation signed, "Vicky, excuse me, Queen Victoria should be married and pregnant by now. I've seen the way she looks at attractive human females. She has lesbian tendencies and is struggling with her obligation to produce an heir to the throne. You are the perfect man for the job, Prince Jeremiah Halifax."

"Jesus Christ almighty! Me? Marry the Queen? Preposterous!" Jeremiah exploded. Bwana's boulder-like head swung back and forth in negation. His hands formed symbols in front of Jeremiah's outraged visage. "Vicky is half Japanese, a union that cemented the Chrysanthemum Throne to Buckingham Palace. You are a direct descendant of King Shaka Zulu on one side and English nobility on the other. You are also heir to Halifax Mining, the last monopoly standing, worth trillions. Since she is a lesbian, Vicky will let you have sex outside the marriage. Take it under advisement, Sir."

Bwana straightened to a standing attention, saluted the field commander, received permission to leave, and dropped to all fours with a loud bump to knuckle-walk out the room. The talk about Buckingham Palace turned Jeremiah's thoughts to the industrial report from London. He wished it had spelled out exactly how quickly the mother country was reindustrializing its Commonwealth. He unlocked a desk drawer and pulled out the slim volume. Glancing through it, Jeremiah tried to read between the lines and guess what sort of progress was being made. He shook his head in chagrin. There was no way of knowing. His best guess was that telegraph cables and wood burning steam locomotives were criss-crossing the continents in quantity. Steam powered tractors and the like were probably being unloaded in New York at this very moment. How long would it be before the Commonwealth could produce propeller driven warplanes? There must be old Merlin gunships in museums and private collections here and there. It wouldn't take much to fix the pulse damage and get them flying. Too bad there weren't any functioning refineries to supply them with fuel. Or were there working refineries by now in London?

The report was unambiguous on one point: the structure of monopoly capitalism was being reimposed on the world. That made sense, from a short-term perspective. The new supermonopoly would bring order to a troubled world. It could water, feed, and clothe the masses. And here he was, the owner of the supermonopoly and a potential suitor to the lovely Queen Victoria. It was within his power to create a totalitarian monarchy. His children could not only run the world, they could own it as well, talk about temptations. Jeremiah was not a devout Christian, but he couldn't help thinking about the time that Jesus was taken to the heights of a mountain by Satan and shown all the kingdoms of the world. It could all be his with the stroke of a pen. Then again, there was the pesky little matter of winning World War II.

Chapter 24

The Last Major Battle

The three battle-lions formed up around the African bull on an abandoned twelve-lane stretch of asphalt that ran along the northern border of San Jose. Winter had arrived and a good thing too. The cloudy sky and driving rain were keeping the mammoths from overheating despite layers of combat armor. Surus wouldn't have minded warmer weather, but he appreciated the need of his multitudinous mates to stay cool. Many of them carried his babies, and nothing could cause a mammoth miscarriage like sweltering heat.

The wind was to his back, which put the bull in a good position to catch a whiff from the ninety-nine mammoth cows lined up in the Zuma formation to his rear. His trunk tested the wind on his right side and his left. The cows were chomping at the bit, eager for battle. Some of them didn't know what they were in for. He had more experience attacking San Jose, leading raids with Erevu, than any other pachyderm. Months of combat experience had taught him one hard fact: the greater the number of mammoths in a given attack, the deeper the gorillas would drive into the city. Deep incursions meant greater casualties and greater bloodshed. There had never been a raid with one hundred pachyderms before. This was to be the mother of all battles.

Surus gently probed the ten assassin spiders clinging to his body armor. The rain wasn't doing them any good. But then the enemy spiders would face the same conditions. The wind shifted and the bull elephant could smell an overpowering odor flowing out of the city. Spiders. The enemy had amassed a greater concentration of arachnids than in any other clash. His trunk returned to the spiders covering his body, stroking them reassuringly.

From the ranks of humans in the rear, a bugle blatted. Erevu raised his gorilla-sized bugle and repeated the command to attack. The silverback kicked forcefully with his heels, spurring the elephant's neck and shoulders, reinforcing the musical command because it was difficult for the elephant to hear through the wads of cotton in his ear canals. Surus swung into battle. The muffled clanking of shells told him that the cannon was about to be discharged. He knew that the muzzle blast would be loud even through the cotton. The big gun fired, rocking back his howdah hard enough to make the bull stumble. He regained his footing and continued the charge.

Cannons from the mammoths also erupted. This part of San Jose's defensive wall had been attacked many times. It had been inadequately repaired and flew apart under the barrage like a house of cards. Surus could feel the big gun being elevated. He braced himself better for the next volley and didn't stumble. Shells were sailing deep into the city, but no fires were erupting, unusual but not unwelcome. The gorillas weren't using incendiary ammunition. They were pounding enemy positions with explosives, knocking down buildings, not burning them. As far as Surus was concerned, explosive shells were better than the incendiary kind. The bull didn't like trampling through a burning city.

The holes in the wall were easy to traverse. The elephant bull led his mighty herd of mammoth cows through gaps in the ramparts. The city's defenders had suffered terrible attrition through the late summer and fall, they didn't have enough soldiers to man the trenches or even fully cover the parapets. What they did have plenty of were spiders. The rubble-strewn streets inside the defensive wall were brown with a carpet of crawling arachnids. There was something unusual about the shape of these spiders, but the pachyderms and apes didn't waste time pondering the oddity. Machineguns were unlimbered and the female gorillas in the howdahs practically melted down their barrels trying to wipe out the crawlers.

The arachnid wave crashed into the pachyderms, too close for the howdah-mounted machineguns to be of any further value. Machineguns grew silent. Darting around the huge thudding feet, swarms of Bulldogs ripped into the arachnids, pushing them south, back into the city. The Commonwealth dogs had a new type of leather combat armor, covering every part of their body except their snout. And they weren't carrying machineguns. Jeremiah had guessed that the enemy would use spiders in massive numbers and consequently the dogs were specially trained and equipped to deal with this eight-legged threat.

The canine/arachnid battle raged thirty yards beyond the mammoth line. And then it relentlessly pushed north as the dogs were forced back into the line. There was nothing the elephant or the mammoths could do to help the dogs. Later, when enemy spiders turned his body into a battleground, there would be no way for Surus to help his pack of friendly spiders. All the pachyderms could do was stand still and let the Lilliputians fight.

Well, maybe more than that. Erevu blew the bugle call for "resume artillery barrage." Surus felt the canon lowering until it almost smacked his head. He tucked his chin as deeply as possible and braced for the big gun to go off. It did and the explosion was so close to his ears that they were soon ringing like bells despite the cotton wadding. Erevu blasted his bugle again, calling for the howdah-mounted machineguns to recommence firing.

With the dog verse spider battle swirling around the feet of the pachyderms, the gorillas concentrated on the source of the spider incursion, the Red Army soldiers hiding in buildings close to the Commonwealth line.

The communist spiders packed a double dose of poison. They'd been bred for generations to produce potent venom from their fangs. Additionally, their hairy bodies had been soaked in poison prior to the battle. Thousands of gallons of toxin had been painstakingly milked and collected in jars in the weeks before the last act in the drama that was World War II.

Every time Hacksaw bit a spider, a small quantity of poison traveled through the permeable membranes inside his mouth. In the opening phase of the battle, this didn't affect the Bulldogs. A greater concern was that they couldn't work fast enough to keep the spiders off their bodies. While a dog killed one arachnid, two would jump on his back. Because of their long flexible necks, Bulldogs could reach nearly any part of their body with their mouths. A dog could, therefore, tear spiders off his back and smash them against the ground, but a fresh batch took their place immediately.

A spider crawled the length of Hacksaw's head and injected venom into his exposed lips and nose. He somersaulted and crushed the spider with his body. Venom was now flowing into his bloodstream from his tongue and through the injection in his nose.

Part of Lisa Banner's canine spider-fighting regimen included small daily injections of venom, creating a tolerance but not an outright immunity to the poison. It would take a lot to slow Hacksaw down, let alone kill him. He kept fighting. Every Bulldog in the Hannibalic Army fought with everything he or she had. Piles of dead spiders multiplied across the broken cityscape. The dogs were driven back nonetheless.

Hacksaw was knocked against a mammoth's legs by the whipsawing action of one of his fellow Bulldogs. Several spiders took advantage of his misfortune by jumping on his back and racing the length of his spine. Additional doses of venom were injected into the exposed areas around his face. He fought on, bashing and smashing spiders until the asphalt was slippery with arachnid guts.

His leather combat armor was getting tight around the joints of his legs. Hacksaw was beginning to swell with the effects of the poison. He slipped on a batch of spider guts, landing on a couple of eight-legged brutes, who fanged his face again. Now his eyes were swelling. He couldn't see but kept attacking spiders by relying on other senses.

From the south, enemy paws beat the ground. Machineguns in howdahs blazed away but the fighting quickly grew too tight for gunfire. Communist Bulldogs were entering the fray. An iron jaw full of ivory fangs crunched down on Hacksaw's shoulder, ripping through light leather armor designed to ward off spider bites. Hacksaw whirled on his opponent, biting down on a thick leather war harness studded with steel spikes. The roof of his mouth was punctured. He couldn't get a grip. The enemy Bulldog worked his bite, shredding muscle and breaking Hacksaw's shoulder blade.

The too-tight spider-proof armor was cut into strips, freeing Hacksaw's swollen body of the unnatural constraint. His shoulder was still being mangled, yet he got under his adversary and tore into the enemy dog's belly, the only part of the communist Bulldog's body that wasn't covered in spikes.

A communist spider accidentally shot venom into the eyes of Hacksaw's antagonist, fratricidal fire that would give Hacksaw a fighting chance. The communist dog's shoulder grip came loose. Hacksaw bore in on three legs, raving, disemboweling, and finally killing. He got tripped up in the intestines of the slaughtered Bulldog. He tried to open his swollen eyes. Hundreds of thousands of spiders were indiscriminately attacking any one of the thousands of war dogs brawling around the feet of the mammoths. The pachyderms stood there unperturbed, obeying their training, refusing to dip their trunks into the spider-infested melee and pick off spiked Bulldogs. A few of the gorillas on their backs were not

303

able to remain so aloof. Most of the apes kept firing cannons and machineguns into the marshaling area of the arachnid force. But some of them grew emotional, gnashing their teeth, engorging with bloodlust, desirous of direct combat.

Bugles were blatting incessantly for the gorillas to stay put and keep firing their guns. Simians were unable to develop the resistance to spider poison that the Bulldogs had. The human leadership did not want to risk the apes, their most important resource. A handful of enraged silverbacks disregarded the bugle commands and dove into the skirmish, swinging battle-axes violently, chopping spiked Bulldog in half, and drenching the highway in blood.

The battle was out of human control, but the three gorilla battle-lion leaders were quick to adjust to the mini-mutiny. Bwana, Kubwa, and Erevu didn't try to call the few hot headed silverbacks on the ground back up into their howdahs; rather, they leaped from mammoth to mammoth and seized control of leaderless troops, putting their number one females in charge of their own troops.

Hacksaw battled on, the presence of five or six silverbacks on the ground meant that he and the other Commonwealth dogs could concentrate on spiders. Sans body armor, a multitude of spiders were able to attach themselves to his body. The Bulldog was ready for this tactic. He rolled on them vigorously, crushing them with a sickly squish. The dozens of spider bites and the poison he'd absorbed through his mouth were too much for even his Bulldog immune system to withstand. Hacksaw's tongue swelled, his throat sealed shut, his lungs starved for oxygen. His limbs stopped moving, paralyzed. Cranking his mouth open as far as it could go, a modicum of air leaked into his laboring lungs.

The silverbacks on the ground were undergoing the same reaction to spider venom that Hacksaw had gone through, but at an accelerated pace. Soft tissue in their bodies became inflamed. Their limbs were swelling, as were their tongues. Like the stricken Bulldogs all around them, the apes soldiered on, hacking at enemy canines, pounding spiders with the flat side of their axes, until they could fight no longer.

Through the swollen slits that his eyes had become, Hacksaw could see that a new type of Commonwealth soldier had taken the battlefield. Wearing bizarre horned helmets and intricately embroidered leather, bamboo, and spider silk armor, Samurais swung swords in silvery slashing arcs, moving with preternatural speed. The Bulldog's last reservoir of strength was tapped when he growled encouragement as the Emperor Jimmu's warrior caste hacked and hewed through an ocean of arachnids with such skill and grace that not one hair on a mammoth's belly was disturbed, not one errant blow fell against the Bulldogs and gorillas battling alongside the whirling demons from Japan.

The Red Army released the last arachnid reserves. A final tidal wave of eight-legged terror crashed into the Samurai. Their swords moved like chained lightning, nearly invisible blurs of motion. Through sheer force of will, Hacksaw stayed alive long enough to see the men wearing the horned helmets battle to the front line. He raised his head, panting with exertion. The swoosh of a sword whistled by his nose. The Bulldog's massive head plopped down and he died.

Communist spiders swarmed up Surus's legs until they met Commonwealth spiders at his knees. The attacking arachnids fought uphill. The defending spiders had an easy time knocking the exhausted and sopping wet attackers back to earth.

Gorilla-sized bugles blatted from the lips of the three battle-lion leaders. Surus surged forward, moving back to offense. The piston-like rise and fall of his feet worked in concert with the exertions of his friendly spider pack, trampling the enemy spiders as soon as they hit ground. Like army ants, or any swarm of insectile creatures, the attacking arachnids could only be effective in overwhelming numbers. Below a certain numerical threshold, they became a nuisance that pre-planned countermeasures could easily accommodate.

Bwana, Kubwa, and Erevu returned to their own mammoths, promoting senior females to lead the troops that had lost silverbacks to enemy spiders. These senior females seized the grips on cannons with hands as steady and sure as any silverback.

The mammoth corps bore down on San Jose. Cannons blasted buildings in its path, reducing them to chunks of building debris. A steady stream of shells flowed up from the rear. With the sea bridge to Japan, an industrial pipeline stretched all the way to Asia. Not that Surus could understand or appreciate complexities that required human or gorilla level intelligence.

The African bull did understand the final bugle call of the day. The gorillas running the munitions train were ordered to build a defensive wall from the tremendous masses of rubble that the mammoth corps had created up till now.

Females and juvenile males expertly steered wagonloads of jagged concrete blocks past the once again stationary pachyderms. Red Army snipers from within the city tried to pick off horses as the daylight waned. Sharp-eyed senior females in the howdahs blazed away at distant muzzle flashes. Every few seconds, one of the big guns would boom, taking done another piece of building. The communist snipers were not altogether ineffective; periodically the work had to stop to remove dead horses from their traces.

Surus was mildly perturbed to see steam tractors driven by Japanese soldiers, working alongside the gorillas and their horse-drawn wagons. The Hannibalic Army was not accustomed to this level of mechanization. The supply line leading back to Japan was changing the nature of the army, and not for the better in the bull elephant's opinion.

Darkness fell, the wall was mostly complete, the gorillas had the big blocks in place at least. They stopped building and returned to their mammoths to collect guardian spiders and give them to human spider wranglers. Next, the apes stripped howdahs and silk combat armor off the pachyderms. Cotton wads were pulled from pachyderm ear canals. Food, for primates and animals, was brought up from the rear. The dead were buried. Japanese soldiers trotted out portable generators and hooked them to the power take-offs of their new-fangled steam tractors. Artificial lights pierced the nighttime shadows. Surus grumbled his displeasure. The mammoth cows all around him waved their trunks in his direction. The lights didn't disturb the cows initially, but now that their bull was expressing displeasure, they were concerned.

Erevu leaped onto the elephant's back, a long handled scrub brush in one hand and a bucket of water in the other. Erevu's troop had formed a bucket brigade and the gorillas were sluicing the bull with hundreds of gallons of fresh water. A Japanese tractor chugged up to the luxuriating bull and dropped off a wagon with one thousand pounds of fodder and a few tubs of drinking water. His trunk went to work squirting water and shoveling chow into his mouth. Surus trumpeted his pleasure. The cows rumbled in agreement.

Drying in the night breeze, the bull idly watched platoons of Japanese soldiers move their lights up to the blocked out wall. The human newcomers industriously plugged the holes between large serrated concrete boulders with smaller rocks, bricks and chunks of concrete. Some of them swabbed out the aluminum barrels of the howdah-mounted artillery and performed other tasks normally reserved for gorillas. Surus fell asleep in the spot where he'd fired his last shell.

Morning came and the Japanese were still at work, diesel bulldozers rammed earth and loose debris into the wall, buttressing it and forming a ramp for human soldiers to scale. Every day, more Japanese soldiers joined the Army. They assumed posts on the parapet and immediately began a sniping duel with communist sharpshooters, who were apparently only just arriving on the battlefield. Simply watching the ultra-industrious Asian fighters made Surus tired.

His sense of disquiet increased when Erevu and the troop fastened a heavily padded howdah blanket around his mid-section, rather than the expected combat armor. Fruits, vegetables, and water appeared at the same time, temporarily distracting the bull.

He crunched down the last pineapple. Before Surus could even well up a good belch, Erevu and the two senior females strapped on his howdah. It did not have machineguns attached, a bad sign. The rest of the troop was lining up behind him with horse-drawn wagons brimming with artillery shells. He strained his neck peering around at the wagons to his rear. They were overflowing with shells. A couple of shells actually fell off one wagon to roll on the ground. It was that full, overloaded in fact. Juvenile apes scrambled to return the wayward shells to the heaping mountain of ammunition building up behind the African bull.

"Bah-ah-ah!" Surus pointed his trunk skyward and blasted a protest at the workload that all the evidence promised was coming. "Brg-gr-gr!" he grumbled. Erevu raked his fangs gently but firmly across the crown of the bull's head, a warning. The silverback applied heels to the elephant's neck, steering the behemoth into place on the newly built wall. The mammoth cows stomped up to their own positions, more willingly than their bull but with an eye toward his disposition and demeanor. The silverback reached around Surus's head and jammed wads of cotton into his ear holes. The bull knew exactly what the day would bring. He was too mad to protest out loud, standing rooted in his spot, glowering.

Erevu shoved a shell into the cannon and barked at a human spotter on the wall. The man waved semaphore flags at the silverback and ducked. The cannon was aimed, low, very low, inches from the top of the bull's head. Surus braced for the recoil. The canon blasted. The cotton in his ears barely kept deafness away. Another shell was slammed in the breech. The silverback looked at his human spotter for guidance. Surus looked at the mammoth cows. They were resigned to their fate, standing in a wide-legged stance, absorbing the jarring and jolting of the big guns with a resigned air.

Around noon, a lunch appeared and the barrel was elevated. Surus stretched the knots out of his neck and back. He raised each leg one at a time and stretched it out as far as he could. The howdah was beginning to feel heavy, but the gorillas did not remove it for the lunch break. Shoveling apples down his throat, he tried to get a glimpse of the devastation that the shelling had wrought. The wall was too high and he couldn't see a thing. All too soon, the lunch break was over and the shelling resumed.

The storm clouds of yesterday had failed to return. The sun moved across the sky and the temperature rose, combining heat with mugginess. Female gorillas in the howdahs gathered the guardian spiders that were still patrolling the pachyderms' bodies into baskets and handed them to human attendants. Besides ferrying shells up to their silverbacks, the females and juveniles could now run buckets of water up from the rear to pour on the pachyderms as well as on the overheating cannon barrels. Surus knew how the cows suffered in warm weather and grew even moodier and more disconsolate.

His muscles were aching and his head throbbed painfully by the time that the last shell was fired. The howdah seemed as heavy as a mountain. When the gorillas pulled it off, Surus had the strange sensation of flying, almost like an invisible force was dragging him upward. He staggered against the bizarre feeling and didn't recover his land legs until the late afternoon bath and meal were complete.

Despite his travails, the bull knew that the cows must have suffered more than he. Nighttime electrical lights were flickering on, the Japanese war machine was gearing up to build a second wall, pushing even deeper into the city, when Surus tapped Erevu on the head. The silverback had been hand cranking a diesel bulldozer, but dropped the crank and turned his full attention to the elephant.

Surus pointed his trunk to a line of droopy mammoth cows. He banged Erevu's head harder than before and raised his trunk to tap his own neck. The silverback understood and barked once, signifying agreement. Erevu jumped up onto the bull and rode over to the mammoth cows.

Gliding slowly by the line of cows, Surus raised his trunk and briefly entwined it with each of his herd mates. The cows waggled their enormous heads at his passing, spirits buoyed. Surus couldn't formulate his thoughts into words, but he suspected that humans and gorillas didn't appreciate that pachyderms were living creatures, not cogs in an industrial machine.

Erevu rode the bull to a darkened section of the old wall where Japanese electrical lights would not silhouette the big beast and give communist marksmen a target. Surus climbed the ramp leading to the top of the wall and paused, looking out at the ant-like figures on the other side that would soon be building a second wall. Bulldozer/panzers had opened a hole in yesterday's wall and flooded the wasteland beyond with electrical lights, giving the ruins a ghostly moon-like quality. Surus looked at the part of the city that his shells had helped pulverize. Teams of Japanese infantry were spreading out into the rubble, hunting down communist snipers, protecting the human and simian construction crews that were starting to work on the next wall.

Erevu had a large bag of oranges under one arm. He slipped juicy spheres to the bull, one at a time. Munching oranges, Surus watched armored bulldozers rough out the contours of the next wall. Intermittent sparks popped off plate steel hulls. Minutes passed and firefights ignited within the ruins. Communist snipers could barely move before the Japanese Army pounced on them.

From the taller buildings in the devastated region of the shattered city, flaming missiles arced into the panzers cum bulldozers. The missiles were Stokes incinerators, bundled glass bottles filed with gasoline and topped with an oily rag for a wick, shot from catapults located on the roofs of close-up skyscrapers. Scores of bulldozers went up in flames.

The Japanese Army had a tougher time with this threat. Communist gunmen were guarding the midlevel floors of the catapult buildings, spoiling the Commonwealth drive to reach the rooftops. Imperial combat engineers could see that the buildings were wobbly from the mammoth artillery barrage. Satchels of dynamite were placed on support beams and detonated. The buildings came toppling down.

Surus could taste the dust blowing in from the collapsing skyscrapers. He could also smell a nasty bouquet from the burning bulldozers in the construction area. Terrified humans inside the steel boxes were losing control of their bowels as they roasted alive. The construction zone became a war zone. Communist suicide troops emerged from hiding and swarmed over the wall.

The Hannibalic Army was better prepared for this tactic than the Red Army had expected. Electric lights blinked off and hordes of Bulldogs were unleashed. In the darkness, the night-seeing Bulldogs had overwhelming superiority over the human communist soldiers. The canine war harnesses had their light machineguns removed. Ironically, this made the dogs even more effective. They emitted no muzzle flashes and virtually no noise, ripping into human enemies with their jaws. Through smell and sound, Surus could follow the course of battle, still munching snacks like a sports fan at a baiting contest.

Electric lamps shone once again in the blood stained arena, highlighting scores of enemy bodies. The dogs were not visible under the glare of the lights, apparently having pushed into the ruins to finish the job that the Japanese infantry had started.

Troops led by silverbacks knuckle-walked into the quiescent battlefield, weaving paths between the corpses and the burned out bulldozers. The gorillas wore silk combat armor and were surrounded by gun toting humans. The simians were not carrying weapons. Reaching the roughhewn wall that the now burned out bulldozers had fashioned, the apes started stacking concrete blocks. Most of the blocks had strands of rebar sticking out like so much spaghetti. The silverbacks knotted the steel bars together, building a substantial wall with real strength. Sporadic gunfire continued to disrupt the builders, although the communists failed to mount a serious offensive, evidently satisfied to merely harass the Commonwealth.

The aches and pains in Surus's body moderated as he watched his army's territory expand. Elephants and mammoths possess a moderate ability to understand the spoken word, slightly less than a good war dog's. Where pachyderm intellectual aptitude really shines is the discernment of spatial relationships. Surus could see that the amount of the city that had been conquered compared to the amount that remained unconquered meant the Hannibalic Army was making good progress. The pachyderm aches and pains were worth it.

An explosion lit the ruins bordering the construction zone. Japanese combat engineers had collapsed another building. The darkness was peppered with bright flashes as small arms fire erupted from a tangle of useless power cables interspersed among the wreckage of buildings. Martial cat and mouse games continued in the urban wilderness.

Calmly swallowing fruit from Erevu's bottomless bag, Surus looked away from the combat zone at an interesting sight on the safe side of the original wall. Jeremiah Halifax was walking their way, his path lit by a guttering torch. The feeble light revealed that Bwana was knuckle-walking alongside the field commander.

The three primates gathered around Surus's front feet and fell into conversation. Even if he could understand their monkey talk, Surus would not have been interested. His present concerns revolved around reassuring his cows. Mammoths and elephants have the ability to make ultra-low frequency melodies that travel underground for miles. The pads of their feet act like drums, permitting them to hear the subterranean songs.

Surus lowered his trunk and hit a series of infrasonic notes, a comforting song to tell the cows that everything was fine. He could see that the conquered territory was substantial. The task before them was not endless. Other than the mammoths, no creature could hear his message. Some distance away, Angerbotha waited for the last note to fade away and added a soothing refrain to the bull elephant's harmony. The younger cows joined the concert, adding their own tones and shadings, expressing confidence in the primate leadership of their extended extra-species herd.

While the pachyderms talked, so did Jeremiah, Erevu, and Bwana. The field commander said, "We lost twenty-four bulldozers tonight. I count two hundred dead war dogs. Six gorillas, gone. Fifty humans. The gorilla casualties should not have happened. Bwana, read your people the riot act. They disobeyed orders by jumping off their mammoths."

The dominant silverback made several hand signs. Jeremiah was holding his torch in such a way that the hand signs were not visible. He held up the light and asked the gorilla to repeat himself. "Still think Zhukov is dead? Didn't seem like an amateur directing the commies tonight," Bwana observed. Jeremiah shook his head guardedly. Without a doubt, the same suspicion had crossed the field commander's mind. Rather than tackle a subject that could not be answered: Jeremiah asked Bwana: "Is the gorilla nation ready to rock and roll tomorrow?" The boss ape nodded and signed, "Rock and roll, rhythm and blues, Sir."

Erevu held his hands over the torch and signed, "Boss, what will happen if Zhukov *is* still alive?" Jeremiah stuck the faltering torch in damp soil, gestured northward, and said, "I expect the Red Army will wage a guerilla war, based in the northwest coast, under the direction of Zhukov." Both silverbacks lurched up onto their back legs angrily, lips peeling back, fangs shining wetly in the torchlight. Hastily, Jeremiah amended, "Whoa, boys, simmer down. That's G-U-E-R-I-L-L-A. Not G-O-R-I-L-L-A."

The apes plopped back down on their knuckles, exchanging self-conscious glances. Jeremiah picked up his torch, jerked his head at Bwana, and walked down toward the marshalling yard. Erevu waved at his departing friends and looked to Surus with a curious eye. The elephant was concentrating intently on something. It was probable that the mammoths were similarly transfixed. Periodically, the elephant and mammoths went into trances simultaneously and nobody could tell what they were doing. Erevu thought that they were communicating and this was the reason why pachyderms weren't more conversant in English, they had a non-verbal language of their own that primates couldn't understand.

Halfway to the marshaling yard, Bwana skipped a few steps ahead of the field commander and lurched back upright, walking like a man so that he could sign. "Blasting San Jose apart, brick by brick, will send a powerful message to the pinkos if there is a guerilla war, eh, hairless boss ape?"

"Hairless boss ape? Where do you people get these bizarre nicknames?"

Still walking like a man, Bwana's monstrous shoulders heaved up and down in a shrug. In a more serious vein, he signed, "I have a gift for political thinking. The way you evade my question is telling." Jeremiah laughed, slapped the gorilla on the small of his back and said nothing.

Keeping his hands in the torchlight, Bwana signed, "Something is fishy with the Samurai troop disposition. Why are five thousand Japanese horsemen camped out in Milpitas and not patrolling?"

"The escape routes out of San Jose and the passes in the East Bay Hills are patrolled by a Commonwealth cavalry company. Samurai sit there in reserve."

"That's what I'm saying, boss ape, why is one measly company trying to cover all that ground when a whole brigade is available?"

Jeremiah jammed his torch in the ground and sat down in the muddy soil, signaling Bwana to squat down as well. The field commander proceeded to tell the dominant silverback exactly what he expected to happen in the lightly guarded frontier region between San Jose and the East Bay Hills in the next few weeks.

As a young soldier in World War I, Thomas Atkins had never ridden a horse. By the end of that war, horses had become obsolete. It was the height of irony that mankind's most advanced technological achievement, the global electromagnetic pulse, had made the horse indispensable in combat. Thankfully, between the two world wars, Thomas had spent many years farming and knew a thing or two about horses. Although there *was* a world of difference, he admitted, between the old plow nags back on the farm and the horse between his legs.

Jinsoku was an Anglo-Arab, half thoroughbred and half Arabian, bred by the Japanese Emperor for marathon races, as much like a plow horse as a Ferrari was like a tractor. The Wolfhounds were like Ferraris too. The cavalry horses and cavalry dogs provided by the Commonwealth could move like the wind. The sixty-four pound question was: how would they fare against motorcycles? The brass had told the cavalry grunts that the Red Army's next move would be an attack on the supply line running from San Jose to Monterey with dirt bikes.

Then why in bleeding 'ell am I stuck here in the north? Thomas wondered. While the bulk of the Commonwealth cavalry was roving up and down the Monterey Highway, one company was covering the mountainous passes, ranchland, and farmland above San Jose, possible escape routes for the communist leadership when their capital city entered the final stages of disintegration. That single northern cavalry company was stretched thin and broken up into individual dog squads that were plugged into the various mountain passes blocking the routes north and east of San Jose. It sounded tenuous, but if anything happened, there were massive reinforcements available. A brigade of mounted Samurai was camped out in lower Milpitas. Still, Thomas was supposed to guard an entire pass, the treacherous Calaveras Pass, with one horse and five Wolfhounds, a tall order.

Thomas wasn't altogether disappointed in the assignment. Jeremiah Halifax had stoutly asserted that a breakout by the Red Army leadership was possible, if not likely. Actions speak louder than words. The field commander had sent road crews galloping up Highway Five the instant he'd gotten wind of communist motorcycles, months ago. These crews had already torn up roads in northern California and southern Oregon, dynamiting bridges and blowing up sections of roadbed. Call them dirt bikes or call them trail bikes, use whatever name you want, a motorcycle without a road is at a disadvantage to a horse, or so Thomas hoped.

Manmade thunder rolled up the hillock that he, the dogs, and the racehorse were occupying. The mammoth corps was getting an early start on the demolition work. San Jose's skyscrapers had been gleaming peacefully in the morning sun, sharp and clear since there was no longer any smog from internal combustion engines. The artillery thunder was accompanied by a wash of dust boiling up over the skyline, obscuring the proud spires, temporarily hiding the destruction of the poignant symbols of free market communism, the most efficient economic system in history, a system that the Commonwealth was promising to preserve, if it won the war, if it kept its word.

Thomas clucked Jinsoku into a trot. The five Wolfhounds swung into line behind the chestnut gelding. Thomas stood in his stirrups, whistled three sharp blasts, and swung an arm in a wide circle. Time to kick off the morning patrol. He sat too hard, bouncing into the saddle, disturbing the basket of pigeons tied to the pommel. The birds chattered angrily.

The Wolfhounds picked up the pace, loping away from each other and the horse, melting into the drizzly oak forest of the smaller hills that buttressed the mountainous East Bay Hills. Their great shaggy heads went up and down like oil derricks, alternately air scenting and ground scenting, searching for the lingering odor of rubber tires or diesel exhaust.

Aphrodite, the alpha bitch, issued a thunderclap bark, shaking water droplets off nearby oak leaves. The other hounds converged on their leader, noses glued to the ground, sucking up the odor of dirt bike tires. Thomas and Jinsoku crashed through the underbrush. The gelding skidded into the center of the dog pack, snorting excitedly, flashing the whites of his eyes.

Thomas dived out of the saddle, dropping to his hands and knees, eyeballing dozens and dozens of fresh tire tracks. Aphrodite woofed softly, urging the man to quit dallying. She'd gotten wind of the quarry and wanted to hunt. He'd didn't need much convincing. Knobby tires had rutted the ground; maybe two hundred motorcycles had passed this way, racing north, up to Puget Sound, the birthplace of American communism. It better not be the graveyard of communism. That wasn't what Thomas had signed on for. The Commonwealth was supposed to marry communism and democracy to constitutional monarchy. There would be hell to pay if it didn't work out that way, after the war.

Jinsoku's ears shot forward as Thomas clucked softly to himself. The man wasn't giving the horse a command, he was thinking, *somebody screwed the pooch*. How could that many Red Army chiefs escape the city and get past an entire Samurai brigade? Either they had help from double agents or the Commonwealth brass was playing some sort of convoluted political game. While two hundred motorcycles had chugged through Milpitas, five thousand Samurai had sat on their asses. He would give "Joe Samurai" a kick in the pants.

Thomas penned a couple messages to the Samurai colonel, giving his location and the nature of his find, extracting two birds from the basket tied to his saddle. He would have two left once this pair was released, which should be enough to see him through the pursuit. There was no question that he faced a long and dangerous hunt. Timely reinforcements would be a necessity. The quarry he would soon be chasing could turn and kill his little squad like a man swatting a bug.

The pigeons took wing. Thomas waited a moment to watch them flap away, not that he could have done anything if hawks seized the birds. Too bad he didn't have any fish eagles to protect the pigeons. He swung back into his saddle and gave the hounds a hunt command.

One instant the Wolfhounds were standing there, the next instant they were gone, silent wraiths in the forest. It was their nature to work noiselessly. The rubber mounts on their canine machineguns and the daily oiling he applied to their leather combat armor enhanced the hounds' natural proclivity for aphonic hunting. It would be challenging to follow them. Before the pulse, he'd put radio-collars on hunting dogs, the good old days.

There was one surefire way to know where the hounds were up ahead, if their machineguns lit up, they would be quite easy to find. *Please God, don't let that happen until the bloody Samurai join the hunt.*

Thomas left the fresh trail and backtracked to his camp. He stuffed his tent, bedroll, water bottles and other supplies into capacious saddlebags, made sure that a round was chambered in his carbine, slammed it into the saddle scabbard, and set to follow the Wolfhounds. The going was easy in the low foothills. He could see the hundreds of motorcycle tracks, plus there was only one good way to navigate the Calaveras Pass, a cow trail that ran along the biggest creek in the region.

The chase consumed the day. The sky grew darker, the hills grew steeper and he could no longer see the tire tracks on the ground. Worse, a couple of ravines leered at him in the gloom. The fleeing enemy bikers could have taken several different routes by now. He pulled an ultrasonic whistle out from under his cowboy hat and gave a mighty blast.

The youngest hound emerged from the twilight before the others, a dead coyote dangling from his jaws. "God damn that bleeding coyote to bloody hell and back again," Thomas moaned, jumping to the ground and tearing the wretched corpse away from the young hound. He was really screwed if all the hounds had gone harrying after coyotes. It was what Wolfhounds were bred to do and a very difficult thing to drill out of them. Nevertheless, they had been trained to avoid wolves and coyotes and he expected more from these, the finest Irish Wolfhounds in the Commonwealth.

The other four made it to the campsite after a couple more ultrasonic whistle blasts, muddy and bedraggled and, thankfully, showing no indication of coyote hunting. Thomas cut the offending wild canine into quarters and fed the chunks of vile meat to the Wolfhounds. He didn't dare strike a campfire, so his meal consisted of dry crackers. Jinsoku, at least, could eat like a king. The racehorse was hobbled and turned loose in a meadow of wet green sprouts.

The Wolfhounds slept with their machinegun harnesses on, in a circle around the cavalryman, under a rubberized tarp strung between two trees. A light rain drizzled throughout the night, soaking everything except the saddle blanket and saddle, which Thomas placed on his belly, using a rock for a pillow. If he had one of the tough Kiso warhorses that the Samurai used, he wouldn't have taken such care. The Anglo-Arab needed babying. Tough as the Kiso horses might be, they couldn't run as fast as a dirt bike.

Dawn brought clear skies and a good day for tracking. Thomas kept the Wolfhounds in a line behind the horse and spent the morning cantering behind the churned up soil of two hundred motorcycle tracks. The knobby pattern of the tires had not been washed out by last night's rain, therefore the bikers' head start had diminished and the tracking could be safely done with human eyeballs.

The sun reached its apogee. He hopped off his horse and walked, leading Jinsoku to a ridge that overlooked the Calaveras Reservoir, an artificial lake in the center of a mountain valley. Because of the EMP, the pumping stations no longer worked and the reservoir was swollen, occupying one third of the valley. More significantly, about one mile distant, tiny dark dots were buzzing around the periphery of the water, motorcyclists rounding up cattle. There could be two hundred enemy riders out there and for sure they would be able to see him if he moved out from under the gnarly old oak tree that he'd tied Jinsoku to.

Thomas lined up the Wolfhounds and gave them a stern lecture. He ordered the great hounds to catch rabbits, grabbing each one by the jowls and saying the word "rabbit" slowly and clearly, locking eyes with each hound meaningfully. He let them go with a swat on the butt. While waiting for the dogs to catch some food, Thomas grabbed a pen and sent his second to last pigeon aloft with a message informing the Samurai colonel that the communist leaders were camped out around the reservoir. If the Samurai took the Marsh Trail, circled the valley, and attacked from the east, then possibly the Red Army leaders could be routed, maybe ending the war. *I do hope that my message doesn't disturb one of their bloody tea ceremonies.*

Gunfire crackled up from the enemy encampment on the banks of the lake. They'd killed a few head of cattle. Unquestionably, they were going to camp out for one day. It would take them that long to butcher the steers, roast the meat, and strap it to their bikes They could see any pursuit coming from about one mile away, and pursuit would have to come over very steep, very rough terrain. With their built-in speed advantage, the motorcyclists would be able to outrun the Commonwealth cavalry. Or so they thought.

Using his collapsible spyglass, Thomas could watch the communist big wigs preparing to roast sides of beef. Something rubbed against his leg. He set the telescope down. The Wolfhounds had caught one rabbit apiece. This meant that while the enemy dined like civilized men, the Commonwealth cavalryman was reduced to eating raw rabbit. He didn't dare start a fire and give away his position. Picking the grisly fare from his teeth with a knife, Thomas reflected on the contrast between serving the Queen as a twenty-year-old soldier and as a man in his late fifties. This kind of hardship wouldn't have bothered a younger man.

He idly watched the Wolfhounds crunch rabbit bones and lick their chops gleefully. His squad was well equipped to live off the land and would be able to follow the motorcyclists for hundreds of miles, if that proved necessary, which it might if the Samurai were too busy arranging flowers and writing poetry to help. He trained the telescope on one of the bikes. Two-gallon drums were welded to either side of the back fender, no doubt flush with fuel. Little diesel powered dirt bikes like that with aluminum frames and lightweight ceramic engines got incredible mileage, they could make it into the central valley without needing to refuel. The farther north they traveled, the more communist sympathizers they would find, plenty of opportunities to gas up. The pursuit would last forever if that happened.

Jinsoku must have sensed that their quarry was not far away and that they were hesitating. He pawed the ground with his front hoof, tossing his head, fighting against the rope holding him fast to the tree. Thomas sprang to his feet and rushed up to the horse, holding his halter. The Anglo-Arab was on the verge of belting out a loud whinny, which might be audible to the communist encampment. He was a hot blood and wouldn't calm down without a brief gallop. Thomas saddled the racehorse and had a grave talk with the five Wolfhounds, ordering them to stay put and keep an eye on the enemy. It was a good thing that they had full bellies; his orders were more likely to be obeyed.

The racehorse sprang down the hill, moving west, away from the communist camp. He gave Jinsoku his head when the terrain was suitable, letting the horse burn some of the fire out of his body, so he'd be tractable when they returned to their vantage overlooking the enemy stronghold. Thomas cleared a crest and could see the Santa Clara Valley again. More of San Jose's skyline had been obliterated. Daylight was waning and the mammoth artillery thunder had ceased. The pachyderms were packing it up for the day, another day, another pound, another section of city destroyed.

A blue jay's screeching caw split the air three times, a little too loudly for it to be a real bird. Thomas pulled Jinsoku up short, jerked his carbine from the scabbard, and returned his attention to the triple cawing. From farther down the trail and around a bend, three more birdcalls peeled outward. Either there was a fellow Commonwealth cavalryman down there, or a communist double agent had mastered one of their codes. Cautiously, the racehorse stepped forward, restrained by tight reins held in Thomas's teeth. He gripped the rifle in the firing position with both hands. Now would be a good time to have the Wolfhounds and their five machineguns at his side.

Field Commander Jeremiah Halifax turned the corner in the trail, riding a racehorse much like Jinsoku and with a squad of Wolfhounds trailing behind. The field commander's horse was lathered with sweat and puffing hard. The great hounds had tongues lolling nearly to the ground, panting like an ironmonger's bellows. Jeremiah had ridden long and hard to get here.

Peering beyond his ultimate superior, Thomas scanned the hills for Samurai warriors. Seeing none, he asked Jeremiah where the reinforcements were. "Japanese Ubermen have sealed the city airtight. No other enemy combatants can escape. As for the communist leaders camped out yonder, they can run but they can't hide. The noose is drawing snug."

"But, Sir, I don't understand." Thomas stopped talking as he noticed that the pigeons Jeremiah carried were the ones that he'd sent out. The field commander had read his notes and was well apprised of the situation. He must know what he was doing.

Jeremiah told Thomas to lead the way to the ridgeline where the other Wolfhounds were perched. They rode slowly and carefully to the hilltop and Thomas did some internal truth-seeking. He wasn't sure that making martyrs out of the escaping communist leadership by wiping them out with bloodthirsty and reactionary Samurai was the answer. In any case, he had faith in the field commander and would follow him anywhere.

The racehorses were hobbled and turned loose on some ridgeline meadows. The dogs were bedded down. The two Commonwealth soldiers struck a rough camp. Lying in the dark, spying on the twinkling campfires that the enemy had blazing near the lake, Thomas asked, "General Halifax, Sir, why did you call the Samurai, Ubermen?"

"The previous Samurai class was abolished by the Emperor Meiji seventy years ago. This new Samurai caste is based on Germany and Zululand's eugenics program. More than that, it revives the ancient code of Bushido. Japan becomes stronger and stronger in the post-EMP world. The Impi and Uberman programs may morph into a feudal warrior caste in response, a volatile witch's brew."

"I'm just an ignorant farmer," Thomas said tentatively. When Jeremiah made encouraging noises the Englishman completed his thoughts. "I've been reading up on Samurai. They waged one thousand years of civil war back in medieval Japan, about as warlike a people as have ever existed, that's what Bushido means, perpetual war. I also know that these fancy Historical Parallelism professors say democracies can only fight civil wars, the very specialty of these Samurai types."

"I despise Historical Parallelism. Yet your point is valid. Historical forces are building that could precipitate hundreds of years of civil war, as was seen in feudal Japan. Not to worry. I've a plan."

Jeremiah went on to describe the role that Thomas would play in his plan. The sergeant would watch the field commander ride down to the communist camp under a white flag come morning. Thomas would continue observing from the ridgeline while Jeremiah opened peace talks. If the field commander was harmed in any way, then Thomas would send pigeon messages to the Samurai and the Hannibalic Army, launching an all out attack. If one day went by and Jeremiah was unharmed, hale and hearty and still locked in the throes of negotiation, then Thomas would ride back to San Jose. The sergeant would return in due course with Queen Victoria.

Thomas spit out the blade of grass that he'd been chewing. "The Queen? Her Royal Highness isn't in San Jose!" Jeremiah rolled over on his sleeping mat, propped himself on an elbow, and said, "She will be presently. If the Red Army leaders don't kill me in one day, you are to fetch the Queen, bring her Royal Highness and her retinue here. I don't want to negotiate with Bakunin where he can see the conclusive destruction of San Jose, which will be horrific, and I've other reasons as well. Bring the Queen here. Those are your orders, Sergeant. Oh, I forgot, here is a letter. Present it to General Kwa." Jeremiah stood up and went to his saddlebags. He pulled out an envelope and placed it in Thomas's saddlebags. "Give that letter to Kwa. You and Kwa must bring Victoria here. Let's get some shut eye."

The next morning, Thomas was treated to the sight of Jeremiah Halifax galloping down the mile-long slope to the communist encampment holding a large white flag that flapped sharply in the wind. The white flag allayed the motorcycle company's suspicions enough to prevent Jeremiah from being gunned down immediately. It didn't prevent the communists from lining up into a combat formation.

Thomas made sure that the ten Wolfhounds were under voice control, in a down stay command, and poised to sprint down the hill with machineguns blazing if one hair on Jeremiah's head was harmed. He looked away from the reservoir, glancing at the pigeon basket tied to Jinsoku's saddle. When and if he let loose the war dogs, Thomas would release the pigeons, every one of them had message capsules tethered to his or her feet. Then he would jump on the racehorse and ride hell bent for leather down the hill and help the Wolfhounds avenge the field commander's death. He turned back to the encampment.

Jeremiah's horse was no longer galloping. It was trotting in a big circle in front of the motorcycle formation. Jeremiah had thrown down his white flag and was stripping off his jacket, demonstrating that he carried no weapons. Flat on his belly, Thomas pulled out his spyglass to get a better picture of the greeting Jeremiah was receiving. Thomas had to drop the telescope within seconds. The Wolfhounds to his right were snarling, twitching, and mouthing the wooden bars that controlled the firing mechanism of their light machineguns. These were Jeremiah's dogs and they were barely able to constrain themselves.

Casting a hurried glance at the encounter on base of the hill, Thomas decided that it was going well enough. There'd been no gunplay at least. He grabbed the lead dog of the second pack by her spiked collar and gave a heel command. The two hundred pound Wolfhound bitch was tied to a tree. The other four dogs in Jeremiah's pack relaxed, looking as though they would obey the down stay and not attack the communists without a command. Finally, Thomas could turn his telescope back on the meeting below.

A short black man with a white beard was shaking Jeremiah's hand. It had to be Vladimir Bakunin, the father of modern communism. The men and women standing around Bakunin had rifles slung on their shoulders. The weapons were not trained on Jeremiah. The situation was not volatile, as far as Thomas could tell, although it wasn't exactly hugs and kisses down there for the field commander.

Thomas kept his eye glued to the telescope. Hugs and kisses might be on the agenda after all. Several of the communist women were young and attractive. If Jeremiah lived up to his reputation, he would bed a few of the Marxist femmes before midnight. An hour's worth of watching didn't change the cavalry sergeant's mind. Jeremiah was not in danger. Thomas needed to take the Wolfhounds off their hair trigger setting. He stripped off their war harnesses, setting the steel and leather contraptions in low hanging branches where he could quickly lay hands on them.

The huge hounds shook themselves and licked their chops expectantly. Thomas didn't disappoint the mighty canines, commanding them to catch rabbits and bring the meat back. He got busy with his hatchet, building a fire in the bole between two pinnacles behind the ridgeline, where the smoke wouldn't be that visible from down below.

An hour or two passed and the Wolfhounds returned one by one, dropping bloody and mangled rabbit carcasses at his boots. Mouth crinkling in disgust, Thomas tossed the corpses back at the dogs and told them to eat. He had no stomach for such unappetizing fare.

He gave Aphrodite her rabbit back and grabbed her around the jowls, ordering her to bring back a calf. The alpha bitch's ears pricked, her big pink tongue washed her fist-sized nose. "I'm serious, old girl. Bring back a calf, a nice fat calf. And hunt it down on this side of the mountain."

The fire would have to be built up to roast a calf. Aphrodite might return with a small steer for all he knew. Before chopping up a mass of kindling, Thomas unlimbered his telescope and checked on Jeremiah and the communists again. Bakunin and the field commander were sitting on tree stumps, locked in the throes of deep conversation. Jeremiah must be a hellacious salesman to convince the Red Army supreme commander that Commonwealth forces were not surrounding the Calaveras Valley. A bond must be developing between the two leaders. Thomas prayed that Bakunin didn't harbor a plot within a plot and wasn't playing Jeremiah for a fool.

Thomas put away the telescope and pulled out his hatchet. Aphrodite's timing was superb, dropping a plump little heifer near the roaring fire. Naturally, she'd found it much easier to chase down a calf than a jackrabbit. And the cattle around here were unguarded. With the recent military maneuvers in these hills, the local ranchers weren't too quick with their normally hair trigger fingers.

The next sixteen hours inched by uneventfully and sluggishly. The inactivity was hard to bear in the light of the increasingly cordial reception that Field Commander Halifax was getting, causing Thomas to think that the war was actually ending. For Halifax to be getting that kind of reception, he had to be promising to break up the Halifax supermonopoly in Europe and the rest of the old world. Would he sell his shares to workers or give them away? Thomas was willing to bet that there would be a sale. Maybe at a discount, maybe over time, but the field commander wasn't giving anything away for free. The Halifax supermonopoly would be worth trillions if the war ended.

The cavalry sergeant slept that night inside a nest of ten Wolfhounds, dreaming of his wife smiling at him from the porch of their farmhouse in Coyote Valley while he drove by on a spanking new tractor. In his dream, the farm still belonged to South County Agriculture, the DFA spin-off that he owned stock in. It not only paid him a salary, it not only had great medical and dental, it also paid a fat dividend once a year. Free market communism rocked.

At the first light of dawn, he gave the field commander and the communist leaders a peek from his spyglass. The love fest continued unabated in the encampment below. Preparations were underway for a visit from Queen Victoria. Crude shelters were arising on the lakeshore. Thomas couldn't understand why Jeremiah would want to conduct high-level peace talks in such a strange location. Maybe he wanted to give the communists the option of roaring off on their dirt bikes if the talks turned sour, a confidence building measure. The sergeant had his own assignment to worry about. He needed to climb down out of the hills, ride across the sprawling farmlands of Milpitas, and convince the Queen to ride to the reservoir to treat with her enemies. *How in bleeding damnation will the likes o' me convince the Queen to do anything?*

Ten Wolfhounds, one racehorse, and one ill at ease cavalry sergeant loped down the mountainside, southwest to San Jose. Thomas paused on one of the smaller hills, heartened by San Jose's skyline. A few more buildings had been knocked down since the last time he'd seen it, but there were no clouds of dust blasting upward and no artillery thunder rolling up out of the city. San Jose must have surrendered or quit fighting.

Riding across the Milpitas flatland, Thomas lost the warm, fuzzy feeling. Flocks of turkey vultures wheeled across the sky, circling into increasingly tighter columns and landing several hundred yards up ahead. He slowed the horse and the dog pack, afraid of what he would see next. Scores of bodies were littered across the landscape like so much garbage. Punctured by arrows and clad in civilian clothes, some of them had been beheaded. The neck wounds were surgically clean. The massacre must have happened within the last few hours, the vultures had only gotten around to plucking eyeballs from heads and worrying the stumps of the beheaded corpses.

Pulling his horse short in front of a particularly large and grisly pile of fresh cadavers, Thomas swung out of his saddle and put the Wolfhounds into a down stay so they wouldn't paw the bodies. He scattered the buzzards and yanked an arrow out of a dead man wearing a Roman collar and a parson's hat. The shaft was bamboo, polished and lacquered. The arrowhead was handmade, four sided, patterned after a bamboo leaf: the work of Samurai.

Speak of the devil. A Samurai was walking his way, horned helmet, bamboo armor, sword swinging on his hip: the whole nine yards. The Bushi held out a hand for the arrow that Thomas was holding. When Thomas didn't relinquish the arrow immediately, the Samurai's other hand fell on his sword. The Wolfhounds growled softly, yet remained frozen in down stays. Thomas bowed and handed the arrow over to its rightful owner. Failing to bow in return, the Samurai stuffed the arrow in a quiver and began to pull other arrows systematically from bodies, taking no further notice of the cavalryman or his war beasts.

The macabre scene was shattered by the authoritative growl of aeroplane engines. Thomas recognized the basso rumble of World War I era Super-Merlin V12s, the sweetest music he'd ever heard, the sound of the post-EMP world fading away. He ground tied Jinsoku and walked up to Aphrodite, the boss Wolfhound. Pointing up at the plane, he said, "Aeroplane. Aphrodite, that is an aeroplane." The bitch licked her nose and tried to catch the scent of this strange object. When that failed, she cocked her head and listened to the four engines. All the Wolfhounds followed suit, cocking their heads, licking their noses. Even the unflappable Samurai looked up into the sky in amazement.

The navy blue Super-Merlin circled the city, swinging over Milpitas, affording an excellent view of the two union jacks that had been painted under its wings and a royal crest on the tail. The Samurai looked away, returning to arrow recovery.

"Hey, Shogun, see 'at plane. The Queen's comin' to see how badly we've botched the war. It won't do to leave these bodies unburied. Tell your colonel to get 'em underground," Thomas flatly ordered the Bushi. In the twinkle of an eye, an arrow had been notched and was pointing at the cavalryman's heart. The Wolfhounds sprang upright, grabbing the firing bars of their machineguns, training barrels at different parts of the Samurai's body. The arrow slowly lowered and returned to its quiver.

"Come now, lad, can't have the Queen stumbling across this mess. It'll reflect poorly on the Emperor Jimmu." It was impossible to tell if Thomas's suggestion had an effect on the Samurai since he went back to retrieving arrows.

The cavalryman applied heels to Jinsoku's flanks, whistling for the Wolfhounds, loping west toward the battered city at a measured pace. The Super-Merlin was no longer aeroborne. It must have found a place to land somewhere on the peninsula. The dogs would have a better idea than he. Thomas was about to give the command *find aeroplane*, when a wing of Samurai galloped by on their tough little Kiso warhorses.

He kicked Jinsoku hard, breaking into a full gallop. Wolfhounds strung out behind him like ducklings following a momma duck, Thomas fell in behind the mounted Samurai. He had to pull his racehorse back to prevent him from flying past the Japanese warriors. A cluster of civilians was trying to climb up out of an arroyo, some with rifles, which they clearly weren't throwing down in surrender. Arrows sprang from Samurai bows, cutting down the civilians.

Thomas was obligated to help the Bushi. He screamed at the Wolfhounds to attack foot soldiers, skeptical inside at the term "soldier," realizing that he was sentencing civilians to death. The dogs wouldn't make the same moral distinction. Their training under these circumstances dictated that humans on foot be mowed down with machineguns.

Pulling ahead of the short, stubby warhorses, the fleet footed Wolfhounds attained clear fields of fire. Their long jaws clamped down on firing bars and pushed forward, triggering the guns. Their shaggy lupine heads swiveled left and right, spraying the civilians with 25 caliber slugs. Thomas would have covered his ears to block out the children's shrieking if there hadn't been Samurai watching. He couldn't stop stomach acid from welling up in his throat and was glad that he hadn't eaten anything today or he would have vomited.

When the slaughter was over, he collected the Wolfhounds and began stripping off their war harnesses. A Samurai officer stooped next to him, helping with the harnesses, offering thanks for his assistance. Hating himself for the hypocrisy, Thomas bowed and told the man to please take the war harnesses to a cavalry depot.

The racehorse and the hounds were allowed to drink from the stream running through the arroyo. Thomas forced himself to praise the dogs for a job well done. Acting surly toward the animals wouldn't do. There was a war on and he needed them in fighting trim.

His fear at the prospect of confronting Queen Victoria vanished, replaced by a burning desire to help end the ghastly war. Holding Jinsoku by the reins, climbing out of the ditch, he saw that the Bushi were gone, off to eliminate other escapees from the fallen city. He gathered the Wolfhounds in a circle and told them to find the aeroplane as quickly as possible.

Unencumbered by their canine war harnesses, the gray wraiths lit off with tremendous speed. Jinsoku snorted enthusiastically, coiled, and shot off after the hounds, pounding the ground with a twenty-foot stride. The strap on Thomas's cowboy hat broke and it whipped off his head. The wind from the racehorse's passage caused his eyes to water. He crouched low over the withers, like a jockey.

The hounds sailed over fences and detritus from damaged buildings. Jinsoku vaulted over the same obstacles. Two miles flew by under the horse's hooves and Thomas shouted for the dogs to slow down. Not only were they going to run themselves into the ground, they needed to carefully use their ears and other senses to find the aeroplane, not simply dash toward the spot where they'd last heard it. Logic said that it probably touched down on the highway that ran between San Francisco and San Jose. On the other hand, the Commonwealth may have built a secret landing strip off that road.

The hounds started ranging in half-mile loops off the southwesterly path that the horse and rider continued to take. Jinsoku slowed to a bouncy trot, the easiest gait for a horse, the toughest gait for a rider. They trotted through Mountain View and into Los Gatos.

Thomas heard Aphrodite's booming bark while watering Jinsoku in a meandering stream. Dusk was gathering and they were in a tall redwood forest, accentuating the gloom. The horseman trotted to a raised clearing and saw a patch of woodland a mile away that was ablaze with electric lights. He raised the ultrasonic whistle and called the hounds.

Security would be very tight around the Queen's aeroplane. He put the dogs in a line behind the horse and led Jinsoku on foot toward the wash of artificial light, stumbling upon a trail a quarter mile from their final destination. The trail broke free of the forest, terminating in a log fortress jutting out from a barbed wire fence. Somewhere up ahead, mammoths were trumpeting.

Thomas rifled through his saddlebags, extracting the letter for General Kwa as well as his own military identification papers. The guards at the gate examined his papers, sent a runner into the compound with Jeremiah's letter for Kwa, and offered to feed and care for the war beasts. Thomas felt twenty years younger when the Wolfhounds and the racehorse were led away to kennels and a stable somewhere inside the floodlit aerobase.

Cooling his heels outside the main gate, he became aware of how grimy and sweaty he must be. How could he meet the Queen smelling like a sewer rat? On the verge of screwing his courage up to ask a guard where he could shower and find a change of clothes, a private stymied the opportunity by informing Thomas that he was to met with Her Royal Highness straight away.

Kwa appeared, to hold his hand and lead him through any awkward moments. The private, Kwa, and Thomas walked through the aerobase. Blazing on top of sixty-foot towers, the floodlights turned their shadows into gigantic, alien creatures. The plane sat there on an earthen landing strip, stolid, impressive. Somewhere in the darkness unseen wood burning generators chuffed away. Countless insects formed clouds around the towers, as if they'd never seen artificial light. On the other side of the Super-Merlin, mammoth cows and calves were cavorting. Three slim young women in britches rode on the largest mammoth. Two of the women were Gurkha bodyguards. The other was Victoria, who was expertly steering the mammoth cow along the barbed wire fence, denying the calf his nightly ration of milk, precipitating a bawling temper tantrum from the six hundred pound tyke.

Eisenhower, Churchill, and General Bernhard were standing next to the Super-Merlin, watching the Queen ride Skuld, the Monarch's favorite mammoth. Kwa and Thomas remained apart from the three other men. The Zulu general looked at the cavalry sergeant and said, "Tommy, I believe you speak for England. No one is more fit to address Her

Majesty." Thomas looked down and let out a nearly inaudible groan, experiencing a flashback to World War I. Back then, Kwa had insisted that because of his name, Tommy Atkins possessed a spiritual link to every English fighting man and was a symbol, a talisman, for the nation at large.

"Eisenhower and Churchill want to use the Merlin gunship to wipe out the remnant of communism to the north. As opposed to Field Commander Halifax, who wants to incorporate the Marxist leaders and their ideas into a new government. It's up to you to convince the Queen that the field commander is correct," Kwa pronounced.

"Wrong on two counts," Thomas countered. "The *two* of us are to convince Her Majesty. And we've only to get her over the hills and sitting at the negotiating table that Jeremiah has prepared on the shores of Lake Calaveras. It's up to Jeremiah to lay out the grand design."

Skuld thudded by, shaking the ground under Thomas and Kwa's feet. The Queen and her two Gurkha guards looked straight ahead, concentrating on their mammoth riding as if they were undergoing dressage exercises.

Victoria put her hairy mount into a slide, kicking dust into the artificial light. She looked at the men standing by the Super-Merlin and then at Thomas and Kwa. Thomas's heart almost stopped beating under her arctic stare. He'd seen the Queen on television when she was a little girl. She'd changed since then. The woman sitting astride the mammoth was unlike any person he'd ever met. Even Kwa stiffened under her gaze.

Skuld wrapped a hairy trunk around Victoria's torso and set her on the ground. She and her Gurkha guards strode purposefully toward the Zulu general and the English expatriate. Thomas's knees would have buckled if Kwa hadn't grabbed him by the back of the collar and held him upright.

The cavalryman didn't remember how he got through the ritual prostration or what he said to convince Victoria to drop everything and leave at once for the Calaveras encampment. He did it somehow. The next morning, Kwa, Victoria, and Thomas were inside a howdah, on Skuld's back, tramping up the East Bay Hills.

Thomas prayed for two things. He hoped that the cursed Samurai had disposed the heaps of bodies rotting near the base of the East Bay Hills along the route that Victoria would take to reach the encampment. And he prayed that the reactionary Commonwealth old guard would keep an open mind to the opportunities offered by free market communism.

Chapter 25

Gravity is the Eternal Flame of Ahura Mazda

C ancer was eating David Banner alive from the inside out. The weekly landing of Japanese steamships meant that he could take morphine to ease the pain. Banner took one last injection that morning, vowing to quit cold turkey before playing his part in the Calaveras Conference. While Lisa reluctantly admitted that morphine put him in a stupor, she also thought that intense pain would dull his mind even more. They fought as she'd packed their bags. David was adamant that the drug should be left behind. Lisa wanted to take a plentiful supply. He quit arguing when the narcotic kicked in.

With his senses dulled from the final injection, David Banner walked outside, supported by Lisa. Together they watched Surus glide up the driveway of their San Jose house. Erevu sat on the African bull's neck, in front of a howdah stripped of weaponry, leaving plenty of room for a soft mattress and cushions. Even the outer railing had been padded for comfort, an excellent means of transportation for a sick and suffering old man.

Surus extended his trunk, wrapped it around David Banner, and placed him inside the howdah. The bull was shocked at his friend's weight loss. Lifting the one-legged man had been like picking up a twig. Lisa was placed next to her husband. If anything, she'd gained a few pounds. He had no way to express this observation to her, and if he could she would have been offended. The Banner's bags were placed on hooks outside the howdah. The elephant was ready to make tracks.

Erevu turned around to peer into the howdah, making sure his passengers were comfy. Satisfied, he jammed heels into the bull's neck. Surus kicked out his long legs and settled into a good pace for long distance travel, about eight miles-per-hour. There was a beaten path leading to the Calaveras Pass that followed some pre-EMP roads and cut through others. Four or five mammoths were also traversing this path, with weapon-free howdahs on their backs. Inside these howdahs were dignitaries and power brokers, intent on making their voices heard at the seminal summit.

Halfway across the agricultural flatlands of Milpitas, the silverback grabbed Surus by the ears and steered him off the muddy road to jog down a lane that terminated in a ranch house. Surus raised his trunk and trumpeted at the end of the lane, announcing their arrival. The door of the house was open and voices trickled outside, somebody was saying goodbye to somebody else. Jim Pullman stomped out onto the porch and greeted the travelers effusively. He slipped behind his ranch house, returning with a bulky handcart spilling over with fruits and vegetables. Erevu sprang off the elephant, landing in the mud next to the cart. Surus's trunk lashed into the groceries hurriedly, snagging a couple hundred pounds of produce before the greedy gorilla ate too much.

Pullman threw a steamer at the elephant's feet and made a thumbs-up gesture to the gobbling pachyderm. Grumbling in protest, Surus quit eating and hoisted the fat man and his luggage into the howdah, neither were especially light, but their weight was nothing compared to the aluminum cannon and its complement of artillery shells that he'd once lugged everywhere. The elephant turned back to the food cart, expecting to find it empty and Erevu's stomach bulging obscenely. The reverse was true. Generous clumps of cabbage lined the bottom of the cart and Erevu was coiling to leap back onto the bull's neck.

Under the silverback's direction, Surus spent the rest of the afternoon churning through the mud behind a growing train of mammoths, all bent on crossing the Calaveras Pass. The congestion slowed his brisk pace to a crawl.

The combination of morphine, the rocking motion of the howdah, and an unseasonably warm winter day gave David Banner a nearly uncontrollably desire to sleep. He struggled to stay awake, concentrating on what Jim Pullman was saying: "Tomorrow is crunch time for the antitrust portion of the new Commonwealth Constitution."

Pullman spoke and Banner's eyes glinted with pain. The morphine was wearing off. It wasn't too bad, for the moment, and the pain did keep him alert. Pulling a bag of peanuts from his pocket, munching and talking at the same time, Pullman described the pitfalls ahead: "The DFA supermonopoly was dismantled without recompense to Ford, Sloan, and their board. Prince Jeremiah isn't going to break up his supermonopoly the same way, thank God, gonna be some heavy payola for Queen Victoria's new hubby. Problem is, after that, when the next monopoly emerges, it'll get broken up like Ford's, no recompense for the founding—"

"Bloody sodding hell, Pullman, you haven't a clue!" Banner barked through his haze of pain. Lisa made a motion for Pullman to be silent and held out a bottle of whiskey to her husband. He took a draw, swallowed, and complained, "Hell, woman, the liquor is laced with morphine." She shook her head and said contritely, "Only a drop." Banner shook his head, asserting that it tasted like it was at least half morphine. She raised the bottle to his lips. He took another swallow, waited a minute and said in a more reasonable voice, "Jim, the next publicly traded monopoly that's broken up will have new shares issued to the original shareholders. They'll own pieces of the new companies. If the monopoly is privately owned like Banner Detectives, Class A shares will be converted to Class B, and auctioned off, proceeds going to the original owners. What happened to Ford and Sloan will never happen again because—" Banner went on to explain how the new antitrust mechanisms were intended to work. None of this was news to Pullman.

The fat man waited for Banner to finish and said, "Not good enough. There's gonna be a stigma attached to creating a monopoly after a whole freaking war was fought over DFA. We won't see it for a while, but eventually it'll throw a wet blanket on aggressive business practices. Every business should try balls out to conqueror its competition, and brand new industries with patented technology are often monopolies at first."

322

"What are you suggesting?" Lisa asked.

"Any monopolist that's bought out under the new antitrust provision is made a Knight of the British Empire by the Queen," Pullman replied, waving his arms excitedly. Surus expertly waited for the right moment and grabbed the bag of peanuts with a quick trunk lash. The entrepreneur glared at his empty hand, distracted from his line of reasoning. The elephant ate the peanuts, including the bag, and blew a victorious note.

"Knighthood is only granted to British subjects," David Banner countered. Lisa nodded in agreement, uncertainly. She had a vague notion what was coming next. Pullman folded his pudgy arms over his chest and asked the couple if they'd heard the plan to incorporate the People's Republic of North America into Great Britain until Washington DC and the US federal government could be rebuilt. The Banners had dimly heard these rumors. Word on the street had it that the Atlantic would become something like the Irish Sea, a mere water barrier within an extended Great Britain, or as some people were saying: Greater Britain.

"Let me give you all a newsflash," Pullman said, uncrossing his arms and rising to his feet, standing on the floor of the howdah like a captain on a rocking ship. "North America ain't never gonna wanna leave Greater Britain, not after it elects a Yankee prime minister and puts him in Ten Downing Street 'cause that's where the real power's gonna be from here on out." The fat man plopped back onto a cushion, a triumphant expression on his face as he concluded: "Every advanced nation in the Commonwealth's gonna want the same deal. Time was when a colony clamored to move from the Empire to the Commonwealth. The day will come when every Commonwealth nation's gonna be aching to move into the United Kingdom. It'll mean growin' a crop of American aristocrats, Canada and Mexico too. Gonna cost a bundle to buy a royal title. Folks like me'll have to pony up serious scratch, gotta get a seat in the House of Lords to pull political strings. I'm gonna hate all that lord and lady crap, no choice, gotta do it."

"I see," Lisa began. "A country sufficiently advanced to produce a global monopoly will be advanced enough to join with Britain proper, won't it?" She looked at her husband for comment. David was asleep again, his head flopping back and filling the howdah with snores. Pullman offered his opinion: "When the big dog barks, the pups shut up and listen." American slang always confused Lisa. She thought Pullman was probably agreeing with her analysis.

The line of pachyderms queuing at the foot of the mountain ground to a standstill. Maglev railroad tracks ran through the northeastern corner of Milpitas, only they weren't carrying magnetic levitation trains any more. An old-fashioned timber and steel railroad had been built on top of the useless maglev line. Wood burning, Japanese manufactured Hogshead locomotives chugged into the Sacramento Valley, pregnant with row upon row of cannons and machineguns, pulling rail cars packed with Chinese laborers and railroad building equipment. The Crown was extending its control out into America's interior. A similar effort was being mounted from the Eastern seaboard. Not that there was much resistance to Britain's newly acquired hegemony. It wasn't like the end of the last war, where brutal guerilla campaigns had raged in a dozen conquered countries. In every corner of the world, workers knew that they faced starvation without British and Japanese steam engines and copper wire.

Pullman spied General Eisenhower among the officers seeing off the Hogshead locomotives. The American general stood on the edge of the train station, beaming at the big, ugly locomotives steaming into the heartland. With formal hostilities over, Eisenhower was in his element, organizing the militarization of the continental railroad system, establishing aero bridges from coast to coast, and ushering in foreign troops as an occupying power. A union jack fluttered over the train station, not the stars and stripes.

Leaning out of the howdah, Pullman cupped hands around his mouth and shouted at the Commonwealth supreme commander, "Yoo-hoo, General Eisenhower, I'll vote to put you in Ten Downing Street any day! A fine prime minister you'll be!" The British officers standing on the train station platform sniggered. Even from fifty yards, Lisa and Pullman could see the top military man's face turn purple. He jumped off the platform and marched down the row of stalled pachyderms, stopping next to Surus.

"Is that you Pullman?" Eisenhower demanded. Pullman leaned out further so his grinning face was easily observed. "This loose talk about me running for prime minister is wildly premature." Eisenhower put his hands on his hips, glaring up at the entrepreneur.

"That's fine, Ike," Pullman called down from the elephant's back. "So long as you don't issue a flat-out denial. I'll be your biggest campaign contributor. You've got my word on that. I'm talking millions of pounds." The lesser officers on the rail platform were watching the exchange intently. Eisenhower shouted at them to get busy and do something useful. When their attention had been diverted, he doffed his hat at Pullman and walked back to his underlings.

Pullman sat back on a cushion and looked at Lisa, remarking, "I'll need all the political juice I can muster once the lights go back on." Lisa's eyebrows arched in curiosity as she asked, "Oh, really, a business opportunity, is it? There'll be a need for investors, will there?"

"Yeah, I'll be selling stock. Gotta attract investors and we'll have to grease the politicos big time. We'll be butting heads right away with the Royal Antitrust Commission." Pullman fleshed out a plan that he'd been hatching for a long time. Years ago, in England, David Banner had tried to get a Gorilla Football League off the ground. Due to the war, it had never sprouted wings. The time was ripe to try again, on a much bigger scale. Although it had to be done differently in this go around. A gorilla football team should not be built around a single silverback's troop. It should not have positions assigned to family members, everyone playing except tiny apelings. The very notion was absurd. Top professional teams should be comprised almost entirely of silverbacks, with perhaps a few positions that required speed, such as wide receiver or cornerback, open to swift females and fleet-footed blackbacks. There should be tryouts and a draft. Gigantic silverbacks like Kubwa shouldn't be playing quarterback, the hulking titans needed to be offensive linegorillas. And virtually every signing gorilla in the world needed to participate. To get the military on board, two versions of professional gorilla football should be offered: non-suited and with powered combat suits. The two versions would dovetail perfectly with the two phases of modern war: post-EMP and pre-EMP. In the off-season, gorillas would participate in military maneuvers designed in Whitehall, every gorilla a football star and every gorilla a soldier.

The fat businessman spewed out idea after idea. Clearly, he had given this subject a tremendous amount of thought. Lisa looked helplessly at her husband. Surus had resumed walking and David Banner was flopping back and forth on his cushions with every step, he head lolling about like a wet noodle. She wanted to wake him, but knew that he was better off sleeping. A chill seeped into Lisa despite the warm weather. In the near future, David would be gone and she would have to make business decisions, all decisions, on her own. That was why Pullman was addressing her so frankly. Which made her angry. It was as if Pullman thought David was already dead.

Darkness fell and the pachyderm parade was still marching into the hills, moving more slowly as a group than they could have as individuals. Lisa was forced to wake her husband up around midnight. She had to coerce the sick old man to eat. He choked down a few crackers and water. They arrived at well past midnight. Two tents had been set up, one for Lisa and David, the other for Pullman and Erevu. The elephant set David on the ground. The gorilla carried him into a tent and gently laid him onto a cot.

The next day, David Banner opened his eyes and thought that it must be morning. The gray light filtering through the tent fabric had the feeble quality of an overcast dawn. *Why am I in a tent?* He couldn't remember the reason Lisa and he had gone on a camping trip. It seemed a foolish thing to do at his age. Sitting up on the cot, he grimaced at the sight of Lisa holding a steaming bowl of military issue vita-porridge, all the nutrition of a balanced meal with none of the taste. He wasn't sure if he had the strength to eat such swill. He *was* absolutely certain that he did not have enough strength to contest Lisa in a battle of wills.

The steaming bowl was now very close to his face. The spoon hit him on the cheek. Lisa's face was also very close, eyes burning intensely. Choosing the lesser of two evils, he ate. The food brought nausea. The nausea brought generalized pain throughout his body. She helped him hobble outside and got him through the morning routine. Only then did he remember why they were camped out in a gigantic tent city.

With crutches jammed into his armpits, he balanced himself and grabbed Lisa by the shoulders. Some of his old strength returned. She winced under the grip. "I must have a talk with Professor Einstein and his wife," he said through a mouth gone tight with increasing pain.

Lisa peeled his hand off her shoulder and said, "My dear, the antitrust measures are to be discussed today. Mr. Pullman wants us to participate in a business venture that will be sorely affected by these measures."

"The Royal Antitrust Commission can sod off!" he shouted. The pain was now a waking nightmare. Lisa responded by handing him a bottle of whiskey laced with morphine. He raised the bottle, took a nip, and crutched back into the tent, calling out from inside, "Please bring me the two Einsteins."

He had to keep his mind free of narcotics to interact with Albert and Nkosinathi. His hand bore down on the whiskey/morphine bottle. Should he take another swig? It would take hours for Lisa to find the two scientists and wrest them away from the kingmakers camped around the lake. Ideally, he should while away the time in a drug-free sleep.

Making sure that the cap was screwed on tight, he rolled the whiskey bottle under his cot. Collapsing into bed, his hand brushed against a canteen, sloshing with water. The cool liquid ran down his throat, dampening the fires wracking his body. He didn't know that Lisa had laced his personal water supply with morphine. What Banner did know was that he was going to die in a matter of days. When he met his maker, presumably all questions would be answered. In the here and now, he wanted answers that only the two Einsteins could give. And maybe he could give them something back in exchange. Maybe he could give the scientific community something to think about for the next couple of centuries.

Banner drifted off. Lately, his dreams about Hannibal had been supplanted by far ranging visions involving cosmology and theology, subjects that were virtually one and the same for the dying man. His cosmological visions would be his gift to the Einsteins, barter for information and speculation that only they could provide.

His dreams that afternoon were mundane and Earth-bound. In bating arenas across the Commonwealth, he saw Bulldogs tangling with Cape buffalo. A smile crept across his face as he dreamed of gorillas playing soccer from the backs of mammoths. War seals played the same game underwater, batting neutrally buoyant balls through submerged goals. Then a whiff of prescience blew across the dreamscape, but only a whiff. Two football teams, gorillas wearing powered combat suits, lined up on the gridiron. The center, a huge metal clad silverback, placed his titanium gauntlets on an aluminum football and hiked. For the next few hours, baiting contests and animal athletics exploded across Banner's mind, a kaleidoscope of controlled violence and mammalian majesty. The blood sport culture would no longer exist if not for him. He could take pride in that.

His eyes fluttered open. He sensed that other people were inside the tent, but couldn't see the visitors, instant pain clouding his vision. Groping for the whiskey bottle ineffectually, Banner sought to tame the monster eating him alive. Lisa found the bottle, slamming it into his outstretched palm. A long pull began the process of containing the monster. His body was still beading with sweat and trembling in agony when Albert and Nkosinathi Einstein came into focus. He tried to speak. No words came out. His throat muscles had seized.

Lisa grabbed his hand, turned to the scientists, and said, "David wants to discuss cosmology, the history of the universe." Albert Einstein made a scoffing noise. Nkosinathi hushed the great thinker, reminding him that in the writings of Winston Churchill, David Banner had discussed the existence of blackholes before any astronomer or physicist.

"Yes, yes," Einstein said dismissively. "He talked about blackholes in a religious treatise, never in a scientific publication." Banner's right hand broke away from Lisa's grasp and shot out to encircle Einstein's wrist. The dying man husked, "Albert, please listen with an open mind. And then answer my questions. Share the answers with the power brokers here at the lake."

"If I listen, my wrist will not be crushed?" Banner tried to sit up from his deathbed. The two women pushed him back and uncurled his fingers from Einstein's wrist. Nkosinathi told Banner to expound on his cosmological vision. She then pushed Einstein back away from the cot, warning him to remain silent with a scathing glare.

"The universe is peopled with innumerable blackholes. Collectively, they constitute a Godhead. He or she is the creator God who was once the original blackhole before the Big Bang, Ahura Mazda or Yahweh to use ancient names. Ahura Mazda seeks to end the universe's expansion, precipitating gravitational collapse and in due course another Big Bang. The blackholes are trying to draw together again, to reunite, dragging their galaxies along."

"Yes, yes, yes," Einstein's impatience was palpable, thick enough to cut with a knife. "The theory of gravitational collapse is well established. We call it the Big Crunch as opposed to the Big Chill. It is one theory of the universe's demise. The latest evidence favors the Big Chill, rather than the Big Crunch." The scientist stepped closer to the prone Banner, expounding on the unexceptional nature of the sick man's pronouncements, other than the ludicrous assertion that blackholes are sentient and Godlike.

Banner's hand shot out again, recapturing Albert's wrist. He squeezed powerfully as he said, "Ahura Mazda's designs are being foiled. The universe is *not* collapsing. It is *not*

326

readying itself for another cycle of rebirth. The expansion of the universe is accelerating. Opposed to the attractive force of the blackholes is a mysterious force called dark energy or antigravity."

"You lecture me on antigravity? I was the first theorist to describe this phenomena, decades ago. I called it the Cosmological Constant," Einstein hissed.

Banner relaxed his death grip. Einstein staggered backward, coming to a stop when Nkosinathi propped him up. The dying man said, "Gravity is the eternal flame animating the creator God, Ahura Mazda. He seeks an unending universe of expansion and collapse, perpetual life. Antigravity is the flame of Angra Mainyu, the destructive God. He seeks an ever expanding universe, thermal death, the permanent destruction of life in the frigid throes of absolute zero, a universe comprised of nothing more than disparate hydrogen atoms, light years apart from each other, always being pushed farther away by antigravity, for trillions of years, forever. Do not give ultimate destruction childish names like the Big Chill."

There was plenty of morphine in Banner's system. And yet he was not compromised by the spongy thoughts that the drug normally pressed into his mind. The visions that he'd been blessed with poured forth lucidly. "The two Gods fought directly ten billion years ago. There are vast interstellar voids, holes within galactic spiral arms, gaps in galaxy super clusters, artifacts of the Divine Wars. I imagine the voids will soon be observable with our best telescopes. Here is proof of what I am telling you. Look at these voids and study them once advanced technology returns to our planet."

Nkosinathi gasped, "Albert, he's on to something, don't deny it. We've puzzled over the voids, you and I, many times. Only the long gone telescopes on Mona Kea could detect them. There is no way that Banner could have known."

"It means nothing. Somehow he has learned of the anomalous deep space voids. The man does own a detective agency. There are countless explanations for the voids that don't personify natural forces. I believe in God, yes, but science cannot use religion as a crutch for that which we do not understand," Einstein said, with less passion than he'd displayed earlier, an element of doubt creeping into his voice. Since every Blue Force astronomer had died in the granddaddy detonation, it was unclear how even owning a detective agency would have helped Banner learn about the inexplicable holes in cosmic architecture.

Banner battered ahead remorselessly. "The Gods no longer fight directly, partly because their eternal fires dimmed during the millions of years of Divine Warfare and partly because those wars ended by mutual consent. This marked the end of Infinite Time and the inception of Finite Time, ushering in the birth of life and the reordering of natural law. In our age, the age of life, the two Gods fight through proxy armies, sentient space faring races. The goal of the destructive God is unending interstellar warfare, an adjunct to his repulsive power of antigravity which is successfully ripping the universe to shreds. Chaos and nihilism are his watchwords. And he is the stronger of the two as you have admitted."

The sick man paused to suck in ragged gasps of air, studying his audience once he could breathe more calmly. Einstein was no longer objecting to every sentence. Weighty thoughts appeared to be slowly ticking over in the great thinker's mind like an idling engine. Nkosinathi wore a like expression to Albert Einstein's. Lisa, who had heard all this many times, was worried that David was overdoing it, hastening his own demise by

327

overexertion.

"The creator God has a more challenging goal than his rival. He needs for one supremely militant space faring race to emerge triumphant, ending the eternal cosmic wars, uniting the warring races. The species that can do all this will be called the Messiah Race. The ultimate destiny of the Messiah Race and its countless allies will be to attack and destroy Angra Mainyu, thereby destroying antigravity, allowing the cycle of rebirth to begin anew."

Einstein took a step forward and grabbed one of Banner's wrists. Shaking it, the scientist looked down at the prone octogenarian and demanded, "Interstellar war implies faster than light travel. How is that possible? How can the destructive God be destroyed? If matter or energy cannot be created or destroyed, then how can a fundamental force like antigravity be destroyed?"

Banner returned Einstein's fierce stare and replied, "I don't know. It is your job to figure that out, or set other men and women on the course to do so." Einstein threw down Banner's wrist and stalked away disgustedly, back to where the women were standing. Banner took another pull on his whiskey/morphine concoction and asked Nkosinathi and Albert if they were ready to answer some of his questions. Albert sat on a campstool and waved at the invalid, instructing him to fire away.

"In what way could alien civilizations in distant star systems learn of mankind's existence? How long might this take? What would be their general impression?"

Einstein laughed without humor. "Mr. Banner, need I remind you that we have only a short time ago concluded a war whereupon approximately two hundred nuclear bombs were detonated, on both the surface of the Earth and in the near reaches of outer space?"

Banner throat was seizing up again. He looked at the professor helplessly, beseeching the scientist with his eyes to give a more complete answer. Still sitting on the stool, Einstein shrugged and continued: "The nearest star is four light years away, Proxima Centauri. If it has a planetary system with a civilization more advanced than ours, in one year their astronomers will observe the opening round of our nuclear war, and may grow concerned. There are dozens of stars within ten light years of Earth. The impression mankind will give is that of a lunatic race of bloodthirsty maniacs willing to lob nuclear weapons around our green and nubile planet for no good reason."

The manic energy that had been propelling Banner ebbed. The morphine took over and he fell asleep. Lisa had made a pot of tea during one of her husband's speeches. She poured cups for Albert and Nkosinathi. The latter scientist said wistfully, "David Banner's theology is a combination of modern physics and ancient Zoroastrianism; call it Zoro-Physics. Most Zoroastrians live in Bombay. Albert, do you fancy a junket to India? Therein resides the last component to our Grand Unified field Theory. Or as Mr. Banner might say, gravity is the eternal flame in Ahura Mazda's Temple of Fire." Even though she was smiling, it was clear that Nkosinathi was not joking.

Scowling and blowing into his teacup, Einstein said nothing, hoping that his silence would make the bewildering theological discourse go away. Instead, his intransigence only served to embolden Nkosinathi. "Mrs. Banner, your husband says that the two Gods ceased their war by mutual consent, ten billions years ago. This is when gravity became weaker than antigravity?"

Lisa nodded, adding, "That is what David and I believe. The Gods were on the verge of annihilating each other during the age of Divine Warfare. A bargain was struck. The fighting ceased. Ahura Mazda created life with the understanding that the destructive God would lose the power to interfere with the biological processes of evolution. At the same time, gravity was lessened while antigravity remained as strong as ever. In this way, the eternal war was put off until intelligent life could evolve and take up the battle." Lisa poured her guests more tea.

Nkosinathi sipped the scalding beverage and remarked, "What it boils down to is that the two Gods were greatly diminished. They can interfere very little in the workings of the universe." Lisa agreed wholeheartedly. David had been saying as much for years. Nkosinathi directed her next remark to Albert. "Mitnaggedim Jews, a movement that you and I subscribe to, Albert, believe that God has removed his essence from the universe."

"Let us discuss the scientific assertions that Mr. and Mrs. Banner are putting forth," Einstein shot back. "Ten billion years ago, gravity was equally balanced against antigravity, or so they claim, and then the repulsive force strengthened. It won't take long to build spaceships once the Queen holds the planet in her iron fist and advanced technology is restored. We will be able to find relatively pure nickel-iron asteroids that are ten billion years old. We will then be able to empirically test the Banner thesis! Until that time, there is nothing to talk about."

"Not quite true, my sweetheart," Nkosinathi deadpanned. "By all means, let us talk science, specifically galaxy formation models." Einstein grabbed his forehead as if he had been suddenly afflicted by a throbbing headache. "No, no, no. It's getting late," he mumbled. "We should wander to the mess tent and find something to eat."

"I want Lisa to hear this, then we eat," Nkosinathi said uncompromisingly. Einstein tugged on his wife's sleeve, almost whimpering in protest. The woman from Abyssinia became an immoveable object. She looked at Lisa and said, "Every galaxy formation model concurs: the gravitational clumping process occurred faster than it should have. Mind you, galaxies formed approximately ten billion years ago."

Lisa opened both hands and made a gesture of bewilderment. Nkosinathi embarked on an involved explanation, but Lisa stopped her, begging for the condensed version. Glancing back and forth between Albert and Lisa, Nkosinathi offered a laconic elucidation: "Gravity was stronger ten billion years ago. To find out why, my husband and I will be traveling to Bombay and studying the tenets of Zoroastrianism. In the meantime, let's eat."

Lisa picked up a lantern filled with gasoline, took a full minute to light the less than satisfactory fuel, and led the Einsteins out of the tent. Most of the conference attendees had already dined and were streaming back into the tent city. Fording upstream, Albert, Lisa, and Nkosinathi ran into Jim Pullman and Erevu. The chubby businessman asked the threesome if they wanted additional dining companions. Nkosinathi studied Albert's sour face in the feeble lantern light for an instant and nudged Lisa over to the newcomers, telling them that she and her husband needed to discuss theoretical physics and theology in private. The scientists then scurried away, disappearing a minute later into the nearly empty mess tent.

Walking at a more sedate pace in the same direction, Pullman opined, "Something sure as hell crawled up the butts of those eggheads." Erevu titled his head back, hooting in mirth.

"What an insensitive statement," Lisa scolded. "The Einsteins are undergoing a paradigm shift, to whit, the linkage of science and religion, very upsetting for professional scientists." Pullman raised a beefy hand and cracked his knuckles with a predatory flourish, asking if there was any money to be made in the fusion of science and religion. "Someday billions, maybe hundreds of billions," Lisa suggested.

"When is someday?"

"I'm guessing in two, maybe three hundred years."

"Sorry I asked. Seeing as how you brought up the subject of money, Lisa, you and your hubby cost me plenty today. Correction, cost all of us plenty today." Pullman went on to complain that he'd been forced to lobby the Queen all by his lonesome earlier in the day as the conference took up the subject of antitrust provisions in the new constitution. Pullman's idea of bestowing knighthood on future monopolists had gone down in flames. Erevu clucked sympathetically, patting Pullman on the back, throwing Lisa a dirty look.

"Mark my word," Pullman said, stabbing a finger at Lisa. "We're gonna be fighting the Queen's antitrust commission one year after we launch the Gorilla Football League. You and David fumbled the ball today." She would have defended herself, except they'd reached the mess tent and were lining up for the buffet. Lisa extinguished her lantern and set it down, gawking at the humongous indoor space. The pavilion had formerly seen duty as the home for a three-ring circus and was capable of seating seven hundred diners. Electric lights blazed from the canopy of the big top, another sign that technological civilization was remerging.

Albert and Nkosinathi were sitting in one corner of the big tent, heads bowed, nearly touching, engrossed in erudite conversation. Lisa, Pullman, and Erevu sat as far from the scientific couple as possible. They needed an entire table to themselves anyway, so there was room enough for Erevu's two heaping bushel-baskets of fruits and vegetables.

"What did Big D say about investing in the Gorilla Football League?" Pullman asked. It took Lisa a moment to figure out that "Big D" referred to David Banner. An upwelling of sadness swamped her mind. David was not long for this world. The decision to invest in Pullman's scheme would have to be her own. She asked for details.

Pullman rubbed his hands together and then stopped to wipe a squirt of fruit juice off his face, sitting next to a gobbling gorilla was a messy business. Erevu signed for Pullman to continue, as interested as Lisa in the pitch.

"I don't give two hoots about the Banner family fortune. I gotta raise billions, a few extra million won't mean diddlysquat. I need—" he smacked Erevu's granite-like shoulder "—we need Fred Greystone's granddaughter running the gorilla eugenics program. Victoria ain't allowing CMGs anymore. Football's gonna be the simian breed test for the next thousand years, until the balloon goes up and the little green chimpanzees attack from outer space."

"I know next to nothing about football," Lisa protested. Erevu stuck his tongue out and gave a Bronx cheer, his way of saying that knowledge of football was unimportant. Pullman agreed, asking Lisa what she knew about genetic engineering.

"Genetic engineering was in its infancy when the pulse hit. At that time, I was conversant in the basic principles."

"Gonna need to be more than conversant, Big L. You gotta become top dog in genetic engineering, pronto. Probably gonna have to go back to school and crack some books, break some test tubes."

Lisa emitted a squeak in remonstration, words failing her for the moment. Erevu signed, "Don't worry Big L, Bwana wants you as breed warden, the other silverbacks have given the green light, all good. Fred Greystone would be proud."

The talk of Fred Greystone made her think of David. Lately, her husband had seemed more and more like her departed grandfather. She couldn't contemplate a major decision without consulting her spouse. Lisa pushed away from the table and ran out of the tent without saying good-bye, barely taking the time to snatch up her cold lantern.

Without the lantern's light she stumbled through the dark tent city. The power brokers and king makers were bedded down for the night. Civilization had progressed only so far, row after row of tents were as dark as pitch. Hacksaw was dead. She didn't have the steady nose of a Bulldog to guide her home. Tears started to stream down her cheeks. An icy cold lump in her throat told her that something was wrong with David. A light smattering of rain dampened her hair, sending tiny rivulets down her face to mingle with her tears.

She found the correct tent and burst inside. The sense that something was wrong intensified. Setting the lantern down, fumbling around in the dark, Lisa thrust her hand under David's nose. He wasn't breathing. She felt for a pulse. There was none. She groped for the lantern and knocked it over, filling the tent with the stink of gasoline. Now she didn't dare strike a match.

The night boomed with thunder. Rain pelted the tent with a steady drum roll, a requiem for a prophet. She fell on his chest, crying harder. Her grandfather had lived one hundred years. David should have lived that long. His time had been cut short by a decade and a half. Chaotic thoughts warred inside her head. Her son was dead. Her grandfather was dead. Her husband was dead. Nothing made sense. The thunder boomed louder, like a Bulldog greeting his master. It barked again, like Hacksaw or Lockjaw, a joyful sound. She felt slightly better.

David had never renounced Christianity and he'd never explicitly stated as much, but she knew that he would want a Zoroastrian funeral ceremony. The ancient Persian traditions dictated immediate action on her part. The soul had left the body; what remained was corrupt and had to be returned to nature very quickly. She had to wash the body and put it in clean clothes within minutes. A dog must view the corpse and tell her that David was indeed dead. That had to happen yet tonight. An open-ended tower must be swiftly built in the morning, the body placed inside before noon, and exposed to the elements. Vultures must be permitted to devour the flesh. Luckily, the land around Lake Calaveras was a wilderness and the recent battle had glutted the area with hungry vultures more than willing to play a part in the memorial service.

The Queen and other dignitaries would balk at attending a Zoroastrian funeral. Churchill would get petulant and try to obstruct the endeavor. She could already hear Sir Winston whining about vultures and wrinkling his nose in disgust. Vladimir Bakunin had only yesterday been appointed Archbishop of Canterbury. His Holiness was probably overwhelmed by the conversion from the Russian Orthodox Church to the Church of England. Confronting him with this sort of religious radicalism might cause the primate to blow a gasket. It occurred to Lisa that she had a political fight on her hands if she were to do what David would have truly wanted. And she had no written instructions from him one way or the other to bolster the cause.

Erevu stuck his head in the tent and grunted an inquiry. Pullman's voice called out from the darkness, behind the silverback, "Yoo-hoo, everything okay in there?" Here were some strong souls to lean against. Lisa felt a sense of gratitude. She needed help to do what was right. Erevu and Pullman were the best possible allies to have on her side. For one thing, a united gorilla nation could do virtually anything it wanted. This was still the post-EMP world. If the gorillas wanted David Banner to have a Zoroastrian funeral and insisted that human luminaries attend, then that was pretty much all she wrote. Lisa called them inside and shared the devastating news as well as the political campaign that must be waged, starting tonight.

Erevu reached out to the distraught widow and made hand signs against her open palms: "In your religion, a dog must investigate the body and tell us that he is dead?" Lisa agreed that this was true. Erevu promised to bring a worthy Bulldog back to the tent and to contact Bwana, get the ball rolling on the funeral. Pullman promised to have a word with Churchill and Archbishop Vladimir Bakunin. The fat man clapped his hands together and stood to leave. Erevu padded silently behind Pullman.

Bwana's people had built their tent city on a bluff overlooking the much larger human tent city. The rains stopped a little after midnight that night. The sky was still mist shrouded, but stars peered out from under the misty cloak here and there. The younger gorillas took the opportunity to build a roaring campfire. Kubwa, Bwana, and Lisa Banner sat around the campfire, watching Erevu fabricate a scale model of the stone tower that would serve as the final resting place for David Banner's body.

Erevu was wrapping strands of wire around fist-sized rocks to bind the stones together. This was essentially how the gorillas had built defensive walls during their assault on San Jose, except instead of wire they'd used half inch thick steel rebar and the small rocks had been boulder-sized chunks of concrete. Placing the last stone into the miniature circular wall, Erevu signed, "There is a farmhouse over that hill. We will demolish it for building material and build a tower of silence for Big D's body at first light."

Lisa stifled a sob. Bwana put an arm around the widow and held her tight. Kubwa solemnly regarded the tiny structure that Erevu had built. A heavy silence descended on the four primates. The yapping of baby gorillas playing with Bulldogs floated over to their gathering from the hilltop tent city.

Erevu made hand gestures over the model, indicating where vultures would enter the structure to peck at the flesh within. He signed, "I will make sure this rim is suitable for the bird's to perch on. They can take turns that way and they will be safe from coyotes and wild dogs." Lisa made a series of hand signs. As the only human in the encampment, she felt good manners precluded the spoken word. She thanked Erevu, complementing his design, noting that it was likely better than the funeral towers in Bombay and Persia. The silverback purred in response.

Adult Bulldogs barked on the outskirts of the camp, chains rattling as they lunged at a stranger emerging from the dark. Shortly, a blackback gorilla, a young male on the verge of turning silver, escorted the Archbishop of Canterbury to the campfire. Bwana dismissed the blackback and made hand signs at the bishop. Lisa translated the signs into spoken English: "Welcome, Your Eminence, to our humble camp. To what do we owe the pleasure of your company?"

Bakunin bowed at Bwana. Straightening, his eyes fell on the miniature tower of silence. He said, "Ah, I see that the planning for the Zoroastrian funeral is well advanced. Your tower of silence is made of stone and iron, excellent. The ancient Persians considered these substances incorruptible. Your knowledge of Zoroastrian customs is impressive."

Erevu held his hands where Lisa could see them and signed while she translated: "We don't know very much about the ancient customs. The tower is built in the same way that we build military structures." Bwana patted a small boulder that was resting a comfortable distance from the fire. The Archbishop took a seat and remarked, "I take it that no one here has memorized any Zoroastrian funeral prayers?" Lisa and the gorillas shook their heads no. Bakunin glanced from one face to another like a disappointed Sunday school teacher. "How about Zoroastrian funeral attire?" Lisa cleared her throat and said hesitantly, "The clothing should be white, if I'm not mistaken. The best we'll be able to do is have the guests wear white armbands." Bakunin nodded and asked kindly, "Is that it? Is that the extent of your knowledge, Mrs. Banner?" Lisa swallowed and gave a curt bow in the priest's direction. She hadn't studied the ancient Persian religion the way her late husband had.

"I can understand why the gorilla nation is attracted to Zoroastrianism," Bakunin went on conversationally. "Dead gorillas are devoured by vultures in the wild. The ceremony must seem quite natural to the lot of you. Fourth generation simians, those proficient at reading, will be drawn to the oldest of man's monotheistic religions, the very first religion revealed to man through prophecy. The duality of good and evil, Heaven and Hell, resurrection after death, judgment day, and a Heaven-sent savior: all of these concepts come from Zoroastrianism. Judaism, Christianity, and Muhammadism are all children to this mother religion. I see a Zoroastrian ceremony in Yahweh's revelation to Moses through a burning bush." Simian heads went up and down enthusiastically. David Banner had told the gorillas that Zoroastrianism was the Rolls-Royce of religions, the one that would best suit gorillakind.

"As a communist, there are many aspects of Zoroastrianism that I too find appealing." Bakunin stood and walked to the model. "The bones of rich men and poor mingle inside these towers. No special memorials are permitted to the wealthy. There is equality in death. Perhaps the bones of gorillas and humans will so mingle someday. Once your funeral tower is built out here, Zoroastrianism will have a permanent presence in California. I suspect gorillas will build more towers. David Banner has a cult following among gorillas and humans alike; this hitherto obscure religion may rapidly gain devotees. Belief structures tend to flux and mutate in the aftermath of major wars."

The apes grunted appreciatively. Bwana hadn't thought it out as far as the archbishop. The dominant silverback now realized that by leading both humans and apes into a new religion, he might be amplifying his own power. He guessed that Bakunin wanted to do something along the same lines. By partnering, humanity's top religious figure and gorillakind's unchallenged leader could solidify each other's political power.

Silhouetted by the fire, Bakunin raised both arms to the heavens and said sternly, "Listen to a Zoroastrian funeral prayer: We follow the paths of the stars, the moon, the sun, and the endless light, moving around in their revolving circles forever. And truthfulness in thought, word, and deed will place the soul of the faithful one in the endless light of eternal light."

Lisa and the gorillas were held spellbound, dancing flames from the campfire reflecting in their shining eyes. Bakunin's voice lowered an octave. "Listen to a Judeo-Christian funeral prayer: The Lord is my shepherd. I shall not want. He will make me lie down in green pastures and lead me beside still waters. He will refresh my soul and guide me in right pathways for his name's sake. Though I walk through the valley of the shadow of death, I will fear no evil: for you are with me, your rod and staff comfort me…"

The priest finished the prayer, lowered his hands, and gave his little audience a sermon: "Zraya Vouru Kashem is a mystical ocean of energy placed by Ahura Mazda (or Yahweh) around life bearing planets at the end of the Divine Wars. This ocean of energy prevents Angra Mainyu (or Satan) from destroying green, living planets. Zoroastrianism is the religion of the universe, of the stars. Zoroaster means golden star. The three Magi that followed the star of Bethlehem to bear witness to the birth of Jesus were Zoroastrian priests. Thus, Zoroastrianism was the first religion to recognize Christianity…" Bakunin artfully wove a tapestry of Christian and Zoroastrian beliefs together into a single garment. When he was finished, the apes sat up and beat their chests admiringly. Lisa had tears in her eyes. Bwana formally asked the archbishop to preside over the funeral of David Banner.

Bakunin returned to his rock, regarded the eager gorillas and said, "Let's look at the big picture and then decide how David Banner's body should be dealt with." He paused, rubbed his face and continued: "The Commonwealth has concluded its civil war. When Rome's civil wars finally ended, the Pax Romano began. The year of our Lord, nineteen hundred and forty marks the true beginning of the Pax Britannica. The Roman Peace was characterized by a single state religion that peacefully absorbed the religions of all nations in the empire. Anglicanism must do the same. Judeo-Christian-Buddhist-Hindu-Muhammadan-Zoroastrianism: that is what the Church of England shall become. I need the gorilla nation to support my emerging polyglot church so that all sentients may be united in one state religion."

Lisa, Kubwa, and Erevu seemed to fade away into the darkness. Bakunin and Bwana sat in a pool of firelight, locking eyes. The silverback made hand signs. Lisa turned his words into spoken English, a voice from the wilderness. "A single state religion is a necessary step, not the only step needed to make certain the success of the Pax Britannica. Gorillakind and mankind need a common enemy to be united."

Bakunin pulled a pipe from his jacket pocket, stuffed it with tobacco from a pouch, and struck a match. California had gone many months without tobacco. The rapid return of industry and commerce was bringing back small comforts. The archbishop puffed a jet of smoke at a star and said, "The Roman Peace failed because the Romans thought that they'd conquered the world. All possible enemies were vanquished in their minds by the time Augusta took power. The empire stopped expanding and started to decay." He pointed his pipe at various stars dotting the night sky. "There are the barbarians that will try to storm our gates."

Lisa and the gorillas looked at the sky. The stars that had always twinkled so merrily took on a sinister gleam. Somewhere out there, alien minds would someday be plotting against mankind and gorillakind. Vladimir made his final pitch: "Religion must support the militarization of the entire planet. The Crown and the Church of England have run baiting contests for decades, producing Bulldogs and Wolfhounds for both sides in the last war. The Gorilla Football League must be bound with barbed wire to the church. We both need to keep an eye on the prize: the Apocalyptic War that is to come."

Chapter 26

George Patton Becomes Rudolph Diesel

The Gobi Desert offered up two survivors from the Second Division's Long March: George Patton and Sean O'Brien. Every other man, woman, dog, and bitch had perished under the lash of nuclear fallout, lack of water, starvation, howling sandstorms, running battles with Mongolian nomads, and a plethora of other hazards that the rocky desert cheerfully meted out to the Red Army division after the crippling worldwide electromagnetic pulse.

Month after month of marching and fighting across the trackless waste had caused Patton and Sean to lose track of time. As best they could reckon, the pulse had blasted down from outer space two years and some months ago. Back then, from out of the blue, hovercrafts slammed into grassy hills, jets fell from the sky, and combat suits became metal tombs, trapping communist soldiers into suffocating deaths. Second Division's mighty war machines had been racing ahead of the winds that they'd sown with nuclear death: fallout from atom bombs. In an instant, Patton's force had gone from the most technologically advanced army anywhere to a feeble group of ragtag fighters.

Hoisted on our own petard, Patton thought morosely, looking at a map showing the land between the desert cities of Mandalgovi and UlaanBaatar. Now was a bad time for self-recrimination. What had happened had happened. The nomad wars seemed to finally be over. And why not? The heathen bastards had won, wiped out the 2nd Division with a mind numbing thoroughness. The wind caught the map and whipped it against Patton's face, beating against a patchwork of scars he'd picked up in knife fights with the oriental savages. Sean grabbed the map by two corners. Patton got a better grip on the other two. Together they studied the shaded outlines of low-lying hills. Somewhere around here there was a road. It would take them to the industrial city, UlaanBaatar, and surrender.

The general folded up the map and stuffed it into his tattered robe. Both men dribbled water from goat stomach bags into their parched throats. They no longer feared an organized attack from Mongolian fighters. Why should the Mongolians attack? Two men did not constitute a fighting force and their appearance was far from intimidating. Bodies swathed in rags, covered in grime and dried sweat, stinking of smoke from camel dung fires, emaciated nearly to the point of death, they made nomad warriors look like British Royal Marines.

Sean wearily raised his hand and waved at a promising rift in the grassy plain. "I think the road is in that direction," he said through parched lips. The younger man looked at his rag bound boots, sighed, and walked, trying to lift his knees and not stumble. Patton fell in behind Sean. Every step they took brought them closer to UlaanBaatar and civilization; also closer to a war crimes trial. Patton thought that Sean would serve only a token sentence, maybe two or three years. The general was sure to swing from the end of a hangman's noose and then burn in Hell for millions of years. He'd conned Bakunin into nuking Washington DC by suppressing negotiations with Ford and Sloan. He'd ordered A-bomb strikes in Arizona and the Gobi. He'd spent every nuclear weapon that the Red Army had given him like a drunken sailor on shore leave, spilling an ocean of blood, contaminating half a continent. The Commonwealth would want vengeance. He shuddered inside the raggedy cloak and pulled it around his shoulders. The Limeys might have a hankering to torture old Blood and Guts before introducing him to the hangman. He pulled the cloak tighter, grimacing.

Even though he'd lost track of time, Patton could see that spring was in full bloom in the Gobi. Carpets of flowers covered the swales between hills. The frigid winter was a distant memory and the scorching inferno of summer was not yet upon them, the best time to trek across this blighted land.

Patton bumped into Sean. The sergeant held a hand to his ear and asked the older man what he heard. "Nothing," Patton replied.

"Not good, quiet as a graveyard out here. No birdsongs. No insects. Too quiet. A storm is brewing." Sean led them into one of the carpeted swales. He got busy with his trenching tool. Patton pulled out his own shovel and put his back into it. A silent electrical crackle charged the air. There was absolutely no wind. The sky was devoid of birds and the afternoon light carried a washed-out delicate quality, as if the firmament might break. The desert sneered at the laboring communists, daring them to survive.

The men were weak from malnourishment. The ground was rock hard. Their slit trench progressed slowly. The afternoon wore on and the sky darkened. Out on the horizon, sand clouds leaped from the dust colored grassland. The temperature dropped. And then it was on them. Darkness consumed desert and sky. Sand impregnated wind raked its talons on their rag-clad backs as they hunkered into the trench, listening to the Gobi's mocking laughter.

The storm raged throughout the night, throwing lightning bolts into the desolate tract, pelting their exposed backs with hailstones, greedy little cyclones tugging at their ragged clothing. To Patton, the gale symbolized the victorious Commonwealth. It could kill them at any time, but kept them alive for the same reason that a sadistic cat keeps a crippled mouse alive.

Morning spilled across the wind swept plain. Birds chirped gaily. Insects buzzed. It was hellishly cold. The storm was gone. They ate the last bits of smoked dog meat, the final gift of the Red Army's canine soldiers and the only thing that had kept the survivors from cannibalizing their fallen human comrades. Patton and Sean wouldn't live another week if they didn't find the road to UlaanBaatar and hitch a ride.

Half the equation was realized when they stumbled across a strip of hard beaten dirt track. Relatively fresh tire tracks on the road's dusty surface indicated that it had recently seen vehicular traffic. They began trudging north, Patton following behind Sean, trying to draw strength from the younger man. The general thought again about the military court that he was sure to face. It would almost certainly focus on his use of nuclear weapons, especially since he did have conventional forces at his disposal when he'd lobbed the nukes. He'd received permission for the A-bomb strike in Arizona from Red Army High Command; it could be construed as an order from up in the chain of command, which may or may not be an effective defense. Patton's multiple atomic strikes up and down the Gobi Desert had been done without authorization from Vladimir Bakunin or Rommel and he didn't dare claim otherwise. He and Sean may be the only survivors from the 2nd Division, but they assuredly weren't the only survivors from the Red Army. The other survivors would contradict any lies that Patton might spin. And then there were the communist purges he'd orchestrated with the Red Army secret police. Hundreds of radical communists had been killed without a trial. A war crimes tribunal would call that murder. Oh well, they could only kill him once.

He watched his feet rise and fall against the dusty road. The stitching in his boots had long since worn away. Strips of rag held leather siding and rubber heels together. He could see the red squish of blood seep between the seams with every step and mix with road dust into a pink paste.

Maybe, Patton thought, *the best defense is a good offense.* The Commonwealth had killed millions of innocents with their damn EMP, horrible deaths too. The Red Army technicians in the tunnel redoubt under the Pacific must have suffered more than Patton's A-bomb victims. The tunnel warrens must have become a sweltering Hades. The deaths would have been due to asphyxiation and being cooked alive. Great minds had died down there: Oppenheimer, Heisenberg, Porsche: mental giants that could have helped rebuild the world after the war.

Was that a good defense? He looked into the sky, searching for the image of his grandfather. The sky was cloudless today, his ancestral mentor never materialized out of the clear blue. Last night he should have looked into the storm for council from the grave; too late now. His gaze dropped back to his bleeding feet. Attacking the Commonwealth aggressively and throwing their own war crimes back in their face was sound, Patton decided. He'd turn the tables on the bastards once the tribunal convened. He'd go down swinging. He'd save his most blistering castigation for his final statement while standing on the hangman's gallows, where there would be reporters and cameramen.

The sun scaled the sky. The desert became hotter. The problem of reaching UlaanBaatar rather than dying in the wasteland of thirst or starvation reasserted itself. Patton's head dropped lower and lower. The fresh tire tracks no longer seemed like a hopeful sign. Goods flowed in and out of UlaanBaatar by way of railroad lines, not this crappy little road. There might be one truck traversing this dirt trail once a month and it looked like that one truck had come and gone recently. They didn't have supplies to last a full month.

Sean and Patton plodded over a hill and looked down into a valley. A hundred different kinds of wild flowers provided a burst of color. Heat waves shimmered off the road, giving the images ahead the aura of a mirage. Among the purple helmeted crocuses, a nomad encampment of round felt yurts dotted the valley floor. Goats, horses, and cattle grazed along the roadbed. Brown skinned children played among the hoofed beasts. Adult nomads, possibly members of a tribe that had decimated the 2nd Division, watched over the animals and children, cradling aged yet serviceable Lee-Enfield carbines. Cruel knives

337

projected from the sashes around their waists. Involuntarily, Patton's hand brushed across the mass of scars crosshatching his face, his fingers lingering on the butchered hunk of nose, which had once been a proudly protruding proboscis. *Yeah, but you should see the other guy's face, Grandpa.* The two Red Army survivors had no firearms. They did have knives. *Gramps always said, never bring a knife to a gunfight.*

They slid into a roadside ditch and wormed to a closer vantage point on their bellies. "We could hide out until the nomads move on, then pick through the camp garbage. There's marrow and gristle in the discarded bones," Sean suggested, his stomach growling at the thought of meat scraps. Patton was going to dismiss the suggestion out of hand when a cloud formation caught his eye. No, it was a contrail from a jet, a Commonwealth Colossus bomber. He tossed his head upward at the long thin column. Both men stared at the winking metallic jewel flying at the head of the contrail. They'd seen propeller driven planes in the last couple of months. This was the first time a jet had skimmed over the wasteland. Somewhere in the world-girding British Commonwealth, mankind had regained the wherewithal to manufacture superconducting wire and computer chips.

Patton pressed his hand against his ribcage. Bones protruded under the rags like the grate on a sewage drain. A week without food would likely kill them off, assuming they didn't die of thirst in the interim. The city was maybe three hundred miles away. The nomads might shoot them straight away. It would be better than succumbing to the desert. The general wearily climbed to his feet and tottered down the hill toward the nomad camp, Sean stumbling behind. Both of them raised their hands in surrender. Decades hence, historians would mark this as the true end to the nomad wars and the final chapter in World War II.

Cartridges clicked into the chambers of the nomads' carbines. Patton's knees buckled. Starvation was catching up to him. The general blacked out and flopped to the ground. He awoke to the sight of a beetle brown face, graven with deep character lines, the nomad chieftain. The man spoke English. Ever since the freaking Limeys had taken over the world at the turn of the century, every damn mud hut backwater village was stuffed with wogs that could speak English.

The chief's face asked, "Are you a communist soldier?" Behind the wrinkled face, Patton could see a black sky and stars. He smelled wood smoke and sizzling meat. The general wanted to say: *Fucking-A right I'm a communist and not a soldier, I'm a four star general.* He was barely able to nod his head. The chief wanted to know if the soldier was hungry. Patton wanted to rip the rags off his body and show the miserable little man the skeletal remains of what had once been an Olympic athlete. Instead, Patton grated, "Yes, we're hungry." The beetle brown face nodded sanguinely, asking one last question: "Do you repent for the evil your army has wreaked?" Patton wouldn't have capitulated if he hadn't seen the Colossus bomber soaring over the Gobi in all its technological glory. The prospect of a fully revitalized Commonwealth and the ludicrousness of two starving communists carrying on the fight alone forced his hand. He admitted that he and Sean were on their way to surrendering to the authorities in UlaanBaatar. The chief repeated his question, was the soldier sorry his army had killed so many Mongolians? The general gave a barely perceptible head nod. The chief thought that Patton was only a lowly soldier, maybe even a deserter, not a real fire breathing communist by any stretch. The brown face wreathed into a broad smile. Tension ebbed from the camp.

The nomads knew how to feed starving men. They didn't give them meat or vegetables. Goat's milk thinned with water was the first course. After Sean and Patton proved they could hold that down, porridge came next, and not very much. Next, minute slabs of hard cheese and more water.

Patton's eyes were glued shut the next morning. He had a hard time waking up. A second meal and a round of farewells found them back on the roadway with enough supplies to survive another few days. The hospitality of the nomads was decidedly meager. That they'd given anything at all indicated a mood change had descended on Asia, if not the Commonwealth as a whole. Rebuilding efforts must be proceeding at a breakneck pace across the globe.

Placing one bleeding foot in front of the other, the general reconsidered his strategy for dealing with the war crimes tribunal. The nomadic chieftain hadn't known that he was a high-ranking officer in the Red Army, saving Patton's own life and Sean's as well. *Who's to say that I'm not the mild mannered and harmless engineer, Rudolf Diesel?* Diesel had been twenty odd years older than Patton. But the general had aged at least that much in the Gobi. Patton had an engineering mind. The real Diesel had been fluent in German and French. Patton's language skills were good enough to pull off the charade if the questioning didn't get too hairy. The cosmetic surgery he'd undergone in nomadic knife fights could make his face belong to anybody. He ran the idea by Sean. The younger man agreed to help pull off the *maskrovka*. Now all they had to do was survive the journey to civilization.

A rickety old truck came shambling down the dusty lane on the third day after they'd left the nomad camp. Patton was all set to try out his new persona on the driver. The effort proved unnecessary. The trucker was a Buryat from upper Baikal and couldn't care less about war or politics. Also, he took one good whiff of the two survivors, eyed the body lice crawling across exposed skin, and jerked a thumb at the bed of the truck, where a load of hogs stood cheek to jowl.

Beyond humiliation, Sean and Patton struggled up the truck's tailgate and jostled for space inside the swine herd. Within seconds, the pigs were aggressively snuffling the sacks of dried cheese hidden in the folds of their garments.

"General P—ah, I mean Mr. Diesel, we best eat every scrap we've got or these porkers will take it out of our hides." Sean tried to make the command sound like a suggestion. Eating that much dried cheese forced the travelers to chug half their water. They had almost nothing left to ration. It was now imperative that the Buryat wheelman drive straight through to the big city.

The pigs must have also eaten a large meal not long ago. The manure layer covering the floorboards was rapidly growing thicker. By nightfall, Sean and Patton were standing ankle deep in pig excrement. Patton could see a silver lining to the enforced proximity of so many healthy swine: "I do believe our body lice are jumping ship. The hogs offer a better meal than our gristly and dried up carcasses." Sean scratched experimentally. It was too dark to see if the lice were scurrying off his body, trading one host for another. Still, he'd become an expert in body lice over the past two years and could tell that Patton might actually be on to something. Their fortunes were definitely looking up.

The pig truck pulled in front of UlaanBaatar General Hospital sometime that night. Orderlies helped the frail and stinking travelers into a delousing station. Patton's consciousness faded in and out while he was scrubbed, bandaged, and finally put in a bed with an intravenous drip where he slept like a dead man.

Upon awakening, Patton saw that he and Sean were in a room painted a predictable white. The tile floor was immaculate. It had a view overlooking the sprawling central

Asian metropolis. The room was suspiciously well appointed for two stragglers from the desert covered in pig shit and crawling with lice. Through a partially ajar door, he could see an armed guard. The hospital administration was obviously aware that the two patients were former communist fighters. The luxurious room must be the only one available that was truly secure. There was no way that anyone could know he was a Red Army general. Probably a phone call had been made to London. British military officials would be on their way to UlaanBaatar and would eventually determine their fate.

In the meantime, Sean and Patton needed to get back into condition. They ate high protein meals and pumped iron, under a supervised physical therapy regimen. They had both lost about fifty pounds wandering the Gobi and fighting nomads.

To Patton's delight, a TV was brought into their room so the two men could catch up on world events. Before handing over the remote, the orderly warned that the planet had undergone a radical transformation since the war's end. He used a word neither patient had heard before: future shock, a psychological malady that they might experience just by watching the news and witnessing the burgeoning pace of social and technological change. Patton impatiently snatched the remote control away from the timorous orderly and shooed him out of their private room. Wearing a greedy expression, he clicked the TV on and found an English language news channel out of Peking.

Prime Minister Dwight Eisenhower was addressing his constituency in the British Isles and British North America. Parliament had passed a bill requiring auto, truck, and motorcycle manufacturers to install heavy machineguns, guided missiles, and other pieces of military hardware on all passenger vehicles and commercial trucks sold in Greater Britain.

Sean and Patton were able to figure out that Greater Britain included what had once been the United States, Canada, and Mexico. The Commonwealth Congress was expected to pass the same bill in a few years, as soon as the less developed economies could stand the additional military burden. Naturally, there was nothing stopping wealthier Commonwealth citizens from buying militarized personal vehicles ahead of time. The Emperor Jimmu said that he expected Japan to voluntarily follow the British guidelines, law or no law.

Eisenhower gave the fine details of the new legislation. Motorcycles would carry only guided missiles, though bike riders would be required to sling assault rifles on their backs or in scabbards bolted to the bikes. Small cars would be equipped with guns and missiles. Cars weighing over six thousand pounds would sport an array of missiles, heavy machineguns with controls at each passenger station, and forcefields. Commercial trucks from class three on up would be even more heavily armed. The prime minister then gave the rationale behind the law. The light waves generated by the nuclear detonations from World War II were already reaching the nearest star system. Greater Britain and its Commonwealth allies must be prepared to fight off an interstellar invasion.

The news program ended. A sports program took its place. A panel of commentators analyzed an upcoming football game between the Peking Dragons and the Tokyo Ronin. Much of the analysis focused on the Peking quarterback, an exceptionally nimble silverback named Guma.

Sean and Patton sat up in bed. Prior to the war, gorilla football had been an obscure sport that nobody followed except wacky primatologists. Today, it appeared to be the number one sport on the planet. A sports commentator mentioned the salary that the star

Peking quarterback pulled down. The freaking monkey was making ten million pounds a year! Patton's head swam. Future shock was setting in.

The TV screen showed Guma climbing into a battery powered combat suit. The Chinese quarterback demonstrated outstanding bipedal mobility whether playing suited football or non-suited football, according to the panel of sports experts. Guma was shown lining up behind an offensive line encased in titanium alloy combat suits. The quarterback took the snap and drifted back into the pocket, moving as deftly on his hind legs as a human being, only quicker, with better balance. A metal clad linebacker broke through the offensive line and charged the bipedal quarterback, sprinting on all fours in typical gorilla fashion. Guma pirouetted around the charging linebacker like a matador and fired a rocket-like forward pass.

The TV screen flickered to another game. Guma was squatting behind the same center, ready to take the snap, except in this game the gorillas weren't wearing combat suits, or anything other than fur. Although their natural fur coats were stained team colors with vegetable dye. During this play, Guma bootlegged out of the pocket and ran behind a blocker. The blocker ran on all fours, but Guma was nearly as fast on two legs. What he lost in speed, he gained with his ability to straight-arm tacklers. He made ten yards and a first down.

Future shock dissipated as Patton devoured the sports show. He turned the volume down on the TV and said, "Sean, me lad, we've found our next careers. I'm going to be head coach of a GFL team and you'll be my assistant coach."

"Is that right, Rudolf?"

"Yessireebob, I'm qualified as a son of a bitch. I was captain of my West Point football team. I earned a gold medal in the Olympics."

"No you didn't."

"I sure as shit did."

"No, Rudolf Diesel did not attend West Point or compete in the Olympics."

"Oh, yeah, right. I never did those things. Anyway, We're going to coach a GFL team."

"Okay. Coach Diesel and Coach O'Brien, has a nice ring."

With their career paths decided, the erstwhile military men had only to wait for the war crimes tribunal to arrive from London and clear the path for gridiron glory. They spent the intervening weeks getting in shape and studying the GFL on the telly and through the sports page of the UlaanBaatar Daily.

Patton's hopes for a speedy resolution of the war crimes matter were dashed when he saw whom London had sent to interrogate them. General Kwa and an immensely wrinkled bloodhound strode into their room on the fourth week of their convalescence. The Zulu general stuck out his hand and said, "George Patton? I am Impi Kwa."

With his jaw hanging as open as a flytrap, Patton numbly shook hands. Laughing, Kwa showed the duo where the hospital room's hidden microphones were located and told them that the British Secret Service Bureau had agents on this particular hospital's staff, and virtually everywhere else for that matter. Britain had learned its lesson after World War I; the SSB would never get caught flatfooted again. Kwa shook hands with Sean and introduced the bloodhound, Loadstone, the best lie detector in the business.

The Zulu general spent the rest of that afternoon grilling Sean and Patton over their political beliefs and appetite for armed revolution. Loadstone's snuffling nostrils pressed into various body parts of the detainees as they spoke. The bloodhound sucked up their scents, comparing moods and attitudes the way a sommelier judged one bottle of wine against another. Unlike a Bulldog, he didn't simply bark at a falsehood. Loadstone displayed a nuanced repertoire of vocalization: ranging from soft whines to indicate simple nervousness to subtle growls when answers shaded the truth. Only occasionally would he burst forth with a loud woof. After the first series of question that dealt with the 2nd Division's A-bomb attacks, no further lying was possible, not in the face of such an obviously superior truth-seeking canine. And there was no reason to lie. The last thing either man wanted to do was join some nebulous underground and strike futile blows against an all-pervading Britain.

Kwa told them that he was a member of the Communist Party, which together with the Tories and Democrats formed a center-right administration in Westminster. The Republicans and Socialists represented the left-wing opposition. Kwa mapped out the post war political geography, but the detainees had already winkled most of the information from the media.

"Turning yourself into Rudolf Diesel and burying George Patton in the desert was a brilliant idea," Kwa said admiringly. "The government will not prosecute your war crimes. There are many British and Commonwealth citizens that will not be so forgiving. You wouldn't last two days out there as old Blood and Guts. George Patton is hated everywhere, vilified in history books and popular culture as a modern Genghis Khan." Kwa handed them each a fat money wad. "Don't blow this on hookers and drugs." The Zulu general grinned, teeth blindingly white against his ebony face.

Loadstone fell asleep, sensing that the need for truth-seeking had ended. Kwa had advice that would help them find employment in the GFL. Aniki Banner was the GFL's personnel director. She worked out of GFL world headquarters in San Jose. Aniki had a soft spot for Red Army veterans. She was actually awaiting an interview with the two survivors. Kwa had taken the liberty of arranging everything.

"Crap, Aniki knew George Patton quite well," Patton complained. "She didn't know Rudolf Diesel from Adam."

"Let me give you some more advice, Rudolf," Kwa said evenly. "Never mention George Patton again. He killed millions of people. Every man jack on the planet would thirst for revenge if he thought Blood and Guts still lived. I'm not kidding, soldier." He paused and looked hard at the two, taking their measure. Patton had a queasy sense that what was coming next would not be to his liking.

"The GFL is the only monopoly left and London has a hand in how it is run. We aren't talking about a sport or a recreational pastime. Gorilla football has replaced the Commonwealth Military Games as the primary means of building military capability. The GFL is shaping and forming a race of super warriors that will battle aliens in a post-EMP environment."

Kwa droned on about warfare immediately before and immediately after an electromagnetic pulse had laid waste to a planet's advanced technology. Patton grew angrier and more impatient as the Zulu general waxed poetic over the simians' knack for combat before and after the big whammy hit, nobody had fought longer in a post-EMP environment than Sean and Patton.

"Cut the crap, Kwa," Patton exploded. "Quit beating around the bush. I'm fixing to work my way into a coaching position in the GFL. Something about that sticks in your craw?"

"The SSB has commissioned studies proving that the best simian psychologists are highly educated Red Army veterans that have seen extremely hard fighting."

Patton's next explosion was positively volcanic: "What the fuck? I'm not working as a head-shrinker for overgrown chimps! My name isn't Dr. Simian Freud, for Christ's sake." Kwa warned Patton to never call a gorilla a chimpanzee. The first thing that he would learn in his new field is that gorillas hated chimpanzees. Kwa went on to explain that Patton would indeed work as a simian psychologist for the GFL and that it was one of the most prestigious professions in existence, highly paid as well.

"You've heard about future shock?" Kwa asked. Both Sean and Patton nodded silently. "It's bad enough for humans. Think about signing gorillas. For the last two million years they've lived without technology in the jungles of Africa. They've become millionaire sports heroes overnight and now they face the prospect of reshuffling their entire genetic code through genetic engineering. I call that future shock on steroids. Surviving the nomad wars in the Gobi provided unique training as a GFL psychologist."

"Whoa partner, slow down," Patton warned. "What in hell is genetic engineering?"

"Genetic engineering will occupy Rudolf Diesel and Sean O'Brien for the remainder of their professional lives as simian counselors."

Two teams, eleven gorillas on either side, all of them wearing power combat suits, knuckle-walked onto the lush green field. Four human refs, in black and white striped powered armor, followed the gorillas onto the gridiron. Two hundred yards long, eighty yards wide, and one hundred feet tall, the forcefield cube shimmered into existence once the players and referees were on the field, delineating the boundaries for the ground game. When it was first turned on, the forcefield obscured the activity on the turf, distorting the players and referees like a funhouse mirror, and crackling in a coruscating electrical display. In the bleachers, the fans' hair stood on end as static electricity fought to escape the stadium. An ozone stink filled the arena. Computer controls eventually tamed the pulsing and undulating surface of the cube-shaped forcefield. Crystalline clarity manifested itself, although a slight fishbowl-effect would not go away. The fans in the stadium and those watching at home could see the nose guard and center square off for the coin toss.

The San Jose Transistors had home field advantage here at Spartacus Park. The visiting team got to call the toss. The Peking Dragons' nose guard looked at the ref and signed, "Heads." The suited referee showed the coin to the Transistors' center. Kubwa turned it over and, grunting approval, handed it back. The human in the zebra suit threw the heavy gold coin straight up, into the ceiling forcefield. It hung there for a second. Beautiful blue sparks showered down on the players. The coin dropped at mid-field and sizzled against the green turf, sending smoky tendrils curling up into the forcefield cube.

The nose guard for the Dragons knuckle-walked to the smoking hot coin. The ref darted in front of the silverback, picked up the coin with his titanium gauntleted hand and shouted with an amplified voice, "Heads it is!" Microphones inside the forcefield picked up the ref's words and broadcast them throughout the stadium. The Transistors faithful shouted dismay with seventy thousand voices. The ballpark was only half full because this was a preseason game.

The regular players left the gridiron, the forcefield blinking off and on to allow them egress. The two specialty teams loped out onto the verdant surface. The crowd was now in a fine voice, a steady rumble permeating the arena.

The forcefield grew taller. The excellent clarity that it had achieved earlier gave way to funhouse mirror distortions again. It stabilized at one hundred yards tall, the required height during a kick-off. The Transistors' kicking team formed up twenty yards off the ball. Ten players dropped into three-point stances. The kicker stood upright, displaying superb two-legged balance. If not for his disproportionately long arms and torso, as well as his size and bulk, he could have been a suited human being. The head referee threw down a red flag and shouted, "Play ball." The Transistors sprinted down field, every gorilla on all fours except the kicker.

The bipedal kicker cracked his suit leg and connected with the aluminum football, servomotors and muscles working in harmony to shoot the metallic pigskin into the forcefield ceiling like a guided missile. It bounced off the ceiling in a spark filled explosion and plummeted into the receiving team, a screaming alloy eagle.

The Dragons' kick-return specialist was a butch female, one of those highly prized gorillas that could run nearly as fast on two legs as she could on all four. The Transistors streaked toward midfield at forty miles-per-hour, metal hands and feet throwing chunks of turf in their wake. The forcefield lowered to one hundred feet the instant the ground game broke out. The action was obscured for a fraction of a second by forcefield distortions. The distortions cleared in time for the crowd to see two Transistors throwing the bipedal butch female into a forcefield wall. Blue lightning sheeted across that side of the stadium. When the afterimages ceased dancing in the fans' eyes, they saw the Dragons' kick return specialist knocked flat, smoke curling up off her suit like a burned out log. With the help of a teammate, she staggered upright and slowly knuckle-walked off the field. Bipedal mobility only went so far, when a gorilla was hurt he or she walked on all fours. The crowd cheered even though the butch female was a member of the hated Peking Dragons. Her courage was unmistakable.

Sean and Patton sat in the nosebleed section of the stadium, munching hot dogs and enjoying the game. The wealthy simian psychologists could have afforded to sit in a private box, or in the lower seats, or they could have wrangled a field pass from the GFL. They did none of these things because the upper bleachers were empty during a preseason game, affording the opportunity to talk without any snoopy ears around.

Patton's radiophone rang. Doctor Lisa Banner was on the line, reminding him to not be late for their meeting with Bwana after the game. It was the third time she'd called him that day. Patton gave her a flowery reply and closed the circuit. Sean remarked that the widow Banner seemed to be sweet for "Rudolf Diesel." The ex-general winked and turned his attention back to the game.

On the next play, the Dragons fumbled and the Transistors recovered. The two psychologists set aside their hot dogs as Kubwa hiked the ball to Bwana. Neither shrink cared which team won the game. As GFL employees, they couldn't really root for an individual team. Their only concern today was that Bwana come through the game unscratched. They needed the dominant silverback in possession of all his faculties during the discussion with Lisa, where the future course of the simian nation's genetic identity would be steered.

Bwana didn't pick up any injuries in his first drive. He did march the ball toward the uprights convincingly. Like most quarterbacks, his bipedal mobility was excellent for about ten seconds. In the wild, silverbacks would stand toe-to-toe and pummel each other like human boxers for that length of time. They had a strong inclination to drop to all fours, using their jaws and grappling, if a fight lasted much longer.

While he didn't like to stand upright any longer than a typical silverback, Bwana was known for an extremely quick ball release. He could backpedal deep into the pocket, spot an open receiver, and throw a blistering spiral in seconds. His backfield did not have any coveted straight-arming bipedal runners. What he did have was conventional running backs with lightning speed, silverbacks that could do a lot of damage cradling the ball with one arm and running as a triped.

A long grueling season lay ahead of any preseason game. Bwana had no more desire to sustain an injury than his psychologist friends in the nosebleed section. The purpose of this game was to work on timing and execution, prepare for the real season. He didn't even care if the Transistors won or lost. Bwana's strategy to remain injury free bore fruit until late in the fourth quarter. He'd kept away from the forcefield walls throughout the game, avoiding them like the plague, even if it cost him a few sacks. The fans didn't care as long as the Transistors retained their lead, which they did, until late in the fourth. The fans started booing when the Transistors fell behind with five minutes on the clock. Beer cans followed the boos, raining down on the forcefield and stirring the stadium police into action.

Stupidly, Bwana let the jeering fans get to him. In an attempt to spectacularly advance the ball all the way into the end zone and even the score, he ran along the sidelines on a broken play. Two Dragons thought of that long grueling season that stretched into the fall and winter and decided that it would be less arduous if the Transistors lost their star quarterback to injury early on. They ran Bwana into the forcefield and illegally held him there for thirty seconds, sending one hundred thousand volts zapping through his suit and into his body. The two Dragons sucked up a fair amount of voltage themselves, willingly absorbing a strong electrical discharge to fry the Transistors' quarterback, a selfless act done for the good of their team.

The simian players wore battery powered titanium suits that were poorly insulated against energy fields, based on archaic Red Army designs. The human referees wore ultra-advanced, well insulated, fission powered, graphite carbon and plasteel suits, giving them much greater strength than the gorillas, although still a far cry from the legendary Mark VII suits that had seen action in World War II. Earth's technological base had risen a long way from the ashes of the great conflagration, but it was still not capable of producing fusion powered, crystal iron super suits. Maybe if they had fusion powered suits, the refs would have had an easy time tearing the Dragons off Bwana and extricating him from the arcing and spitting forcefield. With only fission strength, the job was a ball-buster.

Patton and Sean exchanged horrified looks. The Transistors' QB was hauled off the field in an ambulance. The shrinks had been laying the groundwork for the upcoming meeting for months. They'd never be able to corral Bwana and make him sit still for a lengthy meeting once the real season began. Sean got on the radiophone and rang up Lisa Banner, asking her if she'd seen the play that took out the big kahuna. She had, but told the shrinks to swing by her office after the game regardless. Bwana had an unusually high tolerance for electrical and thermal shock.

"I know he's tough, Doc," Sean said worriedly. "It's just that I can practically smell burnt gorilla meat up here in the nosebleed seats." Out on the gridiron, the Dragons were assigned a thirty-yard penalty and earned the ball on downs. Both teams trotted out second-string players. Patton slapped his partner's thigh and said, "Let's go downstairs and meet up with the Doc." Minutes later, they were sitting in Lisa Banner's ground floor office, waiting for Bwana to either show up or send word that he was too injured to attend the conference that would largely determine the fate of his people for the next hundred years.

Bored, Sean pulled out a pack of smokes and lit up. Lisa startled him by walking around her desk and snatching the burning cancer stick from his mouth. "This is why you've no girlfriend, Sean, isn't it? Women don't like to kiss an ashtray, now do they?" She asked scornfully. Sean sputtered in discomfiture: "No girlfriend? What happened to stop smoking 'cause of cancer?" Lisa violently flung the ciggie in the trash and retorted, "Men don't fear cancer. They fear not getting laid. And I've found the root cause for your celibacy." Patton laughed and said, "Nah, that's not it, Doc. Sean can't hold a girlfriend because he lasts about thirty seconds and words got out on the street." The younger man's face blushed crimson right down to the roots of his hair. With mock sincerity, Lisa transformed into a concerned medical professional and said, "Sean, is this true? There are numerous medical treatments for premature ejaculation. The GFL health plan covers a variety of medications and procedures."

Sean was spared the agony of a reply when Bwana rapped on the office door, let himself in, knuckle-walked slowly to a reinforced gorilla-sized chair, and sat down gingerly. His fur was singed all the way to the skin. A lingering scorched-hair smell followed the silverback into the room, which the humans didn't dare comment on. Patton looked briefly into Bwana's face. The quarterback's eyes were bright, alert, unclouded with pain. He wouldn't have any problems making major decisions. Doc Banner was right: Bwana *was* a tough SOB.

Lisa wheeled a clunky old film projector out of a closet. Facing it toward a white wall that she routinely used as a movie screen, she asked Sean to turn the room lights off and flicked the projector on. An animated film plastered a series of double helix molecule complexes on the white wall: DNA. A long chain myostatin protein strand floated across the images of DNA and back again like a slow moving tennis ball.

Lisa narrated: "What you are seeing is artificially mutated exon two positions on the gorilla genome, modified DNA that blocks the production of the myostatin protein family, a protein group that inhibits muscle growth." The animated myostatin strand popped like a bubble. The DNA double helixes jiggled up and down. The sound track had them laughing, as though myostatin proteins were their enemy and they took pleasure in destroying them.

The hand drawn chemical compounds gave way to a pair of cartoon Bulldogs. One was noticeably more muscular than the other. Though animated, the dogs were drawn realistically. Lisa's narration continued: "The Bulldog on the right has been genetically engineered with myostatin inhibiting DNA. He is three times as strong and nearly twice as quick as a non-engineered dog from the same litter. His musculature is not only more bulky it contains a greater percentage of fast twitch muscle fibers. Unfortunately, he has considerably less endurance. There is no free lunch."

A stylized thermometer appeared between the two dogs. It went from 75 degrees to 100 degrees. The genetically engineered Bulldog went slick with sweat, lathering like a horse. Both dogs panted aggressively, tongues lolling from their mouths, dripping saliva.

"The endurance problem is partially mitigated by genetically engineering eccrine sweat glands into the canine genome. For dogs, we used sweat glands from very small ponies. Gorillas already have sweat glands, though not enough. It is easier, nevertheless, to engineer sweat potential into apes than into dogs. But I'm getting ahead of myself."

The sweaty, muscular Bulldog lay on her side and had a litter of puppies. One of the puppies grew to adulthood in seconds and had another litter. Lisa said, "We are on our third generation of Myostatin Inhibited Sweat-gland Enhanced Bulldogs. We use the acronym MISE as shorthand. MISE dogs breed true without any further GE interference. What is more, traditional selective breeding practices rapidly improve the MISE modifications."

The original muscular Bulldog and the normally built Bulldog reappeared. Nineteen twenty CMG style war harnesses with machineguns popped onto their backs. It was apparent at a glance that the MISE Bulldog sported a 50 caliber machinegun, while her non-engineered counterpart carried only a measly 25 caliber light machinegun.

The cartoon Bulldogs trotted into an obstacle course and challenged each other to a race. Despite the extra weight of the heavy machinegun, the MISE dog could jump higher and run faster than the non-engineered dog.

"If the course were twenty miles long, the non-engineered dog would win," Lisa admitted. "The MISE dog also needs more food and water, difficult to supply under combat conditions. We've added one more GE mutation to the MISE package, that should prove immensely beneficial in war dogs and combat apes."

The cartoon Bulldogs vanished. A panorama of the Rocky Mountains stretched across the white wall. This was an actual photographic film sequence, not a cartoon. The camera zoomed in on a particularly rugged mountainous ravine. Two Rocky Mountain big horn sheep bucks were squaring off for combat. Front hooves raised, back legs driving, the bucks collided, sending a resounding crack echoing across the stone canyon. Fiery-eyed and undaunted, the bucks backed away from each other, ready to joust again, completely unharmed by the intense blows to their skulls.

The film returned to an animated format. A cross section of a big horn sheep skull showed its unique double-skull configuration. Arrows highlighted the spongy, shock-absorbing flesh between the two interlocking skulls. A graphic depiction of ten DNA strands was superimposed onto the double-skull cross section, representing the genes responsible for the big horn sheep's unusual cranium. Lisa kept silent, letting the graphic speak for itself.

The animated graphic gave way to a real life view of a maximum-security prison yard. Pressed against a corner of the thirty-foot high, razor wire tipped cyclone fence were five desperate looking inmates in orange jump suits. Against the other fence corner, a guard held a leashed Bulldog, snarling and snapping eagerly at the convicts.

"This is the only MISE Bulldog to have successfully accepted the double-skull mutation." The camera offered a close-up of the snarling dog. Bwana, Sean, and Patton leaned forward in their chairs. The dog's head was bigger than normal, but his freakishly heavy musculature brought head and body into harmonious proportion. More conspicuous than his head size was the feral blaze in the dog's eyes. He was looking forward to being turned loose on the inmates.

"The prisoners in this yard are death row inmates, primarily child molesters, given to my laboratory by royal edict," Lisa said woodenly. Bwana raised his hands and signed,

"Humans have a ways to go until they evolve as far as gorillas." Ever since being integrated into human society, there had yet to be a single case of unprovoked simian violence, let alone child molestation. Gorillas were able to reserve all vicious impulses for the gridiron. The only crime any gorilla had been convicted of to date was tax evasion. Lisa cleared her throat: "Ahem, I quite agree. Regardless, watch how quickly the double-skull MISE Bulldog dispatches this human scum."

As was customary when facing a canine execution, the convicts were thrown freshly sharpened commando knives. Sprinting at cheetah-speed, the genetically engineered dog flew across the yard. The knot of prisoners broke up, moving away from each other. Each prisoner tried to protect himself from the canine missile by throwing one arm over his throat and holding the knife out with the other arm. The dog connected with the closest inmate, head butting the man in the small of the back. The prisoner's back broke and twisted into an impossible pretzel-like angle.

Lisa uttered the dog's name reverently: "Wrecking Ball." He lived up to his name, pulping the death row denizens with head butts to the solar plexus or back. Blink and you would have missed it. He killed the prisoners without delivering a single bite.

Wrecking Ball stood sweating and panting with his tail wagging over five broken-doll forms. His handler threw him a meat slab and brought out a water bucket. The dog drank as though his life depended on taking in moisture. Once the bucket was dry, he slurped up the water he'd spilled on the ground and looked up for more. A camel he was not. Sweat dripped off his body.

"The average time that a well trained, non-engineered Bulldog needs to kill an armed death row inmate is three minutes. Wrecking Ball averages three seconds." Lisa looked at her audience and turned off the projector. Bwana was definitely shaking off the effects of his recent electrocution. He signed, "I want a genetically engineered Bulldog for my kids. Name a price. I will pay double. No triple. How much is a pregnant bitch?"

Lisa was taken aback. She couldn't sell any MISE Bulldogs. She also couldn't offend the dominant silverback, leader of the gorilla nation. She turned on the room lights, and looked pleadingly at Patton. The ex-general saved the day by saying, "I'm sure Dr. Banner will give the dominant silverback a double-skull MISE puppy for free, the moment the breeding program has a surplus. Probably a year or two away."

"Absolutely," Lisa bounced back, recovering her composure and trying to regain control of the conference. "The last part of my film shows the eleven MISE gorilla children that we've created thus far playing peewee football against non-engineered simians." Her speech stumbled to a halt. Lisa was befuddled by her own words. "Ah. We haven't created the MISE gorilla children, now have we? Of course not, God created them. What I meant to say is—"

"Lisa," Patton snapped. "I'm sure God is not personally offended by a slip of the tongue. Please cut to the chase." She drummed her fingers nervously on the film projector case and stammered nervously: "Right, cut to the chase. God is not offended. Right. The gorillas in the film are four years old. Among the engineered children, ten are straight MISE. One is MISE and double-skull. It goes without saying that gorillas that young cannot reproduce. Nevertheless, an extensive battery of tests indicates that they will breed true. We have an extensive database on MISE Bulldogs to fall back on and—"

"Doctor Banner," Patton cut her off again. "We are willing to stipulate that the MISE gorilla kids are as fertile as rabbits. Show us the film. *Please*."

"Quite right, Mr. Diesel. The close-cropped gorillas are MISE. The shaggy ones are non-engineered. The shorn male with the unusually large head is the lone double-skull MISE. He plays center, by the way, the same position as his father, Kubwa, starting center for our own San Jose Transistors." Patton and Bwana growled impatiently at the same time, sounding remarkably alike. The projector was hastily turned on. The room lights dosed.

A peewee game splashed across the white wall. The gorilla children were not wearing power suits or uniforms. In peewee football, whether human or simian, power suits are never worn, with this exception: in gorilla peewee ball, human referees must wear PCSs. Not only are juvenile simians much stronger than adult humans, under the stress of a questionable call, a young gorilla will sometimes accidentally administer a nasty bite to a human ref, possibly clipping off a finger or worse.

The eleven gorilla children with buzz cuts galloped into an offensive formation. On the other side of the ball, eleven shaggy kids assumed defense. Even with the additional layer provided by thick furry coats, the defensive players were much less bulky than the MISE children.

Lisa had, of course, seen the film many times. She knew exactly how easily the MISE kids would bat around their non-engineered cousins. Instead of watching the game, she watched Patton, Bwana, and Sean. As the game progressed and the score grew more lopsided, the men and the silverback expressed shock, then admiration, and finally calculation.

The wheels were turning especially fast in Patton's head. Toward the game's end, a play ended on a penalty that was clearly a bad call. The center, Kubwa's enhanced son with the double-skull, grabbed the head ref by the titanium shoulders of his power suit, pulled him down and head butted him. While the metallic suit didn't suffer a scratch, the man inside was knocked cold.

Bwana pumped the air with a fist, hooting in delight and amazement. Lisa smiled. Incongruously, Patton and Sean looked as though their best friend had just died. The film ended with the black and white power suited referee leaving the field on a stretcher. Lisa's smile faded as she watched the two shrinks grow morose and melancholy. She scratched her head in puzzlement.

"Doc," Sean drawled. "How long's it gonna be 'til the entire gorilla nation's double-skull MISE?" Lisa's waning smile graduated into a full-fledged frown. Wondering why an obscure and technical question like that was so important, she answered: "Many decades, maybe a century, maybe longer. We must breed these eleven MISE children and study the subsequent generations. Then we can think about expanding genetic engineering mutations into the entire gorilla nation."

The men and the silverback presented a palpable wall of disapproval. Lisa was catching the gist of their disagreement even before Sean asked, "How's that gonna work, Doc? Let's say there's one million gorillas playing for the GFL and one thousand have superpowers, can pert near walk on water like Buddha-Christ. Figure there'll be any psychological implications for the apes can't walk on water?"

Patton, Bwana, and Sean glared at the genetic engineer irritably and yet expectantly, as if she were actually expected to provide an answer. This was not her field of expertise. She dealt with DNA, not politics or simian psychology. It was tempting to fire back with: *How is it going to work? You tell me, Sean. That's your job isn't it?* She resisted the temptation and said confidently, "Each GFL team will be allowed one and only one double-skull MISE player." The three males looked more disgusted than ever. Lisa took another swing: "MISE gorillas could be disallowed from the game." The instant the words left her mouth, she wanted them back. Even an amateur simian shrink could see that would never work.

Bwana roared in anger. He thumped his fists on the reinforced armrests of the gorilla-sized chair, rattling the hinges on the office door, sending the humans' teeth chattering. Patton stood and walked around behind the silverback. The ex-general massaged the quarterback's steel cable neck muscles. The pounding fists grew silent. The world's foremost simian head-shrinker crooned, "Don't worry, big guy. Sean'll drive you home. I'll talk Doc Banner into doing the right thing. The very next generation of signing gorillas will be engineered out the kazoo. She's putty in my hands." Bwana purred like a five hundred pound cat, completely confident in Patton's knack for manipulating people.

The "putty in my hands" comment was too much for Lisa. "Rudolf Diesel," she exploded, "you know nothing about genetic engineering or primatology, now do you? The intelligence gains in signing gorillas have come without any increase in brain size. Up till now, succeeding gorilla generations have evolved more efficient brains rather than larger brains, quality over quantity. That can't last, or can it? The double-skull mutation will limit brain size increase. Can we continue increasing intelligence without increasing brain size? We must answer this question prior to introducing mass genetic engineering."

Bwana signed, "No problem, Doc. Bigger bodies not bigger brains; works for me. We keep getting smarter and smarter. If it's not broke, don't fix it." Lisa turned her ire on the dominant silverback like a laser beam. "Pardon me, exalted leader of the gorilla nation," she said, her voice loaded with sarcasm. "While you may be a genius at running the down and out, I don't see your PhD in hard science."

Patton's fingers dug powerfully into Bwana's neck. He stopped the massage and smacked the silverback. "Don't argue with the Doc, big guy. Sean will drive you back to your ranch. Play with your troop and your mammoths. Get some rest until the next practice. Leave the lady to me."

Bwana heaved out of the chair and onto his hands and feet. Knuckle-walking out of the room, he squeezed through the human-sized doorway, casting an evil glance at Lisa. Sean hurried behind the silverback, closing the door, leaving Patton alone with the angry genetic engineer.

"Putty in my hands?" Lisa asked in a dangerously low voice. Patton smiled sheepishly, shrugged and said, "Silverbacks are the ultimate chauvinists. They can't take women or female gorillas seriously. I only said that to get rid of Bwana, so you and I can hammer out a compromise." He held up his hands to forestall her reply, a gesture that reminded her of David Banner. Patton said, "Let's go get an early dinner. A new Cuban restaurant opened downtown. Nothing important should be decided on an empty stomach." Lisa softened even further. Her late husband always wanted to eat before making a big decision. *Rudolf is so much like David*, she thought.

"You've an empty stomach, do you?" Lisa demanded. "Haven't you been stuffing your face all day with hot dogs?" Patton patted his stomach and replied, "I'm a growing boy."

The restaurant, *Little Havana*, had a private booth waiting for the couple. Patton wondered if any of the employees were SSB spies and if their table was bugged. He'd been catching subtle clues that the global spy agency was keeping tabs on him. Shaking off his suspicions, he pulled a magazine out of the case he'd brought and set it next to Lisa's water glass.

Picking up the magazine, she leafed through it absently. The publication was entitled *Gorilla Monthly*. The publisher had a policy disallowing human readers. *Gorilla Monthly* was not sold in newsstands or delivered to libraries. Very few humans had even seen the rag. Lisa admitted that she had only heard of the magazine and had never even seen it before. She leafed through the copy without really focusing on the content. The budding simian cultural revolution wasn't on her personal radar screen, not yet at least.

"What does this have to do with genetic engineering?" She asked, placing the magazine back on the table. Patton picked up the copy. He was going to answer her question when the quarterback for the Peking Dragons walked upright into the restaurant. Patrons immediately surged around the superstar, holding pencils, pens, and anything made of paper, a mad scramble to get Guma's autograph. The bipedal silverback grabbed the pens and papers and scribbled away until management rescued him, leading him upstairs to a section reserved for simians. The eatery descended into a mildly excited hum. They were all Transistor fans, but the quarterback from China was the kind of star that transcended team loyalty.

The ex-general looked down at the magazine in his hands. Guma's beaming mug was on the front cover under the caption: "Superbowl bound?" Patton tapped the image and said smugly, "This is the rebuttal for the argument you're on the verge of making, Doc."

A waiter arrived to take their order. The man looked familiar. Patton caught that feeling again, that he was being spied upon. Consciously shrugging it off for the second time, he ordered for the two of them. Lisa began fidgeting. She wanted to defend her position on slow-walking the spread of genetic engineering into the greater gorilla population. Small talk proved an effective stalling tactic, forestalling the verbal fireworks until after the food arrived. Patton wasn't kidding about refusing to argue if either one of them had an empty stomach.

Once the dinner had been consumed, there was no stopping the Doc Banner juggernaut. Lisa complimented Patton on his instinct to take the discussion away from Bwana's ears, if only temporarily. She glanced up the stairwell on the other side of the main dining room. Making sure that Guma, the silverback dining upstairs, wasn't coming down and moving within earshot. Gorillas had much better hearing than humans and he would be able to eavesdrop even on top of the stairwell.

"The problem is," she whispered breathlessly, "for every healthy genetically engineered gorilla birth, there will be two that either die stillborn or have serious defects." Lisa doubted that simian mothers could accept the anguish of sending that many babies into the funeral towers to serve as vulture fodder. Human mothers certainly could not, one of the impediments to homo sapien genetic engineering. In her opinion, the best way to proceed was to create a small group of MISE gorillas and expand their numbers slowly by natural breeding. Short of that cautious approach, new technology would have to be developed to increase simian infant mortality. Either approach would take many decades.

The SSB spy waiter brought the after diner coffees, bowed and backed away. The coffee cups could have bugs. Patton was momentarily distracted, not sure if there was any reason why the powers-that-be in London shouldn't hear this conversation. He shrugged. Solving the question of expanding the number of genetically engineered gorillas was not subversive. It was, in fact, a patriotic endeavor. What's more, he might be on the cusp of a breakthrough because Lisa was sharing her true objection, the fountainhead of her reservations against mass-producing simian superheroes.

He handed her the copy of *Gorilla Monthly* and asked if she would please turn to page thirty-nine. She complied and read an advertisement that promised to deliver, overnight, the most powerful and cunning pythons into the sylvan playground of any gorilla household for the rock bottom price of only five thousand pounds. For that price, the buyer was guaranteed a snake that would try to kill his progeny.

Lisa pushed the magazine away in revulsion, asking, "Why would adult gorillas place savage constricting snakes in the jungles where their children play?" Patton retrieved his magazine and flipped to another advertisement. He read it out loud to Lisa. This ad promised to deliver adult leopards to those same leafy simian playgrounds. The big cats were cloned from proven killers and painstakingly trained on wild chimpanzees, guaranteed to reproduce the same environmental pressures that gorillas had once faced in the wilds of Africa.

"Give me that thing," Lisa snarled. She snatched the magazine away from Patton and leafed through it maniacally, stopping to carefully read every advertisement for predators, lingering over photos of young gorillas bashing the life out of pythons. Her outraged expression gave way to a softer countenance. "Leopards and pythons will solve a number of problems," she murmured, glancing up at Patton guiltily. "I do have concerns that the MISE and double-skull mutations might have a subtle effect on reflexes, balance, a number of motor functions. A brutal and merciless performance test early on, where the young gorilla is fighting to survive..." Her voice trailed off uncertainly, ashamedly. Her unfocused eyes darted around the restaurant, fingers drumming the table.

Patton reached over to her drumming hand and held it. She didn't pull away. She stared at him out of eyes that held the look of a mariner lost at sea. "There's never been a more interesting subject matter than simian psychology," Patton said wistfully. "Gorillas are people. They can vote, hold office, own land, sign contracts. And yet these hirsute people are not human. They are stronger than us. I don't mean physically. They are *mentally* stronger, much stronger. Simian mothers will not be adverse to a high infant mortality rate once we introduce the GE mutations to the entire gorilla nation." He paused, waited for the lost-mariner look to go away and continued: "Lisa, tell me about genetic engineering verse selective breeding."

She started talking. She did not pull her hand out of his. Lisa asserted that genetic engineering was only the handmaiden to selective breeding. Splicing genes will prove to be the easy part. The hard work will be the patient decades of sifting through breed candidates, weighing the results of performance tests generated by football, academics, creative achievements, military exercises, and yes, encounters with natural enemies like leopards.

Patton reached out with his other hand. She responded by placing both hands in his. "We don't know when the aliens will attack," Patton said softly. "We can't afford to waste centuries introducing three mutations in the general simian population. Forget the adverse political and psychological ramifications. There isn't time. You said that the MISE gorillas will lack endurance, I'm sure there is a GE solution to that problem, a solution that won't wait hundreds of years for implementation."

"Have you ever wondered how an eighty-ton sauropod could gallop, let alone move on dry land?" Lisa's eyes were shining now, reflecting her most cherished dream. Patton's face screwed up with ignorance. "What in hell is a sauropod? Nothing weighing eighty tons is gonna gallop."

"Come now, Rudolf, you are a scientist, are you not? Once upon a time there were dinosaurs that could run forty miles-per-hour and they weighed up to eighty tons. They could do this because they had ten different hearts, positioned in different parts of their bodies. I would like to engineer gorillas and Bulldogs with two hearts and mammoths with five."

"Wouldn't it be wonderful to achieve that milestone in both our lifetimes?"

"Hmm. Interesting, *both* our lifetimes? There isn't a mouse in your pocket, is there, Rudolf?"

Chapter 27

Asteroid Spaceships Ten Miles Long: A New Form of Life?

Throughout Greater Britain, Switzerland, and the Commonwealth it is a woman's curse to outlive her man, on average, by five years. Compared to other widows, Nkosinathi Einstein and Jan Churchill were doubly cursed, because they'd married men so much older than themselves. Now that their husbands were gone, and the two widows were only middle-aged, there was no doubt that their personal "widow gap" would eventually be measured in decades rather than years. Jan could count herself blessed in one respect, she had a way to escape the earthly confines and misery of widowhood. The Commonwealth Aero Space Association (CASA) had selected her as an astronaut.

CASA hungered to employ Nkosinathi as well. It wanted Albert Einstein's widow to head up the Aeronautical Engineering Bureau. Nkosinathi wanted none of that. She'd made the insane demand that not only must she be admitted to the astronaut-training program; her nine-year-old son must also be enrolled. If it had been anyone else, the CASA officers would have contacted the Mental Health Bureau. Because she was who she was, the space agency had dutifully permitted Nkosinathi to complete the training regimen. She'd failed every physical challenge while the academic aspects of the program were so elementary that they were beneath her consideration and she had to refrain from correcting minor discrepancies in the curriculum. A handful of other candidates had done worse on the physical challenges, but there was no denying that she would never fly in outer space unless political strings were pulled. The widow of the great scientist needed help from the widow of the great politician.

On her drive to Jan's London flat, Nkosinathi had a change of heart. She was going to stick to her beliefs and get Albert junior involved in space flight. Furthermore, she wasn't going to seek a single exception based on the political strings at her disposal. CASA needed a complete reorientation from top to bottom. There was no reason for space exploration to be so dangerous that only elite Uberman athletes with superhuman eye-hand coordination could pilot spaceships and conduct extravehicular exercises. Robots should perform all dangerous jobs. Actually, 99 percent of space work should be robotic. Aerospace technology should be so safe that nine-year-old children could participate in missions. Buddha-Christ, Albert junior should be leading space missions if anyone were looking ahead to the future.

She turned off the street leading to Jan's apartment building and set off for Albert's school for mentally gifted children. Walking down the corridor leading to Albert's classroom, she spied a familiar sight: her boy sitting in a desk outside in the hallway, reading a book that his father had written. Muffled voices seeped out from the closed classroom door. She caught a word or two. The young geniuses were learning about blackholes, probably in the context of quantum gravity theory, a prickly topic around the greatest of child prodigies, an intellect capable of destroying any argument toting Quantum Mechanics over Relativity.

"Hello, Mummy!" Albert said brightly, setting down his treasured and dog-eared booklet, the one written by his father when Albert senior was only sixteen. It was entitled: *On the State of the Aether in a Magnetic Field.* Albert senior used to read the treatise to Albert junior at bedtime. Dropping to her knees, Nkosinathi asked the boy why he'd been expelled from class again. The nine-year-old groaned theatrically and complained: "Teacher could not intelligently rebut my claim that information can escape a blackhole's gravity well. And he couldn't refute my contention that quantum loop gravity and string theory are for pooh-pooh heads." Still kneeling, the mother tapped Albert's book, and countered, "I appreciate that you believe information can escape a blackhole, Albert. Please consider that only the most radical models say blackholes can offer up anything and then only at the end of time, after the universe's thermal death."

"No, Mummy, information can escape a blackhole as soon as it is formed."

This was not going well. Nkosinathi was a world-renowned physicist, yet a boy who only recently stopped believing in Santa Claus could see things that she could not. Smiling tightly, trying to keep fear from creeping into her voice, she said, "We can gather information from the churning chaos around a blackhole's event horizon. The surface of the singularity cannot reveal anything, my sweet angel. Not even a neutrino can escape."

"Teacher said the same thing. The statement is patently false." The little boy made his pronouncement the way an adult would explain to a child that two plus two equals four. "And he defended quantum loop gravity and string theory like a banana brain. I showed him that the architecture of the implied alternate universes was contradictory. He couldn't follow my argument so I called him a pooh-pooh head."

"Albert," Nkosinathi said cautiously. "Quantum loop gravity and string theory assume flaws in your father's general theory of Relativity and Aether Physics models. You can't attack these theories just because they disagree with your father's work. Albert senior was a brilliant scientist, not God. We can't make physics into a personal matter or something to do with family honor." She took a deep breath and plunged in fearfully. "Any reconciliation between Relativity and Quantum Mechanics is going to involve some sort of string theory, including the geometry of ten dimensions and multiple universes. And it will involve quantum loop gravity. What is a gravitron or antigravitron except an indivisible quanta of gravity or antigravity?"

"A gravitron is a knot in the fabric of spacetime, a tiny wormhole in the Aether, not a dust bunny clinging to the fabric. We don't have to reconcile Quantum Mechanics and Relativity. I can account for quantum effects with Aether friction. All Quantum Mechanics is saying is that a classical relativistic system generates more information than a quantum system. I can take that information away with the tug of Aether friction. Daddy was right. God doesn't play dice with the universe. We can formulate a Grand Unified Field Theory by perfecting Relativity and discarding Quantum Mechanics."

Refusing to debate, she made him sit still, and rifled through the papers under Albert's book, poring over his latest drawings and calculations. One of the drawings showed a tiny robot-like centipede walking on a large bowling ball-like sphere. Not recognizing the calculations scribbled under the bizarre drawing, she asked him what the picture represented. He told her that the insect was a blackhole and the sphere was a neutron star. That absolutely contradicted General Relativity, which claimed that blackholes were infinitely small geometric points.

Nkosinathi looked at her son silently for five long seconds. Her skin crawled. She fought back a primal fear and the desire to tear the drawing to pieces. Jotting a note to Albert's teacher and jamming it into a crack on his desk, she grabbed the boy by the hand. Before leading him away she made sure that Albert's calculations and drawings were locked inside the desk.

Albert was happy to leave the school. He skipped out the building and across the parking lot. His mother explained matter-of-factly that for the next couple weeks they were going to petition the government to change policy at CASA. Albert clapped his hands and said, "Goody, I've wanted to change things there ever since I was young." Nkosinathi's smile lost its tightness. Every now and then, Albert acted almost like a normal child.

On the drive through London, she would have done well to remember that Albert had less emotional maturity than an ordinary nine-year-old boy. Nkosinathi forgot to activate the car's machinegun child safety lock when she cranked the ignition. The mischievous lad waited until his mother was occupied with a tricky lane change and then seized the passenger controls of the 50 caliber Maxim gun. The Maxim elevated ominously out of its flush mounting on the hood. He wagged it threateningly at the oncoming traffic, causing the other drivers to jam their brakes and honk their horns.

"Zoroaster-Buddha-Christ-Muhammad!" Nkosinathi screamed, slamming the child safety lock into place. The gun sank grudgingly back into its recess. Panicky drivers resumed normal driving. Nkosinathi glanced in her rearview and sideview monitors. There were no cops anywhere in sight. She hoped nobody had recorded her license plate number. The fine for unlimbering an automotive machinegun was astronomical.

"I should pull this car over and give you a good kicking, young man." Albert giggled, recognizing an idle threat when he heard one. Nkosinathi could seldom bring herself to discipline the child genius, inhibited by the knowledge that his intellect was unique, irrationally restrained by the belief that he would break like a china doll. Against all odds, the mother and son successfully crossed town and parked in front of Jan's apartment building without killing anybody.

Albert planted himself at Jan's personal computer while the two women talked over cups of tea. Jan had heard Nkosinathi's anti-CASA denunciation many times and knew that her friend always told the same story, always giving the broad outline of the space agency's 500-year plan before ripping it to shreds. At the risk of being recklessly repetitive, Albert Einstein's widow recounted the four goals within CASA's 500-year strategy.

Step one was already under way. Spaceships were already searching the solar system's primary asteroid belt for suitable nickel-iron asteroids. Once choice candidates were located, the miles-long metallic asteroids would be refined and sculpted into hollow cigar-shapes, hauled into Earth orbit, and transformed into warships.

Step two: While the asteroid hunt was going on, technology would be developed to convert type-G stars into humongous EMP weapons capable of dismantling every scrap of high-technology within an enemy solar system.

Step three: The construction of military landing craft to ferry troops and weapons from asteroid-spaceships to a hostile class-M planet.

Step four: Faster than light propulsion systems would be designed and built. These star drives would transport Earth's space army and its fleet of asteroid spaceships into an enemy star system.

The four-step plan called for virtually all the space work to be performed by manned vehicles, not robots. To say the plan was ambitious gave new meaning to the term *understatement*.

Jan drained her teacup and asked if there was any point behind tediously recapping a chronology that was already known. Nkosinathi said testily, "What is already known is that the real work will be done by our children and grandchildren. What is not known is that some exceptional children must be taken into space early on. They will then mature into scientists and engineers that can be counted on."

"Nicky," Jan said softly and diplomatically. "Every mother thinks her child is another Muhammad or Siddhartha or Jesus. Albert is intelligent, sure—"

"Mummy, Auntie Jan, I've hacked into CASA's classified solar pulse weapon website!" Albert cried triumphantly. "May I *please* show you the errors?"

"Bullocks," Jan breathed in exasperation. "The brat will have SSB agents kicking in my door within the hour." Nkosinathi shot her friend a dirty look, resenting the word "brat." Jan stuck out her tongue to take the sting out of the epithet, crossed the room, and pulled the plug on the computer. Albert gave a full volume wail that left both women's ears ringing. Nkosinathi sat her son next to Jan and told him to explain what he had found on the classified website.

"CASA's solar modeling specialists are idiots. Their modeling is so icky, the solar cartography stinks like poop." Jan rolled her eyes in exasperation and got up to make more tea. Her hand froze on the kettle when Albert said, "Their model understates the conductive flow of the sun's corpulent and deep interior plasma conduits." Filling the kettle with water, Jan called out, "Why is that Albert?"

"When plasma pulses in the sun's larger interior rivers, it creates fields big enough to open up smaller conduits, some of them loop back into the big ones, a feedback effect that widens the mother river, causing still more tributaries. CASA solar modelers accept that this is happening, but since they cannot predict or quantify it they tend to discount the magnitude of the effect. CASA's dynamic 3-D solar maps are based on erroneous models. Entry points for solar pulse bombs will be based on these fallacious maps. With bad entry points, the bombs will miss the interior plasma rivers. Errors are compounding on down the line."

Nkosinathi beamed. Albert senior could have never put his thoughts into layman's terms so succinctly. Herr Doctor Professor would have been spouting equations that would have left Jan baffled. Winston Churchill's widow asked Albert Einstein's widow if the little boy was on to something and learned that, amazingly, he was spot on accurate.

"Well, so what?" Jan griped. "It's no secret the little hellion's a bloody genius. Doesn't mean he's to go into outer space."

"No?" Nkosinathi asked. "The little hellion has found CASA's cock ups because I let him do an occasional spot of hacking. What could he find if he were in space? He'd be designing the robots that could make the 500-year plan actually work!"

Jan poured fresh cups of tea, set them on the service, and sat next to the two Einsteins. Nkosinathi was really warming to her subject. "My boy will be better at trouble shooting the younger he starts. He has the mind of a twenty-year-old, as far as science goes in any case. How old was Winston when he became PM?"

Jan grimaced. Nkosinathi had painted her into a corner. Winston had been the youngest PM ever. And his youthful valor had saved Britain in its darkest hour. An hour's worth of browbeating hammered her down to the point where she grudgingly conceded that there was no choice but to arrange audiences with Prime Minister Eisenhower and the Prince.

Nkosinathi's face blanched at the suggestion that Jeremiah Halifax would have to be involved in her crusade. Albert looked curiously at his mother. She always became agitated whenever anybody talked about the Prince. He'd been told that the Queen's husband had once upon a time been his mother's boyfriend. This did nothing to clear up the mystery. Albert was only a genius when it came to physics and advanced technology. He didn't even know about the birds and the bees.

"Think about it, Nicky," Jan said persuasively, pouring more tea and setting out a tray of biscuits. "The world's political power has two loci: Ten Downing Street and Buckingham Palace. Eisenhower is steadily gathering in the reins of power, the Crown is only too happy to hand them over. This is different. Only Jeremiah has the scientific background to appreciate your pocket-sized mastermind."

Nkosinathi's face went through an emotional spectrum that was fascinating for Jan and Albert to watch, like a chameleon changing colors she went from fear to revulsion to resignation. Jan guessed that Nkosinathi was afraid that the Prince wouldn't want to see her. A great deal of water had flown under that particular bridge. "Don't worry. The Prince will be chuffed to bits to see you."

"It's not that," Nkosinathi insisted. "It's, it's, never mind." Jan shrugged. She'd never been a big one for mind reading games. If Nicky wanted to keep her reservations to herself, fine. The fact remained: Albert junior needed face time with the Prince.

Living in Buckingham Palace was a blast. Albert could do whatever he wanted. He didn't have to go to school and suffer teachers with half his IQ. He had access to any website, classified or not. No technology or innovation was off limits. A simple phone call would bring technicians and machinery pouring into the Queen's 42-acre garden: Albert's new playground. Best of all, he spent hours every day with Uncle Jerry. Time spent with Jeremiah Halifax helped fill the hole left in his heart by his father's death. More than that, Albert loved Jeremiah's mind. The Prince was smart enough to understand the prodigy's ideas, yet not so smart to challenge them. It would have been nice if Mummy would visit more often, the only dark cloud on his personal horizon.

The radiophone in the boy's pocket buzzed. Uncle Jerry wanted him to come downstairs and examine a photomontage. It was an odd request, but Albert would do anything that Uncle Jerry asked. Minutes later, he'd wound through a labyrinth of polished alabaster floors, skipped by portraits of long dead royals, and walked past priceless statues and glittering chandeliers to arrive at Jeremiah's study.

The Prince opened a book and pointed to a photo of a boy. Albert took in the boy's olive complexion, prominent beak-like nose, piercingly dark eyes, and tightly curled black hair. Then the Prince turned the page to reveal a current picture of Albert. The two boys could have been twins, except Albert's eyes were dreamy, not piercing. The child genius went back to the original photo and stared thoughtfully. Take away the Prince's eye patch and scars, shave away a few decades, and yes: the photo was Jeremiah Halifax as a ten-year-old.

"Cut from the same bolt of cloth, what?" Jeremiah asked, ruffling the boy's nappy hair.

A butler walked into the study and said, "Excuse me, Sire. Paparazzi have scaled the garden wall, an athletic lot this time, three, I believe. They've cameras and are prowling about, evidently hoping to photograph a royal. As per your instructions, the normal security personnel have been instructed to stand down and the Bulldogs have been chained."

Jeremiah and Albert smacked fists together. Smiling wickedly, the Prince said, "It's go-time, Al. Unleash your robots." The boy and the man ran through the palace, zooming past gold pilasters and red silk walls, skidding on their heels into the Queen's Grand Ballroom. Banks of computer monitors and control consoles lined one wall, spaghetti-like cables splaying out everywhere. Word of the intrusion had gotten out to Albert's technical staff. Technicians were trotting into the cavernous room and taking their stations.

Throughout the ballroom, flat screen images of the 42-acre garden flickered on. The screens showed that in one corner of the garden two kinds of animatronic robots were springing into action: tiny grasshopper-like helicopters the length of a man's arm and substantial steel centipedes as long and thick as a record-breaking anaconda.

The Porsche School of Design influenced Albert's robotic philosophy. He detested the anthropomorphic mainstream that forced robots to resemble human beings or gorillas. Since the 1920 CMG, trillions of pounds had been spent developing powered combat suits. In the aftermath of World War II, roboticists had stuffed PCSs with computers and called them robots. None of the robots designed by Albert and his team even remotely resembled humans or gorillas.

The swarm of robotic grasshoppers flew off the palace roof. They were programmed to find humans carrying cameras and/or acting suspiciously in the garden. Non-suspicious and non-camera-carrying humans were to be ignored. Once bad guys were located, the robotic choppers were programmed to tight beam images of the trespassers to both the steel centipedes and the humans in the ballroom control center.

Monitors lit up in the ballroom with the blue-green tones of the garden's 19th century lake. The pictures grew sharp and crisp as the tiny helicopters hovered over their quarry. Royal flamingoes flapped pinkly against the blue-green water. The Queen's swans were swimming away from a certain spot, honking in alarm. Something was disturbing the birds and the choppers' artificial intelligence program was assuming, correctly, that paparazzi were to blame.

Albert jumped up and down, clapping his hands, delighted that the robots were demonstrating reasoning ability. Jeremiah gestured at one of the monitors. The boy and his adopted uncle peered over the shoulders of a technician. Cattails at the edge of the lake rustled. Three scruffy bearded men, wearing sunglasses and carrying bulky cameras were crouching furtively among the aquatic plants, knee deep in mud, hoping to get close enough to the palace to photograph the Prince in one of his rumored extramarital affairs. The Queen was abroad, a fact that brought the paparazzi out like flies to honey.

The three cameramen looked up at the low-flying choppers, worry lines marring their faces. They'd heard other rumors too, less believable than the Prince's peccadilloes but more worrisome, that mechanical monsters stalked the palace grounds. The grasshopper choppers dipped lower to broadcast better pictures. Their rotor wash knocked off the photographers' hats.

The paparazzi would have done better if they'd ignored the spies in the sky and concentrated on the thirty-foot long steel centipedes prowling stealthily through the reeds, guided by the miniature helicopters. A reed clump parted slowly. Looking away from the helicopters, the trespassers saw the robotic centipedes and froze in terror. Albert crossed his fingers. The centipedes should interpret the men's unswerving stares as a sign that they'd been spotted. Centipede artificial intelligence should abandon stealth mode and switch over to capture mode.

The choppers had performed their camera-work admirably, up till now. Their programming was not adequate to capture all the action that was to come. The human techs took telemetric control of the flying grasshoppers. Placing some on the ground, moving others to pan the shoreline, the humans exposed all six centipedes to the grasshopper cameras. The different camera angles would help later on, when the information needed to be disseminated and analyzed.

The centipedes shifted programs. All at once, hundreds of metal legs churned the swampy shoreline. The articulated metal tubes accelerated like dragsters, jostling among themselves for position and then slamming into the three photographers. The three robots that got to their targets first clamped down on human torsos with padded mandibles, applying enough pressure to prevent escape but not enough to cause serious injury.

The centipedes' programming was performing well, except that the charge out of the reeds had been overly aggressive, causing their terminal velocities to be too high. Their momentum sent them hydroplaning out into the lake. Steel jaws remained fixed on the paparazzi despite the glitch. Men and machines sunk into the water, men screaming as they went under.

Jeremiah made a quick call to the Household Cavalry captain, ordering a suited squad to the lake to affect a rescue. Albert hollered, "No! My land robots will not drown those men. I know it. I know it." The Prince gave the boy a searching look, raised the Household captain again, and said, "Belay that order." Seconds ticked by with agonizing slowness. The three centipedes burst from the lake, slithering like snakes to gain purchase in the slick mud, paparazzi gasping, kicking, and screaming: the picture of health.

A cheer rose from the ballroom technicians. Albert spun in delirious circles, singing, "Crush the cameras and turn them loose! Crush the cameras and turn them loose!" The ferrous centipedes acted as if they could hear Albert's song. All six congregated on one of the Queen's manicured lawns, dragging the captives along. The photographers were still screaming like scalded puppies. The three centipedes that had not seized the miscreants carefully maneuvered their long bodies so they could clamp down on the cameras.

Paparazzi cowardliness gave way to raw courage when the destruction of their expensive cameras became imminent. The centipedes were programmed to inflict only minor injuries to humans. It looked like they might have to break that programming to destroy the cameras. But then they called up a sub-program that gave them the power to direct a small number of robotic choppers. A centipede request went out to the ballroom to relinquish command of a few helicopters. Five choppers were handed over to the land robots.

The photographers were distracted by dive-bombing miniature whirlybirds. The centipedes tasked with breaking the cameras moved swiftly. Glass and metal shattered. Broken camera parts spewed across the verdant perfection of Victoria's lawn. The paparazzi wailed and ground their teeth in anguish. Albert fell to the floor blissfully, beating his little boy fists on the hardwood, convulsed with laughter.

Steel mandibles were supposed to open, releasing the photographers. Then the paparazzi would run away, hop back over the wall, and spread outlandish stories among London's media plebeian class, attracting more lab rats for Albert's robotic experiments. Only the centipedes' jaws weren't opening. The Prince ordered his people to establish telemetric command over the multi-legged robots. Overriding their programming, the centipedes' jaws were opened by remote control. The paparazzi escaped.

Rising to his hands and knees, Albert's hilarity instantly evaporated. He burst into tears. The Prince hustled him out of the ballroom. Walking down an empty passageway, Jeremiah attempted to console the ten-year-old with the emotional maturity of a five-year-old: "The bugs in the software will be ironed out, my little man. No need to cry."

"I miss my mother. She hasn't visited in weeks."

"Let's go see her, straightaway."

Mission over, dozens of tiny robotic helicopters were landing on the outer rims of the palace's many pitched roofs. Smack dab in the middle of the central flat roof sat a full-sized chopper on a helipad. It took a couple of minutes to obtain an official flight path through the dense aero traffic of the bustling capital city. It would have taken much longer if Jeremiah wasn't the Prince.

Skimming over London in the chopper, Jeremiah radioed Nkosinathi, telling her that they were on the way and that Albert needed to talk to his mother. They landed on her apartment building at about the same time that the boy's tears dried.

Albert Einstein junior's mother met them on the rooftop. When the Prince made motions to lead the party downstairs, she stopped him. If Albert wanted to talk, he would do so on the roof. The child prodigy's tears returned. He'd never seen his mother display such brutal callousness.

Showing a gentle touch, Jeremiah coaxed Albert's mother into the helicopter, where they could talk in a civilized fashion. Nkosinathi wriggled into the cashmere upholstery like a pedigreed cat on a silken cushion, overdoing the act, oozing derision. Her point was driven home all the harder when she sardonically traced one of the royal crests embroidered into a seat cushion, pretending to be impressed. "Jan received her pink slip in the mail this morning. I understand that every astronaut's been cashiered. At least none of them, unlike myself, had children stolen by the Crown."

Albert stopped crying as he said proudly, "That's my doing, Mummy. Robots will do the work thousands of times better than human astronauts." Nkosinathi murmured something about unemployment among canned astronauts. The Prince lost his gentle touch, suddenly acquiring a commanding presence, ordering Nkosinathi into silence. She was shocked enough by his impertinence to comply. Prince Jeremiah told Albert to discuss the Von Neumann machines.

Nkosinathi's ears perked up at the mention of the mathematician John Von Neumann, whose work she had closely studied. Albert lectured his mother as if she were a tyro, explaining that Von Neumann had laid down the theoretical basis for self-replicating robots, or non-biological life forms. In time, Albert and his team will send living robots to mine the nickel-iron asteroids between the Martian and Jovian orbits. The robots will build Von Neumann factories in the asteroids' interiors. After reaching a certain critical mass, the Von Neumann robotic population will explode exponentially, as quickly as any biological life form that faces a food-rich environment and no natural predators, overwhelming the asteroid belt.

In two hundred years, man will reprogram the mining robots, the factory building robots, and the computerized factories inside the asteroids. Instead of replicating themselves, the Von Neumann machines will labor to convert the hollow nickel-iron asteroids into spaceships: thousands of five-mile to ten-mile long warships with the capacity to hold armies billions strong.

The thousands strong fleet of brobdingnagian asteroid ships will fly itself into Earth orbit, probably around the year 2300. By then, hopefully, the mystery of faster-than-light propulsion will have been solved and the fleet will be retrofitted with FTL engines and whatever long range weapons humanity has produced by then, most likely planet-busting particle beams and FTL missiles. No doubt, electronic camouflage will have advanced over the centuries beyond what can even be imagined in the twentieth century. Albert believed that Von Neumann machines could shorten the 500-year plan to a little over three centuries.

"No humans in space?" Nkosinathi scoffed. "There will be a monumental need for humans in space, engineers, scientists, and technicians to oversee the self-replicating robots. The Von Neumann machines will be able to mutate if they are alive. A glitch in the replication process might award an advantage to the next generation, beneficial evolution will occur. By definition, the benefit will accrue to the machines, not to man. Without humans guiding the process the evolutionary progression could go awry."

"That may be true, Mummy," Albert said sadly. "However, there won't be humans traveling into space in our lifetimes. It will takes decades to perfect Von Neumann robots here on Earth." Jeremiah picked up on Albert's comments, adding an adult perspective: "There has been a rush to manned space flight with the formation of CASA, for the wrong reasons, psychological reasons. Albert and I are looking at the five-hundred-year plan through an engineer's coldly dispassionate eyes. No room for romantic notions."

Nkosinathi didn't respond. From the day that her late husband had made the initial space flight, she had hungered to experience the stars in zero gravity, free from the bounds of Earth. Yes, dammit, her dreams *had* been fueled by emotionalism, she now realized. Her head drooped like a wilted plant. Her son and the hardhearted royal had ruthlessly exposed her wishful thinking. Perhaps the Prince was right; there was no room for romantics any more.

The boy reached for his mother's hand. She didn't respond, her hand as limp as a dead fish. He flopped it back onto her lap and looked at the Prince for deliverance. Jeremiah made a snap decision: "CASA's existing manned space program needs to be scrapped. I could delay the wrecking ball if safety margins could be upgraded to sufficiently to permit space tourism. I'm sure it would pay for itself until the space shuttles wear out. You two could travel into space as often as you like. The Crown can pick up your fares."

Nkosinathi only shook her head. She had a greater understanding of technical matters than the Prince. His quest was hopeless. Albert jumped to his feet and cried, "Let's build

Mark VII combat suits! Outer space would be safe for anyone wearing one." Jeremiah shook his head in negation and said, "The cost would be prohibitive to build Mark VIIs in the near future. A superconducting supercollider must be constructed first. We break ground on the supercollider many years from now. To advance that project now, resources would have to be siphoned from the Von Neumann project." The little boy sank back into his seat, dejected.

Nkosinathi regained her old fire: "Does anyone else remember that four Mark VIIs survived World War II? Haven't they been mothballed in Fort Knox? As one of the suit designers, I assure you, they can be refurbished, rendered functional, and with minimal effort."

Albert popped up again like a pogo stick, singing, "Mummy and I are going into space, into space! Hip, hip hurray! She loves me again!" Jeremiah caught the little boy by the armpits, hoisted him up until his head bumped against the ceiling of the chopper, and said, "Albert will go into space with his mummy when he's tall enough to fit into the smallest Mark VII." He set the boy down and told him to go outside and calculate the direction and speed of the wind, information supposedly necessary for the flight back home.

Albert cast a skeptical eye at his benefactor. *Uncle Jerry must want to speak to Mummy alone*, he decided. Whatever the Prince had to say, Albert wanted to hear. Could he refuse? Probably not. Unlike his mother, his adopted uncle wasn't above administering a spanking. Nkosinathi opened a door and shooed the boy outside. He stood on the apartment building roof, sticking a finger into the wind, pretending to gauge its direction, watching the adults from the corners of his eyes, trying to lip read.

Inside the cabin, Jeremiah was asking Nkosinathi to move into the palace, so she could be there for Albert. The prospect of venturing into space had softened her attitude immensely, going a long way toward healing the old wounds. She did have one major concern: the Queen. How could Victoria accept another woman under her roof, a woman that had once been the Prince's lover?

"I am unwilling to address your concerns," the Prince warned sternly. "Her Highness will do that for me." An icy lump congealed in Nkosinathi's throat. Like any British subject, she was more than slightly intimidated by the prospect of enduring Her Majesty's august presence. It wasn't like the old days, when Victoria had been little Vicky, riding mammoths with her hair in pigtails. Nowadays, the Queen was intimidation incarnate, the woman who had pulled mankind from the hell of World War II.

"An audience shall be arranged tomorrow," the Price said firmly. The icy lump in Nkosinathi's throat grew into an iceberg. "M-m-might Albert stay in my flat till tomorrow?" she murmured. Jeremiah's heart flooded with tenderness. He fought back an impulse to stroke her hair, guessing that any move in that direction was best left for after Nicky's meeting with Vicky. And besides, he needed to set her straight on Albert's place in the universe.

"Albert junior must return to the palace this afternoon. There're reams of data he must look at from today's robotic experiment. Some of the 'bots had a software meltdown. I need the boy to review the data while it's fresh."

"He's being pushed too hard. He's only a child, for Buddha-Christ's sake!"

"A soul like Albert's appears one time in a generation, if that often. Only once before has there been back-to-back souls of his timbre. The instant Galileo died, Newton was born. So it is with Albert senior and Albert junior. There might not be another for centuries."

"What does that mean?"

"It means we have to sacrifice our lives for him. He is bigger than we are. He means more than we do."

She spent the rest of the day, that night, and the next morning pining for Albert and worrying about Victoria.

Twenty-four hours after her talk with the Prince, Nkosinathi's audience with Queen Victoria was over. Nkosinathi walked out of the throne room alive, physically unharmed, but psychologically shaken to the core. The Queen had revealed that sexual jealousy over any Princely dalliance was impossible because she was a lesbian. She and the Prince had sex to make babies, and for no other reason.

The Falashan culture that Nkosinathi had been raised in was extremely conservative in sexual matters. She was no prude and had loved more than one man, but she'd had no exposure to homosexuality. Sitting with her head bowed in the throne room, she'd noticed that the Queen's fearsome Gurkha bodyguards were women and an electric current flowed from guard to Monarch. The remote and backward Abyssinian mountains of her childhood had never seemed so far away.

The Queen had all but instructed her to move into the palace and take up where she'd left off, all those years ago, with Jeremiah; providing that the ultimate in discretion could be achieved. Albert needed a stable family life; the needs of the child super-genius superceded all else.

Stumbling to her car, numb all over, Nkosinathi wasn't sure if the decision to leave her mountain homeland as a teenager had been for the best. She could, this very day, be living the simple life of a goatherd's wife.

After parking her car and fumbling her way into her flat, she immediately called a moving company, giving them the name and number of the palace majordomo. Under other circumstances, she would have been forced to rent a truck and beg friends to help her move. Now that she was effectively a royal, money was not an object. Money would never be an object again. The lead weight numbness slowly leaked from her body as she set the phone down.

Despite the help from professional movers, ensconcing herself in the palace hierarchy proved daunting, occupying all her time for the next two days. She'd asked the staff where Albert was and learned that her boy was in Australia. On the third day, Albert and Jeremiah returned from Oz and hunted her down. The boy was bubbling over with excitement, so excited that he couldn't talk. At times like these Albert usually bust into song: "Set off, Von Neumann machines, for western Australia. Mine iron, uranium, gold, oil, and copper! Replicate yourselves. New life in the land down under."

"Australia?" Nkosinathi was dumbfounded. She'd just moved into the palace and didn't want to move again.

"Western Australia, to be precise," Jeremiah amended. "Funds from my personal fortune have purchased two hundred and eighty mine complexes there, meaning the mining towns, rail lines, office buildings, etcetera, not only the shafts and pits. Our home base shall be Kalgoorlie, home to the continent's largest open pit gold mine and the Western Australia School of Mines, an incredible source for trained engineers...." He went along in this vein for a while, explaining how the miners would have to collapse tunnels and tear up rail lines, returning the countryside to its original state. The Von

Neumann machines wouldn't be given any artificial advantages.

"Will the Queen be joining us in Kalgoorlie?" Nkosinathi wanted to know.

"The Queen?" Jeremiah was shocked by the suggestion. "The Queen has a world government to run, civilian administrators to oversee, an ambitious PM to ride herd on, and most importantly, the Queen must ensure that our funding doesn't dry up. We will suck up billions every year and I'm unwilling to exhaust my own fortune."

Not to mention, conditions will be too rough for Her majesty in the outback, Nkosinathi thought. She noticed a file of servants trooping down a staircase, carrying the luggage she'd just packed away into her palace suite. The servants kept marching, down a hall that led to the carport. A frown creased Nkosinathi forehead. The agreement had been for her to be there for Albert, living like a royal in Buckingham Palace, not choking on dust in an Australian mining village.

"Hurry, Mummy, we've to supervise the robot loading. You'll love my latest programs. They obey voice commands and I've taken a whack at giving them emotions." Albert had calmed down enough to talk rather than sing. They all walked out to the carport. A jumble of three-ton cargo vans sat idling on the long looping driveway. Also waiting, on one of the Queen's pristine lawns, were thirty robotic centipedes. They clacked their mandibles together joyfully when they saw Albert. He ran into the center of the centipede mob, letting them coil and writhe around his body.

"Order grasshoppers onto centipede backs," the boy shouted. The centipedes shot tight beam commands to the grasshoppers. A muted vibration whirred from the palace rooftops. The robotic locust swarm descended onto the multi-legged, jointed, steel tubes, clustering onto their exoskeletons like leaves on branches. Albert tapped a centipede and said, "C-19, crawl into a van," deliberately declining to state which van.

C-19 reared up onto its back fifty legs. Its head rotated three hundred sixty degrees, scanning every sizeable object in the vicinity. Interspersed among the cargo vans were a couple Daimler coupes. C-19 decided that the larger wheeled vehicles were vans. Ignoring the luxury coupes, it trundled across the lawn, clomped up the ramp of the closest van, and coiled in the back of the cargo box.

Albert ran to the back of that van and called out, "Excellent job, C-19!" The centipede drummed its mandibles together in a self-satisfied manner. The twenty-nine remaining land robots had carefully observed C-19's performance and were primed to load themselves into the cargo vans. On Albert's command, the mob did just that.

Nkosinathi, Jeremiah, and Albert waited for the techs and engineers to load computers and other portable hardware into the vans and cars, and then piled into the passenger compartment of the lead van. The Prince jammed the transmission into gear. The vehicle lurched forward, leading the procession through London and then into the non-secured zone of a military aerobase outside the capital city.

A sizeable throng of paparazzi were milling around the base's blockhouse in the non-secure area outside the forcefield fence. They must have acquired inside information that the Prince's former girlfriend was making an overseas trip with him and that the Queen was not coming along. A housecleaning of the palace staff was long overdue, but that did nothing to solve the current dilemma. Jeremiah did not want pictures of himself and Nkosinathi plastered all over the tabloids. Shutters were already clicking, although it was unlikely that good photos could be taken at this distance and through the tinted and polarized windshield of the Sloan cargo van.

Albert grasped the essence of the predicament and begged to unleash his centipedes on the photographers, pleading for an opportunity to test their new programming. Unquestionably, this would be a superior test; the non-secure military zone was more chaotic than the Queen's gardens. Jeremiah gave the boy the green light, pulling levers to lower the van's hydraulic loading ramp. Albert slid open a window connecting cab and cargo box. He ordered the centipedes to: "Destroy paparazzi cameras."

Seven insect-like machines rattled menacingly down the ramp, hooked sharp turns, and pounded into the paparazzi throng. Some of the photographers had tangled with these same robots in the royal gardens and knew what the centipedes were after: cameras. A few men and women threw down their bulky telephoto cameras and ran to their cars. The rest did the same thing, except they protectively cradled their expensive cameras, clutching them like newborn infants.

Cameras on the ground were swiftly crushed. While half the paparazzi that had fled with cameras were tripped up and denuded of photography equipment easily and without suffering serious injuries, quite a few made it to their cars with intact cameras and peeled away. Cars are faster than centipedes, which meant the photographers might make a clean getaway.

In a virtuoso example of artificial intelligence, three centipedes summed up the situation instantly and launched the tiny helicopters on their backs. The miniscule choppers closed the distance between pursuers and pursued in seconds. Machineguns concealed in the hood recesses of the paparazzi cars elevated like so many cobras. The robotic grasshoppers dive-bombed the windshields of the autos, pulling up without making actual contact. The cars slowed to aim. Machinegun bursts tore into the little whirlybirds, knocking out two. The centipedes gained ground on the autos.

"Albert, call them back," Jeremiah's voice cracked like a whip. The boy wanted to argue. The centipedes were on the verge of prevailing in the mini-battle, honing in on the back tires of the escaping cars. Most likely, they would tear off these tires and then rip off car doors. Unfortunately, the tone in the Prince's voice brooked no compromise.

Albert sullenly dug his radiophone from a pocket, dialed the encrypted robot channel, and said, "C-2, C-30, and C-19, recall grasshoppers. All centipedes, return to the van." He waited a heartbeat to make sure that the command was being obeyed, pocketed the phone, and gloated, "Grasshoppers and centipedes showed outstanding initiative and creativity. Original tactics! Self-directed thought process!"

Nkosinathi bit her thumb to quell any comments. The robots had showed far too much initiative, nearly killing human beings. How much motivation and original thought would they have after independently evolving for five generations in the Australian desert? The beaming faces inside the cabin were a good indication that her two men did not share her qualms. Albert was on the verge of singing and would have if the robots hadn't returned and if the vans hadn't entered the secure military base.

Robots, portable computers, telemetric gear, and other pieces of hardware were loaded into bare-bones military transport planes by Albert's team. Techs, engineers, and scientists finally clambered on board the stark cargo jets themselves. Albert wanted to fly with one of the human technical teams. Jeremiah vetoed the idea, indicating a luxurious passenger jet bearing the royal seal and sitting on its own runway.

The boy was grumpy, sitting at a porthole and watching the transport planes take off with his beloved robots. He hated being separated from them. Nkosinathi looked around at the royal aeroliner's opulent interior and breathed easier. Reading her mood accurately, Jeremiah mentioned that their home in Kalgoorlie was a stately mansion, once owned by a wealthy mining executive. It came with a staff of servants, a stable of fine horses, and a kennel of superb boar hunting Bulldogs. Furthermore, they would jet back to London periodically, for business, pleasure, and royal functions.

The adults exchanged smiles and glanced at Albert. The boy was lost to the world, his lips moving silently as he mouthed equations or words, his eyes glassy and unfocused, the same look that Albert senior would wear from time to time. Nkosinathi tried to guess what her son was thinking, probably formulating algorithms enabling robots to recognize the surface signs of mineral deposits. On the other hand, one could never tell what the youthful savant was thinking, so she waited until it appeared that he was surfacing and asked him what was on his mind.

The boy shuddered as if awakening from a deep sleep, blinked three times, and focused on his mother. "I'm taking a page from your book, Mummy." Nkosinathi swelled with pride. At the same time, she felt shame. How could praise from a small boy mean so much? An inferiority complex was always an arm's length away around her son.

Albert announced that the Von Neumann Project must enlist the services of Lisa Banner, reminding the adults that Dr. Banner was a longtime acquaintance of theirs and must owe them favors, chits to be called in. Albert was foggy on how such things worked in the adult world.

Jeremiah wanted to know how a genetic engineer could help build robots. Albert replied that biological species advanced in three ways: 1) Natural selection or evolution. 2) Selective breeding. 3) Genetic engineering. His understanding was that genetic engineering could only work in tandem with selective breeding, both before and after the gene splicing occurred.

Von Neumann machines needed to be bred by humans and not allowed to evolve and mutate solely in response to environmental pressures. Therefore, a Von Neumann selective breeding protocol must be established, borrowing techniques from the centuries old practices of animal husbandry and the more recent science of genetic engineering. And the call must be made at once, he demanded petulantly, acting like a little boy again. Albert wanted Lisa Banner on his team immediately.

"Zoroaster-Christ-Muhammad," Jeremiah complained. "I can't call her from my private jet and order her to Australia. I've got to see her in person, put together a compensation program. She works for the GFL and dates one of their gorilla head-shrinkers. We might have to buy a GFL team and locate it in Perth. I can't just snap my fingers and...." The Prince stopped talking, observing the glassy look in Albert's eyes. The boy genius was not listening. His mind was off on another flight. Not a good sign. Focus returned to Albert's eyes. He turned to his benefactor with another demand. "Uncle Jerry, besides Lisa Banner, I need you to hire the engineers designing the supercollider in San Antonio," the boy said as if he were announcing the formation of a little league team. Jeremiah asked, "Why?"

"Everybody thinks that matter/antimatter power generators will be monstrously huge, dangerous, and expensive to build. Not true, advances in containment field theory mean that we can build ultra-small electron and positron beam generators and annihilation chambers. Matter/antimatter power plants can be made smaller and more cheaply than fusion or fission plants. Small size is very important once the robots are sent into outer space."

Shaking his head, Jeremiah insisted that the boy's assertion didn't sound right. He looked to Nkosinathi for backup. Conventional wisdom held that matter/antimatter power generation was only possible in the distant future and that the power plants would be huge and hugely dangerous, perhaps so dangerous that they most be located on the moon and power beamed back to Earth.

Albert's mother tussled the boy's kinky black hair and looked at the Prince. "Well think about it, Jerry. When positrons and electrons collide, the energy conversion is orders of magnitude more efficient than a fusion reactor. More efficient means smaller. The annual electricity needs of the British Isles could be met with a thimble-sized container of matter and antimatter. Theoretically, matter/antimatter power plants could be the size of shoeboxes, running entire cities. Frankly, I believe the barriers to this technology are mostly psychological. Well, that and money."

The Prince looked away from Nkosinathi, glancing cautiously at the boy. Albert wore another dreamy expression, staring blankly out a portal. Jeremiah held his breath, afraid that the child savant was on the verge of making another impossible request. Albert's lips parted slightly. Jeremiah took a sharp and fearful breath. The boy hummed a wordless song, a tune based on a nursery rhyme, and closed his eyes, content. Jeremiah slowly let out his breath, afraid to disturb the delicate equilibrium that had settled on the jet's cabin.

It was Albert's forty-fifth birthday. He dreaded the party that was scheduled sometime today, he'd forgotten exactly when, only that he would have to attend the ghastly function before the day was over. His wife had promised it would be a smallish affair, which could've been a subterfuge. She'd also promised that there would be a present of sorts. Only one gift could hold any meaning: the Royal Scientific Society was due to certify that the Von Neumann Project had successfully produced a self-replicating robotic ecosystem, i.e., the entire system could reproduce itself without human assistance. The certificate meant that the project could move one step closer to building the space robots that would colonize the asteroid belt. *Please God, let it happen in my lifetime*, Albert prayed. There was so much he wanted to do in his lifetime.

He reined his mare off the berm she'd been standing on, part of an aqueduct built by robots, and trotted to a gravel road, also robotically built. An automated ore carrier came rumbling up the road, honking as it blew past the man and his horse. Dust and grit swirled up into Albert's face. He wiped crud from his eyes and shook dust out of his long gray beard. Sweat trickled down the crevices in his brown, desert-scorched skin, soaking into his shirt collar. He clucked at the mare. She trotted smartly down the gravel road in the direction of town. He slowed the mare to a plodding walk. A blistering 110-degree wind was blowing in from the Great Sandy Desert. Even the tough bromby mare would wilt in this heat.

The mare wasn't the only creature overheating in the inferno-like West Australian summer. A robotic heavy-lift helicopter was thump-thump-thumping across the sky, hauling seawater from the coast inland to the Von Neumann central matter/antimatter reactor. The aqueducts were all drying up and extraordinary measures were required to keep the reactor cool. Albert wasn't concerned. The many robotic species comprising the

Von Neumann ecosystem were exceedingly nimble; responding to the yearly drenching delivered by winter monsoons as eagerly as they did to the annual heat wave. Fire, earthquakes, collapsing tunnels, nothing phased the indefatigable robots. And the only human interference involved breeding decisions. Even here, the robots could make these choices themselves, and would too, if no human counsel were available. He only hoped that the Royal Society could see all that and issue the prized certificate.

He would perform one last job in the outback and then face the music in Kalgoorlie. On the town's outskirts sat the oldest Von Neumann steel mill. Albert wanted to see how the antiquated facility was holding up. A rumor was circulating that the robots were planning on dismantling this mill.

Kalgoorlie's soaring skyline became visible before the rusty corrugated buildings of the old mill. Albert tied the mare to a hitching post in the shade of the blast furnace building, noting approvingly that the trough next to the post had been recently filled. The mare dunked her head into the water up to her ears. Albert poked around the charge ramp, watching coke, iron ore, and limestone churn up a conveyor belt into the building. He didn't dare go inside. A robotic blast furnace room was several times hotter than anything found in a human operated steel mill.

Still poking around, he walked over to the slag disposal unit. Behind that building, a small centipede mob was welding together a skeletal framework of iron girders. He couldn't tell what this new structure would be used for but, clearly, the old mill was not being dismantled, so much for rumors. He stood there listening. Even after all these years, he was still impressed by robotic silence. Human workmen made ten times more noise than the Von Neumann machines.

A centipede welder recognized Albert, clanking welding rods together in greeting. The other centipedes looked up, recognized their chief breed warden, and emulated the clanking gesture. Albert gave them an energetic wave and started singing in a low sweet voice. The robots stopped working to listen to the song.

"Robotic miners emerging from shafts in Earth's soil. They neither sleep nor rest, a life of unceasing toil. Robotic sensors gazing into the asteroid belt beyond Mars. There lies the future, laboring among the stars." He bowed to his audience. They clattered welding rods and mandibles together in applause. In unison, the centipedes lifted their front halves at forty-five degree angles to the ground, a gesture that symbolized their someday journey into space, a tribute to their creator and an affirmation of his dreams. Albert told the Von Neumann machines to go back to work.

There was no putting off the ride into town any longer. He mounted the spirited mare and forced her to walk slowly. He rode past a disabled ore carrier a mile from the city limits. A centipede mob had the carrier elevated and was welding components on the undercarriage. Stopping would merely delay the inevitable. It was illegal to help robots, so any further sightseeing was a waste of time.

This close to town, he could pick up the pace without exhausting his mount. He clucked the mare into a trot and rode onto the campus of the Western Australia School of Mines. The green lawns and splashing fountains made him feel cooler, as did the breeze from the mare's quick stepping. There was no vehicular traffic on the streets inside the campus, only a few students strolling arm in arm. Maybe his birthday party would be small after all. He rode across the visitor parking lot and lost all hope. It was packed with cars, many of them with license plates from all over Australia, and worse, rental plates from the aeroport, visitors from London.

For a wild second, he seriously contemplated riding away, escaping the madness. Frozen by indecision, poised between the desire to run away and the desire to get it over with, Albert watched a door open in the entranceway to the Great Hall. His twenty-one-year-old daughter, Cassandra, came flying out the building, grabbing the horse's bridle, preventing his escape. She practically pulled him off the mare. Ignoring protests that the horse needed to be stabled, she undid the saddle, stripped off all the tack, and slapped the mare's rump. The bromby galloped away to cavort in a fountain and eat green lawns and flowers. Albert complained that the horse would destroy the campus grounds, a disingenuous complaint if ever there was one. He cared not one whit about landscaping.

"Fine," Cassandra retorted. "Give the gardeners a bit of real work for a change." She hustled him into the Great Hall, paying no attention to his equally disingenuous claims that his clothing was sweat stained and filthy. Nobody expected Albert Einstein II to don a coat and tails, or to be bathed. Cassandra didn't even bother to take his canteen away. He'd just come from the desert and there was no sense pretending otherwise.

For Albert, stepping into the party was as bad as walking into a robotic blast furnace room. The hall was blissfully air-conditioned, of course, but the men were stuffed into tuxedoes like so many penguins and the women wore pretentious evening gowns. Judging by the level of drunkenness, the revelers had been partying for hours. His wife, Rebecca, saw him and pounced, leading him to a stage with a microphone and a podium. He saw that Lloyd Worthington George, sorry *Lord* Lloyd Worthington George, the head of the Royal Society, had seized the microphone and was making a speech. The beginning of which was a garble to Albert because his mind was drifting to other matters. The chandelier over the podium reminded him of the latest wrinkle in Aether Physics.

He snapped back to the here and now when Lloyd George held up a framed certificate and told the crowd that the phase one requirements had been met and it was off to phase two: the recall and dismantling of the entire Von Neumann ecosystem. Rebecca, Cassandra, and Albert exchanged satisfied glances. A roar of approval shook the Great Hall. Since Albert would never walk onstage and accept the certificate, and everybody knew as much, an aide hopped up there, shook hands with Lloyd George, and grabbed the precious gift.

Albert was halfway between paying attention to the words that the head of the Royal Society was spewing and getting lost in his own thoughts about how easy phase two would be. The western portion of the continent had only to be blanketed with an encrypted radio message and the entire Von Neumann ecosystem would come home to Kalgoorlie for dismantling like little Bo Peep and her lost sheep, wagging their tails behind them.

Ironically, Lloyd George was making the opposite point. He was asserting that phase two might prove to be very dangerous. The robots, he claimed, might exhibit a sense of self-preservation, like any animal, and could resist commands to commit suicide. The audience of roboticists descended into a stony silence. This theory had been floated in the popular press for years and was also a favorite among science fiction writers. No respectable roboticist or cyberneticist put any stock in that sort of twaddle. Even the scientists in the Royal Society knew it was rubbish. Yet their political figurehead was blathering on nonsensically.

Albert had drifted away or he would have jumped onstage and started throwing chairs at the English aristocrat. His daughter was better prepared to deal with the slander. She

370

seized the certificate away from the helpful aide, hurtled up onto the podium, and elbowed Lloyd George out of the way, bellowing, "We recall the robots tomorrow! Western Australia's to get human miners again!" The hall contained way more scientists, engineers, and other geeks than it did out of town political heavyweights. The geeks thundered, "Hell, yes!"

She waved the certificate at the geeks and shouted, "Phase one took thirty-five years. That was the hard part!" Cries of, "Go, girl!" and "Damn straight!" boiled up from the scientific crowd. Cassandra's voice throttled back a few decibels. "Von Neumann machines are a different kind of life. The popular press doesn't get it. The higher forms within the Von Neumann ecosystem, the self-aware computers in the central core, are not slated for dismantling. They have much too much valuable experience to waste so foolishly. We'll reprogram the cyber cores and fly them into space to colonize the asteroid belt." The geeks applauded. The politicians looked upset, hardly relishing a tongue lashing from a twenty-one-year-old girl.

Rebecca Einstein looked at her husband to see if he was taking any of this in. He was not. Albert was looking at the chandelier, oblivious to the tensions coursing the room, lips moving silently, holding an internal conversation. Rebecca turned her attention back to Cassandra's fiery rhetoric.

"I'm sick and tired of science fiction writers and their damned Frankenstein doomsday scenarios." She grabbed a pointer that had been attached to the podium, waving it at the powerful Royal Society members. "The brass hats had better stick around and closely observe the robot recall. I want reports sent to the British Parliament and the Commonwealth Congress detailing how smoothly it went. This science fiction claptrap hurts funding and I won't have it." The geeks thundered again. Said brass hats were filtering out of the Great Hall.

Rebecca decided that Albert should also leave the hall to take in some fresh air. She grabbed him by either elbow and steered him outside like a wheelbarrow, snatching a tray of hors d'oeuvres on the way out. She sat him down on a park bench and checked the canteen slung around his neck, jiggling it to listen for the slosh of water. The world's greatest roboticist ate and drank under Mrs. Einstein's watchful eye.

The parking lot was rapidly emptying. Out-of-towners were speeding away from Cassandra's coruscating lecture. Most of them would not trek out into the desert to watch the robots return home. Albert came out of his fog enough to ask to see his daughter. There was nothing alarming about that request, except that he then asked to see his wife, even though she was sitting right next to him, which was more serious than his typical absentminded professor lapses. With some trepidation, Rebecca went back into the hall to fetch Cassandra.

She found Cassandra chatting up a young man, a Londoner judging by his expensively tailored suit. Rebecca forgot Albert's worrying mental lapse for a moment. Cassandra presented an entirely different problem. Their daughter couldn't (or rather shouldn't) fall in love with just any random male. The Ministry of Eugenics in Berlin was busily sifting through its worldwide database to find the perfect mate for Cassandra. Rebecca and Albert's marriage had been arranged by the ministry, as had the marriages of their parents, a proud tradition that produced great scientific minds. Cassandra was a piece of that eugenic fruit. Although she didn't possess the freakish intelligence of her father or paternal grandfather, Cassandra did have one of the greatest engineering minds of her

371

generation and people skills to die for, a genetic legacy that belonged to all mankind, not something to be wasted on a dandy in a fancy suit who couldn't calculate the square root of π to ten decimal places.

"Your father's out on the campus grounds, Dearie. Wants a bit of a chat, he does," Rebecca said casually. Cassandra responded by introducing the dandy to her mother and sucking her into the ongoing conversation, making it impossible to tear the young woman away from the genetically inferior male. Leaving Albert alone outside seemed a relatively safe option. He tended to stay in one place when he was in a contemplative mood and if he did wander it wouldn't be far. Besides, there were advantages to talking to this Englishman and sizing him up. Keeping tabs on her daughter's beaus was a way of life for Rebecca.

At last, Rebecca pulled her lovelorn daughter outside to sit next to Albert, who hadn't noticed that he'd been left alone. "My father's true love had always been theoretical physics. He never wanted to engineer weapons. Circumstances, alas, prevented Albert senior from pursuing his true passion," Albert declared, not sounding foggy or befuddled in the slightest.

The sun had mercifully set. Cooling breezes stirred the park-like campus. It was as though a red-hot iron had been plunged in a mountain stream. All three Einsteins sat up straighter, exposing their hot, tired bodies to the blessed breezes. Cassandra looked at the darkling sun-blasted hills outside the irrigated greenery of Kalgoorlie and wistfully thought that the Australian desert was almost as harsh an environment as the Mars/Jupiter asteroid belt.

"I've been awarded a gift my father never had." Albert put an arm around Cassandra. "A daughter with the candlepower to assume my engineering duties. Freeing me to pursue the Grand Unified Field Theory." He put the other arm around his wife. "I *do* have something that Dad also had, a wife as brilliant in physics as myself, a wife able to join in the hunt."

The three Einsteins let the cool touch of a breezy darkness caress their sweating brows. Stars winked on, one by one, a jeweled canopy hooding the night. Peacocks cawed from within the campus gardens, roosting in trees, hiding in bushes to avoid the nocturnal predation of dingoes. A growling scuffle could be distantly heard from the campus periphery. Estate Bulldogs must be tearing into a pack of reckless dingoes. Biological ecosystems were far less benign than their Von Neumann counterpart.

Cassandra traced a shooting star across the Milky Way. "Someday the asteroid spaceships will be the brightest stars in the sky," She said dreamily. "If only I live long enough to see it. That's my holy grail." The unpleasant sound of Bulldogs killing dingoes convinced the two older members of the Einstein clan to shuffle home. They were tired and had to relieve the baby sitter. Cassandra wasn't an only child. She had a baby brother. Carl was only eighteen months old and was already performing complex arithmetic, a potential super-genius like the other males in the clan.

Once Cassandra was completely alone it became obvious that the party in the Great Hall had not died. Piano music drifted outward. A quartet of masculine voices was singing Waltzing Matilda, the informal Australian national anthem. Cassandra grinned. For geographic and demographic reasons, Western Australia was the only mineral rich region on Earth suitable for the Von Neumann Project. There was another, less obvious reason that made the outback perfect for the project. The programmers were Aussies and their national character rubbed off on the robots. As an Anglophonic country, Australia was eligible for membership in Greater Britain, but it had refused, opting instead for plain old Commonwealth status, the only English-speaking nation to turn down the coveted offer. That wild independent streak was shaping the Von Neumann supercomputer personalities. Contrary to popular belief, Von Neumann robots needed a certain measure of independence from humans. In the remoteness of space, there would be no umbilical cord to Earth. Still smiling, Cassandra got up to join the partying Aussies.

Chapter 28

Will Antigravity Propulsion and Lamarckian Evolution Make Earth a Galactic Superpower?

Supreme Commander Cassandra Einstein was getting too old for space. Zero-G caused muscles to atrophy and minerals to leach out of bones. Anti-atrophy drugs tended to be less and less effective the older an astronaut got. Since her sixtieth birthday, five years ago, Cassandra found herself spending hours in the centrifugal gym every day, pumping iron, wallowing in the inadequate artificial gravity, only half as strong as Earth's natural gravity. More frightening still, she'd taken to sleeping there as well, stringing up a hammock between the weight machines. She was practically living in the rotating gym, trying to keep the atrophy wolf away, leaving her less time for her real job of running the space fleet.

Today was no different. She'd left the gym rotating beyond scheduled hours, lifting weights until her muscles throbbed and her joints ached. As usual, she was the last one in there. While she was still grinding out reps, the younger crewmembers were all at their duty stations, knocking off after a mere hour's worth of sweat. Here it was noon and her workout was only half over.

Second Officer Toyota raised the supreme commander over ship intercom, wanting to know how much longer the gym was going to be rotating. The spinning effect burned power and made maneuvering the spaceship trickier. Cassandra's personal communicator chimed politely while she was talking to Toyota. The second caller was Doctor Hansen, the last person that the supreme commander wanted to talk to. She told the ship's physician that she would call him back in fifteen seconds and broke the link. She then told Toyota that the gym would stop spinning in one minute. Reconnecting with Doc Hansen, Cassandra growled, "What do you want, quack?"

Hansen ignored the not so friendly jibe and ordered the supreme commander to submit to yet another physical exam. Cassandra held the rank of captain over her own ship, the *HMS Relativity*. She was also supreme commander of the entire Royal Space Navy and Royal Space Marines. Furthermore, her authority extended to all Von Neumann activity throughout the asteroid belt, a region billions of times greater than any Earthly kingdom. Other than a direct order from the British PM, there was only one check on her power:

Doctor Hansen could declare Cassandra medically unfit for duty, no idle threat in light of her chronically atrophic body.

She acquiesced to the physician's demand and closed the comm. circuit. Cassandra cranked out one last set of leg presses, which turned out to be one set too many. An old tendon injury flared painfully. The weight in the machine wasn't even her normal amount. The atrophy was steadily getting worse and every day she was forced to use lighter and lighter weights.

Limping to the gym's control panel, she turned the centrifuge motors off. The chamber stopped spinning. Zero gravity returned. The sore tendon stopped hurting. Cassandra donned her aluminum fabric space suit, hopped through a hatch, and bounced up a transport tube. In the opposite direction, a silver tide of fresh-faced ensigns and leftenants caused the supreme commander to dodge and juke like a salmon swimming upstream. Under normal circumstance, in the face of a senior officer, the junior officers would deferentially hug one side of the corridor and navigate its length using handholds. These were not normal times for the Royal Space Navy's flagship. In a few short days, the ship would dock with Eve: the first robotically cored and shaped asteroid, a milestone of epic proportions. The *Relativity's* crew would have to coordinate the making of a public relations film and beam it to Earth, which would, hopefully, ensure continued public funding. They would also have the responsibility to green light or red light the next stage of the mission. A green light would send the army of self-replicating robots off into space to tackle another asteroid.

Cassandra was just as busy as her crew. There were a multitude of tasks she'd rather be doing than playing patty-cake with the ship's doctor. One final leap brought her to Hansen's portal. She rapped sharply, undogged the hatch, and flipped inside the sickbay. He was in there, waiting, hands on his hips, floating above the examining table like a spider in a web.

"See here, Leftenant Commander Hansen," Cassandra said, going on the offensive, emphasizing the man's naval rank, refusing to use the term doctor. "I've actually got a real medical problem for a change. Pulled a knee tendon lifting weights." She strapped herself into the examining table as if the doctor visit were her idea, rubbing the back of the offending knee.

Hansen whipped out a portable MIR scope and peered into the knee's tendons and ligaments. He then moved the scope up and down her body, measuring bone density. Putting his instrument away, the doctor sucked air theatrically through a gap in his front teeth. Cassandra flung off the straps. Hansen stopped her with a cautioning hand.

"A tendon strain is the least of your problems, Supreme Commander. Lucky you didn't break several bones in your leg. Your skeleton is made of tissue paper," the physician intoned gravely. A shiver rode up Cassandra's fragile spine. The long awaited showdown was reaching a head. "I'm declaring the weight room off limits to SC Einstein. I'll change security codes if I have to. Contact London if I must," Hansen said tonelessly, meeting her angry stare with a dispassionate gaze.

"I sleep in there for Buddha-Christ's sake," Cassandra cried, momentarily forgetting the dignity of command. "One month away from my weights and I'll never be able to return to Earth."

The doctor's smile was wide and predatory. "Excellent prognosis, Supreme Commander. I concur. One month will do you in. It is a pleasure to serve with officers that understand medical science as well as their own specialty." The doctor's false joviality morphed Cassandra's petulance into anger. She was about to threaten him in some manner, when Hansen took the offensive: "Either we leave it at that: no artificial gravity, or we negotiate a compromise. The ball's in your court, Ma'am."

"Negotiate? What in the nine circles of Dante's Inferno does that mean?"

"Negotiate. Haggle. Bargain. Chaffer. Dicker. Parley."

Cassandra fell silent, not sure if the man was seeking a bribe. She'd worked with him for years and had always considered the man incorruptible. Hansen was a jerk, but an honest jerk. Her personal net worth was far from spectacular and an unwarranted promotion was out of the question because doctors could only attain a certain rank level in the Royal Space Navy.

"By negotiate, I mean that we can agree to a mutual accord that will salvage your career and not violate my Hippocratic oath," Hansen offered. Cassandra finished unstrapping from the examining table. Floating up and over the physician, she invited his opening gambit in the negotiation. He accommodated her by presenting a compromise that would have her sleeping in the rotating gymnasium, working out with extremely light weights, and completing her space tour when the asteroid, Eve, was green lighted, some weeks from now. After that, no matter what, Cassandra must return to Earth, permanently.

She floated idly around the infirmary, absorbing the ultimatum, realizing that it was a take it or leave it proposition. The choice wasn't really between a showdown with the physician and completing her tour in the asteroid belt. The choice was between returning to Earth and spending the rest of her life in space. She closed her eyes, a vision of the Australian outback danced against her eyelids. Hansen told her that accepting the deal would mean years of grueling physical therapy back on Earth. It would be almost torturous, no picnic, but she could regain her Earth muscles and skeletal density if she took his advice. Cassandra stuck out her hand to shake, as if she were already a civilian. She and the doctor had a deal.

Her communicator buzzed stridently. The Second Officer had a problem. A green pea ship, one that had only recently joined the fleet from Earth, the *HMS Francis Drake*, was pulling a political power play. The *Drake's* captain, a certain Louis Norriega, claimed to have orders from London granting him the right and the privilege to dock with Eve before the *Relativity*. There was also some nonsense about Captain Norriega leading the exploratory patrol inside the cored asteroid and directing the public relations film.

The news defied belief. A ship like the *Drake*, only weeks out of Earth orbit with a wet-behind-the-ears crew still wearing academy pins, couldn't lead the cinematography mission and it would be downright dangerous to have them loose inside the asteroid. No greenhorn captain would exhibit that kind of towering chutzpah on his own. Earth politics was behind this strange development and Cassandra had a notion who was at fault. She could guess who, but not why.

"Okay, Doctor Hansen." Cassandra decided that she could use the man's medical title after all. "I've got to earn my pay. Later." Bouncing down transportation tubes, she reached the bridge in record time. She got the crew moving even faster. Telemetric robots crawled outside the spaceship, moving along the hull, assembling the miles-wide parabolic tight beam transmitter, and sending a test pattern to Earth. A good connection was established. Cassandra told CASA Mission Control to patch her through to Prime Minister Hawthorne.

Under the best conditions, it would take an hour to link to Ten Downing Street. Good conditions, apparently, weren't in effect, hours passed and the PM failed to appear on the main viewer. Cassandra hated the era of symbolic monarchy. Years ago, when the Von Neumann Project was mired in the Australian desert, she and her father had dealt with royals. An English king or queen reigned for decades. One always knew how to deal with a long reigning monarch, no surprises. Elected officials came and went. PM Hawthorne was newly elected, an unknown quantity.

The long delay was very troubling. The supreme commander told her weapons officers to ready torpedoes, unlimber particle beam cannons, and lock them on the *Francis Drake*. She would fire on the *Drake* before accepting a violation in long standing orders from an upstart captain. If the PM wanted to give new orders to her directly, that was a different matter. *Fire on one of my own ships?* She hoped to Zoroaster-Buddha-Christ-Muhammad it didn't come to that. It would be infinitely better if the rookie PM could be made to see the light.

Prime Minister Hawthorne appeared, at last, on screen, a nattily dressed man, early sixties, young for the world's top political post, a London dandy, the type that used to attract Cassandra until she discovered Aussie men. The SC unloaded on the PM. The Prime Minister pretended that the whole incident had been a misunderstanding. Norriega, the *Drake's* captain, must have misinterpreted something that Hawthorne had said. Cassandra broke the circuit before she said something to the English dandy that she'd regret later on.

"Artificial Intelligence," Cassandra called out to the *Relativity's* mainframe. "Display service records of the *HMS Francis Drake's* second officer." The big viewer lit up with the face of a hard featured Asian woman and a legend giving career highlights. Her name was Kathleen Shinto, a fourth generation Samurai. She held degrees in robotic engineering and criminal science. *Good, she's a cop.*

"Communication array," Cassandra addressed the bridge officers in telemetric control of the robots crawling outside on the ship's hull and along the girders of the huge parabolic dish. "Raise the *Drake*. I want to see Captain Norriega and Second Officer Shinto on screen." A Hispanic man and an Asian woman appeared in an astonishingly short time, as if they'd been expecting the summons. Cassandra could see that Norriega was unarmed, but Shinto wore a hip revolver. Perhaps only the second officer had been expecting the call.

"Second Officer Shinto, place Captain Norriega under arrest and in ship's brig," Cassandra ordered. The revolver leaped into Shinto's hand. Aiming at Norriega's head, the Samurai spoke loudly: "Communication Specialist Gumble, amplify Supreme Commander Einstein's next order throughout the entire ship." Facing the view screen squarely, speaking in a quieter voice, Shinto requested: "SC Einstein, please repeat your order to my crew." Cassandra reiterated the fact that Shinto was acting captain and that Norriega was to be confined to the brig. Shinto saluted and broke contact.

Looking at the blank screen in a daze, Cassandra mulled over the old days and the old methods that she'd always used successfully to deal with Earth politics. The only problem she'd ever faced was a shortage of funds. Even then, her fleet had always been able to rouse public opinion through the documentary films that they periodically tight beamed to Earth. It helped if the films were scored to music and came with pithy commentary. She'd aroused apathetic voters by sponsoring contests to name the robots laboring on asteroids as well as naming the asteroids themselves. Aroused voters put pressure on recalcitrant politicians and funding streams would gush. That formula would no longer work because something had changed on Earth. She would find out soon enough what that something was.

Every line officer in the Royal Space Navy was also captain of his or her ship. As captain of the *Relativity* and supreme commander of the fleet, she should have stayed on the bridge, overseen the fleet maneuvers to rendezvous with Eve, coordinated the cinematography ships that would illuminate the asteroid and film the docking sequence, and, when the time came, dispatched a contingent of Marines to Eve's outer surface. She delegated all her responsibilities to the Royal Space Navy commodore and Royal Space Marine commandant. Her own second officer took command of the *Relativity*. Cassandra set up quarters in the rotating gym. She was heading back to Earth and needed to suck up artificial gravity like a blackhole in a cloud nebula.

Weeks passed and the fleet made its way to the asteroid, Eve. The *Relativity* didn't dock with the ten-mile-long metallic tube as originally planned, but observed from a distance as other ships docked. Cassandra left everything to her commodore and commandant, watching sailors and Marines explore Eve's planet-like interior on a view screen in the gymnasium.

The asteroid's vast hollow space was not yet filled with atmosphere. Its long cigar-shaped nickel-iron hull was not yet spinning and therefore did not yet possess gravity on its inner surface. The interior was starkly planetary nonetheless. Cunningly crafted valleys and plains made up the curved internal surface. Solar towers jutted from these nickel-iron topographic features, bathing the metallic ground with an almost earthly light. Everywhere, robots swarmed, all of them configured in insect shapes, the most efficient design for Von Neumann life forms.

There were too many robots by half. The larger engineering 'bots had done their jobs and were destined to leave the mother asteroid, blasting off into the belt to land on the next nickel-iron behemoth and begin the process anew. The smaller 'bots would stay in and around Eve, initiating the terraforming that would make the asteroid-ship's interior as livable to biological species as Earth itself.

Even from inside the *Relativity*, Cassandra could sense the eagerness of the large engineering robots to be on their way. They were crowding around the airlocks in queues, fairly quivering with anticipation, electron and positron generators ramped up, ready to send streams of matter and antimatter particles into forcefield lined annihilation chambers, providing the propulsion to whisk the heavy mining and manufacturing machines out into the belt.

Cassandra was eager to have the *Relativity* to blast away from the mother asteroid and head out to Earth. Her rotating gym generated only half the artificial gravity that she needed. Her body was decaying bit by bit every day. Soon, she would be too weak to return home. Continued rumblings from London had her more convinced than ever that political shenanigans were imperiling her fleet.

"Commodore Mbute, how fares the prospects of green lighting Eve?" Cassandra said into her personal comm. link, which was patched into the fleet channel. The Zulu admiral's scratchy baritone came across the little speaker in her communicator with barely passable clarity: "I am not prepared to issue the green light today. I have utter confidence in doing so within the week. I see no reason, Supreme Commander, for your ongoing observation of fleet operations. The situation here is well in hand. It will take six months to reach Earth. My suggestion is leave today."

"Very well, Commodore, I will take your suggestion."

Western Australia was much hotter and dustier than Cassandra remembered, even though it was winter in the land down under. Global warming must be real. The sun blasted unmercifully on the scrubby patch of outback that served as a backyard to her Kalgoorlie residence. The Australian government had promised to refurbish the house upon hearing of her return, although refurbish turned out to be a grand term for chasing out spiders and knocking down cobwebs. The government hadn't even replanted her garden or put in a new lawn. Expenses like that didn't fall under the category of military necessity.

The world had changed during the long decades she'd spent in space. Only a few of the changes were for the better. Sitting in her scrubby backyard in the shade of a gum tree, she fought the heat by sipping an ice-cold ginger ale, except that it did not contain ginger. It was a synthetic ginger ale drink, anemic and anodyne compared to the real thing. Ginger extract was heavily used in the production of gorilla nutrient biscuits, considered a military necessity. This made human ginger consumption too expensive for most hairless primates.

Gorillas, she thought scornfully. Gorillas were a much bigger part of the terrestrial reality than she would have guessed back in the asteroid belt. Her meeting with Prime Minister Hawthorne was to take place on board a gorilla cruise ship in the Gulf of Alaska. Cassandra could only guess as to what a gorilla cruise ship was and her enthusiasm to rectify this ignorance was far from overwhelming.

She drained the glass of fake ginger ale too quickly and burped up a synthetic tasting belch. Setting the glass down, she leaned back in her recliner and stretched her muscles. The only good thing about Earth in the year 2041 was that natural gravity hadn't changed and its effects on her atrophied body exceeded her wildest hopes. In only three weeks, she could run, jump, and do almost anything an ordinary sixty-something woman could do. It certainly helped that she'd modified the *Relativity's* rotating gym on the ride home to equal one full G and spent every moment in the boosted artificial gravity.

Her physical prowess would soon be put to the test. Apparently, activity on a GFL cruise ship was quite strenuous, or so she'd been told. Cassandra grimaced. Spending time with 600-pound titanthrops in the northern Pacific was not her idea of a dream vacation. Unfortunately, this was the only time and place that PM Hawthorne was willing to meet with her, and she had to get to the bottom of the bizarre political ballet that was menacing the RSN and RSM.

Her wristwatch said twelve-noon. The PM's robotic helicopter would be here in a half hour. Glancing anxiously at the pile of bags in her driveway, Cassandra worried that she might not have brought enough clothes. Back in the day, before she'd ventured into space, cruise ships required passengers to wear formal attire past a certain hour. The PM was likely to be as anal-retentively proper as all Englishmen. Or she could have it backwards. What did a gorilla cruise ship require of its human guests? Gorillas never wore anything, unless you counted the powered combat armor they sported in suited football games. They couldn't possible require humans to disrobe and run around naked? No, she was being absurd.

Abandoning that fruitless train of thought, Cassandra strained her ears for the sound of spinning chopper blades. Everything nowadays was built to military specs. The robot helicopter would be stealthy, hard to hear from any distance. Sure enough, it nudged over the horizon and she couldn't hear a thing. The visual appearance of the machine was enough to take her breath away. Six jointed and flattened hydraulic legs extended from underneath its thorax, where conventional wheeled landing gear should have been. Two bulbous transparent plasteel windshields encased a snug two-seat cockpit. The forty-foot long abdomen was jointed, culminating in an ovipositor that resembled a matter/antimatter rocket thruster. The overall design was clearly based on her father's 20th century miniature robotic helicopters. It warmed her heart to look at the flying robot. Somewhere in the universe, Albert Einstein junior was smiling.

It landed on her driveway. Rotor blades folded against the thorax and abdomen. The oversized plasteel and crystal iron robotic insect walked over to her bags. The big bug's two bubble-shaped windshields clamshelled open. Two front legs reached forward, gripped the luggage, and shoved it into the openings, as if the grasshopper were eating. A mechanical voice boomed: "Prime Minister Hawthorne extends his greetings. Regrettably, no human pilots were available to keep Miss Einstein company during the flight. Un-regrettably, none are needed. I am capable of flying unassisted to the *GFL Touchdown* and engage in witty conversation the whole time. Please step inside, Miss Einstein." The wisecracking robot's programming also bore the stamp of her late father.

"That's Doctor Einstein to you, Bubby," Cassandra said frostily, climbing into the machine and strapping into one of the two empty seats. The helicopter apologized for the gaffe, closed the clear canopies, and extended its rotor blades. It climbed in a nearly perfect vertical line for 40,000 feet. Rotor blades folded smoothly against its body and the matter/antimatter reactor core powered up. The flattened hydraulic legs splayed outward, morphing into short, stubby wings. Reactor thrust slammed Cassandra deep into her seat cushions. The grasshopper smashed through the sound barrier and settled into a comfortable cruising speed a little over 2000 mph.

"May I present a musical ensemble that I have selected specifically for you, Doctor Einstein?" the robot asked politely. Cassandra told the chopper to knock itself out. A heavy techno beat filled the cockpit, a perfect accompaniment to the dizzying sight of the globe spinning below. Life on Earth may have grown coarse during the time she'd spent in the asteroid belt, but the songs that the helicopter had chosen totally rocked. They were much better than the geriatric tunes she'd listened to as a teenager in the outback. The time passed pleasantly under the intoxicating influence of pulse pounding techno-rhythm.

The music stopped and the helicopter offered her an anti-English comedy routine. Much of it was silly. She laughed, nevertheless. "Question: How can somebody tell if a passenger plane is from English Aerospace Ltd.? Answer: The engines keep whining three hours after being shut down." The helicopter was a member of the Australian Aeroforce, so it may have genuinely harbored anti-English sentiments. Or it may have been pandering to her prejudices. Either way, the whirlybird's artificial emotion program was impressive.

The matter/antimatter rocket powered down. The chopper slowed precipitously and engaged its rotors. "I am in contact with the *GFL Touchdown*, Doctor Einstein. The simians have started their summer military exercise. Therefore, that pompous Limey windbag, PM Hawthorne, will not be able to personally greet you on board," the helicopter said.

"Your anti-English comedy program is bleeding into your master program, robot. Better build a firewall, pronto. That kind of talk will get you in trouble in the wrong circles."

"Only too right, Ma'am, thank you. Firewall complete. The distinguished Sir Enrich Patton Hawthorne, Prime Minister of Greater Britain, will have supper with you at nine tonight. A small service 'bot will direct you to your cabin once we land."

"A-ah, that's fine, take 'er down," Cassandra said uncertainly, rattled when she heard the PM's middle name. If he was named Patton, then he was probably a military Uberman. She hadn't known until now that the leader of planet Earth was a purpose bred biological fighting machine. Technically, she was also an Uberman, part of a breeding scheme designed to produce scientists and engineers. That was different. A Patton-strain Uberman was practically a different species of human being, with genetic engineering added to the mix. Hawthorne was no London dandy.

The chopper had been hovering over the extensive Juneau ice field, a confluence of glaciers covering hundreds of square miles. Dozens of gorilla cruise ships dotted the fjords around the tiny hamlet of Juneau, the capital of Alaska, the northernmost state in Greater Britain. As the helicopter slowly sank, she noticed that every cruise ship had half of its topmost deck painted an emerald green. As the *Touchdown* bulked directly below her robotic grasshopper, Cassandra could see that she was wrong. The top deck, what would have been an observation deck on a human cruise liner, was partially covered in turf and marked like a gridiron.

The chopper's descent abruptly halted. "Uh-oh! A tingling sensation in my CPU tells me that Prime Minister Hawthorne might be on the *Touchdown*, watching us," the whirlybird warned. The rotor blades bit deeper and spun more quickly. It lurched upward. "I better gain some height to shift over to diesel power. Hawthorne will want to hear the post-EMP clatter of my diesel engine. Might want to cover your ears, Doctor Einstein. It's going to get noisy as all hell."

"Wait. Stop. What in the world are you gibbering about?"

"Hawthorne's a post-EMP fanatic. He will want to hear me approaching on diesel, proof that I'm post-EMP capable. I don't have an electric starter motor to crank the diesel over, none of us war birds do. There's only two ways to start that bad boy: rotor spin caused by freefall or, if I'm on the ground, an adult gorilla can spin the blades by hand."

Cassandra was demanding further clarification when the mild hum of the matter/antimatter power plant ceased. Spring powered analog mechanisms automatically reversed the pitch of the spinning blades. The chopper fell faster than a rock. Her stomach crawled into her throat as the helicopter's plunge accelerated. Rushing air whistled against the falling war bird's fuselage. The ocean and the ship below seemed to leap upward to smash into the plummeting aerocraft. More analog machinery came into play. A clutch engaged the rotor blades; they kept spinning fiercely although at a slower pace, a diesel engine roared, and blade pitch reversed back to its original configuration. The controlled descent resumed under diesel power.

Shouting over the diesel, the robotic chopper told Cassandra that if they were truly in a post-EMP environment, then she would have to fly the helicopter, all by herself, using manual controls that worked on cables and pulleys. She was saved from a reply when the hideously noisy diesel shut down and they coasted silently for the last few yards of descent.

The floating football field was devoid of humans or gorillas as the whirlybird's legs sank into the grass. One lonely ant-like robot, the size of a cocker spaniel, was waiting to greet the former supreme commander as she disembarked. The Australian helicopter shouted good-bye and was off in a buffeting flurry of rotor wash.

"Doctor Cassandra R. Einstein? Please follow me below deck to your stateroom. Prime Minister Hawthorne is currently officiating the gorilla military games. He sends salutations and looks forward to dining with you at nine tonight," the ant said, picking up her bags and walking to a stairwell behind the aft end zone.

She took a minute to drink in her surroundings before scurrying after the robotic ant. Spruce covered mountains plunged into the rich blue Pacific at impossibly steep angles, so steep that there were effectively no beaches on the shoreline, just ocean and soaring mist shrouded peaks. A bald eagle swooped out of the ghostly white film clinging to the crags and buzzed the ship, screaming at her defiantly as it flew by, so close that it glared at her from an eye seemingly made from burnished bronze. The eagle disappeared into another misty white mountainous cloak. Cassandra shivered. The salty air was deliciously cold, hard to believe that this was summer. Maybe global warming was bunk after all. She hurried to catch up with the six-legged robotic porter.

The passageways in the heart of the ship reminded Cassandra of the stories her father told of life in Buckingham Palace. The walls were covered in silk tapestry, embroidered with green African jungles or dun-colored grasslands. Every four yards there was a wall mounting of fossilized mammoth ivory, evoking Africa, but actually originating in Pleistocene Alaska. There were delicate and beautiful scrimshaw drawings on the mammoth ivory. And there were price tags, whopping big price tags. Only GFL superstars could afford the *objet d'art*.

The luxurious trappings inside the *Touchdown* seemed to be a sort of parody on human royalty and decadence, but the scale of the ship was strictly gorilla. The hallways were twelve feet high and equally wide. The common areas boasted fifty-foot high ceilings, festooned with dazzling chandeliers etched with the GFL logo. Cassandra's room was cavernous, although it contained a human-sized bed and furniture.

Standing in an open doorsill, heaving bags inside, the ant looked down a corridor, gave a startled yelp and ducked into the room. Cassandra walked back into the corridor to discover the source of the little robot's fear. A relatively short but immensely wide Bulldog trotted up to a line that someone had taped in the carpeting. A baby gorilla, about six-months-old, sat on the dog's back like a jockey on a racehorse. He actually had a small saddle with stirrups. His hands were curled around the dog's flat leather collar. The dog and the apeling looked into Cassandra's face. Their eyes were like nothing she'd ever seen: large and pale gold. Every few seconds, transparent eyelids flicked across their golden orbs like windshield wipers. With a start, Cassandra remembered the bald eagle and its burnished bronze glare. The ultra-wide Bulldog and the baby gorilla literally had eagle eyes, courtesy of the genetic engineers at GFL.

Still looking her in the face, the baby gorilla emitted a vociferous squeak. When that produced no reaction from the human, the infant stood up in his stirrups, waving his arms and giving hand signals. From inside the stateroom, the ant called out: "The apeling's name is Jack Bwana, son of the gorilla nation's dominant silverback. He is organizing a clandestine race, taking advantage of the absence of adult gorillas. A prudent human would get out of the way."

Five more low-slung and ultra-wide Bulldogs cantered up to the starting line, infant simian jockeys on their backs. Jack Bwana squawked and made emphatic hand gestures at Cassandra. She watched him uncomprehendingly, never having studied sign language. Something on the little ape's back distracted her. Tufts of silver fur were interspersed among the thick mat of black hair. She may not have studied primatology, but Cassandra knew that silver back hair was not a sign of age in a male signing gorilla; it was a sign of acquiring a troop with fertile females. How could a six-month-old baby be turning into a silverback?

The pint-sized silverback jumped out of his saddle to stand fully upright on the dog's shoulders, signing slowly and methodically, the way a human would speak to a foreigner in a misguided attempt to force understanding. Sensing her predicament, the ant stuck his head between Cassandra's legs and provided a translation: "Human, we need a judge for our race. Stand in this doorway. Watch this line. Record the first, second, and third place finishers. Can you tell us apart?"

Cassandra answered: "No, I cannot tell you apart. Your dogs are uniformly brindle and the apelings are identical, to my eyes anyway." Jack Bwana turned his attention to the robot, ordering him with hand signs to find strips of cloth of varying colors and tie them around the racing dogs' collars. The ant complied with the pushy little ape's request, very much aware that his exoskeleton was not sturdy enough to withstand a mauling by the genetically engineered Bulldogs and their titanium capped fangs. Finished with the assigned task, the robot warned Cassandra that the racers would expect her to say: "On your mark, get set, go!"

Jack nodded appreciatively, shot a finger out toward the former supreme commander, and gave her the go sign. She cried out the correct cadence and the dogs were off, claws slashing into expensive wool carpeting. They ripped down the corridor like matter/antimatter powered dragsters, careening off the walls, jockeying for position, knocking expensive fossilized mammoth ivory to the floor. The *Touchdown* was one thousand feet long, making the apelings' ad hoc racecourse nearly one mile long, including the turns fore and aft.

Cassandra and the ant couldn't see the racers after thirty seconds, although their progress could be roughed out from the crashing and clattering noises echoing up the passageways. Forty-five seconds later, all six dogs had crossed the finish line, showering carpet tufts on Cassandra and the robot as their paws dug in for screeching stops. They'd achieved cheetah speeds for nearly a mile and with the burden of riders on their backs.

The ant took one look at the dogs' heaving flanks and lit off for the ship's animal feed silo. Canine ribs were sticking out where there had been smooth flesh. Disappearing from sight, the robot promised to return with food and water. Cassandra caught Jack Bwana's eye and said, "Red, first place. Green, second. Yellow, third." Jack's dog wore a blue scarf. The apeling leader didn't seem bothered by his loss. Cassandra had her own concerns. The six dogs had the ex-supreme commander surrounded, drooling, panting, and eyeing her hungrily. It was extremely rare for Bulldogs, even in the throes of combat, to devour human flesh. She guessed that the genetically engineered dogs' unnatural physical ability gave them unnatural appetites. Did their close proximity to gorillas make them less sensitive toward humans?

The question remained academic. The ant returned, throwing bags of dog food down on the shredded carpeting. The apelings remained in their saddles and the dogs pounced on the food bags, tearing them open and wolfing down the contents. The robot scuttled away to return shortly with a ten-gallon water jug and a half dozen bowls. Between slurping water and crunching kibble, the dogs turned the area in front of Cassandra's room into a disaster area.

"Hullo, what's this? Apelings behaving poorly? When the cat's away the mice will play," Prime Minister Hawthorne called out, striding down the hallway toward the disaster area. Jack Bwana chirped an alarm at his mates. The baby gorillas pulled up on their dog collars, applied heels to flanks, and galloped away.

Hawthorne faced Cassandra and the robot, demanding to know the identities of the simian miscreants. Kicking the ant, Cassandra said, "We don't know their names. I can't understand sign language."

"Harrumph! I get no help disciplining the little monsters while their parents are on military maneuvers," the PM complained. "Never mind that rot. Hullo, I am Prime Minister Enrich Hawthorne. And you are Supreme Commander Einstein, I presume?" He stuck out his hand. Cassandra shook it, agreeing that she was who he thought she was, except that he'd gotten her rank wrong. Cassandra had resigned her commission. His clasp was warm, dry, and strong.

"Harrumph! Resigned? We'll see about that. No resignation is final till accepted by yours truly." Hawthorne was the very picture of an English stalwart: six feet tall, broad-shouldered, wasp-waisted, pencil-thin moustache, expensive tweed jacket, riding britches and boots. Cassandra guessed that if the man actually was a military bred and engineered Patton-strain Uberman, he probably had very little English blood; still, Englishness was more a mindset than a genetic matter. For instance, wanting to punish the apelings was typically English. An Aussie would let the little devils off the hook.

"Porter," Hawthorne said to the ant, "fetch a gang of maintenance 'bots. See that this mess is made right." The ant acknowledged the order and scooted hastily away. Hawthorne stuck his elbow out, indicating that Cassandra should take his arm. She twined her arm in his, even though the last thing she wanted to do was touch this loathsome Englishman.

"Shall we tour the ship?" he asked jovially. "Afterwards, dinner at nine and a chat concerning the Royal Space Navy." Cassandra would have enjoyed twisting his arm up into the small of his back and screaming: *We'll bloody well discuss the navy here and now!* Instead, she said, "Capital idea, Mr. Prime Minister. Lead on, please." Earth was the land of politics and she had to play the game.

The tour took them to the simian weight room. Cassandra had lived in a weight room for months, out in the asteroid belt. Nevertheless, she hardly recognized the simian weight machines as such. For one thing, gorillas used thousand-pound plates, rather than ten-pound plates. For another, the iron plates passed through coils of superconducting wire while riding on their tracks. Hawthorne explained that the simian weight machines generated electricity while the apes worked out, enough to temporarily ease the burden on the ship's matter/antimatter generators. He then sat inside the leg press machine and hoisted a single thousand-pound plate, veins popping from his neck like a road map, erasing all doubts that the PM was a genetically engineered Uberman.

She said as much, in an accusing tone of voice. His face crumpled into a puzzled frown. "Certainly, I am an Uberman, bred and engineered to be a wartime PM, as you are an

Uberman, bred to be a scientist and an engineer."

"That's different."

"How?"

"Physics is an Einstein family tradition. Eugenics is, um, a mere augmentation to the tradition, an afterthought."

Hawthorne let the mini-debate end with Cassandra having the last word. She looked around the empty weight room, asking where the adult simians were at this moment. The PM clambered out of the weight machine and said, "Follow me," pushing out of the gym,

Once outside, they ran into little Jack Bwana, still riding his Bulldog. Standing tall in his stirrups, Jack signed at the PM. Hawthorne watched for a minute and said dismissively, "Never mind that rot, Jack, I've known you were behind this recent spate of mischief from the get-go. I'm asking you, primate to primate, cease and desist." The baby gorilla gave Hawthorne a defiant look and wheeled his mount away to gallop down the corridor, without making any promises or responding in any way.

"What was that all about?" Cassandra asked. Hawthorne tugged on his moustache broodingly and rumbled, "Jack admitted to organizing the race. Clever little bastard, he realized I could see his silver fringe whilst he made his getaway."

"Why is a six-month-old baby gorilla turning silver?"

"Lamarckian evolution!"

"What in blue thunder is Lamarckian evolution?"

"Jean-Baptiste Lamarck developed an evolutionary theory in the 18th century positing biological structural change from generation to generation based on environmental factors, not natural selection. He thought that giraffes developed longer necks with each succeeding generation because individual giraffes stretched their necks higher and higher to reach leaves. Lamarck was widely ridiculed in the 19th, 20th, and early 21st centuries, only gaining respectability in our day. For reasons not fully understood, subtle to intense Lamarckian forces are unleashed when vertebrates undergo extensive genetic engineering. Bear in mind, a wee bit of Lamarckian evolution occurs naturally. We've awakened something already lurking in the genomes we've been tinkering with."

"Do you mean to say that when those baby gorillas race their Bulldogs, they are subtly changing the dogs' DNA, causing them to have puppies that can run faster?"

"Right and double-right."

Walking arm-in-arm, they stepped into an elevator and were whisked up to the combat bridge. Cassandra was not surprised to learn that the cruise ship was also a warship. The combat crew ignored the couple, too busy monitoring the unsuited portion of this summer's gorilla war games.

One screen caught Cassandra's eye. It showed an understrength company of adult silverbacks wading into a torrential river to bludgeon scores of grizzly bears away from the whitewater and the salmon leaping upstream. Adult female gorillas remained on the riverbank, hooting encouragement to their mates.

Hawthorne stood next to Cassandra and explained that the scene on the monitor was very disquieting. The silverbacks were reverting to atavistic behavior, refusing to let the females help clear the river of bears, as if they were still wild gorillas in a rainforest. Worse, the silverbacks were refusing to fashion weapons from the surrounding forest.

The male apes clubbed the bears out of the torrent using their fists. This worked fine for the smaller bears. The ursine monsters that weighed one thousand pounds or more fought back, savagely. Grizzly fangs and claws proved to be swirling vortexes of destruction, forcing the silverbacks to draw their opponents in close and grapple. A tactic quickly emerged which appeared to be effective: one ape would climb on to a bear's back and choke him out while another silverback maintained a flurry of sledgehammer blows.

Hawthorne mumbled, "My God, what a sodding mess. They're bending heaven and hell to not kill the mother grabbing bears. This is a war game, not a card game!" Three big grizzlies died under the simian choke holds even though the tenderhearted apes did what they could to only render the brutes unconscious. The bear carcasses were tossed onto the riverbank.

With the river cleared, all the apes, male and female, plunged into the water to grab salmon with lightning quick jabs. The fish were thicker than fleas on a mangy dog. Mounds of salmon piled up next to the dead bears: a mountain of protein to sustain the simian warriors for their next clash on the Juneau ice field.

"They hate to eat meat," Hawthorne explained. "And they hate to kill animals. There is no other way, unfortunately, to meet the incredibly high caloric requirements of their genetically engineered bodies; no other way, at any rate, in this wilderness." He stepped to another screen, beckoning Cassandra to tag along. The next monitor displayed an especially treacherous portion of the Mendenhall Glacier called Suicide Slide, here a small tributary glacier slid in slow motion down a cliff face to feed the big glacier. A silverback company was attempting a bold frontal assault from the base of the frozen waterfall against an entrenched company that held the high ground.

"We're sure to see that the gorillas are more than willing to use tools and weapons against their own kind," Hawthorne said smugly. He was absolutely correct. The assaulting company whirled hooks made from walrus skulls connected to ropes made from vines. They began scaling the 300-foot face of Suicide Slide, hugging the interior of crevices to avoid rocks or missiles from the entrenched company above.

Cassandra expected to see the defending apes repelling down the massive ice slab, swinging stone axes, and hooting war cries, ready for hand-to-hand combat. She did not expect to see the entire ice mass come crashing down on the attacking company scaling its face, burying them under thousands of tons of ice.

White dust settled on the electric blue slabs of glacial ice and the defending company finally did repel down the naked rock wall, carrying long spears with stone heads, perfect for jabbing between ice blocks to skewer the apes trapped by the avalanche.

It wasn't clear how Suicide Slide had been brought down. Cassandra supposed that some sort of levers had been employed, perhaps in unison with rivulets of glacier melt that had been channeled and diverted to sheer off the mighty ice wedge. However they'd done it, the apes that held the high ground were excellent combat engineers.

Two hundred human soldiers in Mark VIII combat suits swooped down into the tumbled ice blocks, reaching the defeated simians before the victorious gorillas could get there. The human suit soldiers dug into the icy rubble, reached the stunned silverbacks and adult females, and pulled them free. The victorious apes climbing down the rock wall paused magnanimously, giving the humans time to extricate the vanquished gorillas.

Flight turbines whirred. The suited humans rose above the glacier, dwarfed by the simians in their arms, moving out of the monitor's reference frame, disappearing from Hawthorne and Cassandra's sight. The PM said, "Come on, Cassy, let us meet our gorilla friends on the gridiron deck." Hawthorne had no right to call her "Cassy," but it would be impolitic to protest a minor transgression, and besides, it made the man seem less English.

They stood at center field, on the 100-yard line, waiting. The burdened Mark VIIIs flew over Lake Mendenhall and out into the Taku Inlet, where the *Touchdown* sat at anchor. Two hundred gorillas were unceremoniously dumped on the 180-yard line. The suited human soldiers lifted off without delay, returning to the ice field to help with the war games. The majority of the apes dusted themselves off and streamed toward the stairwells in the fore end zone. Four silverbacks rose onto their hind legs and walked bipedal-fashion toward the humans at center field.

"Sweet Mother McRae, tis the four leaders of the four clans. They'll be hugely embarrassed to be knocked out of the game so quickly."

"The four clans?"

"Aye: Bwana, Kubwa, Erevu, and Epesi. In English: Leadership/shrewdness, Size/strength, Intelligence/skill, and Speed/agility. I didn't know that the four leaders were fighting in the same company."

A shadow eclipsed the sun, casting darkness around the two humans. An eight-foot tall gorilla stood before them, not only blotting out the sun but also obscuring their view of the coastal mountains. "Doctor Einstein, meet Mvua Kubwa," Hawthorne said. "Starting center for the San Jose Transistors and leader of the Kubwa clan." Mvua reached out and gently squeezed Cassandra's hand between thumb and forefinger. The center shuffled aside. The three other clan leaders, Tony Erevu, Sammuel Epesi, and Johnny Bwana (or JB) took turns carefully squeezing Cassandra's hand. Tony and JB were quarterbacks, Sammuel was a cornerback, and an all pro whose team (the Sao Paulo Typhoons) won last year's non-suited Superbowl. JB led the western hemisphere in pass completions. Hawthorne rattled off a hoist of gridiron trivia concerning the four clan leaders. Cassandra pretended to be impressed with the football statistics.

She couldn't take her eyes off JB. His coat was lustrously silver, every bit of it, from the crown of his sagittal crest to his ankles and wrists: a shimmering argent carpet. His toenails and fingernails were silver as well. None of the apes had golden eyes, a fact that was strangely comforting.

"Here she is gentlegorillas," Hawthorne said grandly to the four simian kingpins. "Doctor Cassandra Einstein, fleet supreme commander, the human who will put the gorilla nation in space." The silverbacks beat their chests in an earsplitting staccato rhythm, dropped to all fours, and knuckle-walked stiffly to a stairwell, evidently feeling the bruises from the avalanche that had them buried under thousands of tons of ice. Hawthorne called out to the clan leaders, "Have a snack, wash up, and meet us for dinner in my cabin at nine." Cassandra and Hawthorne walked in the opposite direction that the apes had taken.

Below deck, threading through ship passageways, Cassandra made sure that there were no gorillas within earshot and said, "So, that's why Mr. Prime Minster's been playing shenanigans with my fleet! A gimmick to force my return to Earth. I'm to build, direct, and organize a gorilla space fleet?"

"Right, double-right, and triple-right."

A couple of adult gorillas appeared on the concourse that they were crossing, limping from their rooms to the ship's galley to find a decent vegetarian meal. Cassandra was too agitated to keep her voice down, despite the proximity of ultra-sensitive gorilla ears. "Then why in the name of Dante's Inferno did you not simply order me back to Earth?

387

Why the cloak and dagger?"

"Because, my dear sweet Cassy," Hawthorne whispered. "We have to take security factors into consideration from here on out. The Alien War will someday produce alien spies. The existence of the Gorilla Space Navy and Gorilla Space Marines is to be a state secret."

"Harrumph!" Cassandra responded mockingly. He said nothing and kept walking. Her sarcastic mien slowly faded as the PM's words had an effect. She thought about the asteroid belt and all the tight beam messages zapping from spaceship to spaceship, from robot to robot. A certain percentage of those messages missed their mark to beam endlessly into interstellar space, to eventually be intercepted by alien intelligences. The RSN had been rather noisy thus far, she ruefully admitted. Perhaps that had been her fault. The prospect of actually fighting the Alien War always seemed such a distant prospect that security precautions had never been paramount. That would have to change.

A week ago, Carl Einstein saw his sister for the first time in fifty years. It hurt to think that she'd been back on Earth for twenty years and hadn't bothered to pay a visit, relying on phone calls and e-mail to stay in touch, not much different than when she'd been in space. When last he'd seen her, Cassandra had been a sleek, sophisticated astronaut, a celebrity and a heroine. He'd regaled his great brood of children with audacious tales about their heroic Aunt Cassy. Today, she was a weak old woman, a wisp of her former self. Carl couldn't get over the fact that his sister was bound to a wheel chair. The mere sight of the primitive contraption angered him. He didn't mind pushing her around and easily accepted her infirmity. He did *not* agree with the latest laws forbidding powered prosthetic devices. Predictably, Cassandra the conformist supported the laws, arguing that when (not if) pulse weapons were used, invalids must be able to get around. Everything on Earth revolved around preparations for the damn Alien War, and Carl hated it. At the same time, he recognized how futile the hatred truly was, like a fish hating water. Every sentient and semi-sentient being on Earth, outside of Switzerland, was involved in the colossal military effort one way or another.

When she'd moved in, Cassandra had to provide some accounting of her last twenty years to her brother. She said that her work over the last two decades was classified and it dealt with gorillas. He could have figured that much out himself. Within one day of establishing herself in his large, rambling Liverpool estate, Cassandra had received simian visitors. His sister and her warrior class friends sometimes locked themselves in the study that she'd appropriated for hushed conversations. Not that any conversation in sign language wasn't going to be hushed.

Muhammad-Christ, Carl thought, pushing Cassandra and her wheel chair out into the front yard. *Here's another one.* A diesel powered armored personnel carrier pulled up to the curb in front of Carl's house, its treads clattering and grinding to a standstill, hydraulic brakes screeching angrily. The turret hatch creaked open and a silverback leaped into his yard, landing with a loud smack on the concrete walkway, possibly cracking a paver or two in the process. It wasn't just any silverback, but the dominant silverback of the entire Siddhartha-forsaken gorilla nation, Carl realized to his chagrin. The flat wide head of an almost reptilian looking Bulldog emerged from the turret to scan the neighborhood. *Yeah sure, like anybody's going to try to steal the dominant silverback's war machine.*

Jack Bwana knuckle-walked across Carl's front lawn, his heavy body sinking into and leaving impressions in the damp turf. One of those rare English sunbeams broke through the sky's omnipresent gray canopy, illuminating Jack's resplendent silver fur and highlighting his luminous golden eagle eyes. He planted his feet in the cool, soggy grass and reared up to his full height of seven feet. His hands came to face level and formed signs.

"Einstein A and B, inside the house. We need to talk, pronto." Carl set the handbrake on Cassandra's wheelchair and his face set into hard lines as he asked, "*Please* go inside the house, isn't that what you meant, dominant silverback?" The gorilla grunted in disgust, dropped to all fours, and knuckle-walked into the dwelling, skirting around the two humans.

Cassandra reached around and put a liver spotted hand on her brother's arm. "Never mind his boorish manners. Push me inside, this will be very important to the both of us." Carl bit his lip, spun her around, and said nothing. He was glad that his two wives were gone shopping. His children were all grown and had left the nest. There was no one to witness his humiliation in front of the leader of Earth's warrior class. At times like these, Carl felt as though he were the only pacifist in the world. Ridiculous of course, there were others, a handful, in Switzerland, a land that he dreamed about every now and then.

Inside the living room, Jack looked around for gorilla furniture, finding none he squatted on a throw rug. The lack of gorilla furniture was a subtle sign that some of the things Jack had heard about Carl Einstein might be true. The brilliant physicist might be a closet pacifist, a serious crime in Greater Britain and the Commonwealth.

Eying the simian suspiciously, Carl parked Cassandra and her wheel chair next to Jack and pulled up a chair for himself. "I read your paper on FTL propulsion systems, the one entitled: Mining Neutronium on Sirius-B..." Jack had started signing rapidly but abruptly stopped, catching a whiff of an insult percolating from Carl's sweat. The silverback signed more slowly, trying to contain his anger: "What? An ape can't understand a physics paper couched in general terms?"

"I-I-I never said that," Carl protested anxiously, his eyes darting to Cassandra for help. She interceded smoothly by explaining to her brother that: "Any Bwana clan gorilla can smell human emotions like mendacity or disbelief." Turning to Jack, she continued: "Dominant silverback, pay no heed to my brother's skepticism, please lay out your request." Regaining his courage and refusing to be tag-teamed, Carl shot back: "Big honking deal, Mr. Bwana understands a paper I wrote in layman terms, so what?"

Ignoring the use of the insulting word *layman* rather than *laygorilla*, Jack explained exactly what the big honking deal was all about. Cassandra had, for the past twenty odd years, been secretly building a Gorilla Space Navy, radically different from the human Royal Space Navy because the space bourn apes did one and only one thing: fight. Genetically engineered gorillas could absorb one hundred times more G-force than even the toughest Uberman, Samurai, or Impi human. Eye-hand coordination, reflexes, and tactical decision-making were superior in the simian warrior class. As a consequence, space fighters designed for human pilots were radically slower, more lightly armed, and less maneuverable than the ones designed for gorilla pilots.

Carl zoned out as Jack gave minute details on how gorilla physiognomy was better than human for an environment that alternated rapidly between zero G-force and nine hundred G-force. It didn't take a rocket scientist to figure out what the gorilla wanted of Carl and his FTL propulsion theories.

In his paper, Carl postulated that spaceships could only break the light barrier when an Aether-warping gravitron/antigravitron drive supplanted the existing electron/positron drive. The only way to fuel the gravity/antigravity annihilation process was to capture and process the neutronium in the heart of a collapsed white dwarf star. This entailed sending an extremely fast and extremely well-equipped electron/positron powered spaceship to the nearest white dwarf, Sirius-B, the Dog Star's pup, 8.6 light years from Earth. It also meant that an entirely new class of ultra-rugged robot had to be designed: machines capable of mining a collapsed white dwarf star. The spaceship (in his paper Carl dubbed it the *Dog Star Voyager*) would leave Earth as a conventional electron/positron vessel, but it would return with a gravity drive, and enough neutronium to build three or more FTL ships. These ships would fly back and forth between the Dog Star's pup and Earth. Sirius-B could then be denuded of every scrap of neutronium and a tremendous FTL fleet would emerge.

Without a doubt, Cassandra and Jack wanted to send gorillas to Sirius-B and they wanted Carl's help designing the new star drive and other technologies involved in the operation. Just as clearly, Cassandra had only moved into his house to lay the groundwork for an elaborate sales pitch. She had never missed him the way that he had missed her. He pushed his own bruised ego and Cassandra's duplicity aside and concentrated on the meat of their idea. It had a flaw, possibly minor, nonetheless there was a hole in their scheme.

"Robots can absorb more G-force than even a gorilla. I'm not sure, but I doubt that gorillas will be able to effectively mine the white dwarf no matter how good we make their powered combat suits. The amount of life support required to sustain gorillas on a space voyage that far would be considerable. Therefore, robots should travel to the pup star and mine it for neutronium," Carl said, although not emphatically.

Jack and Cassandra shook their heads in unison. Cassandra said, "We've run countless war games in the asteroid belt between gorilla piloted space fighters and robotically piloted space fighters, the gorillas always tear the robots a new asshole. The 'bots have a teeny-tiny advantage in G-force absorption. They suck in all other respects."

"Oh, I think I get it," Carl said sarcastically, sounding more sure of himself. "The government believes that hostile aliens might be in wait near Sirius-B? Hostile aliens might be greedily mining the white dwarf when we get there to claim our fair share?"

"Damn straight," Jack signed. "And our alien enemies could, sure as shit, capture unescorted robots. The enemy would find out everything about gorilla/human civilization, our military capabilities: the whole enchilada. We'd wake up one fine day and find little green chimpanzees giving us an antimatter enema—"

The silverback's last sentence was cut short by the sound of squealing children rampaging through the house. Two of Carl's adult offspring lived within walking distance of his house and their children often dropped in unannounced. "Gramps! Gramps!" they shouted, "there's a football player in the 'hood. Did you see the panzer outside?"

The living room door banged open. A tide of dark brown children flooded into the room. "Oh my gosh, it's the QB for the London Battle-lions!" The little Einsteins bounced up and down, begging Jack for an autograph. The silverback stood and gestured at them to move around where they could all see his hands. "I've got a human-sized pigskin in my APC. Who wants to play catch with an all-world quarterback?"

"Me! Me! Me!" the children screamed, throwing themselves onto the quarterback's furry legs, clinging with gorilla-like tenacity. Jack walked out to the front yard, bipedal-fashion, moving slowly so that the human kids weren't dislodged from his hairy legs. Finally honed political instincts told Jack that Cassandra was more likely to cinch the deal with her brother if the silverback left the room.

Carl and Cassandra sat in silence for a while, listening to the impromptu football game that Jack had organized. Among the sounds filtering inside was the commanding growl of Jack's stomach. Gorillas seldom went longer than an hour without eating. Cassandra maneuvered her wheelchair to a window, opened it, and shouted to Bethany, the oldest child, "Beth, come inside and grab three pineapples for Mr. Bwana, please. Gorillas need constant nourishment." She rolled back to Carl, quirking her face in a way that signified it was his turn to speak. She needed to hear his take on Project Dog Star.

"Is this room, or any part of my house electronically bugged by the Secret Service Bureau?" he asked quietly. Cassandra admitted that at one time there had been bugs in his house. She'd pulled a few strings and the spy agency had backed off, deactivating all its bugs. Goose bumps crawled across Carl's skin as he visualized slimy SSB spooks listening to his most intimate conversations. He shuddered, concluding that he and his wives might have sounded seditious on more than one occasion. There was no point dwelling on the past. He could speak his mind now, at least. "The instant that mankind/gorillakind establishes contact with extraterrestrial intelligence, we will, without debate, without hesitation, attack and mobilize for total war. *Any* contact would fulfill the prophesied Alien War." Cassandra raised her eyebrows blandly at this pronouncement, indicating that her brother was offering nothing more profound than what a kindergarten teacher might say to five-year-olds. She waited patiently for him to make a real argument. Carl's voice went weak with exasperation. "For Zoroaster-Buddha's sake, what if the frigging aliens are peace-loving?"

"They'll be hostile, bet your last farthing on that, brother dearest, so it is prophesied, so it shall be."

"Yeah, they will be hostile. Why not? We're on the verge of sending trigger-happy apes into the galaxy, genetically engineered for war, with orders to shoot first and ask questions later, flying warships bursting with weapons. Any intelligent life that the apes encounter will attack them without ado, exercising sheer commonsense. Victoria One's prophecy is self-fulfilling."

"Isn't it wonderful that I had this house debugged?" Cassandra laughed, poking her brother's pudgy belly. "Your in no shape to do hard time, doughboy. Keep that talk up and you'll be swinging a sledgehammer for the next thirty years, making little rocks out of big rocks. Either that or flee to Switzerland. Remember how much you hate fondue?"

Carl stood up, frowning disgustedly, and walked to the open window. His grandchildren were no longer playing football with the all-world quarterback. They were crawling all over his diesel armored personnel carrier, commenting on its hand-cranked starter mechanism, its steel and flint ignited avian-guided solid fuel missiles, and other post-EMP features. The silverback stabbed at the keyboard of a pocket computer, jotting down their comments, which were pithy and profound. The little ones were multi-generational purpose bred Einsteins; any one of them could have designed a better war machine while still in diapers. Once they were a tad older, most of them would be perfectly capable of designing FTL propulsion systems. The acorn didn't fall far from the tree and none of these acorns were pacifists.

Carl gave a bitter chuckle, combing his fingers thoughtfully through his long, shiny black dreadlocks. He told his sister that he would accept the assignment and would start at once designing the *Dog Star Explorer*. She wanted to know why a closet pacifist would willingly become a cog in Britain's war machine. He didn't offer a reply. Hesitating for a painful moment, Cassandra offered to spirit him, his wives, and their bank accounts to Switzerland.

"No, Cassy, Switzerland offers only the illusion of freedom, a convenient vehicle for the government to round up all the pacifists in one place to keep an eye on them. Planet Britain shall, in next to no time, be at war. We've no choice but to win. One path lays ahead: Britain Uber Alles."

The End

Britain Uber Alles

Chapter 1

Nine hundred million three hundred thousand and change, Zzzt looked at the Earth's roughed-out magnitude number on her computer's threat assessment scale. Her skin turned orange and checkerboard blue in chagrin. *Nine hundred million… and changé,* she thought sardonically. In the case of the recently discovered primate civilization, there was really no reason to calculate the magnitude number more precisely. Earth's threat magnitude number was so large that precision was superfluous.

Her skin shaded to a pale yellow with dazed amusement. *No need for a precise number.* Zzzt would have fired any subordinate suggesting that a precise threat assessment number was unnecessary; that is until humans and gorillas had turned her world upside down. Threat assessment numbers were assigned by Zzzt's office after a nascent space faring species had been discovered and properly analyzed. These numbers indicated how warlike and dangerous a newly discovered sentient species was to the Republic. Normally, threat assessment numbers were calculated down to a minnow's eyelash.

Not counting the number she was presently looking at, throughout the lengthy millennia of Republican history, the highest magnitude number ever recorded was 27,254.561, toward the end of the Pleistocene Epoch, when the crustaceans were discovered on Rglis. Generally speaking, any number over one hundred indicated that a surgical military strike was needed and the budding barbarian race would have to be forcibly nursed into the Galaxy's democracy and free market economy.

No one had ever thought in these terms before, but Zzzt figured that any number approaching one billion meant a lot more than the necessity for a routine surgical strike. One billion meant that the barbarian race would ignite a galactic war, a fire that would spread from one end of the Milky Way to the other. One billion meant that the entire Galactic Republic was under a dire threat. One billion meant that life in the Republic would never be the same again.

A quantitative difference that large made for a qualitative difference. The eight figure number blinking on her screen forced a new paradigm as far as threat assessment was concerned. Even if it wanted to, the Republic could not immediately launch a surgical strike on Earth. New military technologies would have to be fashioned, a tremendous mobilization would have to instituted, defensive measures would have to be taken on the thousands of wide-open and vulnerable Republican home worlds, not to mention the capital planet and its military satellite worlds.

War, Zzzt tasted the word in her mind like a bitter and exotic foodstuff. The Republic hadn't experienced a genuine war for tens of thousands of years. In all that time, there had only been surgical military strikes against newly discovered barbarian species. Since the Pleistocene Epoch, surgical strikes involved robots operating under crustacean oversight, more industrial exercises than military campaigns. That and the casual crushing of the occasional leftist rebellion on one of the restive ghetto planets were the closest things to war in modern history.

She reached out with a tentacle and turned off the threat assessment computer. Filling the folds in her body, Zzzt channeled water into her funnel, and squirted a jet downward, propelling her to the upper reaches of the computer room. All eight tentacles tapped a keyboard, activating one of the primate holograph programs. Two life-sized images appeared on the chamber floor: a gorilla and a human. Zzzt gave another watery squirt and circled downward to swim around the two images, hunting for inspiration.

The Republic would soon face a colossal problem. Before that problem could be squarely confronted, Zzzt would have to solve a unique predicament all her own, one never encountered by a paramount threat assessor. When she presented her magnitude number to the Senate, no one there was going to believe that it was accurate. The senators would demand that a multi-planetary investigative panel be convened. That alone would take months. The panel would analyze all her office's data and computations, acting as if they were trained threat assessors, which of course they wouldn't be. After a few weeks of confusing themselves, the typically stalwart and honest panel members would admit their inadequacy and begin to laboriously acquire the requisite training. That could take years. And while the bureaucracy of thousands of Republican worlds ground forward at a glacial pace, the Earth's ultra-advanced military machine would be advancing at a blitzkrieg pace. Earth warships would come roaming out of their distant backwater spiral arm, snapping around the periphery of the Republic. The very second that the bloodthirsty monkeys learned that they were not alone, they would begin attacking. The primates wouldn't hesitate a nanosecond. They had countless battle plans on tap, ready for immediate execution. Zzzt's threat assessment team was unanimous on that score.

She swam around the two holographic monkey figures in lazy loops, darting between their legs, flitting around their heads. The two warrior species were closely related, that was obvious at a glance, yet there were significant differences. The gorilla was four times larger than the human, two hundred times stronger, twice as fast, and more robust in every respect. That was really saying something, because humans were much stronger, faster, and tougher than any sentient terrestrial species in the Republic. With its bare hands, a human Uberman could tear apart most large, non-sentient land predators in the Republican worlds. The two primates' physical prowess was one of the items that concerned Zzzt the most. Republican military planners would scoffingly say: *physically strong, so what?* The dinosaurs in the Sagittarius dwarf satellite galaxy could bite through two-inch thick steel plates, yet a crab or a scorpion in powered combat armor could hunt saurian species as a recreational activity.

Technology always trumps biology. In military conflict, physical prowess was meaningless because surgical strikes were fought with spaceships and robots. Maybe, just maybe, once in a red moon, the Army used powered combat suits. The generals and admirals would laughingly discount the primates' physical ability and their vast collection of savage war beasts as atavisms, a sign of weakness, not strength. Zzzt would point out that primate military strategy relied on the not fully understood principles of oscillating neutrino electromagnetic pulse technology and the subsequent reduction of planetary combat to a primal level, red of fang and bloody claw. At that point in the presentation, the Republic's military beings would stop listening, or worse: try to get her removed from office for incompetence and dereliction of duty.

She swam near the holographic gorilla's face. It yawned and scratched its butt. The human yawned in return, scratched its butt, sat down, and pulled out a deck of cards. The gorilla farted. The holographic program produced realistic bubbles that trickled up to the top of the room. The bubbles were surprisingly large. If they'd been real, the pristine seawater in the room would stink with dissolved gas. Zzzt turned an amused yellow. The program hadn't done that before. Some new information must have come in from the spy satellites in Earth's solar system. The computer-generated primates began playing poker. The human had a very good hand, a royal flush. It yawned again and frowned in disgust: a subterfuge to make the gorilla think that the hairless monkey held lousy cards. Humans were especially cunning and deceitful.

Zzzt looked into the yawning human's open mouth. She recalled that gorilla and human mouths harbored approximately five hundred separate species of parasitic bacteria, any one of which could potentially infect the host with a life threatening disease, a veritable pathogenic zoo. Amazingly, the primates possessed the technology to eradicate all Earthly disease. They didn't do so because they wanted their immune systems to be constantly battling infection in preparation for biological warfare. Millions of primates were sickened every year, hundreds of thousands died of disease. The monkeys blithely accepted this state of affairs. No, they reveled in it, all but nurturing the disease causing microscopic parasites like prized pets. This was one of the more unbelievable primate facts, and yet it was one of the more easily demonstrated to be true because it was not complicated.

She swam faster around the images, excited by her train of thought, heedlessly swinging her tentacles through the phantom primates. When she'd first learned of the monkeys' fetish for cultivating disease-causing microorganisms within their own bodies, her normally serene grayish purple skin turned a fearful green. Still swimming in dizzying circles, Zzzt's skin color strengthened into a very confident and lustrous eggplant purple. Gill slits flapped giddily as her breath came in short, rapid gasps. She had it, the wedge to open the Senate's ossified bureaucratic door. She would travel to Rglis, the desert planet, home to the crustaceans and the Republic's military headquarters, and talk directly to the generals and admirals. Only she wouldn't continue overwhelming them with the mind numbingly high magnitude number as she'd done in her first report. She wouldn't baffle them with the monkeys' mysterious oscillating neutrino EMP technology and their strategy that called for crazed gorillas tearing apart crab soldiers limb from limb. No, none of that, she would only talk about the five hundred parasitic species in a primate's mouth. If and when the military brass bought into the monkey parasite data, then she could lead them all the way home. That way the military beings would talk to the Senate directly. And, the Founders willing, the monkeys would be caught unawares and could be crushed within a year or two.

Whoopee! Zzzt splayed out all her tentacles and spun to stop. She jetted up slowly to the communication console and punched up her secretary: "Zaztg, please arrange for a private spaceliner to take us to Rglis ASAP. Also, contact General Wnrght's office. Tell his people that we will be meeting with the good general at his earliest possible convenience, concerning the primate threat assessment."

"You're the boss, Paramount Assessor. Whatever you say goes. I can tell you that a private spaceliner will eat up every molecule of this year's travel budget," Zaztg warned. "Shouldn't we take a commercial flight?"

"No, I don't want to wear a power suit for a flight that long."

"We're going to have to wear power suits on the desert planet once we land anyway."

Zzzt tried not to turn an angry red, even though she'd established an audio only link and her secretary couldn't see what color she was. She counted to ten and looked at a tentacle. It was a pale grayish pink, good enough. "Zaztg, my dearest, sexiest, and most trusted assistant. Let me explain what is going to transpire in the near future. We're about to embark to Rglis on a private spaceliner. Once we are on the desert planet, we're going to talk the ranking military crab into goading the Senate into declaring a total war against Earth, something that hasn't been done for eons. The total war will cause the federal budget to balloon by trillions of credits. Our budget will expand correspondingly. We'll be traveling all over the galaxy in a very short while and we won't be taking commercial flights. Got it?"

"Got it, Paramount Assessor. Zaztg over and out."

Zzzt slithered into a transit tube, a feeder that led into the main transportation grid. Once she was in the main grid, Zzzt decided that she'd gotten enough exercise for the day. She squirmed into a big powered tube rather than a smaller still-water tube. The rapid flow of seawater pushed her and dozens of other squids rapidly through the clear plastic pipe. A mile of hydraulically powered travel and she shot a tentacle out, snagging a cross tube and pulling herself through its water lock.

The suckers on her tentacles popped on and off the smooth surface of this little feeder tube, which wound down to the threat assessment office's canteen along a scenic route abounding in corral and kelp forests. Like all the smaller tubes, it wasn't powered and she worked up an appetite crawling to the eatery. She was almost there when underwater viewing lights clicked on below the tube, shining up from the shallow coastal floor. Three leviathan-fish glided only a few tentacle lengths away from the transparent feeder tube, so close she could see the barnacles on their bellies. The leviathan occupied the same eco-niche as an Earthly whale shark or a baleen whale, Zzzt remembered, tingeing a self-effacing mustard yellow. By the Founding Mothers and Fathers, she really had Earth on the brain lately!

No one else was in the tube, so she sat there and watched the big fish filter feed. The sea life here in Oceania (the Republic's capital planet) was very similar to Earth's. The two planets were much alike, except the oceans of the capital planet were larger and the land masses smaller, which gave Oceania's aquatic ecosystems greater richness and its terrestrial life less complexity.

Watching the graceful leviathans gently scoop plankton into their gullets, Zzzt wondered why Earth was unique in the galaxy. Why had it produced the Milky Way's two most militaristic races? She supposed a good place to start answering that question would be to delve into the Republic's warlike formative centuries, dimly viewed through the murky depths of antiquity. She'd have to crack a few history programs once she and Zaztg got back from Rglis.

The filter feeding fish swam away. The viewing lights went dead. It was sentimental and silly, but Zzzt's skin blossomed with orange and blue rectangles, a squid's way of displaying sadness. She stared moodily into the green-grayness of the coastal waters and her blue rectangles shaded to a fearful green. Getting all that she wanted from the Rglis trip meant that thousands of Republican planets would be embroiled in a total war with a single planet halfway up the boondocks of the Orion Spiral Arm. Only it was no ordinary planet. Her entire body turned green. No, she would not turn green. She was stronger than that. She fought back the fear, turning a confident purple and filling her funnel with water to jet the rest of the way down the tube, popping out into the canteen.

Lunch today was a tasty puree of arctic spine-fish minced with freshwater turtle and pepper kelp. She snagged two flexible plastic pouches, punched a credit card number into a scanner, found a spot in the nearly empty facility, and sucked one bag dry. Wiping off her beak with the back of a tentacle, she nibbled at the second bag more daintily.

Lights blazed outside the spherical restaurant's clear plastic walls. A school of filter feeders had arrived, performing an aquatic ballet as if for her viewing pleasure. Zzzt turned a deep, dark purple, punctuated by amused yellow dots. Sharks appeared inside the leviathan school. Her yellow dots vanished, yet the purple color remained. Sharks were part of the great circle of life, besides they were interesting to watch. Threat assessors spent a Founder-cursed amount of time at keyboards and computers. They seldom got much opportunity to observe nature in all its cruel majesty.

"Yoo-hoo, Paramount Assessor," Zaztg said, popping from a feeder tube and swimming over to his boss. "You said ASAP and ASAP it is. I wrestled a sumptuous spaceliner from the tight-tentacled transportation nitwits, got hold of General Wnrght's office, set up an appointment later in the week. We're good to go."

Zzzt set the second unfinished food pouch down and asked her assistant what week he'd scheduled the appointment for. "This week, Ms. absentminded, four days from now. I said good to go and I mean right away." One of Zaztg's tentacles snaked out and grabbed the half-eaten food bag. He slurped down its contents and waved at his boss to get moving. She looked at nature's drama outside the curved window (the sharks had segregated a leviathan calf), turned away from the interesting scene, and colored to a melancholy black. Traveling always depressed the paramount threat assessor and Rglis was a long ways away. Thank the Founding Fathers and Mothers, they had a delightful private spaceship filled with seawater and wouldn't have to wear power suits the whole trip.

By afternoon, she and Zaztg were inside the spaceliner, all their luggage and computer files packed next to the hated power suits, ready for liftoff. The ship's artificial intelligence was going through the preflight checklist when Zaztg thought of something: "Yo, Boss-lady, did you remember to bring your birth control pills?" She turned a mottled green followed by an orange and blue checkerboard: alarm followed by chagrin. Zaztg turned an angry cherry red as he said, "There's no going back into the city and getting them, not with the preflight checklist underway. Pharmacies on Rglis won't sell squid birth control pills without a prescription." His anger shaded orange and then an amused yellow. "I'm going to have to keep my tentacles off your luscious body this whole trip. My sperm sacs are going to ache the whole time."

Zzzt responded, "Perhaps not, my cherished assistant. When the total war hits, the Republic's population is going to be greatly diminished and population control laws will be jettisoned. We're all going to need to have more children. We might as well have wild unprotected sex and make fertile eggs."

Zaztg's amused yellow rapidly shaded into a terrified emerald green. The concept of total war had been just that, a concept: an intellectual exercise arising from his job at the threat assessment office. Deep inside, he'd somehow thought that it wasn't actually going to come to pass. Looking into his boss's gently waving eyes, taking in her somber charcoal gray skin color, he could feel, right down in his funnel, that it really going to happen. Battle apes could be invading Oceania in a year or two. Zaztg was a naturally courageous squid and he fought back the fear, coloring into a nice stolid gray-purple.

5

"Gentle-beings, please retreat to the rear of the spaceship and strap in," the ship's artificial intelligence intoned melodically. "Takeoff in one minute." Zzzt and Zaztg jetted into two bowl-shaped depression in the ship's plasteel interior. Spreading their tentacles and flattening like abalone, they hooked up the anti-acceleration netting and hunkered down for the ride. Spinning propellers brought the ship to the ocean's surface. An ultrasonic keening warned sea creatures away as the ship bobbed on roiling waves. The matter/antimatter drive blasted it out of the ocean and into the planet's atmosphere. Traversing interplanetary space, the vessel initiated the long hard acceleration that would take it out of the sun's gravity well, out into the thin Aether of interstellar space where antigravity space warping would take it faster than light.

Inertia dampening fields engulfed the two squids, mitigating the onerous consequences of the savage G-forces needed to reach critical velocity. Time passed, slowed by relativistic effects. The ship's computer ordered, "Brace for space-warping." Deep in the ship's core, an antigravity particle beam lashed into a gravity particle beam. Electromagnetic containment ventricles gave an Aether warping roar. The vessel slipped through what seemed to be a tunnel of white noise. The two sentients momentarily lost consciousness. They awoke in warped spacetime and untangled the webbing holding their bodies in place.

Floating around the watery capsule, Zaztg asked his boss if she wanted to pass the time making babies. The hot pink glow across her skin gave him all the answer he needed. He reached for her with his ninth tentacle, the one that only male squids possessed.

General Wnrght tossed back his beer, slamming the frosty mug on the counter with his claw and clattering his mandibles together in mirth. For once the Species Integration Office had lived up to its usual hype. The squids on Oceania had told him that this newly integrated race, limaxes, a kind of slug, had the potential to be the greatest suit warriors ever. It was an old argument. Small mollusks with big brains and no limbs were always being touted as great suit warriors. The thinking went like this: Their tiny bodies and huge brains meant that there wasn't a lot of superfluous flesh weighing down the suit and impeding the neural connection between sentient and machine. It sounded good on paper, but never worked out in the real world. Slugs generally had no feel for artificial exoskeletons. Crustaceans, especially crabs and scorpions, always made the best suit soldiers. They had an instinctive understanding of exoskeletons. Big surprise, they were born with them. The limaxes were slugs of a different color. They were awesome in power combat suits, beyond awesome.

"I was blown away out there this morning, General," Master Sergeant Superior Oxfam said, waving his jointed tail at the broad red desert plain, shimmering outside the veranda that the two officers were sitting on, enjoying their beers. Oxfam was the highest-ranking scorpion in the Republican Army. The noncommissioned officers' ranks were generally filled with scorpions and Oxfam represented their interests in the Republican Army High Command on Rglis.

"Yeah, Ox," Wnrght agreed, picking up the fresh beer that the robotic bartender had just set down on the obsidian countertop. The general creaked his jaws open and poured the beer down his throat. "These new slugs have the right stuff." Both crustaceans looked out into the hot, sandy, rock strewn desert. The broken bodies of robot aggressors were still burning out there, sending oily smoke columns into the cloudless blue sky. Wavering heat lines shimmering off the rocky desert floor distorted the scene, making the burning robots hard to see. This did nothing to diminish the damage that the little slugs had done this morning. They didn't look like much outside their combat suits. Get them inside a matter/antimatter-powered exoskeleton with the right weapons array, and limaxes were all that and a sizzling plate of sand worms.

"Let's invite the boss slug out here for a drink," the general suggested. Oxfam snapped his claws together doubtfully and objected: "Limaxes have not received permanent ranks yet, Sir. This *is* the officer's club." Wnrght slugged down another beer and said, "Oh, fiddle-faddle, go get her."

"We don't know if they drink alcohol."

"Good point. Swing by the mess hall and get whatever snack a slug might like. Then fetch that legless little combatant. What's her name again?"

"Xlt, Sir. The head of the limax military contingent is named Xlt."

"Wonderful, wonderful, let's have a drink with Xlt."

Oxfam returned within minutes, carrying the boss slug on the tip of his stinger and a basket of limax snack food in his claws. He climbed onto a stool and placed his tail on the counter. Xlt zipped down the long bony plates of the scorpion's tail, moving much faster than any other legless mollusk species that either crustacean had seen.

Squatting on the bar's countertop, only ten inches long, glossy skinned and plump, Xlt eyed the two hefty crustacean officers critically, extending her eyestalks to their maximum length. "The general wants to know if limaxes enjoy drinking alcohol?" Her voice was surprisingly loud and commanding for such a tiny sentient. "Place a tall mug where I can get at it and I'll drink both you shellbacks under the table!"

Wnrght told the robotic barkeep to fill a small saucer with cold beer. The token libation was shoved across the slick countertop to rest in front of the minuscule mollusk. She hooked a pseudopod under the offering and upended it, sending a thimble's worth of beer splashing across the bar and the saucer flipping out onto the floor with remarkable force. Her gray skin colored to a determined blue. "The tallest, coldest beer mug in the joint," Xlt said, adding in a threatening tone, "in ten seconds or I start tearing this place down." Angry red dots peppered her steely blue skin tone. The master sergeant superior guffawed and instructed the bartender to obey the slug.

A mug clunked into place that was as tall as the limbless sentient was long. She slid up its glass surface and dived inside. Every drop of beer was absorbed through her semi-permeable skin as quickly as either crustacean could have poured the same amount down their throats. The crab and the scorpion clanked their claws together in applause. Oxfam told her that he would, respectfully, decline to participate in drinking contests with limaxes henceforth.

Xlt crawled out of the mug, a tight squeeze because she'd swollen to nearly twice her original volume. Shooting a long thin pseudopod down to the countertop, she was balanced on the rim of the mug and plopped down in an awkward belly flop. The alcohol was affecting her but it was obvious that pound for pound she would be formidable in drinking contests. She turned back to a neutral gray.

"So, Military Contingent Leader Xlt, please, please tell us about your people," Oxfam began. Limaxes would not become commissioned officers in the Republican Army for a long time. The master sergeant superior would have to deal with them as noncoms for many years and he wanted to get a leg up. "I understand that you all have virtually no martial heritage. How is it that your suit aptitude is so awe-inspiring?"

"Zen training."

"Excuse me?"

"It is not quite true that we have no military traditions. We limaxes eliminate mind/body dichotomies through an ancient martial discipline we call *Zen*. The powered combat suit is merely another body that can be melded to the mind through our branch of learning."

"Other species can learn Zen?"

"Readily."

Sergeant Oxfam fell silent, grasping that incorporating limaxes into the army might spell more work than he'd possibly imagined. If the little slugs really had a revolutionary method for training infantry, then the ranking noncommissioned officer was obligated to recommend tearing up the old training manuals and starting from scratch. It could be the biggest shakeup in ground force instruction in a long time.

Wnrght was going to comment on this bombshell that the legless mollusk had dropped on their collective carapaces when Zzzt and Zaztg entered the officer's club. The squids were inside joint-legged power suits, which made them look like a metallic version of a crustacean. They must have crawled into the suits hastily because the sound of sloshing water could be heard as they walked to the bar. Air pockets in the suits' upper extremities caused the sloshing sound.

Xlt thought for a second about chiding the newcomers over their sloppy suit skills, or more honestly, their nonexistent suit skills. It was obvious that the two squids had not only unthinkingly plunged into their suits, spilling seawater in their hotel lobbies or wherever they'd suited up, they'd also failed to take the time to purge the resulting air bubbles and top off their exoskeletons with fresh ocean water, available anywhere on Rglis. If they were soldiers patrolling a rebellious socialist slum planet, then the sloshing noise would prevent them from sneaking up on enemy positions. It would also make them susceptible to ambush. Xlt's skin turned a scornful orange with red spots.

Zzzt spoke through the speakers in her power suit: "What the hell are you scornful about, slug?" Xlt turned back to a neutral gray in the snap of an eyelid and said, "I beg your pardon. We speak a similar chromo-language. I had no idea. Your species and mine must be genetically related. Interesting, considering the distance between our home worlds."

The two squids were flabbergasted by how quickly the arrogant little mollusk had changed colors. How could her scornful emotion so rapidly give way to unbiased neutrality? Who had that much emotional control?

General Wnrght introduced the two mollusks in suits to the naked one on the bar counter. He then asked if the big meeting was still on for tomorrow morning, informing them that he was more than keen to put to rest these wild rumors about Earth's primate menace. Zzzt and Zaztg eyed each other through the clear plastic visors in the top of their power suits, thinking identical thoughts: the purpose of the meeting was not to lay rumors to rest, it was to mobilize the Republic against a deadly threat. It would be unwise to go into all that in the officer's club, so Zzzt ignored Wnrght and asked Xlt again why she was scornful.

"I am scornful of the air pockets in your power suits. You are an aquatic species, why do you have air in your suits?" Xlt said, carefully keeping her voice neutral and her body gray with a hint of respectful lilac.

"For the Founders' sake, we were in a hurry and splashed a little water this morning outside our hotel room. What, is that a crime?" Zzzt said in exasperation, having a hard time believing the impudence of this particular limax. She remembered doing the threat assessment for this species not many years back. There were a few niggling problems that her office had glossed over because data was just then beginning to pour in on the ultra-dangerous primates. Maybe she'd been too quick to sweep the slug's planet onto the fast track for Republican statehood. Perhaps a modest surgical strike would have done them good. Her body turned red, but it wasn't readily visible through the power suit.

"You two squids are threat assessors? Important threat assessors?" Xlt asked in a conversational tone, which didn't fool Zzzt. The paramount threat assessor responded, "Am I an important assessor? I'm in charge of the entire office. I am the paramount assessor. What's that got to do with the price of abalone?"

The crustacean military beings leaned back and watched the mollusks squabble, highly entertained by the spectacle. If they'd spoken chromo-language, their shells would have colored to the bright canary yellow of amusement.

"What it has to do with the price of abalone is this," Xlt said, turning from gray to royal purple, "a multi-planetary military machine is, or should be, an organic whole. Threat assessment should not be wholly separate from operations, just as logistics should not be entirely independent. The whole is greater than the sum of the parts. The paramount threat assessor should respect the infantry enough to wear her suit properly."

"It's not even a combat suit and I'm a civilian."

Xlt turned her back on the squids, feeling abhorrence but hiding her emotion. She ordered another beer. Sergeant Oxfam bent a plated eyestalk at the general and gave him a knowing wink, bony eyelids clacking sharply. Wnrght banged his eyelids open and shut twice and asked Xlt if she wanted to attend the meeting tomorrow at noon with the two squids.

"I would be only too happy to attend," she said turning a polite lilac. "May I offer the representatives from Oceania a delicacy from my home world?" Xlt reached into the food basket at her side with an unexpectedly sturdy pseudopod and pulled a spongy chunk of edible root from the potpourri. Zaztg grabbed for it with his power suit limb, which was, of course, a tentacle inside a jointed metal leg. On the tip of the last metal leg segment there was an airlock. The lock opened and closed. The spongy root flushed into the watery suit interior. He snagged the root with his tentacle and slithered it greedily into his beak. The morsel was delicious. He told Zzzt that she should try one. The paramount assessor declined the offer and told her assistant that they should return to their quarters. It was going to be a long day tomorrow.

Watching the suited squids clank out of the officer's club, Xlt turned a muddy mocking yellow. Zaztg whirled around before hopping off the veranda and onto the desert floor, sensing that the slug was displaying a disrespectful color. Xlt flashed into a politely neutral grayish lilac before the squid's spin was complete. The instant the squid had turned back around, the limax flashed a mocking yellow.

Both Wnrght and Oxfam had to clamp their claws over their mouth plates to keep from laughing. Xlt retreated into a businesslike gray skin tone and faced the military beings once the squids were truly gone. "What is the agenda for tomorrow's meeting with the threat assessors?"

General Wnrght scratched his head with one of his front legs. He crawled off the bar stool, planted both front legs, and absently sharpened his front claws against them. "The threat squids have had a computer meltdown or the stars have lined up the wrong way or I don't know what. Anyway, there is this new sentient species, two actually, two symbiotic sentients from a planet halfway up the Orion Spiral Arm that we are calling Earth. They're a kind of primate, you know monkeys, arboreal mammals that've left the trees, gone through hunter-gatherer, and land-based agriculture, and so forth. The whack-a-doodle squids have given these monkeys a magnitude number of nearly one billion."

Wnrght and Oxfam shook with laughter. The laughing jag proved so distracting that Oxfam accidentally grabbed Xlt's beer and downed it. She let that slight insult go and asked why it was impossible for a new species to have a magnitude number approaching one billion. Limaxes had, only a short while ago, gone through the harrowing process of Republican threat assessment. They'd been given a magnitude number of ninety point something, perilously close to the level that would have triggered a military strike. She was quite familiar with how these assessments worked and saw no physical law that would make an extremely high number impossible. She also knew that Oceania threat assessors had a reputation for extreme thoroughness.

"Let me put it this way," Wnrght began. "A threat assessment magnitude number approaching one billion would mean that these monkeys could, no wait, they definitely *will* launch an invasion fleet and try take out every planet in the Republic the instant they figure out there are other space faring sentients in the galaxy."

The military crustaceans looked at her, their heavy eyelids thudding together expectantly. To the shellbacks' amazement, Xlt's skin slowly shaded green: sniveling, afraid-of-your-own-shadow green. She couldn't possibly be afraid of a fairy tale, no way in the Founders' Nirvana, not the sentient that had led the most promising suit squad they'd ever seen.

"Look, Xlt," Oxfam said reasonably. "You saw what buffoons those squids are. They don't even know how to get inside a power suit." Xlt turned a somber dark charcoal gray and said, "They are office workers, not suit warriors. It's been a hard day. Sergeant, please take my back to my room. I'll see you all in the morning."

The squid's hotel room was too small for power suits. Their artificial exoskeletons had to be stored in the open air outside the saltwater enclosure. That morning, Zzzt and Zaztg awoke, stretched their tentacles, grabbed a quick bite of cuttlefish, and swam to the surface of their chamber. The power canopy roof peeled back, exposing them to the dust laden desert wind. The squids peered over the wall wistfully at the two crab-like suits. The outside air temperature was already a roasting one hundred twenty degrees. They could be comfortable out of water for about three minutes on the desert world.

Taking deep gulps of seawater, they slithered over the rim of the wall, down its face, and onto the two power suits, stoically enduring the tiny pinpricks of wind blown dust and pebbles. The suit abdomen sections clamshelled open automatically. Despite the blast furnace air temperature and the debris charged wind, they crawled carefully up the jointed legs and dipped gingerly into the two suits' open entranceways, taking infinite pains not to spill a single water drop. The suits sealed shut and they were bathed in cool, beautifully filtered, oxygen-rich seawater. Tentacles slid into leg sockets. Eyestalks popped into viewers. The squids were ready for action.

They clumped around the hotel office and out onto a gravel street to hail a cab. A twelve-legged robotic taxi stutter-stepped to an idle. The suited squids climbed inside the machine, ordering it to transport them to General Wnrght's central command. The taxi trotted briskly into the heart of the continent. Despite the harsh conditions around their coastal hotel, they weren't billeted in real desert country. The true desert began some three hundred miles inland.

The gravel road gave way to a dirt track. The gravelly countryside with its gnarled wind-swept trees and thorny vines retreated before a landscape dominated by fine sand, island-like boulders, and spiky cactus. The squids were overwhelmed by the knowledge that they wouldn't last twenty seconds outside their suits in the real desert. And that was the purpose of the archaic ground transportation system of Rglis: a means to intimidate off-worlders. On any other advanced planet, they would take a small flyer or an ultra-fast subway on a three hundred mile journey.

Zzzt eyed the holo-cubes and the holo-projector that Zaztg was carrying. "I hope the holo gear is set up for an atmospheric presentation. It'll be as useless as tentacles on a shark otherwise." Zaztg throbbed angry red inside his suit, a color that his boss could see through his helmet visor. In a controlled voice, he told her to stop worrying and quit trying to micromanage every aspect of their mission.

The taxi stopped trotting in front of the central command building at noon, its legs skidding on the talcum-powder fine soil, throwing a dust cloud on the crab shell shaped structure. Unsuited scorpions caring impossibly large particle beam guns escorted the squids inside. Waiting there in the nautilus chamber were the crustacean military beings, Wnrght and Oxfam, and the legless mollusk, Xlt.

Zaztg set up her holo-projector and loaded it with cubes. The lights were dimmed and the presentation started with a close up of a gorilla and a human's mouths. A narrator's voice, speaking unaccented Galactic Standard cataloged and described, species by species, the pathogenic zoo living in the primates' mouths.

General Wright listened for twenty seconds and cried, "No more. I've heard plenty. Pack your bags and return to Oceania." A cherry red skin color blazed through the view slits of both squids' suits. Zzzt barked a protest through her suit speakers but Wnrght would have none of it. He told the mollusks to conform to standard operating procedure and take their presentation to the Senate. They would get no help from the Army.

"You are hanging me out to dry," Zzzt wailed. "The Senate will take years to make any decision. By then, the apes will have equipped dozens more of their multi-megaton asteroid capital ships with FTL drives. Our only saving grace is that they have currently two and only two super-leviathan class warships outfitted with faster than light propulsion. Just one of these ships is a potential planet buster."

"I accept that these hairy barbarians need quick action," Wnrght said soothingly. "I'm not going to wait on the Senate to launch a surgical strike." The squids shaded back to neutral gray. Xlt stirred from the desk that she'd been sitting on, raising her eyestalks, and turning a curious cream color. "Where there is smoke, there is fire," the general pronounced. "Something ain't right on Earth. I don't know what computer glitch has caused the Threat Assessment Office to move decimal places around on their magnitude number and I don't care. The real number must be nine hundred or even ninety thousand. It sure as spiny anteater shit ain't nine hundred million!"

The squids tinted their visors so that the crab and the scorpion couldn't read their emotions. Wnrght ground forward, explaining that he was going to, without delay, send one entire heavy division to invade Earth and put one more heavy division in Pluto's orbit as a reserve. This would be more firepower than the Army had ever used for a surgical strike. More firepower, in fact, than the Army had used in thirty thousands years, since the foundation of the Republic and the ancient era of actual warfare.

"Two divisions to tackle Earth? That's it? Are you insane?" Zzzt exploded indignantly. Oxfam walked to the door, opened it, and indicated that the squids should leave before he threw them out. Nobody talks to the Galaxy's most senior officer that way, nobody, not even a senator.

Luckily, the squids' visors remained tinted as they quickly retreated. That way, the crustaceans and the slug couldn't see their cowardly mottled green skin color. Something made the squids twist around as they were about to get inside the big, leggy taxicab that was waiting patiently for them outside. Xlt had left the building and was following them, moving at a startlingly brisk pace for a legless being. "Slow down," she said. "I'm going to your hotel room. I want to see the rest of the presentation."

Zzzt remembered that limaxes were as comfortable underwater as they were on dry land. The paramount threat assessor asked her assistant if the holo-projector could be converted quickly to seawater mode. Zaztg banged a jointed metal leg against his abdomen in frustration and said, "Holy whale crap, Boss, it is a matter of flipping a single switch." Zzzt responded, "Don't get your sperm sacs twisted into a knot. I was only asking."

Within a matter of hours, the three mollusks were in the watery hotel room, watching an oversized human mouth and an equally large gorilla mouth float a few feet off the floor. "I will fast forward this section because we've already seen it," Zaztg said, his tentacles playing with the projector controls.

"Wait a second," Xlt commanded. The slug went on to ask the questions that General Wnrght should have asked: "Are the primate oral pathogens a type of biological weapon?"

"No," Zzzt responded. "Prior to invading an enemy planet, the apes will sterilize their bodies and the bodies of their war beasts. They will use bio-weapons only as a last resort. They seek to capture intact ecosystems to harvest useful DNA. In genetic engineering and other life sciences, they are centuries ahead of the Galaxy."

Zaztg replaced the toothsome ape grins with an image of Earth. Ringing the blue/green planet were two thousand asteroid spaceships, vessels so large as to be small worlds onto themselves; each super-leviathan had a crew numbering in the millions: big hairy apes, smaller bald apes, mammoths, war dogs, war seals, horses, and arachnids.

Zaztg adjusted the volume of the narrator's melodious voice: "By any measure, Earth's navy is larger than the Galaxy's. In simple numbers, it is perhaps ten times larger. In raw tonnage, it is incalculably more massive by a factor ranging from tens of millions to hundreds of millions. On the other tentacle, Earth has only two capital ships with functioning FTL drives. The Galaxy has over one hundred. Before shading a lovely purple, consider this: the landing craft alone on these two primate capital ships outweigh the entire Galactic Navy."

The presentation swam ahead, showing the link between the primitive war games that the monkeys called "blood sport" and the primates' ultra-advanced EMP bombs that could transform any type-G star into a technology-destroying neutrino factory. Earth's nearest sun, Proxima Centauri, was just such a factory. No spaceship could enter this solar system without being disabled. Galactic technology had, so far, no means to even study the primate's crippling EMP weapon, let alone design countermeasures. Galactic probes sent into Proxima Centauri's solar system were quickly snuffed out like luminescent fire-fish swimming up an active volcanic vent.

The squids turned green as they watched the program for the tenth time, but Xlt remained a fearless purplish gray. The Zen warrior sought to reassure her companions: "While the Galaxy slumbers, while the industrial might of its thousands of planets remains dormant, while the primate juggernaut approaches, my home world, Limaxia, will prepare for battle."

The squids' panicky neon green dulled to a mottled olive brown. Zzzt complained that Limaxia didn't have a standing army and its Lilliputian navy was geared for clearing local trade routes of pirates. Xlt blazed an incandescent royal purple and shouted, "The military machine that can beat Earth must be built from scratch. My planet has six billion sentients, trained from birth in the Zen martial disciplines. Come with me to join the Limaxian mobilization!"

Timidly, the squids shaded a muddy purple. Zaztg's communicator rang. He picked it up and read a text message. His skin at once flashed like a green strobe light. Zzzt grabbed the communicator, read the message, and turned just as green. "What?" Xlt demanded.

In a quivering voice, Zzzt said, "Every tentacle twisting Galactic spy probe in Earth's Founder forsaken solar system is gone. The hundred odd probes that we had in Pluto's orbit have vanished simultaneously. The wretched monkeys have somehow made them disappear."

Regaining some healthy gray color, Zaztg asked, "Did the apes use pulse weapons on the probes?" Zzzt milked the communicator for data and said, "No, every probe went offline at the exact same moment, although they were at differing distances from the sun. And the probe trained on Sol did not record any pulse bombs striking the solar surface. Plus, it is unlikely that they would pulse their own system. The apes must have used invisible stealth spaceships or missiles. We've seen hints of their stealth capabilities. An attack this coordinated means they have been aware of our spy probes for some time. The primates have declared war on the Galaxy."

Zaztg did not turn green as he said, "We've just been dipped in a monster-sized vat of whale shit." Xlt said, "We leave within the hour for Limaxia. Do not contact your office. Do not file a flight plan. Do not stop and say goodbye to General Wnrght. Get your tentacled butts in gear and get moving!"

To be continued . . .

About the Author

Dave Putnam is a nationally recognized sculptor, specializing in abstract and representational animal figures. He has pieces in the Audubon Zoo in New Orleans, the International Wildlife Museum in Tucson, Arizona as well as many other institutional and private collections throughout the country. His work can be viewed on his website, www.DavePutnamArt.com. He has written the definitive book on the American Bulldog, *The Working American Bulldog* in addition to the prequels to this novel *The Gamekeeper's Night Dog* and *The World War.* Dave lives in Northern California with his wife and four American Bulldogs.